CRITICAL ACCLAIM FOR

Minette Walters

CW 01655018

The Ice House

'Terrific first novel with a high Rendellesque frisson count' *The Times*

The Sculptress

'A devastatingly effective novel' *Observer*

The Scold's Bridle

'A gothic puzzle of great intricacy and psychological power' *Sunday Times*

The Dark Room

'A marvellous, dramatically intelligent novel. It shimmers with suspense, ambiguity and a deep unholy joy' *Daily Mail*

The Echo

'It grips like steel . . . Passion, compassion, intelligence and romance are what Walters offers with no quarter for squeamish cowards' *Mail on Sunday*

The Breaker

'Stands head and shoulders above the vast majority of crime novels . . . Existing fans will love *The Breaker*, new readers will be instant converts' *Express*

The Shape of Snakes

'Breaking all the rules of popular fiction, Minette Walters asks as much of her readers as many literary novelists, and yet she offers them a book as gripping as any thriller' *Times Literary Supplement*

Acid Row

'Humane intelligence enables Walters to twist and turn her plot . . . *Acid Rain* is a breathtaking achievement' *Daily Telegraph*

Fox Evil

'*Fox Evil* is the work of a writer at the peak of her confidence and supreme ability' *The Times*

Disordered Minds

'A powerful, acute and vivid work from a staggeringly talented writer' *Observer*

The Devil's Feather

'Suffused with an aura of lurking menace . . . This is high-octane, on-the-edge stuff, at which Walters excels . . . engrossing reading' *The Times*

The Sculptress

With her debut, *The Ice House*, Minette Walters won the Crime Writers' Association John Creasey Award for the best first crime novel of 1992. Rapidly establishing a reputation as one of the most exciting crime novelists writing today, her second novel, *The Sculptress*, was acclaimed by critics as one of the most compelling and powerful novels of the year and won the Edgar Allan Poe Award for the best crime novel published in America in 1993. In 1994 Minette Walters achieved a unique triple when *The Scold's Bridle* was awarded the CWA Gold Dagger for best crime novel of the year. Her following five novels, *The Dark Room*, *The Echo*, *The Breaker*, *The Shape of Snakes* and *Acid Row* were also published to further critical acclaim throughout the world and her ninth novel, *Fox Evil*, won the 2003 CWA Gold Dagger for Fiction.

Minette Walters lives in Dorset with her husband and two children. Her latest novel, *The Devil's Feather*, is available in Pan paperback.

Also by Minette Walters in Pan Books

The Ice House
The Scold's Bridle
The Dark Room
The Echo
The Breaker
The Shape of Snakes
Acid Row
Fox Evil
Disordered Minds
The Tinder Box
The Devil's Feather
Chickenfeed (Quick Reads)

MINETTE WALTERS

THE Sculptress

PAN BOOKS

First published 1993 by Macmillan

This edition published 2007 by Pan Books
an imprint of Pan Macmillan Ltd
Pan Macmillan, 20 New Wharf Road, London N1 9RR
Basingstoke and Oxford
Associated companies throughout the world
www.panmacmillan.com

Reissued 1998

ISBN 978-0-330-45725-5

Copyright © Minette Walters 1993

The right of Minette Walters to be identified as the
author of this work has been asserted by her in accordance
with the Copyright, Designs and Patents Act 1988.

Grateful acknowledgement is made to Encyclopaedia Britannica,
Inc., for permission to quote from *Encyclopaedia Britannica*,
15th edition (1992), 12:535.

All rights reserved. No part of this publication may be
reproduced, stored in or introduced into a retrieval system, or
transmitted, in any form or by any means (electronic, mechanical,
photocopying, recording or otherwise), without the prior written
permission of the publisher. Any person who does any unauthorized
act in relation to this publication may be liable to criminal
prosecution and civil claims for damages.

1 3 5 7 9 8 6 4 2

A CIP catalogue record for this book is available from
the British Library.

Phototypeset by Intype London Ltd
Printed and bound in Great Britain
by Mackays of Chatham plc, Chatham, Kent

This book is sold subject to the condition that it shall not,
by way of trade or otherwise, be lent, resold, hired out,
or otherwise circulated without the publisher's prior consent
in any form of binding or cover other than that in which
it is published and without a similar condition including this
condition being imposed on the subsequent purchaser.

Visit **www.panmacmillan.com** to read more about all our books and to buy
them. You will also find features, author interviews and news of any author
events, and you can sign up for e-newsletters so that you're always first to hear
about our new releases.

For Roland and Philip

Prologue

Southern Evening Herald, January, 1988

Twenty-Five Years for Brutal Murders

At Winchester Crown Court yesterday, Olive Martin, 23, of 22 Leven Road, Dawlington, was sentenced to life imprisonment for the brutal murders of her mother and sister, with a recommendation that she serve twenty-five years. The judge, who referred to Martin as 'a monster without a grain of humanity', said that nothing could excuse the savagery she had shown to two defenceless women. The murder of a mother by her daughter was the most unnatural of crimes and demanded the strongest penalty that the law could impose. The murder of a sister by a sister was no less heinous. 'Martin's butchery of the bodies,' he went on, 'was an unforgivable and barbarous desecration that will rank in the annals of crime as an act of supreme evil.' Martin showed no emotion as sentence was passed. . .

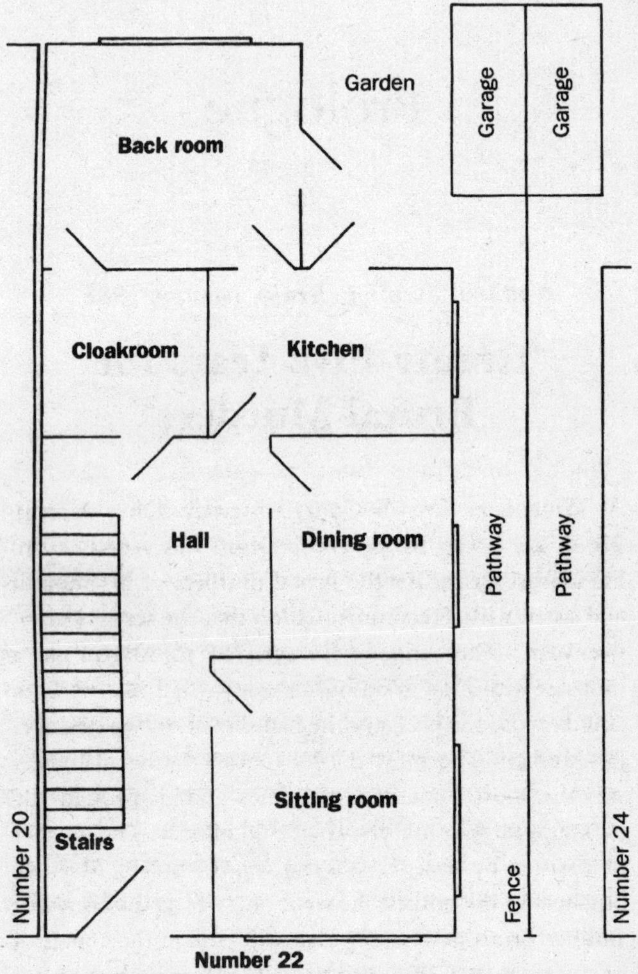

Ground-floor plan of Number 22 Leven Road, Dawlington, Southampton, as it was at the time of the murders. Drawn by the present owner for Miss Rosalind Leigh.

One

IT WAS IMPOSSIBLE to see her approach without a shudder of distaste. She was a grotesque parody of a woman, so fat that her feet and hands and head protruded absurdly from the huge slab of her body like tiny disproportionate afterthoughts. Dirty blonde hair clung damp and thin to her scalp, black patches of sweat spread beneath her armpits. Clearly, walking was painful. She shuffled forward on the insides of her feet, legs forced apart by the thrust of one gigantic thigh against another, balance precarious. And with every movement, however small, the fabric of her dress strained ominously as the weight of her flesh shifted. She had, it seemed, no redeeming features. Even her eyes, a deep blue, were all but lost in the ugly folds of pitted white lard.

Strange that after so long she was still an object of curiosity. People who saw her every day watched her progress down that corridor as if for the first time. What was it that fascinated them? The sheer size of a woman who stood five feet eleven and weighed over twenty-six stones? Her reputation? Disgust? There were no smiles. Most watched impassively as she passed, fearful perhaps of attracting her attention. She had carved her mother and sister into little pieces and rearranged the bits in bloody abstract on her kitchen floor. Few who saw her could forget it. In view of the horrific nature of the crime and the fear that her huge brooding figure had instilled in everyone who had sat in the courtroom she had been sentenced to life with a recommendation that she serve a minimum of twenty-five years. What made her unusual, apart from the crime itself, was that she had pleaded guilty and refused to offer a defence.

She was known inside the prison walls as the Sculptress. Her real name was Olive Martin.

Rosalind Leigh, waiting by the door of the interview room, ran her tongue around the inside of her mouth. Her revulsion was immediate as if Olive's evil had reached out and touched her. *My God*, she was thinking, and the thought alarmed her, *I can't go through with this.* But she had, of course, no choice. The gates of the prison were locked on her, as a visitor, just as securely as they were locked on the inmates. She pressed a shaking hand to her thigh where the muscles were jumping uncontrollably. Behind her, her all but empty briefcase, a testament to her lack of preparation for this meeting, screamed derision at her ill-considered assumption that conversation with Olive could develop like any other. It had never occurred to her, not for one moment, that fear might stifle her inventiveness.

Lizzie Borden took an axe and gave her mother forty whacks. When she saw what she had done, she gave her father forty-one. The rhyme churned in her brain, over and over, numbingly repetitive. *Olive Martin took an axe and gave her mother forty whacks. When she saw what she had done she gave her sister forty-one . . .*

Roz stepped away from the door and forced herself to smile. 'Hello, Olive. I'm Rosalind Leigh. Nice to meet you at last.' She held out her hand and shook the other's warmly, in the hope, perhaps, that by demonstrating an unprejudiced friendliness she could quell her dislike. Olive's touch was token only, a brief brush of unresponsive fingers. 'Thank you.' Roz spoke to the hovering prison officer briskly. 'I'll take it from here. We have the Governor's permission to talk for an hour.' *Lizzie Borden took an axe . . .* Tell her you've changed your mind. *Olive Martin took an axe and gave her mother forty whacks . . .* I can't go through with this!

The uniformed woman shrugged. 'OK.' She dropped the welded metal chair she was carrying carelessly on to the floor and steadied it against her knee. 'You'll need this. Anything else in there will collapse the minute she sits on it.' She laughed amiably. An attractive woman. 'She got wedged in the flaming toilet last year and it took four men to pull her out again. You'd never get her up on your own.'

Roz manoeuvred the chair awkwardly through the doorway. She felt at a disadvantage, like the friend of warring partners being pressured into taking sides. *But Olive intimidated her in a way the prison officer never could.* 'You will see me using a tape-recorder during this interview,' she snapped, nervousness clipping the words brusquely. 'The Governor has agreed to it. I trust that's in order.'

There was a short silence. The prison officer raised an eyebrow. 'If you say so. Presumably someone's taken the trouble to get the Sculptress's agreement. Any problems, like, for example, she objects violently' – she drew a finger across her throat before tapping the pane of glass beside the door which allowed the officers a clear view of the room – 'then bang on the window. Assuming she lets you, of course.' She smiled coolly. 'You've read the rules, I hope. You bring nothing in for her, you take nothing out. She can smoke your cigarettes in the interview room but she can't take any away with her. You do not pass messages for her, in or out, without the Governor's permission. If in doubt about anything, you refer it to one of the officers. Clear?'

Bitch, thought Roz angrily. 'Yes, thank you.' But it wasn't anger she felt, of course, it was fear. Fear of being shut up in a confined space with this monstrous creature who stank of fat woman's sweat and showed no emotion in her grotesquely bloated face.

'Good.' The officer walked away with a broad wink at a colleague.

Roz stared after her. 'Come in, Olive.' She chose the chair furthest from the door deliberately. It was a statement of confidence. She was so damn nervous she needed a wee.

The idea for the book had been delivered as an ultimatum by her agent. 'Your publisher is about to wash his hands of you, Roz. His precise words were, "She has a week to commit herself to something that will sell or I shall remove her from our lists." And, though I hate to rub your nose in it, I am within a whisker of doing the same thing.' Iris's face softened a little. Berating Roz, she felt, was like beating your head against a brick wall, painful and completely ineffective. She was, she knew, the woman's best friend – her *only* friend, she thought sometimes. The barrier of barbed wire that Roz had erected around herself had deterred all but the most determined. People rarely even asked after her these days. With an inward sigh, Iris threw caution to the winds. 'Look, sweetheart, you really can't go on like this. It's unhealthy to shut yourself away and brood. Did you think about what I suggested last time?'

Roz wasn't listening. 'I'm sorry,' she murmured,

her eyes maddeningly vacant. She saw the irritation on Iris's face and forced herself to concentrate. Iris, she thought, had been lecturing again. But really, Roz wondered, why did she bother? Other people's concern was so exhausting, for her and for them.

'Did you ring that psychiatrist I recommended?' Iris demanded bluntly.

'No, there's no need. I'm fine.' She studied the immaculately made-up face, which had changed very little in fifteen years. Someone had once told Iris Fielding that she looked like Elizabeth Taylor in *Cleopatra*. 'A week's too short,' Roz said, referring to her publisher. 'Tell him a month.'

Iris flicked a piece of paper across her desk. 'You've run out of room to manoeuvre, I'm afraid. He's not even prepared to give you a choice of subject. He wants Olive Martin. Here's the name and address of her solicitor. Find out why she wasn't sent to Broadmoor or Rampton. Find out why she refused to offer a defence. And find out what made her commit the murders in the first place. There's a story there somewhere.' She watched the frown on Roz's face deepen and shrugged. 'I know. It's not your sort of thing, but you've brought this on yourself. I've been pressing you for months to produce an outline. Now it's this or nothing. To tell you the truth, I think he's done it on purpose. If you write it, it will sell, if you refuse to write it because it's pure sensationalism, then he's found a good excuse to drop you.'

Roz's reaction surprised her. 'OK,' she said mildly, taking the piece of paper and tucking it into her handbag.

'I thought you'd refuse.'

'Why?'

'Because of the way the tabloids sensationalized what happened to *you*.'

Roz shrugged. 'Maybe it's time someone showed them how to handle human tragedy with dignity.' She wouldn't write it, of course – she had no intention of writing anything any more – but she gave Iris an encouraging smile. 'I've never met a murderess before.'

Roz's application to visit Olive Martin for the purposes of research was passed on by the Prison Governor to the Home Office. It was several weeks before permission was given in a grudging processed letter from a civil servant. While Martin had consented to the visits, she reserved the right at any time to withdraw consent, without reason and without prejudice. It was emphasized that the visits had been authorized only on the understanding that there would be no breaches of the prison regulations, that the Governor's word would be final in all circumstances, and that Ms Leigh would be held liable should she contribute in any way to an undermining of prison discipline.

Roz found it hard to look at Olive. Good manners and the woman's ugliness precluded staring and the monstrous face was so flat, so unresponsive, that her eyes kept sliding off it like butter off a baked potato. Olive, for her part, watched Roz greedily. Attractive looks put no such limitations on staring – quite the reverse, they invite it – and Roz was, in any case, a novelty. Visitors were rare in Olive's life, particularly ones who came without the reforming baggage of missionary zeal.

After the cumbersome business of getting her seated, Roz gestured towards the tape-recorder. 'If you remember, I mentioned in my second letter that I'd like to record our chats. I presumed when the Governor gave permission for it that you'd agreed.' Her voice was pitched too high.

Olive shrugged a kind of acquiescence.

'You've no objections, then?'

A shake of the head.

'Fine. I'm switching on now. Date, Monday, April twelve. Conversation with Olive Martin.' She consulted her all too sketchy list of questions. 'Let's start with some factual details. When were you born?'

No answer.

Roz looked up with an encouraging smile, only to be confronted by the woman's unblinking scrutiny. 'Well,' she said, 'I think I have that detail already. Let's see. Eighth of September, nineteen sixty-four, which makes you twenty-eight. Am I right?' No response. 'And you were born in Southampton General, the first of Gwen and Robert Martin's two daughters. Your sister, Amber, came along two years later on the fifteenth of July, nineteen sixty-six. Were you pleased about that? Or would you rather have had a brother?' Nothing.

Roz did not look up this time. She could feel the weight of the woman's eyes upon her. 'Your parents liked colours, obviously. I wonder what they would have called Amber if she'd been a boy?' She gave a nervous giggle. 'Red? Ginger? Perhaps it was a good thing the baby was another girl.' She listened to herself in disgust. *Goddamnit, why the hell did I agree to this!* Her bladder was hurting.

A fat finger reached out and switched off the tape-recorder. Roz watched it with a horrible fascination. 'There's no need to be so frightened,' said a deep, surprisingly cultured voice. 'Miss Henderson was teasing you. They all know I'm completely harmless. If I wasn't, I'd be in Broadmoor.' A strange rumbling noise vibrated the air. A laugh? Roz wondered. 'Stands to reason, really.' The finger hovered over the switches. 'You see, I do what normal people do when I have objections to something. I express them.' The finger moved to *Record* and gently pushed the button. 'Had Amber been a boy they would have called him Jeremy after my mother's father. Colour didn't come into it. In actual fact, Amber was christened Alison. I called her Amber because, at the age of two, I couldn't get my tongue round the "*l*" or the "*s*". It suited her. She had lovely honey-blonde hair, and as she grew up she always answered to Amber and never to Alison. She was very pretty.'

Roz waited a moment until she was sure she had her voice under control. 'Sorry.'

'That's all right. I'm used to it. Everyone is afraid at first.'

'Does that upset you?'

A flicker of amusement twitched the fatness round her eyes. 'Would it upset you?'

'Yes.'

'Well, then. Have you got a cigarette?'

'Sure.' Roz took an unopened pack from her brief-case and pushed it across the table with a box of matches. 'Help yourself. I don't smoke.'

'You would if you were in here. Everyone smokes in here.' She fumbled her way into the cigarette packet and lit up with a sigh of contentment. 'How old are you?'

'Thirty-six.'

'Married?'

'Divorced.'

'Children?'

Roz shook her head. 'I'm not the maternal type.'

'Is that why you got divorced?'

'Probably. I was more interested in my career. We went our separate ways very amicably.' Absurd, she thought, to bother with pain management in front of

Olive but the trouble was that if you told a lie often enough it became a truth, and the hurt only returned occasionally, in those strange, disorientating moments of wakening when she thought she was still at home with a warm body wrapped in her arms, hugging, loving, laughing.

Olive blew a smoke ring into the air. 'I'd have liked children. I got pregnant once but my mother persuaded me to get rid of it. I wish I hadn't now. I keep wondering what sex it was. I dream about my baby sometimes.' She gazed at the ceiling for a moment, following the wisp of smoke. 'Poor little thing. I was told by a woman in here that they wash them down the sink – you know, when they've vacuumed them out of you.'

Roz watched the big lips suck wetly on the tiny cigarette and thought of foetuses being vacuumed out of wombs. 'I didn't know that.'

'About the sink?'

'No. That you'd had an abortion.'

Olive's face was impassive. 'Do you know anything about me?'

'Not much.'

'Who've you asked?'

'Your solicitor.'

Another wheeze rumbled up through the caverns of her chest. 'I didn't know I had one.'

'Peter Crew,' said Roz with a frown, pulling a letter from her briefcase.

'Oh, him.' Olive's tone was contemptuous. 'He's a creep.' She spoke with undisguised venom.

'He says here he's your solicitor.'

'So? Governments say they care. I haven't heard a word from him in four years. I told him to get stuffed when he came up with his wonderful idea to get me an indefinite stay at Broadmoor. Slimy little sod. He didn't like me. He'd have wet himself with excitement if he could have got me certified.'

'He says' – Roz skimmed through the letter without thinking – 'ah, yes, here it is. "Unfortunately Olive failed to grasp that a plea of diminished responsibility would have ensured her receiving the sort of help in a secure psychiatric unit that would, in all probability, have meant her release into society within, at the most, fifteen years. It has always been obvious to me—" ' She came to an abrupt stop as sweat broke out across her back. *Any problems like, for example, she objects violently* . . . Was she completely out of her mind? She smiled weakly. 'Frankly, the rest is irrelevant.'

' "It has always been obvious to me that Olive is psychologically disturbed, possibly to the point of paranoid schizophrenia or psychopathy." Is that what it says?' Olive stood the glowing butt of her cigarette on the table and took another from the packet. 'I don't say I wasn't tempted. Assuming I could have got the court to accept that I was temporarily insane when I did it, I would almost certainly be a free woman by now. Have you seen my psychological reports?' Roz shook her head. 'Apart from an unremitting compulsion to eat, which is generally considered abnormal – one psychiatrist dubbed it a tendency to severe self-abuse – I am classified "normal".' She blew out the match with a gust of amusement. 'Whatever normal means. You've probably got more hang-ups than I have but I assume you fall into a "normal" psychological profile.'

'I wouldn't know,' said Roz, fascinated. 'I've never been analysed.' *I'm too frightened of what they might find.*

'You get used to it in a place like this. I reckon they do it to keep their hand in and it's probably more fun talking to a mother-hacker than a boring old depressive. I've had five different psychiatrists put me through the hoops. They love labels. It makes the filing system easier when they're trying to sort out what to do with us. I create problems for them. I'm sane but dangerous, so where the hell do they put me? An open prison's out of the question in case I get out and do it again. The public wouldn't like that.'

Roz held up the letter. 'You say you were tempted. Why didn't you go along with it if you thought there was a chance of getting out earlier?'

Olive didn't answer immediately but smoothed the shapeless dress across her thighs. 'We make choices. They're not always right but, once made, we have to live with them. I was very ignorant before I came here. Now I'm streetwise.' She inhaled a lungful of smoke. 'Psychologists, policemen, prison officers, judges, they were all out of the same mould. Men in authority with complete control of my life. Supposing I'd pleaded diminished responsibility and they'd said this girl can never get better. Lock the door and throw away the key. Twenty-five years amongst sane people was so much more attractive to me than a whole life with mad ones.'

'And what do you think now?'

'You learn, don't you? We get some real nut cases in here before they're transferred on. They're not so bad. Most of them can see the funny side.' She balanced a second dog-end next to her first. 'And I'll tell you something else, they're a damn sight less critical than the sane ones. When you look like me, you appreciate that.' She scrutinized Roz from between sparse blonde eyelashes. 'That's not to say I'd have pleaded differently had I been more *au fait* with the system. I still think it would have been immoral to claim I didn't know what I was doing when I knew perfectly well.'

Roz made no comment. What can you say to a woman who dismembers her mother and sister and then calmly splits hairs over the morality of special pleading?

Olive guessed what she was thinking and gave her wheezy laugh. 'It makes sense to me. By my own standards, I've done nothing wrong. It's only the law, those standards set by society, that I've transgressed.'

There was a certain biblical flourish about that last phrase, and Roz remembered that today was Easter Monday. 'Do you believe in God?'

'No. I'm a pagan. I believe in natural forces. Worshipping the sun makes sense. Worshipping an invisible entity doesn't.'

'What about Jesus Christ? He wasn't invisible.'

'But he wasn't God either.' Olive shrugged. 'He was a prophet, like Billy Graham. Can you swallow the garbage of the Trinity? I mean, either there's one God or there's a mountainful of them. It just depends on how imaginative you feel. I, for one, have no cause to celebrate that Christ is Risen.'

Roz, whose faith was dead, could sympathize with Olive's cynicism. 'So, if I understand you correctly, you're saying there is no absolute right or wrong, only individual conscience and the law.' Olive nodded. 'And your conscience isn't troubling you because you don't think you've done anything wrong.'

Olive looked at her with approval. 'That's it.'

Roz chewed her bottom lip in thought. 'Which means you believe your mother and sister deserved to die.' She frowned. 'Well, I don't understand, then. Why didn't you put up a defence at your trial?'

'I had no defence.'

'Provocation. Mental cruelty. Neglect. They must

have done *something* if you felt you were justified in killing them.'

Olive took another cigarette from the pack but didn't answer.

'Well?'

The intense scrutiny again. This time Roz held her gaze.

'Well?' she persisted.

Abruptly, Olive rapped the window pane with the back of her hand. 'I'm ready now, Miss Henderson,' she called out.

Roz looked at her in surprise. 'We've forty minutes yet.'

'I've talked enough.'

'I'm sorry. I've obviously upset you.' She waited. 'It was unintentional.'

Olive still didn't answer but sat impassively until the Officer came in. Then she grasped the edge of the table and, with a shove from behind, heaved herself to her feet. The cigarette, unlit, clung to her lower lip like a string of cotton wool. 'I'll see you next week,' she said, easing crabwise through the door and shambling off down the corridor with Miss Henderson and the metal chair in tow.

Roz sat on for several minutes, watching them through the window. Why had Olive balked at the mention of justification? Roz felt unreasonably cheated – it was one of the few questions she had wanted an answer to – and yet . . . Like the first stirrings of long dormant sap, her curiosity began to reawaken. God knows, there was no sense to it – she and Olive were as different as two women could be – but she had to admit an odd liking for the woman.

She snapped her briefcase closed and never noticed that her pencil was missing.

Iris had left a breathy message on the answerphone. 'Ring me with all the dirt . . . Is she perfectly ghastly? If she's as mad and as fat as her solicitor said, she must be terrifying. I'm agog to hear the gory details. If you don't phone, I shall come round to the flat and make a nuisance of myself . . .'

Roz poured herself a gin and tonic and wondered if Iris's insensitivity was inherited or acquired. She dialled her number. 'I'm phoning because it's the lesser of two evils. If I had to watch you drooling your disgusting prurience all over my carpet, I should be sick.' Mrs Antrobus, her bossy white cat, slithered round her legs, stiff tailed and purring. Roz winked down at her. She and Mrs Antrobus had a relationship of long standing, in which Mrs Antrobus wore the trousers and Roz knew her place. There was no persuading Mrs A. to do anything she didn't want.

'Oh, goody. You liked her, then?'

'What a revolting woman you are.' She took a sip

from her glass. 'I'm not sure that *like* is quite the word I would use.'

'How fat is she?'

'Grotesque. And it's sad, not funny.'

'Did she talk?'

'Yes. She has a very pukka accent and she's a bit of an intellectual. Not at all what I expected. Very sane, by the way.'

'I thought the solicitor said she was a psychopath.'

'He did. I'm going to see him tomorrow. I want to know who gave him that idea. According to Olive, five psychiatrists have diagnosed her normal.'

'She might be lying.'

'She's not. I checked with the Governor afterwards.' Roz reached down to scoop Mrs Antrobus against her chest. The cat, purring noisily, licked her nose. It was only cupboard love. She was hungry. 'Still, I wouldn't get too excited about this, if I were you. Olive may refuse to see me again.'

'Why, and what's that awful row?' demanded Iris.

'Mrs Antrobus.'

'Oh God! The mangy cat.' Iris was diverted. 'It sounds as if you've got the builders in. What on earth are you doing to it?'

'Loving it. She's the only thing that makes this hideous flat worth coming back to.'

'You're mad,' said Iris, whose contempt for cats was matched only by her contempt for authors. 'I can't think why you wanted to rent it in the first place. Use the money from the divorce and get something decent. Why might Olive refuse to see you?'

'She's unpredictable. Got very angry with me suddenly and called a halt to the interview.'

She heard Iris's indrawn gasp. 'Roz, you wretch! You haven't blown it, I hope.'

Roz grinned into the receiver. 'I'm not sure. We'll just have to wait and see. Got to go now. Bye-ee.' She hung up smartly on Iris's angry squeaking and went into the kitchen to feed Mrs Antrobus. When the phone rang again, she picked up her gin, moved into her bedroom, and started typing.

Olive took the pencil she had stolen from Roz and stood it carefully alongside the small clay figure of a woman that was propped up at the back of her chest of drawers. Her moist lips worked involuntarily, chewing, sucking, as she studied the figure critically. It was crudely executed, a lump of dried grey clay, unfired and unglazed but, like a fertility symbol from a less sophisticated age, its femininity was powerful. She selected a red marker from a jar and carefully coloured in the slab of hair about the face, then, changing to a green marker, filled in on the torso a rough representation of the silk shirtwaisted dress that Roz had been wearing.

To an observer her actions would have appeared

childish. She cradled the figure in her hands like a tiny doll, crooning over it, before replacing it beside the pencil which, too faintly for the human nose, still carried the scent of Rosalind Leigh.

Two

PETER CREW'S OFFICE was in the centre of Southampton, in a street where estate agents predominated. It was a sign of the times, thought Roz, as she walked past them, that they were largely empty. Depression had settled on them, as on everything else, like a dark immovable cloud.

Peter Crew was a gangling man of indeterminate age, with faded eyes and a blond toupee parted at the side. His own hair, a yellowish white, hung beneath it like a dirty net curtain. Every so often, he lifted the edge of the hair-piece and poked a finger underneath to scratch his scalp. The inevitable result of so much ill-considered stretching was that the toupee gaped perpetually in a small peak above his nose. It looked, Roz thought, like a large chicken perched on top of his head. She rather sympathized with Olive's contempt for him.

He smiled at her request to tape their conversation, a studied lift of the lips which lacked sincerity. 'As you please.' He folded his hands on his desk. 'So, Miss Leigh, you've already seen my client. How was she?'

'She was surprised to hear she still had a solicitor.'

'I don't follow,'

'According to Olive, she hasn't heard from you in four years. Are you still representing her?'

His face assumed a look of comical dismay but, like his smile, it lacked conviction. 'Good Heavens. Is it as long as that? Surely not. Didn't I write to her last year?'

'You tell me, Mr Crew.'

He fussed to a cabinet in the corner and flicked through the files. 'Here we are. Olive Martin. Dear me, you're right. Four years. Mind you,' he said sharply, 'there's been no communication from her either.' He pulled out the file and brought it across to his desk. 'The law is a costly business, Miss Leigh. We don't send letters for fun, you know.'

Roz lifted an eyebrow. 'Who's paying, then? I assumed she was on Legal Aid.'

He adjusted his yellow hat. 'Her father paid, though, frankly, I'm not sure what the position would be now. He's dead, you know.'

'I didn't know.'

'Heart attack a year ago. It was three days before anyone found him. Messy business. We're still trying to sort out the estate.' He lit a cigarette and then abandoned it on the edge of an overflowing ashtray.

Roz pencilled a doodle on her notepad. 'Does Olive know her father's dead?'

He was surprised. 'Of course she does.'

'Who told her? Obviously, your firm didn't write.'

He eyed her with the sudden suspicion of an unwary rambler coming upon a snake in the grass. 'I telephoned the prison and spoke to the Governor. I thought it would be less upsetting for Olive if the news was given personally.' He became alarmed. 'Are you saying she's never been told?'

'No. I just wondered why, if her father had money to leave, there's been no correspondence with Olive. Who's the beneficiary?'

Mr Crew shook his head. 'I can't reveal that. It's not Olive, naturally.'

'Why naturally?'

He tut-tutted crossly. 'Why do you think, young woman? She murdered his wife and younger daughter and condemned the poor man to live out his last years in the house where it happened. It was completely unsaleable. Have you any idea how tragic his life became? He was a recluse, never went out, never received visitors. It was only because there were milk bottles on the doorstep that anyone realized there was something wrong. As I say, he'd been dead for three days. Of course he wasn't going to leave money to Olive.'

Roz shrugged. 'Then why did he pay her legal bills? That's hardly consistent, is it?'

He ignored the question. 'There would have been difficulties, in any case. Olive would not have been allowed to benefit financially from the murder of her mother and her sister.'

Roz conceded the point. 'Did he leave much?'

'Surprisingly, yes. He made a tidy sum on the stock market.' His eyes held a wistful regret as he scratched vigorously under his toupee. 'Whether through luck or good judgement he sold everything just before Black Monday. The estate is now valued at half a million pounds.'

'My God!' She was silent for a moment. 'Does Olive know?'

'Certainly, if she reads the newspapers. The amount has been published and, because of the murders, it found its way into the tabloids.'

'Has it gone to the beneficiary yet?'

He frowned heavily, his brows jutting. 'I'm afraid I'm not at liberty to discuss that. The terms of the will preclude it.'

Roz shrugged and tapped her teeth with her pencil. 'Black Monday was October eighty-seven. The murders happened on September ninth, eighty-seven. That's odd, don't you think?'

'In what way?'

'I'd expect him to be so shell-shocked that stocks and shares would be the last thing he'd worry about.'

'Conversely,' said Mr Crew reasonably, 'that very fact would demand that he find something to occupy his mind. He was semi-retired after the murders. Perhaps the financial pages were his only remaining interest.' He looked at his watch. 'Time presses. Was there anything else?'

It was on the tip of Roz's tongue to ask why, if Robert Martin had made a killing on the stock exchange, he had chosen to live out his days in an unsaleable house. Surely a man worth half a million could have afforded to move, irrespective of what his property was worth? What, she wondered, was in that house to make Martin sacrifice himself to it? But she sensed Crew's hostility to her and decided that discretion was the better part of valour. This man was one of the few sources of corroborative information open to her and she would need him again, even though his sympathies clearly lay more with the father than the daughter. 'Just one or two more questions this morning.' She smiled pleasantly, a studied use of charm as insincere as his. 'I'm still feeling my way on this, Mr Crew. To tell you the truth, I'm not yet convinced there's a book in it.' And what an understatement that was. She wasn't intending to write anything. Or was she?

He steepled his fingers and tapped them together impatiently. 'If you remember, Miss Leigh, I made that very point in my letter to you.'

She nodded gravely, pandering to his ego. 'And as I told you, I don't want to write Olive's story simply to cover the pages with lurid details of what she did.

But one part of your letter implied an angle that might be worth pursuing. You advised her to plead not guilty to murder on the grounds of diminished responsibility. Had that succeeded, you suggested, she would have been found guilty of manslaughter and would, in all probability, have been sentenced to indefinite detention. I think you went on to estimate ten to fifteen years in a secure unit if she had been given psychiatric treatment and had responded favourably to it.'

'That is correct,' he agreed. 'And I think it was a reasonable estimate. Certainly she would have served nothing like the twenty-five year sentence the judge recommended she serve.'

'But she rejected your advice. Do you know why?'

'Yes. She had a morbid fear of being locked up with mad people and she misunderstood the nature of indefinite detention. She was convinced that it meant endless, and, try as we might, we could not persuade her otherwise.'

'In that case, why didn't you lodge a not guilty plea on her behalf? The very fact that she couldn't grasp what you were telling her implies that she wasn't capable of pleading for herself. You must have thought she had a defence or you wouldn't have suggested it.'

He smiled grimly. 'I don't quite understand why, Miss Leigh, but you seem to have decided that we failed Olive in some way.' He scribbled a name and address on a piece of paper. 'I suggest you talk to this man before you come to any more erroneous conclusions.' He flicked the paper in her direction. 'He's the barrister we briefed for her defence. Graham Deedes. In the event, she outmanoeuvred us and he was never called to defend her.'

'But why? How could she outmanoeuvre you?' She frowned. 'I'm sorry if I sound critical, Mr Crew, and please believe me, you are wrong in assuming I have reached any unfavourable conclusions.' But was that really true? she wondered. 'I am simply a perplexed onlooker asking questions. If this Deedes was in a position to raise serious doubts over her quote *sanity* unquote, then surely he should have insisted that the court hear her defence whether she wanted it or not. Not to put too fine a point on it, if she was bonkers then the system had a duty to recognize the fact, even if she herself thought she was sane.'

He relented a little. 'You're using very emotive language, Miss Leigh – there was never a question of pleading insanity, only diminished responsibility – but I do take your point. I used the word outmanoeuvred advisedly. The simple truth is that a few weeks before the scheduled date of her trial, Olive wrote to the Home Secretary demanding to know whether she had the right to plead guilty or whether, under British law, this right was denied her. She claimed that undue pressure was being brought to bear to force a lengthy trial that would do nothing to help her but only prolong the agony for her father. The trial date was postponed while tests were carried out to discover if she was fit to plead. She was ruled eminently fit and was allowed to plead guilty.'

'Good Lord!' Roz chewed her lower lip. 'Good Lord!' she said again. 'Were they right?'

'Of course.' He noticed the forgotten cigarette with a curl of ash dripping from its end and, with a gesture of annoyance, stubbed it out. 'She knew exactly what the consequences would be. They even told her what sort of sentence to expect. Nor would prison have come as any surprise to her. She spent four months on remand before the trial. Frankly, even had she agreed to defend herself the result would still have been the same. The evidence for a plea of diminished responsibility was very flimsy. I doubt we could have swung a jury.'

'And yet in your letter you said that, in spite of everything, you are still convinced she's a psychopath. Why?'

He fingered the file on his desk. 'I saw the photographs of Gwen and Amber's bodies, taken before their removal from the kitchen. It was a slaughterhouse running with blood, the most horrifying scene I have ever witnessed. Nothing will ever convince me that a psychologically stable personality could wreak such atrocity on anyone, let alone on a mother and sister.' He rubbed his eyes. 'No, despite what the psychiatrists say – and you must remember, Miss Leigh, that whether or not psychopathy is a diagnosable disease is under constant debate – Olive Martin is a dangerous woman. I advise you to be extremely wary in your dealings with her.'

Roz switched off her tape-recorder and reached for her briefcase. 'I suppose there's no doubt that she did it.'

He stared at her as if she had said something dirty. 'None at all,' he snapped. 'What are you implying?'

'It just occurs to me that a simple explanation for the discrepancy between the psychiatric evidence of Olive's normality and the quite *ab*normal nature of the crime is that she didn't do it but is covering for whoever did.' She stood up and gave a small shrug in face of his tight-lipped expression. 'It was just a thought. I agree it makes little sense, but nothing about this case makes much sense. I mean, if she really *is* a psychopathic murderess she wouldn't have cared tuppence about putting her father through the mill of a trial. Thank you for your time, Mr Crew. I can see myself out.'

He held up a hand to hold her back. 'Have you read her statement, Miss Leigh?'

'Not yet. Your office promised to send it to me.'

He sorted through the file and took out some stapled sheets of paper. 'This is a copy you may keep,' he told her, passing the pages across the desk. 'I urge you to read it before you go any further. It will persuade you, I think, as it persuaded me, of Olive's guilt.'

Roz picked up the papers. 'You really don't like her, do you?'

His eyes hardened. 'I have no feelings for her, one way or the other. I merely question society's rationale in keeping her alive. She kills people. Don't forget that, Miss Leigh. Good day to you.'

It took Roz an hour and a half to drive back to her flat in London and for most of that time Crew's words – *She kills people* – obscured all other thoughts. She took them out of context and wrote them large across the screen of her mind, dwelling on them with a kind of grim satisfaction.

It was later, curled up in an armchair, that she realized the journey home was a complete blank. She had no recollection, even, of leaving Southampton, a city she wasn't familiar with. *She* could have killed someone, crushing them under the wheels of her car, and she wouldn't have been able to remember when or how it happened. She stared out of her sitting-room window at the dismal grey façades opposite, and she wondered quite seriously about the nature of diminished responsibility.

Statement made by Olive Martin
9.9.87 – 9.30 p.m.
Present: DS Hawksley, DS Wyatt,
E.P. Crew (Solicitor)

My name is Olive Martin. I was born on 8th September, 1964. I live at 22 Leven Road, Dawlington, Southampton. I am employed as a clerk in the Department of Health and Social Security in Dawlington High Street. Yesterday was my birthday. I am twenty-three years old. I have always lived at home. My relationship with my mother and sister has never been close. I get on well with my father. I weigh eighteen and a half stone and my mother and sister have always teased me about it. Their nickname for me was Fattie-Hattie, after Hattie Jacques, the actress. I am sensitive to being laughed at for my size.

Nothing was planned for my birthday and that upset me. My mother said I wasn't a child any more and that I must organize my own treats. I decided to show her I was capable of doing something on my own. I arranged to have today off work with the idea of taking the train to London and spending the day sight-seeing. I did not organize the treat for yesterday, my birthday, in case she had planned a surprise for the evening which is what she did for my sister's twenty-first birthday in July. She did not. We all spent the evening quietly watching television. I went to bed feeling very upset. My parents gave me a pale pink jumper for my birthday present. It was very unflattering and I didn't like it. My sister gave me some new slippers which I did like.

I woke up feeling nervous about going to London on my own. I asked Amber, my sister, to phone in sick and come with me. She has been working in *Glitzy*, a fashion boutique in Dawlington, for about a month. My mother got very angry about this and stopped her. We had an argument over breakfast and my father left for work in the middle of it. He is fifty-five and works three days a week, as a book-keeper for a private haulage company. For many years he owned his own garage. He sold it in 1985 because he had no son to take it over.

The argument became very heated after he left, with my mother blaming me for leading Amber astray. She kept calling me Fattie and laughing at me for being too wet to go to London alone. She said I had been a disappointment to her from the day I was born. Her shouting gave me a headache. I was still very upset that she had done nothing for my birthday and I was jealous because she had given Amber a birthday party.

I went to the drawer and took out the rolling pin. I hit her with it to make her be quiet, then I hit her again when she started screaming. I might have stopped then but Amber started screaming because of what I had done. I had to hit her too. I have never liked noise.

I made myself a cup of tea and waited. I thought I had knocked them out. They were both lying on the floor. After an hour I wondered if they were dead. They were very pale and hadn't moved. I know that if you hold a mirror to someone's mouth and there is no mist on it afterwards it means they are dead. I used the mirror from my handbag. I held it to their mouths for a long time but there was no mist. Nothing.

I became frightened and wondered how to hide the bodies. At first, I thought of putting them in the attic, but they were too heavy to carry upstairs. Then I decided the sea would be the best place as it's only two miles from our house, but I can't drive and, anyway, my father had taken the car. It seemed to me that if I could make them smaller I could fit them into suitcases and carry them that way. I have cut chickens into portions many times. I thought it would be easy to do the same thing with Amber and my mother. I used an axe that we kept in the garage and a carving knife from the kitchen drawer.

It wasn't at all like cutting up chickens. I was tired by two o'clock and I had only managed to take off the heads and the legs and three of the arms. There was a lot of blood and my hands kept slipping. I knew my father would be home soon and that I could never finish by then as I still had to carry the pieces to the sea. I realized it would be better to ring the police and admit what I had done. I felt much happier once I had made this decision.

It never occurred to me to leave the house and pretend that someone else had done it. I don't know why except that my mind was set on hiding the bodies. That's all I thought about. I did not enjoy cutting them up. I had to undress them so I could see where the joints were. I did not know I'd mixed the pieces up. I rearranged them out of decency, but there was so much blood that I couldn't tell which body was which. I must have put my mother's head on Amber's body by mistake. I acted alone.

I am sorry for what I have done. I lost my temper and behaved stupidly. I confirm that everything written here is true.

Signed – OLIVE MARTIN

The statement was a photocopy, covering three typed sheets of A4. On the reverse of the last sheet was a photocopied extract from what was presumably the pathologist's report. It was brief, just a concluding paragraph, and there was no indication to show who had written it.

The injuries to the heads are entirely consistent with a blow or blows from a heavy solid object. These were inflicted before death and were not fatal. While there is no forensic evidence to suggest that the rolling pin was the weapon used, there is none to prove it wasn't. Death in both cases was caused by severance of the carotid artery during the decapitation process. Examination of the axe revealed considerable rusting beneath the blood stains. It is highly probable that it was blunt before it was used to dismember the bodies. The extensive bruising around the cuts on Amber Martin's neck and trunk indicate three or four strikes with an axe before the carving knife was used to cut the throat. It is unlikely that she ever regained consciousness. In Mrs Gwen Martin's case, however, the lacerations to her hands and forearms, inflicted before death, are consistent with her regaining consciousness and trying to defend herself. Two stabbing incisions below the jawline imply two failed attempts before her throat was successfully cut with the knife. These attacks were carried out with savage ferocity.

Roz read the pages through then put them on the table beside her and stared into the middle distance. She felt very cold. *Olive Martin took an axe* . . . Oh, God! No wonder Mr Crew called her a psychopath. Three or four strikes with a blunted axe and Amber was still alive! Bile rose in her throat, nauseous, bitter, gagging. *She must stop thinking about it.* But she couldn't, of course. The muffled thuds of metal bouncing off soft flesh boomed loudly in her brain.

How dark and shadowy the flat was. She reached out abruptly and snapped on a table lamp but the light did nothing to dispel the vivid pictures that crowded her imagination, nightmare visions of a madwoman, frenzied by blood-lust. And the bodies . . .

How far had she committed herself to writing this book? Had she signed anything? Had she received an advance. She couldn't remember and a cold fist of panic squeezed her insides. She was living in a twilight world where so little mattered that day followed day with nothing to distinguish their passing. She thrust herself out of her chair and paced about the floor, cursing Iris for bouncing her, cursing herself for her own insanity, and cursing Mr Crew for not sending her the statement when she'd first written to him.

She seized the telephone and dialled Iris's number. 'Have I signed anything on the Olive Martin book? Why? Because I damn well can't write it, that's why. The woman scares the bloody shit out of me and I am not visiting her again.'

'I thought you liked her.' Iris spoke calmly through a mouthful of supper.

Roz ignored this comment. 'I've got her statement here and the pathologist's report, or his conclusions at least. I should have read them first. I'm not doing it. I will not glorify what she did by writing a book about it. My God, Iris, they were alive when she cut their heads off. Her poor wretched mother tried to ward off the axe. It's making me sick just thinking about it.'

'OK.'

'OK what?'

'Don't write it.'

Roz's eyes narrowed suspiciously. 'I thought you'd argue at least.'

'Why? One thing I've learnt in this business is that you can't force people to write. Correction. You can if you're persistent and manipulative enough, but the result is always below par.' Roz heard her take a drink. 'In any case, Jenny Atherton sent me the first ten chapters of her new book this morning. It's all good stuff on the inherent dangers of a poor self-image, with obesity as number one confidence crippler. She's unearthed a positive goldmine of film and television personalities who've all sunk to untold depths since gaining weight and being forced off camera. It's disgustingly tasteless, of course, like all Jenny's books, but it'll sell. I think you should send all your gen – sorry about the pun – to her. Olive would make rather a dramatic conclusion, don't you think, particularly if we can get a photograph of her in her cell.'

'No chance.'

'No chance of getting a photograph? Shame.'

'No chance of my sending anything to Jenny Atherton. Honestly, Iris,' she stormed, losing her temper, 'you really are beneath contempt. You should be working for the gutter press. You believe in exploiting anyone just as long as they bring in the cash. Jenny Atherton is the last person I'd allow near Olive.'

'Can't see why,' said Iris, now chewing heartily on something. 'I mean if you don't want to write about her and you're refusing ever to visit her again because she makes you sick, why cavil at somebody else having a bash?'

'It's the principle.'

'Can't see it, old thing. Sounds more like dog in the manger to me. Listen, I can't dally. We've got people in. At least let me tell Jenny that Olive's up for grabs. She can start from scratch. It's not as though you've got very far, is it?'

'I've changed my mind,' Roz snapped. 'I will do it. Goodbye.' She slammed the receiver down.

At the other end of the line, Iris winked at her husband. 'And you accuse me of not caring,' she murmured. 'Now, what could have been more caring than that?'

'Hobnailed boots,' Gerry Fielding suggested acidly.

Roz read Olive's statement again. 'My relationship with my mother and sister was never close.' She reached for her tape-recorder and rewound the tape, flicking to and fro till she found the piece she wanted. 'I called her Amber because, at the age of two, I couldn't get my tongue round the "*l*" or the "*s*". It suited her. She had lovely honey-blonde hair, and as she grew up she always answered to Amber and never to Alison. She was very pretty . . .'

It meant nothing of course, in itself. There was no unwritten law that said psychopaths were incapable of pretending. Rather the reverse, in fact. But there was a definite softening of the voice when she spoke about her sister, a tenderness which from anyone else Roz would have interpreted as love. And why hadn't she mentioned the fight with her mother? Really, that was very odd. It could well have been her justification for what she did that day.

The chaplain, quite unaware that Olive was behind him, started violently as a large hand fell on his shoulder. It wasn't the first time she had crept up on him and he wondered again, as he had wondered before, how she managed to do it. Her normal gait was a painful shuffle which set his teeth on edge every time he heard its approach. He steeled himself and turned with a friendly smile. 'Why, Olive, how nice to see you. What brings you to the chapel?'

The bald eyes were amused. 'Did I frighten you?'

'You startled me. I didn't hear you coming.'

'Probably because you weren't listening. You must listen first if you want to hear, Chaplain. Surely they taught you that much at theological college. God talks in a whisper at the best of times.'

It would be easier, he thought sometimes, if he

could despise Olive. But he had never been able to. He feared and disliked her but he did not despise her. 'What can I do for you?'

'You had some new diaries delivered this morning. I'd like one.'

'Are you sure, Olive? These are no different from the others. They still have a religious text for every day of the year and last time I gave you one you tore it up.'

She shrugged. 'But I need a diary so I'm prepared to tolerate the little homilies.'

'They're in the vestry.'

'I know.'

She had not come for a diary. That much he could guess. But what did she plan to steal from the chapel while his back was turned? What *was* there to steal except Bibles and prayer books?

A candle, he told the Governor afterwards. Olive Martin took a six-inch candle from the altar. But she, of course, denied it, and though her cell was searched from top to bottom, the candle was never found.

Three

GRAHAM DEEDES WAS young, harassed, and black. He saw Roz's surprise as she came into his room, and he frowned his irritation. 'I had no idea black barristers were such a rarity, Miss Leigh.'

'Why do you say that?' she asked curiously, sitting down in the chair he indicated.

'You looked surprised.'

'I am, but not by your colour. You're much younger than I expected.'

'Thirty-three,' he said. 'Not so young.'

'No, but when you were briefed to appear for Olive Martin you can only have been twenty-six or twenty-seven. That *is* young for a murder trial.'

'True,' he agreed, 'but I was only the junior. The QC was considerably older.'

'But you did most of the preparation?'

He nodded. 'Such as there was. It was a very unusual case.'

She took her tape-recorder from her bag. 'Have you any objections to being recorded?'

'Not if you intend to talk about Olive Martin.'

'I do.'

He chuckled. 'Then I've no objections, for the simple reason that I can tell you virtually nothing about her. I saw the woman once, on the day she was sentenced, and I never even spoke to her.'

'But I understood you were preparing a diminished responsibility defence. Didn't you meet her in the course of doing that?'

'No, she refused to see me. I did all my work from material her solicitor sent me.' He smiled ruefully. 'Which wasn't much, I have to say. We would, quite literally, have been laughed out of court if we'd had to proceed, so I was quite relieved when the judge ruled her guilty plea admissible.'

'What arguments would you have used if you had been called?'

'We planned two different approaches.' Deedes considered for a moment. 'One, that the balance of her mind was temporarily disturbed – as far as I recall it was the day after her birthday and she was deeply upset because instead of paying her attention the family teased her about being fat.' He raised his eyebrows in query and Roz nodded. 'In addition, I believe, she made a reference in her statement to not liking noise. We did manage to find a doctor who was prepared to give evidence that noise can cause such violent distress in some people that they may act out of character in trying to stop it. There was no psychiatric or medical evidence, however, to prove that Olive was of this type.' He tapped his forefingers together. 'Two, we were going to work backwards from the appalling savagery of the crime and invite the court to draw what we hoped to persuade them was an inescapable inference – that Olive was a psychopath. We hadn't a cat's chance on the balance of her mind argument, but the psychopathy' – he made a see-saw motion with one hand – 'maybe. We found a professor of psychology who was prepared to stick his neck out after seeing the photographs of the bodies.'

'But did he ever *talk* to her?'

He shook his head. 'There wasn't time and she wouldn't have seen him anyway. She was quite determined to plead guilty. I assume Mr Crew told you that she wrote to the Home Office demanding an independent psychiatric report to prove that she was competent to plead?' Roz nodded. 'After that there was really nothing we could do. It was an extraordinary business,' he mused. 'Most defendants fall over themselves to come up with excuses.'

'Mr Crew seems convinced she's a psychopath.'

'I think I'd agree with him.'

'Because of what she did to Amber and her mother? You don't have any other evidence?'

'No. Isn't that enough?'

'Then how do you explain that five psychiatrists

have all diagnosed her normal?' Roz looked up. 'She's had several sessions, as far as I can gather, in the prison.'

'Who told you this? Olive?' He looked sceptical.

'Yes, but I spoke to the Governor afterwards and she verified it.'

He shrugged. 'I wouldn't place too much reliance on it. You'd have to see the reports. It depends who wrote them and why they were testing her.'

'Still, it's odd, don't you think?'

'In what way?'

'You'd expect some measurable level of sociopathic behaviour over a period of time if she was a psychopath.'

'Not necessarily. Prison may be the sort of controlled environment that suits her. Or perhaps her particular psychopathy was directed against her family. Something brought it on that day and once rid of them, she settled down.' He shrugged again. 'Who knows? Psychiatry is hardly an exact science.' He was silent for a moment. 'In my experience, well-adjusted people don't hack their mothers and their sisters to death. You do know they were still alive when she set to with the axe?' He smiled grimly. 'She knew it, too. Don't imagine she didn't.'

Roz frowned. 'There is another explanation,' she said slowly, 'but the trouble is, while it fits the facts, it's too absurd to be credible.'

He waited. 'Well?' he asked at last.

'Olive didn't do it.' She saw his amused disbelief and hurried on. 'I'm not saying I go along with it, I'm just saying that it fits the facts.'

'*Your* facts,' he pointed out gently. 'It seems to me you're being a little selective in what you choose to believe.'

'Maybe.' Roz remembered her extremes of mood of the previous evening.

He watched her for a moment. 'She knew a great deal about the murders for someone who wasn't responsible for them.'

'Do you think so?'

'Of course. Don't you?'

'She doesn't say anything about her mother trying to ward off the axe and the carving knife. But that must have been the most frightening part. Why didn't she mention it?'

'Shame. Embarrassment. Traumatic amnesia. You'd be surprised how many murderers blot what they've done from their memories. Sometimes it's years before they come to terms with their guilt. In any case, I doubt the struggle with her mother was as frightening for Olive as you suggest. Gwen Martin was a tiny woman, five feet at the most, I would think. Physically, Olive took after her father, so containing her mother would have been easy for her.' He saw the hesitation in Roz's eyes. 'Let me put a question to *you*. Why would Olive confess to two murders she didn't commit?'

'Because people do.'

'Not when they have their lawyers present, Miss Leigh. I accept that it happened, which is why new rules were introduced governing the taking of evidence, but Olive did not fall into the category of either forced confession or having her confession subsequently tampered with. She had legal representation throughout. So I repeat, why would she confess to something she didn't do?'

'To protect someone else?' She was relieved they weren't in court. He was a bruising cross-examiner.

'Who?'

She shook her head. 'I don't know.'

'There was no one else except her father, and he was at work. The police had him thoroughly checked and his alibi was unbreakable.'

'There was Olive's lover.'

He stared at her.

'She told me she'd had an abortion. Presumably, then, she must have had a lover.'

He found that very entertaining. 'Poor Olive.' He laughed. 'Well, I guess an abortion is as good a way as any of keeping her end up. Especially' – he laughed again – 'if everyone believes her. I shouldn't be too gullible, if I were you.'

She smiled coldly. 'Perhaps it's you who is being gullible by subscribing to the cheap male view that a woman like Olive could not attract a lover.'

Deedes studied her set face and wondered what

was driving her. 'You're right, Miss Leigh, it was cheap, and I apologise.' He raised his hands briefly, then dropped them again. 'But this is the first I have heard about an abortion. Let's just say it strikes me as a little unlikely. And somewhat convenient, perhaps? It's not something you can ever really check, is it, not without Olive's permission. If laymen were allowed to browse through other people's medical records some very delicate secrets might be exposed.'

Roz regretted her waspish remark. Deedes was a nicer man than Crew and hadn't deserved it. 'Olive mentioned an abortion. *I* assumed the lover. But perhaps she was raped. Babies can be conceived as easily in hate as in love.'

He shrugged. 'Beware of being used, Miss Leigh. Olive Martin dominated the court the day she appeared in it. I had the impression then, and still have it, that it was *we* who were dancing to *her* tune not she to ours.'

Dawlington was a small eastern suburb of Southampton, once an isolated village, now swallowed up in the great urban expansion of the twentieth century. It maintained an identity of a sort by the busy trunk-roads that gave it tarmac boundaries but, even so, the place was easy to miss. Only a tired peeling shop sign, advertising *Dawlington Newsagents*, alerted Roz to the fact that she had left one suburb and entered another. She drew into the kerb before a left-hand turning and consulted her map. She was, presumably, in the High Street and the road to the left – she squinted at the sign – was Ainsley Street. She ran her finger across the grid. 'Ainsley Street,' she muttered. 'Come on, you bugger, where are you? OK. Leven Road. First right, second left.' With a glance in her driving mirror, she pulled out into the traffic and turned right.

Olive's story, she thought, grew odder by the minute, as she studied number twenty-two, Leven Road, from her parked car. Mr Crew had said the house was unsaleable. She had imagined something out of a Gothic novel, twelve months of dereliction and decay since the death of Robert Martin, a house condemned by the haunting horror in its kitchen. Instead, the reality was a cheerful little semi, freshly painted, with pink, white, and red geraniums nodding in boxes beneath its windows. Who, she wondered, had bought it? Who was brave enough (or ghoulish enough?) to live with the ghosts of that tragic family? She double-checked the address from press cuttings she had put together that morning in the archives basement of the local newspaper. There was no mistake. A black and white photograph of 'The House of Horror' showed this same neat semi, but without its window-boxes.

She climbed out of the car and crossed the road. The house remained stubbornly silent to her ring on the doorbell, so she went next door and tried there. A young woman answered with a sleepy toddler clinging round her neck. 'Yes?'

'Hello,' said Roz, 'I'm sorry to bother you.' She indicated towards her right. 'It's your neighbours I really want to talk to but there's no one in. Have you any idea when they might be back?'

The young woman thrust out a hip to support the child more easily and subjected Roz to a penetrating glare. 'There's nothing to see, you know. You're wasting your time.'

'I'm sorry?'

'They pulled the innards out of the house and revamped the whole of the inside. They've done it up nice. There's nothing to see, no blood stains, no spirits roaming about, nothing.' She pressed the child's head against her shoulder, a casual, proprietary gesture, a statement of tender motherhood at odds with the hostility in her voice. 'You want to know what I think? You should see a psychiatrist. It's the likes of you who're the real sick people of society.' She prepared to close the door.

Roz raised her palms in a gesture of surrender. She smiled sheepishly. 'I haven't come to gawp,' she said. 'My name is Rosalind Leigh and I'm working in co-operation with the late Mr Martin's solicitor.'

The woman eyed her suspiciously. 'Oh, yeah? What's his name?'

'Peter Crew.'

'You could of got it from the paper.'

'I have a letter from him. May I show it to you? It will prove I am who I say I am.'

'Go on then.'

'It's in the car. I'll fetch it.' She retrieved her brief-case hurriedly from the boot, but when she got back, the door was closed. She rang several times and waited for ten minutes on the doorstep, but it was obvious the young woman had no intention of answering. From a room above came the wail of a baby. Roz listened to the mother's soothing tones as she climbed the stairs, then, thoroughly annoyed with herself, she retreated to the car and pondered her next step.

The press cuttings were disappointing. It was names she wanted, names of friends or neighbours, even old school teachers, who could give her back-ground detail. But the local newspaper had, like the nationals, sensationalized the crime's horror without uncovering any details about Olive's life or why she might have done it. There were the usual quotes from 'neighbours' – all anonymous and all wise after the event – but they were so uniformly unenlightening that Roz suspected imaginative journalism at work.

> 'No, I'm not surprised,' said a neighbour, 'shocked and appalled, yes, but not surprised. She was a strange girl, unfriendly, kept herself to herself. Not like the sister. She was the attractive, outgoing one. We all liked Amber.' 'The parents found her very

difficult. She wouldn't mix or make friends. She was shy, I suppose, because of her size but she had a way of looking at you that wasn't normal.'

Beyond the sensationalism, there had been nothing to write about. There was no police investigation to report – Olive had phoned them herself, had confessed to the crime in the presence of her solicitor, and had been charged with murder. Because she had pleaded guilty there had been no salacious details from a lengthy trial, no names of friends or associates to draw on, and her sentencing had rated a single paragraph under the headline: twenty-five years for brutal murders. A conspiracy of journalistic apathy seemed to surround the whole event. Of the five cardinal Ws of the journalist's creed – Where?, When?, What?, Who?, and Why? – the first four had been amply covered. Everyone knew what had happened, who had done it, where, and when. But no one, it seemed, knew why. Nor, and this was the real puzzle, had anyone actually asked. Could teasing alone really drive a young woman to such a pitch of anger that she would hack her family to pieces?

With a sigh, Roz switched on the radio and fed Pavarotti into the tape-deck. Bad choice, she thought, as 'Nessun Dorma' flooded the car and brought back bitter memories of a summer she would rather forget. Strange how a piece of music could be so evocative, but then the path to separation had been choreographed around the television screen with 'Nessun Dorma' triggering the stops and starts of their rows. She could remember every detail of every World Cup football match. They were the only peaceful periods in a summer of war. How much better, she thought wearily, if she had called a halt then instead of dragging the misery out to its far more terrible conclusion.

A net curtain, in the semi to the right, number 24, twitched behind a Neighbourhood Watch sticker which proclaimed itself loudly against the glass. A case, Roz wondered, of locking the stable door after the horse had bolted? Or was that same net curtain twitching the day Olive wielded her chopper? Two garages filled the gap between the houses, but it was possible the occupants had heard something. '*Olive Martin took an axe and gave her mother forty whacks . . .*' The words circled in her brain as they had done, on and off, for days.

She resumed her contemplation of number 22, but watched the net curtain out of the corner of her eye. It moved again, plucked by prying fingers, and she felt unreasonably irritated by the busybody spying on her. It was an empty, wasted life that had time to stand and stare. What sort of interfering old bitch inhabited there, she wondered? The frustrated spinster who got off on voyeurism? Or the bored and boring wife with nothing better to do than find fault? Then something clicked inside her head, a realignment of thought like the points on a railway line. Just the sort of busybody she wanted, of course, but why had that not occurred to her immediately? Really, she worried about herself. She spent so much time in neutral now, just listening to the footfalls, leading nowhere, that echoed in her memory.

A frail old man opened the door, a small, shrunken person with transparent skin and bowed shoulders. 'Come in, come in,' he said, standing back and ushering her into his corridor. 'I heard what you said to Mrs Blair. She won't talk to you, and I'll tell you something else, it wouldn't help you if she did. They only came four years ago when the first youngster was on the way. Didn't know the family at all and, as far as I know, never spoke to poor old Bob. What shall I say? She's got a nerve. Typical of today's youngsters. Always wanting something for nothing.' He muttered on, leading the way into his living room. 'Resents living in a goldfish bowl but forgets that they got the house for a pittance just because it *was* a goldfish bowl. Ted and Dorothy Clarke virtually gave the place away because they couldn't stand it any longer. What shall I say? Ungrateful girl. Imagine what it's like for those of us who've always lived here. No bargains for us. We have to put up with it, don't we? Sit down. Sit down.'

'Thank you.'

'You're from Mr Crew, you say. They found the child yet?' He stared into her face with disconcertingly bright blue eyes.

Roz stared back, her mind racing. 'That's not my province,' she said carefully, 'so I'm not sure where they are on that one. I'm conducting a follow-up of Olive's case. You did know that Mr Crew is still representing her?'

'What's to represent?' he asked. His eyes strayed in disappointment. 'Poor little Amber. They should never have made her give it up. I said it would cause trouble.'

Roz sat very still and stared at the worn carpet.

'People don't listen, of course,' he said crossly. 'You give them well-meant advice and they tell you you're interfering. What shall I say? I could see where it would lead.' He fell into a resentful silence.

'You're talking about the child,' said Roz at last.

He looked at her curiously. 'If they'd found him, you'd know.'

It was a boy, then. 'Oh, yes.'

'Bob did his best but there's rules about these things. They'd signed him away, given up their stake, so to speak. You'd think it was different where money's concerned, but there's no contest for the likes of us against the government. What shall I say? They're all thieves.'

Roz made what she could of this speech. Was he talking about Mr Martin's will? Was this child

(Amber's child?) the beneficiary? On the pretext of looking for a handkerchief, she opened her bag and surreptitiously switched on her tape-recorder. This conversation, she felt, was going to be tortuous. 'You mean,' she tried tentatively, 'that the government will get the money?'

'Course.'

She nodded wisely. 'Things aren't exactly stacked in our favour.'

'Never are. Damn thieves. Take every last penny off you. And what for? To make sure the skivers go on breeding like rabbits at the expense of the rest of us. Makes you sick. There's a woman in the council houses has five children, and all by different fathers. What shall I say? They're all worthless. Is that the sort of breeding stock we want in this country? Good-for-nothings, with not a brain between them. Where's the sense in encouraging a woman like that? Should have sterilized her and put a stop to it.'

Roz was noncommittal, unwilling to be drawn down a cul-de-sac, even more unwilling to antagonize him. 'I'm sure you're right.'

'Course I'm right, and it'll be the death of the species. Before the dole, she'd have starved to death and her brood with her, and quite right too. What shall I say? It's the survival of the fittest in this world. There's no other species mollycoddles its rotten apples the way we do, and certainly none that pays its rotten apples to produce more rotten apples. Makes you sick. How many children have you got?'

Roz smiled faintly. 'None, I'm afraid. I'm not married.'

'See what I mean?' He cleared his throat noisily. 'Makes you sick. What shall I say? It's your sort, decent sort, should have the children.'

'How many do you have, Mr – er—?' She made a play of consulting her diary, as if looking for his name.

'Hayes. Mr Hayes. Two lads. Fine boys. Grown up now, of course. Only the one granddaughter,' he added morosely. 'It's not right. I keep telling them they've a duty to their class but I could be pissing in the wind – excuse my French – for all the good it does.' His face set into familiar lines of irritation. His obsession was clearly a deep-seated one.

Roz knew she had to take the plunge or one hobby horse would follow another as inexorably as night follows day. 'You're a very perceptive man, Mr Hayes. Why were you so sure that making Amber give up her son would cause trouble?'

'Stands to reason there'd come a time when he was wanted again. It's sod's law, isn't it? The minute you throw something out, that's the minute you find you needed it after all. But it's too late by then. It's gone. My wife was one, forever throwing things away, pots of paint, carpet, and two years later you needed to patch. Me, I hoard. What shall I say? I value everything.'

'So, are you saying Mr Martin wasn't bothered about his grandson before the murders?'

He touched the end of his nose with thumb and forefinger. 'Who's to say? He kept his own counsel, did Bob. It was Gwen who insisted on signing the kid away. Wouldn't have it in the house. Understandable, I suppose, in view of Amber's age.'

'How old was she?'

He frowned. 'I thought Mr Crew knew all this.'

She smiled. 'He does but, as I told you, it's not my province. I'm just interested, that's all. It seems so tragic.'

'It is that. Thirteen,' he said wistfully. 'She was thirteen. Poor little kid. Didn't know anything about anything. Some lout at the school was responsible.' He jerked his head towards the back of his house. 'Parkway Comprehensive.'

'Is that the school Amber and Olive went to?'

'Hah!' His old eyes were amused. 'Gwen wouldn't have stood for that. She sent them to the posh Convent where they learnt their times tables and didn't learn the facts of life.'

'Why didn't Amber have an abortion? Were they Catholics?' She thought again about Olive and foetuses being washed down the sink.

'They didn't know she was pregnant, did they? Thought it was puppy fat.' He cackled suddenly. 'Rushed her off to hospital with suspected appendicitis and out pops a bouncing baby boy. They got away with it, too. Best kept secret I've ever come across. Even the nuns didn't know.'

'But you knew,' she prompted.

'The wife guessed,' he said owlishly. 'It was obvious something untoward had happened, and not appendicitis neither. Gwen was well-nigh hysterical the night it happened and my Jeannie put two and two together. Still, we know how to keep our mouths shut. No reason to make life harder for the kid. It wasn't her fault.'

Roz did some rapid mental arithmetic. Amber was two years younger than Olive which would have made her twenty-six if she were still alive. 'Her son's thirteen,' she said, 'and due to inherit half a million pounds. I wonder why Mr Crew can't find him. There must be records of the adoption.'

'I heard they'd found traces.' The old man clicked his false teeth with disappointment. 'But, there, it was probably just rumour, Brown Australia,' he muttered with disgust, as if that explained everything. 'I ask you.'

Roz allowed this cryptic remark to pass unchallenged. Time enough to puzzle over it later without claiming ignorance yet again. 'Tell me about Olive,' she invited. 'Were you surprised that she did what she did?'

'I hardly knew the girl.' He sucked his teeth. 'And you don't feel surprised when people you know get hacked to death, young lady, you feel bloody sick. It did for my Jeannie. She was never the same afterwards, died a couple of years later.'

'I'm sorry.'

He nodded, but it was clearly an old wound that had healed. 'Used to see the child come and go but she wasn't a great talker. Shy, I suppose.'

'Because she was fat?'

He pursed his lips thoughtfully. 'Maybe. Jeannie said she was teased a lot, but I've known fat girls who've been the life and soul of the party. It was her nature, I think, to look on the black side. Never laughed much. No sense of humour. That sort doesn't make friends easily.'

'And Amber did?'

'Oh, yes. She was very popular.' He glanced back down the passages of time. 'She was a pretty girl.'

'Was Olive jealous of her?'

'Jealous?' Mr Hayes looked surprised. 'I've never thought about it. What shall I say? They always seemed very fond of each other.'

Roz shrugged her bewilderment. 'Then why did Olive kill her? And why mutilate the bodies? It's very odd.'

He scowled suspiciously. 'I thought you were representing her. You should know if anyone does.'

'She won't say.'

He stared out of the window. 'Well, then.'

Well then what? 'Do you know why?'

'Jeannie reckoned it was hormones.'

'Hormones?' Roz echoed blankly. 'What sort of hormones?'

'You know.' He looked embarrassed. 'Monthly ones.'

'Ah.' PMT? she wondered. But it was hardly a subject she could pursue with him. He was of a generation where menstruation was never mentioned. 'Did Mr Martin ever say why he thought she did it?'

He shook his head. 'The subject didn't arise. What shall I say? We saw very little of him afterwards. He talked about his will once or twice, and the child – it was all he thought about.' He cleared his throat again. 'He became a recluse, you know. Wouldn't have anyone in the house, not even the Clarkes, and there was a time when Ted and he were close as brothers.' His mouth turned down at the corners. 'It was Ted started it, mind. Took against Bob for some reason and wouldn't go in. And others followed suit, of course, the way they do. Reckon I was his only friend at the end. It was me as realized something was wrong, seeing the milk bottles outside.'

'But why did he stay? He was rich enough to let number twenty-two go for peanuts. You'd have thought he'd go anywhere rather than stay with the ghosts of his family.'

Mr Hayes muttered to himself. 'Never understood it myself. Perhaps he wanted his friends about him.'

'You said the Clarkes moved. Where did they go?'

He shook his head. 'No idea. They upped and went

one morning without a word to anyone. A removal van took out their furniture three days later and the house stood empty for a year till the Blairs bought it. Never heard a word from them since. No forwarding address. Nothing. What shall I say? We were good friends, the six of us, and I'm the only one left now. Strange business.'

Very strange, thought Roz. 'Can you remember which estate agent sold the house?'

'Peterson's, but you won't learn anything from them. Little Hitlers,' he said, 'all bursting with self-importance. Told me to mind my own business when I went in and asked what was what. It's a free world, I pointed out, no reason why a man shouldn't ask after his friends, but oh, no, they had instructions of confidentiality or some such rubbish. What shall I say? Made out it was me the Clarkes were cutting their ties with. Hah! More likely Bob, I told them, or ghosts. And they said if I spread those sort of rumours, they'd take action. You know who I blame. The estate agents' federation, if there is one, which I doubt . . .' He rambled on, venting his spleen out of loneliness and frustration.

Roz felt sorry for him. 'Do you see much of your sons?' she asked when he drew to a halt.

'Now and then.'

'How old are they?'

'Forties,' he said after a moment's thought.

'What did they think of Olive and Amber?'

He pinched his nose again and waggled it from side to side. 'Never knew them. Left home long before either of the girls reached their teens.'

'They didn't baby-sit or anything like that?'

'My lads? You wouldn't catch them baby-sitting.' His old eyes moistened, and he nodded towards the sideboard where photographs of two young men in uniform crowded the surface. 'Fine boys. Soldiers.' He thrust out his chest. 'Took my advice and joined up. Mind, they're out of jobs now, what with the bloomin' regiment being cut from under them. It makes you sick when you think them and me's served Queen and country for nigh on fifty years between us. Did I tell you I was in the desert during the war?' He looked vacantly about the room. 'There's a photograph somewhere of Churchill and Monty in a jeep. We all got one, us boys who were out there. Worth a bob or two, I should think. Now where is it?' He became agitated.

Roz picked up her briefcase. 'Don't worry about it now, Mr Hayes. Perhaps I could see it next time I come.'

'You coming back?'

'I'd like to, if it's no trouble.' She took a card from her handbag, flicking the switch on the recorder at the same time. 'That's my name and telephone number. Rosalind Leigh. It's a London number but I'll be down here regularly over the next few weeks, so if you feel like a chat' – she smiled encouragingly and stood up – 'give me a ring.'

He regarded her with astonishment. 'A chat. Goodness me. A youngster like you has better things to do with her time.'

Too right, she thought, but I do need information. Her smile, like Mr Crew's, was false. 'I'll be seeing you then, Mr Hayes.'

He pushed himself awkwardly out of his chair and held out a marbled hand. 'It's been a pleasure meeting you, Miss Leigh. What shall I say? It's not often an old man sees charming young ladies out of the blue.'

He spoke with such sincerity that she felt chastened by her own lack of it. Why, oh why, she wondered, was the human condition so damn bloody?

Four

ROZ FOUND THE local convent with the help of a policeman. 'That'll be St Angela's,' he told her. 'Left at the traffic lights and left again. Large red-brick building set back from the road. You can't miss it. It's the only decent piece of architecture still standing round there.'

It reared in solid Victorian magnificence above its surrounding clutter of cheap concrete obsolescence, a monument to education in a way that none of the modern prefabricated schools could ever be. Roz entered the front door with a sense of familiarity, for this was a schooling she recognized. Glimpses through classroom doors of desks, blackboards, shelves of books, attentive girls in neat uniforms. A place of quiet learning, where parents could dictate the sort of education their daughters received simply by threatening to remove the pupils and withhold the fees. And whenever parents had that power the requirements were always the same: discipline, structure, results.

She peeped through a window into what was obviously the library. Well, well, no wonder Gwen had insisted on sending the girls here. Roz would put money on Parkway Comprehensive being an unruly bedlam where English, History, Religion and Geography were all taught as the single subject of General Studies, spelling was an anachronism, French an extra-curricular activity, Latin unheard of, and Science a series of chats about the greenhouse effect. . .

'Can I help you?'

She turned with a smile. 'I hope so.'

A smart woman in her late fifties had paused in front of a door marked Secretary. 'Are you a prospective parent?'

'I wish I were. It's a lovely school. No children,' she explained at the woman's look of puzzled enquiry.

'I see. So how can I help you?'

Roz took out one of her cards. 'Rosalind Leigh,' she introduced herself. 'Would it be possible for me to talk to the headmistress?'

'Now?' said the woman in surprise.

'Yes, if she's free. If not, I can make an appointment and come back later.'

The woman took the card and read it closely. 'May I ask what you want to talk about?'

Roz shrugged. 'Just some general information about the school and the sort of girls who come here.'

'Would you be the Rosalind Leigh who wrote *Through the Looking Glass* by any chance?'

Roz nodded. *Through the Looking Glass*, her last book and her best, had sold well and won some excellent reviews. A study of the changing perceptions of female beauty down the ages, she wondered now how she had ever managed to summon the energy to write it. A labour of love, she thought, because the subject had fascinated her.

'I've read it.' The other smiled. 'I agreed with very few of your conclusions but it was extremely thought-provoking none the less. You write lovely prose, but I'm sure you know that.'

Roz laughed. She felt an immediate liking for the woman. 'At least you're honest.'

The other looked at her watch. 'Come into my office. I have some parents to see in half an hour, but I'm happy to give you general information until then. This way.' She opened the secretary's door and ushered Roz through to an adjoining office. 'Sit down, do. Coffee?'

'Please.' Roz took the chair indicated and watched her busy herself with a kettle and some cups. 'Are you the headmistress?'

'I am.'

'They were always nuns in my day.'

'So you're a convent girl. I thought you might be. Milk?'

'Black and no sugar, please.'

She placed a steaming cup on the desk in front of Roz and sat down opposite her. 'In fact I am a nun.

Sister Bridget. My order gave up wearing the habit quite some time ago. We found it tended to create an artificial barrier between us and the rest of society.' She chuckled. 'I don't know what it is about religious uniforms, but people try to avoid you if they can. I suppose they feel they have to be on their best behaviour. It's very frustrating. The conversation is often so stilted.'

Roz crossed her legs and relaxed into the chair. She was unaware of it but her eyes betrayed her. They brimmed with all the warmth and humour that, a year ago, had been the outward expression of her personality. Bitterness, it seemed, could only corrode so far. 'It's probably guilt,' she said. 'We have to guard our tongues in case we provoke the sermon we know we deserve.' She sipped the coffee. 'What made you think I was a convent girl?'

'Your book. You get very hot under the collar about established religions. I guessed you were either a lapsed Jew or a lapsed Catholic. The Protestant yoke is easier to discard, being far less oppressive in the first place.'

'In fact I wasn't a lapsed anything when I wrote *Through the Looking Glass*,' said Roz mildly. 'I was a good Catholic still.'

Sister Bridget interpreted the cynicism in her voice. 'But not now.'

'No. God died on me.' She smiled slightly at the look of understanding on the other woman's face.

'You read about it, I suppose. I can't applaud your taste in newspapers.'

'I'm an educator, my dear. We take the tabloids here as well as the broadsheets.' She didn't drop her gaze or show embarrassment, for which Roz was grateful. 'Yes, I read about it and I would have punished God, too. It was very cruel of Him.'

Roz nodded. 'If I remember right,' she said, reverting to her book, 'religion is confined to only one chapter of my book. Why did you find my conclusions so hard to agree with?'

'Because they are all drawn from a single premiss. As I can't accept the premiss, then I can't agree with the conclusions.'

Roz wrinkled her brow. 'Which premiss?'

'That beauty is only skin deep.'

Roz was surprised. 'And you don't think that's true?'

'No, not as a general rule.'

'I'm speechless. And you a nun!'

'Being a nun has nothing to do with it. I'm streetwise.'

It was an unconscious echo of Olive. 'You really believe that beautiful people are beautiful all the way through? I can't accept that. By the same token ugly people are ugly all the way through.'

'You're putting words into my mouth, my dear.' Sister Bridget was amused. 'I am simply questioning the idea that beauty is a surface quality.' She cradled her coffee cup in her hands. 'It's a comfortable thought, of course – it means we can all feel good about ourselves – but beauty, like wealth, is a moral asset. The wealthy can afford to be law abiding, generous and kind. The very poor cannot. Even kindness is a struggle when you don't know where your next penny is coming from.' She gave a quirky smile. 'Poverty is only uplifting when you can choose it.'

'I wouldn't disagree with that, but I don't see the connection between beauty and wealth.'

'Beauty cushions you against the negative emotions that loneliness and rejection inspire. Beautiful people are prized – they always have been, you made that point yourself – so they have less reason to be spiteful, less reason to be jealous, less reason to covet what they can't have. They tend to be the focus of all those emotions, rarely the instigators of them.' She shrugged. 'You will always have exceptions – most of them you uncovered in your book – but, in my experience, if a person is attractive then that attractiveness runs deep. You can argue which comes first, the inner beauty or the outer, but they do tend to walk together.'

'So if you're rich and beautiful the pearly gates will swing open for you?' She smiled cynically. 'That's a somewhat radical philosophy for a Christian, isn't it? I thought Jesus preached the exact opposite. Something like it's easier for a camel to pass through the eye of a needle than for a rich man to enter the kingdom of heaven.'

Sister Bridget laughed good-humouredly. 'Yours was obviously an excellent convent.' She stirred her coffee absent-mindedly with a biro. 'Yes, He did say that but, if you put it in context, it supports my view, I think, rather than detracts from it. If you remember, a wealthy young man asked Him how he could have eternal life. Jesus said: keep the commandments. The youth answered: I have kept them, since childhood, but what more can I do. If you want to be perfect, said Jesus – and I emphasize the *perfect* – sell all you have and give it to the poor, *then* follow me. The young man went away sorrowing because he had many possessions and could not bring himself to sell them. It was then Jesus made the reference to the camel and the eye of the needle. He was, you see, talking about perfection, not goodness.' She sucked the end of her biro. 'In fairness to the young man, I have always assumed that to sell his possessions would have meant selling houses and businesses with tenants and employees in them, so the moral dilemma would have been a difficult one. But what I think Jesus was saying was this: so far you have been a good man, but to test how good you really are, reduce yourself to abject poverty. Perfection is to follow me and keep the commandments when you are so poor that stealing and lying are a way of life if you want to be sure of waking up the next morning. An impossible goal.' She sipped her coffee. 'I could be wrong, of course.' There was a twinkle in her eye.

'Well, I'm not going to argue the toss with you on that,' said Roz bluntly. 'I suspect I'd be on a hiding to nothing. But I reckon you're on very bumpy ground with your beauty is a moral asset argument. What about the pitfalls of vanity and arrogance? And how do you explain that some of the nicest people I know are, by no stretch of the imagination, beautiful?'

Sister Bridget laughed again, a happy sound. 'You keep twisting my words. I have never said that to be nice you have to be beautiful. I merely dispute your assertion that beautiful people are *not* nice. My observation is that very often they are. At the risk of labouring the point, they can afford to be.'

'Then we're back to my previous question. Does that mean ugly people are very often not nice?'

'It doesn't follow, you know, any more than saying poor people are invariably wicked. It just means the tests are harder.' She cocked her head on one side. 'Take Olive and Amber as a case in point. After all, that's why you've really come to see me. Amber led a charmed life. She was quite the loveliest child I've ever seen and with a nature to match. Everyone adored her. Olive, on the other hand, was universally unpopular. She had few redeeming features. She was greedy, deceitful, and often cruel. I found her very hard to like.'

Roz made no attempt to deny her interest. The

conversation had, in any case, been about them from the beginning. 'Then you were being tested as much as she was. Did you fail? Was it impossible to like her?'

'It was very difficult until Amber joined the school. Olive's best quality was that she loved her sister, without reserve and quite unselfishly. It was really rather touching. She fussed over Amber like a mother hen, often ignoring her own interests to promote Amber's. I've never seen such affection between sisters.'

'So why did she kill her?'

'Why indeed? It's time that question was asked.' The older woman drummed her fingers impatiently on the desk. 'I visit her when I can. She won't tell me, and the only explanation I can offer is that her love, which was obsessional, turned to a hate that was equally obsessional. Have you met Olive?'

Roz nodded.

'What did you make of her?'

'She's bright.'

'Yes, she is. She could have gone to university if only the then headmistress had managed to persuade her mother of the advantages. I was a lowly teacher in those days.' She sighed. 'But Mrs Martin was a decided woman, and Olive very much under her thumb. There was nothing we, as a school, could do to make her change her mind. The two girls left together, Olive with three good A-levels and Amber with four rather indifferent O-levels.' She sighed again. 'Poor Olive. She went to work as a cashier in a supermarket while Amber, I believe, tried her hand at hairdressing.'

'Which supermarket was it?'

'Pettit's in the High Street. But the place went out of business years ago. It's an off-licence now.'

'She was working at the local DHSS, wasn't she, at the time of the murders?'

'Yes and doing very well, I believe. Her mother pushed her into it, of course.' Sister Bridget reflected for a moment. 'Funnily enough, I bumped into Olive quite by chance just a week or so before the murders. I was pleased to see her. She looked' – she paused – 'happy. Yes, I think happy is exactly the word for it.'

Roz let the silence drift while she busied herself with her own thoughts. There was so much about this story that didn't make sense. 'Did she get on with her mother?' she asked at last.

'I don't know. I always had the impression she preferred her father. It was Mrs Martin who wore the trousers, of course. If there were choices to be made, it was invariably she who made them. She was very domineering, but I don't recall Olive voicing any antagonism towards her. She was a difficult woman to talk to. Very correct, always. She appeared to watch every word she said in case she gave herself away.' She shook her head. 'But I never did find out what it was that needed hiding.'

There was a knock on the connecting door and a

woman popped her head inside. 'Mr and Mrs Barker are waiting, Sister. Are you ready for them?'

'Two minutes, Betty.' She smiled at Roz. 'I'm sorry. I'm not sure I've been very helpful. Olive had one friend while she was here, not a friend as you or I would know it, but a girl with whom she talked rather more than she did with any of the others. Her married name is Wright – Geraldine Wright – and she lives in a village called Wooling about ten miles north of here. If she's willing to talk to you then I'm sure she can tell you more than I have. The name of her house is Oaktrees.'

Roz jotted down the details in her diary. 'Why do I have the feeling you were expecting me?'

'Olive showed me your letter the last time I saw her.'

Roz stood up, gathering her briefcase and handbag together. She regarded the other woman thoughtfully. 'It may be that the only book I can write is a cruel one.'

'I don't think so.'

'No, I don't think so either.' She paused by the door. 'I've enjoyed meeting you.'

'Come and see me again,' said Sister Bridget. 'I'd like to know how you get on.'

Roz nodded. 'I suppose there's no doubt that she did it?'

'I really don't know,' said the other woman slowly. 'I've wondered, of course. The whole thing is so shocking that it *is* hard to accept.' She seemed to come to a conclusion. 'Be very careful, my dear. The only certainty about Olive is that she lies about almost everything.'

Roz jotted down the name of the arresting officer from the press clippings and called in at the police station on her way back to London. 'I'm looking for a DS Hawksley,' she told the young constable behind the front desk. 'He was with this division in nineteen eighty-seven. Is he still here?'

He shook his head. 'Jacked it in, twelve – eighteen months ago.' He leaned his elbows on the counter and eyed her over with an approving glance. 'Will I do instead?'

Her lips curved involuntarily. 'Perhaps you can tell me where he went?'

'Sure. He opened a restaurant in Wenceslas Street. Lives in the flat above it.'

'And how do I find Wenceslas Street?'

'Well, now' – he rubbed his jaw thoughtfully – 'by far the easiest way is to hang around for half an hour till the end of my shift. I'll take you.'

She laughed. 'And what would your girlfriend say to that?'

'A ruddy mouthful. She's got a tongue like a chain-saw.' He winked. 'I won't tell her if you won't.'

'Sorry, sunshine. I'm shackled to a husband who

hates policemen only marginally less than he hates toy-boys.' Lies were always easier.

He grinned. 'Turn left out of the station and Wenceslas Street is about a mile down on the left. There's an empty shop on the corner. The Sergeant's restaurant is bang next door to it. It's called the Poacher.' He tapped his pencil on the desk. 'Are you planning to eat there?'

'No,' she said, 'it's purely business. I don't intend to hang around.'

He nodded approval. 'Wise woman. The Sergeant's not much of a cook. He'd have done better to stick with policing.'

She had to pass the restaurant to reach the London road. Rather reluctantly she pulled into its abandoned car park and climbed out of the car. She was tired, she hadn't planned on talking to Hawksley that day, and the young constable's light-hearted flirtation depressed her because it had left her cold.

The Poacher was an attractive red-brick building, set back from the road with the car park in front. Leaded bay windows curved out on either side of a solid oak door and wistaria, heavy with buds, grew in profusion across the whole façade. Like St Angela's Convent it was at odds with its surroundings. The shops on either side, both apparently empty, their windows a repository for advertising stickers, complemented each other in cheap post-war pragmatism but did nothing for the old faded beauty in their midst. Worse, a thoughtless council had allowed a previous owner to erect a two-storey extension behind the red-brick frontage, and it gloomed above the restaurant's tiled roof in dirty pebble-dashed concrete. An attempt had been made to divert the wistaria across the roof but, starved of sunlight by the jutting property to the right, the probing tendrils showed little enthusiasm for reaching up to veil the dreary elevation.

Roz pushed open the door and went inside. The place was dark and deserted. Empty tables in an empty room, she thought despondently. Like her. Like her life. She was on the point of calling out, but thought better of it. It was all so peaceful and she was in no hurry. She tiptoed across the floor and took a stool at a bar in the corner. A smell of cooking lingered on the air, garlicky, tempting, reminding her that she hadn't eaten all day. She waited a long time, unseen and unheard, a trespasser upon another's silence. She thought about leaving, unobtrusively, as she had come, but it was strangely restful and her head drooped against her hand. Depression, an all too constant companion, folded its arms around her again, and turned her mind, as it often did, to death. She would do it one day. Sleeping pills or the car. The car, always the car. Alone, at night, in the rain. So easy just to turn the wheel and find a peaceful oblivion. It would be justice of a sort. Her head hurt where the hate swelled and throbbed inside it. God, what a mess she had become. If only someone could lance her destructive anger and let the poison go. Was Iris right? Should she see a psychiatrist? Without warning, the terrible unhappiness burst like a flood inside her, threatening to spill out in tears.

'Oh, shit!' she muttered furiously, dashing at her eyes with the palms of her hands. She scrabbled in her bag for her car keys. 'Shit! Shit! And more bloody shit! Where the hell are you?'

A slight movement caught her attention and she lifted her head abruptly. A shadowy stranger leant against the back counter, quietly polishing a glass and watching her.

She blushed furiously and looked away. 'How long have you been there?' she demanded angrily.

'Long enough.'

She retrieved her keys from the inside of her diary and glared at him briefly. 'What's that supposed to mean?'

He shrugged. 'Long enough.'

'Yes, well, you're obviously not open yet, so I'll be on my way.' She pushed herself off the stool.

'Suit yourself,' he said with supreme indifference. 'I was just about to have a glass of wine. You can go or you can join me. I'm easy either way.' He turned his back on her and uncorked a bottle. The colour receded from her cheeks.

'Are you Sergeant Hawksley?'

He lifted the cork to his nose and sniffed it appreciatively. 'I was, once. Now I'm just plain Hal.' He turned round and poured the wine into two glasses. 'Who's asking?'

She opened her bag again. 'I've got a card somewhere.'

'A voice would do just as well.' He pushed one of the glasses towards her.

'Rosalind Leigh,' she said shortly, propping the card against the telephone on the bar.

She stared at him in the semi-darkness, her embarrassment temporarily forgotten. He was hardly a run of the mill restaurateur. If she had any sense, she thought, she would take to her heels now. He hadn't shaved and his dark suit hung in rumpled folds as if he'd slept in it. He had no tie and half the buttons on his shirt were missing, revealing a mass of tight black curls on his chest. A swelling contusion on his upper left cheek was rapidly closing the eye above it, and thick dried blood encrusted both nostrils. He raised his glass with an ironic smile. 'To your good health, Rosalind. Welcome to the Poacher.' There was a lilt to his voice, a touch of Geordie, tempered by long association with the South.

'It might be more sensible to drink to your good

health,' she said bluntly. 'You look as though you need it.'

'To us then. May we both get the better of whatever ails us.'

'Which, in your case, would appear to be a steam-roller.'

He fingered the spreading bruise. 'Not far off,' he agreed. 'And you? What ails you?'

'Nothing,' she said lightly. 'I'm fine.'

'Sure you are.' His dark eyes rested kindly on her for a moment. 'You're half alive and I'm half dead.' He drained his glass and filled it again. 'What did you want with Sergeant Hawksley?'

She glanced about the room. 'Shouldn't you be opening up?'

'What for?'

She shrugged. 'Customers.'

'Customers,' he echoed thoughtfully. 'Now there's a beautiful word.' He gave a ghost of a chuckle. 'They're an endangered species, or haven't you heard? The last time I saw a customer was three days ago, a skinny little runt with a rucksack on his back who was scratching about in search of a vegetarian omelette and decaffeinated coffee.' He fell silent.

'Depressing.'

'Yes.'

She eased herself on to the stool again. 'It's not your fault,' she said sympathetically. 'It's the recession. Everyone's going under. Your neighbours already have, by the look of it.' She gestured towards the door.

He reached up and flicked a switch at the side of the bar. Muted lamplight glowed around the walls, bringing a sparkle to the glasses on the tables. She looked at him with alarm. The contusion on his cheek was the least of his problems. Bright red blood was seeping from a scab above his ear and running down his neck. He seemed unaware of it. 'Who did you say you were?' His dark eyes searched hers for a moment then moved past her to search the room.

'Rosalind Leigh. I think I should call an ambulance,' she said helplessly. 'You're bleeding.'

She had a strange feeling of being outside herself, quite remote from this extraordinary situation. Who was this man? Not her responsibility, certainly. She was a simple bystander who had stumbled upon him by accident. 'I'll call your wife,' she said.

He gave a lop-sided grin. 'Why not? She always enjoyed a good laugh. Presumably she still does.' He reached for a tea-towel and held it to his head. 'Don't worry, I'm not going to die on you. Head wounds always look worse than they are. You're very beautiful. "From the east to western Ind, No jewel is like Rosalind." '

'It's Roz and I'd rather you didn't quote that,' she said sharply. 'It annoys me.'

He shrugged. '*As You Like It.*'

She sucked in an angry breath. 'I suppose you think that's original.'

'A tender nerve, I see. Who are we talking about?' He looked at her ring finger. 'Husband? Ex-husband? Boyfriend?'

She ignored him. 'Is there anyone else here? Someone in the kitchen? You should have that cut cleaned.' She wrinkled her nose. 'In fact you should have this *place* cleaned. It stinks of fish.' The smell, once noticed, was appalling.

'Are you always this rude?' he asked curiously. He rinsed the tea-towel under a tap and watched the blood run out of it. 'It's me,' he said matter of factly. 'I went for a ride on a ton of mackerel. Not a pleasant experience.' He gripped the edge of the small sink and stood staring into it, head lowered in exhaustion, like a bull before the *coup de grâce* of the matador.

'Are you all right?' Roz watched him with a perplexed frown creasing her forehead. She didn't know what to do. It wasn't her problem, she kept telling herself, but she couldn't just walk away from it. Supposing he passed out? 'Surely there's someone I can call,' she insisted. 'A friend. A neighbour. Where do you live?' But she knew that. In the flat above, the young policeman had said.

'Jesus, woman,' he growled, 'give it a rest, for Christ's sake.'

'I'm only trying to help.'

'Is that what you call it? It sounded more like

nagging to me.' He was alert suddenly, listening to something she couldn't hear.

'What's the matter?' she asked, alarmed by his expression.

'Did you lock the door after you?'

She stared at him. 'No. Of course I didn't.'

He dowsed the lights and padded across to the entrance door, almost invisible in the sudden darkness. She heard the sound of bolts being thrust home.

'Look—' she began, getting off her stool.

He loomed up beside her and put an arm around her shoulder and a finger to her lips. 'Quiet, woman.' He held her motionless.

'But—'

'Quiet!'

A car's headlamps swept across the windows, slicing the darkness with white light. The engine throbbed in neutral for a moment or two, then the gears engaged and the vehicle drove away. Roz tried to draw away but Hawksley's arm only gripped her more firmly. 'Not yet,' he whispered.

They stood in silent immobility among the tables, statues at a spectral feast. Roz shook herself free angrily. 'This is absolutely absurd,' she hissed. 'I don't know what on earth is going on but I'm not staying like this for the rest of the night. Who was in that car?'

'Customers,' he said regretfully.

'You're mad.'

He took her hand. 'Come on,' he whispered, 'we'll go upstairs.'

'We will not,' she said, snatching her hand away. 'My God, doesn't anyone think about anything except screwing these days.'

Amused laughter fanned her face. 'Who said anything about screwing?'

'I'm going.'

'I'll see you out.'

She took a deep breath. 'Why do you want to go upstairs?'

'My flat's up there and I need a bath.'

'So what do you want me for?'

He sighed. 'If you remember, Rosalind, it was you who came in here asking for me. I've never met a woman who was so damn prickly.'

'Prickly!' she stuttered. 'My God, that's rich. You stink to high heaven, you've obviously been in a fight, you plunge us into total darkness, moan about not having any customers and then turn them away when they do come, make me sit for five minutes without moving, try to manhandle me upstairs . . .' She paused for breath. 'I think I'm going to be sick,' she blurted out.

'Oh, great! That's all I need.' He took her hand again. 'Come on. I'm not going to rape you. To tell you the truth I haven't the strength at the moment. What's wrong?'

She stumbled after him. 'I haven't eaten all day.'

'Join the club.' He led her through the darkened kitchen and unlocked a side door, reaching past her to switch on some lights. 'Up the stairs,' he told her, 'and the bathroom's on the right.'

She could hear him double-locking the door behind her as she collapsed on the lavatory seat and pressed her head between her knees, waiting for the waves of nausea to pass.

The light came on. 'Here. Drink this. It's water.' Hawksley squatted on the floor in front of her and looked into her white face. She had skin like creamy alabaster and eyes as dark as sloes. A very cold beauty, he thought. 'Do you want to talk about it?'

'What?'

'Whatever's making you so unhappy.'

She sipped the water. 'I'm not unhappy. I'm hungry.'

He put his hands on his knees and pushed himself upright. 'OK. Let's eat. How does sirloin steak sound?'

She smiled weakly. 'Wonderful.'

'Thank God for that! I've got a freezer full of the flaming stuff. How do you like it?'

'Rare but—'

'But what?'

She pulled a face. 'I think it's the smell that's making me sick.' She put her hands to her mouth. 'I'm sorry but I really think it would be better if you got cleaned up first. Mackerel-flavoured sirloin doesn't appeal over much.'

He sniffed at his sleeve. 'You don't notice it after a while.' He turned the taps on full and emptied bath foam into the running water. 'There's only the one loo, I'm afraid, so if you're going to puke you'd better stay there.' He started to undress.

She stood up hurriedly. 'I'll wait outside.'

He dropped his jacket on to the floor and unbuttoned his shirt. 'Just don't be sick all over my carpets,' he called after her. 'There's a sink in the kitchen. Use that.' He was easing the shirt carefully off his shoulders, unaware that she was still behind him, and she stared in horror at the blackened scabs all over his back.

'What happened to you?'

He pulled the shirt back on. 'Nothing. Scoot. Make yourself a sandwich. There's bread on the side and cheese in the fridge.' He saw her expression. 'It looks worse than it is,' he said prosaically. 'Bruising always does.'

'What happened?'

He held her gaze. 'Let's just say I fell off my bike.'

With a contemptuous smile, Olive extracted the candle from its hiding place. They had given up body searches after a woman haemorrhaged in front of one of the Board of Visitors following a particularly aggressive probing of her vagina for illicit drugs. The Visitor had been a MAN. (Olive always thought of men in capital letters.) No woman would have fallen for it. But MEN, of course, were different. Menstruation disturbed them, particularly if the blood flowed freely enough to stain the woman's clothes.

The candle was soft from the warmth of her body and she pulled off the end and began to mould it. Her memory was good. She had no doubt of her ability to imbue the tiny figure with a distinct individuality. This one would be a MAN.

Roz, preparing sandwiches in the kitchen, looked towards the bathroom door. The prospect of questioning Hawksley about the Olive Martin case unnerved her suddenly. Crew had become very annoyed when she questioned *him*; and Crew was a civilized man – in so far as he did not look as if he'd spent half an hour in a dark alley having the shit beaten out of him by Arnold Schwarzenegger. She wondered about Hawksley. Would he be annoyed when he learnt that she was delving into a case he had been involved with? The idea was an uncomfortable one.

There was a bottle of champagne in the fridge. On the rather naïve assumption that another injection of alcohol might make Hawksley more amenable, Roz put it on a tray with the sandwiches and a couple of glasses.

'Were you saving the champagne?' she asked brightly – *too brightly?* – placing the tray on the lavatory seat lid and turning round.

He was lying in a welter of foam, black hair slicked back, face cleaned and relaxed, eyes closed. ''Fraid so,' he said.

'Oh.' She was apologetic. 'I'll put it back then.'

He opened one eye. 'I was saving it for my birthday.'

'And when's that?'

'Tonight.'

She gave an involuntary laugh. 'I don't believe you. What's the date?'

'The sixteenth.'

Her eyes danced wickedly. 'I still don't believe you. How old are you?' She was unprepared for his look of amused recognition and couldn't stop the adolescent flush that tinged her pale cheeks. He thought she was flirting with him. *Well – dammit! – maybe she was.* She had grown weary of suffocating under the weight of her own misery.

'Forty. The big four-o.' He pushed himself into a sitting position and beckoned for the bottle. 'Well, well, this is jolly.' His lips twitched humorously. 'I wasn't expecting company or I'd have dressed for the occasion.' He unbound the wire and eased out the cork, losing only a dribble of bubbly into the foam before filling the glasses that she held out to him. He lowered the bottle to the floor and took a glass. 'To life,' he said, clinking hers.

'To life. Happy birthday.'

His eyes watched her briefly, before closing again as he leant his head against the back of the bath. 'Eat a sandwich,' he murmured. 'There's nothing worse than champagne on an empty stomach.'

'I've had three already. Sorry I couldn't wait for the sirloin. You have one.' She put the tray beside the bottle and left him to help himself. 'Do you have a laundry basket or something?' she asked, stirring the heap of stinking clothes with her toe.

'They're not worth saving. I'll chuck 'em out.'

'I can do that.'

He yawned. 'Bin bags. Second cupboard on the left in the kitchen.'

She carried the bundle at arm's length and sealed the lot into three layers of clean white plastic. It took only a few minutes but when she went back he was asleep, his glass clasped in loose fingers against his chest.

She removed it carefully and put it on the floor. What now? she wondered. She might have been his sister, so unaroused was he by her presence. Go or stay? She had an absurd longing to sit quietly and watch him sleep but she was nervous of waking him.

He would never understand her need to be at peace, just briefly, with a man.

Her eyes softened. It was a nice face. No amount of battering and bruising could hide the laughter lines, and she knew that if she let it it would grow on her and make her pleased to see it. She turned away abruptly. She had been nurturing her bitterness too long to give it up as easily as this. God had not been punished enough.

She retrieved her handbag from where she'd dropped it beside the lavatory and tiptoed down the stairs. But the door was locked and the key was missing. She felt more foolish than concerned, like the embarrassed eavesdropper trapped inside a room whose only object is to escape without being noticed. He must have put the wretched thing in his pocket. She crept back up to the kitchen to scrabble through the dirty clothes bundle but the pockets were all empty. Perplexed, she stared about the work surfaces, searched the tables in the sitting-room and bedroom. If keys existed, they were well hidden. With a sigh of frustration, she pulled back a curtain to see if there was another way out, a fire escape or a balcony, and found herself gazing on a window full of bars. She tried another window and another. All were barred.

Predictably, anger took over.

Without pausing to consider the wisdom of what she was doing, she stormed into the bathroom and shook him violently. 'You bastard!' she snapped. 'What the hell do you think you're playing at! What are you? Some kind of Bluebeard. I want to get out of here. Now!'

He was hardly awake before he'd smashed the champagne bottle against the tiled wall, caught her by the hair, and thrust the jagged glass against her neck. His bloodshot eyes blazed into hers before a sort of recognition dawned and he let her go, pushing her away from him. 'You stupid bitch,' he snarled. 'Don't you ever do that again.' He rubbed his face vigorously to clear it of sleep.

She was very shaken. 'I want to go.'

'So what's stopping you?'

'You've hidden the key.'

He looked at her for a moment, then started to soap himself. 'It's on the architrave above the door. Turn it twice. It's a double lock.'

'Your windows are all barred.'

'They are indeed.' He splashed water on his face. 'Goodbye, Ms Leigh.'

'Goodbye.' She made a weak gesture of apology. 'I'm sorry. I thought I was a prisoner.'

He pulled out the plug and tugged a towel off the rail. 'You are.'

'But – you said the key—'

'Goodbye, Ms Leigh.' He splayed his hand against the door and pushed it to, forcing her out.

*

She should not be driving. The thought hammered in her head like a migraine, a despairing reminder that self-preservation was the first of all the human instincts. But he was right. She *was* a prisoner and the yearning to escape was too strong. So easy, she thought, so very, very easy. Successive headlamps grew from tiny distant pinpoints to huge white suns, sweeping through her windscreen with a beautiful and blinding iridescence, drawing her eyes into the heart of their brilliance. The urge to turn the wheel towards the lights was insistent. How painless the transition would be at the moment of blindness and how bright eternity. *So easy . . . so easy . . . so easy . . .*

Five

OLIVE TOOK A cigarette and lit it greedily. 'You're late. I was afraid you wouldn't come.' She sucked down the smoke. 'I've been dying for a bloody fag.' Her hands and shift were filthy with what looked like dried clay.

'Aren't you allowed cigarettes?'

'Only what you can buy with your earnings. I always run out before the end of the week.' She rubbed the backs of her hands vigorously and showered the table with small grey flakes.

'What is that?' Roz asked.

'Clay.' Olive left the cigarette in her mouth and set to work, plucking the smears from her bosom. 'Why do you think they call me the Sculptress?'

Roz was about to say something tactless, but thought better of it. 'What do you make?'

'People.'

'What sort of people? Imaginary people or people you know?'

There was a brief hesitation. 'Both.' She held Roz's gaze. 'I made one of you.'

Roz watched her for a moment. 'Well, I just hope you don't decide to stick pins into it,' she said with a faint smile. 'Judging by the way I feel today, somebody else is at that already.'

A flicker of amusement crossed Olive's face. She abandoned the smears and fixed Roz with her penetrating stare. 'So what's wrong with you.'

Roz had spent a weekend in limbo, analysing and re-analysing until her brain was on fire. 'Nothing. Just a headache, that's all.' And that was true as far as it went. Her situation hadn't altered. She was still a prisoner.

Olive screwed her eyes against the smoke. 'Changed your mind about the book?'

'No.'

'OK. Fire away.'

Roz switched on the tape-recorder. 'Second conversation with Olive Martin. Date: Monday, April nineteen. Tell me about Sergeant Hawksley, Olive, the policeman who arrested you. Did you get to know him well? How did he treat you?'

If the big woman was surprised by the question, she didn't show it, but then she didn't show anything very much. She thought for some moments. 'Was he the dark-haired one? Hal, I think they called him.'

Roz nodded.

'He was all right.'

'Did he bully you?'

'He was all right.' She drew on her cigarette and stared stolidly across the table. 'Have you spoken to him?'

'Yes.'

'Did he tell you he threw up when he saw the bodies?' There was an edge to her voice. Of amusement? Roz wondered. Somehow, amusement didn't quite square.

'No,' she said. 'He didn't mention that.'

'He wasn't the only one.' A short silence. 'I offered to make them a pot of tea but the kettle was in the kitchen.' She transferred her gaze to the ceiling, aware, perhaps, of having said something tasteless. 'Matter of fact, I liked him. He was the only one who talked to me. I might have been deaf and dumb for all the interest the others showed. He gave me a sandwich at the police station. He was all right.'

Roz nodded. 'Tell me what happened.'

Olive took another cigarette and lit it from the old one. 'They arrested me.'

'No. I mean before that.'

'I called the police station, gave my address, and said the bodies were in the kitchen.'

'And before that?'

Olive didn't answer.

Roz tried a different tack. 'The ninth of September, eighty-seven, was a Wednesday. According to your statement you killed and dismembered Amber and your mother in the morning and early afternoon.' She watched the woman closely. 'Did none of the neighbours hear anything, come and investigate?'

There was a tiny movement at the corner of one eye, a tic, hardly noticeable amidst the fat. 'It's a man, isn't it?' said Olive gently.

Roz was puzzled. 'What's a man?'

Sympathy peeped out from between the puffy, bald lids. 'It's one of the few advantages of being in a place like this. No men to make your life a misery. You get the odd bit of bother, of course, husbands and boyfriends playing up on the outside, but you don't get the anguish of a daily relationship.' She pursed her lips in recollection. 'I always envied the nuns, you know. It's so much easier when you don't have to compete.'

Roz played with her pencil. Olive was too canny to discuss a man in her own life, she thought, assuming there had ever been one. *Had she told the truth about her abortion?* 'But less rewarding,' she said.

A rumble issued from the other side of the table. 'Some reward you're getting. You know what my father's favourite expression was? The game is not worth the candle. He used to drive my mother mad with it. But it's true in your case. Whoever it is you're after, he's not doing you any good.'

Roz drew a doodle on her pad, a fat cherub inside a balloon. Was the abortion a fantasy, a perverted link in Olive's mind with Amber's unwanted son? There was a long silence. She pencilled in the cherub's smile and spoke without thinking. 'Not whoever,' she said, 'whatever. It's what I want, not who I want.' She regretted it as soon as she'd said it. 'It's not important.'

Again there was no response and she began to find Olive's silences oppressive. It was a waiting game, a trap to make her speak. And then what? The toe-curling embarrassment of stammered apologies.

She bent her head. 'Let's go back to the day of the murders,' she suggested.

A meaty hand suddenly covered hers and stroked the fingers affectionately. 'I know about despair. I've felt it often. If you keep it bottled up, it feeds on itself like a cancer.'

There was no insistence in Olive's touch. It was a display of friendship, supportive, undemanding. Roz squeezed the fat, warm fingers in acknowledgement then withdrew her hand. *It's not despair*, she was going to say, *just overwork and tiredness.* 'I'd like to do what you did,' she said in a monotone, 'and kill someone.' There was a long silence. Her own statement had shocked her. 'I shouldn't have said that.'

'Why not? It's the truth.'

'I doubt it. I haven't the guts to kill anyone.'

Olive stared at her. 'That doesn't stop you wanting to,' she said reasonably.

'No. But if you can't summon the guts then I don't think the will is really there.' She smiled distantly. 'I can't even find the guts to kill myself and sometimes I see that as the only sensible option.'

'Why?'

Roz's eyes were over bright. 'I hurt,' she said simply. 'I've been hurting for months.' *But why was she telling Olive all this instead of the nice safe psychiatrist Iris had recommended?* Because Olive would understand.

'Who do you want dead?' The question vibrated in the air between them like a tolled bell.

Roz thought about the wisdom of answering. 'My ex-husband,' she said.

'Because he left you?'

'No.'

'What did he do?'

But Roz shook her head. 'If I tell you, you'll try to persuade me I'm wrong to hate him.' She gave a strange laugh. 'And I need to hate him. Sometimes I think it's the only thing that's keeping me alive.'

'Yes,' said Olive evenly. 'I can understand that.' She breathed on the window and drew a gallows in the mist with her finger. 'You loved him once.' It was a statement, expecting no reply, but Roz felt compelled to answer.

'I can't remember now.'

'You must have done.' The fat woman's voice became a croon. 'You can't hate what you never loved, you can only dislike it and avoid it. Real hate, like real love, consumes you.' With a sweep of her large palm she wiped the gallows from the window. 'I suppose,' she went on, matter of factly, 'you came to see me to find out whether murder is worth it.'

'I don't know,' Roz said honestly. 'Half the time I'm in limbo, the other half I'm obsessed by anger. The only thing I'm sure of is that I'm slowly falling apart.'

Olive shrugged. 'Because it's inside your head. Like I said, it's bad to keep things bottled up. It's a pity you're not a Catholic. You could go to confession and feel better immediately.'

Such a simple solution had never occurred to Roz. 'I was a Catholic, once. I suppose I still am.'

Olive took another cigarette and placed it reverently between her lips like a consecrated wafer. 'Obsessions,' she murmured, reaching for a match, 'are invariably destructive. That, at least, I have learnt.' She spoke sympathetically. 'You need more time before you can talk about it. I understand. You think I'll pick at the scab and make you bleed again.'

Roz nodded.

'You don't trust people. You're right. Trust has a way of rebounding. I know about these things.'

Roz watched her light the cigarette. 'What was your obsession?'

She flicked Roz a strangely intimate look but didn't answer.

'I needn't write this book, you know, not if you don't want me to.'

Olive smoothed her thin blonde hair with the back of her thumb. 'It'll upset Sister Bridget if we give up now. I know you've seen her.'

'Does that matter?'

Olive shrugged. 'It might upset *you* if we give up now. Does *that* matter?'

She smiled suddenly and her whole face brightened. How very *nice* she looked, thought Roz. 'Maybe, maybe not,' she said. 'I'm not convinced myself that I want to write it.'

'Why not?'

Roz pulled a face. 'I should hate to turn you into a freak side-show.'

'Aren't I that already?'

'In here perhaps. Not outside. They've forgotten all about you outside. It may be better to leave it that way.'

'What would persuade you to write it?'

'If you tell me why.'

The silence grew between them. Ominous. 'Have they found my nephew?' Olive asked at last.

'I don't think so.' Roz frowned. 'How did you know they were looking for him?'

Olive gave a hearty chuckle. 'Cell telegraph. Everyone knows everything in here. There's bugger-all else to do except mind other people's business, and we all have solicitors and we all read the newspapers and everyone talks. I could have guessed anyway. My father left a lot of money. He would always leave it to family if he could.'

'I spoke to one of your neighbours, a Mr Hayes. Do you remember him?' Olive nodded. 'If I understood him right, Amber's child was adopted by some people called Brown who've since emigrated to Australia. I assume that's why Mr Crew's firm is having so much difficulty in tracing him. Big place, common name.' She waited for a moment but Olive didn't say anything. 'Why do you want to know? Does it make a difference to you whether he's found or not?'

'Maybe,' she said heavily.

'Why?'

Olive shook her head.

'Do you want him found?'

The door crashed open, startling them both. 'Time's up, Sculptress. Come on, let's be having you.' The officer's voice boomed about the peaceful room, tearing the fabric of their precarious intimacy. Roz saw her own irritation reflected in Olive's eyes. But the moment was lost.

She gave an involuntary wink. 'It's true what they say, you know. Time does fly when you're enjoying yourself. I'll see you next week.' The huge woman lumbered awkwardly to her feet.

'My father was a very lazy man, which is why he let my mother rule the roost.' She rested a hand against the door jamb to balance herself. 'His other favourite saying, because it annoyed her so much, was:

never do today what can always be done tomorrow.' She smiled faintly. 'As a result, of course, he was completely contemptible. The only allegiance he recognized was his allegiance to himself, but it was allegiance without responsibility. He should have studied existentialism.' Her tongue lingered on the word. 'He would have learnt something about man's imperative to choose and act wisely. We are all masters of our fate, Roz, including you.' She nodded briefly then turned away, drawing the prison officer and the metal chair into her laborious, shuffling wake.

Now what, Roz wondered, watching them, was that supposed to mean?

'Mrs Wright?'

'Yes?' The young woman held the front door half open, a restraining hand hooked into her growling dog's collar. She was pretty in a colourless sort of way, pale and fine drawn with large grey eyes and a swinging bob of straw-gold hair.

Roz offered her card. 'I'm writing a book about Olive Martin. Sister Bridget at your old convent school suggested you might be prepared to talk to me. She said you were the closest friend Olive had there.'

Geraldine Wright made a pretence of reading the card then offered it back again. 'I don't think so, thank you.' She said it in the sort of tone she might have used to a Jehovah's Witness. She prepared to close the door.

Roz held it open with her hand. 'May I ask why not?'

'I'd rather not be involved.'

'I don't need to mention you by name.' She smiled encouragingly. 'Please, Mrs Wright. I won't embarrass you. That's not the way I work. It's information I'm after, not exposure. No one will ever know you were connected with her, not through me or my book at least.' She saw a slight hesitancy in the other woman's eyes. 'Ring Sister Bridget,' she urged. 'I know she'll vouch for me.'

'Oh, I suppose it's all right. But only for half an hour. I have to collect the children at three thirty.' She opened the door wide and pulled the dog away from it. 'Come in. The sitting room's on the left. I'll have to shut Boomer in the kitchen or he won't leave us alone.'

Roz walked through into the sitting room, a pleasant, sunny space with wide patio doors opening out on to a small terrace. Beyond, a neat garden, carefully tended, merged effortlessly into a green field with distant cows. 'It's a lovely view,' she said as Mrs Wright joined her.

'We were lucky to get it,' said the other woman with some pride. 'The house was rather out of our price range, but the previous owner took a bridging loan on another property just before the interest rates went through the roof. He was so keen to be shot of this one we got it for twenty-five thousand less than he was asking. We're very happy here.'

'I'm not surprised,' said Roz warmly. 'It's a beautiful part of the world.'

'Let's sit down.' She lowered herself gracefully into an armchair. 'I'm not ashamed of my friendship with Olive,' she excused herself. 'I just don't like talking about it. People are so persistent. They simply won't accept that I knew nothing about the murders.' She examined her painted fingernails. 'I hadn't seen her, you know, for at least three years before it happened and I certainly haven't seen her since. I really can't think what I can tell you that will be of any use.'

Roz made no attempt to record the conversation. She was afraid of scaring the woman. 'Tell me what she was like at school,' she said, taking out a pencil and notepad. 'Were you in the same form?'

'Yes, we both stayed on to do A-levels.'

'Did you like her?'

'Not much.' Geraldine sighed. 'That does sound unkind, doesn't it? Look, you really won't use my name, will you? I mean, if there's a chance you will, I just won't say any more. I should hate Olive to know how I really felt about her. It would be so hurtful.'

Of course it would, thought Roz, but why would you care? She took some headed notepaper from her briefcase, wrote two sentences on it and signed it.

' "I, Rosalind Leigh, of the above address, agree to treat all information given to me by Mrs Geraldine Wright of Oaktrees, Wooling, Hants, as confidential. I shall not reveal her as the source of any information, either verbally or in writing, now or at any time in the future." There. Will that do?' She forced a smile. 'You can sue me for a fortune if I break my word.'

'Oh dear, she'll guess it's me. I'm the only one she talked to. At school, anyway.' She took the piece of paper. 'I don't know.'

God, what a ditherer! It occurred to Roz then that Olive may well have found the friendship as unrewarding as Geraldine appeared to have done. 'Let me give you an idea of how I'll use what you tell me, then you'll see there's nothing to worry about. You've just said you didn't like her much. That will end up in the book as something like: "Olive was never popular at school." Can you go along with that?'

The woman brightened. 'Oh, yes. That's absolutely true anyway.'

'OK. Why wasn't she popular?'

'She never really fitted in, I suppose.'

'Why not?'

'Oh dear.' Geraldine shrugged irritatingly. 'Because she was fat, perhaps.'

This was going to be like drawing teeth, slow and extremely painful. 'Did she try to make friends or didn't she bother?'

'She didn't really bother. She hardly ever said

anything, you know, just used to sit and stare at everyone else while they talked. People didn't like that very much. To tell you the truth, I think we were all rather frightened of her. She was very much taller than the rest of us.'

'Was that the only reason she scared you? Her size?'

Geraldine thought back. 'It was a sort of over-all thing. I don't know how to describe it. She was very quiet. You could be talking to someone and you'd turn round to find her standing right behind you, staring at you.'

'Did she bully people?'

'Only if they were nasty to Amber.'

'And did that happen often?'

'No. Everyone liked Amber.'

'OK.' Roz tapped her pencil against her teeth. 'You say you were the only one Olive spoke to. What sort of things did you talk about?'

Geraldine plucked at her skirt. 'Just things,' she said unhelpfully. 'I can't remember now.'

'The sort of things all girls talk about at school.'

'Well, yes, I suppose so.'

Roz gritted her teeth. 'So you discussed sex, and boys, and clothes, and make-up?'

'Well, yes,' she said again.

'I find that hard to believe, Mrs Wright. Not unless she's changed a great deal in ten years. I've met her, you know. She's not remotely interested in trivia and she doesn't like talking about herself. She wants to know about me and what I do.'

'That's probably because she's in prison and you're her only visitor.'

'I'm not, in actual fact. Also, I am told that most prisoners do the exact opposite when someone visits them. They talk about themselves nineteen to the dozen because it's the only time they get a sympathetic hearing.' She raised a speculative eyebrow. 'I think it's Olive's nature to quiz the person she's talking to. I suspect she's always done it, and that's why none of you liked her very much. You probably thought she was nosy.' Pray God, I'm right, she thought, because this one, who's about as manipulable as putty, will say I am regardless.

'How funny,' said Geraldine. 'Now you mention it, she did ask a lot of questions. She was always wanting to know about my parents, whether they held hands and kissed, and whether I'd ever heard them making love.' She turned her mouth down. 'Yes, I remember now, that's why I didn't like her. She was forever trying to find out how often my parents had sex, and she used to push her face up close when she asked, and stare.' She gave a small shudder. 'I used to hate that. She had such greedy eyes.'

'Did you tell her?'

'About my parents?' Geraldine sniggered. 'Not the truth, certainly. I didn't know myself. Whenever she asked, I always said, yes, they'd had sex the night before, just to get away from her. Everyone did. It became a silly sort of game in the end.'

'Why did she want to know?'

The woman shrugged. 'I always thought it was because she had a dirty mind. There's a woman in the village who's just the same. The first thing she says to anyone is, "Tell me all the gossip," and her eyes light up. I hate that sort of thing. She's the last person to hear what's going on, of course. She puts people's backs up.'

Roz thought for a moment. 'Did Olive's parents kiss and cuddle?'

'Lord, no!'

'You're very certain.'

'Well, of course. They loathed each other. My mother said they only stayed together because he was too lazy to move out and she was too mercenary to let him.'

'So Olive was looking for reassurance?'

'I'm sorry?'

'When she asked you about your parents,' said Roz coolly, 'she was looking for reassurance. The poor kid was trying to find out if hers were the only ones who didn't get on.'

'Oh,' said Geraldine in surprise. 'Do you think so?' She made a pretty little moue with her lips. 'No,' she said, 'I'm sure you're wrong. It was the sex bits she wanted to know about. I told you, her eyes had a greedy look.'

Roz let this pass. 'Did she tell lies?'

'Yes, that was another thing.' Memories chased themselves across her face. 'She was always lying. How odd, I'd forgotten that. In the end, you know, nobody ever believed anything she said.'

'What did she lie about?'

'Everything.'

'What in particular? Herself? Other people? Her parents?'

'Everything.' She saw the impatience in Roz's face. 'Oh dear, it's so hard to explain. She told stories. I mean, she couldn't open her mouth without telling stories. Oh dear, let me see now. All right, she used to talk about boyfriends that didn't exist, and she said the family had been on holiday to France one summer but it turned out they'd stayed at home, and she kept talking about her dog, but everyone knew she didn't have a dog.' She pulled a face. 'And she used to cheat, of course, all the time. It was really annoying that. She'd steal your homework out of your satchel when you weren't looking and crib your ideas.'

'She was bright, though, wasn't she? She got three A-levels.'

'She passed them all but I don't think her grades were anything to shout home about.' It was said with a touch of malice. 'Anyway, if she was so bright, why couldn't she get herself a decent job? My mother said it was embarrassing going to Pettit's and being served by Olive.'

Roz looked away from the colourless face to gaze out over the view from the window. She let some moments pass while common sense battled with the angry reproaches that were clamouring inside her head. After all, she thought, she could be wrong. And yet . . . And yet it seemed so clear to her that Olive must have been a deeply unhappy child. She forced herself to smile. 'Olive was obviously closer to you than anyone else, except, perhaps, her sister. Why do you think that was?'

'Oh, goodness, I haven't a clue. My mother says it's because I reminded her of Amber. I couldn't see it myself, but it's true that people who saw the three of us together always assumed Amber was my sister and not Olive's.' She thought back. 'Mother's probably right. Olive stopped following me around quite so much when Amber joined the school.'

'That must have been a relief.' There was a certain acidity in her tone, mercifully lost on Geraldine.

'I suppose so. Except' – she added this as a wistful afterthought – 'nobody dared tease when Olive was with me.'

Roz watched her for a moment. 'Sister Bridget said Olive was devoted to Amber.'

'She was. But then everyone liked Amber.'

'Why?'

Geraldine shrugged. 'She was nice.'

Roz laughed suddenly. 'To be frank, Amber's

beginning to get up my nose. She sounds too damn good to be true. What was so special about her?'

'Oh dear.' She frowned in recollection. 'Mother said it was because she was willing. People put on her, but she never seemed to mind. She smiled a lot, of course.'

Roz drew her cherub doodle on the notepad and thought about the unwanted pregnancy. 'How was she put upon?'

'I suppose she just wanted to please. It was only little things, like lending out her pencils and running errands for the nuns. I needed a clean sports shirt once for a netball match, so I borrowed Amber's. That sort of thing.'

'Without asking?'

Surprisingly, Geraldine blushed. 'You didn't need to, not with Amber. She never minded. It was only Olive who got angry. She was perfectly beastly about that sports shirt.' She looked at the clock. 'I shall have to go. It's getting late.' She stood up. 'I haven't been very helpful, I'm afraid.'

'On the contrary,' said Roz, pushing herself out of her chair, 'you've been extremely helpful. Thank you very much.'

They walked into the hall together.

'Did it never seem odd to you,' Roz asked as Geraldine opened the front door, 'that Olive should kill her sister?'

'Well, yes, of course it did. I was terribly shocked.'

'Shocked enough to wonder if she actually did it? In view of all you've said about their relationship it seems a very unlikely thing for her to do.'

The wide grey eyes clouded with uncertainty. 'How strange. That's just what my mother always said. But if she didn't do it, then why did she say she did?'

'I don't know. Perhaps because she makes a habit of protecting people.' She smiled in a friendly way. 'Would your mother be prepared to talk to me, do you think?'

'Oh Lord, I shouldn't think so. She hates anyone even knowing I was at school with Olive.'

'Will you ask her anyway? And if she agrees, phone me at that number on the card.'

Geraldine shook her head. 'It would be a waste of time. She won't agree.'

'Fair enough.' Roz stepped through the door and on to the gravel. 'What a lovely house this is,' she said with enthusiasm, looking up at the clematis over the porch. 'Where were you living before?'

The other woman grimaced theatrically. 'A nasty modern box on the outskirts of Dawlington.'

Roz laughed. 'So coming here was by way of a culture shock.' She opened the car door. 'Do you ever go back to Dawlington?'

'Oh, yes,' said the other. 'My parents still live there. I see them once a week.'

Roz tossed her bag and briefcase on to the back

seat. 'They must be very proud of you.' She held out a hand. 'Thank you for your time, Mrs Wright, and please don't worry, I shall be very careful how I use the information you've given me.' She lowered herself on to the driver's seat and pulled the door to. 'There's just one last thing,' she said through the open window, her dark eyes guileless. 'Can I have your maiden name so I can cross you off the school list Sister Bridget gave me? I don't want to go troubling you again by mistake.'

'Hopwood,' said Geraldine helpfully.

It wasn't difficult to locate Mrs Hopwood. Roz drove to the library in Dawlington and consulted the local telephone directory. There were three Hopwoods with Dawlington addresses. She made a note of these with their numbers, found a telephone box and rang each in turn, claiming to be an old friend of Geraldine's and asking to speak to her. The first two denied any knowledge of such a person, the last, a man's voice, told her that Geraldine had married and was now living in Wooling. He gave her Geraldine's telephone number and told her, rather sweetly, how nice it had been to talk to her again. Roz smiled as she put down the receiver. Geraldine, she thought, took after her father.

*

This impression was forcibly confirmed when Mrs Hopwood rattled her safety chain into place and opened the front door. She eyed Roz with deep suspicion. 'Yes?' she demanded.

'Mrs Hopwood?'

'Yes.'

Roz had planned a simple cover story but, seeing the hard glint in the woman's eyes, decided to abandon it. Mrs Hopwood was not the type to take kindly to flannel. 'I'm afraid I bamboozled your daughter and your husband into giving away this address,' she said with a slight smile. 'My name's—'

'Rosalind Leigh and you're writing a book about Olive. I know. I've just had Geraldine on the phone. It didn't take her long to put two and two together. I'm sorry but I can't help you. I hardly knew the girl.' But she didn't close the door. Something – curiosity? – kept her there.

'You know her better than I do, Mrs Hopwood.'

'But I haven't chosen to write a book about her, young woman. Nor would I.'

'Not even if you thought she was innocent?'

Mrs Hopwood didn't answer.

'Supposing she didn't do it? You've considered that, haven't you?'

'It's not my affair.' She started to close the door.

'Then whose affair is it, for God's sake?' demanded Roz, suddenly angry. 'Your daughter paints a picture of two sisters, both of whom were so insecure that one told lies and cheated to give herself some status and the other was afraid to say no in case people didn't like her. What the hell was happening to them at home to make them like that? And where were you then? Where was anybody? The only real friend either of them had was the other.' She saw the thin compression of the woman's lips through the gap in the door and she shook her head contemptuously. 'Your daughter misled me, I'm afraid. From something she said I thought you might be a Samaritan.' She smiled coldly. 'I see you're a Pharisee, after all. Goodbye, Mrs Hopwood.'

The other clicked her tongue impatiently. 'You'd better come in, but I'm warning you, I shall insist on a transcript of this interview. I will not have words put into my mouth afterwards simply to fit some sentimental view you have of Olive.'

Roz produced her tape-recorder. 'I'll tape the whole thing. If you have a recorder you can tape it at the same time, or I can send you a copy of mine.'

Mrs Hopwood nodded approval as she unhooked the chain and opened the door. 'We have our own. My husband can set it up while I make a cup of tea. Come in, and wipe your feet, please.'

Ten minutes later they were ready. Mrs Hopwood took natural control. 'The easiest way is for me to tell you everything I remember. When I've finished you can ask me questions. Agreed?'

'Agreed.'

'I said I hardly knew Olive. That's true. She came here perhaps five or six times in all, twice to Geraldine's birthday parties, and on three or four occasions to tea. I didn't take to her. She was a clumsy girl, slow, impossible to talk to, lacking in humour, and, frankly, extremely unattractive. This may sound harsh and unkind but there you are – you can't pretend feelings that you don't have. I wasn't sorry when her friendship with Geraldine died a natural death.' She paused to collect her thoughts.

'After that, I really had very little to do with her. She never came to this house again. I heard stories, of course, from Geraldine and Geraldine's friends. The impression I formed was very much along the lines you set out earlier – a sad, unloved, and unlovely child, who had resorted to boasting about holidays she hadn't taken and boyfriends she didn't have to make up for unhappiness at home. The cheating, I think, was the result of her mother's constant pressure to do well, as indeed was the compulsive eating. She was always plump but during her adolescence her eating habits became pathological. According to Geraldine, she used to steal food from the school kitchen and cram it, in its entirety, into her mouth, as if she were afraid someone would take it away from her before she had finished.

'Now, you would interpret this behaviour, I imagine, as a symptom of a troubled home background.' She looked enquiringly at Roz, who nodded.

'Yes, well, I think I'd agree with you. It wasn't natural, and nor was Amber's submissiveness, although I must stress I never witnessed either girl in action, so to speak. I am relating only what I was told by Geraldine and her friends. In any event, it did trouble me, mostly because I had met Gwen and Robert Martin when I went to collect Geraldine on the few occasions she was invited to their house. They were a very strange couple. They hardly spoke. He lived in a downstairs room at the back of the house and she and the two girls lived at the front. As far as I could make out, virtually all contact between them was conducted through Olive and Amber.' Seeing Roz's expression, she stopped. 'No one's told you this yet?'

Roz shook her head.

'I never did know how many people were aware of it. She kept up appearances, of course, and, frankly, had Geraldine not told me she had seen a bed in Mr Martin's study, I wouldn't have guessed what was going on.' She wrinkled her brow. 'But it's always the way, isn't it? Once you begin to suspect something, then everything you see confirms that suspicion. They were never together, except at the odd parents' evening, and then there would always be a third party with them, usually one of the teachers.' She smiled self-consciously. 'I used to watch them, you know, not out of malice – my husband will confirm that – but just to prove myself wrong.' She shook her head. 'I came to the conclusion that they simply loathed each other. And it wasn't just that they never spoke, they couldn't bring themselves to exchange *anything* – touches, glances – anything. Does that make sense to you?'

'Oh, yes,' said Roz with feeling. 'Hatred has as strong a body language as love.'

'It was she, I think, who was the instigator of it all. I've always assumed he must have had an affair which she found out about, though I must stress I don't know that. He was a nice looking man, very easy to talk to, and, of course, he got out and about with his job. Whereas she, as far as I could see, had no friends at all, a few acquaintances perhaps, but one never came across her socially. She was a very controlled woman, cold and unemotional. Really rather unpleasant. Certainly not the type one could ever grow fond of.' She was silent for a moment. 'Olive was very much her daughter, of course, both in looks and personality, and Amber his. Poor Olive,' she said with genuine compassion. 'She did have very little going for her.'

Mrs Hopwood looked at Roz and sighed heavily. 'You asked me earlier where I was while all this was going on. I was bringing up my own children, my dear, and if you have any yourself you will know it's hard enough to cope with them, let alone interfere with someone else's. I do regret now that I didn't say anything at the time, but, really, what could I have done? In any case, I felt it was the school's responsibility.' She spread her hands. 'But there you are, it's so easy with hindsight, and who could possibly have guessed that Olive would do what she did? I don't suppose anyone realized just how disturbed she was.' She dropped her hands to her lap and looked helplessly at her husband.

Mr Hopwood pondered for a moment. 'Still,' he said slowly, 'there's no point pretending we've ever believed she killed Amber. I went to the police about that, you know, told them I thought it was very unlikely. They said my disquiet was based on out-of-date information.' He sucked his teeth. 'Which of course was true. It was five years or so since we'd had any dealings with the family, and in five years the sisters could well have learned to dislike each other.' He fell silent.

'But if Olive didn't kill Amber,' Roz prompted, 'then who did?'

'Gwen,' he said with surprise, as if it went without saying. He smoothed his white hair. 'We think Olive walked in on her mother battering Amber. That would have been quite enough to send her berserk, assuming she had retained her fondness for the girl.'

'Was Gwen capable of doing such a thing?'

They looked at each other. 'We've always thought so,' said Mr Hopwood. 'She was very hostile towards Amber, probably because Amber was so like her father.'

'What did the police say?' asked Roz.

'I gather Robert Martin had already suggested the same thing. They put it to Olive and she denied it.'

Roz stared at him. 'You're saying Olive's father told the police that he thought his wife had battered his younger daughter to death and that Olive then killed her mother?'

He nodded.

'God!' she breathed. 'His solicitor never said a word about that.' She thought for a moment. 'It implies, you know, that Gwen had battered the child before. No man would make an accusation like that unless he had grounds for it, would he?'

'Perhaps he just shared our disbelief that Olive could kill her sister.'

Roz chewed her thumbnail and stared at the carpet. 'She claimed in her statement that her relationship with her sister had never been close. Now, I might go along with that if I accept that in the years after school they drifted apart, but I can't go along with it if her own father thought they were still so close that Olive would kill to revenge her.' She shook her head. 'I'm damn sure Olive's barrister never got to hear about this. The poor man was trying to conjure a defence out of thin air.' She looked up. 'Why did Robert Martin give up on it? Why did he let her plead guilty? According to her she did it to spare him the anguish of a trial.'

Mr Hopwood shook his head. 'I really couldn't say. We never saw him again. Presumably, he somehow became convinced of her guilt.' He massaged arthritic fingers. 'The problem for all of us is trying to accept that a person we know is capable of doing something so horrible, perhaps because it shows up the fallibility of our judgement. We knew her before it happened. You, I imagine, have met her since. In both cases, we have failed to see the flaw in her character that led her to murder her mother and sister, and we look for excuses. In the end, though, I don't think there are any. It's not as if the police had to beat her confession out of her. As far as I understand it, it was they who insisted she wait till her solicitor was present.'

Roz frowned. 'And yet you're still troubled by it.'

He smiled slightly. 'Only when someone pops up to stir the dregs again. By and large we rarely think about it. There's no getting away from the fact that she signed a confession saying she did it.'

'People are always confessing to crimes they didn't commit,' countered Roz bluntly. 'Timothy Evans was hanged for his confession, while downstairs Christie went on burying his victims under the floorboards. Sister Bridget said Olive lied about everything, you and your daughter have both cited lies she told. What makes you think she was telling the truth in this one instance?'

They didn't say anything.

'I'm so sorry,' said Roz with an apologetic smile. 'I don't mean to harangue you. I just wish I understood what it was all about. There are so many inconsistencies. I mean why, for example, did Robert Martin stay in the house after the deaths? You'd expect him to move heaven and earth to get out of it.'

'You must talk to the police,' said Mr Hopwood. 'They know more about it than anyone.'

'Yes,' Roz said quietly, 'I must.' She picked up her cup and saucer from the floor and put them on the table. 'Can I ask you three more things? Then I'll leave you in peace. First, is there anyone else you can think of who might be able to help me?'

Mrs Hopwood shook her head. 'I really know very little about her after she left school. You'll have to trace the people she worked with.'

'Fair enough. Second, did you know that Amber had a baby when she was thirteen years old?' She read the astonishment in their faces.

'Good Heavens!' said Mrs Hopwood.

'Quite. Third . . .' She paused for a moment, remembering Graham Deedes' amused reaction. Was it fair to make Olive a figure of fun? 'Third,' she repeated firmly, 'Gwen persuaded Olive to have an abortion. Do you know anything about that?'

Mrs Hopwood looked thoughtful. 'Would that have been at the beginning of eighty-seven?'

Roz, unsure how to answer, nodded.

'I was having problems of my own with a prolonged menopause,' said Mrs Hopwood, matter of factly. 'I bumped into her and Gwen quite by chance at the hospital. It was the last time I saw them. Gwen was very jumpy. She tried to pretend they were there for a gynaecological reason of her own but I couldn't help noticing that it was clearly Olive who had the problem. The poor girl was in tears.' She tut-tutted crossly. 'What a mistake not to let her have it. It explains the murders, of course. They must have happened around the time the baby would have been due. No wonder she was disturbed.'

Roz drove back to Leven Road. This time the door to number 22 stood ajar and a young woman was clipping the low hedge that bordered the front garden. Roz drew her car into the kerb and stepped out. 'Hi,' she said, holding out her hand and shaking the other's firmly. Immediate, friendly contact, she hoped, would stop this woman barring the door to her as her neighbour had done. 'I'm Rosalind Leigh. I came the other day but you were out. I can see your time's precious so I won't stop you working, but can we talk while you're doing it?'

The young woman shrugged as she resumed her clipping. 'If you're selling anything, and that includes religion, then you're wasting your time.'

'I want to talk about your house.'

'Oh, Christ!' said the other in disgust. 'Sometimes I wish we'd never bought the flaming thing. What are you? Psychical bloody research? They're all nutters.

They seem to think the kitchen is oozing with ecto-plasm or something equally disgusting.'

'No. Far more earthbound. I'm writing a follow-up report on the Olive Martin case.'

'Why?'

'There are some unanswered questions. Like, for example, why did Robert Martin remain here after the murders?'

'And you're expecting me to answer that?' She snorted. 'I never even met him. He was long dead before we moved in. You should talk to old Hayes' – she jerked her head towards the adjoining garages – 'he's the only one who knew the family.'

'I have talked to him. He doesn't know either.' She glanced towards the open front door but all she could see was an expanse of peach wall and a triangle of russet carpet. 'I gather the house has been gutted and redecorated. Did you do that yourselves or did you buy it after it was done?'

'We did it ourselves. My old man's in the building trade. Or was,' she corrected herself. 'He was made redundant ten, twelve months ago. We were lucky, managed to sell our other house without losing too much, and bought this for a song. Did it without a mortgage, too, so we're not struggling the way some other poor sods are.'

'Has he found another job?' Roz asked sympathetically.

The young woman shook her head. 'Hardly. Building's all he knows and there's precious little of that at the moment. Still, he's trying his best. Can't do more than that, can he?' She lowered the shears. 'I suppose you're wondering if we found anything when we gutted the house.'

Roz nodded. 'Something like that.'

'If we had, we'd have told someone.'

'Of course, but I wouldn't have expected you to find anything incriminating. I was thinking more in terms of impressions. Did the place look loved, for example? Is that why he stayed? Because he loved it?'

The woman shook her head. 'I reckon it was more of a prison. I can't swear to it because I don't know for sure, but my guess is he only used one room and that was the room downstairs at the back, the one that was attached to the kitchen and the cloakroom with its own door into the garden. Maybe he went through to the kitchen to cook, but I doubt it. The connecting door was locked and we never found the key. Plus, there was an ancient Baby Belling still plugged into one of the sockets in that room, which the house clearers couldn't be bothered to take, and my bet is he did all his cooking on that. The garden was nice. I think he lived in the one room and the garden, and never went into the rest of the house at all.'

'Because the door was locked?'

'No, because of the nicotine. The windows were so thick with it that the glass looked yellow. And the ceiling' – she pulled a face – 'was dark brown. The smell of old tobacco was overpowering. He must have smoked non-stop in there. It was disgusting. But there were no nicotine stains anywhere else in the house. If he ever went beyond the connecting door, then it can't have been for very long.'

Roz nodded. 'He died of a heart attack.'

'I'm not surprised.'

'Would you object to my taking a look inside?'

'There's no point. It's completely different. We knocked out any walls that weren't structural and changed the whole layout downstairs. If you want to know what it looked like when he was here, then I'll draw you a plan. But you don't come in. If I say yes to you, then there's no end to it, is there? Any Tom, Dick, or Harry can demand to put his foot through our door.'

'Point taken. A plan would be more helpful, anyway.' She reached into the car for a notepad and pencil and passed it across.

'It's much nicer now,' said the self-possessed young woman, drawing with swift strokes. 'We've opened up the rooms and put some colour into them. Poor Mrs Martin had no idea at all. I think, you know, she was probably rather boring. There.' She passed the notepad back. 'That's the best I can do.'

'Thank you,' said Roz studying the plan. 'Why do you think Mrs Martin was boring?'

'Because everything – walls, doors, ceilings, *everything* – was painted white. It was like an operating theatre, cold and antiseptic, without a spot of colour. And she didn't have pictures either, because there were no marks on the walls.' She shuddered. 'I don't like houses like that. They never look lived in.'

Roz smiled as she glanced up at the red-brick façade. 'I'm glad it's you who bought it. I should think it feels lived in now. I don't believe in ghosts myself.'

'Put it this way, if you want to see ghosts, you'll see them. If you don't, you won't.' She tapped the side of her head. 'It's all in the mind. My old dad used to see pink elephants but no one ever thought *his* house was haunted.'

Roz was laughing as she drove away.

Six

THE CAR PARK of the Poacher was as deserted as before but this time it was three o'clock in the afternoon, lunchtime was over, and the door was bolted. Roz tapped on the window pane but, getting no response, made her way round to the alley at the back where the kitchen door must be. It stood ajar and from inside came the sound of singing.

'Hello,' she called. 'Sergeant Hawksley?' She put her hand on the door to push it wider and almost lost her balance when it was whipped away from her. 'You did that on purpose!' she snapped. 'I could have broken my arm.'

'Good God, woman,' he said in mock disgust. 'Can't you open your mouth without nagging? I'm beginning to think I did my ex-wife an injustice.' He crossed his arms, a fish slice dangling from one hand. 'What do you want this time?'

He had a peculiar talent for putting her at a disadvantage. She bit back an angry retort. 'I'm sorry,' she said instead. 'It's just that I nearly fell over. Look, are you busy at the moment or can I come in and talk to you?' She examined his face warily for signs of further damage but there were none that hadn't been there before.

'I'm busy.'

'What if I came back in an hour? Could you talk then?'

'Maybe.'

She gave a rueful smile. 'I'll try again at four.'

He watched her walk up the alleyway. 'What are you going to do for an hour?' he called after her.

She turned round. 'I expect I'll sit in the car. I've some notes to work on.'

He swung the fish slice. 'I'm cooking *steak au poivre* with some lightly steamed vegetables and potatoes fried in butter.'

'Bully for you,' she said.

'There's enough for two.'

She smiled. 'Is that an invitation or a refined form of torture?'

'It's an invitation.'

She came back slowly. 'Actually, I'm starving.'

A slight smile warmed his face. 'So what's new?' He took her into the kitchen and pulled out a chair at the table. He eyed her critically as he turned the gas up under some simmering pans. 'You look as if you haven't had a square meal in days.'

'I haven't.' She recalled what the young policeman had said. 'Are you a good cook?'

He turned his back on her without answering, and she regretted the question. Talking to Hawksley was almost as intimidating as talking to Olive. She couldn't speak, it seemed, without treading on a nerve. Except for a muted thank you when he poured her a glass of wine she sat in uncomfortable silence for five minutes, wondering how to open the conversation. She was highly doubtful that he would greet her proposed book on Olive with any enthusiasm.

He placed the steaks on warmed plates, surrounded them with fried whole potatoes, steamed mangetout, and baby carrots, and garnished them with the juices from the pan. 'There,' he said, whisking a plate in front of Roz, apparently unaware of her discomfort, 'that'll put some colour in your cheeks.' He sat down and attacked his own plate. 'Well, come on, woman. What are you waiting for?'

'A knife and fork.'

'Ah!' He pulled open a drawer in the table and slid some cutlery across. 'Now, get stuck in and don't yatter while you're eating. Food should be enjoyed for its own sake.'

She needed no further bidding but set to with a will. 'Fabulous,' she said at last, pushing her empty plate to one side with a sigh of contentment. 'Absolutely fabulous.'

He arched a sardonic eyebrow. 'So what's the verdict? Can I cook or can I cook?'

She laughed. 'You can cook. May I ask you something?'

He filled her empty glass. 'If you must.'

'If I hadn't turned up would you have eaten all that yourself?'

'I might have drawn the line at one steak.' He paused. 'Then again I might not. I've no bookings for tonight and they don't keep. I'd probably have eaten them both.'

She heard the trace of bitterness in his voice. 'How much longer can you stay open without customers?' she asked incautiously.

He ignored the question. 'You said you wanted to talk to me,' he reminded her. 'What about?'

She nodded. Apparently, he had no more desire than she to lick wounds in public. 'Olive Martin,' she told him. 'I'm writing a book about her. I believe you were one of the arresting officers.'

He didn't answer immediately but sat looking at her over the rim of his wine glass. 'Why Olive Martin?'

'She interests me.' It was impossible to gauge his reaction.

'Of course.' He shrugged. 'She did something completely horrific. You'd be very unnatural if you didn't find her interesting. Have you met her?'

She nodded.

'And?'

'I like her.'

'Only because you're naïve.' He stretched his long arms towards the ceiling, cracking the joints in his shoulders. 'You steeled yourself to delve in the sewer, expecting to pull out a monster, and you've landed yourself something comparatively pleasant instead. Olive's not unusual in that. Most criminals are pleasant most of the time. Ask any prison officer. They know better than anyone that the penal system relies almost entirely on the goodwill of the prisoners.' His eyes narrowed. 'But Olive hacked two completely innocent women to death. The fact that she presents a human face to you now doesn't make what she did any less horrific.'

'Have I said it does?'

'You're writing a book about her. Even if you castigate her, she will still be something of a celebrity.' He leaned forward, his tone unfriendly. 'But what about her mother and sister? Where is the justice for them in giving their murderer the thrill and the kudos of being written about?'

Roz dropped her eyes. 'It does worry me,' she admitted. 'No, that's wrong.' She looked up. 'It *did* worry me. I'm a little more sure now of where I'm heading. But I take your point about her victims. It's all too easy to focus on Olive. She's alive and they're dead, and the dead are difficult to recreate. You have to rely on what other people tell you, and just as their perceptions at the time were not always accurate, neither are their memories now.' She sighed. 'I still have reservations – there's no point in pretending I don't – but I need to understand what happened that day before I can make up my mind.' She fingered the stem of her wine glass. 'I think I may very well be naïve but I'd need convincing that that is a bad thing. I could argue, with considerable justification, that anyone delving regularly in sewers must come up jaundiced.'

'What's that supposed to mean?' He was amused.

She looked at him again. 'That what Olive did shocks you but doesn't surprise you. You've known, or known of, other people who've done similar things before.'

'So?'

'So you never established *why* she did it. Whereas I, being naïve' – she held his gaze – 'am surprised as well as shocked and I want to know why.'

He frowned. 'It's all in her statement. I can't remember the exact details now, but she resented not being given a birthday party, I think, and then blew a fuse when her mother got angry with her for persuading the sister to ring in sick the next day. Domestic violence erupts over the most trivial things. Olive's motives were rather more substantial than some I've known.'

Roz bent down to open her briefcase. 'I've a copy of her statement here.' She handed it across and waited while he read it through.

'I can't see your problem,' he said at last. 'She makes it clear as crystal why she did it. She got angry, hit them, and then didn't know how to dispose of the bodies.'

'That's what she says, I agree, but it doesn't mean it's *true*. There's at least one blatant lie in that statement and possibly two.' She tapped her pencil on the table. 'In the first paragraph she says that her relationship with her mother and sister had never been close but that's been flatly contradicted by everyone I've spoken to. They all say she was devoted to Amber.'

He frowned again. 'What's the other lie?'

She leaned over with her pencil and put a line by one of the middle paragraphs. 'She says she held a mirror to their lips to see if there was any mist. According to her, there wasn't, so she proceeded to dismember the bodies.' She turned the pages over. 'But here, according to the pathologist, Mrs Martin put up a struggle to defend herself before her throat was cut. Olive makes no mention of that in her statement.'

He shook his head. 'That doesn't mean a damn thing. Either she decided to put a gloss on the whole affair out of belated shame, or shock simply blotted the less acceptable bits out of her memory.'

'And the lie about not getting on with Amber? How do you explain that away?'

'Do I need to? The confession was completely voluntary. We even made her wait until her solicitor arrived to avoid any hint of police pressure.' He drained his glass. 'And you're not going to try and argue that an innocent woman would confess to a crime like this?'

'It's happened before.'

'Only after days of police interrogation and then, when it comes to the trial, they plead not guilty and deny their statement. Olive did neither.' He looked amused. 'Take it from me, she was so damned relieved to get it all off her chest she couldn't confess fast enough.'

'How? Did she deliver a monologue or did you have to ask questions?'

He clasped his hands behind his neck. 'Unless she's changed a great deal I should imagine you've already discovered that Olive doesn't volunteer information easily.' He cocked his head enquiringly. 'We had to ask questions but she answered them readily enough.' He looked thoughtful. 'For most of the time she sat and stared at us as if she were trying to engrave our faces on her memory. To be honest, I live in terror of her getting out and doing to me what she did to her family.'

'Five minutes ago you described her as comparatively pleasant.'

He rubbed his jaw. 'Comparatively pleasant as far as *you* were concerned,' he corrected her. 'But you were expecting something inhuman, which is why you find it difficult to be objective.'

Roz refused to be drawn again down this blind alley. Instead she took her recorder from her briefcase and put it on the table. 'Can I tape this conversation?'

'I haven't agreed to talk to you yet.' He stood up abruptly and filled a kettle with water. 'You'd do better,' he said after a moment, 'to ring Detective Sergeant Wyatt. He was there when she gave her statement, and he's still on the Force. Coffee?'

'Please.' She watched him select a dark Arabica and spoon the grounds into a cafetière. 'I really would rather talk to you,' she said evenly. 'Policemen are notoriously difficult to pin down. It could take me weeks to get an interview with him. I won't quote you, I won't even name you, if you'd rather I didn't, and you can read the final draft before it goes to print.' She gave a hollow laugh. 'Assuming it ever gets that far. What you say may persuade me not to write it.'

He looked at her, absent-mindedly scratching his chest through his shirt, then made up his mind. 'All right. I'll tell you as much as I can remember but you'll have to double-check everything. It's a long time ago and I can't vouch for my memory. Where do I start?'

'With her telephone call to the police.'

He waited for the kettle to boil, then filled the cafetière and placed it on the table. 'It wasn't a 999 call. She looked up the number in the book and dialled the desk.' He shook his head, remembering. 'It started out as a farce because the sergeant on duty couldn't make head or tail of what she was saying.'

He was shrugging into his jacket at the end of his shift when the desk sergeant came in and handed him a piece of paper with an address on it. 'Do me a favour, Hal, and check this out on your way home. It's Leven Road. You virtually pass it. Some madwoman's been bawling down the phone about chicken legs on her kitchen floor.' He pulled a face. 'Wants a policeman to take them away.' He grinned. 'Presumably she's a vegetarian. You're the cookery expert. Sort it out, there's a good chap.'

Hawksley eyed him suspiciously. 'Is this a wind-up?'

'No. Scout's honour.' He chuckled. 'Look, she's obviously a mental case. They're all over the place, poor sods, since the Government chucked 'em on to the streets. Just do as she asks or we'll have her phoning all night. It'll take you five minutes out of your way.'

Olive Martin, red eyed from weeping, opened the door to him. She smelt strongly of B.O. and her bulky shoulders were hunched in unattractive despair. So much blood was smeared over her baggy T-shirt and trousers that it took on the property of an abstract pattern and his eyes hardly registered it. And why should they? He had no premonition of the horror in store. 'D.S. Hawksley,' he said with an encouraging smile, showing her his card. 'You rang the police station.'

She stepped back, holding the door open. 'They're in the kitchen.' She pointed down the corridor. 'On the floor.'

'OK. We'll go down and have a look. What's your name, love?'

'Olive.'

'Right, Olive, you lead the way. Let's see what's upset you.'

Would it have been better to know what was in there? Probably not. He often thought afterwards that he could never have entered the room at all if he'd been told in advance that he was about to step into a human abattoir. He stared in horror at the butchered bodies, the axe, the blood that ran in rivers across the floor, and his shock was so great that he could hardly breathe for the iron fist that thrust against his diaphragm and squeezed the breath from his lungs. The room reeked of blood. He leant against the door jamb and sucked desperately at the sickly, cloying air, before bolting down the corridor and retching over and over again into the tiny patch of front garden.

Olive sat on the stairs and watched him, her fat moon face as white and pasty as his. 'You should have brought a friend,' she told him miserably. 'It wouldn't have been so bad if there'd been two of you.'

He held a handkerchief to his lips as he used his radio to summon assistance. While he spoke he eyed her warily, registering the blood all over her clothes. Nausea choked him. Je-*sus*! JESUS! How mad was she? *Mad enough to take the axe to him?* 'For God's sake, make it quick,' he shouted into the mouthpiece. 'This is an emergency.' He stayed outside, too frightened to go back in.

She looked at him stolidly. 'I won't hurt you. There's nothing to be afraid of.'

He mopped at his forehead. 'Who are they, Olive?'

'My mother and sister.' Her eyes slid to her hands. 'We had a row.'

His mouth was dry with shock and fear. 'Best not talk about it,' he said.

Tears rolled down her fat cheeks. 'I didn't mean it to happen. We had a row. My mother got so angry with me. Should I give my statement now?'

He shook his head. 'There's no hurry.'

She stared at him without blinking, her tears drying in dirty streaks down her face. 'Will you be able to take them away before my father comes home?' she asked him after a minute or two. 'I think it would be better.'

Bile rose in his throat. 'When do you expect him back?'

'He leaves work at three o'clock. He's part-time.'

Hal glanced at his watch, an automatic gesture. His mind was numb. 'It's twenty to now.'

She was very composed. 'Then perhaps a policeman could go there and explain what's happened. It would be better,' she said again. They heard the wail of approaching sirens. 'Please,' she said urgently.

He nodded. 'I'll arrange it. Where does he work?'

'Carters Haulage. It's in the Docks.'

He was passing the message on as two cars, sirens shrieking, swept round the corner and bore down on number 22. Doors flew open all along the road and curious faces peered out. Hal switched off the radio and looked at her. 'All done,' he said. 'You can stop worrying about your father.'

A large tear slipped down her blotchy face. 'Should I make a pot of tea?'

Hal thought of the kitchen. 'Better not.'

The sirens stilled as policemen erupted from the cars. 'I'm sorry to cause so much bother,' she said into the silence.

She spoke very little after that, but only, thought Hal on reflection, because nobody spoke to her. She was packed into the living room, under the eye of a shocked W.P.C., and sat in bovine immobility watching the comings and goings through the open door. If she was aware of the mounting horror that was gathering about her, she didn't show it. Nor, as time passed and the signs of emotion faded from her face, did she display any further grief or remorse for what she had done. Faced with such complete indifference, the consensus view was that she was mad.

'But she wept in front of you,' interrupted Roz. 'Did *you* think she was mad?'

'I spent two hours in that kitchen with the pathologist, trying to work out the order of events from the blood splashes over the floor, the table, the kitchen units. And then, after the photographs had been taken, we embarked on the grisly jigsaw of deciding which bit belonged to which woman. Of course I thought she was mad. No normal person could have done it.'

Roz chewed her pencil. 'That's begging the question, you know. All you're really saying is that the act itself was one of madness. I asked you if, from your experience of her, you thought Olive was mad.'

'And you're splitting hairs. As far as I could see, the two were inextricably linked. Yes, I thought Olive was mad. That's why we were so careful to make sure her solicitor was there when she made her statement. The idea of her getting off on a technicality and spending twelve months in hospital before some idiot psychiatrist decided she was responding well enough to treatment to be allowed out scared us rigid.'

'So did it surprise you when she was judged fit to plead guilty?'

'Yes,' he admitted, 'it did.'

*

At around six o'clock attention switched to Olive. Areas of dried blood were lifted carefully from her arms and each fingernail was minutely scraped before she was taken upstairs to bathe herself and change into clean clothes. Everything she had been wearing was packed into individual polythene bags and loaded into a police van. An inspector drew Hal to one side.

'I gather she's already admitted she did it.'

Hal nodded. 'More or less.'

Roz interrupted again. 'Less is right. If what you said earlier is correct, she did not admit anything. She said they'd had a row, that her mother got angry, and she didn't mean it to happen. She didn't say she had killed them.'

Hal agreed. 'I accept that. But the implication was there which is why I told her not to talk about it. I didn't want her claiming afterwards that she hadn't been properly cautioned.' He sipped his coffee. 'By the same token, she didn't deny killing them, which is the first thing an innocent person would have done, especially as she had their blood all over her.'

'But the point is, you assumed her guilt before you knew it for a fact.'

'She was certainly our prime suspect,' he said drily.

*

The inspector ordered Hal to take Olive down to the station. 'But don't let her say anything until we can get hold of a solicitor. We'll do it by the book. OK?'

Hal nodded again. 'There's a father. He'll be at the nick by now. I sent a car to pick him up from work but I don't know what he's been told.'

'You'd better find out then, and, for Christ's sake, Sergeant, if he doesn't know, then break it to him gently or you'll give the poor sod a heart attack. Find out if he's got a solicitor and if he's willing to have him or her represent his daughter.'

They put a blanket over Olive's head when they took her out to the car. A crowd had gathered, lured by rumours of a hideous crime, and cameramen jostled for a photograph. Boos greeted her appearance and a woman laughed. 'What good's a blanket, boys? You'd need a bloody marquee to cover that fat cow. I'd recognize her legs anywhere. What you done, Olive?'

Roz interrupted again when he jumped the story on to his meeting with Robert Martin at the police station.

'Hang on. Did she say anything in the car?'

He thought for a moment. 'She asked me if I liked her dress. I said I did.'

'Were you being polite?'

'No. It was a vast improvement on the T-shirt and trousers.'

'Because they had blood on them?'

'Probably. No,' he contradicted himself, ruffling his hair, 'because the dress gave her a bit of shape, I suppose, made her look more feminine. Does it matter?'

Roz ignored this. 'Did she say anything else?'

'I think she said something like: "That's good. It's my favourite." '

'But in her statement, she said she was going to London. Why wasn't she wearing the dress when she committed the murders?'

He looked puzzled. 'Because she was going to London in trousers, presumably.'

'No,' said Roz stubbornly. 'If the dress was her favourite, then that's what she would have worn for her trip to town. London was her birthday treat to herself. She probably had dreams of bumping into Mr Right on Waterloo station. It simply wouldn't occur to her to wear anything but her best. You need to be a woman to understand that.'

He was amused. 'But I see hundreds of girls walking around in shapeless trousers and baggy T-shirts, particularly the fat ones. I think they look grotesque but they seem to like it. Presumably they're making a statement about their refusal to pander to conventional standards of beauty. Why should Olive have been any different?'

'Because she wasn't the rebellious type. She lived at home under her mother's thumb, took the job her mother wanted her to take, and was apparently so unused to going out alone for the day that she had to beg her sister to go with her.' She drummed her fingers impatiently on the table. 'I'm right. I know I am. If she wasn't lying about the trip to London then she should have been wearing her dress.'

He was not impressed. 'She was rebellious enough to kill her mother and sister,' he remarked. 'If she could do that, she could certainly go to London in trousers. You're splitting hairs again. Anyway, she might have changed to keep the dress clean.'

'But she definitely intended to go to London? Did you check that?'

'She certainly booked the day off work. We accepted that London was where she was going because, as far as we could establish, she hadn't mentioned her plans to anyone else.'

'Not even to her father?'

'If she did, he didn't remember it.'

Olive waited in an interview room while Hal spoke to her father. It was a difficult conversation. Whether he had schooled himself to it, or whether it was a natural trick of behaviour, Robert Martin reacted little to anything that was said to him. He was a handsome man but, in the way that a Greek sculpture is handsome, he invited admiration but lacked warmth or attraction. His curiously impassive face had an unlined and ageless quality, and only his hands, knotted with arthritis, gave any indication that he had passed his middle years. Once or twice he smoothed his blond hair with the flat of his hand or touched his fingers to his tie, but for all the expression on his plastic features Hal might have been passing the time of day. It was impossible to gauge from his expression how deeply he was shocked or whether, indeed, he was shocked at all.

'Did you like him?' asked Roz.

'Not much. He reminded me of Olive. I don't know where I am with people who hide their feelings. It makes me uncomfortable.'

Roz could identify with that.

Hal kept detail to a minimum, informing him only that the bodies of his wife and one of his daughters had been discovered that afternoon in the kitchen of his house, and that his other daughter, Olive, had given the police reason to believe she had killed them.

Robert Martin crossed his legs and folded his hands calmly in his lap. 'Have you charged her with anything?'

'No. We haven't questioned her either.' He watched the other man closely. 'Frankly, sir, in view of the serious nature of the possible charges we think she should have a solicitor with her.'

'Of course. I'm sure my man, Peter Crew, will come.' Mild enquiry twitched his brows. 'What's the procedure? Should I telephone him?'

Hal was puzzled by the man's composure. He wiped a hand across his face. 'Are you sure you understand what's happened, sir?'

'I believe so. Gwen and Amber are dead and you think Olive murdered them.'

'That's not quite accurate. Olive has implied that she was responsible for their deaths but, until we take a statement from her, I can't say what the charges will be.' He paused for a moment. 'I want you to be quite clear on this, Mr Martin. The Home Office pathologist who examined the scene had no doubts that considerable ferocity was used both before and after death. In due course, I'm afraid to say, we will have to ask you to identify the bodies and you may, when you see them, feel less charitably inclined towards any possible suspect. On that basis, do you have any reservations about your solicitor representing Olive?'

Martin shook his head. 'I would be happier dealing with someone I know.'

'There may be a conflict of interests. Have you considered that?'

'In what way?'

'At the risk of labouring the point, sir,' said Hal

coldly, 'your wife and daughter have been brutally murdered. I imagine you will want the perpetrator prosecuted?' He lifted an eyebrow in enquiry and Martin nodded. 'Then you may well want a solicitor yourself to ensure that the prosecution proceeds to your satisfaction, but if your own solicitor is already representing your daughter, he will be unable to assist you because your interests will conflict with your daughter's.'

'Not if she's innocent.' Martin pinched the crease in his trousers, aligning it with the centre of his knee. 'I am really not concerned with what Olive may have implied, Sergeant Hawksley. There is no conflict of interest in my mind. Establishing her innocence and representing me in pressing for a prosecution can be done by the same solicitor. Now, if you could lend me the use of a telephone, I will ring Peter Crew, and afterwards, perhaps you will allow me to talk to my daughter.'

Hal shook his head. 'I'm sorry, sir, but that won't be possible, not until we've taken a statement from her. You will also be required to make a statement. You may be allowed to speak to her afterwards, but at the moment I can't guarantee it.'

'And that,' he said, recalling the incident, 'was the one and only time he showed any emotion. He looked quite upset, but whether because I'd denied him access to Olive or because I'd told him he'd have to make a statement, I don't know.' He considered for a moment. 'It must have been the denial of access. We went through every minute of that man's day and he came out whiter than white. He worked in an open-plan office with five other people and, apart from the odd trip to the lavatory, he was under someone's eye the whole day. There just wasn't time for him to go home.'

'But you did suspect him?'

'Yes.'

Roz looked interested. 'In spite of Olive's confession?'

He nodded. 'He was so damn cold blooded about it all. Even identifying the bodies didn't faze him.'

Roz thought for a moment. 'There was another conflict of interest which you don't seem to have considered.' She chewed her pencil. 'If Robert Martin was the murderer, he could have used his solicitor to manipulate Olive into confessing. Peter Crew makes no secret of his dislike of her, you know. I think he regrets the abolition of capital punishment.'

Hal folded his arms, then smiled in amusement. 'You'll have to be very careful if you intend to make statements like that in your book, Miss Leigh. Solicitors are not required to like their clients, they merely have to represent them. In any case, Robert Martin dropped out of the frame very rapidly. We toyed with the idea that he killed Gwen and Amber before he went to work and Olive then set about disposing the bodies to protect him, but the numbers didn't add up. He had an alibi even for that. There was a neighbour who saw her husband off to work a few minutes before Martin himself left. Amber and Gwen were alive then because she spoke to them on their doorstep. She remembered asking Amber how she was getting on at Glitzy. They waved as Martin drove away.'

'He could have gone round the corner and come back again.'

'He left home at eight-thirty and arrived at work at nine. We tested the drive and it took half an hour.' He shrugged. 'As I said, he was whiter than white.'

'What about lunch? Could he have gone back then?'

'He had a pint and a sandwich in the local pub with two men from the office.'

'OK. Go on.'

There was little more to tell. In spite of Crew's advice to remain silent, Olive agreed to answer police questions, and at nine-thirty, expressing relief to have got the whole thing off her chest, she signed her statement and was formally charged with the murder of her mother and sister.

Following her remand into custody on the morning of the next day, Hal and Geoff Wyatt were given the task of detailing the police case against her. It was a straightforward collating of pathological, forensic, and police evidence, all of which, upon examination, supported the facts given in Olive's statement. Namely that, acting alone, she had, on the morning of the ninth of September, 1987, murdered her mother and sister by cutting their throats with a carving knife.

Seven

THERE WAS A lengthy silence. Hal splayed his hands on the scrubbed deal table and pushed himself to his feet. 'How about some more coffee?' He watched her industrious pen scribbling across a page of her notebook. 'More coffee?' he repeated.

'Mm. Black, no sugar.' She didn't look up but went on writing.

'Sure, baas. Don't mind me, baas. I'se just de paid help, baas.'

Roz laughed. 'Sorry. Yes, thank you, I'd love some more coffee. Look, if you can just bear with me for a moment, I've a few questions to ask and I'm trying to jot them down while the thing's still fresh.'

He watched her while she wrote. Botticelli's *Venus*, he had thought the first time he saw her, but she was too thin for his liking, hardly more than seven stone and a good five feet six. She made a fabulous clothes'-horse, of course, but there was no softness to hug, no comfort in the tautly strung body. He wondered if her slenderness was a deliberate thing or if she lived on her nerves. The latter, he thought. She was clearly a woman of obsessions if her crusade for Olive was anything to go by. He put a fresh cup of coffee in front of her but stayed standing, cradling his own coffee cup between his hands.

'OK,' she said, sorting out the pages, 'let's start with the kitchen. You say the forensic evidence supported Olive's statement that she acted alone. How?'

He thought back. 'You have to picture that place. It was a slaughter house, and every time she moved she left footprints in the congealing blood. We photographed each one separately and they were all hers, including the bloody prints that her shoes left on the carpet in the hall.' He shrugged. 'There were also bloody palm-prints and fingerprints over most of the surfaces where she had rested her hands. Again all hers. We did raise other fingerprints, admittedly, including about three, I think, which we were never able to match with any of the Martins or their neighbours, but you'd expect that in a kitchen. The gas man, the electricity man, a plumber maybe. There was no blood on them so we inclined to the view that they had been left in the days prior to the murder.'

Roz chewed her pencil. 'And the axe and the knife? I suppose they had only her fingerprints.'

'Actually no. The cutting weapons were so smeared that we couldn't get anything off them at all.' He chuckled at her immediate interest. 'You're chasing red herrings. Wet blood is slippery stuff. It would have been very surprising if we *had* found some perfect prints. The rolling pin had three damn good ones, all hers.'

She made a note. 'I didn't know you could take them off unpolished wood.'

'It was solid glass, two feet long, a massive thing. I suppose if we were surprised by anything it was that the blows she struck with it hadn't killed Gwen and Amber. They were both tiny women. By rights she should have smashed their skulls with it.' He sipped his coffee. 'It leant some credence to her story, in fact, that she only tapped them lightly in the first instance to make them shut up. We were afraid she might use that in her defence to get the charge reduced to manslaughter, the argument being that she slit their throats *only* because she believed they were already dead and she was trying to dismember them in panic. If she could then go on to show that the initial blows with the rolling pin were struck with very little force – well, she might almost have persuaded a jury that the whole thing was a macabre accident. Which is one good reason, by the way, why she never mentioned the fight with her mother. We did push her on that, but she kept insisting that no mist on the mirror meant they were dead.' He pulled a face. 'So I spent a very unpleasant two days working with the pathologist and the bodies, going step by step through what actually happened. We ended up with enough evidence of the fight Gwen put up to save her life to press a murder charge. Poor woman. Her hands and arms were literally cut to ribbons where she had tried to ward off the blows.'

Roz stared into her coffee for some minutes. 'Olive was very kind to me the other day. I can't imagine her doing something like that.'

'You've never seen her in a rage. You might think differently if you had.'

'Have you seen her in a rage?'

'No,' he admitted.

'Well, I find it difficult even to imagine that. I accept she's put on a lot of weight in the last six years but she's a heavy, stolid type. It's highly strung, impatient people who lose their tempers.' She saw his scepticism and laughed. 'I know, I know, amateur psychology of the worst kind. Just two more questions then I'll leave you in peace. What happened to Gwen and Amber's clothes?'

'She burnt them in one of those square wire incinerators in the garden. We retrieved some scraps from the ashes which matched the descriptions that Martin gave of the clothes the two women had been wearing that morning.'

'Why did she do that?'

'To get rid of them, presumably.'

'You didn't ask her?'

He frowned. 'I'm sure we must have done. I can't remember now.'

'There's nothing in her statement about burning clothes.'

He lowered his head in reflection and pressed a thumb and forefinger to his eyelids. 'We asked her why she took their clothes off,' he murmured, 'and she said they had to be naked or she couldn't see where to make the cuts through the joints. I think Geoff then asked her what she had done with the clothes.' He fell silent.

'And?'

He looked up and rubbed his jaw pensively. 'I don't think she gave an answer. If she did, I can't remember it. I have a feeling the information about the scraps in the incinerator came in the next morning when we made a thorough search of the garden.'

'So you asked her then?'

He shook his head. 'I didn't, though I suppose Geoff may have done. Gwen had a floral nylon overall that had melted over a lump of wool and cotton. We had to peel it apart into its constituent elements but there was enough there that was recognizable. Martin ID'd the bits and so did the neighbour.' He stabbed a finger in the air. 'There were some buttons, too. Martin recognized those straightaway as being from the dress his wife had been wearing.'

'But didn't you wonder why Olive took time out to burn the clothes? She could have put them in the suitcases with the bodies and dumped the whole lot in the sea.'

'The incinerator certainly wasn't burning at five o'clock that night or we'd have noticed it; therefore disposing of the clothes must have been one of the first things she did. She wouldn't have seen it as taking time out because at that stage she probably still thought dismembering two bodies would be comparatively easy. Look, she was trying to get rid of evidence. The only reason she panicked and called us in was because her father was coming home. If it had been just the three women living in that house she could have gone through with her plan, and we'd have had the job of trying to identify some bits and pieces of mutilated flesh found floating in the sea off Southampton. She might even have got away with it.'

'I doubt it. The neighbours weren't stupid. They'd have wondered why Gwen and Amber were missing.'

'True,' he conceded. 'What was the other question?'

'Did Olive's hands and arms have a lot of scratches on them from her fight with Gwen?'

He shook his head. 'None. She had some bruising but no scratches.'

Roz stared at him. 'Didn't that strike you as odd? You said Gwen was fighting for her life.'

'She had nothing to scratch with,' he said almost apologetically. 'Her fingernails were bitten to the quick. It was rather pathetic in a woman of her age. All she could do was grip Olive's wrists to try and keep the knife away. That's what the bruises were. Deep finger-marks. We took photographs of them.'

With an abrupt movement Roz squared her papers and dropped them into her briefcase. 'Not much room for doubt then, is there?' she said, picking up her coffee cup.

'None at all. And it wouldn't have made any difference, you know, if she'd kept her mouth shut or pleaded not guilty. She would still have been convicted. The evidence against her was overwhelming. In the end, even her father had to accept that. I felt quite sorry for him then. He became an old man overnight.'

Roz glanced at the tape, which was still running. 'Was he very fond of her?'

'I don't know. He was the most undemonstrative person I've ever met. I got the impression he wasn't fond of any of them but' – he shrugged – 'he certainly took Olive's guilt very badly.'

She drank her coffee. 'Presumably the post-mortem revealed that Amber had had a baby when she was thirteen?'

He nodded.

'Did you pursue that at all? Try and trace the child?'

'We didn't see the need. It had happened eight years before. It was hardly likely to have any bearing on the case.' He waited, but she didn't say anything. 'So? Will you go on with the book?'

'Oh, yes,' she said.

He looked surprised. 'Why?'

'Because there are more inconsistencies now than there were before.' She held up her fingers and ticked them off point by point. 'Why was she crying so much when she telephoned the police station that the desk sergeant couldn't understand what she was saying? Why wasn't she wearing her best dress for London? Why did she burn the clothes? Why did her father think she was innocent? Why wasn't he shocked by Gwen and Amber's deaths? Why did she say she didn't like Amber? Why didn't she mention the fight with her mother if she intended to plead guilty? Why were the blows from the rolling pin so comparatively light? Why? Why? Why?' She dropped her hands to the table with a wry smile. 'They may very well be red herrings but I can't get rid of a gut feeling that there's something wrong. Ultimately, perhaps, I cannot square your and her solicitor's conviction that Olive was mad with the assessments of five psychiatrists who all say she's normal.'

He studied her for some minutes in silence. 'You accused me of assuming her guilt before I knew it for a fact, but you're doing something rather worse. You're assuming her innocence *in spite of* the facts. Supposing you manage to whip up support for her through this book of yours – and in view of the way the judicial system is reeling at the moment, that's not as unlikely as it should be – have you no qualms about releasing someone like her back into society?'

'None at all, if she's innocent.'

'And if she isn't, but you get her out anyway?'

'Then the law is an ass.'

'All right, if she didn't do it, who did?'

'Someone she cared about.' She finished her coffee and switched off the tape. 'Anything else just doesn't make sense.' She shut the recorder into her briefcase and stood up. 'You've been very kind to give up so much of your time. Thank you, and thank you for the lunch.' She held out a hand.

He took it gravely. 'My pleasure, Miss Leigh.' Her fingers, soft and warm in his, moved nervously when he held them too long, and he thought she seemed suddenly rather afraid of him. It was probably for the best. One way and another, she spelt trouble.

She walked to the door. 'Goodbye, Sergeant Hawksley. I hope the business picks up for you.'

He gave a savage smile. 'It will. This is what's known as a temporary blip, I assure you.'

'Good.' She paused. 'There's just one last thing. I understand Robert Martin told you he thought the more likely scenario was that Gwen battered Amber, and Olive then killed Gwen trying to defend her sister. Why did you dismiss that possibility?'

'It didn't hold water. The pathologist established that both throats were cut with the same hand. The size, depth, and angle of the wounds were consistent with one attacker. Gwen wasn't just fighting for herself, you know, she was fighting for Amber, too. Olive is completely ruthless. You would be very foolish to forget that.' He smiled again but the smile didn't reach his eyes. 'If you'll take my advice you'll abandon the whole thing.'

Roz shrugged. 'I tell you what, Sergeant' – she gestured towards the restaurant – 'you mind your business, and I'll mind mine.'

He listened to her heels tapping away down the alley, then reached for the telephone and dialled. 'Geoff,' he snapped into the mouthpiece, 'get down here, will you? We need to talk.' His eyes hardened as he listened to the voice at the other end. 'Like hell it's not your problem. I'm damned if I'll be the fall guy for this one.'

Roz glanced at her watch as she drove away. It was four thirty. If she pushed it she might catch Peter Crew before he went home for the day. She found a parking space in the centre of Southampton and arrived at his office just as he was leaving.

'Mr Crew!' she called, running after him.

He turned with his unconvincing smile, only to frown when he saw who it was. 'I've no time to talk to you now, Miss Leigh. I have an engagement.'

'Let me walk with you,' she urged. 'I won't delay you, I promise.'

He gave a nod of acquiescence and set off again,

the hair of his toupee bobbing in time to his steps. 'My car isn't far.'

Roz did not waste time on pleasantries. 'I gather Mr Martin left his money to Amber's illegitimate son. I have been told' – she stretched the truth like a piece of elastic – 'that he was adopted by some people called Brown who have since emigrated to Australia. Can you tell me if you've made any progress in finding him?'

Mr Crew shot her an annoyed glance. 'Now where did you find that out, I wonder?' His voice clipped the words angrily. 'Has someone in my practice been talking?'

'No,' she assured him. 'I had it from an independent source.'

His eyes narrowed. 'I find that hard to believe. May I ask who it was?'

Roz smiled easily. 'Someone who knew Amber at the time the baby was born.'

'How did they know the name?'

'I've no idea.'

'Robert certainly wouldn't have talked,' he muttered. 'There are rules governing the tracing of adopted children, which he was well aware of, but even allowing for that he was passionate on the subject of secrecy. If the child were to be found he didn't want any publicity surrounding the inheritance. The stigma of the murders could follow the boy all his life.' He shook his head crossly. 'I must insist, Miss

Leigh, that you keep this information to yourself. It would be gross irresponsibility to publish it. It could jeopardize the lad's future.'

'You really do have quite the wrong impression of me,' said Roz pleasantly. 'I approach my work with immense care, and I do not set out to expose people for the sake of it.'

He turned a corner. 'Well, be warned, young lady. I shan't hesitate to take out an injunction against your book if I think it justified.' A gust of wind lifted the toupee's peak and he pressed it firmly to his head like a hat.

Roz, a step or two behind him, scurried alongside. 'Fair enough,' she said, biting back her laughter. 'So, on that basis, could you answer my question? Have you found him yet? Are you anywhere near finding him?'

He padded on doggedly. 'Without wishing to be offensive, Miss Leigh, I don't see how that information can help you. We have just agreed you won't be publishing it.'

She decided to be straight with him. 'Olive knows all about him, knows her father left him his money, knows you're looking for him.' She lifted her hands at his expression of irritation. 'Not, in the first instance, from me, Mr Crew. She's very astute and what she hadn't guessed for herself she picked up on the prison grapevine. She said her father would always leave money to family if he could so it hardly required much imagination to guess that he would try and trace Amber's child. Anyway, whether or not you've had any success seems to matter to her. I hoped you could tell me something that would set her mind at rest.'

He stopped abruptly. 'Does she want him found?'

'I don't know.'

'Hm. Perhaps she thinks the money will come to her in the absence of the named beneficiary?'

Roz showed her surprise. 'I don't think that's ever occurred to her. It couldn't, anyway, could it? You made that point before.'

Mr Crew set off again. 'Robert did not insist that Olive should be kept in the dark. His only instruction was that we should avoid distressing her unnecessarily. Wrongly, perhaps, I assumed that knowledge of the terms of the will *would* distress her. However, if she is already acquainted with them – well, well, you can leave that with me, Miss Leigh. Was there anything else?'

'Yes. Did Robert Martin ever visit her in prison?'

'No. I'm sorry to say he never spoke to her again after she was charged with the murders.'

Roz caught his arm. 'But he thought she was innocent,' she protested with some indignation, 'and he paid her legal bills. Why wouldn't he see her? That was very cruel, wasn't it?'

There was a sharp gleam in the man's eyes. 'Very cruel,' he agreed, 'but not on Robert's part. It was

Olive who refused to see him. It drove him to his death, which, I think, was her intention all along.'

Roz frowned unhappily. 'You and I have very different views of her, Mr Crew. I've only experienced her kindness.' The frown deepened. 'She did know he wanted to see her, I suppose.'

'Of course. As a prosecution witness he had to apply to the Home Office for special permission to visit her, even though she was his daughter. If you contact them they'll verify it for you.' He moved on again and Roz had to run to keep up with him.

'What about the inconsistencies in her statement, Mr Crew? Did you ask her about them?'

'What inconsistencies?'

'Well, for example, the fact that she doesn't mention the fight with her mother but claims Gwen and Amber were dead before she started to dismember them.'

He cast an impatient glance at his watch. 'She was lying.'

Roz caught at his arm again and forced him to stop. 'You were her solicitor,' she said angrily. 'You had a duty to believe her.'

'Don't be naïve, Miss Leigh. I had a duty to *represent* her.' He shook himself free. 'If solicitors were required to believe everything their clients told them there would be little or no legal representation left.' His lips thinned in distaste. 'In any case I did believe her. She said she killed them and I accepted it. I had to. In spite of every attempt I made to suggest she said nothing, she insisted on making her confession.' His eyes bored into hers. 'Are you telling me now that she denies the murders?'

'No,' Roz admitted, 'but I don't think the version she gave the police is the correct one.'

He studied her for a moment. 'Did you talk to Graham Deedes?' She nodded. 'And?'

'He agrees with you.'

'The police?'

She nodded again. 'One of them. He also agrees with you.'

'And doesn't that tell you anything?'

'Not really. Deedes was briefed by you and never even spoke to her and the police have been wrong before.' She brushed a curl of red hair from her face. 'Unfortunately, I don't have your faith in British justice.'

'Obviously not.' Crew smiled coolly. 'But your scepticism is misplaced this time. Good day to you, Miss Leigh.' He loped away up the wind-swept street, the absurd toupee held in place under his hand, his coat-tails whipping about his long legs. He was a comical figure, but Roz did not feel like laughing. For all his idiotic mannerisms he had a certain dignity.

She telephoned St Angela's Convent from a payphone but it was after five o'clock and whoever answered said Sister Bridget had gone home for the evening. She called Directory Enquiries for the DSS number in Dawlington, but, when she tried it, the office had closed for the night and there was no answer. Back in her car she pencilled in a rough timetable for the following morning, then sat for some time with her notebook propped against the steering-wheel, running over in her mind what Crew had told her. But she couldn't concentrate. Her attention kept wandering to the more attractive lure of Hal Hawksley in the Poacher's kitchen.

He had an unnerving trick of catching her eye when she wasn't expecting it, and the shock to her system every time was cataclysmic. She thought 'going weak at the knees' was something invented by romantic authoresses. But the way things were, if she went back to the Poacher, she'd need a Zimmer frame just to make it through the door! *Was she mad?* The man was some sort of gangster. Whoever heard of a restaurant without customers? People had to eat, even in recessions. With a rueful shake of her head, she fired the engine and set off back to London. *What the hell, anyway!* Sod's law predicated that because thoughts of him filled her mind with erotic fantasies his thoughts of her (if he thought about her at all) would be anything but libidinous.

London, when she reached it, was fittingly clogged

and oppressive with Thursday night rush-hour traffic.

An older motherly inmate, elected by the others, paused nervously by the open door. The Sculptress terrified her but, as the girls kept saying, she was the only one Olive would talk to. You remind her of her mother, they all said. The idea alarmed her, but she *was* curious. She watched the huge brooding figure, clumsily rolling a cigarette paper around a meagre sprinkling of tobacco, for several moments before she spoke. 'Hey, Sculptress! Who's the redhead you're seeing?'

Except for a brief flick of her eyes, Olive ignored her.

'Here, have one of mine.' She fished a pack of Silk Cut from her pocket and proffered it. The response was immediate. Like a dog responding to the ringing tap of its dinner plate, Olive shuffled across the floor and took one, secreting it in the folds of her dress somewhere. 'So who's the redhead?' persisted the other.

'An author. She's writing a book about me.'

'Christ!' said the older woman in disgust. 'What she want to write about you for? I'm the one got bloody stitched up.'

Olive stared at her. 'Maybe I did, too.'

'Oh, sure,' the other sniggered, tapping her thigh. 'Now pull the other one. It's got frigging bells on.'

A wheeze of amusement gusted from Olive's lips. 'Well, you know what they say: you can fool some of the people all of the time and all of the people some of the time . . .' She paused invitingly.

'But not all of the people all of the time,' the woman finished obligingly. She wagged her finger. 'You haven't got a prayer.'

Olive's unblinking eyes held hers. 'So who needs prayers?' She tapped the side of her head. 'Find yourself a gullible journalist, then use a bit more of this. Even *you* might get somewhere. She's an opinion-former. You fool her and she fools everyone else.'

'That stinks!' declared the woman incautiously. 'It's only the bloody psychos they're ever interested in. The rest of us poor sods can go hang ourselves for all they care.'

Something rather unpleasant shifted at the back of Olive's tiny eyes. 'Are you calling me a psycho?'

The woman smiled weakly and retreated a step. 'Hey, Sculptress, it was a slip of the tongue.' She held up her hands. 'OK? No harm done.' She was sweating as she walked away.

Behind her, using her bulk to obscure what she was doing from prying eyes, Olive took the clay figure she was working on from her bottom drawer and set her ponderous fingers to moulding the child on its mother's lap. Whether it was intentional or whether she hadn't the skill to do it differently, the mother's crude hands, barely disinterred from the clay, seemed to be smothering the life from the baby's plump, round body.

Olive crooned quietly to herself as she worked. Behind the mother and child, a series of figures, like grey gingerbread men, lined the back of the table. Two or three had lost their heads.

He sat slumped on the steps outside the front door of her block of flats, smelling of beer, his head buried in his hands. Roz stared at him for several seconds, her face blank of expression. 'What are you doing here?'

He had been crying, she saw. 'We need to talk,' he said. 'You never talk to me.'

She didn't bother to answer. Her ex-husband was very drunk. There was nothing they could say that hadn't been said a hundred times before. She was so tired of his messages on her answerphone, tired of the letters, tired of the hatred that knotted inside her when she heard his voice or saw his handwriting.

He plucked at her skirt as she tried to pass, clinging to it like a child. 'Please, Roz. I'm too pissed to go home.'

She took him upstairs out of an absurd sense of past duty. 'But you can't stay,' she told him, pushing him on to the sofa. 'I'll ring Jessica and get her to come and collect you.'

'Sam's sick,' he muttered. 'She won't leave him.'

Roz shrugged unsympathetically. 'Then I'll call a cab.'

'No.' He reached down and jerked the jackplug from its socket. 'I'm staying.

There was a raw edge to his voice which was a warning, if she had chosen to heed it, that he was in no mood to be trifled with. But they had been married too long and had had too many bruising rows for her to allow him to dictate terms. She had only contempt for him now. 'Please yourself,' she said. 'I'll go to a hotel.'

He stumbled to the door and stood with his back to it. 'It wasn't my fault, Roz. It was an accident. For God's sake, will you stop punishing me?'

Eight

ROZ CLOSED HER eyes and saw again the tattered, pale face of her five-year-old daughter, as ugly in death as she had been beautiful in life, her skin ripped and torn by the exploding glass of the windscreen. Could she have accepted it more easily, she wondered as she had wondered so many times before, if Rupert had died too? Could she have forgiven him, dead, as she could not forgive him, alive? 'I never see you,' she said with a tight smile, 'so how can I be punishing you? You're drunk and you're being ridiculous. Neither of which conditions is any way out of the ordinary.' He had an unhealthy and uncared-for look which fuelled her scorn and made her impatient. 'Oh, for God's sake,' she snapped, 'just get out, will you? I don't feel anything for you any more and, to be honest, I don't think I ever did.' But that wasn't true, not really. 'You can't hate what you never loved,' Olive had said.

Tears slithered down his drink-sodden face. 'I weep for her every day, you know.'

'Do you, Rupert? I don't. I haven't the energy.'

'Then you didn't love her as much as I loved her,' he sobbed, his body heaving to control itself.

Roz's lips curled contemptuously. 'Really? Then why your indecent haste to provide her replacement? I worked it out, you know. You must have impregnated your precious Jessica within a week of walking away unscathed from the – *accident*.' She larded the word with sarcasm. 'Is Sam a good replacement, Rupert? Does he wind your hair round his finger the way Alice used to do? Does he laugh like her? Does he wait by the door for you and hug your knees and say: "Mummy, Mummy, Daddy's home"?' Her anger made her voice brittle. 'Does he, Rupert? Is he everything Alice was and more? Or is he nothing like her and that's why you have to weep for her every day?'

'He's a baby, for Christ's sake.' He clenched his fists, her hatred mirrored in his eyes. 'God, you're a fucking bitch, Roz. I never set out to replace her. How could I? Alice was Alice. I couldn't bring her back.'

She turned away to look out of the window. 'No.'

'Then why do you blame Sam? It wasn't his fault either. He doesn't even know he had a half-sister.'

'I don't blame Sam.' She stared at a couple, lit by orange light, on the other side of the road. They held each other tenderly, stroking hair, stroking arms, kissing. How naïve they were. They thought love was kind. 'I resent him.'

She heard him blunder against her coffee table. 'That's just bloody spite,' he slurred.

'Yes,' she said quietly, more to herself than to him, her breath misting the glass, 'but I don't see why you should be happy when I am not? You killed my daughter but you got away with it because the law said you'd suffered enough. I've suffered far more and my only crime was to let my adulterous husband have access to his daughter because I knew she loved him and I didn't want to see her unhappy.'

'If you'd only been more understanding,' he wept, 'it would never have happened. It was your fault, Roz. You're the one who really killed her.' She didn't hear his approach. She was turning back into the room when his fist smashed against her face.

It was a shabby, sordid fight. Where words had failed them – the very predictability of their conversations meant they were always forearmed – they hit and scratched instead in a brutish desire to hurt. It was a curiously passionless exercise, motivated more by feelings of guilt than by hate or revenge, for at the back of both their minds was the knowledge that it was the failure of their marriage, the war they had conducted between themselves, that had led Rupert to accelerate away in frustrated anger with their daughter, unstrapped, upon the back seat. And who could have foreseen the car that would hurtle out of control across a central reservation and, under the force of its impact, toss a helpless five-year-old through shards of broken glass, smashing her fragile skull as she went? An act of God, according to the insurance company. But for Roz, at least, it had been God's final act. He and Alice had perished together.

Rupert was the first to stay his hand, aware, perhaps, that the fight was an unequal one or because, quite simply, he had sobered up. He crawled away to sit huddled in a corner. Roz fingered the tenderness round her mouth and licked blood from her lips, then closed her eyes and sat for several minutes in restful silence, her murderous anger assuaged. They should have done this a long time ago. She felt at peace for the first time in months, as if she had exorcised her own guilt in some way. She should, she knew, have gone out to the car that day and strapped Alice into the seat herself, but instead she had slammed the front door on them both and retreated to the kitchen to nurse her hurt pride with a bottle of gin and an orgy of tearing up photographs. Perhaps, after all, she had needed to be punished too. Her guilt had never been expiated. Her own atonement, a private rending of herself, had brought about her disintegration and not her redemption.

Enough, she saw now, was enough. *'We are all masters of our fate, Roz, including you.'*

She pushed herself gingerly to her feet, located the jackplug and inserted it back into its socket. She glanced at Rupert for a moment, then dialled Jessica. 'It's Roz,' she said. 'Rupert's here and he needs collecting, I'm afraid.' She heard the sigh at the other end of the line. 'It's the last time, Jessica, I promise.' She gave a hint of a laugh. 'We've declared a truce. No more recriminations. OK, half an hour. He'll be waiting for you downstairs.' She replaced the receiver. 'I mean it, Rupert. It's over. It was an accident. Let's stop blaming each other and find some peace at last.'

Iris Fielding's insensitivity was legendary but even she was shocked by the sight of Roz's battered face the next day. 'God, you look awful!' she said bluntly, making straight for the drinks cabinet and pouring herself a brandy. As an afterthought she poured one for Roz. 'Who did it?'

Roz closed the door and limped back to the sofa.

Iris drained her glass. 'Was it Rupert?' She proffered the second glass to Roz who shook her head to the brandy and the question.

'Of course it wasn't Rupert.' She lowered herself carefully on to the sofa, half lying, half sitting, while Mrs Antrobus stalked across the soft fluff of her dressing-gowned chest to butt her chin with an affectionate head. 'Could you feed Mrs A. for me? There's an opened tin in the fridge.'

Iris glowered at Mrs Antrobus. 'Horrible flea-bitten creature. Where were you when your mistress needed you?' But she disappeared into the kitchen and rattled a saucer anyway. 'Are you sure it wasn't Rupert?' she asked again when she re-emerged.

'No. Not his style at all. The fights we have are entirely verbal and infinitely more bruising.'

Iris looked thoughtful. 'You've always told me how supportive he's been.'

'I lied.'

Iris looked even more thoughtful. 'So who was it?'

'Some creep I picked up at a wine bar. He was more fanciable with his clothes on than off, so I told him to get stuffed and he took exception.' She saw a question in Iris's eyes and smiled cynically through her split lip. 'No, he didn't rape me. My virtue is intact. I defended it with my face.'

'Hm. Well, far be it from me to criticize, my love, but wouldn't it have been more sensible to defend your face with your virtue? I'm not a great believer in fighting over lost causes.' She drank Roz's brandy. 'Did you call the police?'

'No.'

'A doctor?'

'No.' She put a hand on the telephone. 'And you're not calling them either.'

Iris shrugged. 'So what have you been doing all morning?'

'Trying to work out how I could get by without calling anyone. At midday, I realized I couldn't. I've used all my aspirin, I've no food in the house, and

I'm not going out looking like this.' She raised bruised and suspiciously bright eyes. 'So I thought of the least shockable and the most egocentric person I know and I telephoned her. You'll have to go out shopping for me, Iris. I need enough to last me a week.'

Iris was amused. 'I would never deny that I'm egocentric but why is that important?'

Roz bared her teeth. 'Because you're so wrapped up in yourself you'll have forgotten all about this by the time you get home. Plus, you're not going to pressure me into doing the right thing and nailing the little bastard. It wouldn't reflect well on your agency if one of your authors was in the habit of bringing home pick-ups from wine bars.' She clenched both hands over the telephone and Iris watched her knuckles whiten under the strain.

'True,' she agreed calmly.

Roz relaxed a little. 'I really couldn't bear it, you know, if this got out, and it will if doctors or the police are involved. You know the bloody press as well as I do. Any excuse, and they'll plaster their front pages all over again with pictures of Alice in the wreckage.' Poor little Alice. Malign providence had put a freelance photographer beside the dual carriageway when she was tossed like a rag doll from Rupert's car. His dramatic shots – published, according to the tabloid editors, as a tragic reminder to other families of the importance of wearing seat belts – had been

Alice's most lasting memorial. 'You can imagine the sordid parallels they'll draw. MOTHER DISFIGURED LIKE DAUGHTER. I couldn't survive it a second time.' She fished in her pocket and produced a shopping list. 'I'll write you a cheque when you come back. And whatever you do, don't forget the aspirin. I'm in agony.'

Iris tucked the shopping list into her bag. 'Keys,' she said, holding out her hand. 'You can go to bed while I'm out. I'll let myself back in.'

Roz pointed to her keys on a shelf by the door. 'Thank you,' she said, 'and, Iris—' She didn't finish.

'And, Iris, what?'

She made an attempt at a wry grimace but abandoned it because it was too painful. 'And, Iris, I'm sorry.'

'So am I, old thing.' She gave an airy wave and let herself out of the flat.

For reasons best known to herself, Iris returned a couple of hours later with the shopping and a suitcase. 'Don't look at me like that,' she said severely, administering aspirin in a glass of water. 'I intend to keep an eye on you for a day or two. For entirely mercenary purposes, of course. I like to guard my investments closely. And anyway,' she scratched under Mrs Antrobus's chin, 'someone's got to feed this revolting moggy for you. You'll only start howling if it dies of starvation.'

Roz, depressed and very lonely, was touched.

Detective Sergeant Geoff Wyatt toyed unhappily with his wine glass. His stomach was playing up, he was very tired, it was Saturday, he would rather have been at a Saints' football match, and the sight of Hal tucking into a plateful of rare steak needled him. 'Look,' he said, trying to keep the irritation out of his voice, 'I hear what you're saying but evidence is evidence. What are you expecting me to do? Tamper with it?'

'It's hardly evidence if it was tampered with at the outset,' Hal snapped. 'It was a frame, for Christ's sake.' He pushed his plate away. 'You should have had some,' he said acidly. 'It might have improved your temper.'

Wyatt looked away. 'There's nothing wrong with my temper and I ate before I got here.' He lit a cigarette and glanced towards the door into the restaurant. 'I've never felt comfortable in kitchens, not since seeing those women on Olive's floor. Too many murder weapons and too much bloody meat about the place. Couldn't we go next door?'

'Don't be a fool,' said Hal curtly. 'Damn it, Geoff, you owe me a few one way and another.'

Wyatt sighed. 'How's it going to help you if I get suspended for doing dodgy favours for an ex-copper?'

'I'm not asking for dodgy favours. Just get the pressure taken off. Give me a breathing space.'

'How?'

'You could start by persuading the Inspector to back off.'

'And that's not dodgy?' His mouth turned down. 'Anyway, I've tried. He's not playing. He's new, he's honest, and he doesn't like anyone who bends the rules, particularly policemen.' He tapped ash on the floor. 'You should never have left the Force, Hal. I did warn you. It's very lonely outside.'

Hal rubbed his unshaven face. 'It wouldn't be so bad if my erstwhile colleagues didn't keep treating me like a criminal.'

Wyatt stared at the remains of the steak on Hal's plate. He felt very queasy. 'Well, if it comes to that, you shouldn't have been so damn careless, then they wouldn't have to.'

Hal's eyes narrowed unpleasantly. 'One of these days you're going to wish you hadn't said that.'

With a shrug, Wyatt ground his cigarette against his shoe and tossed the butt into the sink. 'Can't see it, old son. I've been shitting my backside off ever since the Inspector rumbled you. It's made me ill, it really has.' He pushed back his chair and stood up. 'Why the hell did you have to cut corners instead of doing it by the book the way you were supposed to?'

Hal nodded towards the door. 'Out,' he said, 'before I rip your two-faced head off.'

'What about that check you wanted me to run?'

Hal fished in his pocket and removed a piece of paper. 'That's her name and address. See if there's anything on her.'

'Like what?'

Hal shrugged. 'Anything that will give me a lever. This book she's writing is too well timed.' He frowned. 'And I don't believe in coincidence.'

One of the few advantages of being fat was that it was easier to hide things. Another bulge here or there passed unnoticed and the soft cavity between Olive's breasts could accommodate itself to almost anything. In any case, she had noticed very early on that the officers preferred not to search her too diligently on the rare occasions when they thought it necessary. She had assumed at first that they were frightened of her, but she soon came to recognize that it was her fatness that inhibited them. Politically correct thinking within the prison service meant that while they were free to say what they liked about her behind her back they had to guard their tongues in her presence and treat her with a modicum of respect. Thus the helpful legacy of her anguished tears during strip-searches at the beginning, when her huge, repulsive body shook with distress, was a reluctance on the part of the screws now to do anything more than a perfunctory running of their hands down the sides of her shift.

But she had problems. Her small family of wax figures, absurdly cheerful in their painted cottonwool wigs and strips of dark material which she had wound around them like miniature suits, kept softening against the warmth of her skin and losing their shape. With infinite patience, she set her awkward fingers to remoulding them, first removing the pins which skewered the wigs to each of the heads. She wondered idly if the one of Roz's husband looked anything like him.

'What a ghastly place this is,' said Iris, gazing critically about the bleak grey walls of Roz's flat from her place on the vinyl sofa. 'Haven't you ever felt the urge to liven it up a bit?'

'No. I'm just passing through. It's a waiting room.'

'You've been here twelve months. I can't think why you don't use the money from the divorce and buy yourself a house.'

Roz rested her head against the back of her chair. 'I like waiting rooms. You can be idle in them without feeling guilty. There's nothing to do except wait.'

Thoughtfully, Iris put a cigarette between her brilliant red lips. 'What are you waiting for?'

'I don't know.'

She flicked a lighter to the tip of her cigarette while her penetrating eye-lined gaze fixed uncomfortably on Roz. 'One thing does puzzle me,' she said. 'If it wasn't Rupert, then why did he leave another tearful message on my answerphone, telling me he had behaved badly?'

'Another?' Roz stared at her hands. 'Does that mean he's done it before?'

'With tedious regularity.'

'You've never mentioned it.'

'You've never asked me.'

Roz digested this for some moments in silence, then let out a long sigh. 'I've been realizing recently how dependent I've become on him.' She touched her sore lip. 'His dependence hasn't changed, of course. It's the same as it always was, a constant demand for reassurance. Don't worry, Rupert. It's not your fault, Rupert. Everything will be all right, Rupert.' She spoke the words without emphasis. 'It's why he prefers women. Women are more sympathetic.' She fell silent.

'How does that make you dependent on him?'

Roz gave a slight smile. 'He's never left me alone long enough to let me think straight. I've been angry for months.' She shrugged. 'It's very destructive. You can't concentrate on anything because the anger won't go away. I tear his letters up without reading them, because I know what they'll say, but his handwriting sets my teeth on edge. If I see him or hear him, I start shaking.' She gave a hollow laugh. 'You can become obsessed by hatred, I think. I could have moved a long time ago but, instead, I stay here waiting for Rupert to make me angry. That's how I'm dependent on him. It's a prison of sorts.'

Iris wiped her cigarette end round the rim of an ashtray. Roz was telling her nothing she hadn't worked out for herself a long time ago, but she had never been able to put it into words for the simple reason that Roz had never let her. She wondered what had happened to bring the barbed wire down. Clearly, it was nothing to do with Rupert, however much Roz might like to think it was. 'So how are you going to break out of this prison? Have you decided?'

'Not yet.'

'Perhaps you should do what Olive has done,' said Iris mildly.

'And what's that?'

'Let someone else in.'

Olive waited by her cell door for two hours. One of the officers, wondering why, paused to talk to her. 'Everything all right, Sculptress?'

The fat woman's eyes fixed on her. 'What day is it?' she demanded.

'Monday.'

'That's what I thought.' She sounded angry.

The officer frowned. 'Are you sure there's nothing wrong?'

'There's nothing.'

'Were you expecting a visitor?'

'No. I'm hungry. What's for tea?'

'Pizza.' Reassured, the officer moved on. It made sense. There were few hours in the day when Olive *wasn't* hungry, and the threat of withholding her meals was often the only way to control her. A medical officer had tried to persuade her once of the benefits of dieting. He had come away very shaken and never tried again. Olive craved food in the way others craved heroin.

In the end Iris stayed for a week and filled the sterile waiting room of Roz's life with the raucous baggage of hers. She ran up a colossal telephone bill phoning her clients and customers at home and abroad, piled the tables with magazines, dropped ash all over the floor, imported armfuls of flowers which she abandoned in the sink when she couldn't find a vase, left the washing-up in tottering stacks on the kitchen work-tops, and regaled Roz, when she wasn't doing something else, with her seemingly inexhaustible flow of anecdotes.

Roz said her farewells on the following Thursday afternoon with some relief and rather more regret. If nothing else, Iris had shown her that a solitary life was emotionally, mentally, and spiritually deadening. There was, after all, only so much that one mind could encompass, and obsessions grew when ideas went unchallenged.

Olive's destruction of her cell that night took the prison by surprise. It was ten minutes before the duty governor was alerted and another ten before a response was possible. It required eight officers to restrain her. They forced her to the ground and brought their combined weight to bear on her, but as one remarked later: 'It was like trying to contain a bull elephant.'

She had wreaked complete havoc on everything. Even the lavatory bowl had shattered under a mighty blow from her welded metal chair which, bent and buckled, had been discarded amongst the shards of porcelain. The few possessions which had adorned her chest of drawers lay broken across the floor and anything that could be lifted had been hurled in fury against the walls. A poster of Madonna, ripped limb from limb, lay butchered on the floor.

Her rage, even under sedation, continued long into the night from the confines of an unfurnished cell, designed to cool the tempers of ungovernable inmates.

'What the hell's got into her?' demanded the duty governor.

'God knows,' said a shaken officer. 'I've always said she should be in Broadmoor. I don't care what the psychiatrists say, she's completely mad. They've no business to leave her here and expect us to look after her.'

They listened to the muffled bellowings from

behind the locked door. 'BI-ITCH! BI-ITCH! BI-ITCH!'

The duty governor frowned. 'Who's she talking about?'

The officer winced. 'One of us, I should think. I wish we could get her transferred. She puts the wind up me, she really does.'

'She'll be fine again tomorrow.'

'Which is why she puts the wind up me. You never know where you are with her.' She tucked her hair back into place. 'You noticed none of her clay figures were touched except the ones she's already mutilated?' She smiled cynically. 'And have you seen that mother and child she's working on? The mother's only smothering her baby, for God's sake. It's obscene. Presumably it's supposed to be Mary and Jesus.' She sighed. 'What do I tell her? No breakfast if she doesn't calm down?'

'It's always worked in the past. Let's hope nothing's changed.'

Nine

THE FOLLOWING MORNING, a week later than planned, Roz was shown through to a clerical supervisor at the Social Security office in Dawlington. He regarded her scabby lip and dark glasses with only mild curiosity and she realized that for him her appearance was nothing unusual. She introduced herself and sat down. 'I telephoned yesterday,' she reminded him.

He nodded. 'Some problem that goes back over six years, you said.' He tapped his forefingers on the desk. 'I should stress we're unlikely to be able to help. We've enough trouble chasing current cases, let alone delving into old records.'

'But you were here six years ago?'

'Seven years in June,' he said without enthusiasm. 'It won't help, I'm afraid. I don't remember you or your circumstances.'

'You wouldn't.' She smiled apologetically. 'I was a little economical with the truth on the telephone. I'm not a consumer. I'm an author. I'm writing a book about Olive Martin. I need to talk to someone who knew her when she worked here and I didn't want a straight refusal down the phone.'

He looked amused, glad perhaps that he was spared an impossible search for lost benefits. 'She was the fat girl down the corridor. I didn't even know what her name was until it appeared in the paper. As far as I remember, I never exchanged more than a dozen words with her. You probably know more about her than I do.' He crossed his arms. 'You should have said what you wanted. You could have saved yourself a drive.'

Roz took out her notebook. 'That doesn't matter. It's names I need. People who did speak to her. Is there anyone else who's been here as long as you?'

'A few, but no one who was friendly with Olive. A couple of reporters came round at the time of the murders and there wasn't a soul who admitted to passing anything more than the time of day with her.'

Roz felt his distrust. 'And who can blame them?' she said cheerfully. 'Presumably it was the gutter press looking for a juicy headline. I HELD THE HAND OF A MONSTER or something equally tasteless. Only publicity seekers or idiots allow themselves to be used by Wapping to boost their grubby profits.'

'And your book won't make a profit?' There was a dry inflection in his voice.

She smiled. 'A very modest one by newspaper standards.' She pushed her dark glasses to the top of her head, revealing her eyes and the yellow rings around them. 'I'll be honest with you. I was dragooned into this research by an irritable agent demanding copy. I found the subject distasteful and was prepared to abandon it after a token meeting with Olive.' She looked at him, turning her pencil between her fingers. 'Then I discovered that Olive was human and very likeable, so I kept going. And almost everyone I've spoken to has given a similar answer to you. They hardly knew her, they never talked to her, she was just the fat girl down the corridor. Now, I could write my book on that theme alone, how social ostracism led a lonely, unloved girl to turn in a fit of frenzied anger on her teasing family. But I'm not going to because I don't think it's true. I believe there's been a miscarriage of justice. I believe Olive is innocent.'

Surprised, he reassessed her. 'It shocked us rigid when we heard what she'd done,' he admitted.

'Because you thought it out of character?'

'Totally out of character.' He thought back. 'She was a good worker, brighter than most, and she didn't clock-watch like some of them. OK, she was never going to set the world alight, but she was reliable and willing and she didn't make waves or get involved in office politics. She was here about eighteen months and while no one would have claimed her as a bosom friend she made no enemies either. She was one of those people you only think about when you want something done and then you remember them with relief because you know they'll do it. You know the type?'

She nodded. 'Boring but dependable.'

'In a nutshell, yes.'

'Did she tell you anything about her private life?'

He shook his head again. 'It was true what I said at the beginning. Our paths rarely crossed. Any contact we had was work related and even that was minimal. Most of what I've just told you was synthesized from the amazed reactions of the few who did know her.'

'Can you give me their names?'

'I'm not sure I can remember.' He looked doubtful. 'Olive would know them better than I do. Why don't you ask her?'

Because she won't tell me. She won't tell me anything. 'Because,' she said instead, 'I don't want to hurt her.' She saw his look of puzzlement and sighed. 'Supposing doors get slammed in my face and I'm given the cold shoulder by Olive's so-called friends. She's bound to ask me how I got on, and how would I answer her? Sorry, Olive, as far as they're concerned you're dead and buried. I couldn't do that.'

He accepted this. 'All right, there is someone who might be willing to help you but I'm not prepared to give you her name without her permission. She's elderly, retired now, and she may not want to be involved. If you give me five minutes, I'll telephone and see how she feels about talking to you.'

'Was she fond of Olive?'

'As much as anyone was.'

'Then will you tell her that I don't believe Olive murdered her mother and sister and that's why I'm writing the book.' She stood up. 'And please impress on her that it's desperately important I talk to someone who knew her at the time. So far I've only managed to trace one old school friend and a teacher.' She walked to the door. 'I'll wait outside.'

True to his word, he was five minutes. He joined her in the corridor and gave her a piece of paper with a name and address on it. 'Her name's Lily Gainsborough. She was the cleaner-cum-tea-lady in the good old days before privatized cleaning and automatic coffee machines. She retired three years ago at the age of seventy, lives in sheltered accommodation in Pryde Street.' He gave her directions. 'She's expecting you.' Roz thanked him. 'Give my regards to Olive when you see her,' he said, shaking her hand. 'I had more hair and less flab six years ago, so a description won't be much use, but she might remember my name. Most people do.'

Roz chuckled. His name was Michael Jackson.

'Of course I remember Olive. Called her "Dumpling", didn't I, and she called me "Flower". Get it, dear? Because of my name, Lily. There wasn't an ounce of harm in her. I never believed what they said she done and I wrote and told her so when I heard where they'd sent her. She wrote me back and said I was wrong, it was all her fault and she had to pay the penalty.' Old wise eyes peered short-sightedly at Roz. 'I understood what she meant, even if no one else did. She never did it but it wouldn't have happened if she'd not done what she shouldn't have. More tea, dear?'

'Thank you.' Roz held out her cup and waited while the frail old lady hefted a large stainless steel teapot. A relic from her job on the tea trolley? The tea was thick and charged with tannin, and Roz could hardly bring herself to drink it. She accepted another indigestible scone. 'What did she do that she shouldn't have?'

'Upset her mum, that's what. Took up with one of the O'Brien boys, didn't she?'

'Which one?'

'Ah, well, that I'm not too sure about. I've always thought it was the baby, young Gary – mind, I only saw them together once and those boys are very alike. Could have been any of them.'

'How many are there?'

'Now you're asking.' Lily pursed her mouth into a wrinkled rosebud. 'It's a big family. Can't keep track of them. Their mum must be a grandmother twenty times over and I doubt she's reached sixty yet.

Gyppos, dear. Bad apples the lot of them. In and out of prison that regular you'd think they owned the place. The mum included. Taught them to steal soon as they could walk. The kids kept being taken off her, of course, but never for very long. Always found their way home. Young Gary was sent to a boarding school – approved schools, they was called in my day – did quite well by all accounts.' She crumbled a scone on her plate. 'Till he went home, that is. She had him back on the thieving quicker than you can say knife.'

Roz thought for a moment. 'Did Olive tell you she was going out with one of them?'

'Not in so many words.' She tapped her forehead. 'Put two and two together, didn't I? She was that pleased with herself, lost some weight, bought some pretty dresses from that boutique her sister went to work in, dabbed some colour on her face. Made herself look quite bonny, didn't she? Stood to reason there was a man behind it somewhere. Asked her once who it was and she just smiled and said, "No names no pack drill, Flower, because Mummy would have a fit if she ever found out." And then, two or three days later, I came across her with one of the O'Brien boys. Her face gave her away, as sunny as the day is long it was. That was him all right – the one she was soppy over – but he turned away as I passed, and I never did know exactly which O'Brien he was.'

'But what made you think it was an O'Brien anyway?'

'The uniform,' said Lily. 'They all wore the same uniform.'

'They were in the Army?' asked Roz in surprise.

'Leathers, they call them.'

'Oh, I see. You mean they're bikers, they ride motorbikes.'

'That's it. Hell's Angels.'

Roz drew her brows together in a perplexed frown. She had told Hal with absolute conviction that Olive was not the rebellious type. But Hell's Angels, for God's sake! Could a convent girl get more rebellious than that? 'Are you sure about this, Lily?'

'Well, as to being sure, I don't know as I'm sure about anything any more. There was a time when I was sure that governments knew better how to run things than I did. Can't say as I do these days. There was a time when I was sure that if God was in his heaven all would be right with the world. Can't say as I think that now. If God's there, dear, He's blind, deaf, and dumb, far as I'm concerned. But, yes, I am sure my poor Dumpling had fallen for one of the O'Briens. You'd only to look at her to see she was head over heels in love with the lad.' She compressed her lips. 'Bad business. Bad business.'

Roz sipped the bitter tea. 'And you think it was the O'Brien lad who murdered Olive's mother and sister?'

'Must have been, mustn't it? As I said, dear, bad apples.'

'Did you tell the police any of this?' asked Roz curiously.

'I might have done if they'd asked, but I didn't see no point in volunteering the information. If Dumpling wanted them kept out, then that was her affair. And, to tell you the truth, I wasn't that keen to run up against them. Stick together, they do, and my Frank had passed on not many months before. Wouldn't have stood a chance if they'd come looking, would I?'

'Where do they live?'

'The Barrow Estate, back of the High Street. Council likes to keep 'em together, under their eye so to speak. It's a shocking place. Not an honest family there, and they're not all O'Briens neither. Den of thieves, that's what it is.'

Roz took another thoughtful sip from her cup. 'Are you prepared to let me use this information, Lily? You do realize that if there's anything in it it could help Olive.'

'Course I do, dear. Why would I tell you otherwise?'

'The police would become involved. They'd want to talk to you.'

'I know that.'

'In which case your name would be out, and the O'Briens could still come looking for you.'

The old eyes appraised her shrewdly. 'You're only a slip of a thing, dear, but you've survived a beating by the look of it. Reckon I can too. In any case,' she went on stoutly, 'I've spent six years feeling bad about not speaking up, and I was that glad when young Mick phoned and said you was coming, you wouldn't believe. You go ahead, dear, and don't mind about me. It's safer here, anyway, than my old place. They could have set the whole thing alight and I'd have been dead long before anyone'd have thought of phoning for help.'

If Roz had expected to see a chapter of Hell's Angels rampaging about the Barrow Estate she was disappointed. At lunchtime on a Friday it was an unexceptional place, where only the odd dog barked and young women, in ones and twos, pushed babies in prams piled high with shopping for the weekend. Like too many council estates there was a naked and uncared for look about it, a recognition that what it offered was not what its tenants wanted. If individuality was present in these dull uniform walls then it was inside, away from view. But Roz doubted its existence. She had a sense of empty spaces marking time where people waited for somebody else to offer them something better. Like her, she thought. Like her flat.

As she drove away she passed a large school, advertising itself with a tired sign beside the gate. Parkway Comprehensive. Children milled about the tarmac, the sound of their voices loud in the warm air. Roz slowed the car to watch them for a moment. Groups of children played the same games whichever school they went to, but she could see why Gwen had turned her nose up at Parkway and had sent her girls to the convent. Its close proximity to the Barrow Estate would worry even the most liberal of parents, and Gwen certainly wasn't that. But it was ironic, if what Lily and Mr Hayes had said was true, that both Gwen's daughters had succumbed to the attractions of this other world. Was that in spite of or because of their mother? she wondered.

She told herself she needed a tame policeman to give her the low-down on the O'Briens, and her road led inevitably to the Poacher. Being lunchtime the door to the restaurant was unlocked, but the tables were as empty as ever. She selected one well away from the window and sat down, her dark glasses firmly in place.

'You won't need those,' said Hawksley's amused voice from the kitchen doorway. 'I don't intend to put the lights on.'

She smiled, but did not remove the glasses. 'I'd like to order some lunch.'

'OK.' He held the door wide. 'Come into the kitchen. It's more comfortable in there.'

'No, I'll have it in here.' She stood up. 'At the table in the window. I'd like the door open and' – she looked for amplifiers and found them – 'some loud music, preferably jazz. Let's liven the place up a bit. Nobody wants to eat in a morgue, for God's sake.' She seated herself in the window.

'No,' he said, an odd inflection in his voice. 'If you want lunch, you eat it in here with me. Otherwise, you go somewhere else.'

She studied him thoughtfully. 'This has nothing to do with the recession, has it?'

'What hasn't?'

'Your non-existent customers.'

He gestured towards the kitchen. 'Are you going or staying?'

'Staying,' she said, standing up. What was this all about? she wondered.

'It's really none of your concern, Miss Leigh,' he murmured, reading her mind. 'I suggest you stick to what you know and leave me to deal with my affairs in my own way.' Geoff had phoned through the results of his check the previous Monday. 'She's kosher,' he had said. 'A London-based author. Divorced. Had a daughter who died in a car accident. No previous connections with anyone in the area. Sorry, Hal.'

'OK,' Roz said mildly, 'but you must admit it's very intriguing. I was effectively warned off eating here by a policeman when I went to the station to find out where you were. I've been wondering why ever since. With friends like that you don't really need enemies, do you?'

His smile didn't reach his eyes. 'Then you're very

brave to accept my hospitality a second time.' He held the door wide.

She walked past him into the kitchen. 'Just greedy,' she said. 'You're a better cook than I am. In any case, I intend to pay for what I eat unless, of course' – her smile didn't reach her eyes either – 'this isn't a restaurant at all, but a front for something else.'

That amused him. 'You've an overactive imagination.' He pulled out a chair for her.

'Maybe,' she said, sitting down. 'But I've never met a restaurateur before who barricades himself behind bars, presides over empty tables, has no staff, and looms up in the dark looking like something that's been fed through a mincing machine.' She arched her eyebrows. 'If you didn't cook so well, I'd be even more inclined to think this wasn't a restaurant.'

He leaned forward abruptly and removed her dark glasses, folding them and laying them on the table. 'And what should I deduce from this?' he said, unexpectedly moved by the damage done to her beautiful eyes. 'That you're not a writer because someone's left his handprints all over your face?' He frowned suddenly. 'It wasn't Olive, was it?'

She looked surprised. 'Of course not.'

'Who was it, then?'

She dropped her gaze. 'No one. It's not important.'

He waited for a moment. 'Is it someone you care about?'

'No.' She clasped her hands loosely on the table top. 'Rather the reverse. It's someone I don't care about.' She looked up with a half smile. 'Who beat you up, Sergeant? Someone *you* care about?'

He pulled open a fridge door and examined its contents. 'One of these days your passion for poking your nose into other people's business is going to get you into trouble. What do you fancy? Lamb?'

'I really came to see you for some more information,' she told him over coffee.

Humour creased his eyes. He really was extraordinarily attractive, she thought, wistfully aware that the attraction was all one way. Lunch had been a friendly but distant meal, with a large sign between them saying: so far and no further. 'Go on, then.'

'Do you know the O'Brien family? They live on the Barrow Estate.'

'Everyone knows the O'Briens.' He frowned at her. 'But if there's a connection between them and Olive I'll eat my hat.'

'You're going to have galloping indigestion then,' she said acidly. 'I've been told she was going out with one of the sons at the time of the murders. Probably Gary, the youngest. What's he like? Have you met him?'

He linked his hands behind his head. 'Someone's winding you up,' he murmured. 'Gary is marginally brighter than the rest of them, but I'd guess his educational level is still about fourteen years old. They are the most useless, inadequate bunch I've ever come across. The only thing they know how to do is petty thieving and they don't even do that very well. There's Ma O'Brien and about nine children, mostly boys, all grown up now, and, when they're not in prison, they play box and cox in a three-bedroomed house on the estate.'

'Aren't any of them married?'

'Not for long. Divorce is more prevalent in that family than marriage. The wives usually make other arrangements while their men are inside.' He flexed his laced fingers. 'They produce a lot of babies, though, if the fact that a third generation of O'Briens has started appearing regularly in the juvenile courts is anything to go by.' He shook his head. 'Someone's winding you up,' he said again. 'For all her sins Olive wasn't stupid and she'd have to have been brain-dead to fall for a jerk like Gary O'Brien.'

'Are they really as bad as that?' she asked him curiously. 'Or is this police animosity?'

He smiled. 'I'm not police, remember? But they're that bad,' he assured her. 'Every patch has families like the O'Briens. Sometimes, if you're really unlucky, you get an estateful of them, like the Barrow Estate, when the council decides to lump all its bad apples into one basket and then expects the wretched police to throw a cordon round it.' He gave a humourless laugh. 'It's one of the reasons I left the Force. I got sick to death of being sent out to sweep up society's messes. It's not the police who create these ghettos, it's the councils and the governments, and ultimately society itself.'

'Sounds reasonable to me,' she said. 'In that case why do you despise the O'Briens so much? They sound as if they need help and support rather than condemnation.'

He shrugged. 'I suppose it's because they've already had more help and support than you or I will ever be offered. They take everything society gives them and then demand more. There's no quid pro quo with people like that. They put nothing in to compensate for what they've had out. Society owes them a living and, by God, they make sure society pays, usually in the shape of some poor old woman who has all her savings stolen.' His lips thinned. 'If you'd arrested those worthless shits as often as I have, you'd despise them, too. I don't deny they represent an underclass of society's making, but I resent their unwillingness to try and rise above it.' He saw her frown. 'You look very disapproving. Have I offended your liberal sensibilities?'

'No,' she said with a twinkle in her eye. 'I was just thinking how like Mr Hayes you sound. Remember him? "What shall I say?" ' – she mimicked the old man's soft burr – ' "They should all be strung up from the nearest lamppost and shot." ' She smiled when he laughed.

'My sympathies with the criminal classes are a trifle frayed at the moment,' he said after a moment. 'More accurately, my sympathies in general are frayed.'

'Classic symptoms of stress,' she said lightly, watching him. 'Under pressure we always reserve our compassion for ourselves.'

He didn't answer.

'You said the O'Briens are inadequate,' Roz prompted. 'Perhaps they can't rise above their situation.'

'I believed that once,' he admitted, toying with his empty wine glass, 'when I first joined the police force, but you have to be very naïve to go on believing it. They're professional thieves who simply don't subscribe to the same values as the rest of us hold. It's not a case of *can't*, but more a case of *won't*. Different ball game entirely.' He smiled at her. 'And if you're a policeman who wants to hold on to the few drops of human kindness that remain to you, you get out quick the minute you realize that. Otherwise you end up as unprincipled as the people you're arresting.'

Curiouser and curiouser, thought Roz. So he had little sympathy left for the police either. He gave the impression of a man under siege, isolated and angry within the walls of his castle. But why should his friends in the police have abandoned him? Presumably he had had some. 'Have any of the O'Briens been charged with murder or GBH?'

'No. As I said, they're thieves. Shoplifting, pick-pocketing, house burglaries, cars, that sort of thing. Old Ma acts as a fence whenever she can get her hands on stolen property but they're not violent.'

'I was told they're all Hell's Angels.'

He gave her an amused look. 'You've been given some very duff information. Are you toying with the idea, perhaps, that Gary did the murders and Olive was so besotted with him that she took the rap on his behalf?'

'It doesn't sound very plausible, does it?'

'About as plausible as little green men on Mars. Apart from anything else, Gary is scared of his own shadow. He was challenged once during a burglary – he didn't think anyone was in the house – and he burst into tears. He could no more have cut Gwen's throat while she was struggling with him than you or I could. Or for that matter, than his brothers could. They're skinny little foxes, not ravening wolves. Who on earth have you been talking to? Someone with a sense of humour, obviously.'

She shrugged, suddenly out of patience with him. 'It's not important. Offhand, do you know the O'Briens' address? It would save me having to look it up.'

He grinned. 'You're not planning on going there?'

'Of course I am,' she said, annoyed by his amusement. 'It's the most promising lead I've had. And now that I know they're not axe-wielding Hell's Angels, I'm not so worried about it. So what's their address?'

'I'll come with you.'

'Think again, sunshine,' she said roundly. 'I don't want you queering my pitch. Are you going to give me the address or must I look it up?'

'Number seven, Baytree Avenue. You can't miss it. It's the only house in that road with a satellite dish. Nicked for sure.'

'Thank you.' She reached for her handbag. 'Now, if we can just settle my bill, I'll leave you in peace.'

He unfolded himself from his chair and walked round to draw hers back. 'On the house,' he said.

She stood up and regarded him gravely. 'But I'd like to pay. I didn't come here at lunchtime just to scrounge off you and, anyway' – she smiled – 'how else can I show my appreciation of your cooking? Money always speaks louder than words. I can say it was fabulous, like the last time, but I might just be being polite.'

He raised a hand as if he was going to touch her, then dropped it abruptly. 'I'll see you out,' was all he said.

Ten

ROZ DROVE PAST the house three times before she could pluck up enough courage to get out and try the door. In the end it was pride that led her up the path. Hal's amusement had goaded her. A tarpaulined motorbike was parked neatly on a patch of grass beside the fence.

The door was opened by a bony little woman with a sharp, scowling face, her thin lips drawn down in a permanently dissatisfied bow. 'Yes?' she snapped.

'Mrs O'Brien?'

''Oo's asking?'

Roz produced a card. 'My name's Rosalind Leigh.' The sound of a television blared out from an inner room.

The woman glanced at the card but didn't take it. 'Well, what do you want? If it's the rent, I put it in the post yesterday.' She folded her arms across her thin chest and dared Roz to dispute this piece of information.

'I'm not from the council, Mrs O'Brien.' It occurred to her that the woman couldn't read. Apart from her telephone number and address, Roz's card had only her name and her profession on it. Author, it stated clearly. She took a flyer. 'I work for a small independent television company,' she said brightly, her mind searching rapidly for some plausible but tempting bait. 'I'm researching the difficulties faced by single parents with large families. We are particularly interested in talking to a mother who has problems keeping her sons out of trouble. Society is very quick to point the finger in these situations and we feel it's time to redress the balance.' She saw the lack of comprehension on the woman's face. 'We'd like to give the mother a chance to give her side of the story,' she explained. 'There seems to be a common pattern of continual harassment and interference from people in authority – social services, the council, the police. Most mothers we've spoken to feel that if they'd been left alone they wouldn't have had the problems.'

A gleam of interest lit the other's eyes. 'That's true enough.'

'Are you willing to take part?'

'Maybe. 'Oo sent you?'

'We've been conducting some research in the local courts,' she said glibly. 'The name O'Brien popped up quite frequently.'

'Not surprised. Will I get paid?'

'Certainly. I'd need to talk to you for about an

hour now to get a rough idea of your views. For that you will receive an immediate cash payment of fifty pounds.' Ma would turn her nose up at anything less, she thought. 'Then, if we think your contribution is valuable and if you agree to be filmed, we will pay you at the same hourly rate while the cameras are here.'

Ma O'Brien pursed her meagre lips and proceeded to splatter aitches about the place. 'Han hundred,' she said, 'hand h'I'll do it.'

Roz shook her head. Fifty pounds would clean her out anyway. 'Sorry. It's a standard fee. I'm not authorized to pay any more.' She shrugged. 'Never mind. Thank you for your time, Mrs O'Brien. I've three other families on my list. I'm sure one of them will jump at the chance to get their own back at authority and earn some money while they're doing it.' She turned away. 'Look out for the programme,' she called over her shoulder. 'You'll probably see some of your neighbours on it.'

'Not so 'asty, Mrs. Did I say no? Course I didn't. But I'd be a mug not to try for more hif there was more to be 'ad. Come in. Come in. What d'you say your name was?'

'Rosalind Leigh.' She followed Ma into a sitting room and took a chair while the little woman turned off the television and flicked aimlessly at some non-existent dust on the set. 'This is a nice room,' said Roz, careful to keep the surprise from her voice. A three-piece suite of good quality burgundy leather ringed a pale Chinese rug in pinks and greys.

'All bought and paid for,' snapped Ma.

Roz didn't doubt her for a moment. If the police spent as much time in her house as Hal had implied, then she was hardly likely to furnish it with hot goods. She took out her tape-recorder. 'How do you feel about my recording this conversation? It'll be a useful gauge for the sound man when he comes to set levels for filming, but if the microphone puts you off then I'm quite happy to make notes instead.'

'Get on with you,' she said, perching on the sofa. 'I'm not afraid of microphones. We've got a karaoke next door. You gonna ask questions or what?'

'That's probably easiest, isn't it? Let's start with when you first came to this house.'

'Ah, well, now, they was built twenty year ago, near enough, and we was the first family hin. There was six of us, including my old man, but 'e got nicked shortly after and we never seen 'im again. The old bastard buggered hoff when they let 'im out.'

'So you had four children?'

'Four in the 'ouse, five in care. Bloody hinterference, like you said. Kept taking the poor little nippers hoff me, they did. Makes you sick, it really does. They wanted their ma, not some do-good foster mother who was only in it for the money.' She hugged herself. 'I always got them back, mind. They'd turn up on my doorstep, regular as clockwork, no matter 'ow many times they was taken away. The council's tried everything to break us up, threatened me with a one-roomed flat even.' She sniffed. ''Arassment, like you said. I remember one time . . .'

She required little prompting to tell her story but rambled on with remarkable fluency for nearly three-quarters of an hour. Roz was fascinated. Privately she dismissed at least fifty per cent of what she was hearing, principally because Ma blithely maintained that her boys were and always had been innocent victims of police frames. Even the most gullible of listeners would have found that difficult to swallow. Nevertheless, there was a dogged affection in her voice whenever she referred to her family and Roz wondered if she was really as callous as Lily had painted her. She certainly portrayed herself as a hapless victim of circumstances beyond her control, though whether this was something she genuinely believed or whether she was saying what she thought Roz wanted to hear, Roz couldn't tell. Ma, she decided, was a great deal smarter than she let on.

'Right, Mrs O'Brien, let me see if I've got it right,' she said at last, interrupting the flow. 'You've got two daughters, both of whom are single parents like you, and both of whom have been housed by the council. You have seven sons. Three are currently in prison, one is living with his girlfriend, and the remaining three live here. Your oldest child is Peter, who's thirty-six, and your youngest is Gary, who's twenty-five.'

She whistled. 'That was some going. Nine babies in eleven years.'

'Two sets of twins in the middle. Boy and a girl each time. Mind, it was 'ard work.'

Unmitigated drudgery, thought Roz. 'Did you want them?' she asked curiously. 'I can't think of anything worse than having nine children.'

'Never 'ad much say in it, dear. There weren't no abortion in my day.'

'Didn't you use contraceptives?'

To her surprise, the old woman blushed. 'Couldn't get the 'ang of them,' she snapped. 'The old man tried a rubber once but didn't like it and wouldn't do it again. Old bugger. No skin off 'is nose if I kept falling.'

It was on the tip of Roz's tongue to ask why Ma couldn't get the hang of contraceptives when the penny dropped. If she couldn't read and she was too embarrassed to ask how to use them, they'd have been useless to her. Good God, she thought, a little education would have saved the country a fortune where this family was concerned. 'That's men for you,' she said lightly. 'I noticed a motorbike outside. Does that belong to one of the boys?'

'Bought and paid for,' came the belligerent refrain. 'It's Gary's. Motorbike mad, 'e is. There was a time when three of the boys 'ad bikes, now it's just Gary. They was all working for one of them messenger companies till the bloody coppers went round and got them sacked. Victimization, pure and simple. 'Ow's a man to work hif the police keep waving 'is record under the boss's noses. Course, they lost the bikes. They was buying them on the never-never and they couldn't keep up the payments.'

Roz made sympathetic noises. 'When was that? Recently?'

'Year of the gales. I remember the electricity was off when the boys came 'ome to say they'd been given the push. We'd got one blooming candle.' She firmed her lips. 'Bloody awful night, that was. Depressing.'

Roz kept her expression as neutral as she could. Was Lily right, after all, and Hal wrong? 'The nineteen eight-seven gales,' she said. 'The first ones.'

'That's it. Mind, it 'appened again two years later. No electricity for a week the second time, hand you get no compensation for the 'ardship neither. I tried and the buggers told me hif I didn't pay what I owed they'd cut me hoff for good and all.'

'Did the police give a reason for getting your boys the sack?' asked Roz.

'Hah!' Ma sniffed. 'They never give reasons for nothing. It was victimization, like I said.'

'Did they work for the messenger company long?'

Old eyes regarded her suspiciously. 'You're mighty interested all of a sudden.'

Roz smiled ingenuously. 'Only because this was an occasion when three of your family were trying to go straight and build careers for themselves. It would make good television if we could show that they were denied that opportunity because of police harassment. Presumably it was a local firm they were working for?'

'Southampton.' Ma's mouth became an inverted horseshoe. 'Bloody silly name it 'ad too. Called their-selves Wells-Fargo. Still, the boss was a ruddy cowboy so maybe it wasn't so silly after all.'

Roz suppressed a smile. 'Is it still in business?'

'Last I 'eard, it was. That's it. You've 'ad your 'our.'

'Thank you, Mrs O'Brien.' She patted the tape-recorder. 'If the producers like what they hear I might need to come back and talk to your sons. Would that be acceptable, do you think?'

'Don't see why not. Can't see them sneezing at fifty quid apiece.' Ma held out her hand.

Dutifully, Roz took two twenty-pound notes and a ten from her wallet and laid them on the wrinkled palm. Then she started to gather her things together. 'I hear Dawlington's quite famous,' she remarked chattily.

'Oh yeah?'

'I was told Olive Martin murdered her mother and sister about half a mile down the road.'

'Oh, 'er,' said Ma dismissively, standing up. 'Strange girl. Knew 'er quite well at one time. Used to clean for the mother when she and 'er sister were nippers. She took a real fancy to Gary. Used to pretend 'e was 'er doll whenever I took 'im halong with me. There was only three years between them but she was nearly twice as big as my skinny little runt. Strange girl.'

Roz busied herself with sorting out her briefcase. 'It must have been a shock hearing about the murders then. If you knew the family, that is.'

'Can't say I gave it much thought. I was only there six month. Never liked *'er.* She only took me on for a bit of snobbery, then got rid of me the minute she found hout my old man was in the nick.'

'What was Olive like as a child. Was she violent to your Gary?'

Ma cackled. 'Used to dress 'im up in 'er sister's frocks. God, 'e looked a sight. Like I said, she treated 'im like a doll.'

Roz snapped the locks on her briefcase and stood up. 'Were you surprised she became a murderess?'

'No more surprised by that than by anything else. There's nowt so queer as folk.' She escorted Roz to the front door and stood, arms akimbo, waiting for her to leave.

'It might make an interesting introduction to the programme,' Roz mused, 'the fact that Gary was a doll-substitute for a notorious murderess. Does he remember her?'

Ma cackled again. 'Course 'e remembers 'er. Carried messages between 'er and 'er fancy man, didn't 'e, when she was workin' for the Social.'

*

Roz made a beeline for the nearest telephone. Ma O'Brien either wouldn't or couldn't elaborate on her tantalizing statement and had closed the door abruptly when pressed for information on Gary's whereabouts. Roz dialled Directory Enquiries and asked for Wells-Fargo in Southampton, then used her last fifty pence to call the number she was given. A bored female voice on the other end gave her the company's address and some directions on how to find it. 'We close in forty minutes,' was the woman's parting shot.

By dint of parking on a double yellow line and shrugging off the prospect of a parking ticket Roz made it to the Wells-Fargo office with ten minutes to spare. It was a dingy place, approached through a doorway between two shops and up a flight of uncarpeted stairs. Two anaemic Busy Lizzies and an ancient Pirelli calendar were the only spots of colour against the yellowed walls. The bored female voice resolved itself into a bored-looking middle-aged woman who was counting the seconds to the start of her weekend.

'We don't often see customers,' she remarked, filing her nails. 'I mean if they can bring their package here they might just as well deliver it themselves.' It was an accusation, as if she felt Roz were wasting company time. She abandoned her nails and held out a hand. 'What is it and where's it for?'

'I'm not a customer,' said Roz. 'I'm an author and I'm hoping you can give me some information for a book I'm writing.' Stirrings of interest animated the other's face so Roz pulled forward a chair and sat down. 'How long have you been working here?'

'Too long. What sort of book?'

Roz watched her closely. 'Do you remember Olive Martin? She murdered her mother and sister in Dawlington six years ago.' She saw immediate recognition in the woman's eyes. 'I'm writing a book about her.'

The woman returned to her nails but didn't say anything.

'Did you know her?'

'God, no.'

'Did you know *of* her? Before the murders, that is. I've been told one of your messengers delivered letters to her.' It was true enough. The only trouble was that she didn't know if Gary was working for Wells-Fargo when he did it.

A door to an inner office opened and a man fussed out. He looked at Roz. 'Did this lady want to see me, Marnie?' His fingers ran involuntarily up and down his tie, playing it like a clarinet.

The nail file vanished from sight. 'No, Mr Wheelan. She's an old friend of mine. Popped in to see if I've time for a drink before I go home.' She stared hard at Roz, her eyes demanding support. There was a curious intimacy in her expression as if she and Roz already shared a secret.

Roz smiled amiably and glanced at her watch. 'It's

nearly six now,' she said. 'Half an hour won't delay you too much, will it?'

The man made shooing motions with his hands. 'You two get on then. I'll lock up tonight.' He paused in the doorway, his forehead wrinkling anxiously. 'You didn't forget to send someone to Hasler's, did you?'

'No, Mr Wheelan. Eddy went two hours ago.'

'Good, good. Have a nice weekend. What about Prestwick's?'

'All done, Mr Wheelan. There's nothing outstanding.' Marnie raised her eyes to heaven as he closed the door behind him. 'He drives me mad,' she muttered. 'Fuss, fuss, fuss, all the time. Come on, quick, before he changes his mind. Friday evenings are always the worst.' She scurried across to the door and started down the stairs. 'He hates weekends, that's his trouble, thinks the business is going to fold because we have two consecutive days without orders. He's paranoid. Had me working Saturday mornings last year till he realized we were simply sitting around twiddling our thumbs because none of the offices we deal with open on a Saturday.' She pushed through the bottom door and stepped out on to the pavement. 'Look, we can forget about that drink. I'd like to get home in reasonable time for once.' She looked at Roz, measuring the other's reaction.

Roz shrugged. 'Fine. I'll go and talk to Mr Wheelan about Olive Martin. He doesn't seem to be in any hurry.'

Marnie tapped her foot impatiently. 'You'll get me sacked.'

'*You* talk to me then.'

There was a long pause while the other woman considered her options. 'I'll tell you what I know, as long as you keep it to yourself,' she said at last. 'Is that a deal? It's not going to help you one little bit, so you won't need to use it.'

'Suits me,' said Roz.

'We'll talk as we walk. The station's this way. If we hurry I might be able to catch the six thirty.'

Roz caught her arm to hold her back. 'My car's over there,' she said. 'I'll drive you instead.' She took Marnie across the road and unlocked the passenger door. 'OK,' she said, getting in the other side and starting the engine. 'Fire away.'

'I did know of her, or at least I knew of *an* Olive Martin. I can't swear it's the same one because I never saw her, but the description sounded right when I read about her in the newspaper. I've always assumed it was the same person.'

'Who gave you her description?' asked Roz, turning into the main road.

'There's no point asking questions,' snapped Marnie. 'It'll just take longer. Let me tell the story my way.' She collected her thoughts. 'I said back there that we hardly ever see customers. Sometimes office managers come in to suss out what sort of operation we run, but normally it's all done by telephone. Somebody wants something delivered, they phone us and we dispatch a rider, simple as that. Well, one lunchtime, when Wheelan was out getting his sandwiches, this man came into the office. He had a letter that he wanted delivered that afternoon to a Miss Olive Martin. He was prepared to pay over the odds if the dispatch rider would hang around outside where she worked and give it to her quietly as she was leaving. He was absolutely adamant that it wasn't to be taken inside and said he was sure I understood why.'

Roz forgot herself. 'And did you?'

'I assumed they were having an affair and that neither of them wanted people asking questions. Anyway, he gave me a twenty-quid note for the one letter, and we're talking six years ago, remember, plus a very good description of Olive Martin, right down to the clothes she was wearing that day. Well, I thought it was a one-off and as that old bastard Wheelan pays peanuts at the best of times, I pocketed the cash and didn't bother to record the transaction. Instead, I got one of our riders who lived in Dawlington to do it freelance, as it were, on his way home. He got ten for doing virtually nothing and I kept the other ten.' She motioned with her hand. 'You take the next right at the traffic lights and then right at the roundabout.'

Roz put on her indicator. 'Was that Gary O'Brien?'

Marnie nodded. 'I suppose the little sod's been talking.'

'Something like that,' said Roz, avoiding a direct answer. 'Did Gary ever meet this man?'

'No, only Olive. It turned out he'd known her before – she used to look after him when he was a child or something – so he had no trouble recognizing her and didn't bungle the job by trying to give the letter to the wrong woman. Which, considering what an oaf he was, I thought he might do. Pull in here.' She glanced at her watch as Roz drew to a halt. 'That's grand. OK, well, the upshot of the whole thing going so smoothly was that Olive's bloke started to use us quite regularly. All in all we must have delivered about ten letters in the six months before the murders. I think he realized we were doing it on the side because he always came in at lunchtime after Wheelan had gone out. I reckon he used to wait until he saw the old fool leave.' She shrugged. 'It stopped with the murders and I've never seen him since. And that's all I can tell you except that Gary got really nervous after Olive was arrested and said we should keep our mouths shut about what we knew or the police would be down on us like a ton of bricks. Well, I wasn't keen to say anything anyway, not because of the police but because of Wheelan. He'd have burst a blood vessel if he'd found out we'd been running a bit of private enterprise behind his back.'

'But didn't the police turn up anyway about a month later to warn Wheelan against the O'Brien brothers?'

Marnie looked surprised. 'Who told you that?'

'Gary's mother.'

'First I've heard of it. As far as I know they just got bored. Gary wasn't so bad because he loved his motorbike but the other two were the most work-shy creeps I've ever come across. In the end they were skiving off so often that Wheelan sacked the lot. It's about the only decision he's ever made that I agreed with. God, they were unreliable.' She checked her watch again. 'To tell you the truth it amazed me that Gary delivered Olive's letters so conscientiously. I did wonder if he had a bit of a yen for her himself.' She opened the car door. 'I'll have to go.'

'Hang on,' said Roz sharply. 'Who was this man?'

'No idea. We dealt in cash and he never gave his name.'

'What did he look like?'

'I'll miss my train.'

Roz leant across and pulled the door to. 'You've got ten minutes and if you don't give me a decent description I'll go straight back to your office and spill the beans to Wheelan.'

Marnie shrugged petulantly. 'He was fifty-odd, old enough to be her father if the age they gave for her in the paper was right. Quite good-looking in a smarmy sort of way, very clean cut and conservative. He had a posh accent. He smoked. He always wore a suit and tie. He was about six foot and he had blond hair. He never said very much, just sort of waited for me to speak, never smiled, never got excited. I remember his eyes because they didn't go with his hair. They were very dark brown. And that's it,' she said firmly. 'I don't know any more about him and I don't know anything at all about her.'

'Would you recognize him from a photograph?'

'Probably. Do you know him then?'

Roz drummed her fingers on the steering-wheel. 'It doesn't make any sense but it sounds exactly like her father.'

Eleven

THE OFFICER ON the gate checked Roz's name against his list the following Monday, then picked up the telephone. 'The Governor wants to see you,' he said, dialling a number.

'What for?'

'I wouldn't know, miss.' He spoke into the telephone. 'Miss Leigh's here for Martin. There's a note that she's to see the Governor first. Yes. Will do.' He pointed with his pencil. 'Straight through the first set of gates and you'll be met the other side.'

It was horribly reminiscent of being hauled before the headmistress at school, thought Roz, waiting nervously in the secretary's office. She was trying to remember if she'd broken any rule. *Bring nothing in and take nothing out. Don't pass messages.* But she had done that, of course, when she spoke to Crew about the will. The slimy little toad must have ratted on her!

'You can go in now,' the secretary told her.

The Governor gestured towards a chair. 'Sit down, Miss Leigh.'

Roz lowered herself into the easy chair, hoping she looked less guilty than she felt. 'I wasn't expecting to see you.'

'No.' She studied Roz for a moment or two, then seemed to reach a decision. 'There's no point beating about the bush. Olive has had her privileges suspended and we think you may be the indirect cause of the suspension. According to the log-book you didn't come in last week, and I'm told Olive was very upset about it. Three days later she destroyed her cell and had to be sedated.' She saw Roz's surprise. 'She's been very volatile ever since and, under the circumstances, I am not happy about letting you back in. I think it's something I need to discuss with the Home Office.'

God! Poor old Olive! Why on earth didn't I have the sense to phone? Roz folded her hands in her lap and collected her thoughts rapidly. 'If it was three days before she did anything, what makes you think it was because of my not turning up? Did she say it was?'

'No, but we're stumped for any other explanation and I'm not prepared to risk your safety.'

Roz mulled this over for a moment or two. 'Let's assume for a moment you're right – though I should emphasize that I don't think you are – then if I don't show up again won't that distress her even more?' She leaned forward. 'Either way it would be more sensible to let me talk to her. If it *was* to do with my non-appearance then I can reassure her and calm her down; if it *wasn't*, then I see no reason why I should be punished with Home Office delays and wasted journeys when I haven't contributed to Olive's disturbance.'

The Governor gave a slight smile. 'You're very confident.'

'I've no reason not to be.'

It was the Governor's turn to reflect. She studied Roz in silence for some time. 'Let's be clear,' she said finally, 'about what sort of woman Olive really is.' She tapped her pencil on the desk. 'I told you when you first came here that there was no psychiatric evidence of psychopathy. That was true. It means that when Olive butchered her mother and sister she was completely sane. She knew exactly what she was doing, she understood the consequences of her act, and she was prepared to go ahead with it, despite those consequences. It also means – and this is peculiarly relevant to you – that she cannot be cured because there is nothing to cure. Under similar circumstances – unhappiness, low self-image, betrayal, in other words whatever triggers her anger – she would do the same thing again with the same disregard for the consequences because, in simple terms, having weighed them up, she would consider the consequences worth the action. I would add, and again this is peculiarly relevant to you, that the consequences are far less daunting to her now than they would have been six years ago. On the whole Olive enjoys being in prison. She has security, she has respect, and she has people to talk to. Outside, she would have none of them. And she knows it.'

It *was* like being up before her old headmistress. The confident voice of authority. 'So what you're saying is that she would have no qualms about taking a swipe at me because an additional sentence would only mean a longer stay here? And she would welcome that?'

'In effect, yes.'

'You're wrong,' said Roz bluntly. 'Not about her sanity. I agree with you, she's as sane as you or I. But you're wrong about her being a danger to me. I'm writing a book about her and she wants that book written. If it *is* me she's angry with, and I stress again that I don't think it is, then her interpretation of my non-appearance last week may be that I've lost interest, and it would be very poor psychology to let her go on thinking it.' She composed her arguments. 'You have a notice at the gate, presumably all prisons do. It's a declaration of policy. If I remember right, it includes something about helping prison inmates to lead law-abiding lives both inside prison and outside. If that has any meaning at all, and isn't simply a piece of decorative wallpaper to appease the reformers, then how can you justify provoking further punishable outbursts from Olive by denying her visits which the

Home Office has already approved?' She fell silent, worried about saying too much. However reasonable the woman might be, she could not afford to have her authority challenged. Few people could.

'Why does Olive want this book written?' asked the Governor mildly. 'She hasn't sought public notoriety before and you're not the first author to show an interest in her. We had several applications in the early days. She refused them all.'

'I don't know,' said Roz honestly. 'Perhaps it has something to do with her father's death. She claimed that one of her reasons for pleading guilty was to avoid putting him through the mill of a trial.' She shrugged. 'Presumably she felt a book would have been just as devastating to him, so waited till he died.'

The Governor was more cynical. 'Alternatively, while he was alive, her father was in a position to contest what she said; dead, he cannot. However, that is no concern of mine. My concern is with the ordered running of my prison.' She tapped her fingers impatiently on her desk. She had no desire at all to be drawn into a three-cornered dispute between herself, the Home Office, and Roz, but time-consuming correspondence with civil servants would pale into insignificance beside the murder of a civilian inside her prison. She had hoped to persuade Roz to abort the visit herself. She was surprised and, if the truth be told, rather intrigued by her own failure. *What was*

Rosalind Leigh getting right in her relationship with Olive that the rest of them were getting wrong? 'You may talk to her for half an hour,' she said abruptly, 'in the Legal Visits room, which is larger than the one you are used to. There will be two male officers present throughout the interview. Should either you or Olive breach any regulation of this prison, your visits will cease immediately and I will personally ensure that they will never resume. Is that understood, Miss Leigh?'

'Yes.'

The other nodded. 'I'm curious, you know. Are you raising her expectations by telling her your book will get her released?'

'No. Apart from anything else, she won't talk to me about the murders.' Roz reached for her briefcase.

'Then why are you so confident you're safe with her?'

'Because as far as I can make out I'm the only outsider she's met who's not frightened of her.'

Privately, she retracted that statement as Olive was ushered into the Legal Visits room by two large male officers who then retreated to the door behind Olive's back and stationed themselves on either side of it. The woman's look of dislike was chilling, and Roz recalled Hal saying to her that she might think differently about Olive if she ever saw her in a rage.

'Hi.' She held Olive's gaze. 'The Governor has allowed me to see you, but we're on trial, both of us. If we misbehave today my visits will be stopped. Do you understand?'

BITCH, Olive mouthed, unseen by the officers. FUCKING BITCH. But was she referring to Roz or the Governor? Roz couldn't tell.

'I'm sorry I didn't make it last Monday.' She touched her lip where the ugly scab still showed. 'I got thrashed by my miserable husband.' She forced a smile. 'I couldn't go out for a week, Olive, not even for you. I do have some pride, you know.'

Olive examined her stolidly for a second or two then dropped her eyes to the cigarette packet on the table. She plucked greedily at a cigarette and popped it between her fat lips. 'I've been on the block,' she said, flaring a match to the tip. 'The bastards wouldn't let me smoke. And they've been starving me.' She threw a baleful glance behind her. 'Bastards! Did you kill him?'

Roz followed her gaze. Every word she and Olive said would be reported back. 'Of course not.'

Olive smoothed the limp, greasy hair from her forehead with the hand that held the cigarette. A streak of nicotine staining along her parting showed she had done it many times before. 'I didn't think you would,' she said contemptuously. 'It's not as easy as it looks on the telly. You've heard what I did?'

'Yes.'

'So why have they let you see me?'

'Because I told the Governor that whatever you had done was nothing to do with me. Which it wasn't, was it?' She pressed one of Olive's feet with hers under the table. 'Presumably somebody else upset you?'

'Bloody Chaplain,' said Olive morosely. A bald eyelid drooped in a wink. 'Told me that God would do the rock'n'roll in heaven if I got down on my knees and said: "Alleluiah, I repent." Stupid sod. He's always trying to make religion relevant to modern criminals with low IQs. We can't cope with "There will be much rejoicing in heaven over one sinner that repenteth", so we get God will do the fucking rock'n'roll instead.' She listened with some satisfaction to the snorts of amusement behind her, then her eyes narrowed. I TRUSTED YOU, she mouthed at Roz.

Roz nodded. 'I assumed it was something like that.' She watched Olive's meaty fingers play with the tiny cigarette. 'But it was rude of me not to phone the prison and ask them to pass on a message. I had the mother and father of all headaches most of last week. You'll have to put it down to that.'

'I know you did.'

Roz frowned. 'How?'

With a flick of her fingers Olive squeezed the glowing head from the cigarette and dropped it into an ashtray on the table. 'Elementary, my dear Watson. Your ex gave you two black eyes if all that yellow round them isn't some weird sort of make-up. And headaches usually accompany black eyes.' But she was bored with the subject and fished an envelope abruptly from her pocket. She held it above her head. 'Mr Allenby, sir. Are you going to let me show this to the lady?'

'What is it?' asked one of the men, stepping forward.

'Letter from my solicitor.'

He took it from her raised hand, ignoring the two-fingered salute she gave him, and skimmed through it. 'I've no objections,' he said, placing it on the table and returning to his place by the door.

Olive prodded it towards Roz. 'Read it. He says the chances of tracing my nephew are virtually nil.' She reached for another cigarette, her eyes watching Roz closely. There was a strange awareness in them as if she knew something that Roz didn't, and Roz found it disturbing. Olive, it seemed, now held the initiative in this unnatural glasshouse relationship of theirs but why and when she had taken it, Roz couldn't begin to fathom. It was she, wasn't it, who had engineered this meeting against the odds?

Surprisingly, Crew had handwritten his letter in a neat, sloping script, and Roz could only assume he had composed it out of office hours and decided not to waste company time and money by having it typed. She found that oddly offensive.

Dear Olive,

I understand from Miss Rosalind Leigh that you are acquainted with some of the terms of your late father's will, principally those concerning Amber's illegitimate son. The bulk of the estate has been left in trust to the child although other provisions have been made in the event of failure on our part to trace him. Thus far, my people have met with little success and it is fair to say that we are increasingly pessimistic about our chances. We have established that your nephew emigrated to Australia with his family some twelve years ago when he was little more than a baby but, following their move from a rented flat in Sydney where they remained for the first six months, the trail goes cold. Unfortunately the child's adopted surname is a common one and we have no guarantee that he and his family remained in Australia. Nor can we rule out the possibility that the family decided to add to their name or change it entirely. Carefully worded advertisements in several Australian newspapers have produced no response.

Your father was most insistent that we should be circumspect in how we traced the child. His view, which I endorsed wholeheartedly, was that great damage could be done if there was any publicity associated with the bequest. He was very conscious of the shock his grandson might suffer if he learnt through an incontinent media campaign of his tragic association with the Martin family. For this reason, we have kept and will continue to keep your nephew's name a closely guarded secret. We are pressing on with our enquiries but, as your father stipulated a limited period for searches, the likelihood is that I, as executor, will be obliged to adopt the alternative provisions specified. These are a range of donations to hospitals and charities which care entirely for the needs and welfare of children.

Although your father never instructed me to keep the terms of his will from you, he was very concerned that you should not be distressed by them. It was for this reason that I thought it wiser to keep you in ignorance of his intentions. Had I known that you were already in possession of some of the facts, I should have corresponded sooner.

Trusting you are in good health,
Yours sincerely,
Peter Crew

Roz refolded the letter and pushed it back to Olive. 'You said last time that it mattered to you if your nephew was found, but you didn't enlarge on it.' She glanced towards the two officers, but they were showing little interest in anything except the floor.

She leaned forward and lowered her voice. 'Are you going to talk to me about it now?'

Olive jammed her cigarette angrily into the ashtray. She made no attempt to keep her voice down. 'My father was a terrible MAN.' Even in speech the word carried capital letters. 'I couldn't see it at the time but I've had years to think about it and I can see it now.' She nodded towards the letter. 'His conscience was troubling him. That's why he wrote that will. It was his way of feeling good about himself after the appalling damage he'd done. Why else would he leave his money to Amber's baby when he never cared shit for Amber herself?'

Roz looked at her curiously. 'Are you saying your father did the murders?' she murmured.

Olive snorted. 'I'm saying, why use Amber's baby to whitewash himself?'

'What had he done that needed whitewashing?'

But Olive didn't answer.

Roz waited a moment, then tried a different tack. 'You said your father would always leave money to family if he could. Does that mean there's other family he could have left it to? Or did you hope he'd leave it to you?'

Olive shook her head. 'There's no one. Both my parents were only children. And he couldn't leave it to me, could me?' She slammed her fist on the table, her voice rising furiously. 'Otherwise everyone would kill their fucking families!' The great ugly face leered at Roz. YOU WANTED TO, mouthed the sausage lips.

'Keep the volume down, Sculptress,' said Mr Allenby mildly, 'or the visit finishes now.'

Roz pressed a finger and thumb to her eyelids where she could feel her headache coming back. *Olive Martin took an axe* – she tried to thrust the thought away, but it wouldn't go – *and gave her mother forty whacks.* 'I don't understand why the will makes you so angry,' she said, forcing her voice to sound steady. 'If family was important to him who else is there except his grandson?'

Olive stared at the table, her jaw jutting aggressively. 'It's the principle,' she muttered. 'Dad's dead. What does it matter now what people think?'

Roz recalled something Mrs Hopwood had said. *'I've always assumed he must have had an affair . . .'* She took a shot in the dark. 'Do you have a half-brother or sister somewhere? Is that what you're trying to tell me?'

Olive found this amusing. 'Hardly. He'd have to have had a mistress for that and he didn't like women.' She gave a sardonic laugh. 'He did like MEN though.' Again the strange emphasis on the word.

Roz was very taken aback. 'Are you saying he was a homosexual?'

'I'm saying,' said Olive with exaggerated patience, 'that the only person I ever saw make Dad's face light up was our next-door neighbour, Mr Clarke. Dad used to get quite skittish whenever he was around.' She lit another cigarette. 'I thought it was rather sweet at the time, but only because I was too bloody thick to recognize a couple of queens when I saw them. Now I just think it was sick. It's no wonder my mother hated the Clarkes.'

'They moved after the murders,' said Roz thoughtfully. 'Vanished one morning without leaving a forwarding address. No one knows what happened to them or where they went.'

'Doesn't surprise me. I expect *she* was behind it.'

'Mrs Clarke?'

'She never liked him coming round to our house. He used to hop across the fence at the back and he and Dad would shut themselves in Dad's room and not come out for hours. I should think it must have worried her sick after the murders when Dad was all alone in the house.'

Images, gleaned from things people had said, chased themselves across Roz's mind. Robert Martin's vanity and his Peter Pan looks; he and Ted Clarke being as close as brothers; the room at the back with the bed in it; Gwen's keeping up appearances; her frigid flinching from her husband; the secret that needed hiding. It all made sense, she thought, but did it affect anything if Olive hadn't known it at the time?

'Was Mr Clarke his only lover, do you think?'

'How would I know? Probably not,' she went on,

contradicting herself immediately. 'He had his own back door in that room he used. He could have been out after rent-boys every night for all any of us would have known about it. I hate him.' She looked as if she were about to erupt again but Roz's look of alarm gave her pause. 'I hated him,' she repeated, before lapsing into silence.

'Because he killed Gwen and Amber?' asked Roz for the second time.

But Olive was dismissive: 'He was at work all day. Everyone knows that.'

Olive Martin took an axe . . . Are you raising her expectations by telling her your book will get her out? 'Did your lover kill them?' She felt she was being clumsy, asking the wrong questions, in the wrong way, at the wrong time.

Olive sniggered. 'What makes you think I had a lover?'

'Someone made you pregnant.'

'Oh, that.' She was scornful. 'I lied about the abortion. I wanted the girls here to think I was attractive once.' She spoke loudly as if intent on the officers hearing everything.

A cold fist of certainty squeezed at Roz's heart. Deedes had warned her of this four weeks ago. 'Then who was the man who sent you letters via Gary O'Brien?' she asked. 'Wasn't he your lover?'

Olive's eyes glittered like snakes' eyes. 'He was Amber's lover.'

Roz stared at her. 'But why would he send letters to you?'

'Because Amber was too frightened to receive them herself. She was a coward.' There was a brief pause. 'Like my father.'

'What was she frightened of?'

'My mother.'

'What was your father frightened of?'

'My mother.'

'And were you frightened of your mother?'

'No.'

'Who was Amber's lover?'

'I don't know. She never told me.'

'What was in his letters?'

'Love, I expect. Everyone loved Amber.'

'Including you?'

'Oh, yes.'

'And your mother. Did she love Amber?'

'Of course.'

'That's not what Mrs Hopwood says.'

Olive shrugged. 'What would she know about it? She hardly knew us. She was always fussing over her precious Geraldine.' A sly smile crept about her mouth, making her ugly. 'What does anybody know about it now except me?'

Roz could feel the scales peeling from her eyes in slow and terrible disillusionment. 'Is that why you waited till your father died before you would talk to anyone? So that there'd be no one left to contradict you?'

Olive stared at her with undisguised dislike then, with a careless gesture – hidden from the officers' eyes but all too visible to Roz – she removed a tiny clay doll from her pocket and turned the long pin that was piercing the doll's head. Red hair. Green dress. It required little imagination on Roz's part to endow the clay with a personality. She gave a hollow laugh. 'I'm a sceptic, Olive. It's like religion. It only works if you believe in it.'

'I believe in it.'

'Then more fool you.' She stood up abruptly and walked to the door, nodding to Mr Allenby to let her out. What had induced her to believe the woman innocent in the first place? And why, for Christ's sake, had she picked on a bloody murderess to fill the void that Alice had left in her heart?

She stopped at a payphone and dialled St Angela's Convent. It was Sister Bridget herself who answered. 'How may I help?' asked her comfortable lilting voice.

Roz smiled weakly into the receiver. 'You could say: "Come on down, Roz, I'll give you an hour to listen to your woes." '

Sister Bridget's light chuckle lost none of its warmth by transmission down the wire. 'Come on down, dear. I've a whole evening free and I like nothing better than listening. Are the woes so bad?'

'Yes. I think Olive did it.'

'Not so bad. You're no worse off than when you started. I live in the house next to the school. It's called Donegal. Totally inappropriate, of course, but rather charming. Join me as soon as you can. We'll have supper together.'

There was a strained note in Roz's voice. 'Do you believe in black magic, Sister?'

'Should I?'

'Olive is sticking pins into a clay image of me.'

'Good Lord!'

'And I've got a headache.'

'I'm not surprised. If I had just had my faith in someone shattered, I would have a headache, too. What an absurd creature she is! Presumably it's her way of trying to regain some semblance of control. Prison is soul destroying in that respect.' She tut-tutted in annoyance. 'Really quite absurd, and I've always had such a high esteem for Olive's intellect. I'll expect you when I see you, my dear.'

Roz listened to the click at the other end, then cradled the receiver against her chest. *Thank God for Sister Bridget* . . . She put the receiver back with two hands that trembled. *Oh, Jesus, Jesus, Jesus! THANK GOD FOR SISTER BRIDGET* . . .

*

Supper was a simple affair of soup, scrambled eggs on toast, fresh fruit and cheese, with Roz's contribution of a light sparkling wine. They ate in the dining room, looking out over the tiny walled garden where climbing plants tumbled their vigorous new growth in glossy green cascades. It took Roz two hours to run through all her notes and give Sister Bridget a complete account of everything she had discovered.

Sister Bridget, rather more rosy-cheeked than usual, sat in contemplative silence for a long time after Roz had finished. If she noticed the bruises on the other woman's face, she did not remark on them. 'You know, my dear,' she said at last, 'if I'm surprised by anything it is your sudden certainty that Olive is guilty. I can see nothing in what she said to make you overturn your previous conviction that she was innocent.' She raised mildly enquiring eyebrows.

'It was the sly way she smiled when she talked about being the only one who knew anything,' said Roz tiredly. 'There was something so unpleasantly knowing about it. Does that make sense?'

'Not really. The Olive I see has a permanently sly look. I wish she could be as open with me as she seems to have been with you, but I'm afraid she will always regard me as the guardian of her morals. It makes it harder for her to be honest.' She paused for a moment. 'Are you sure you're not simply reacting to her hostility towards you? It's so much easier to believe well of people who like us, and Olive made no secret of her liking for you on the two previous occasions you went to see her.'

'Probably.' Roz sighed. 'But that just means I'm as naïve as everyone keeps accusing me of being.' *Most criminals are pleasant most of the time*, Hal had said.

'I think you probably are naïve,' agreed Sister Bridget, 'which is why you've ferreted out information that none of the cynical professionals thought worth bothering with. Naïvety has its uses, just like everything else.'

'Not when it encourages you to believe lies, it doesn't,' said Roz with feeling. 'I was so sure she had told me the truth about the abortion, and if anything set me questioning her guilt it was that. A secret lover floating around, a rapist even' – she shrugged – 'either would have made a hell of a difference to her case. If he didn't do the murders himself, he might well have provoked them in some way. She cut that ground from under me when she told me the abortion was a lie.'

Sister Bridget looked at her closely for a moment. 'But when did she lie? When she told you about the abortion or, today, when she denied it?'

'Not today,' said Roz decisively. 'Her denial had a ring of truth which her admission never had.'

'I wonder. Don't forget, you were inclined to believe her the first time. Since when, everyone, except Geraldine's mother, has poured cold water on the idea. Subconsciously, you've been slowly conditioned to reject the idea that Olive could have had a sexual relationship with a man. That's made you very quick to accept that what she told you today was the truth.'

'Only because it makes more sense.'

Sister Bridget chuckled. 'It makes more sense to believe that Olive's confession was true but you've highlighted too many inconsistencies to take it at face value. She tells lies, you know that. The trick is to sort out fact from fiction.'

'But why does she lie?' asked Roz in sudden exasperation. 'What good does it do her?'

'If we knew that, we'd have the answer to everything. She lied as a child to shore up the image she wanted to project and to shield herself and Amber from her mother's angry disappointment. She was afraid of rejection. It's why most of us lie, after all. Perhaps she keeps on with it for the same reasons.'

'But her mother and Amber are dead,' Roz pointed out, 'and isn't her image diminished by denying she had a lover?'

Sister Bridget sipped her wine. She didn't respond directly. 'She may, of course, have done it to get her own back. I suppose you've considered that. I can't help feeling she's adopted you as a surrogate Amber or a surrogate Gwen.'

'And look what happened to them.' Roz winced. 'Getting her own back for what, anyway?'

'For missing a visit. You said that upset her.'

'I had good reason.'

'I'm sure you did.' The kind eyes rested on the bruises. 'That's not to say Olive believed you or, if she did, that a week of resentment could be cast off so easily. She may, quite simply, have wanted to spite you in the only way she could, by hurting you. And she's succeeded. You *are* hurt.'

'Yes,' Roz admitted, 'I am. I believed in her. But I'm the one who's feeling rejected, not Olive.'

'Of course. Which is exactly what she wanted to achieve.'

'Even if it means I walk away and abandon her for good?'

'Spite is rarely sensible, Roz.' She shook her head. 'Poor Olive. She must be quite desperate at the moment if she's resorting to clay dolls and outbursts of anger. I wonder what's brought it on. She's been very tetchy with me, too, these last few months.'

'Her father's death,' said Roz. 'There's nothing else.'

Sister Bridget sighed. 'What a tragic life his was. One does wonder what he did to deserve it.' She fell silent. 'I am disinclined to believe,' she went on after a moment, 'that this man who sent the letters was Amber's lover. I think I told you that I bumped into Olive shortly before the murders. I was surprised to see how nice she looked. She was still very big, of course, but she had taken such trouble with her appearance that she looked quite pretty. A different girl entirely from the one who'd been at St Angela's. Such transformations never come about in a vacuum. There's always a reason for them and, in my experience, the reason is usually a man. Then, you know, there is Amber's character to consider. She was never as bright as her sister and she lacked Olive's independence and maturity. I would be very surprised if, at the age of twenty-one, she had been able to sustain an affair with anybody for as long as six months.'

'But you said yourself, men can bring about amazing transformations. Perhaps she changed under his influence.'

'I can't deny that, but if he was Amber's lover, then I can point to a very definite lie that Olive has told you. She would know exactly what was in the letters, either because Amber would have told her or because she would have found a way to open them. She always pried into things that weren't her concern. It sounds so churlish to say it now, but we all had to be very careful of our personal possessions while Olive was at St Angela's. Address books and diaries, in particular, drew her like magnets.'

'Marnie at Wells-Fargo thought Gary O'Brien had a yen for Olive. Perhaps *he* was the man she was dressing up for.'

'Perhaps.'

They sat in silence for some time watching twilight fall. Sister Bridget's cat, a threadbare tabby of advanced years, had curled in a ball on Roz's lap, and she stroked it mechanically in time to its purrs with the same careless affection that she bestowed on Mrs Antrobus. 'I wish,' she murmured, 'there was some independent way of finding out whether or not she had the abortion, but I'd never be allowed within spitting distance of her medical records. Not without her permission, and probably not even then.'

'And supposing it turns out that she didn't have an abortion? Would that tell you anything? It doesn't mean she didn't have a man in her life.'

'No,' agreed Roz, 'but by the same token if she *did* have an abortion then there can be no doubt there *was* a man. I'd be so much more confident about pressing ahead if I knew a lover existed.'

Sister Bridget's perceptive eyes remained on her too long for comfort. 'And so much more confident about dropping the whole thing if you can be convinced he didn't. I think, my dear, you should have more faith in your ability to judge people. Instinct is as good a guide as written evidence.'

'But my instinct at the moment tells me she's guilty as hell.'

'Oh, I don't think so.' Her companion's light laughter rang about the room. 'If it did you wouldn't have driven all these miles to talk to me. You could have sought out your friendly policeman. He would have approved your change of heart.' Her eyes danced. 'I, on the other hand, am the one person you know who could be relied on to fight Olive's corner.'

Roz smiled. 'Does that mean you now think she didn't do it?'

Sister Bridget stared out of the window. 'No,' she said frankly. 'I'm still in two minds.'

'Thanks,' said Roz with heavy irony, 'and you expect me to have faith. That's a bit two-faced, isn't it?'

'Very. But you were chosen, Roz, and I wasn't.'

Roz arrived back at her flat around midnight. The telephone was ringing as she let herself in but after three or four bells the answerphone took over. Iris, she thought. No one else would call at such an unearthly hour, not even Rupert. She had no intention of speaking to her but, out of curiosity, she flicked the switch on the machine to hear Iris leave her message.

'I wonder where you are,' slurred Hal's voice, slack with drink and tiredness. 'I've been calling for hours. I'm drunk as a skunk, woman, and it's your fault. You're too bloody thin, but what the hell!' He gave a baritone chuckle. 'I'm drowning in shit here, Roz. Me and Olive both. Mad, bad and dangerous to know.' He sighed. '*From East to western Ind, no jewel is like Rosalind*. Who are you, anyway? Nemesis? You lied, you know. You said you'd leave me in peace.' There was the sound of a crash. 'Je-*sus*!' he roared into the telephone. 'I've dropped the bloody bottle.' The line was cut abruptly.

Roz wondered if her grin looked as idiotic as it felt. She switched the answerphone back to automatic and went to bed. She fell asleep almost immediately.

The phone rang again at nine o'clock the next morning. 'Roz?' asked his sober, guarded voice.

'Speaking.'

'It's Hal Hawksley.'

'Hi,' she said cheerfully. 'I didn't know you knew my number.'

'You gave me your card, remember.'

'Oh, yes. What can I do for you?'

'I tried you yesterday, left a message on your answerphone.'

She smiled into the receiver. 'Sorry,' she told him, 'the tape's on the blink. All I got was my ear-drums pierced by high-pitched crackling. Has something happened?'

His relief was audible. 'No.' There was a brief pause. 'I just wondered how you got on with the O'Briens.'

'I saw Ma. It cost me fifty quid but it was worth it. Are you busy today or can I come and chew your ear off again? I need a couple of favours: a photograph of Olive's father and access to her medical records.'

He was happy talking details. 'No chance on the

latter,' he told her. 'Olive can demand to see them but you'd have more chance breaking into Parkhurst than breaking into NHS files. I might be able to get hold of a photograph of him, though, if I can persuade Geoff Wyatt to take a photocopy of the one on file.'

'What about pictures of Gwen and Amber? Could he get photocopies of them too?'

'Depends how strong your stomach is. The only ones I remember are the post-mortem shots. You'll have to get on to Martin's executors if you want pictures of them alive.'

'OK, but I'd still like to see the post-mortem ones if that's possible. I won't try to publish them without the proper authority,' she promised.

'You'd have a job. Police photocopies are usually the worst you'll ever see. If your publisher can make a decent negative out of them, he probably deserves a medal. I'll see what I can do. What time will you get here?'

'Early afternoon? There's someone I need to see first. Could you get me a copy of Olive as well?'

'Probably.' He was silent for a moment. 'High-pitched crackling. Are you sure that's all you heard?'

Twelve

PETERSON'S ESTATE AGENCY in Dawlington High Street maintained a brave front, with glossy photographs turning enticingly in the window and bright lights inviting the punters in. But, like the estate agents in Southampton centre, the recession had taken its toll here, too, and one neat young man presided over four desks in the despondent knowledge that another day would pass without a single house sale. He jerked to his feet with robotic cheerfulness as the door opened, his teeth glittering in a salesman's smile.

Roz shook her head to avoid raising false hopes. 'I'm sorry,' she said apologetically. 'I haven't come to buy anything.'

He gave an easy laugh. 'Ah, well. Selling perhaps?'

'Not that either.'

'Very wise.' He pulled out a chair for her. 'It's still a buyer's market. You only sell at the moment if you're desperate to move.' He resumed his chair on the other side of the desk. 'How can I help?'

Roz gave him a card. 'I'm trying to trace some people called Clarke who sold their house through this agency three or four years ago and moved out of the area. None of their neighbours knows where they went. I was hoping you might be able to tell me.'

He pulled a face. 'Before my time, I'm afraid. What was the address of the house?'

'Number twenty, Leven Road.'

'I could look it up, I suppose. The file will be out the back if it hasn't been binned.' He looked at the empty desks. 'Unfortunately there's no one to cover for me at the moment so I won't be able to do it until this evening. Unless—' He glanced at Roz's card again. 'I see you live in London. Have you ever thought about buying a second property on the south coast, Mrs Leigh? We have a lot of authors down here. They like to escape to the peace and quiet of the country.'

Her mouth twitched. 'Miss Leigh. And I don't even own a first property. I live in rented accommodation.'

He spun his chair and pulled out a drawer in the filing cabinet behind him. 'Then let me suggest a mutually beneficial arrangement.' His fingers ran nimbly through the files, selecting a succession of printed pages. 'You read these while I search out that information for you. If a customer comes into the shop, offer them a seat and call for me. Ditto, if the phone rings.' He nodded to a back door. 'I'll leave that open. Just call "Matt" and I'll hear you. Fair?'

'I'm happy if you are,' she said, 'but I'm not planning on buying anything.'

'That's fine.' He walked across to the door. 'Mind you, there's one property there that would fit you like a glove. It's called Bayview, but don't be put off by the name. I shan't be long.'

Roz fingered through the pages reluctantly as if just touching them might induce her to part with her money. He had the soft insidiousness of an insurance salesman. Anyway, she told herself with some amusement, she couldn't possibly live in a house called Bayview. It conjured up too many images of net-curtained guest-houses with beak-nosed landladies in nylon overalls and lacklustre signs saying vacancies propped against the downstairs windows.

She came to it finally at the bottom of the pile and the reality, of course, was very different. A small whitewashed coastguard's cottage, the last of a group of four, perched on a cliff near Swanage on the Isle of Purbeck. Two up, two down. Unpretentious. Charming. Beside the sea. She looked at the price.

'Well?' asked Matt, returning a few minutes later with a folder under one arm. 'What do you think?'

'Assuming I could afford it, which I can't, I think I'd freeze to death in the winter from winds lashing in off the sea and be driven mad in the summer by streams of tourists wandering along the coastal path. According to your blurb it passes only a matter of yards from the fence. And that's ignoring the fact that I'd be rubbing shoulders with the inhabitants of the other three cottages, day in, day out, plus the frightening prospect of knowing that sooner or later the cliff will slip and take my very expensive cottage with it.'

He chuckled good-humouredly. 'I knew you'd like it. I'd have bought it myself if it wasn't too far to travel each day. The cottage at the other end has a retired couple in it in their seventies and the two in the middle are weekend cottages. They are situated in the middle of a small headland, well away from the cliff edges, and, frankly, the bricks will crumble long before the foundations do. As for the wind and the tourists, well, it's to the east of Swanage so it's sheltered from the prevailing winds, and the sort of tourists who walk that coastal path are not the sort to disturb your peace, simply because there is no public access beside these cottages. The nearest one is four miles away and you don't get noisy children or drunken lager louts tackling that sort of hike for the fun of it. Which leaves' – his boyish face split into a carefree smile – 'the problem of cost.'

Roz giggled. 'Don't tell me. The owners are so desperate to get rid of it they're prepared to give it away.'

'As a matter of fact, yes. Liquidity problems with

their business and this is only a weekend retreat. They'll take a twenty-thousand reduction if someone can come up with cash. Can you?'

Roz closed her eyes and thought of her fifty per cent share of the proceeds of divorce, sitting on deposit. Yes, she thought, I can. 'This is absurd,' she said impatiently. 'I didn't come in to buy anything. I'll hate it. It'll be far too small. And why on earth have you got it on your books? It's miles away.'

'We have a reciprocal arrangement with our other branches.' He had hooked his fish. Now he let her swim a little. 'Let's see what this file can tell us.' He drew it forward and opened it. 'Twenty, Leven Road. Owners: Mr and Mrs Clarke. Instructions: quick sale wanted; carpets and curtains included in asking price. Bought by Mr and Mrs Blair. Completion date: twenty-fifth Feb., eighty-nine.' He looked surprised 'They didn't pay very much for it.'

'It was vacant for a year,' said Roz, 'which would probably explain the low price. Does it give a forwarding address for the Clarkes?'

He read on: 'It says here: "Vendors have asked Peterson's not to divulge any information about their new whereabouts." I wonder why.'

'They fell out with their neighbours,' said Roz, economical as ever with the truth. 'But they must have given a forwarding address,' she remarked reasonably, 'or they wouldn't have asked for it to be withheld.'

He turned over several pages then carefully closed the file, leaving his finger to mark a place. 'We're talking professional ethics here, Miss Leigh. I am employed by Peterson's, and Peterson's were asked to respect the Clarkes' confidence. It would be very wrong to abuse a client's trust.'

Roz thought for a moment. 'Is there anything from Peterson's in writing saying they agreed to honour the Clarkes' request?'

'No.'

'Then I don't see that you're bound by anything. Confidences cannot be inherited. If they could, they would no longer be confidences.'

He smiled. 'That's a very fine distinction.'

'Yes.' She picked up the details of Bayview. 'Supposing I said I wanted to view this cottage at three o'clock this afternoon? Could you arrange it for me, using that telephone over there' – she nodded to the furthest desk – 'while I stay here looking through these other house details?'

'I could, but I'd take it very badly if you failed to keep the appointment.'

'My word's my bond,' she assured him. 'If I say I'm going to do something I always do it.'

He stood up, letting the file fall open on the desk. 'Then I'll phone our Swanage branch,' he told her. 'You will have to collect the key from them.'

'Thank you.' She waited until his back was turned,

then swung the file round and jotted down the Clarkes' address on her pad. Salisbury, she noted.

A few minutes later Matt resumed his seat and gave her a map of Swanage with Peterson's estate agency marked with a cross. 'Mr Richards is expecting you at three o'clock.' With a lazy flick of his hand he closed the Clarkes' file. 'I trust you will find your dealings with him as mutually satisfactory as you have found your dealings with me.'

Roz laughed. 'And I hope I don't, or I shall be considerably poorer by this evening.'

Roz approached the Poacher by the alleyway at the back and knocked on the kitchen door. 'You're early,' said Hal, opening it.

'I know, but I have to be in Swanage by three and if I don't leave fairly soon I won't make it. Have you any customers?'

He gave her a withering smile. 'I haven't even bothered to open up.'

She chose to ignore the sarcasm. 'Then come with me,' she said. 'Forget this place for a few hours.'

He didn't exactly jump at the invitation. 'What's in Swanage?'

She handed him the details of Bayview. 'A "des. res." overlooking the sea. I've committed myself to looking at it and I could do with some moral support or I might end up buying the wretched thing.'

'Then don't go.'

'I have to. It's by way of a quid pro quo,' she said obliquely. 'Come with me,' she urged, 'and say no whenever I look like saying yes. I'm a sucker for a soft sell and I've always wanted to live on a cliff by the sea and own a dog and go beachcombing.'

He looked at the price. 'Can you afford it?' he asked curiously.

'Just about.'

'Rich lady,' he said. 'Writing is obviously very profitable.'

'Hardly. That was by way of a pay-off.'

'Pay-off for what?' he asked, his eyes veiled.

'It's not important.'

'Nothing ever is in your life.'

She shrugged. 'So you don't want to come? Ah, well, it was only a thought. I'll go on my own.' She looked lonely suddenly.

He glanced behind him towards the restaurant, then abruptly reached his jacket off the back of the door. 'I'll come,' he told her, 'but I'm damned if I'll say no. It sounds like paradise, and the second best piece of advice my mother ever gave me was never get between a woman and what she wants.' He pulled the door to and locked it.

'And what was the best piece of advice?'

He dropped a casual arm across her shoulders – *could she really be as lonely as she looked? The thought saddened him* – and walked her up the alleyway. 'That happiness is no laughing matter.'

She gave a throaty chuckle. 'What's that supposed to mean?'

'It means, woman, that the pursuit of happiness deserves weighty consideration. It's the be-all and end-all of existence. Where is the sense in living if you're not enjoying it?'

'Earning Brownie points for the great hereafter, suffering being good for the soul and all that.'

'If you say so,' he said cheerfully. 'Shall we go in my car? It'll give you a chance to test out your theory.' He led her to an ancient Ford Cortina estate and unlocked the passenger door, pulling it half-open on screaming hinges.

'What theory?' she asked, squeezing inelegantly through the gap.

He shut the door. 'You'll soon find out,' he murmured.

They arrived with half an hour to spare. Hal drew into a parking space on the sea front and rubbed his hands. 'Let's have some fish and chips. We passed a kiosk about a hundred yards back and I'm ravenous. It's the fresh air that does it.'

Roz's head, tortoise-like, emerged from the collar of her jacket, slowly easing its frozen jaw and skewering him with gimlet eyes. 'Has this heap of junk got an MOT?' she grated.

'Of course it's got an MOT.' He slapped the steering-wheel. 'She's sound as a bell, just lacks a window or two. You get used to it after a while.'

'A window or two!' she spluttered. 'As far as I can see it hasn't got any windows at all except for the front one. I think I've caught pneumonia.'

'There's no pleasing some women. You wouldn't be whingeing like this if I'd whisked you down to the seaside on a beautiful sunny day in an open-topped cabriolet. You're being snotty-nosed just because it's a Cortina.' He gave an evil chuckle. 'And what about suffering being good for the soul? It's done bugger all for yours, my girl.'

She thrust the screeching door open as far as it would go and crawled out. 'For your information, Hawksley, it is *not* a beautiful sunny day' – she giggled – 'in fact it will probably turn out to be the coldest May day this century. And *had* this been a convertible, we could have stopped to put the top up. In any case, why aren't there any windows?'

He tucked her into the crook of his arm and set off towards the fish and chip kiosk. 'Someone smashed them,' he said matter of factly. 'I haven't bothered to replace them because there's a good chance it will happen again.'

She rubbed the end of her nose to restore the circulation. 'I suppose you're in hock to loan sharks.'

'And if I am?'

She thought of her money on deposit, untouched, going nowhere. 'I might be able to broker you out of your difficulties,' she suggested tentatively.

He frowned. 'Is this charity, Roz, or an offer to negotiate?'

'It's not charity,' she assured him. 'My accountant would have a fit if I offered charity.'

He dropped his arm abruptly. 'Why would you want to negotiate on my behalf? You don't know a damn thing about me.' He sounded angry.

She shrugged. 'I know you're in deep shit, Hawksley. I'm offering to help you out of it. Is that so terrible?' She walked on.

Hal, a step or two behind, cursed himself roundly. What sort of fool lowered his defences just because a woman looked lonely? But loneliness, of course, was the one thing guaranteed to strike a chord. There must have been times when he hadn't been lonely but he was damned, at the moment, if he could remember them.

Roz's delight in the cottage, masked by an unconvincing smile of bored indifference, announced itself loudly as she stared wide-eyed at the views from the windows, noted the double-glazing, admitted grudgingly that, yes, she had always liked open fireplaces, and, yes, she was quite surprised by the size of the rooms. She *had* expected them to be smaller. She poked for several minutes round the patioed garden, said it was a pity there wasn't a greenhouse, then, rather belatedly, obscured her enthusiasm behind a pair of dark glasses to examine a small rose-covered outhouse which was used by the present owners as a third bedroom, but which might, she supposed, at a pinch, serve as a sort of study–library.

Hal and Mr Richards sat on cast-iron chairs in front of the french windows, talking idly about very little and watching her. Mr Richards, thoroughly intimidated by Hal's brusque one-word answers, scented a sale but contained his excitement rather better than Roz.

He stood up when Roz had finished her inspection and, with a disarming smile, offered her his chair. 'I should perhaps have mentioned, Miss Leigh, that the present owners will consider selling the furniture with the house assuming, of course, a satisfactory price can be arranged. I understand none of it is more than four years old and the wear and tear has been minimal with weekend occupation only.' He glanced at his watch. 'Why don't I give you fifteen minutes to talk it over? I'll go for a stroll along the cliff path.' He vanished tactfully through the french windows and a moment later they heard the front door close.

Roz took off her glasses and looked at Hal. Her eyes were childlike in their enthusiasm. 'What do you think? Furniture, too. Isn't it fabulous?'

His lips twitched involuntarily. *Could this be acting?* It was damn good if it was. 'It depends what you want it for.'

'To live in,' she said. 'It would be so easy to work here.' She looked towards the sea. 'I've always loved the sound of waves.' She turned to him. 'What do you think? Should I buy it?'

He was curious. 'Will my opinion make a difference?'

'Probably.'

'Why?'

'Because common sense tells me it would be a mad thing to do. It's miles from everyone I know, and it's expensive for what it is, a pokey little two up, two down. There must be better ways of investing my money.' She studied his set face and wondered why her earlier offer to help had made him so hostile. He was a strange man, she thought. So very approachable as long as she steered clear of talking about the Poacher.

He looked past her towards the cliff-top where Mr Richards was just visible, sitting on a rock and having a quiet smoke. 'Buy it,' he said. 'You can afford it.' His dark face broke into a smile. 'Live dangerously. Do what you've always wanted to do. How did John Masefield put it? "I must down to the seas again, for the call of the running tide/Is a wild call and a clear call that may not be denied." So, live on your cliff by the sea and go beachcombing with your dog. As I said, it sounds like paradise.'

She smiled back, her dark eyes full of humour. 'But the trouble with paradise was that it was boring, which is why, when the one-eyed trouser-snake appeared, Eve was so damn keen to bite into the apple of knowledge.' He was a different man when he laughed. She caught a glimpse of the Hal Hawksley, hail-fellow-well-met, boon companion, who could, were his tables ever full, preside with confident conviviality among them. She threw caution to the winds. 'I wish you'd let me help you. I'd be lonely here. And where's the sense in paying a fortune to be lonely on a cliff?'

His eyes veiled abruptly. 'You really are free with your money, aren't you? Exactly what are you suggesting? A buy-out? A partnership? What?'

God, he was prickly! And he had accused her of it once. 'Does it matter? I'm offering to bail you out of whatever mess you're in.'

His eyes narrowed. 'The only certain thing you know about me, Roz, is that my restaurant is failing. Why would an intelligent woman want to throw good money after bad?'

Why indeed? She would never be able to explain it to her accountant whose idea of sensible living was minimum risk-taking, clean balance sheets, and tax advantageous pension plans. How would she even begin? 'There's this man, Charles, who reduces me to jelly every time I see him. But he's a damn good cook and he loves his restaurant and there's no logical reason why it should be going down the pan. I keep trying to lend him money but he throws it back in my face every time.' Charles would have her certified. She swung her bag on to her shoulder. 'Forget I mentioned it,' she said. 'It's obviously a sore nerve, though I can't imagine why.'

She started to get up but he caught her wrist in a grip of iron and held her in her seat. 'Is this another set-up, Roz?'

She stared at him. 'You're hurting me.' He released her abruptly. 'What are you talking about?' she asked, massaging her wrist.

'You came back.' He rubbed his face vigorously with both hands as if he were in pain. 'Why the hell do you keep coming back?'

She was incensed. 'Because you phoned,' she said. 'I wouldn't have come if you hadn't phoned. God, you're arrogant. They come two a penny like you in London, you know.'

His eyes narrowed dangerously. 'Then offer your money to them,' he said, 'and stop patronizing me.'

Tight-lipped, they took their leave of Mr Richards with false promises of phoning the next day, and drove off up the narrow coast road towards Wareham. Hal, all too conscious of the darkening clouds and the reduction in speed that wet tarmac would enforce on him, concentrated on his driving. Roz, crushed by his hostility which, like a tropical storm, had blown out of nowhere, withdrew into hurt silence. Hal had been gratuitously cruel, and knew it, but he was gripped by his own certainty that this trip had been engineered to get him out of the Poacher. And *God* was Roz good. She had every damn thing: looks, humour, intellect, and just enough vulnerability to appeal to his stupid chivalry. But *he* had phoned *her. Fool, Hawksley!* She would have come back, anyway. Someone had to offer him the stinking money. *Sh-i-it!* He slammed his fist against the steering-wheel. 'Why did you want me to come with you?' he demanded into the silence.

'You're a free agent,' she pointed out caustically. 'You didn't have to come.'

It started to rain as they reached Wareham, slanting stair-rods that drove in through the open windows.

'Oh, great!' announced Roz, clutching her jacket about her throat. 'The perfect end to a perfect day. I'll be soaked. I should have come on my own in my own car. I could hardly have had less fun, could I?'

'Why didn't you then? Why drag me out on a wild-goose chase?'

'Believe it or not,' she said icily, 'I was trying to do you a favour. I thought it would be good for you to escape for a couple of hours. I was wrong. You're even more touchy away from the place than you are in it.' He took a corner too fast and threw her against the door, grazing her leather jacket against the buckled chromium window strip. 'For God's sake,' she snapped crossly. 'This jacket cost me a fortune.'

He pulled into the kerb with a screech of rubber. 'OK,' he snarled, 'let's see what we can do to protect it.' He reached across her to take a book of road maps out of the dashboard pocket.

'What good will that do?'

'It will tell me where the nearest station is.' He thumbed through the pages. 'There's one in Wareham and the line goes to Southampton. You can take a taxi back to your car at the other end.' He fished out his wallet. 'That should be enough to pay your way.' He dropped a twenty-pound note into her lap then swung the car on to the road again. 'It's off to the right at the next roundabout.'

'You're a real sweetheart, Hawksley. Didn't your mother teach you any manners along with her little aphorisms about women and life?'

'Don't push your luck,' he growled. 'I'm on a very short fuse at the moment and it doesn't take much to rile me. I spent five years of marriage being criticized for every damn thing I did. I'm not about to repeat the experience.' He drew up in front of the station. 'Go home,' he told her, wiping a weary hand across his damp face. 'I'm doing you a favour.'

She put the twenty-pound note on the dashboard and reached for her handbag. 'Yes,' she agreed mildly, 'I think you probably are. If your wife stuck it out for five years, she must have been a saint.' She pushed the door open on its screaming hinges and eased round it, then bent down to look through the window, thrusting her middle finger into the air. 'Go screw yourself, Sergeant. Presumably it's the only thing that gives you any pleasure. Let's face it, no one else could ever be good enough.'

'Got it in one, Miss Leigh.' He nodded a curt farewell, then spun the wheel in a U-turn. As he drove away the twenty-pound note whipped like a bitter recrimination from the window and fell with the rain into the gutter.

Hal was cold and wet by the time he reached Dawlington, and his already evil temper was not improved to find her car still parked at the end of the alleyway where she had left it. He glanced past it, between the buildings, and saw that the back door of the Poacher stood ajar, the wood in splinters where a crowbar had been used to wrench it free of its frame. OH, *Jesus*! She *had* set him up. He knew a moment of total desolation – he was not as immune as he thought himself – before the need to act took over.

He was too angry for common sense, too angry to take even elementary precautions. He ran on light feet, thrust the door wide and weighed in with flailing fists, punching, kicking, gouging, oblivious to the blows that landed on his arms and shoulders, intent only on causing maximum damage to the bastards who were destroying him.

Roz, arriving thirty minutes later with Hal's sodden twenty-pound note clutched in one hand and a blistering letter of denunciation in the other, stared in disbelief at what she saw. The kitchen looked like a scene from Beirut in the aftermath of war. Deserted and destroyed. The table, up-ended, leant drunkenly against the oven, two of its legs wrenched free. Chairs, in pieces, lay amongst shards of broken crockery and jagged glass. And the fridge, tilted forward and balanced precariously on its open door, had poured its contents across the quarry tiling in streams of milk and congealed stock. She held a trembling hand to her lips. Here and there, splashes of bright red blood had tinged the spreading milk pink.

She looked wildly up the alleyway, but there was no one in sight. *What to do?* 'Hal!' she called, but her voice was little more than a whisper. 'Hal!' This time it rose out of control and, in the silence that followed, she thought she heard a sound from the other side of the swing doors into the restaurant. She stuffed the letter and the money into her pockets and reached inside the door for one of the table legs. 'I've called the police,' she shouted, croaky with fear. 'They're on their way.'

The door swung open and Hal emerged with a

bottle of wine. He nodded at the table leg. 'What are you planning to do with that?'

She let her arm fall. 'Have you gone mad? Did you do all this?'

'Am I likely to have done it?'

'Olive did.' She stared about her. 'This is just what Olive did. Lost her temper and destroyed her room. She had all her privileges taken away.'

'You're babbling.' He found a couple of glasses in an intact wall cupboard and filled them from the bottle. 'Here.' His dark eyes watched her closely. '*Have* you called the police?'

'No.' Her teeth chattered against the wine glass. 'I thought if you were a burglar you'd run away. Your hand's bleeding.'

'I know.' He took the table leg away from her and put it on top of the oven, then pulled forward the only intact chair from behind the back door and pressed her into it. 'What were you going to do if the burglar ran out this way?'

'Hit him, I suppose.' Her fear was beginning to subside. 'Is this what you thought I'd set you up for?'

'Yes.'

'God!' She didn't know what else to say. She watched while he found a broom and started to sweep the mess towards one corner. 'Shouldn't you leave that?'

'What for?'

'The police.'

He eyed her curiously. 'You said you hadn't called them.'

She digested this in silence for several seconds, then put her glass on the floor beside her. 'This is all a bit heavy for me.' She took the twenty-pound note from her pocket, but left the letter where it was. 'I only came back to give you this.' She held it out as she stood up. 'I'm sorry,' she said with an apologetic smile.

'What for?'

'Making you angry. I seem to have a knack for making people angry at the moment.' He moved towards her to take the money, but stopped abruptly at her look of alarm.

'Goddamnit, woman, do you think *I* did this?'

But he was speaking to thin air. Roz had taken to her heels down the alleyway and the twenty-pound note, once again, fluttered to the ground.

Thirteen

ROZ'S SLEEP THAT night was intermittent, fitful dozing between turbulent dreams. Olive with an axe, hacking kitchen tables to pieces. *I didn't think you would . . . it's not as easy as it looks on the telly . . .* Hal's fingers on her wrist, but his face the gleeful face of her brother as he gave her Chinese burns as a child. *Goddamnit, woman, do you think I did this . . .* Olive hanging from the gallows, her face the slimy grey of wet clay. *Have you no qualms about releasing someone like her back into society . . .* A priest with the eyes of Sister Bridget. *It's a pity you're not a Catholic . . . You could go to confession and feel better immediately . . . You keep offering me money . . . The law is an ass . . . Have you called the police . . .*

She woke in the morning to the sound of the phone ringing in her sitting room. Her head was splitting. She snatched up the receiver to shut off the noise. 'Who is it?'

'Well, that's a nice welcome, I must say,' remarked Iris. 'What's eating you?'

'Nothing. What do you want?'

'Shall I phone off,' said Iris sweetly, 'and call you back again in half an hour when you've remembered that I'm your friend and not some piece of dog's dirt that you've just scraped off your shoe?'

'Sorry. You woke me. I didn't sleep very well.'

'M'm, well, I've just had your editor on the phone pressing me for a date – and I don't mean an invitation to dinner. He wants a rough idea of when the book will be ready.'

Roz made a face into the receiver. 'I haven't started writing it yet.'

'Then you'd better get a move on, my darling, because I've told him it will be finished by Christmas.'

'Oh, Iris, for Heaven's sake. That's only six months away and I'm no further forward than the last time I spoke to you. Olive clams up every time we get to the murders. In fact I—'

'Seven months,' Iris cut in. 'Go and grill that dodgy policeman again. He sounds absolutely frightful and I'll bet you anything you like he framed her. They all do it. It boosts their quotas. The buzz word is productivity, darling, something that is temporarily absent from your vocabulary.'

*

Mrs Clarke listened to Roz's introductory speech about her book on Olive with an expression of complete horror. 'How did you find us?' she asked in a quavering voice. For no particular reason, Roz had pictured her in her fifties or early sixties. She was unprepared for this old woman, closer in age to Mr Hayes than to the age Robert and Gwen Martin would have been if they were still alive.

'It wasn't difficult,' she hedged.

'I've been so afraid.'

It was an odd reaction but Roz let it pass. 'Can I come in? I won't take up much of your time, I promise.'

'I couldn't possibly speak to you. I'm alone. Edward is shopping.'

'Please, Mrs Clarke,' she begged, her voice catching under the strain of her tiredness. It had taken two and a half hours to drive to Salisbury and locate their house. 'I've come such a long way to see you.'

The woman smiled suddenly and held the door wide. 'Come in. Come in. Edward made some cakes specially. He'll be so thrilled you found us.'

With a puzzled frown, Roz stepped inside. 'Thank you.'

'You remember Pussy, of course' – she waved at an ancient cat curled beneath a radiator – 'or was she after your time? I forget things, you know. We'll sit in the lounge. Edward,' she called, 'Mary's here.'

There was no response. 'Edward's gone shopping,' said Roz.

'Oh, yes.' She looked at Roz in confusion. 'Do I know you?'

'I'm a friend of Olive's.'

'I'm a friend of Olive's,' mimicked the old lady. 'I'm a friend of Olive's.' She lowered herself on to the sofa. 'Sit down. Edward's made some cakes specially. I remember Olive. We were at school together. She had long pigtails which the boys used to pull. Such wicked boys. I wonder what happened to them.' She looked at Roz again. 'Do I know you?'

Roz sat awkwardly in an armchair, weighing the ethics of questioning a vulnerable old woman with senile dementia. 'I'm a friend of Olive Martin,' she prompted. 'Gwen and Robert's daughter.' She studied the vacant blue eyes but there was no reaction. She was relieved. Ethics became irrelevant when asking questions was a nonsense. She smiled encouragingly. 'Tell me about Salisbury. Do you like living here?'

Their conversation was an exhausting one, filled with silences, chanting repetition, and strange inconsequential references that left Roz struggling to follow the thread. Twice, she had to divert Mrs Clarke from a sudden realization that she was a stranger, fearing that if she left she would find it impossible to get back in to talk to Edward. With part of her mind she wondered how he coped. Could you go on loving an empty shell when your love was neither reciprocated nor appreciated? Could there ever be enough flashes of lucidity to make the loneliness of caring worthwhile?

Her eye was drawn again and again to the wedding photograph above the mantelpiece. They had married comparatively late, she thought, judging by their ages. He looked to be in his forties, with most of his hair already missing. She looked a little older. But they stood shoulder to shoulder, laughing together out of the frame, two happy, healthy people, with not a care in the world, unaware – and how could they be? – that she carried the seeds of dementia. It was cruel to make a comparison but Roz couldn't help herself. Beside the celluloid woman, so alive, so vivid, so substantial, the real Mrs Clarke was a colourless, trembling shadow. Was this, Roz wondered, why Edward and Robert Martin had become lovers? She found the whole experience immensely depressing and when, at last, the sound of a key grated in the lock, it came like the welcome patter of rain on drought-hardened earth.

'Mary's come to see us,' said Mrs Clarke brightly as her husband entered the room. 'We've been waiting for cakes.'

Roz stood up and handed Mr Clarke one of her cards. 'I did tell her who I was,' she said quietly, 'but it seemed kinder to be Mary.'

He was old, like his wife, and entirely bald, but he still carried himself erect with shoulders squared. He towered above the woman on the sofa who shrank away from him in sudden fear, muttering to herself. Roz wondered if he ever lost his temper with her.

'I really don't leave her alone very often,' he answered defensively, as if she had accused him of it, 'but the shopping has to be done. Everyone's so busy and it's not fair to keep asking the neighbours.' He ran a hand across his bald head and read the card. 'I thought you were Social Services,' he said, this time accusing *her*. 'Author? We don't want an author. What good would an author be to us?'

'I was hoping you could help me.'

'I don't know the first thing about writing. Who gave you my name?'

'Olive did,' said Mrs Clarke. 'She's a friend of Olive's.'

He was shocked. 'Oh, no!' he said. 'No, no, no! You'll have to leave. I'm not having that dragged up again. It's an outrage. How did you get hold of this address?'

'No, no, no!' chanted his wife. 'It's an outrage. No, no, no!'

Roz held her breath and counted to ten, not sure if her sanity or her control would slip first. 'How on earth do you cope?' The words tumbled out as involuntarily as Mrs Clarke's did. 'I'm sorry.' She saw the strain in his face. 'That was unforgivably rude.'

'It's not so bad when we're alone. I just switch

off.' He sighed. 'Why have you come? I thought we'd put all that behind us. There's nothing I can do for Olive. Robert tried to help her at the time but it was all thrown back in his face. Why has she sent you here?'

'It's an outrage,' muttered the old woman.

'She hasn't. I'm here off my own bat. Look,' she said, glancing at Mrs Clarke, 'is there somewhere we can talk privately?'

'There's nothing to talk about.'

'But there is,' she said. 'You were a friend of Robert's. You must have known the family better than anyone. I'm writing a book' – she remembered belatedly that her explanations had been given to Mrs Clarke – 'and I can't do it if no one will tell me about Gwen and Robert.'

She had shocked him again. 'Gutter journalism,' he spat. 'I won't have anything to do with it. Leave now, or I shall call the police.'

Mrs Clarke gave a whimper of fear. 'Not the police. No, no, no. I'm afraid of the police.' She peered at the stranger. 'I'm afraid of the police.'

With reason, thought Roz, wondering if the shock of the murders had brought on the dementia. Was that why they had moved away? She picked up her briefcase and handbag. 'I'm no gutter journalist, Mr Clarke. I'm trying to help Olive.'

'She's beyond help. We all are.' He glanced at his wife. 'Olive destroyed everything.'

'I disagree.'

'Please go.'

The thin reedy voice of the old woman broke in on them. 'I never saw Gwen and Amber that day,' she cried plaintively. 'I lied. I lied, Edward.'

He closed his eyes. 'Oh, God,' he murmured, 'what did I ever do to deserve this?' His voice vibrated with repressed dislike.

'Which day?' Roz pressed.

But the moment of lucidity, if that is what it was, had passed. 'We've been waiting for cakes.'

Irritation and something else – relief? – passed across his face. 'She's senile,' he told Roz. 'Her mind's gone. You can't rely on anything she says. I'll show you out.'

Roz didn't move. 'Which day, Mrs Clarke?' she asked gently.

'The day the police came. I said I saw them but I didn't.' She furrowed her brow in perplexity. 'Do I know you?'

Mr Clarke seized Roz roughly by the arm and manhandled her towards the front door. 'Get out of my house!' he stormed. 'Haven't we suffered enough at the hands of that family?' He thrust her into the street and slammed the door.

Roz rubbed her arm reflectively. Edward Clarke, in spite of his age, was a good deal stronger than he looked.

*

She turned the problem in her mind throughout the long drive home. She was caught in the same dilemma that Olive kept posing her, the dilemma of belief. Was Mrs Clarke telling the truth? Had she lied to the police that day or was her senile recollection faulty? And if she had lied, did it make a difference?

Roz pictured herself in the Poacher's kitchen, listening to Hal talking about Robert Martin's alibi. 'We did wonder if he might have killed Gwen and Amber before he went to work and Olive then attempted to dispose of the bodies to protect him, but the numbers didn't add up. He had an alibi even for that. There was a neighbour who saw her husband off to work a few minutes before Martin himself left. Amber and Gwen were alive then because she spoke to them on their doorstep. She remembered asking Amber how she was getting on at Glitzy. They waved as Martin drove away.'

Mrs Clarke, thought Roz, it had to be. But how remiss of her not to question that statement before? Was it likely that Gwen and Amber would wave goodbye to Robert when so little love was lost between husband and wife? A sentence from Olive's statement pierced her thoughts like a sharp knife. *'We had an argument over breakfast and my father left for work in the middle of it.'*

So Mrs Clarke had been telling lies. But why? Why give Robert an alibi when, according to Olive, she saw him as a threat?

'There was a neighbour who saw her husband off to work a few minutes before Martin himself left . . .'

God, but she'd been blind. The alibi was Edward's.

She phoned Iris in a fever of excitement from a pay phone. 'I've cracked it, old thing. I know who did it and it wasn't Olive.'

'There you are, you see. Always trust your agent's instincts. I've had a fiver on you with Gerry. He'll be sick as a parrot about losing. So who did do it?'

'The neighbour, Edward Clarke. He was Robert Martin's lover. I think he killed Gwen and Amber out of jealousy.' Breathlessly, she rattled off her story. 'Mind you, I've still got to find a way of proving it.'

There was a lengthy silence at the other end.

'Are you still there?'

'Yes, I was just mourning my five pounds. I know you're excited, darling, but you'll have to sober up and give it a little more thought. If this Edward chopped up Gwen and Amber before Robert went to work, wouldn't Robert have stumbled across the bits in the kitchen?'

'Perhaps they did it together?'

'Then why didn't they kill Olive as well? Not to mention the small matter of why on earth Olive would want to shield her father's homosexual lover. It would make much more sense if Mrs Clarke lied to give Robert an alibi.'

'Why?'

'They were having a raging affair,' declared Iris. 'Mrs C. guessed Robert had done his wife in to give himself a free hand with her and lied through her teeth to protect him. You don't know for sure he was a homosexual. The schoolfriend's mother didn't think he was. Is Mrs C. attractive?'

'Not now. She was once.'

'There you are, then.'

'Why did Robert kill Amber?'

'Because she was there,' said Iris simply. 'I expect she woke up when she heard the fight and came downstairs. Robert would have had no option but to kill her as well. Then he skedaddled and left poor old Olive, who slept through it all, to face the music.'

Somewhat reluctantly, Roz went to see Olive.

'I wasn't expecting you, not after—' Olive left the rest of the sentence unsaid. 'Well, you know.' She smiled shyly.

They were back in their old room, unsupervised. The Governor's qualms, it seemed, had been laid to rest along with Olive's hostility. Really, thought Roz, the prison system never ceased to surprise her. She had foreseen enormous problems, particularly as it was a Wednesday and not her normal day, but there had been none. Access to Olive was once more unrestricted. She pushed forward the cigarette packet. 'You seem to be *persona grata* again,' she said.

Olive accepted a cigarette. 'With you, too?'

Roz arched an eyebrow. 'I felt better after my headache had gone.' She saw distress on the fat face. 'I'm teasing,' she said gently. 'And it was my fault anyway. I should have phoned. Have you had all your privileges restored?'

'Yes. They're pretty decent really, once you calm down.'

'Good.' Roz switched on her tape-recorder. 'I've been to see your next-door neighbours, the Clarkes.'

Olive studied her through the flame of the match, then tipped it thoughtfully towards her cigarette. 'And?'

'Mrs Clarke lied about seeing your mother and sister on the morning of the murders.'

'How do you know?'

'She told me.'

Olive wedged the cigarette firmly between her lips and drew in a lungful of smoke. 'Mrs Clarke's been senile for years,' she said bluntly. 'She had a thing about germs, used to rush about every morning scrubbing the furniture with Domestos and hoovering like mad. People who didn't know them thought she was the char. She always called me Mary which was her mother's name. I should imagine she's completely loopy by now.'

Roz shook her head in frustration. 'She is, but I'll swear she was lucid when she admitted lying. She's frightened of her husband, though.'

Olive looked surprised. 'She was never frightened of him before. If anything, he was more frightened of her. What did he say when she told you she'd lied?'

'He was furious. Ordered me out of the house.' She made a wry face. 'We got off to a bad start. He thought I was from the Social Services, spying on him.'

A wheeze of amusement eddied up through Olive's throat. 'Poor Mr Clarke.'

'You said your father liked him. Did *you*?'

She shrugged indifference. 'I didn't know him well enough to like him or dislike him. I suppose I felt sorry for him because of his wife. He had to retire early to look after her.'

Roz mulled this over. 'But he was still working at the time of the murders?'

'He carried on a small accountancy business from home. Other people's tax returns mostly.' She tapped ash on to the floor. 'Mrs Clarke set fire to their living room once. He was afraid to leave her alone after that. She was very demanding but my mother said most of it was an act to keep him tied to her apron strings.'

'Was that true, do you think?'

'I expect so.' She stood the cigarette on its end, as

was her habit, and took another. 'My mother was usually right.'

'Did they have children?'

Olive shook her head. 'I don't think so. I never saw any.' She pursed her lips. '*He* was the child. It was quite funny sometimes watching him scurrying about, doing what he was told, saying sorry when he got it wrong. Amber called him Puddleglum because he was wet and miserable.' She chuckled. 'I'd forgotten that until this minute. It suited him at the time. Does it still?'

Roz thought of his grip on her arms. 'He didn't strike me as being particularly wet,' she said. 'Miserable, yes.'

Olive studied her with her curiously penetrating gaze. 'Why have you come back?' she asked gently. 'You didn't intend to on Monday.'

'What makes you say that?'

'I saw it in your face. You thought I was guilty.'

'Yes.'

Olive nodded. 'It upset me. I hadn't realized what a difference it made to have someone believe I didn't do it. Politicians call it the feel-good factor.' Roz saw dampness on the pale lashes. 'You get used to being viewed as a monster. Sometimes I believe it myself.' She placed one of her disproportionate hands between her huge breasts. 'I thought my heart would burst when you left. Silly, isn't it?' Tears welled in her eyes.

'I can't remember being so upset about anything before.'

Roz waited a moment but Olive didn't go on. 'Sister Bridget knocked some sense into me,' she said.

A glow, like a rising candle flame, lit the fat woman's face. 'Sister Bridget?' she echoed in amazement. 'Does she think I didn't do it? I never guessed. I thought she came out of Christian duty.'

Oh hell, thought Roz, what does a lie matter? 'Of course she thinks you didn't do it. Why else would she keep pushing me so hard?' She watched the tremulous pleasure bring a sort of beauty to the awful ugliness that was Olive, and she thought, I've burnt my boats. I can never again ask her if she's guilty or if she's telling me the truth because, if I do, her poor heart *will* burst.

'I didn't do it,' said Olive, reading her expression.

Roz leaned forward. 'Then who did?'

'I don't know now. I thought I did at the time.' She stood her second cigarette beside the first and watched it die. 'At the time it all made sense,' she murmured, her mind groping into the past.

'Who did you think it was?' asked Roz after a while. 'Someone you loved?'

But Olive shook her head. 'I couldn't bear to be laughed at. In so many ways it's easier to be feared. At least it means people respect you.' She looked at Roz. 'I'm really quite happy here. Can you understand that?'

'Yes,' said Roz slowly, remembering what the Governor had said. 'Oddly enough, I can.'

'If you hadn't sought me out, I could have survived. I'm institutionalized. Existence without effort. I really don't know that I could cope on the outside.' She smoothed her hands down her massive thighs. 'People will laugh, Roz.'

It was a question more than a statement and Roz didn't have an answer, or not the reassuring answer that Olive wanted. People *would* laugh, she thought. There was an intrinsic absurdity about this grotesque woman loving so deeply that she would brand herself a murderess to protect her lover.

'I'm not giving up now,' she said firmly. 'A battery hen is born to exist. You were born to live.' She levelled her pen at Olive. 'And if you don't know the difference between existence and living then read the Declaration of Independence. Living means Liberty and the Pursuit of Happiness. You deny yourself both by staying here.'

'Where would I go? What would I do?' She wrung her hands. 'In all my life I've never lived on my own. I couldn't bear it, not now, not with everyone knowing.'

'Knowing what?'

Olive shook her head.

'Why can't you tell me?'

'Because,' said Olive heavily, 'you wouldn't believe me. No one ever does when I tell the truth.' She rapped on the glass to attract a prison officer's attention. 'You must find out for yourself. It's the only way you'll ever really know.'

'And if I can't?'

'I'm no worse off than I was before. I can live with myself, and that's all that really matters.'

Yes, thought Roz, at the end of the day it probably was. 'Just tell me one thing, Olive. Have you lied to me?'

'Yes.'

'Why?'

The door opened and Olive heaved herself upright with the customary shove from behind. 'Sometimes, it's safer.'

The telephone was ringing as she opened the door to the flat. 'Hi,' she said, thrusting it under her chin and taking off her jacket. 'Rosalind Leigh.' *Pray God it wasn't Rupert.*

'It's Hal. I've been ringing all day. Where the hell have you been?' He sounded worried.

'Chasing clues.' She leant her back against the wall for support. 'What's it to you, anyway?'

'I'm not psychotic, Roz.'

'You damn well behaved like it yesterday.'

'Just because I didn't call the police?'

'Among other things. It's what normal people do

when their property's been smashed up. Unless they've done it themselves, of course.'

'What other things?'

'You were bloody rude. I was only trying to help.'

He laughed softly. 'I keep seeing you standing by my door with that table leg. You're a hell of a gutsy lady. Shit scared, but gutsy. I've got those photographs for you. Do you still want them?'

'Yes.'

'Are you brave enough to collect them or do you want me to post them?'

'It's not bravery that's required, Hawksley, it's thick bloody skin. I'm tired of being needled.' She smiled to herself at the pun. 'Which reminds me, was it Mrs Clarke who said Gwen and Amber were alive after Robert went to work?'

There was a slight pause while he tried to see a connection. He couldn't. 'Yes, if she was the one in the attached semi.'

'She was lying. She says now that she didn't see them, which means Robert Martin's alibi is worthless. He could have done it before he went to work.'

'Why would she give Robert Martin an alibi?'

'I don't know. I'm trying to work it out. I thought at first she was alibiing her own husband, but that doesn't hold water. Apart from anything else, Olive tells me he was already retired so he wouldn't have gone to work anyway. Can you remember checking Mrs Clarke's statement?'

'Was Clarke the accountant? Yes?' He thought for a moment. 'OK, he ran most of his business from home but he also looked after the books of several small firms in the area. That week he was doing the accounts of a central heating contractor in Portswood. He was there all day. We checked. He didn't get home until after we had the place barricaded. I remember the fuss he made about having to park his car at the other end of the road. Elderly man, bald, with glasses. That the one?'

'Yes,' she said, 'but what he and Robert did during the day is irrelevant if Gwen and Amber were dead before either of the men left for work.'

'How reliable is Mrs Clarke?'

'Not very,' she admitted. 'What was the earliest estimate of death according to your pathologist?'

He was unusually evasive. 'I can't remember now.'

'Try,' she pressed him. 'You suspected Robert enough to check his alibi so he can't have been ruled out immediately on the forensic evidence.'

'I can't remember,' he said again. 'But if Robert did it, then why didn't he kill Olive as well? And why didn't she try and stop him? There must have been a hell of a row going on. She couldn't possibly have avoided hearing something. It's not that big a house.'

'Perhaps she wasn't there.'

*

The Chaplain made his weekly visit to Olive's room. 'That's good,' he said, watching her bring curl to the mother's hair with the point of a matchstick. 'Is it Mary and Jesus?'

She looked at him with amusement. 'The mother is suffocating her baby,' she said baldly. 'Is it likely to be Mary and Jesus?'

He shrugged. 'I've seen many stranger things that pass for religious art. Who is it?'

'It's Woman,' said Olive. 'Eve with all her faces.'

He was interested. 'But you haven't given her a face.'

Olive twisted the sculpture on its base and he saw that what he had taken to be curls at the side of the mother's hair was in fact a crude delineation of eyes, nose and mouth. She twisted it the other way and the same rough representation stared out from that side as well. 'Two-faced,' said Olive, 'and quite unable to look you in the eye.' She picked up a pencil and shoved it between the mother's thighs. 'But it doesn't matter. Not to MAN.' She leered unpleasantly. 'MAN doesn't look at the mantelpiece when he's poking the fire.'

Hal had mended the back door and the kitchen table, which stood in its customary place once more in the middle of the room. The floor was scrubbed clean, wall units repaired, fridge upright, even some chairs had been imported from the restaurant and placed neatly about the table. Hal himself looked completely exhausted.

'Have you had any sleep at all?' she asked him.

'Not much. I've been working round the clock.'

'Well, you've performed miracles.' She gazed about her. 'So who's coming to dinner? The Queen? She could eat it off the floor.'

To her surprise he caught her hand and lifted it to his lips, turning it to kiss the palm. It was an unexpectedly delicate gesture from such a hard man. 'Thank you.'

She was at a loss. 'What for?' she asked helplessly.

He released her hand with a smile. 'Saying the right things.' For a moment she thought he was going to elaborate, but all he said was: 'The photographs are on the table.'

Olive's was a mug-shot, stark and brutally unflattering. Gwen and Amber's shocked her as he had said they would. They were the stuff of nightmares and she understood for the first time why everyone had said Olive was a psychopath. She turned them over and concentrated on the head and shoulders' shot of Robert Martin. Olive was there in the eyes and mouth, and she had a fleeting impression of what might lie beneath the layers of lard if Olive could ever summon the will-power to shed it. Her father was a very handsome man.

'What are you going to do with them?'

She told him about the man who sent letters to

Olive. 'The description fits her father,' she said. 'The woman at Wells-Fargo said she'd recognize him from a photograph.'

'Why on earth should her father have sent her secret letters?'

'To set her up as a scapegoat for the murders.'

He was sceptical. 'You're plucking at straws. What about the ones of Gwen and Amber?'

'I don't know yet. I'm tempted to show them to Olive to shock her out of her apathy.'

He raised an eyebrow. 'I'd think twice about that if I were you. She's an unknown quantity, and you may not know her as well as you think you do. She could very easily turn nasty if you present her with her own handiwork.'

She smiled briefly. 'I know her better than I know you.' She tucked the photographs into her handbag and stepped out into the alleyway. 'The odd thing is you're very alike, you and Olive. You demand trust but you don't give it.'

He wiped a weary hand around his two-day growth of stubble. 'Trust is a two-edged sword, Roz. It can make you extremely vulnerable. I wish you'd remember that from time to time.'

Fourteen

MARNIE STUDIED THE photograph of Robert Martin for several seconds then shook her head. 'No,' she said, 'that wasn't him. He wasn't so good looking and he had different hair, thicker, not swept back, more to the side. Anyway, I told you, he had dark brown eyes, almost black. These eyes are light. Is this her father?'

Roz nodded.

Marnie handed the photograph back. 'My mother always said, never trust a man whose earlobes are lower than his mouth. It's the sign of a criminal. Look at his.'

Roz looked. She hadn't noticed it before because of the way his hair swept over them, but Martin's ears were almost unnaturally out of symmetry with the rest of his face. 'Did your mother know any criminals?'

Marnie snorted. 'Of course she didn't. It's just an old wives' tale.' She cocked her head to look at the picture again. 'Anyway, if there was something in it he'd be a Category A by now.'

'He's dead.'

'Perhaps he passed the gene on to his daughter. She's Category A all right.' She got busy with her nail file. 'Where did you get it, as a matter of interest?'

'The photograph? Why do you ask?'

Marnie tapped the top right-hand corner with her file. 'I know where it was taken.'

Roz looked where she was pointing. In the background beyond Martin's head was part of a lampshade with a pattern of inverted *y*s round its base. 'In his house, presumably.'

'Doubt it. Look at the sign round the shade. There's only one place anywhere near here has shades like that.'

The *y*s were lambdas, Roz realized, the international symbol of homosexuality. 'Where?'

'It's a pub near the waterfront. Goes in for drag acts.' Marnie giggled. 'It's a gay knocking-shop.'

'What's it called?'

Marnie giggled again. 'The White Cock.'

The landlord recognized the photograph immediately. 'Mark Agnew,' he told her. 'Used to come here a lot. But I haven't seen him in the last twelve months. What happened to him?'

'He died.'

The landlord pulled a long face. 'I shall have to go straight,' he said with weary gallows humour. 'What with AIDS and the recession I've hardly any customers left.'

Roz smiled sympathetically. 'If it's any consolation I don't think he died of AIDS.'

'Well, it is some consolation, lovey. He put himself about a bit, did Mark.'

Mrs O'Brien regarded her with deep displeasure. Time and her naturally suspicious nature had persuaded her that Roz was nothing to do with television but had come to worm information out of her about her sons. 'You've got a flaming cheek, I must say.'

'Oh,' said Roz with obvious disappointment, 'have you changed your mind about the programme?' Lies, she thought, worked if you kept repeating them.

'Programme, my arse. You're a bloody snooper. What you after? That's what I want to know.'

Roz took Mr Crew's letter out of her briefcase and handed it to the woman. 'I explained it as well as I could last time, but these are the terms of my contract with the television company. If you read it, you'll see that it sets out quite clearly the aims and objectives of the programme they want to make.' She pointed to Crew's signature. 'That's the director. He listened to the tape we made and liked what he heard. He'll be disappointed if you back out now.'

Ma O'Brien, presented with written evidence, was impressed. She frowned intelligently at the unintelligible words. 'Well,' she said, 'a contract makes a difference. You should of shown me this last time.' She folded it, preparatory to putting it in her pocket.

Roz smiled. 'Unfortunately,' she said, whisking it from Ma's fingers, 'this is the only copy I have and I need it for tax and legal purposes. If it's lost, none of us will get paid. May I come in?'

Ma compressed her lips. 'No reason not to, I suppose.' But suspicion died hard. 'I'm not hanswering hanything fishy, mind.'

'Of course not.' She walked into the sitting room. 'Is any of your family at home? I'd like to include them if possible. The more rounded the picture the better.'

Ma gave it some thought. '*Mike!*' she yelled suddenly. 'Get yourself down. There's a lady wants to talk to you. *Nipper!* In 'ere.'

Roz, who was only interested in talking to Gary, saw fifty-pound notes flying out the window by the bucket-load. She smiled with resignation as two skinny young men joined their mother on the sofa. 'Hi,' she said brightly, 'my name's Rosalind Leigh and I represent a television company which is putting together a programme on social deprivation . . .'

'I told them,' said Ma, cutting her short. 'No need for the sales pitch. Fifty quid per 'ead. That's right, isn't it?'

'As long as I get my money's worth. I'll need another good hour of chat and I'm only really prepared to pay fifty apiece if I can talk to your eldest son, Peter, and your youngest son, Gary. That way I get the broadest viewpoint possible. I want to know what difference it made to your older children being fostered out.'

'Well, you've got Gary,' said Ma, prodding the unprepossessing figure on her left, 'young Nipper 'ere. Pete's in the nick so you'll 'ave to make do with Mike. 'E's number three and spent as much time being fostered as Pete did.'

'Right, let's get on then.' She unfolded her list of carefully prepared questions and switched on her tape-recorder. The two 'boys', she noticed, had perfectly proportioned ears.

She spent the first half-hour talking to Mike, encouraging him to reminisce about his childhood in foster homes, his education (or, more accurately, lack of it through persistent truanting) and his early troubles with the police. He was a taciturn man, lacking even elementary social skills, who found it hard to articulate his thoughts. He made a poor impression and Roz, containing her impatience behind a forced smile, wondered if he could possibly have turned out any worse if Social Services had left him in the care of his mother. Somehow she doubted it. Ma, for all her sins and his, loved him, and to be loved was the cornerstone of confidence.

She turned with some relief to Gary, who had been listening to the conversation with a lively interest. 'I gather you didn't leave home till you were twelve,' she said, consulting her notes, 'when you were sent to a boarding school. Why was that?'

He grinned. 'Truanting, nicking, same as my brothers, only Parkway said I was worse and got me sent off to Chapman 'Ouse. It was OK. I learnt a bit. Got two CSEs before I jacked it in.'

She thought the truth was probably the exact opposite, and that Parkway had said he was a cut above his brothers and worth putting some extra effort into. 'That's good. Did the CSEs make it easier to find a job?'

She might have been talking about a trip to the moon for all the relevance a job seemed to have in his life. 'I never tried. We were doing all right.'

She remembered something Hal had said. 'They simply don't subscribe to the same values that the rest of us hold.' 'You didn't want a job?' she asked curiously.

He shook his head. 'Did *you*, when you left school?'

'Yes,' she said, surprised by the question. 'I couldn't wait to leave home.'

He shrugged, as perplexed by her ambition as she was perplexed by his lack of it. 'We've always stuck together,' he said. 'The dole goes a lot further if it's pooled. You didn't get on with your parents then?'

'Not enough to want to live with them.'

'Ah, well,' he said sympathetically, 'that would explain it then.'

Absurdly, Roz found herself envying him. 'Your mother told me you worked as a motorbike courier at one point. Did you enjoy that?'

'So-so. It was all right at the beginning but there's no fun driving a bike in town and it was all town work. It wouldn't 'ave been so bad if the bastard who ran it 'ad paid us enough to cover the cost of the bikes.' He shook his head. ''E was a mean sod. We 'ad 'em took off us after six months and that was it. No bikes, no work.'

Roz had now heard three different versions of how the O'Brien boys had lost their jobs at Wells-Fargo. Were any of them true, she wondered, or was it that they were all true, but seen from different perspectives? Truth, she thought, was not the absolute she had once believed it to be. 'Your mother told me,' she said with a look of innocent amusement, 'that you had a brush with a murderess while you were doing that job.'

'You mean Olive Martin?' Whatever qualms he had had on the matter at the time of the murders had obviously disappeared. 'Funny business, that. I used to deliver letters to her on a Friday evening from some bloke she was keen on, then – wham! – she did her folks in. Bloody shocked me to tell you the truth. 'Ad no idea she was a nutter.'

'But she must have been to hack her mother and sister to pieces.'

'Yeah.' He looked thoughtful. 'Never did understand it. She was all right. I knew 'er as a kid. She was all right then, as well. It was the bloody mother who was the cow and the stuck-up sister. Christ, she was a 'orrible little swine.'

Roz hid her surprise. *Everyone loved Amber.* How often had she heard that said? 'Maybe Olive had had enough and just snapped one day. It happens.'

'Oh,' he said with a dismissive shrug, 'that's not the bit I don't understand. It's why she didn't just go off with 'er fancy man instead. I mean, even if 'e was married, 'e could've set her up in a flat somewhere. 'E wasn't short of a bob or two judging by what 'e paid to have the letters delivered. Twenty quid a throw. 'E must have been bloody rolling in it.'

She chewed her pencil. 'Maybe she didn't do it,' she mused. 'Maybe the police got the wrong person. Let's face it, it wouldn't be the first time.'

Ma compressed her lips. 'They're all corrupt,' she said. 'Nick anyone for anythink these days. You don't want to be Irish in this country. You've no 'ope if you're Irish.'

'Still,' said Roz, looking at Gary, 'if Olive didn't do it, who did?'

'I'm not saying it wasn't 'er,' he said sharply. 'She

went guilty so she must of done it. All I'm saying is she didn't *need* to do it.'

Roz gave a careless shrug. 'Just lost her temper and didn't think. You'll probably find the sister provoked her. You said she was horrible.'

Surprisingly, it was Mike who spoke. 'Street angel, 'ouse devil,' he said. 'Like our Tracey.'

Roz smiled at him. 'What does that mean?'

Ma elucidated. 'A bitch to your family, a perfect darling to everybody else. But our Tracey's nothing like Amber Martin. I always said that child would come a cropper and I was right. You can't face two ways all your life and expect to get away with it.'

Roz showed her curiosity. 'You really did know the family quite well then. I thought you only worked there a short while.'

'So I did, but Amber took a fancy to one of the boys later' – she paused – 'though I'm blowed if I can remember at the moment which one. Was it you, Nipper?'

He shook his head.

'Chris,' said Mike.

'That's right,' agreed Ma, 'took a real shine to 'im and 'im to 'er. She'd sit in this room, pleased as punch with herself, making sheep's eyes at 'im and she can't 'ave been more than twelve or thirteen. 'E was – what? – fifteen, sixteen but, of course, any attention at that age is flattering and she was a pretty girl, I'll say that for 'er, *and* looked older than she was. Anyway, we saw the real Amber then. She treated Chris like a king and the rest of us like something the cat'd brought in. She had a tongue on 'er like I've never heard. Bitch, bitch, bitch, all the time.' She looked thoroughly indignant. 'Can't think 'ow I kept my 'ands off 'er but I did, for Chris's sake. Besotted, 'e was, poor lad. 'Er mother didn't know, of course. Put a stop to it straight away the minute she found out.'

Roz hoped her expression was less revealing than it felt. Did that make Chris O'Brien the father of Amber's illegitimate child? It made sense. Mr Hayes had referred to a lad from Parkway Comprehensive being responsible, and if Gwen had put a stop to the relationship then she would have known who to blame when a baby appeared. It would also explain the secrecy surrounding Robert Martin's efforts to trace his grandchild. Presumably the O'Briens had no idea that Chris had fathered a son nor that the son, if he could be found, was worth half a million pounds.

'It's fascinating,' she murmured, searching desperately for something to say. 'I've never met anyone so closely associated with a murder. Was Chris upset when Amber was killed?'

'No,' said Ma with an unfeeling chuckle. ''E 'adn't seen 'er in years. Gary was more upset for Olive, weren't you, love?'

He was watching Roz closely. 'Not really,' he said bluntly. 'I was jumpy about being roped in on it. I mean, I'd seen quite a bit of 'er one way and another.

Reckoned the cops'd be rounding up everyone she knew and grilling them.' He shook his head. ''Er bloke got off lightly. 'E'd've been 'auled in and no mistake if she'd named a few names to try and get off.'

'Did you ever meet him?'

'No.' His face became suddenly sly and he stared at Roz with an expression that said he saw right through her. 'I know where he took her for sex, though.' He gave a conspiratorial smile. 'What's it worth to you?'

She stared back. 'How do you know?'

'The silly sod used self-sticking envelopes. They're a doddle to open. I read one of the letters.'

'Did he sign it? Do you know his name?'

Gary shook his head. 'Something beginning with P. "All my love, P", was how it finished.'

Roz didn't bother with further pretence. 'Another fifty pounds,' she said, 'on top of the hundred and fifty I've already agreed to. But that's it. I'll be cleaned out.'

'OK.' He held out his hand in unconscious mimicry of his mother. 'Money up front.'

She took out her wallet and emptied it. 'Two hundred pounds.' She counted it on to his palm.

'I knew you wasn't from the television,' said Ma in disgust. 'I bloody knew it.'

'Well?' Roz demanded of Gary.

'It was on for Sunday at the Belvedere Hotel in

Farraday Street. "All my love, P." That's the Farraday Street in Southampton, in case you didn't know.'

The route to Southampton took Roz along Dawlington High Street. She had passed Glitzy boutique before the name registered, and nearly caused a pile-up by standing on her brakes in the middle of the road. With a cheerful wave to the furious man behind her, who was mouthing imprecations against women drivers, she drew into a side street and found a parking space.

Glitzy was something of a misnomer, she thought, as she pushed open the door. She had expected designer wear or, at the very least, clothes from the more expensive end of the market. But then, she was used to London boutiques. Glitzy catered very definitely for the cheaper end of the market, wisely recognizing that their customers would be predominantly teenage girls without the wherewithal or the transport to go shopping in the more stylish parts of Southampton.

Roz sought out the manager, a woman in her thirties with a splendid hairdo backcombed into a blonde beehive on top of her head. Roz handed her one of her cards and ran through her spiel about her book on Olive Martin. 'I'm trying to find someone who knew the sister, Amber,' she said, 'and I'm told she worked here during the month before she was murdered. Were you here then? Or do you know anyone who was?'

'No, love, sorry. Staff turns over very quickly in a place like this, young girls normally, doing a short stint till something better comes up. I don't even know who was manager then. You'll have to get on to the owners. I can give you their address,' she finished helpfully.

'Thank you. It's worth a shot, I suppose.'

The woman took her over to the cash desk and sorted through a card index. 'Funny, I remember those murders, but I never put two and two together. You know, that the sister had worked here.'

'She wasn't here very long and I'm not sure it was even reported. The press was more interested in Olive than in Amber.'

'Yeah.' She took out a card. 'Amber. It's not that common a name, is it?'

'I suppose not. It was a nickname, anyway. Her real name was Alison.'

The woman nodded. 'I've been here three years and for three years I've been pressing to have the staff toilet redecorated. The recession's their excuse for not doing it, same as it's their excuse for any wretched thing, from cuts in wages to cheap imported stock that's not even stitched properly. Anyway, the toilet's tiled and that's an expensive job, apparently, chipping off the old ones to put up new.' Roz smiled politely. 'Don't worry, love, it's to the point and I'm getting there. The reason I want new tiles is that someone took a chisel or something similar to the old ones. They scratched graffiti into the surface and then filled in the scratches with some sort of indelible ink. I've tried everything to get it out, bleach, oven cleaner, paint remover, you name it, love, I've tried it.' She shook her head. 'It can't be shifted. And why? Because whoever did it gouged so deep they cut right through the ceramic, and the china clay underneath just goes on absorbing dirt and stains. Every time I look at it, it gives me the shivers. Pure hate, that's what it was done with.'

'What does the graffiti say?'

'I'll show you. It's at the back.' She negotiated a couple of doors, then pushed open another and stood aside to let Roz pass. 'There. It sucks, doesn't it? And, you know, I've always wondered who Amber was. But it must be the sister, mustn't it? Like I say, Amber's not that common a name.'

It was the same two words, repeated ten or eleven times across the tiles, a violent inversion of the hearts and arrows that more usually adorned lavatory walls. **HATES AMBER . . . HATES AMBER . . . HATES AMBER.**

'I wonder who did it?' murmured Roz.

'Someone very sick, I should think. They certainly didn't want her to know, seeing how they've left their name off the front.'

'It depends how you read it,' said Roz thoughtfully.

'If it were set out neatly for you in a circle it would say Amber hates Amber hates Amber ad infinitum.'

The Belvedere was a typical back-street hotel, two substantial semis knocked together and entered via a flight of steps and a pillared front door. The place had an air of neglect as if its customers – sales reps for the main part – had deserted it. Roz rang the bell at the reception desk and waited.

A woman in her fifties emerged from a room at the back, all smiles. 'Good afternoon, madam. Welcome to the Belvedere.' She pulled the registration book towards her. 'Is it a room you're after?'

What terrible things recessions were, thought Roz. How long could people maintain this sad veneer of confident optimism when the reality was empty order books? 'I'm sorry,' she said. 'I'm afraid it isn't.' She handed over one of her cards. 'I'm a freelance journalist and I think someone I'm writing about may have stayed here. I was hoping you could identify her photograph for me.'

The woman tapped a finger on the book then pushed it away. 'Will what you write be published?'

Roz nodded.

'And will the Belvedere be mentioned if whoever it is did stay here?'

'Not if you'd rather it wasn't.'

'My dear, how little you know about the hotel

trade. Any publicity would be welcome at the moment.'

Roz laughed as she placed the photograph of Olive on the desk. 'If she came it would have been during the summer of eighty-seven. Were you here then?'

'We were.' The woman spoke with regret. 'We bought in eighty-six when the economy was booming.' She took a pair of glasses from her pocket and popped them on her nose, leaning forward to examine the photograph. 'Oh, yes, I remember her very well. Big girl. She and her husband came most Sundays during that summer. Used to book the room for the day and go home in the evening.' She sighed. 'It was a wonderful arrangement. We were always able to let the room again for the Sunday night. Double pay for one twenty-four-hour period.' She heaved another sigh. 'Chance'd be a fine thing now. I wish we could sell, I really do, but what with so many of the small hotels going bankrupt we wouldn't even get what we paid for it. Soldier on, that's all we can do.'

Roz brought her back to Olive by tapping the photograph. 'What did she and her husband call themselves?'

The woman was amused. 'The usual, I should think. Smith or Brown.'

'Did they sign in?'

'Oh, yes. We're very particular about our register.'

'Could I take a look?'

'Don't see why not.' She opened a cupboard under

the desk and sorted out the register for 1987. 'Now, let me see. Ah, here we are. Mr and Mrs Lewis. Well, well, they were more imaginative than most.' She twisted the book so that Roz could look at it.

She gazed at the neat script and thought: Got you, you bastard. 'This is the man's handwriting.' She knew already.

'Oh, yes,' said the woman. 'He always signed. She was a lot younger than he was and very shy, particularly at the beginning. She gained in confidence as time passed, they always do, but she never put herself forward. Who is she?'

Roz wondered if the woman would be so keen to help once she knew, but there was no point in keeping it from her. She would learn all the details the minute the book appeared. 'Her name's Olive Martin.'

'Never heard of her.'

'She's serving a life sentence for murdering her mother and sister.'

'Good lord! Is she the one who—' She made chopping motions with her hands. Roz nodded. 'Good Lord!'

'Do you still want the Belvedere mentioned?'

'Do I heck!' She beamed broadly. 'Of course I do! A murderess in our hotel. Fancy! We'll have a plaque put up in the bedroom. What are you writing exactly? A book? A magazine article? We'll provide photographs of the hotel and the room she stayed in. Well, well, I must say. How exciting! If only I'd known.'

Roz laughed. It was a cold-bloodedly ghoulish display of pleasure at another's misfortune but she couldn't find it in her heart to criticize. Only a fool would look a gift horse in the mouth. 'Before you get too excited,' she warned, 'the book probably won't be published for another year and it will be an exoneration of Olive, not a further condemnation. You see, I believe she's innocent.'

'Better and better. We'll have the book on sale in the foyer. I knew our luck had to turn eventually.' She beamed at Roz. 'Tell Olive she can stay here free of charge for as long as she likes the minute she gets out of prison. We always look after our regulars. Now, my dear, anything else I can help you with?'

'Do you have a photocopying machine?'

'We do. Every mod. con. here, you know.'

'Then may I have a copy of this entry in the register? And perhaps you could also give me a description of Mr Lewis.'

She pursed her lips. 'He wasn't very memorable. Early fifties. Blond, always wore a dark suit, a smoker. Any good?'

'Maybe. Did his hair look natural? Can you remember?'

The woman chuckled. 'There now, I'd forgotten. It never occurred to me till I took them in some tea one day and surprised him adjusting his wig in the mirror. I laughed afterwards, I can tell you. But it was a good one. I wouldn't have guessed just by looking at him. You know him then?'

Roz nodded. 'Would you recognize him from a photograph?'

'I'll try. I can usually remember a face when I see it.'

'Visitor for you, Sculptress.' The officer was in the room before Olive had time to hide what she was doing. 'Come on. Get a move on.'

Olive swept her wax figures into one hand and crushed them together in her palm. 'Who is it?'

'The nun.' She looked at Olive's closed fist. 'What have you got there?'

'Just plasticine.' She uncurled her fingers. The wax figures, carefully painted and clothed in coloured scraps, had merged into a multi-coloured mash, unidentifiable now as the altar candle they had sprung from.

'Well, leave it there. The nun's come to talk to you, not watch you play with plasticine.'

Hal was asleep at the kitchen table, body rigidly upright, arms resting on the table, head nodding towards his chest. Roz watched him for a moment through the window, then tapped lightly on the glass. His eyes, red-rimmed with exhaustion, snapped open to look at her and she was shocked by the extent of his relief when he saw who it was.

He let her in. 'I hoped you wouldn't come back,' he said, his face drawn with fatigue.

'What are you so frightened of?' she asked.

He looked at her with something like despair. 'Go home,' he said, 'this is none of your business.' He went to the sink and ran the cold-water tap, dowsing his head and gasping as the icy stream hit the back of his neck.

From the floor above came a sudden violent hammering.

Roz leapt a foot in the air. '*Oh, my God!* What was that?'

He reached out and gripped her arm, pushing her towards the door. 'Go home,' he ordered. 'Now! I don't want to have to force you, Roz.'

But she stood her ground. 'What's going on? What was that noise?'

'So help me,' he said grimly, 'I will do you some damage if you don't leave now.' But in outright contradiction to the words, he suddenly put his hands on either side of her face and kissed her. 'Oh, God!' he groaned, smoothing the tumbled hair from her eyes. 'I do not want you involved, Roz. *I do not want you involved.*'

She was about to say something when over his shoulder she saw the door into the restaurant swing open. 'Too late,' she said, turning him round. 'We've got company.'

Hal, horribly unprepared, showed his teeth in a wolfish grin. 'I've been expecting you,' he drawled. With a proprietary arm he eased Roz behind him and prepared to defend what was his.

There were four of them, large anonymous men in ski-masks. They said nothing, just weighed in indiscriminately with baseball bats, using Hal as a human target. It happened so fast that Roz was a spectator to their grisly sport almost before she realized it. She, it seemed, was too insignificant to concern them.

Her first angry impulse was to catch out at a flailing arm but the battering she had had at the hands of Rupert two weeks before persuaded her to use her brain instead. With trembling fingers she opened her handbag and removed the three-inch hatpin she had taken to carrying with her, thrusting it upwards into the buttock of the man nearest her. It drove in up to its ornate jade head and a soft groan issued from his mouth as he stood, completely paralysed with shock, the baseball bat slipping to the floor from his slackening fingers. No one noticed, except her.

With an exclamation of triumph she dived on it and brought it up in a swinging arc to smash against the man's balls. He sat on the floor and started to scream.

'I've got one, Hal,' she panted. 'I've got a bat.'

'Then use it, for Christ's sake,' he bellowed, going down under a rain of blows.

'Oh God!' Legs, she thought. She knelt on one knee, swiped at the nearest pair of trousers and crowed with triumph when she made contact. She took another swipe only to have her head jerked up as a hand seized her by the hair and started to pull it out by the roots. Shock and pain flooded her eyes with stinging tears.

Hal, on his hands and knees on the floor, his head protected by his shoulders, was only vaguely aware that the rapidity of the blows beating against his back had lessened. His brain was concentrated on the high-pitched screaming which he thought was coming from Roz. His anger was colossal, triggering such a surge of adrenalin that he exploded to his feet in an all-consuming fury and threw himself at the first man he saw, bearing him back against the gleaming ovens where a saucepan of fish stock bubbled gently. Oblivious to the blow which crashed with the force of a bus between his shoulder blades he bent his victim in an arc over the rings, grabbed the saucepan and upended the boiling liquid over the masked head.

He swung round to face the fourth man and fended off another blow with his forearm before smashing the cast-iron base of the saucepan into the side of an unprotected jaw. The eyes behind the mask registered the briefest glimmer of surprise before rolling helplessly into their sockets. The man was unconscious before he hit the floor.

Exhausted, Hal looked about for Roz. It was a moment or two before he found her, so disorientated was he by the noise of screaming which seemed to be filling the kitchen from every side. He shook his head to clear the fog and looked towards the door. He saw her almost immediately, her neck trapped in the hooked arm of the only man left with any fight in him. Her eyes were closed and her head lolled alarmingly to one side. 'If you make a move,' the man told Hal between jerky breaths, 'I'll break her neck.'

A hatred, so primeval that he couldn't control it, erupted like hot lava in Hal's brain. His actions were instinctive. He lowered his head and charged.

Fifteen

ROZ SWAM UP to a strange twilight world between oblivion and consciousness. She knew she was there in the room but she felt apart from it as if she were watching what was going on from behind thickened glass. Sound was muted. She had a vague memory of fingers clamping round her throat. And afterwards? She wasn't sure. It had, she thought, been very peaceful.

Hal's face loomed over her. 'Are you all right?' he asked from a great distance.

'Fine,' she murmured happily.

He smacked her on the cheek with the flat of his hand. 'That's my girl,' he told her, his voice muffled by cotton wool. 'Come on, now. Snap out of it. I need some help.'

She glared at him. 'I'll be up in a minute,' she said with dignity.

He hauled her to her feet. 'Now,' he said firmly, 'or we'll be back where we started.' He thrust a baseball bat into her hand. 'I am going to tie them up but you've got to protect my back while I'm doing it. I don't want one of these bastards surprising me.' He looked into her dazed eyes. 'Come on, Roz,' he said savagely, shaking her. 'Pull yourself together and show a bit of character.'

She took a deep breath. 'Has anyone ever told you what a complete and utter turd you are? I nearly died.'

'You fainted,' he said unemotionally, but his eyes were twinkling. 'Hit anything that moves,' he instructed her, 'except the one with his head under the tap. He's in enough agony already.'

Reality came rushing in on wings of sound. Moans and groans and running water. There *was* a man with his head under the tap. She caught a movement out of the corner of her eye and swung the baseball bat in terrified reaction, ramming home the hatpin that its unfortunate recipient was gingerly plucking from his bottom. His screams of reawakened agony were pitiful.

'Oh God!' she cried. 'I've done something awful.' Tears sprang into her eyes.

Hal finished trussing her putative killer, who had been knocked cold by his frenzied charge, and moved on to the other unconscious figure, winding twine expertly about the wrists and ankles. 'What's he yelling for anyway?' he demanded, tethering his victim to the table for good measure.

'He's got a pin in his bottom,' said Roz, her teeth chattering uncontrollably.

Hal approached the man warily. 'What sort of pin?'

'My mother's hatpin.' She gagged. 'I think I'm going to be sick.'

He saw the green ornamental head protruding from the man's Levis and felt a tiny twinge of sympathy. It didn't last. He left it there while he bound the man's wrists and ankles and tethered him, like his friend, to the table. It was almost as an afterthought that he gripped the jade and yanked the hatpin, grinning, from the quivering buttock. 'You arsehole,' he murmured cheerfully, tucking the pin into the front of his jumper.

'I feel ill,' said Roz.

'Sit down, then.' He took a chair and pressed her into it before moving to the back door and flinging it open. 'Out,' he ordered the man at the sink. 'Get yourself to hospital as fast as you can. If your friends have an ounce of decency they'll keep your name to themselves. If they haven't' – he shrugged – 'you've got about half an hour to get yourself admitted before the police come looking for you.'

The man needed no persuading. He launched himself into the fresh air of the alleyway and took to his heels.

With a groan of exhaustion, Hal shut the door and slithered to the floor. 'I need a rest. Do me a favour, sweetheart, and take off their masks. Let's see what we've got.'

Roz's head was aching intolerably where the roots of her hair had been loosened. She looked at him with burning eyes in a pasty white face. 'For your information, Hawksley,' she said icily, 'I'm just about out on my feet. It may have escaped your notice, but if it hadn't been for me you wouldn't have *got* anything.'

He gave a mighty yawn and winced as pain seared around his chest and back. Fractured ribs, he thought tiredly. 'I'll tell you this for free, Roz. As far as I'm concerned you are the most wonderful woman God ever made and I'll marry you if you'll have me.' He smiled sweetly. 'But at the moment I'm bushed. Be kind. Get off your high horse and take their ski-masks off.'

' "Words, words, mere words",' she murmured, but she did as he asked. The side of his face was already thickening where a baseball bat had split the skin. What the hell sort of state must his back be in? Covered in weals, probably, like the last time. 'Do you know any of them?' She studied the slack features of the unconscious man by the door. She had a fleeting impression she knew him, but his head moved and the impression vanished.

'No.' He'd seen her frown of brief recognition. 'Do you?'

'I thought I did,' she said slowly. 'Just for a

moment.' She shook her head. 'No. He probably reminded me of someone on the telly.'

Hal pushed himself to his feet and padded over to the sink, his stiffening body protesting at every step. He filled a bowl with water and sloshed it into the gaping mouth, watching the eyes flicker open. They were instantly alert, wary, guarded, all of which told Hal he wasn't likely to get anywhere by asking questions.

With a shrug of resignation, he looked at Roz. 'I need a favour.'

She nodded.

'There's a phonebox about two hundred yards down the main road. Take your car to it, dial 999, tell them the Poacher's been broken into, and then go home. Don't give your name. I'll call you the minute I can.'

'I'd rather stay.'

'I know.' His face softened. She was wearing her lonely look again. He reached out and ran the back of a finger down the line of her cheek. 'Trust me. I *will* call.'

She took a deep breath. 'How long do you want?'

He'd make it up to her one day, he thought. 'Fifteen minutes before you phone.'

She retrieved her handbag from the floor, cramming the contents inside and zippering it closed. 'Fifteen minutes,' she echoed, pulling the door open and stepping outside. She stared at him for a long moment then shut the door and walked away.

Hal waited until her footsteps faded. 'This,' he said gently, reaching for the hatpin, 'is going to be extremely painful.' He grasped the man's hair and forced him down until his face was flat against the floor. 'And I haven't got time for games.' He placed the weight of one knee across the man's shoulders then prised a finger straight in one of the bound fists and pushed the point of the hatpin between the flesh and the nail. He felt the finger flinch. 'You've got five seconds to tell me what the hell is going on before I push it home. One. Two. Three. Four. Five.' He breathed deeply through his nose, closed his eyes and shoved.

The man screamed.

Hal caught 'Foreclosures. You're costing money on the foreclosures' before a ton weight descended on the back of his head.

Sister Bridget, as imperturbable as ever, ushered Roz into her sitting room and sat her in a chair with a glass of brandy. Clearly Roz had been in another fight. Her clothes were filthy and dishevelled, her hair was a mess, and splotchy red marks on her neck and face looked very like the imprint of fingers. Someone, it seemed, was using her as a target for his spleen, though why she chose to put up with it Sister Bridget couldn't begin to imagine. Roz was as far removed from Dickens' Nancy as anyone could be, and had quite enough independence of spirit to reject the degrading life that a Bill Sykes offered.

She waited placidly while wave after wave of giggles spluttered from Roz's mouth.

'Do you want to tell me about it?' she asked at last, when Roz had composed herself enough to dab at her eyes.

Roz blew her nose. 'I don't think I can,' she said. 'It wasn't at all funny.' Laughter welled in her eyes again and she held the handkerchief to her mouth. 'I'm sorry to be a nuisance but I was afraid I'd have an accident if I tried to drive home. I think it's what's known as an adrenalin high.'

Privately, Sister Bridget decided it was a product of delayed shock, the natural healing process of mind over traumatized body. 'I'm pleased to have you here. Tell me how you're progressing on the Olive front. I saw her today but she wasn't very communicative.'

Grateful for something to take her mind off the Poacher, Roz told her. 'She did have a lover. I've found the hotel they used.' She peered at the brandy glass. 'It was the Belvedere in Farraday Street. They went there on Sundays during the summer of eighty-seven.' She took a sip from the glass then placed it hurriedly on the table beside her and slumped back into the chair, pressing shaking fingers to her temples.

'I'm terribly sorry,' she said, 'but I don't feel at all well. I've got the mother and father of all headaches.'

'I should imagine you have,' said Sister Bridget, rather more tartly than she had intended.

Roz massaged her aching temples. 'This ape tried to pull my hair out,' she murmured. 'I think that's what's done it.' She pressed an experimental hand to the back of her head and winced. 'There's some codeine in my handbag. You couldn't find them for me, could you? I think my head is about to explode.' She giggled hysterically. 'Olive must be sticking pins into me again.'

Tut-tutting with motherly concern, Sister Bridget administered three with a glass of water. 'I'm sorry, my dear,' she said severely, 'but I'm really very shocked. I can't forgive any man who treats a woman like a chattel and, harsh though it may sound, I find it almost as difficult to forgive the woman. Better to live without a man at all than to live with one who is only interested in the degradation of the spirit.'

Roz squinted through one half-closed eyelid, unable to take the glare of light from the window. How indignant the other woman looked, puffing her chest like a pouter pigeon. Hysteria nudged about her diaphragm again. 'You're very harsh all of a sudden. I doubt Olive saw it as degradation. Rather the reverse, I should think.'

'I'm not talking about Olive, my dear, I'm talking

about you. This ape you referred to. He isn't worth it. Surely you can see that?'

Roz shook with helpless laughter. 'I'm so sorry,' she said at last. 'You must think me incredibly rude. The trouble is I've been on an emotional rollercoaster for months.' She dabbed at her eyes and blew her nose. 'You must blame Olive for this. She's been a godsend. She's made me feel useful again.'

She saw the polite bewilderment on the other's face and sighed inwardly. Really, she thought, it was so much easier to tell lies. They were one dimensional and uncomplicated. '*I'm fine . . . Everything's fine . . . I like waiting rooms . . . Rupert's been very supportive over Alice . . . We went our separate ways amicably . . .*' It was the tangled web of truth, woven deep into the fragile stuff of character, that made life difficult. She wasn't even sure now what was true and what wasn't. Had she really hated Rupert that much? She couldn't imagine where she had found the energy. All she could really remember was how stifling the last twelve months had been.

'I'm completely infatuated,' she went on wildly as if that explained anything, 'but I've no idea if what I feel is genuine or just pie in the sky hoping.' She shook her head. 'I suppose one never really knows.'

'Oh, my dear,' said Sister Bridget, 'do be careful. Infatuation is a very poor substitute for love. It withers as easily as it flourishes. Love – *real* love – takes time to grow, and how can it do that in an atmosphere of brutality?'

'That's hardly his fault. I could have run away, I suppose, but I'm glad I didn't. I'm sure they'd have killed him if he'd been alone.'

Sister Bridget sighed. 'We seem to be talking at cross purposes. Do I gather the ape is not the man you're infatuated with?'

With streaming eyes, Roz wondered if there was any truth in the phrase *to die laughing*.

'You're very brave,' said Sister Bridget. 'I'd have assumed he was up to no good and run a mile.'

'Perhaps he is. I'm a very poor judge of character, you know.'

Sister Bridget laughed to herself. 'Well, it all sounds very exciting,' she said with a twinge of envy, taking Roz's dress from the tumble-drier and laying it on the ironing board. 'The only man who ever showed any interest in me was a bank clerk who lived three doors away from my parents. He was skin and bone, poor chap, with an enormous Adam's apple that crawled about his throat like a large pink beetle. I simply couldn't bear him. The Church was far more attractive.' She wet her finger and tapped it against the iron.

Roz, wrapped in an old flannelette nightie, smiled. 'And is it still?'

'Not always. But I wouldn't be human if I didn't have regrets.'

'Have you ever been in love?'

'Good Heavens, yes. More often than you have, I expect. Purely platonically, of course. I meet some very attractive fathers in my job.'

Roz chuckled. 'What sort of fathers? The cassocked variety or the ones in trousers?'

Sister Bridget's eyes danced wickedly. 'All I will say, as long as you promise not to quote me, is that I've always found cassocks a little off-putting and, with all the divorces there are these days, I spend more time talking to single men than, frankly, is good for a nun.'

'If things ever work out,' said Roz wistfully, 'and I have another daughter, I'll put her in your school so fast you won't know what hit you.'

'I shall look forward to it.'

'No. I don't believe in miracles. I did once.'

'I'll pray for you,' said Sister Bridget. 'It's time I had something to get my teeth into. I prayed for Olive and look what God sent me.'

'Now you're going to make me cry.'

She woke in the morning with brilliant sunlight bathing her face through a gap in Sister Bridget's spare-room curtains. It was too bright to look at so she cuddled down into the warmth of the duvet and listened instead. Ripples of birdsong swelled in glorious chorus from tiny feathered throats in the garden, and somewhere a radio murmured the news, but too low for her to make out the words. The smell of grilled bacon drifted tantalizingly from the kitchen downstairs, urging her to get up. She tingled with half-remembered vitality and wondered why she had allowed herself to stumble for so long through the blind fog of her depression. Life, she thought, was fabulous and the desire to live it too insistent to be ignored.

She waved goodbye to Sister Bridget, pointed the car towards the Poacher and switched on her stereo, feeding in Pavarotti. It was a very deliberate laying of a ghost. The rich voice surged in the speakers and she listened to it without regret.

The restaurant was deserted, no answer front or back to her knocking. She drove to the payphone she had used the night before and dialled the number, letting it ring for a long time in case Hal was asleep. When he didn't reply, she replaced the receiver and returned to her car. She wasn't concerned – frankly, Hal could look after himself rather better than any other man she had known – and she had more urgent fish to fry. From the dashboard pocket she took an expensive automatic camera with a powerful zoom lens – a legacy of the divorce – and checked it for film. Then, switching on the ignition, she drew out into the traffic.

She had to wait two hours, crouched uncomfortably on the back seat of her car, but she was well rewarded for her patience. When Olive's Svengali finally emerged from his front door he paused for a second or two and presented her with a perfect shot of his face. Magnified by the zoom lens, the dark eyes bored straight through her as she took the picture before they turned away to glance down between the avenue of trees to check for oncoming traffic. She felt the hairs pricking on the back of her neck. He couldn't possibly have seen her – the car was facing away from him with the camera lens propped on her handbag in the back window – but she shivered none the less. The photographs of Gwen and Amber's mutilated bodies, lying on the seat beside her, were a terrible reminder that she was stalking a psychopath.

She arrived back at her flat, hot and tired from the sweltering heat of unheralded summer. The wintry feel of three days before had melted into brilliant blue skies with a promise of more heat to come. She opened the windows of the flat and let in the roar of London traffic. More noticeable than usual, it made her think with a brief wistfulness of the peace and beauty of Bayview.

She checked her answerphone for messages while she poured a glass of water, only to find the tape as she had left it, blank. She dialled the Poacher and listened, this time with mounting anxiety, to the vain ringing at the other end. Where on earth was he? She chewed the knuckle of her thumb in frustration then phoned Iris.

'How would Gerry react if you asked him nicely to put on his solicitor's hat' – Gerald Fielding was a partner in a top London legal practice – 'ring Dawlington police station and make some discreet enquiries before everything winds down for the weekend?'

Iris was never one to beat about the bush. 'Why?' she demanded. 'And what's in it for me?'

'My peace of mind. I'm too twitched at the moment to write anything.'

'Hmm. Why?'

'I'm worried about my shady policeman.'

'*Your* shady policeman?' asked Iris suspiciously.

'That's right.'

Iris heard the amusement in her friend's voice. 'Oh, my God,' she said crossly, 'you haven't gone and fallen for him? He's supposed to be a source.'

'He is – of endless erotic fantasy.'

Iris groaned. 'How can you write objectively about

corrupt policemen if you've got the hots for one of them?'

'Who says he's corrupt?'

'He must be, if Olive's innocent. I thought you said he took her confession.'

'It's a pity you're not a Catholic. You could go to confession and feel better immediately . . .'

'Are you still there?' demanded Iris.

'Yes. Will Gerry do it?'

'Why can't you make the call yourself?'

'Because I'm involved and they might recognize my voice. I made them a 999 call.'

Iris groaned again. 'What on earth have you been up to?'

'Nothing criminal, at least I don't think so.' She heard the grunt of horror at the other end. 'Look, all Gerry has to do is ask a few innocent questions.'

'Will he have to lie?'

'A white lie or two.'

'He'll have a fit. You know Gerry. Breaks out in a muck sweat at the mere mention of falsehoods.' She sighed loudly. 'What a pest you are. You realize I shall have to bribe him with promises of good behaviour. My life won't be worth living.'

'You're an angel. Now, these are the only details Gerry needs to know. He's trying to contact his client, Hal Hawksley of the Poacher, Wenceslas Street, Dawlington. He has reason to believe the Poacher has been broken into and wonders if the police know where Hal can be contacted. OK?'

'No, it's not OK, but I'll see what I can do. Will you be in this evening?'

'Yes, twiddling my thumbs.'

'Well, try twiddling them round your keyboard,' said Iris acidly. 'I'm fed up with being the only one who does any meaningful work in this lopsided relationship of ours.'

She had had the film developed at a one-hour booth in her local High Street while she did some shopping. Now she spread the prints over her coffee table and studied them. She put the ones of Svengali, the two close-ups of his face and some full-length shots of his back as he walked away, to one side and smiled at the rest. She had forgotten taking them. Deliberately, she thought. They were of Rupert and Alice playing in the garden on Alice's birthday, a week before the accident. They had declared a truce that day, she remembered, for Alice's sake. And they had kept it, up to a point, although as usual the responsibility for refusing to be drawn had been Roz's. As long as she could keep her cool and smile while Rupert let slip his poisoned darts about Jessica, Jessica's flat, and Jessica's job, everything was hunky-dory. Alice's joy in having her parents back together again shone from the photographs.

Roz pushed them tenderly to one side and rummaged through her carrier bag of shopping, removing some cellophane, a paintbrush, and three tubes of acrylic paint. Then, munching into a pork pie, she set to work.

Every now and then she paused to smile at her daughter. She should have had the film developed before, she told Mrs Antrobus, who had curled contentedly into her lap. The rag doll of the newspapers had never been Alice. *This* was Alice.

'He's legged it,' said Iris baldly down the wire two hours later, 'and Gerry has been threatened with all sorts of nasties if he doesn't reveal his client's whereabouts the minute he knows them. There's a warrant out for the wretched man's arrest. Where on earth do you find these ghastly creatures? You should take up with a nice one, like Gerry,' she said severely, 'who wouldn't dream of beating up women or involving them in criminal activities.'

'I know,' agreed Roz mildly, 'but the nice ones are already taken. Did they mention what the charge is against Hal?'

'*Charges*, more like. Arson, resisting arrest, GBH, absconding from the scene of a crime. You name it, he's done it. If he gets in touch with you, don't bother to let me know. Gerry's already behaving like the man who knew the identity of Jack the Ripper but kept it quiet. He'll have a heart attack if he thinks I know where he is.'

'Mum's the word,' Roz promised.

There was a moment's silence. 'You might do better to hang up if he calls. There's a man in hospital with appalling facial burns, apparently, a policeman with a dislocated jaw, and when they arrived to arrest him he was trying to set fire to his restaurant. He sounds horribly dangerous to me.'

'I think you're probably right,' said Roz slowly, wondering what on earth had happened after she left. 'He's got a lovely arse, too. *Aren't* I the lucky one?'

'Cow!'

Roz laughed. 'Thank Gerry for me. I appreciate his niceness even if you don't.'

She went to sleep on the sofa in case she missed the phone when it rang. It occurred to her that he might not want to trust himself to an answer machine.

But the telephone remained stubbornly silent all weekend.

Sixteen

ON MONDAY MORNING, with the black dog of depression on her shoulder again, Roz went to the Belvedere Hotel and placed the photograph on the desk. 'Is this Mr Lewis?' she asked the proprietress.

The amiable woman popped on her glasses and took a good look. She shook her head apologetically. 'No, dear, I'm sorry. He doesn't ring a bell at all.'

'Try now.' She smoothed the cellophane across the photograph.

'Good heavens. How extraordinary. Yes, that's Mr Lewis all right.'

Marnie agreed. 'That's him. Dirty bugger.' She screwed up her eyes. 'It doesn't flatter him, does it? What would a young girl see in that?'

'I don't know. Uncritical affection perhaps.'

'Who is he?'

'A psychopath,' said Roz.

The other whistled. 'You want to be careful then.'

'Yes.'

Marnie tapped her carmined nails on the desk. 'Sure you don't want to tell me who he is in case you end up in bits on your kitchen floor?' She flicked Roz a speculative glance. There might, she thought, be some money in this somewhere.

Roz caught the glint in the other's eye. 'No thanks,' she said shortly. 'This is one piece of information I intend to keep to myself. I don't fancy my chances if he learns I'm close.'

'I won't blab,' said Marnie with a pout of injured innocence.

'You can't if I don't put temptation your way.' Roz tucked the photograph into her handbag. 'It would be irresponsible, anyway. You're a prime witness. He could just as easily come after *you* and chop *you* into little pieces.' She smiled coldly. 'I should hate to have that on my conscience.'

Roz returned to her car and sat for some minutes staring out of the window. If ever she had needed a tame ex-policeman to guide her through the maze of legal procedure, she thought, it was now. She was an amateur who could all too easily make mistakes and muck up the chances of a future prosecution. And where would that leave Olive? Languishing in prison, presumably. The verdict against her could only be overturned rapidly if someone else was convicted. On its own the seed of reasonable doubt would take years of germination before the Home Office would feel pressured enough to take notice. How long had the Birmingham Six had to wait for justice? The responsibility to get it right was frightening.

But, loath though she was to admit it, what weighed rather more heavily with her was the knowledge that she hadn't the courage to write the book while Olive's psychopathic lover remained at liberty. Try as she might, she could not get the pictures of Gwen and Amber out of her mind.

She slammed her fists against the steering-wheel. Where are you, Hawksley? *You bastard!* I was always there for you.

Graham Deedes, Olive's one-time barrister, walked into his chambers after a long day in court and frowned in irritation to find Roz parked on a seat outside his door. He looked pointedly at his watch. 'I'm in a hurry, Miss Leigh.'

She sighed, unfolding herself from the hard chair. 'Five minutes,' she begged. 'I've been waiting two hours.'

'No, I'm sorry. We have people coming to dinner and I promised my wife I wouldn't be late.' He opened his door and went inside. 'Ring and make an appointment. I'm in court for the next three days but

I may be able to fit you in towards the end of the week.' He prepared to shut her out.

She stood up and leaned her shoulder on the door jamb, holding the door open with one hand. 'Olive did have a lover,' she told him. 'I know who he is and I've had his photograph identified by two witnesses, one of whom is the owner of the hotel that he and Olive used throughout the summer before the murders. I have a witness who bears out Olive's claim to have had an abortion. The date she gave me implies that Olive's baby, had it lived, would have been born around the time of the murders. I have learned that two people, Robert Martin and the father of a friend of Olive's, quite independently of each other, told the police that Olive was incapable of murdering her sister. The scenario they both offered was that Gwen killed Amber – she didn't like Amber, apparently – and Olive killed Gwen. I admit the forensic evidence doesn't support that case but it proves that serious doubts existed even at the time which I don't think were brought to your attention.' She saw the impatience in his face and hurried on. 'For all sorts of reasons, principally because it was her birthday, I do not believe that Olive was in the house on the night before the murders and I *do* believe that Gwen and Amber were killed much earlier than the time Olive claims to have done it. I think Olive returned home some time during the morning or afternoon of the ninth, found the carnage in the kitchen, knew her lover was responsible, and was so overcome with shock and remorse that she confessed to the crime herself. I think she was very unsure of herself, very distressed, and didn't know how to cope when the main prop in her life, her mother, was so suddenly taken from her.'

He took some papers out of his desk and tucked them into his briefcase. He heard so many imaginative defences that he was more polite than interested. 'I assume you're suggesting that Olive and her lover spent her birthday night together in a hotel somewhere.' Roz nodded. 'Have you any proof of that?'

'No. They weren't registered at the hotel they usually used but that's not surprising. It was a special occasion. They may even have come up to London.'

'In that case why should she assume her lover was responsible? They would have gone back together. Even if he'd dropped her at a distance from her house he wouldn't have had time to do what was done.'

'He would if he'd walked out,' said Roz, 'and left her alone in the hotel.'

'Why would he do that?'

'Because she told him that but for her sister's earlier illegitimate baby and her mother's horror of it happening again he would by now be a proud father.'

Deedes looked at his watch. 'What illegitimate baby?'

'The one Amber had when she was thirteen. There's no dispute about that. The child is mentioned in Robert Martin's will. Gwen managed to hush it up but, as she couldn't hope to do the same thing with Olive, she persuaded her to abort.'

He clicked his tongue impatiently. 'This is all highly fanciful, Miss Leigh. As far as I can see, you've absolutely nothing to support these allegations and you can't go into print accusing somebody else of the murders without either some very strong evidence or enough capital behind you to pay a fortune in libel damages.' He looked at his watch again, torn between going and staying. 'Let's suppose for a moment your hypothesis is right. So, where was Olive's father while Gwen and Amber were being butchered in his kitchen? If I remember correctly he was in the house that night and left for work as usual the following morning. Are you suggesting he didn't know what had happened?'

'Yes, that's exactly what I'm suggesting.'

Deedes's pleasant face scowled in perplexity. 'That's absurd.'

'Not if he was never there. The only people who said he *was* were Olive, Robert himself, and the next-door neighbour, and she only mentioned him in the context of claiming that Gwen and Amber were still alive at eight thirty.'

He shook his head in complete bewilderment. 'So everybody's lying? That's too ridiculous. Why should the neighbour lie?'

Roz sighed. 'I know it's hard to swallow. I've had

a lot of time to think about it, so it's easier for me. Robert Martin was a closet homosexual. I've found the gay pub that he used for his pick-ups. He was well known there as Mark Agnew. The landlord recognized his picture immediately. If he was with a lover the night of the murders and went straight to work from there, he wouldn't have known anything about what had happened in the kitchen until he was told by the police.' She raised a cynical eyebrow. 'And he never had to reveal where he really was because Olive, who assumed he must have been in the house, claimed in her statement that she didn't attack her mother until after her father had left.'

'Hang on, hang on,' barked Deedes, as if he were haranguing a difficult witness, 'you can't have it both ways. A minute ago you were suggesting that Olive's lover dashed off in the middle of the night to have it out with Gwen.' He ran a smooth hand over his hair, collecting his thoughts. 'But, as Robert's body wasn't lying in the kitchen when Olive got back, she must have known he hadn't been there. Why claim in her statement he was?'

'Because he should have been. Look, it really doesn't matter what time her lover left her – the middle of the night, early morning – it's irrelevant as far as she was concerned. She didn't have a car, she was probably quite upset about being abandoned, plus she'd taken the day off work, presumably to spend it with her man, so the chances were she didn't get home till after lunch. She must have assumed her lover waited until Robert left for work before going in to tackle Gwen and Amber, so it was quite natural for her to include her father in her statement. He lived and slept downstairs in a back room but it doesn't appear to have occurred to any of them, except possibly Gwen, that he was slipping out at night for casual gay sex.'

He glanced at his watch for a third time. 'It's no good. I shall have to go.' He reached for his coat and folded it over his arm. 'You haven't explained why the neighbour lied.' He ushered her through the door and closed it behind them.

She spoke over her shoulder as she started down the stairs. 'Because I suspect that when the police told her Gwen and Amber had been murdered she jumped to the immediate conclusion that Robert had done it after a row over her husband.' She shrugged at his snort of disbelief. 'She knew all about the strained relationships in that house, knew that her husband spent hours shut up with Robert in the back room, knew jolly well, I should think, that Robert was a homosexual and by inference that her husband was one as well. She must have been beside herself until she heard that Olive had confessed to the murders. The scandal, if Robert had done it for love of Edward, would have been devastating, so, in a rather pathetic attempt to keep him out of it, she said that Gwen and Amber were alive after Edward left for work.' She led him across the hallway. 'Luckily for her the statement was never questioned because it tied in very neatly with what Olive said.'

They pushed through the main doors and walked down the front steps to the pavement. 'Too neatly?' he murmured. 'Olive's version is so simple. Yours is so complicated.'

'The truth always is,' she said with feeling. 'But in actual fact, all three of them only described what was, in effect, a normal Wednesday morning. Not so much neatness, then, as inevitability.'

'I go this way,' he said, pointing up towards Holborn Tube station.

'That's all right. I'll come with you.' She had to walk briskly to keep up with him.

'I don't understand why you're telling me all this, Miss Leigh. The person you should have gone to is Olive's solicitor, Mr Crew.'

She avoided a direct answer. 'You think I've got a case, then?'

He smiled good-humouredly, his teeth very white in his dark face. 'No, you're a long way off that. You may have the *beginnings* of a case. Take it to Mr Crew.'

'You're the barrister,' she persisted doggedly. 'If you were fighting Olive's corner, what would you need to convince a court she's innocent?'

'Proof that she could not have been in the house during the period of time that the murders happened.'

'Or the real murderer?'

'Or the real murderer,' he agreed, 'but I can't see you producing him very easily.'

'Why not?'

'Because there's no evidence against him. Your argument, presumably, is that Olive obscured all the evidence in order to take the blame on herself. She did it very successfully. Everything confirmed her as the guilty party.' He slowed down as they approached the Underground. 'So, unless your hypothetical murderer confesses voluntarily and persuades the police that he knew things that only the murderer could know, there's no way you can overturn Olive's conviction.' He smiled apologetically. 'And I can't see him doing that now, for the simple reason that he didn't do it at the time.'

She telephoned the prison from Holborn Tube station and asked them to tell Olive she wouldn't be in that evening. She had a feeling that things were about to blow up in her face, and the feeling centred on Olive.

It was late by the time she let herself in through the main door of her block. Unusually, the hall was in total darkness. She pressed the time switch to light the stairs and first-floor landing, and sighed when nothing happened. Another power cut, she thought.

She could have predicted it. Black was in tune with her mood. She sorted out the key to her flat, by touch, and groped her way up the stairs, trying to remember if she had any candles left over from the last time. With luck there was one in her kitchen drawer, otherwise this was going to be a long and tedious night.

She was fumbling blindly across her door with both hands, searching for the lock, when something rose up from the floor at her feet and brushed against her.

'*Aa-agh!*' she screamed, beating at it furiously.

Next second she was lifted bodily off the floor while a great palm clamped itself across her mouth. 'Ssh,' hissed Hal in her ear, shaking with laughter. 'It's me.' He kissed her on the nose. '*Ow!*' he roared, letting her go and bending over to clutch himself.

'Serves you right,' she said, scrabbling on the floor for her keys. 'You're lucky I didn't have my hatpin. Ah, got them.' She renewed her search for the lock and found it. 'There.' She tried the lights inside the door but the blackness remained impenetrable. 'Come on,' she said, catching his jacket and pulling him inside. 'I think there's a candle in the kitchen.'

'Everything all right?' called a quavering female voice from the floor upstairs.

'Yes, thank you,' Roz called back. 'I trod on something. How long has the power been off?'

'Half an hour. I've telephoned. There's a fuse gone in a box somewhere. Three hours they said. I told them I wouldn't pay my bill if it was any longer. We should take a stand. Don't you agree?'

'Absolutely,' said Roz, wondering who she was talking to. Mrs Barrett, perhaps. She knew their names from their mail but she rarely saw anyone. ''Bye now.' She closed her door. 'I'll try and find the candle,' she whispered.

'Why are we whispering?' Hal whispered back.

She giggled. 'Because one always does in the dark.'

He stumbled into something. 'This is ridiculous. The street lights aren't out, are they? Your curtains must be closed.'

'Probably.' She pulled open the kitchen drawer. 'I left early this morning.' She felt around the clutter of cotton reels and screwdrivers. 'I think I've found it. Have you any matches?'

'No,' he said patiently, 'otherwise I'd have lit one by now. Do you keep snakes by any chance?'

'Don't be silly. I have a cat.' *But where was Mrs Antrobus?* Her cries should have risen in joyful greeting when the key scraped in the lock. Roz made her way back to the door and groped for her briefcase where she kept the matches that she took in to the prison. She snapped the locks and poked amongst her papers. 'If you can find the sofa,' she told him, 'the curtains are behind it. There's a cord on the left-hand side.'

'I've found something,' he said, 'but it certainly isn't a sofa.'

'What is it?'

'I don't know,' he said cautiously, 'but whatever it is it's rather unpleasant. It's wet and slimy and it's wound itself round my neck. Are you sure you don't keep snakes?'

She gave a nervous laugh. 'Don't be an idiot.' Her fingers knocked against the matchbox and she snatched at it with relief. She struck a match and held it up. Hal was standing in the middle of the room, his head and shoulders swathed in the damp shirt she had washed that morning and hung on a coathanger from the lampshade. She shook with laughter. 'You knew it wasn't a snake,' she said, holding the candle to the spluttering match flame.

He found the cord and swished the curtains back to let in the orange glow from the street lamps outside. With that and the candlelight, the room sprang alive out of the pitch darkness. He gazed about him. Towels, clothes, carrier bags, and photographs lay in clutters on chairs and tables, a duvet sprawled half on and half off the sofa, dirty cups, and empty bags of crisps jostled happily about the floor. 'Well, this is nice,' he said, lifting his foot and prising off the remains of a half-eaten pork pie. 'I can't remember when I felt so much at home.'

'I wasn't expecting you,' she said, taking the pork pie with dignity and dropping it into a waste-paper basket. 'Or at least I thought you'd have the decency to warn me of your arrival with a phone-call first.'

He reached down to stroke the soft ball of white fur that was stretching luxuriously in its warm nest on the duvet. Mrs Antrobus licked his hand in approval before embarking on a comprehensive grooming. 'Do you always sleep on the sofa?' he asked Roz.

'There's no telephone in the bedroom.'

He nodded gravely but didn't say anything.

She moved over to him, the candle tilted to stop the hot wax burning her fingers. 'Oh, God, I'm so pleased to see you. You wouldn't believe. Where did you go? I've been worried sick.'

He lowered his weary forehead and pressed it against her sweet-smelling hair. 'Round and about,' he said, resting his wrists on her shoulders and running the softest of fingers down the lines of her neck.

'There's a warrant out for your arrest,' she said weakly.

'I know.' His lips brushed against her cheek, but so gently that their touch was almost unbearable.

'I'm going to set fire to something,' she groaned.

He reached down to pinch out the candle. 'You already have.' He cupped his strong hands about her bottom and drew her against his erection. 'The question is,' he murmured into the arch of her neck, 'should I have a cold shower before it spreads out of control?'

'Is that a serious question?' *Could* he stop now? *She* couldn't.

'No, a polite one.'

'I'm in agony.'

'You're supposed to be,' he said, his eyes glinting in the orange light. 'Damn it, woman, I've been in agony for weeks.'

Mrs Antrobus, ejected from the duvet, stalked indignantly into the kitchen.

Later, the lights came on, drowning the tiny flame of the candle which, rekindled, had started to splutter in its saucer on the table.

He stroked the hair from Roz's face. 'You are quite the most beautiful woman I've ever seen,' he said.

She smiled wickedly. 'And I thought I was too thin?'

His dark eyes softened 'I knew you were lying about that blasted answerphone.' He ran his hands over her silky arms, gripping them suddenly with urgent fingers. She was completely addictive. He plucked her up and sat her astride his lap. 'I've been dreaming about this.'

'Were they nice dreams?'

'Not a patch on the real thing.'

'Enough,' she said even later, sliding away from him and pulling on her clothes. 'What are you planning to do about this arrest warrant?'

He ignored the question and stirred the photographs on her coffee table. 'Is this your husband?'

'Ex-husband.' She threw him his trousers.

He pulled them on with a sigh, then isolated a close-up of Alice. 'And this must be your daughter,' he said evenly. 'She looks just like you.'

'Looked,' Roz corrected him. 'She's dead.'

She waited for the apology and the change of subject, but Hal smiled and touched a finger to the laughing face. 'She's beautiful.'

'Yes.'

'What was her name?'

'Alice.'

He examined the picture closely. 'I remember falling in love with a little girl just like her when I was six. I was very insecure and I used to ask her every day how much she loved me. She always answered in the same way. She would hold her hands out, like this' – he spread his palms apart, like a fisherman demonstrating the length of a fish – 'and say: this much.'

'Yes,' said Roz, remembering, 'Alice always measured love with her hands. I'd forgotten.'

She tried to take the photograph away, but he moved it out of her reach and tilted it to the light. 'There's a very determined glint in her eyes.'

'She liked her own way.'

'Sensible woman. Did she always get it?'

'Most times. She had very decided views. I remember once . . .' But she fell silent and didn't go on.

Hal shrugged into his shirt and started to button it. 'Like mother, like daughter. I bet she had you wound round her little finger before she could walk. I'd have enjoyed seeing someone get the better of you.'

Roz held a handkerchief to her streaming eyes. 'I'm sorry.'

'What for?'

'Being embarrassing.'

He pulled her against his shoulder and rested his cheek against her hair. What a terrible indictment of Western society it was, that a mother should be afraid to shed tears for her dead daughter in case she embarrassed someone.

'Thank you.' She saw the question in his eyes. 'For listening,' she explained.

'It was no hardship, Roz.' He could sense how insecure she was. 'Are you going to agonize over this all night and wake up tomorrow morning wishing you hadn't told me about Alice?'

He was far too perceptive. She looked away. 'I hate feeling vulnerable.'

'Yes.' He understood that. 'Come here.' He patted

his lap. 'Let me tell you about my vulnerabilities. You've been trying to prise them out of me for weeks. Now it's your turn to have a good laugh at my expense.'

'I won't laugh.'

'Ah!' he murmured. 'So that's what this is all about. You're a cut above me. I'll laugh at yours, but you won't laugh at mine.'

She put her arms about him. 'You're so like Olive.'

'I wish you'd stop comparing me with the madwoman of Dawlington.'

'It's a compliment. She's a very nice person. Like you.'

'I'm not nice, Roz.' He held her face between his hands. 'I'm being prosecuted under the Health and Hygiene regulations. The Environmental Health Inspector's report describes my kitchen as the worst he's ever seen. Ninety-five per cent of the raw meat in the fridge was so rotten it was crawling with maggots. The dry foods should have been in sealed containers, but weren't, and rat droppings were found in all of them. There were open bags of rubbish in the larder. The vegetables had deteriorated so far they had to be discarded, and a live rat was discovered under the cooker.' He arched a weary eyebrow. 'I've lost all my customers because of it, my case comes up in six weeks, and I haven't a leg to stand on.'

Seventeen

ROZ DIDN'T SPEAK for some moments. She had invented a number of scenarios to account for what was happening at the Poacher, but never this. It would certainly explain his lack of customers. Who, in their right mind, would eat in a restaurant where the meat had been found crawling with maggots? She had. Twice. But she hadn't known about the maggots. It would have been more honest of Hal to tell her at the outset, she thought, her stomach protesting mildly over what might have gone into it. She felt his gaze upon her and quelled the treacherous stirrings firmly.

'I don't understand,' she said carefully. 'Is this a genuine prosecution? I mean, you appear to have been tried and judged already. How did your customers know what the Inspector found if the case hasn't been to court? And who are the men in ski-masks?' She gave a puzzled frown. 'I can't believe you'd be such a bloody fool, anyway, as to flout the hygiene regulations. Not to the extent of having an entire fridgeful of rotten meat and live rats running around the floor.' She laughed suddenly with relief and smacked a slender palm against his chest. 'You creep, Hawksley! It's a load of old flannel. You're trying to wind me up.'

He shook his head. 'I wish I were.'

She studied him thoughtfully for a moment then pushed herself off his lap and walked through to the kitchen. He heard the sound of a cork being drawn from a bottle and the clink of glasses. She took longer than she should have, and he recalled how his wife had always done the same thing – disappeared into the kitchen whenever she was hurt or disappointed. He had thought Roz different.

She reappeared finally with a tray. 'OK,' she said firmly, 'I've had a think.'

He didn't say anything.

'I do not believe you'd keep a dirty kitchen,' she told him. 'You're too much of an enthusiast. The Poacher is the fulfilment of a dream, not a financial investment to be milked for all its worth.' She poured him a glass of wine. 'And you accused me a week ago of setting you up again, which would imply you'd been set up before.' She filled the second glass for herself. 'Ergo, the rat and the rotten meat were planted. Am I right?'

'Right.' He sniffed the wine. 'But I would say that, wouldn't I?'

A very sore nerve, she thought. No wonder he didn't trust anyone. She perched on the edge of the sofa. 'Plus,' she went on, ignoring the comment, 'you've been beaten up twice to my knowledge, had your car windows smashed and the Poacher broken into.' She sipped her wine. 'So what do they want from you?'

He eased the still-bruised muscles in his back. 'Presumably they want me out, and fast. But I haven't a clue why or who's behind it. Six weeks ago I was a contented chef, presiding over a healthy little business without a care in the world. Then I came home from the markets at ten o'clock one morning to find my assistant being berated by the Environmental Health Inspector, my kitchen stinking to high heaven of corruption, and me on the wrong end of a prosecution.' He ruffled his hair. 'The restaurant was closed for three days while I cleaned it. My staff never came back after the closure. My customers, predominantly policemen and their families – which, incidentally, is how the news of the Inspector's visit got out – deserted in droves because they reckoned I'd been cutting corners to line my pockets, and the local restaurateurs are accusing me of giving the whole trade a bad name through my lack of professionalism. I've been effectively isolated.'

Roz shook her head. 'Why on earth didn't you report that break-in last Tuesday?'

He sighed. 'What good would it have done me? I couldn't tie it in to the Health Inspector's visit. I decided to work with some live bait instead.' He saw her bewilderment. 'I caught two of them at it, wrecking the place. I think it was a chance thing. They discovered the restaurant was empty and took their opportunity.' He laughed suddenly. 'I was so angry with you that I had them both upstairs, gagged and handcuffed to my window bars, before they even knew what had hit them. But they were a tough pair,' he said with genuine admiration. 'They weren't going to talk.' He shrugged. 'So I sat it out and waited for someone to come looking for them.'

No wonder he had been frightened. 'Why did you decide it was chance that brought them and not me?' she asked curiously. 'I'd have thought it was me every time.'

The laughter lines rayed out around his eyes. 'You didn't see yourself with that table leg. You were so terrified when the kitchen door opened, so relieved when you saw it was me, and so twitched when I told you I hadn't called the police. No one, but no one, is that good.' He took a mouthful of wine and savoured it for a moment. 'I'm in a catch twenty-two. The police don't believe me. They think I'm guilty, but trying to use clout or cunning to wriggle out of the prosecution. Even Geoff Wyatt, who was my partner and who knows me better than anyone, claims to have had the runs since he saw the Inspector's photographs. They all ate there regularly, partly because I gave them discounts and partly out of a genuine desire to see an ex-copper succeed.' He wiped a weary hand across his mouth. 'Now, I'm *persona non grata* and I can't really blame them. They feel they've been conned.'

'Why would you need to con them?'

'The recession.' He sighed. 'Businesses are going down like ninepins. There's no reason mine should have been immune. What's the first thing a restaurateur's likely to do when he's running out of money? Hang on to dodgy food and serve it up in a curry.'

There was a twisted logic to it. 'Won't your staff speak up for you?'

He smiled grimly. 'The two waitresses have agreed to, but the only one whose word might carry weight is my assistant chef, and he was last heard of heading for France.' He stretched his arms towards the ceiling, and winced as pain seared round his ribs. 'It wouldn't do me any good anyway. He must have been bought. Someone had to let whoever framed me into the kitchen and he had the only other key.' His eyes hardened. 'I should have throttled him when I had the chance but I was so damn shell-shocked I didn't put two and two together fast enough. By the time I had, he'd gone.'

Roz chewed her thumb in thought. 'Didn't that man tell you anything after I left? I assumed you were going to use my hatpin on him.'

Her candour brought a smile to his bleak face. 'I did, but he didn't make much sense. "You're costing money on the foreclosures." That's all he said.' He arched an eyebrow. 'Can you make anything of it?'

'Not unless the bank's about to pull the rug from underneath your feet.'

He shook his head. 'I borrowed the absolute minimum. There's no immediate pressure.' He drummed his fingers on the floor. 'Logically, he should have been referring to the businesses on either side of me. They've both gone bankrupt and in each case the lenders have foreclosed.'

'Well, that's it then,' said Roz excitedly. 'Someone wants all three properties. Didn't you ask him who it was and why?'

He rubbed the back of his head in tender recollection. 'I was clobbered before I had the chance. There was obviously a fifth man who went upstairs during the brawl to release Tweedledum and Tweedledee from the window bars. For all I know, it was that hammering we heard. Anyway, by the time I came to, a chip pan was in flames on the stove, the police had arrived in force, and my next-door neighbour was rabbiting on about how he'd had to call an ambulance because I'd tried to boil a customer in fish stock.' He grinned sheepishly. 'It was a blasted nightmare. So I hit the nearest copper and legged it through the restaurant. It was the only thing I could think of.' He looked at her. 'In any case the idea that someone was trying to get hold of the Poacher was the first thing I thought of. I checked out both the adjoining properties five weeks ago and there's no common factor between them. One was bought privately by a small retail chain and the other was sold at auction to an investment company.'

'They could be fronts. Did you go to Companies' House?'

'What do you think I've been doing for the last three days?' He gritted his teeth angrily. 'I've checked every damn register I can think of and I've got sweet FA to show for it. I don't know what the hell's going on except that the court case will be the last nail in the Poacher's coffin and presumably, at that point, someone will make me an offer to buy the place. Rather like you kept doing the other day.'

She let his anger slide past her. She understood it now. 'By which time it will be too late.'

'Precisely.'

They sat in silence for several minutes.

'Why were you beaten up the first time I saw you?' Roz asked at last. 'That must have followed on the Inspector's visit.'

He nodded. 'It was three or four days after I re-opened. They grabbed me off the doorstep when I unlocked the door. Same MO as you witnessed – men in ski-masks with baseball bats – but that time they shoved me in the back of a fish lorry, drove me ten miles into the New Forest, slapped me about a bit, then dumped me by the side of the road with no money and no cards. It took me all afternoon to walk home, because nobody fancied giving me a lift, and at the end of it' – he flicked her a sideways glance – 'I found Botticelli's *Venus* loitering palely among my tables. I really thought my luck had changed until Venus opened her mouth and turned into a Fury.' He ducked to avoid her hand. 'God, woman' – he grinned – 'I was out on my feet and you tore more strips off me than the bastards in the fish lorry. Rape, for Christ's sake! I could hardly put one foot in front of the other.'

'It's your own fault for having bars on your windows. Why do you, as a matter of interest?'

'They were there when I bought it. The chap before me had a wife who sleepwalked. I've been glad of them these last few weeks.'

She reverted to her former question. 'But it doesn't explain why, you know. I mean if the idea of the Inspector's visit was to get you to jack it in quickly, then they should have clobbered you the day you reopened, not four days later. And if they were happy to wait until the court case, then why clobber you at all?'

'I know,' he admitted. 'It made me very suspicious of you. I kept thinking you must be connected with it somehow but I had you checked and you seemed genuine enough.'

'Thanks,' she said drily.

'You'd have done the same.' A frown carved a deep furrow between his brows. 'You must admit it's damned odd the way everything blew up around the time you appeared.'

In all fairness, Roz could see it was. 'But you got stitched up,' she pointed out, 'before you or I had ever heard of each other. It must be coincidence.' She topped up his glass. 'And, anyway, the only common factor between you and me five weeks ago was Olive and you're not suggesting she's behind it. She's hardly confident enough to run a bath on her own, let alone mastermind a conspiracy to defraud you of the Poacher.'

He shrugged impatiently. 'I know. I've been over it a thousand times. None of it makes sense. The only thing I'm sure of is that it's about the neatest operation I've ever come across. I've had the ground cut from under me. I'm the fall guy and I can't even begin to get a fix on who's done it.' He scratched his stubble with weary resignation. 'So, Miss Leigh, how do you feel now about a failed restaurateur with convictions for health violation, GBH, arson, and resisting arrest? Because, barring miracles, that's what I'll be in three weeks.'

Her eyes gleamed above her wine glass. 'Horny.'

He gave an involuntary chuckle. It was the same gleam in the pictured eyes of Alice. 'You look just like your daughter.' He stirred the photographs again. 'You should have them all around the room to remind yourself of how beautiful she was. I would if she'd been mine.' He heard Roz's indrawn breath and glanced at her. 'Sorry. That was insensitive.'

'Don't be an oaf,' she said. 'I've just remembered where I've seen that man before. I knew I knew him. It's one of Mr Hayes's sons. You know, the old man who lived next door to the Martins. He had photographs of the family on his sideboard.' She clapped her hands. 'Is that a miracle, Hawksley, or is it a miracle? Sister Bridget's prayers must be working.'

She sat at her kitchen table and watched Hal work his magic on the meagre contents of her fridge. He had sloughed off his frustration like a used-up skin and was humming contentedly to himself as he interleaved bacon between thin slices of chicken breast and sprinkled them with parsley. 'You're not planning to stick my hatpin into Mr Hayes, are you?' she asked him. 'I'm sure he hasn't a clue what his beastly son's been up to. He's a dear old thing.'

Hal was amused. 'I shouldn't think so.' He covered the dish with silver foil and put it in the oven. 'But I'm damned if I can see at the moment how the jigsaw fits together. Why did Hayes Junior suddenly up the pressure on me if all he had to do was sit tight and wait for my prosecution?'

'Have him arrested and find out,' said Roz reasonably. 'If it was me, I'd have driven straight down, demanded an address off his father, and sent in the fuzz.'

'And you'd have got precisely nowhere.' He thought for a moment. 'You said you made a tape of your conversation with the old man. I'd like to listen to it. I can't believe it's coincidence. There has to be a stronger link. Why did they all get so twitched suddenly and start wielding baseball bats? It doesn't make sense.'

'You can listen to it now.' She brought her briefcase in from the hallway, located the tape, and set the recorder running on the table. 'We were talking about Amber's illegitimate son,' she explained as the old man's voice quavered out. 'He knew all about him, even down to the child's adopted name and what country he's in. Robert Martin's entire estate is his if they can find him.'

Hal listened with rapt attention. 'Brown?' he queried at the end. 'And living in Australia? How do you know he's right?'

'Because Olive's shitty solicitor threatened me with injunctions when I let on I knew.' She frowned. 'Mind you, I've no idea how Mr Hayes found out. Crew won't even give Olive the child's name. He's paranoid about keeping it secret.'

Hal removed a saucepan of rice from the cooker and drained it. 'How much did Robert Martin leave?'

'Half a million.'

'Christ!' He gave a low whistle. 'Christ!' he said

again. 'And it's all on deposit waiting for the child's appearance?'

'Presumably.'

'Who's the executor?'

'The solicitor, Peter Crew.'

Hal spooned the rice into a bowl. 'So what did he say when you tackled him about it? Did he admit they were on the child's track?'

'No. He just kept threatening me with injunctions.' She shrugged. 'But he wrote to Olive and told her the chances were minimal. There's a time limit, apparently, and if the child doesn't turn up the money goes to charity.' She frowned. 'He wrote that letter himself in long hand. I thought he was saving money but, you know, it's far more likely that he didn't want his secretary reading it. She would know if he was telling lies.'

'And meanwhile,' Hal said slowly, 'he is administering the estate and has access to the sort of capital that would be needed to buy up bankrupt businesses.' He stared past her head, his eyes narrowed. 'Plus, he's a solicitor, so probably has inside information on development plans and proposals.' He looked at Roz. 'It would amount to indefinite free credit, as long as no one turned up to claim Robert's money. When did you first go and see Crew?'

She was ahead of him. 'The day before you were beaten up.' Her eyes gleamed excitedly. 'And he was very suspicious of me, kept accusing me of jumping to unfavourable conclusions about his handling of Olive's case. I've got it all on tape.' She scrabbled through her cassettes. 'He said Olive couldn't inherit because she would not be allowed to benefit from Gwen and Amber's death. But, you know, if Olive were innocent' – she pounced triumphantly on the tape – 'it would be a whole new ball game. She could get leave to appeal against the will. And I remember saying to him at the end of the interview that one explanation for the discrepancies between the abnormality of the crime and the normality of Olive's psychiatric tests was that she didn't do it. God, it fits, doesn't it? First he learns that Amber's son is likely to surface and then I turn up, aggressively taking Olive's side. The Poacher must be awfully important to him.'

Hal took the chicken from the oven and put it on the table with the rice. 'You do realize your dear old man must be in it up to his neck? Crew would never have given him chapter and verse on Amber's child unless Hayes has some kind of hold on him.'

She stared at him for a long moment, then removed the Svengali photographs from her briefcase. 'Perhaps he knows Crew is using Robert's money. Or perhaps,' she said slowly, 'he knows who really murdered Gwen and Amber. Either or both could ruin Crew.' She fanned the pictures across the table. 'He was Olive's lover,' she said simply, 'and if I could find out so easily then so could anyone else. Including the police. You let her down, Hal, all of you. It's a betrayal of justice to assume someone's guilt before it's proved.'

Watery blue eyes regarded Roz with undisguised pleasure. 'Well, well. You came back. Come in. Come in.' He peered past her, frowning at Hal in half-recognition. 'Surely we've met before. What shall I say? I never forget a face. Now when could that have been?'

Hal shook the old man's hand. 'Six years ago,' he said pleasantly. 'I was on the Olive Martin case. Sergeant Hawksley.' The hand fluttered weakly in his, like a tiny bird, but only from old age and decrepitude, Hal thought.

Mr Hayes nodded vigorously. 'I remember now. Unhappy circumstances.' He fussed ahead of them into the sitting room. 'Sit down. Sit down. Any news?' He took a firm chair and sat bolt upright his head cocked enquiringly to one side. On the sideboard behind him his violent son smiled disarmingly into the camera.

Roz took her notebook from her handbag and switched on her recorder again. They had reached a mutual decision that Roz should ask the questions. For, as Hal had pointed out: 'If he knows anything, he's more likely to let it slip while talking to a – what shall I say? – charming young lady about Olive.'

'In fact,' she said in a gossipy voice which grated

on Hal but clearly appealed to Mr Hayes, 'there's quite a bit of news one way and another. Where would you like me to begin? With Olive? Or with Amber's baby?' She gave him an approving look. 'You were quite right about them finding traces, you know, in spite of there being thousands of Browns in Australia.'

'Ah,' he said, rubbing his hands, 'I knew they were close. That mean the lad will get the money? What shall I say? It's what Bob wanted. Fair upset him, it did, to think the government would get it all.'

'He made alternative provisions, you know, in case the boy wasn't found. It'll go to various children's charities.'

The old man's mouth compressed into a split of disgust. 'And we all know what sort of children they'll be. The worthless sort. The sort as are never going to make anything of theirselves but live off the rest of us till they drop. And you know who I blame. The social workers. They're namby-pamby when it comes to telling a woman she's had more children than's good for her.'

'Quite,' Roz interrupted hurriedly, reining in the inevitable hobby horse. She tapped her pencil on her notepad. 'Do you remember telling me that your wife thought Olive committed the murders because of hormones?'

He pursed his lips at the abrupt change of subject. 'Maybe.'

'Did your wife say that because she knew Olive had had an abortion the previous Christmas?'

'Maybe.'

'Do you know who the father was, Mr Hayes?'

He shook his head. 'Someone she met through work, we were told. Silly girl. Only did it to cock a snook at Amber.' He fingered his ancient mouth. 'Or that's what I reckoned anyway. Amber had a lot of boyfriends.'

So much for Mr Hayes and Crew in a conspiracy of silence, thought Roz. 'When did you find out about it?'

'Gwen told my Jeannie. She was that upset. Thought Olive was going to up and get married and abandon them all. It would have done for Gwen, that would. She couldn't have coped on her own.'

'Coped with what?'

'Everything,' he said vaguely.

'Housework, you mean?'

'Housework, cooking, bills, shopping. Everything. Olive did everything.'

'What did Gwen do?'

He didn't answer immediately, but seemed to be weighing something in his mind. He glanced across at Hal. 'You lot never did ask many questions. I might have said something if you had.'

Hal eased himself in his chair. 'At the time it was clear cut,' he said carefully. 'But Miss Leigh has unearthed a number of discrepancies which do tend to throw a different light on the affair. What would you have told us, had you been asked?'

Mr Hayes sucked at his false teeth. 'Well, for one thing, Gwen Martin drank too much. She had troubles, I can't deny that, kept up a good front, I can't deny that either, but she was a bad mother. She married beneath herself and it made her bitter. Felt life had dealt her a bad hand and she took it out on Bob and the girls. My Jeannie always said if it hadn't been for Olive the family would have fallen apart years before. It made us sick, of course, what she did, but everyone turns eventually and she was badly put upon one way and another. She shouldn't have killed them, though. Can't forgive that.'

'No,' said Roz thoughtfully. 'So what did Gwen do all day while the other three were out at work?'

The marbled hands fluttered a contradiction. 'Amber was at home more often than not. Work-shy, that one. Never stayed anywhere very long. Used to drive her mother mad listening to pop records at full blast and inviting boys up to her bedroom. She was a pretty girl but my Jeannie said she was difficult. Couldn't see it myself.' He smiled reminiscently. 'She was always charming to me. I had a soft spot for little Amber. But she got on with men, I think, better than she got on with women.' He peered at Roz. 'You asked me about Gwen. What shall I say, Miss Leigh? She kept up appearances. If you knocked on the door she was always smartly dressed, always held herself well, always spoke with icy correctness, but as often as not she was drunk as a lord. Strange woman. Never did know why she took to the bottle, unless it was the business of Amber's baby. She was a lot worse afterwards.'

Roz drew her cherub doodle. 'Robert Martin was an active homosexual but didn't want anyone to know,' she said bluntly. 'Perhaps that's what she found difficult to cope with.'

Mr Hayes sniffed. 'She drove him to it,' he said. 'There was nothing wrong with Bob that a loving wife wouldn't have put right. The two girls were his all right, so there was nothing untoward in the locker at the beginning, if you get my meaning. It was her turned him off women. She was frigid.'

Roz let that pass. Mr Hayes was too set in his views to see that what he said was nonsense and, in any case, there was probably some truth in the idea that Gwen was frigid. Roz found it difficult to believe that Robert Martin could ever have got as far as the altar with a woman who had a normal sexual drive. Her very normality would have been a threat to him. 'But if she was mourning Amber's baby,' she said in feigned puzzlement, 'I don't understand why she didn't try and get him back or at least establish contact with him? Presumably she knew who had adopted him or she wouldn't have been able to tell your Jeannie his name.'

He tut-tutted impatiently. 'It wasn't Jeannie told

me the name, it was my son, Stewart, six, seven weeks back. Knew I'd be interested, seeing as how me and Bob were pals.' He wagged a finger at her. 'You don't know much about adoption, that's for sure. Once you sign 'em away, that's it. You're not given a dossier. Gwen never knew who'd got him.'

Roz smiled easily. 'Does your son work for Mr Crew, then? I've not come across him. I thought he took after you and became a soldier.'

'Blooming Army didn't want him any more, did they?' he muttered crossly. 'Cutbacks there, like everywhere else. What shall I say? So much for loyalty to Queen and country. Course he doesn't work for Mr Crew. He's running a small security firm with his brother, but there's precious little work.' He flexed his arthritic fingers in annoyance. 'Trained soldiers and the best they can get is nightwatchmen jobs. Their wives aren't happy, not by a long chalk.'

Roz gritted her teeth behind another ingenuous smile. 'So how did he know the child's name?'

Archly, Mr Hayes tapped the side of his nose. 'No names no pack drill, young lady. Always best.'

Hal leaned forward aggressively and held up a hand. 'One moment, please, Miss Leigh.' He drew his brows together in a ferocious scowl. 'You do realize, Mr Hayes, that if your son doesn't work for Mr Crew then, strictly speaking, he's committed an offence by being in receipt of confidential information. The legal profession is bound by the same codes as the medical profession and if someone in Mr Crew's practice is talking to outsiders, then both he and the police would want to know about it.'

'Bah!' the old man snorted contemptuously. 'You never change, you lot. What shall I say? Quick as lightning to bang up the innocent while the bloody thieves wander around, free as birds, nicking anything they feel like nicking. You should do what you're being paid for, Sergeant, and not go round threatening old men. It was Mr Crew himself gave out that information. He told my lad and my lad told me. How's he supposed to know it's confidential if the blooming solicitor's telling everyone? Stands to reason he'd pass it on, seeing as how I was the only friend Bob had at the end.' He glared suspiciously from Hal to Roz. 'What you bring a policeman for, anyway?'

'Because there's some doubt of Olive's guilt,' said Roz glibly, wondering if being economical with the truth constituted deliberate impersonation of a police officer. 'This gentleman is holding a watching brief while I talk to people.'

'I see,' said Mr Hayes. But it was obvious he didn't.

'I'm nearly finished.' She smiled brightly. 'I found the Clarkes, by the way. Had a chat with them a week or so ago. Poor Mrs Clarke is completely senile now.'

The watery eyes looked amused. 'That doesn't surprise me. She was pretty far gone when I knew her. I sometimes thought my Jeannie was the only sensible woman in the road.'

'I gather Mr Clarke had to stay at home to look after her?' She raised her eyebrows in enquiry. 'But he spent more time with Robert than he spent with her. How friendly were they, Mr Hayes? Do you know?'

It was obvious he understood the point of her question. He chose – out of delicacy? – not to answer it. 'Good friends,' he muttered, 'and who can blame them? Bob's wife was a dipso and Ted's was the silliest creature I've ever met. Cleaned the house from top to bottom every day.' He gave a grunt of contempt. 'Hygiene mad, she was. Used to walk around in nothing but an overall, no undies in case she spread germs, swabbing everything with disinfectant.' He chuckled suddenly. 'Remember once she scrubbed the dining table with neat Domestos to sterilize it. Hah! Ted was hopping mad. He'd just paid for the thing to be french polished after Dorothy's last effort with boiling water. And now she's completely senile, you say. Not surprised. Not surprised at all.'

Roz sat with her pencil poised above her notepad. 'And can you say,' she asked after a moment, 'if Ted and Bob were lovers?'

'No. It weren't none of my business.'

'OK.' She gathered her things together. 'Thank you, Mr Hayes. I don't know if there's anything Mr Hawksley wants to ask you.' She looked at Hal.

He stood up. 'Only the name of your son's security firm, Mr Hayes.'

The old man eyed him suspiciously. 'What you want that for?'

'Just so I can put a quiet word in the right ear about the leak of privileged information.' He smiled coldly. 'Otherwise I shall have to report it and then there'll be an official complaint.' He shrugged. 'Don't worry. You have my word I won't make an issue out of it, not unless I have to.'

'The word of a policeman, eh? That's not something I'd want to rely on. Certainly not.'

Hal buttoned his jacket. 'It'll have to go through official channels then, and it'll be an inspector coming to see you next time.'

'What shall I say? Blooming blackmail, that's all this is. STC Security, Bell Street, Southampton. There now. Let's see if your word's worth something.'

Hal looked past him towards the photograph of his son. 'Thank you, Mr Hayes,' he said pleasantly. 'You've been very helpful.'

Eighteen

ROZ WALKED BACK to the car deep in thought. 'What's up?' Hal asked her.

'Just something he said.' She put her bag on the roof and stared into the middle distance, trying to pick up an elusive thread. 'It's no good. I'll have to go back through my notes.' She unlocked the door. 'So what do we do now? Go to the police?' She released Hal's door and he climbed in beside her.

'No. We'd be there all day answering questions and there's no guarantee they'd act at the end of it.' He thought for a moment. 'And it's no good tackling Crew either. If we're going to nail him we'll have to do it through Stewart Hayes and his security firm.'

Roz winced. 'We? Listen, Hawksley, I've already had my hair pulled out once by that gorilla. I'm not sure I fancy it a second time.' She meant it, too.

Hal put his hand on her shoulder and gave it a reassuring squeeze. 'If it's any consolation, I don't think I fancy it much either.' He could smell the scent of soap on her face and with a sigh he moved away. 'But we've got to get it settled one way or another,' he said coolly. 'I can't stand much more of this.'

Her insecurities resurfaced. 'Much more of what?'

'Sitting around in confined spaces with you,' he growled. 'It requires too much blasted self-control. Come on. Let's grasp the nettle. I'll phone Geoff Wyatt and see if I can persuade him to hold my hand while I offer the Poacher for sale.'

'Wouldn't it be easier just to have Hayes arrested?'

'What for?'

'Breaking and entering.'

'On what evidence?'

'Me,' she said. 'I can identify him.'

'He'll have an alibi by now.' He flicked a strand of hair from her cheek with a gesture of casual affection. 'We need to tempt Crew into the open.'

It was Roz's turn to sigh. In the cold light of morning, she was having doubts. 'It's all guesswork, Hal. Crew could be squeaky clean as far as the Poacher's concerned. Mr Hayes likes to give the impression he knows more than he does. It makes him feel important.'

'But it's the only scenario that makes sense.' He stroked his jaw and smiled at her with a confidence he didn't really feel. 'My nose is twitching. It's always a good sign.'

'Of what?'

'That I'm on the right track.'

'You'll lose the Poacher if you're wrong.'

'I'll lose it anyway.' He drummed his fingers on the dashboard. 'Come on,' he said abruptly. 'Let's go. Head for the city centre. Bell Street runs parallel with the main shopping area. We'll stop at the first telephone we see. And keep your eyes peeled for an electrical goods shop.'

She fired the engine and pulled out into the road. 'Why?'

'You'll find out.'

He dialled Dawlington police station and asked to be put through to Geoff Wyatt. 'It's Hal.' He let the angry recriminations run for a moment, then broke in. 'Save your breath. I'm trying to sort it now, but I need your help. What do you have on STC Security in Bell Street? No, I'll wait.' He propped the receiver under his chin and took out a notepad. 'OK. Hayes. Ex-Army. Clean as a whistle. You're sure? Right. Can you meet me there in half an hour?' More squeaks. 'For old time's sake, that's why. No, you bastard, I don't give a monkey's toss if you still feel sick. At the very least, you owe me for Sally. Half an hour.' He hung up.

Roz examined her fingernails with studied uninterest. 'Who's Sally?' she asked.

'My ex.'

'Why does he owe you for her?'

'He married her.'

'God!' She hadn't expected that.

He smiled at her startled expression. 'He did me a favour but doesn't know it. He thinks it's why I left the Force. His guilt is huge and extremely useful at times like this.'

'That's cruel.'

He lifted an eyebrow. 'It hurt at the time.'

'Sorry,' she said regretfully. 'I keep forgetting we both have pasts.'

He pulled her against him. 'The marriage was long dead, and Geoff didn't set out to poach Sally. He's a decent sort. He held her hand out of friendship, and ended up with more than he bargained for. And that's genuine gratitude talking, Roz, not bitterness.' He kissed her nose. 'Poor bastard. He had no idea what he was signing on for.'

'Olive's revenge,' she said slowly.

He frowned as he dialled Directory Enquiries. 'I don't follow.'

Roz gave a hollow laugh. 'She makes clay figures in her room and then sticks pins into them. She did one of me when she was angry with me. I had a migraine for a week.'

'When was that? Yes,' he said into the phone, 'STC Security, Southampton, please.'

'A couple of weeks ago.'

'Someone beat you up a couple of weeks ago,' he

pointed out. 'That's why you had a migraine.' He wrote a number on his pad and hung up.

'My ex-husband,' she agreed. 'I told Olive I wanted to kill him and he turned up out of the blue. I could have killed him, too, if I'd had a knife, or been better prepared. I was angry enough.' She shrugged. 'And then there's you and Crew and the Poacher, and Wyatt taking your wife, and her father dying. All people she blames for what's happened to her.'

He looked surprised. 'You don't really believe that, do you?'

She laughed. 'No, of course I don't.' But she did. Only she knew how much her head had hurt when Olive turned the pin.

'STC Security,' said a woman's bright voice at the other end of the wire.

Hal looked at Roz as he spoke. 'Good morning. I'd like to discuss security arrangements for my restaurant with Mr Stewart Hayes.'

'I'm not sure he's available to talk at the moment, sir.'

'He will be for me. Try his number and tell him that Hal Hawksley of the Poacher is on the line.'

'One moment, please.'

Several moments passed before she came back to him. 'Mr Hayes will talk to you now, Mr Hawksley.'

A bluff, friendly voice swelled down the wire. 'Good morning, Mr Hawksley. How may I help you?'

'You can't, Mr Hayes, but I can help you. You have a window of opportunity which will stay open for the length of time it takes me to reach your office. Roughly half an hour.'

'I don't understand.'

'I'm prepared to sell the Poacher, but at my price, and today. That's the only offer you'll ever get.'

There was a short silence. 'I'm not in the market for buying restaurants, Mr Hawksley.'

'But Mr Crew is, so I suggest you consult with him before you allow the window to close.'

There was another silence. 'I don't know any Mr Crew.'

Hal ignored this. 'Tell him the Olive Martin case is about to blow wide open.' He gave Roz a broad wink. 'She is already taking legal advice from another solicitor and is expected to lodge an appeal against the terms of her father's will within seven days on the grounds that she is innocent. Crew buys the Poacher today, at my price, or he doesn't buy it at all. You have half an hour, Mr Hayes.' He hung up.

Geoff was waiting on the pavement when they arrived. 'You didn't mention you were bringing company,' he said suspiciously, bending down to look through the open passenger window.

Hal introduced them. 'Sergeant Wyatt, Miss Rosalind Leigh.'

'Jesus, Hal,' he said in disgust. 'What on earth do you want to bring her for?'

'I fancy her.'

Geoff shook his head in exasperation. 'You're mad.'

Hal opened the door and got out. 'I trust you're referring to my motives in bringing her here. If I thought you were impugning my choice, I'd bop you on the nose.' He looked across the roof at Roz who had got out on the other side and was locking her door. 'I think you should stay in the car.'

'Why?'

'You might get your hair pulled.'

'So might you.'

'It's my battle.'

'And mine, if I'm really thinking of making this relationship permanent. Anyway, you need me. I'm the one with the Tampax.'

'They won't work.'

Roz chuckled at the expression on Geoff's face. 'They will. Trust me.'

Hal tipped a finger at Wyatt. 'Now you know why I brought her.'

'You're both bloody mad.' Geoff dropped his cigarette butt on to the pavement and ground it out beneath his heel. 'So what do you want me for? By rights I should be arresting you.' He eyed Roz curiously. 'I suppose he's told you everything.'

'I shouldn't think so,' she said cheerfully, walking round the back of the car. 'I only learnt half an hour ago that his ex-wife's name was Sally and you married her. So, on that basis, there must be an awful lot more still to come.'

'I was referring,' he said sourly, 'to the numerous prosecutions he's about to face when this little farce is over and I take him down the nick.'

'Oh, them.' She gave a dismissive wave. 'Bits of paper, that's all they are.'

Geoff, not altogether happy with his new marital arrangements, watched her amused exchange of glances with Hal and wondered why other people, infinitely less deserving than he, had all the luck. He listened to Hal's instructions for him with a hand pressed to his queasy stomach.

Roz had expected something seedy and run-down like the Wells-Fargo office: instead they walked into a clean, brightly painted reception with an efficient-looking receptionist behind an efficient-looking desk. Someone, she thought, had spent a great deal of money on STC Security. But who? And where had it come from?

Hal favoured the receptionist with his most charming smile. 'Hal Hawksley. Mr Hayes is expecting me.'

'Oh, yes.' She smiled in return. 'He said to show you straight in.' She leaned forward and pointed down the corridor. 'Third door on the left. Perhaps your friends would like to take a seat out here?' She indicated some chairs in the corner.

'Thank you, miss,' said Geoff. 'Don't mind if I do.' He hefted one as he passed and took it with him down the corridor.

'No,' she called, 'I didn't mean take one away.'

He beamed back at her as Hal and Roz disappeared through the third door without knocking and he stationed himself on the chair in the middle of the closed doorway. 'Very comfortable, I must say.' He lit a cigarette and watched, with some amusement, as she picked up the phone and put through a flustered call.

On the other side of the door, Stewart Hayes replaced the receiver. 'I gather from Lisa that you have a minder, Mr Hawksley. Would he be a policeman by any chance?'

'He would.'

'Ah.' He clasped his hands on his desk, apparently unconcerned. 'Sit down, please.' He smiled at Roz and gestured towards a chair.

Fascinated by him, she took it. This was not the man who had tried to strangle her. He was younger, better looking, bluff and friendly like his voice. The brother, she thought, recalling the photographs on the sideboard. He had his father's smile, with all its sincerity, his father's old-world charm, and under different circumstances she would have found him easy to like. Only his eyes, pale and carefully guarded, implied he had something to hide. Hal remained standing.

The smile embraced them both. 'OK, now perhaps you'd like to explain what you said over the telephone. I'll be honest with you' – his tone suggested he was about to be the exact opposite – 'I don't understand why I've been given half an hour to buy a restaurant *from* someone I've never met *for* someone I've never heard of, and all because a self-confessed murderess wants to contest her father's will.'

Hal glanced about the well-appointed office. 'Expensive,' he said. 'You and your brother are doing well.' He fastened speculative eyes on Hayes. 'Your father thinks you're on the breadline.'

Hayes gave a slight frown but didn't say anything.

'So how much does Crew pay for the baseball-bat treatment? It's risky so it won't come cheap.'

The pale eyes showed faint amusement. 'You've lost me, I'm afraid.'

'Your brother was very easy to identify, Hayes. Photographs of him litter your father's sideboard. But then Crew obviously never warned you about the loose cannon on board. Or perhaps you should have warned him. Does he know your father lived next door to Olive Martin?' He saw the other's incomprehension and nodded to Roz. 'This lady is writing a book about her. Crew was Olive's solicitor, I was her arresting officer, and your father was her neighbour.

Miss Leigh has visited us all and she recognized your brother from his snapshot. It is a much smaller world than you ever imagined.'

There was a tiny shift in the pale eyes, a flicker of annoyance. 'Mistaken identity. You'll never prove anything. It's your word against his and he was in Sheffield all last week.'

Hal shrugged well-feigned indifference. 'The window is closing. I came with a genuine offer.' He placed his hands on the desk and leaned forward aggressively. 'I think it runs something like this. Crew has been using Robert Martin's money to buy up bankrupt businesses cheap while he waits for the market to recover, but time's running out on him. Amber's child is not as dead and buried as he thought, and Olive is about to become a *cause célèbre* when Miss Leigh proves her innocent. Either she or her nephew, whoever gets in first, will demand a reckoning of Robert Martin's executor, namely Crew. But the recession has dragged on rather longer than he thought it would and he's in danger of being caught with his hands in the till. He needs to shift some property to make up the shortfall in his books.' He raised an eyebrow. 'What plans are there for the corner of Wenceslas Street, I wonder? A supermarket? Flats? Offices? He needs the Poacher to clinch the deal. I'm offering it to him. Today.'

Hayes wasn't so easily intimidated. 'The way I hear it, Hawksley, your restaurant is about to close anyway.

When it does, it will become a liability to you. At which point it will not be you who dictates terms, but whoever is willing to take it off your hands.'

Hal grinned and backed off. 'I'd say that rather depends on who goes down the chute first. Crew faces total extinction if his misappropriation of the Martin money comes to light before my bank decides to foreclose on the Poacher. Crew's taking a hell of a risk if he's backing me to lose.' He nodded to the telephone. 'He can save himself by clinching a deal on the Poacher today. Talk to him.'

Hayes pondered for a moment, then transferred his gaze to Roz. 'I presume you have a tape-recorder in your handbag, Miss Leigh. Would you oblige me by letting me have a look?'

Roz glanced up at Hal, and he nodded. She placed the bag with a bad grace on the desk in front of her.

'Thank you,' said Hayes politely. He opened it and removed the tape-recorder, making a cursory examination of the remaining contents of the handbag before snapping the recorder open and removing the cassette. He pulled the tape from between the rollers and cut it into pieces with a pair of scissors, then he stood up. 'You first, Hawksley. Let's just make sure there are no other little surprises.' He ran expert hands over Hal, then did the same with Roz. 'Good.' He gestured towards the door. 'Tell your minder to move his chair back to Reception and wait there.'

He resumed his seat and waited while Hal relayed

the message. After three minutes he used the telephone to establish that Wyatt was out of earshot.

'Now,' he said thoughtfully, 'there seem to be various courses open to me. One is to take you up on your offer.' He picked up a ruler and flexed it between his hands. 'I'm not inclined to do that. You could have put the Poacher on the market at any time in the last six weeks but you didn't, and this sudden urge of yours to sell makes me nervous.' He paused for a moment. 'Two, I can leave things to follow their natural course. The law is a joke and a slow joke at that, and there's only a fifty-fifty chance that Peter Crew's manipulations of Robert Martin's estate will surface before you sink.' He bent the ruler as far as it would go without breaking, then released it abruptly. 'I'm not inclined to do that either. Fifty-fifty is too close to call.' The pale eyes hardened. 'Three, and in many ways this is the most attractive, I can wish an unfortunate accident on the pair of you, thereby killing two birds with one stone.' He flicked a glance at Roz. 'Your death, Miss Leigh, would put Olive and this book you're writing, temporarily at least, on a back burner, and yours, Hawksley, would ensure the Poacher coming on the market. A neat solution, don't you think?'

'Very neat,' agreed Hal. 'But you're not going to do that either. There's still the child in Australia, after all.'

Hayes gave a faint laugh. An echo of his father.

'So what are you going to do?'

'Give you what you came for.'

Hal frowned. 'Which is?'

'Proof that you were framed.' He pulled open a drawer in his desk and removed a transparent polythene folder. Holding it by its top corners he shook the contents – a page of headed notepaper, showing creases where it had once been crumpled – on to his desk. The printed address was a house in one of the more expensive parts of Southampton and written across the page in Crew's handwriting were a series of short notes:

Re: Poacher	Cost £s
Pre-culture bad meat, rat excrement etc	1,000
Key b/door + guaranteed exit/France	1,000
Advance for set-up	5,000
If E H prosecution successful	5,000
Poacher foreclosure	80,000?
SUB-TOTAL	92,000
Site offer	750,000
Less Poacher	92,000
Less 1 Wenceslas St	60,000
Less Newby's	73,000
TOTAL	525,000

'It's genuine,' said Hayes, seeing Hal's scepticism. 'Crew's home address, Crew's handwriting' – he tapped the side of the note with his ruler – 'and his fingerprints. It's enough to get you off the hook but whether it's enough to convict Crew I don't know. That's your problem, not mine.'

'Where did you get it?'

But Hayes merely smiled and shook his head. 'I'm an ex-soldier. I like fall-back positions. Let's just say it came into my possession and, realizing its importance, I passed it on to you.'

Hal wondered if Crew knew the sort of man he had hired. Had this been intended for later blackmail? 'I don't get it,' he said frankly. 'Crew is bound to implicate you. So will I. So will Miss Leigh. One way or another you and your brother will get done. Why make it easy for us?'

Hayes didn't answer directly. 'I'm cutting my losses, Hawksley, and giving you your restaurant back. Be grateful.'

'Like hell, I'll be grateful,' said Hal angrily. His eyes narrowed suspiciously. 'Who's behind this foreclosure racket? You or Crew?'

'There's no racket. Foreclosures are a fact of life at the moment,' said the other. 'Anyone with a little capital can acquire property cheaply. Mr Crew was part of a small perfectly legal syndicate. Unfortunately, he used money that didn't belong to him.'

'So you run the syndicate?'

Hayes didn't answer.

'No racket, my arse,' said Hal explosively. 'The Poacher was never going to come on the market yet you still bought up the properties on either side.'

Hayes flexed the ruler again. 'You'd have sold eventually. Restaurants are appallingly vulnerable.' He gave a slight smile. 'Consider what would have happened if Crew had kept his nerve and sat it out till after your prosecution.' His eyes hardened. 'Consider what would have happened if my brother had told me about the approach Crew made to him. You and I would never have had this conversation for the simple reason that you would not have known who to have it with.'

The flesh crept on Hal's neck. 'The hygiene scam was going to happen anyway?'

The ruler, bent beyond endurance, snapped abruptly. Hayes smiled. 'Restaurants are appallingly vulnerable,' he said again. 'I repeat. Be grateful. If you are, the Poacher will flourish.'

'Which is another way of saying we must keep our mouths shut about your involvement.'

'Of course.' He looked almost surprised, as if the question went without asking. 'Because next time, the fire won't be confined to a chip pan, and you' – his pale eyes rested on Roz – 'and your lady friend won't be so lucky. My brother's pride was hurt. He's itching to have another go at the pair of you.' He pointed to the piece of notepaper. 'You can do what you like with Crew. I don't admire men without principle. He's a lawyer. He had a duty to a dead man's estate and he abused it.'

Hal, rather shaken, picked up the page by its corner and tucked it into Roz's handbag. 'You're no better, Hayes. You abused Crew's confidence when you told your father about Amber's child. But for that we'd never have put Crew in the frame.' He waited while Roz stood up and walked to the door. 'And I'll make damn sure he knows that when the police arrest him.'

Hayes was amused. 'Crew won't talk.'

'What's to stop him?'

He drew the broken ruler across his throat. 'The same thing that will stop you, Hawksley. Fear.' The pale eyes raked Roz from head to toe. 'But in Crew's case, it's his grandchildren he loves.'

Geoff followed them out on to the pavement. 'OK,' he ordered, 'give. What the hell's going on here?'

Hal looked at Roz's pale face. 'We need a drink.'

'Oh, no, you don't,' said Geoff aggressively. 'I've paid my dues, Hal, now you pay yours.'

Hal gripped him fiercely above the elbow, digging his fingers into the soft flesh. 'Keep your voice down, you cretin,' he muttered. 'There's a man in there who would take out your liver, eat it in front of you, and then start on your kidneys. And he'd smile while he was doing it. Where's the nearest pub?'

Not until they were settled in a tight corner of the

saloon, with empty tables all around them, was Hal prepared to speak. He delivered the story in clipped, staccato sentences, emphasizing Crew's role but referring to the intruders at the Poacher only as hired thugs. He finished by removing the note from Roz's handbag and laying it carefully on the table between them. 'I want this bastard screwed, Geoff. Don't even think about letting him worm his way out of it.'

Wyatt was sceptical. 'It's not much, is it?'

'It'll do.'

Wyatt slipped the page into his notebook and tucked it into his jacket pocket. 'So where does STC Security fit in?'

'It doesn't. Hayes got hold of that note for me. That's the extent of his firm's involvement.'

'Ten minutes ago he was going to eat my liver.'

'I was thirsty.'

Wyatt shrugged. 'You're giving me precious little to work with. I can't even guarantee you'll win the Environmental Health prosecution. Crew's bound to deny having anything to do with it.'

There was a silence.

'He's right,' said Roz abruptly, removing a packet of Tampax from her bag.

Hal grasped the hand holding the box and pressed it firmly to the table. 'No, Roz,' he said softly. 'Believe it or not, I care more about you than I do about the Poacher or about abstract justice.'

She nodded. 'I know, Hawksley,' Her eyes smiled

into his. 'The trouble is, I care about *you*, too. Which means we're in a bit of a fix. You want to save me and I want to save the Poacher, and the two would seem to be mutually exclusive.' She started to ease her hands from under his. 'So one of us must win this argument, and it's going to be me because this has nothing to do with abstract justice and everything to do with my peace of mind. I shall feel much happier with Stewart Hayes behind bars.' She shook her head as his hands moved to smother hers again. 'I won't be responsible for you losing your restaurant, Hal. You've gone through hell for it, and you can't give it up now.'

But Hal was no Rupert to be browbeaten or cajoled into doing what Roz wanted. 'No,' he said again. 'We're not playing intellectual games here. What Hayes said was *real*. And he's not threatening to kill you, Roz. He's threatening to maim you.' He lifted one hand to her face. 'Men like him don't kill because they don't need to. They cripple or they disfigure, because a live, broken victim is a more potent encouragement to others than a dead one.'

'But if he's convicted—' she began.

'You're being naïve again,' he cut in gently, smoothing the hair from her face. 'Even if he is convicted, which I doubt – ex-Army, first offence, hearsay evidence, Crew denying everything – he won't go to jail for any length of time. The worst that will happen will be twelve months for conspiracy to defraud, of which he'll serve six. More likely he will be given a suspended sentence. It wasn't Stewart who broke into the Poacher with a baseball bat, remember, it was his brother, and you will have to stand up in court and say that.' His eyes were insistent. 'I'm a realist, Roz. We'll go for Crew and raise enough doubts to get the Health charges lifted. After that' – he shrugged – 'I'll gamble that Hayes can be trusted to leave the Poacher alone.'

She was silent for a moment or two. 'Would you act differently if you'd never met me and I wasn't involved? And don't lie to me, Hal, please.'

He nodded. 'Yes,' he admitted. 'I would act differently. But you *are* involved, so the question doesn't arise.'

'OK.' She relaxed her hands under his and smiled. 'Thank you. I feel much happier now.'

'You agree.' Relieved, he lessened his pressure slightly and she seized the opportunity to snatch the Tampax box out of his grasp.

'No,' she said, 'I don't.' She opened the box, removed some truncated cardboard tubes and upended it to disgorge a miniature voice-activated dictaphone. 'With luck' – she turned to Geoff Wyatt – 'this will have enough on it to convict Hayes. It was at full volume, sitting on his desk, so it should have caught him.'

She rewound the tape for a second or two and then pressed 'play'. Hal's voice was muffled by distance: '. . . *another way of saying we must keep our mouths shut about your involvement with the Poacher?*'

Hayes's, clear as a bell. '*Of course. Because next time, the fire won't be confined to the chip pan, and you and your lady friend won't be so lucky. My brother's pride was hurt. He's itching to have another go at the pair of you.*'

Roz switched it off and pushed it across the table towards Wyatt. 'Will it do any good?'

'If there's more like that, it will certainly help with Hal's prosecution, as long as you're prepared to give evidence to support it.'

'I am.'

He cast a glance at his friend, saw the tension on the other's face and turned back to Roz. 'But Hal's right in everything he's said, assuming I've understood the gist correctly. We *are* talking abstract justice here.' He picked up the dictaphone. 'At the end of the day – whatever sentence this man gets – if he still wants to revenge himself on you, he will. And there's nothing the police will be able to do to protect you. So? Are you sure you want me to take this?'

'I'm sure.'

Wyatt looked at Hal again and gave a helpless shrug. 'Sorry, old man. I did my best, but it looks like you've caught a tigress this time.'

Hal gave his baritone chuckle. 'Don't say it, Geoff, because I already know.'

But Wyatt said it anyway. 'You lucky, bloody sod.'

*

Olive sat hunched over her table, working on a new sculpture. Eve and her faces and her baby had collapsed under the weight of a fist, leaving the pencil pointing heavenward like an accusing finger. The Chaplain regarded the new piece thoughtfully. A bulky shape, roughly human and lying on its back, seemed to be struggling from its clay base. Strange, he thought, how Olive, with so little skill, made these figures work. 'What are you sculpting now?'

'MAN.'

He could, he thought, have predicted that. He watched the fingers roll a thick sausage of clay and plant it upright on the base at the figure's head. 'Adam?' he suggested. He had the feeling she was playing a game with him. There had been a surge of sudden activity when he entered her room, as if she had been waiting for him to break hours of stillness.

'Cain.' She selected another pencil and laid it across the top of the clay sausage, parallel with the recumbent man, pressing it down till it was held firmly. 'Faustus. Don Giovanni. Does it matter?'

'Yes, it does,' he said sharply. 'Not all men sell their souls to the devil, any more than all women are two-faced.'

Olive smiled to herself and cut a piece of string from a ball on the table. She made a loop in one end and fastened the other round the tip of the pencil so that the string hung down over the figure's head.

With infinite care, she tightened the loop about a matchstick. 'Well?' she demanded.

The Chaplain frowned. 'I don't know. The gallows?'

She set the matchstick swinging. 'Or the sword of Damocles. It amounts to the same thing when Lucifer owns your soul.'

He perched on the edge of the table and offered her a cigarette. 'It's not Man in general, is it?' he said, flicking his lighter. 'It's someone specific. Am I right?'

'Maybe.'

'Who?'

She fished a letter from her pocket and handed it to him. He spread the single page on the table and read it. It was a standard letter, personalized on a word processor, and very brief.

Dear Miss Martin,

Please be advised that unforeseen circumstances have obliged Mr Peter Crew to take extended leave from this practice. During his absence his clients' affairs will be covered by his partners. Please be assured of our continued assistance.

Yours etc.

The Chaplain looked up. 'I don't understand.'

Olive inhaled deeply then blew a stream of smoke towards the matchstick. It spiralled wildly before slipping from the noose and striking the clay forehead. 'My solicitor's been arrested.'

Startled, he looked at the clay figure. He didn't bother to ask if she was sure. He knew the efficiency of the cell telegraph as well as she did. 'What for?'

'Wickedness.' She stubbed her cigarette into the clay. 'MAN was born to it. Even you, Chaplain.' She peeped at him to watch his reaction.

He chuckled. 'You're probably right. But I do my best to fight it, you know.'

She took another of his cigarettes. 'I shall miss you,' she said unexpectedly.

'When?'

'When they let me out.'

He looked at her with a puzzled smile. 'That's a long way off. We've years yet.'

But she shook her head and mashed the clay into a ball with the dog end in the middle. 'You never asked me who Eve was.'

The game again, he thought. 'I didn't need to, Olive. I knew.'

She smiled scornfully to herself. 'Yes, you would.' She examined him out of the corner of her eye. 'Did you work it out for yourself?' she asked. 'Or did God tell you? Look, my son, Olive strikes her reflection in the clay. Now help her to come to terms with her own duplicity. Well, don't worry, either way I shall remember what you did for me when I get out.'

What did she want from him? Encouragement that

she *would* get out, or rescuing from her lies? He sighed inwardly. Really, it would all be so much easier if he liked her, but he didn't. And *that* was his wickedness.

Nineteen

OLIVE REGARDED ROZ with deep suspicion. Contentment had brought a glow to the other woman's usually pale cheeks. 'You look different,' she said in an accusing tone as if what she saw displeased her.

Roz shook her head. 'No. Everything's the same.' Lies *were* safer sometimes. She was afraid Olive would regard her moving in with the police officer who arrested her as a betrayal. 'Did you get my message last Monday night?'

Olive was at her most unattractive, unwashed hair hanging limply about her colourless face, a smear of tomato ketchup ground into the front of her shift, the smell of her sweat almost unbearable in the small room. She vibrated with irritation, her forehead set in a permanent scowl, ready, it seemed to Roz, to reject anything that was said to her. She didn't answer.

'Is something wrong?' Roz asked evenly.

'I don't want to see you any more.'

Roz turned her pencil in her fingers. 'Why not?'

'I don't have to give a reason.'

'It would be polite,' said Roz in the same even tone. 'I've invested a great deal of time, energy, and affection in you. I thought we were friends.'

Olive's lip curled. 'Friends,' she hissed scathingly. 'We're not friends. You're Miss Wonderful making money out of doing her Lady Muck bit and I'm the poor sap who's being exploited.' She splayed her hands across the table top and tried to get up. 'I don't want you to write your book.'

'Because you'd rather be treated with awe in here than laughed at outside.' Roz shook her head. 'You're a fool, Olive. And a coward as well. I thought you had more guts.'

Olive pursed her fat lips as she struggled to rise. 'I'm not listening,' she said childishly. 'You're trying to make me change my mind.'

'Of course I am.' She rested her cheek against one raised hand. 'I shall write the book whether you want me to or not. I'm not afraid of you, you see. You can instruct a solicitor to take out an injunction to stop me, but he won't succeed because I shall argue that you're innocent, and a court will uphold my right to publish in the interests of natural justice.'

Olive slumped back on to her chair. 'I'll write to a Civil Liberties group. They'll support me.'

'Not when they find out I'm trying to get you released, they won't. They'll support *me*.'

'The Court of Human Rights, then. I'll say what you're doing is an invasion of my privacy.'

'Go ahead. You'll make me a fortune. Everyone will buy the book to find out what the fuss is all about. And if it's argued in a court, whichever one it is, I shall make damn sure this time that the evidence is heard.'

'What evidence?'

'The evidence that proves you didn't do it.'

Olive slammed a meaty fist on to the table. 'I did do it.'

'No, you didn't.'

'I *did*!' roared the fat woman.

'You did not,' said Roz, her eyes flashing with anger. 'When will you face up to the fact that your mother is dead, you silly woman.' She banged the table in her turn. 'She's not there for you any more, Olive, and she never will be, however long you hide in here.'

Two fat tears rolled down Olive's cheeks. 'I don't like you.'

Roz continued brutally. 'You came home, saw what your precious lover had done, and went into shock. And God knows, I don't blame you.' She took the mortuary photographs of Gwen and Amber from her bag and slapped them on the table in front of Olive. 'You adored your mother, didn't you? You always adore the people who need you.'

Olive's anger was enormous. 'That's *crap*, bloody fucking *crap*!'

Roz shook her head. 'I needed you. That's how I know.'

Olive's lip trembled. 'You wanted to know how it felt to kill someone, that's all you needed me for.'

'No.' Roz reached across and took a large, soft hand in hers. 'I needed someone to love. You're very easy to love, Olive.'

The woman tore the hand away and clamped it across her face. 'No one loves me,' she whispered. 'No one's ever loved me.'

'You're wrong,' said Roz firmly. 'I love you. Sister Bridget loves you. And we are not going to abandon you the minute you get out. You must trust us.' She closed her mind on the insidious voice that murmured warnings against a long-term commitment she could never keep and against well-meant lies that could so easily rebound on her. 'Tell me about Amber,' she went on gently. 'Tell me why your mother needed you.'

A sigh of surrender shuddered through the huge frame. 'She wanted her own way all the time, and if she didn't get it she made life hell for everyone. She told lies about things people did to her, spread awful stories, even hurt people sometimes. She poured boiling water down my mother's arm once to punish her, so we used to give in just to make life easy. She was as nice as pie as long as everyone did what she wanted.' She licked the tears from her lips. 'She never took responsibility, you see, but it got worse after the baby was born. Mum said she stopped maturing.'

'To compensate herself?'

'No, to excuse herself.' She twined her fingers in the front of her dress. 'Children get away with behaving badly so Amber went on behaving like a child. She was never told off for getting pregnant. We were too afraid of how she would react.' She wiped her nose with the back of her hand. 'Mum had made up her mind to take her to a psychiatrist. She thought Amber had schizophrenia.' She sighed heavily. 'Then they were killed and it didn't matter any more.'

Roz passed her a Kleenex and waited while she blew her nose. 'Why did she never behave badly at school?'

'She did,' said Olive flatly, 'if people teased her or took her things without asking. I used to have to get quite angry to stop them doing it, but most of the time I made sure no one got on her bad side. She was a lovely person as long as she wasn't crossed. Really,' she insisted, 'a lovely person.'

'The two faces of Eve.'

'Mum certainly thought so.' She took the cigarette packet out of Roz's open briefcase and stripped away the cellophane. 'I used to keep her with me when she wasn't in class. She didn't mind that. The older girls treated her like a pet and that made her feel special.

She had no friends of her own age.' She pulled some cigarettes on to the table and selected one.

'How did she hold down a job? You weren't there to protect her then.'

'She didn't. She never lasted anywhere longer than a month. Most of the time she stayed at home with Mum. She made Mum's life a misery.'

'What about Glitzy?'

Olive struck a match and lit the cigarette. 'The same. She'd only done three weeks and she was already talking about leaving. There was some trouble with the other girls. Amber got one of them sacked or something. I can't remember now. Anyway, that's when Mum said enough was enough, and she'd have to see a psychiatrist.'

Roz sat in thoughtful silence for some moments. 'I know who your lover was,' she said abruptly. 'I know that you spent Sundays at the Belvedere in Farraday Street and that you signed in as Mr and Mrs Lewis. I've had his photograph identified by the owner of the Belvedere and by the receptionist at Wells-Fargo. I think he abandoned you in a hotel the night of your birthday when you told him you had aborted his baby, and that he went straight to Leven Road to have it out with Amber and your mother whom he regarded as jointly responsible for the murder of the son or daughter he had always wanted. I think your father was out of the house that night and that the whole thing got out of hand. I think you came home a long time afterwards, discovered the bodies, and went to pieces because you thought it was all your fault.' She took one of Olive's hands in hers again and squeezed it tightly.

Olive closed her eyes and wept quietly, her soft skin caressing Roz's fingers. 'No,' she said at last, releasing the hand. 'It didn't happen like that. I wish it had. At least I'd know then why I did what I did.' Her eyes were curiously unfocused as if they were turned inwards upon herself. 'We didn't plan anything for my birthday,' she said. 'We couldn't. It wasn't a Sunday and Sundays were the only days we could ever be together. That was when his sister-in-law came over to give him some time away from his wife. They both thought he spent the day at the British Legion.' She smiled but there was no humour in it. 'Poor Edward. He was so afraid they'd find out and turn him off without a penny. It was her house and her money and it made him miserable. Puddleglum was such a good name for him, especially when he wore his silly wig. He looked just like a marshwiggle out of Narnia, tall and skinny and hairy.' She sighed. 'It was supposed to be a disguise, you know, in case anyone saw him. To me, it just looked funny. I liked him much better bald.' She sighed again. '*The Silver Chair* was Amber's and my favourite book when we were children.'

Roz had guessed. 'And you signed in as Mr and Mrs Lewis because it was C. S. Lewis who wrote it.

Were you afraid of Mrs Clarke finding out, or your parents?'

'We were afraid of everyone but mostly of Amber. Jealousy was a disease with her.'

'Did she know about your abortion?'

Olive shook her head. 'Only my mother knew. I never told Edward and I certainly didn't tell Amber. *She* was the only one who was allowed to have sex in our house. She did, too. All the time. Mum had to force her to take the pill every night so she didn't get pregnant again.' She pulled a long face. 'Mum was furious when I fell. We both knew Amber would go mad.'

'Is that why you had the abortion?'

'Probably. It seemed the only sensible solution at the time. I regret it now.'

'You'll have other chances.'

'I doubt it.'

'So what did happen that night?' asked Roz after a moment or two.

Olive stared at her unblinkingly through the smoke from her cigarette. 'Amber found the birthday present Edward had given me. It was well hidden but she used to pry into everything.' Her mouth twisted. 'I was always having to put things back that she'd taken. People thought I was the snooper.' She encircled her wrist with finger and thumb. 'It was an identity bracelet with a tiny silver-chair charm on it. He'd had the tag inscribed: u.r.n.a.r.n.i.a. Do you get it? You are

Narnia, Narnia being heaven.' She smiled self-consciously. 'I thought it was wonderful.'

'He was very fond of you.' It was a statement, not a question.

'I made him feel young again.' Tears squeezed from between the bald lids. 'We really didn't harm anyone, just conducted a quiet little affair now and then on Sundays which gave us both something to look forward to.' The tears flowed down her cheeks. 'I wish I hadn't done it now but it was nice to feel special. I never had before and I was so jealous of Amber. She had a lot of boyfriends. She used to take them upstairs. Mum was too frightened of her to say anything.' She sobbed loudly. 'They always laughed at me. I hate being laughed at.'

What a dreadful household it must have been, thought Roz, with each one desperately seeking love but never finding it. Would they have recognized it, anyway, if they had? She waited until Olive had composed herself a little. 'Did your mother know it was Edward?'

'No. I told her it was someone at work. We were very careful. Edward was my father's best friend. It would have devastated everyone if they'd known what we were doing.' She fell silent. 'Well, of course, it did devastate them in the end.'

'They found out.'

The sad head nodded. 'Amber guessed the minute she found the bracelet. I should have known she would. Silver chair, Narnia. The bracelet had to be from Puddleglum.' She sucked in a lungful of smoke.

Roz watched her for a moment. 'What did she do?' she asked when Olive didn't go on.

'What she always did when she was angry. Started a fight. She kept pulling my hair, I remember that. And screaming. Mum and Dad had to tear us apart. I ended up in a tug of war with my father gripping my wrists and tugging one way while Amber tugged my hair the other. All hell broke loose then. She kept yelling that I was having an affair with Mr Clarke.' She stared wretchedly at the table. 'My mother looked as if she was going to be sick – nobody likes the idea of old men getting excited about young girls – I used to see it in the eyes of the woman at the Belvedere.' She turned the cigarette in her fingers. 'But now, you know, I think it was because Mum knew that Edward and my father were doing it as well. That's what really made her sick. Makes *me* sick now.'

'Why didn't you deny it?'

Olive puffed unhappily on her cigarette. 'There was no point. She knew Amber was telling the truth. I suppose it's a kind of instinctive thing. You learn a fact and lots of other little bits and pieces, which didn't make sense at the time, suddenly slot into place. Anyway, all three of them started screeching at me then, my mother in shock, my father in fury.' She shrugged. 'I'd never seen Dad so angry. Mum let out about the abortion and he kept slapping my face and calling me a slut. And Amber kept screaming that he was jealous because he loved Edward, too, and it was so awful' – her eyes welled – 'that I left.' There was a rather comical expression on her face. 'And when I came back the next day there was blood everywhere and Mum and Amber were dead.'

'You stayed out all night?'

Olive nodded. 'And most of the morning.'

'But that's good,' said Roz leaning forward. 'We can prove that. Where did you go?'

'I walked to the beach.' She stared at her hands. 'I was going to kill myself. I wish I had now. I just sat there all night and thought about it instead.'

'Did anyone see you?'

'No. I didn't want to be seen. When it got light I hid behind a dinghy every time I heard someone coming.'

'What time did you get back?'

'About noon. I hadn't had anything to eat and I was hungry.'

'Did you speak to anyone?'

Olive sighed wearily. 'Nobody saw me. If they had I wouldn't be here.'

'How did you get into the house? Did you have a key?'

'Yes.'

'Why?' demanded Roz sharply. 'You said you left. I assumed you just walked out as you were.'

Olive's eyes widened. 'I knew you wouldn't believe

me,' she howled. 'No one believes me when I tell the truth.' She started to cry again.

'I do believe you,' said Roz firmly. 'I just want to get it straight.'

'I went to my room first and got my things. I only went out because they were all making so much noise.' She screwed her face in distress. 'My father was weeping. It was horrible.'

'OK. Go on. You're back at the house.'

'I let myself in and went down to the kitchen to get some food. I stepped in all the blood before I even knew it was there.' She looked at the photograph of her mother and the ready tears sprang into her eyes afresh. 'I really don't like to think about it too much. It makes me sick when I think about it.' Her lower lip wobbled violently.

'OK,' said Roz easily, 'let's concentrate on something else. What made you stay? Why didn't you run out into the road and call for help?'

Olive mopped at her eyes. 'I couldn't move,' she said simply. 'I wanted to, but I couldn't. I just stood there thinking how ashamed my mother would be when people saw her without her clothes on.' Her lip kept wobbling like some grotesque toddler's. 'I felt so ill. I wanted to sit down but there wasn't a chair.' She held her hand to her mouth and swallowed convulsively. 'And then Mrs Clarke started banging on the kitchen window. She kept screaming that God would never forgive my wickedness, and there was dribble coming out of her mouth.' A shudder ran through the big shoulders. 'I knew I had to shut her up because she was making it all so much worse. So I picked up the rolling pin and ran across to the back door.' She sighed. 'But I fell over and she wasn't there any more anyway.'

'Is that when you called the police?'

'No.' The wet face worked horribly. 'I can't remember it all now. I went mad for a bit because I had their blood all over me and I kept scraping my hands to clean them. But everything I touched was bloody.' Her eyes widened at the memory. 'I've always been so clumsy and the floor was slippery. I kept stumbling over them and disturbing them and then I had to touch them to put them back again and there was more blood on me.' The sorrowful eyes flooded again. 'And I thought, this is all my fault. If I'd never been born this would never have happened. I sat down for a long time because I felt sick.'

Roz looked at the bowed head in bewilderment. 'But why didn't you tell the police all this?'

She raised drowned blue eyes to Roz's. 'I was going to, but nobody would talk to me. They all thought I'd done it, you see. And all the time I was thinking how it was all going to come out, about Edward and me, and Edward and my father, and the abortion, and Amber, and her baby, and I thought how much less embarrassing it would be for everyone if I said I did it.'

Roz kept her voice deliberately steady. 'Who did you think had done it?'

Olive looked miserable. 'I didn't think about that for ages.' She hunched her shoulders as if defending herself. 'And then I knew my father had done it and they'd find me guilty whatever happened because he was the only one who could save me.' She plucked at her lips. 'And after that, it was quite a relief just to say what everyone wanted me to say. I didn't want to go home, you see, not with Mum dead, and Edward next door and everyone knowing. I couldn't possibly have gone home.'

'How did you know your father had done it?'

A whimper of pure pain, like a wounded animal's, crooned from Olive's mouth. 'Because Mr Crew was so beastly to me.' Sorrow poured in floods down her cheeks. 'He used to come to our house sometimes and he'd pat me on the shoulder and say: "How's Olive?" But in the police station' – she buried her face in her hands – 'he held a handkerchief to his mouth to stop himself being sick and stood on the other side of the room and said: "Don't say anything to me or the police, or I won't be able to help you." I knew then.'

Roz frowned. 'How? I don't understand.'

'Because Dad was the only person who knew I wasn't there, but he never said a word to Mr Crew before, or to the police afterwards. Dad must have done it or he'd have tried to save me. He let me go to prison because he was a coward.' She sobbed loudly. 'And then he died and left his money to Amber's child when he could have left a letter, saying I was innocent.' She beat her hands against her knees. 'What did it matter once he was dead?'

Roz took the cigarette from Olive's fingers and stood it on the table. 'Why didn't you tell the police you thought it was your father who had done it? Sergeant Hawksley would have listened to you. He already suspected your father.'

The fat woman stared at the table. 'I don't want to tell you.'

'You must, Olive.'

'You'll laugh.'

'Tell me.'

'I was hungry.'

Roz shook her head in perplexity. 'I don't understand.'

'The sergeant brought me a sandwich and said I could have a proper dinner when we'd finished the statement.' Her eyes welled again. 'I hadn't eaten all day and I was so hungry,' she wailed. 'It was quicker when I said what they wanted me to say and then I got my dinner.' She wrung her hands. 'People will laugh, won't they?'

Roz wondered why it had never occurred to her that Olive's insatiable craving for food might have been a contributory factor in her confession. Mrs Hopwood had described her as a compulsive eater and stress would have piled on the agonies of the wretched girl's hunger. 'No,' she said firmly, 'no one will laugh. But why did you insist on pleading guilty at your trial? You could have made a fight of it then. You'd had time to think and get over the shock.'

Olive wiped her eyes. 'It was too late. I'd confessed. I had nothing to fight with except diminished responsibility and I wasn't going to let Mr Crew call me a psychopath. I hate Mr Crew.'

'But if you'd told someone the truth they might have believed you. You've told me and I've believed you.'

Olive shook her head. 'I've told you nothing,' she said simply. 'Everything you know you've found out for yourself. That's why you believe it.' Her eyes flooded again. 'I did try at the beginning, when I first came to prison. I told the Chaplain but he doesn't like me and thought I was telling lies. I'd confessed, you see, and only the guilty confess. The psychiatrists were the most frightening. I thought if I denied the crime and didn't show any remorse, they'd say I was sociopathic and send me to Broadmoor.'

Roz looked at the bent head with compassion. Olive had never really stood a chance. And who was to blame at the end of the day? Mr Crew? Robert Martin? The police? Poor Gwen even, whose dependence on her daughter had mapped Olive's life. Michael Jackson had said it all: 'She was one of those people you only think about when you want something done and then you remember them with relief because you know they'll do it.' It had never been Amber who set out to please, she thought, only Olive, and as a result she had grown completely dependent herself. With no one to tell her what to do she had taken the line of least resistance.

'You'll be hearing this officially in the next few days but I'm damned if you should have to wait for it. Mr Crew is on bail at the moment, charged with embezzlement of your father's money and conspiracy to defraud. He may also be charged with conspiracy to murder.' There was a long pause before Olive looked up.

The strange awareness was back in her eyes, a look of triumphant confirmation that made the hair prickle on the back of Roz's neck. She thought of Sister Bridget's simple assertion of *her* truth: *You were chosen, Roz, and I wasn't.* And Olive's truth? What was Olive's truth?

'I know already.' Idly Olive removed a pin from the front of her dress. 'Prison grapevine,' she explained. 'Mr Crew hired the Hayes brothers to do over Sergeant Hawksley's restaurant. You were there, and you and the Sergeant got beaten up. I'm sorry about that but I'm not sorry about anything else. I never liked Mr Hayes much. He always ignored me and talked to Amber.' She stuck the pin into the tabletop. Bits of dried clay and wax still clung to the head.

Roz arched an eyebrow at the pin. 'It's superstitious rubbish, Olive.'

'You said it works if you believe in it.'

Roz shrugged. 'I was joking.'

'*The Encyclopaedia Britannica* doesn't joke.' Olive chanted in a sing-song voice: 'Page 96, volume 25, general heading: Occultism.' She clapped her hands excitedly like an over-boisterous child and raised her voice to a shout. ' "*Witchcraft worked in Salem because the persons involved believed in it.*" ' She saw the frown of alarm on Roz's face. 'It's all nonsense,' she said calmly. 'Will Mr Crew be convicted?'

'I don't know. He's claiming that your father gave him the go-ahead, as executor, to invest the money while the searches were made for your nephew, and the bugger is' – she smiled grimly – 'if the property market takes off again, which it probably will, his investments look very healthy.' Of the other charges, only the conspiracy to defraud Hal of the Poacher had any chance of sticking, purely because Stewart Hayes's brother, a far weaker character than Stewart, had collapsed under police questioning. 'He's denying everything, but the police seem fairly optimistic they can pin assault charges on both him and the Hayes boys. I'd give anything to get him for negligence where your case was concerned. Was he one of the people you tried to tell the truth to?'

'No,' said Olive regretfully. 'There was no point.

He'd been Dad's solicitor for years. He'd never have believed Dad had done it.'

Roz started to gather her bits and pieces together. 'Your father didn't kill your mother and sister, Olive. He thought *you* did. Gwen and Amber were alive when he went to work the next morning. As far as he was concerned, your statement was completely true.'

'But he knew I wasn't there.'

Roz shook her head. 'I'll never be able to prove it but I don't suppose he even realized you'd gone. He slept downstairs, remember, and I'll bet a pound to a penny you slipped out quietly to avoid attracting attention to yourself. If you'd only agreed to see him, you'd have sorted it out.' She stood up. 'It's water under the bridge, but you shouldn't have punished him, Olive. He was no more guilty than you are. He loved you. He just wasn't very good at showing it. I suspect his only fault was to take too little notice of the clothes women wore.'

Olive shook her head. 'I don't understand.'

'He told the police your mother owned a nylon overall.'

'Why would he do that?'

Roz sighed. 'I suppose because he didn't want to admit he never looked at her. He wasn't a bad man, Olive. He couldn't help his sexuality any more than you or I can help ours. The tragedy for you all was that none of you could talk about it.' She took the pin from the tabletop and wiped the head clean. 'And

I don't believe for one moment that he would ever have blamed you for what happened. Only himself. That's why he went on living in the house. It was his atonement.'

A large tear rolled down Olive's cheek. 'He always said the game wasn't worth the candle.' She held out her hand for the pin. 'If I'd loved him less I'd have hated him less, and it wouldn't be too late now, would it?'

Twenty

HAL WAS DOZING in the car outside, arms crossed, an old cap pulled over his eyes to block out the sun. He raised his head and surveyed Roz lazily from under the brim as she tugged open the driver's door. 'Well?'

She dumped her briefcase on the back seat and slipped in behind the wheel. 'She shot my version down in flames.' She gunned the engine into life and reversed out of the parking slot.

Hal eyed her thoughtfully. 'So where are we going?'

'To tear strips off Edward,' she told him. 'He's had nothing like the punishment he deserves.'

'Is that wise? I thought he was a psychopath.' Hal pulled the cap over his eyes again and settled down for another snooze. 'Still, I'm sure you know what you're doing.' His faith in Roz was unshakeable. She had more bottle than most of the men he knew.

'I do.' She inserted the tape she had just made into the deck and rewound it. 'But you don't, Sergeant, so cock an ear to this. I'm inclined to think it's you I should be tearing strips off. The wretched child – because let's face it, that's all she really is, even now – was starving, and you promised her a "proper dinner" when she'd finished her statement. No wonder she couldn't confess fast enough. If she'd told you she *hadn't* done it you'd have kept her waiting for her food.' She turned the volume up full blast.

It took several rings of the doorbell before Edward Clarke finally opened the door to them on the burglar chain. He gestured angrily for them to go away. 'You have no business here,' he hissed at Roz. 'I shall call the police if you persist in harassing us.'

Hal moved into his line of sight, smiling pleasantly. 'Detective Sergeant Hawksley, Mr Clarke. Dawlington CID. The Olive Martin case. I'm sure you remember me.'

A look of dejected recognition crossed Edward's face. 'I thought we'd done with all that.'

'I'm afraid not. May we come in?'

The man hesitated briefly and Roz wondered if he was going to call Hal's bluff and demand identification. Apparently not. The ingrained British respect for authority ran deep with him. He rattled the chain and opened the door, his shoulders slumped in weary defeat. 'I knew Olive would talk eventually,' he said. 'She wouldn't be human if she didn't.' He showed them into the sitting room. 'But on my word I knew nothing about the murders. If I'd had any idea what she was like, do you really think I'd have befriended her?'

Roz took the chair she had sat in before and surreptitiously switched on the tape-recorder in her handbag. Hal walked to the window and looked out. Mrs Clarke was sitting on the small patio at the back of the house, her face, vacant of expression, turned towards the sun. 'You and Olive were rather more than friends,' he said without hostility, turning back into the room.

'We didn't harm anyone,' said Mr Clarke, unconsciously echoing Olive. Roz wondered how old he was. Seventy? He looked more, worn out by care of his wife perhaps. The rough wig she had painted on cellophane over his photograph had been a revelation. It was quite true that hair made a man look younger. He squeezed his hands between his knees as if unsure what to do with them. 'Or should I say we did not set out with the intention to harm anyone. What Olive did was incomprehensible to me.'

'But you felt no responsibility for it?'

He stared at the carpet, unable to look at either of them. 'I assumed she had always been unstable,' he said.

'Why?'

'Her sister was. I thought it was a genetic thing.'

'So she behaved oddly before the murders?'

'No,' he admitted. 'As I say, I wouldn't have

pursued' – he paused – 'the – relationship – if I had known the kind of person she was.'

Hal changed tack. 'What exactly was your relationship with Olive's father?'

He clamped his knees tighter about his hands. 'Friendly.'

'How friendly?'

Mr Clarke sighed. 'Does it matter now? It was a long time ago and Robert is dead.' His eyes drifted towards the window.

'It matters,' said Hal brusquely.

'We were very friendly.'

'Did you have a sexual relationship?'

'Briefly.' His hands struggled from between his knees and he buried his face in them. 'It sounds so sordid now, but it really wasn't. You have to understand how lonely I was. God knows it's not her fault, but my wife has never been much in the way of a companion. We married late, no children, and her mind has never been strong. I became her nurse and keeper before we'd been married five years, imprisoned in my own house with someone I could barely communicate with.' He swallowed painfully. 'Robert's friendship was all I had and he, as you obviously know, was homosexual. His marriage was as much a prison as mine, though for different reasons.' He pressed the bridge of his nose with a finger and thumb. 'The sexual nature of the relationship was simply a by-product of our dependence on each other. It mattered a great deal to Robert and very much less to me, though I admit that at the time – a period of three or four months only – I genuinely believed myself to be a homosexual.'

'Then you fell in love with Olive?'

'Yes,' said Mr Clarke simply. 'She was very like her father, of course, intelligent, sensitive, really quite charming when she wanted to be, and extraordinarily sympathetic. She made so few demands, unlike my wife.' He sighed. 'It seems strange to say it, in view of what happened later, but she was a very comfortable person to be with.'

'Did Olive know about your relationship with her father?'

'Not from me. She was very naïve in many respects.'

'And Robert didn't know about you and Olive.'

'No.'

'You were playing with fire, Mr Clarke.'

'I didn't plan it, Sergeant. It happened. All I can say in my defence is that I ceased being' – he sought for the right word – 'intimate with Robert the minute I recognized my feelings for Olive. We did not stop being friends, however. That would have been cruel.'

'Bullshit!' said Hal with calculated anger. 'You didn't want to be found out. My guess is you were shafting both of them at the same time and loving every exciting minute of it. And you have the bloody gall to say you don't feel responsible!'

'Why should I?' Clarke said with a flash of spirit. 'My name was never mentioned by either of them. Do you imagine it wouldn't have been if I had unwittingly precipitated the tragedy?'

Roz smiled contemptuously. 'Did you never wonder why Robert Martin wouldn't speak to you after the murders?'

'I assumed he was too distressed.'

'I think you feel a little more than simple distress when you discover that your lover has seduced your daughter,' she said ironically. 'Of course you precipitated it, Mr Clarke, and you knew it. But, by God, you weren't going to say anything. You'd rather see the entire Martin family destroy itself than prejudice your own position.'

'Was that so unreasonable?' he protested. 'They were free to name me. They didn't. How would it have helped if I had spoken out? Gwen and Amber would still have been dead. Olive would still have gone to prison.' He turned to Hal. 'I regret intensely my involvement with the family but I really can't be held responsible if my connection with them led to tragedy. There was nothing illegal about what I did.'

Hal looked out of the window again. 'Tell us why you moved, Mr Clarke. Was it your decision or your wife's?'

He clamped his hands between his knees again. 'It was a joint decision. Life there became unbearable for both of us. We saw ghosts everywhere. A change of environment seemed the only sensible course.'

'Why were you so keen to keep your forwarding address secret?'

Clarke raised haunted eyes. 'To avoid the past catching up with me. I've lived in constant dread of this.' He looked at Roz. 'It's almost a relief to have it out in the open at last. You probably won't believe that.'

She gave a tight smile. 'The police took a statement from your wife on the day of the murders, saying that she saw Gwen and Amber on the doorstep that morning after you and Robert left for work. But when I came here the other day, she said she had lied about it.'

'I can only repeat what I said to you then,' he answered wearily. 'Dorothy's senile. You can't put any reliance on anything she says. She doesn't even know what day it is most of the time.'

'Was she telling the truth five years ago?'

He nodded. 'In so far as saying they were alive when I left for work, yes, she was. Amber was at the window, watching. I saw her myself. She ducked behind the curtain when I waved at her. I remember thinking how odd that was.' He paused. 'As to whether Dorothy saw Robert leave,' he resumed after a moment, 'I don't know. She said she did and I've always understood that Robert had a cast-iron alibi.'

'Has your wife ever mentioned seeing the bodies, Mr Clarke?' asked Hal casually.

'Good God, no.' He sounded genuinely shocked.

'I just wondered why she saw ghosts. She wasn't particularly friendly with Gwen or Amber, was she? Rather the reverse, I'd have thought, in view of the amount of time you spent at the Martins' house.'

'Everyone in that road saw ghosts,' he said bleakly. 'We all knew what Olive had done to those wretched women. It would have required a very dull imagination not to see ghosts.'

'Can you remember what your wife was wearing the morning of the murders?'

He stared at Hal, surprised by the sudden switch. 'Why do you ask?'

'We've had a report that a woman was seen walking down past the Martins' garage.' The lie rolled glibly off his tongue. 'From the description it was too small for Olive but whoever it was was dressed in what looked like a smart black suit. We'd like to trace her. Could it have been your wife?'

The man's relief was palpable. 'No. She never had a black suit.'

'Was she wearing anything black that morning?'

'No. She wore a floral overall.'

'You're very certain.'

'She always wore it, every morning, to do the housework. She used to get dressed after she'd finished. Except Sundays. She didn't do housework on Sundays.'

Hal nodded. 'The same overall every morning? What happened when it got dirty?'

Clarke frowned, puzzled by the line of questioning. 'She had another one, a plain blue one. But she was definitely wearing the floral one on the day of the murders.'

'Which one was she wearing the day after the murders?'

He licked his lips nervously. 'I can't remember.'

'It was the blue one, wasn't it? And she went on wearing the blue one, I suspect, until you or she bought a spare.'

'I can't remember.'

Hal smiled unpleasantly. 'Does she still have her floral overall, Mr Clarke?'

'No,' he whispered. 'It's a long time since she did any housework.'

'What happened to it?'

'I can't remember. We threw out a lot of things before we moved.'

'How did you find the time to do that?' asked Roz. 'Mr Hayes said you upped and left one morning and a removal company turned up three days later to pack your stuff for you.'

'Perhaps I sorted through everything when it came here,' he said rather wildly. 'I can't remember the precise order of things so long afterwards.'

Hal scratched his jaw. 'Did you know,' he murmured evenly, 'that your wife identified some charred remains of a floral overall, found in the incinerator in the Martins' garden, as being part of the clothing that Gwen was wearing the day she was murdered?'

Colour drained from Clarke's face, leaving it an unhealthy grey. 'No, I didn't.' The words were barely audible.

'And those remains were carefully photographed and carefully stored, ready to be produced at a future date if there was ever any dispute over their ownership. Mr Hayes, I'm sure, will be able to tell us whether it was your wife's overall or Gwen's.'

Clarke raised his hands in helpless surrender. 'She told me she'd thrown it away,' he pleaded, 'because the iron had scorched a hole through the front. I believed her. She often did things like that.'

Hal hardly seemed to hear him but went on in the same unemotional voice. 'I very much hope, Mr Clarke, that we will find a way of proving that you knew all along that it was your wife who killed Gwen and Amber. I should like to see you tried and convicted of allowing an innocent girl to go to prison for a crime you knew she hadn't committed, particularly a girl whom you used and abused so shamelessly.'

They could never prove it, of course, but he drew considerable satisfaction from the fear that set Clarke's face working convulsively.

'How could I know? I wondered' – his voice rose

– 'of course I wondered, but Olive confessed.' His eyes strayed beseechingly to Roz. 'Why did Olive confess?'

'Because she was in deep shock, because she was frightened, because she didn't know what else to do, because her mother was dead, and because she had been brought up to keep secrets. She thought her father would save her, but he didn't, because he thought she had done it. *You* could have saved her, but you didn't, because you were afraid of what people would say. The woman at Wells-Fargo could have saved her, but she didn't, because she didn't want to be involved. Her solicitor could have saved her if he had been a kinder man.' She flicked a glance at Hal. 'The police could have saved her if they'd questioned, just once, the value of confession evidence. But it was six years ago, and six years ago, confessions' – she made a ring with her thumb and forefinger – 'were A-OK. But I don't blame them, Mr Clarke. I blame you. For everything. You played at being a homosexual because you were bored with your wife and then you seduced your lover's daughter to prove you weren't the pervert you thought he was.' She stared at him with disdain. 'And that's how I'm going to portray you in the book that will get Olive out of prison. I really despise people like you.'

'You'll destroy me.'

'Yes.'

'Is that what Olive wants? My destruction?'

'I don't know what Olive wants. I only know what I want, which is to get her released. If it means your destruction, then so be it.'

He sat for some moments in silence, his fingers plucking shakily at the creases in his trousers. Then, as if reaching a sudden decision, he looked at Roz. 'I would have spoken if Olive hadn't confessed. But she did, and I assumed like everyone else that she was telling the truth. Presumably you have no desire to prolong her stay in prison? Her release in advance of your book's publication would improve your sales considerably, wouldn't it?'

'Maybe. What are you suggesting?'

His eyes narrowed. 'If I give you the evidence now that will hasten her release, will you in return promise not to divulge my real name or address in the book? You could refer to me by the name Olive called me, Mr Lewis. Do you agree?'

She smiled faintly. What an unbelievable shit he was. He could never hold her to it, of course, but he didn't seem to realize that. And the police would release his name, anyway, if only as Mrs Clarke's husband. 'I agree. As long as it gets Olive out.'

He stood up, taking some keys out of his pocket, and walked over to an ornate Chinese box on the sideboard. He unlocked it and raised the lid, removing something wrapped in tissue paper and handing it to Hal. 'I found it when we moved,' he said. 'She'd hidden it at the bottom of one of her drawers. I swear

I never knew how she got it, but I've always been afraid that Amber must have taunted her with it. She talks about Amber a lot.' He washed his hands in mimicry of Pontius Pilate. 'She calls her the Devil.'

Hal peeled away the tissue paper and looked at what was revealed. A silver bracelet with a tiny silver-chair charm and a tag on which U.R.N.A.R.N.I.A. was barely discernible through a welter of deep angry scratches.

It was almost Christmas before the scales of justice had tipped enough in Olive's favour to allow her to leave the confines of her prison. There would always be doubters, of course, people who would call her the Sculptress till the day she died. After six years the evidence in support of her story was desperately thin. A silver bracelet where it shouldn't have been. Tiny fragments of a burnt floral overall, identified by a senile woman's bitter husband. And, finally, the painstaking reappraisal of the photographic evidence, using sophisticated computer enhancement, which had revealed a smaller, daintier shoe print in the blood beneath a huge ribbed rubber sole mark left by Olive's trainer.

No one would ever know what really happened that day because the truth was locked inside a brain that no longer functioned, and Edward Clarke could not, or would not, shed any light from statements his wife had made in the past. He maintained his complete ignorance of the whole affair, saying that any qualms he might have had had been put to rest by Olive's confession and that the onus for mistakes must lie with her and with the police. The most probable scenario, and the one generally accepted, was that Amber waited until Edward and Robert had left for work and then invited Mrs Clarke into the house to taunt her with the bracelet and the abortion. What happened then was a matter for guesswork but Roz, at least, believed that Mrs Clarke had set about the murders in cold blood and with a clear mind. There was something very calculating about the way she must have donned gloves to perform her butchery and her careful stepping around the blood to avoid leaving too many traces. But most calculating of all was the clever burning of her blood-stained overall amidst Gwen and Amber's clothes and her cool identification of the pieces afterwards as being the overall worn by Gwen that morning. Roz even wondered sometimes if the intention all along had been to implicate Olive. There was no telling now why Mrs Clarke had drawn attention to herself outside the kitchen window, but Roz couldn't help feeling that, had she not done so, Olive might have had enough presence of mind to phone the police immediately before she ran amok in the kitchen and obliterated the evidence that might have exonerated her.

There were to be no disciplinary charges against the police team involved. The chief constable issued a press release, pointing to the recent tightening of police procedure, particularly in relation to confession evidence, but he stressed that as far as Olive's case was concerned the police had taken all available steps to ensure her rights were fully protected. In the circumstances it had been reasonable to assume that her confession was genuine. He took the opportunity to reiterate forcefully the duty imperative on the public never to disturb evidence at the scene of a crime.

Peter Crew's association with the case, particularly in view of his subsequent mishandling of Robert Martin's estate, had attracted considerable and unwelcome interest. At worst he was accused of deliberately engineering Olive's conviction in order to gain access to unlimited funds, and, at best, of bullying an emotionally disturbed young woman at a time when he had a responsibility to safeguard her interests. He denied both accusations strenuously, arguing that he could not have foreseen Robert Martin's success on the stock exchange nor his early death; and claiming that because Olive's story had been remarkably consistent with the forensic evidence he, in the absence of any denials on her part, had, like the police, accepted it as a true statement of fact. He had advised her to say nothing and could not be held liable for her confession. Meanwhile, he remained at liberty on bail, facing the sort of charges that for most of his clients would have resulted in a remand to prison, bullishly declaring his innocence on all counts.

Roz, when she heard what he was saying, was angry enough to waylay him in the street with a local journalist in tow. 'We could argue about liability for ever, Mr Crew, but just explain this to me. If Olive's statement was as consistent with the forensic evidence as you maintain, then why did she claim there was no mist on the mirror at a time when Gwen and Amber were still alive?' She caught his arm as he tried to walk away. 'Why didn't she mention that the axe was too blunt to cut off Amber's head? Why didn't she say she had struck her four times before resorting to the carving knife? Why didn't she describe her fight with her mother and the stabbing incisions she'd made in her mother's throat before cutting it? Why didn't she mention burning the clothes? In fact, try quoting me one detail from Olive's statement that does accord fully with the forensic evidence.'

He shook her off angrily. 'She said she used the axe and the carving knife,' he snapped.

'Neither of which had her fingerprints on them. The forensic evidence did not support her statement.'

'She had their blood all over her.'

'All over is right, Mr Crew. But where does it say in her statement that she rolled in it?'

He tried to walk away but found the journalist blocking his path. 'Footprints,' he said. 'At the time, there were only her footprints.'

'Yes,' said Roz. 'And on that one piece of evidence, which was at odds with all the rest, you made up your mind she was a psychopath and prepared a defence on the grounds of diminished responsibility. Why did you never brief Graham Deedes on the lifelines her poor father was trying to throw her? Why didn't you question your own judgement when she was pronounced fit to plead guilty? Why the hell didn't you treat her like a human being, Mr Crew, instead of a monster?'

He stared at her with dislike. 'Because, Miss Leigh,' he said, 'she *is* a monster. Worse, she's a clever monster. Doesn't it worry you that this wretched woman you've set up to take Olive's place is the only one who's not mentally fit to fight the accusation? And doesn't it worry you that Olive waited till her father died before she would talk to anyone? Mark my words, *he* was the one she intended to smear with her guilt – because he was easy. He was dead. But you gave her Mrs Clarke instead.' He thrust his face angrily into hers. 'The evidence you've unearthed raises doubts, but no more. Computer-enhanced photography is as open to interpretation as the nature of psychopathy.' He shook his head. 'Olive will get out because of it, of course. The law has become very flabby in the last few years. But I was there when she told her story and, as I made clear to you at the start, Olive Martin is a dangerous woman. She's after her father's money. You've been led by the nose, Miss Leigh.'

'She's not half as dangerous as you, Mr Crew. At least she's never paid to have people's businesses destroyed and their lives threatened. You're a cheap crook.'

Crew shrugged. 'If that appears in print, Miss Leigh, I shall sue you for defamation, and it will cost you considerably more in legal fees than it will cost me. I suggest you remember that.'

The journalist watched him walk away. 'He's doing a Robert Maxwell on you.'

'That's the law for you,' said Roz in disgust. 'It's nothing but a big stick if you know how to use it or you're rich enough to employ someone else to use it for you.'

'You don't think he's right about Olive, do you?'

'Of course not,' said Roz angrily, sensing his doubt. 'But at least you know now what she was up against. This country is mad if it assumes that the presence of a solicitor during an interview will automatically protect a prisoner's rights. They are just as fallible, just as lazy, and just as crooked as the rest of us. It cost the Law Society millions last year to compensate clients for their solicitors' misdeeds.'

*

The book was scheduled to come out within a month of Olive's release. Roz had finished it in record time amidst the peace and seclusion of Bayview, which she bought on impulse when she discovered it was impossible to work above the continuous noise of people enjoying their food in the restaurant downstairs. The Poacher had been relaunched in a whirl of somewhat exaggerated publicity featuring Hal as the heroic underdog fighting the evil of organized crime. His association with the Olive Martin case, particularly his latter efforts to help in securing her release, had only added to the hype. He applauded Roz's decision to buy Bayview. Making love against the back-drop of the ocean was a vast improvement on the metal bars at the Poacher.

And she was safer there.

Hal had discovered within himself a capacity for caring that he hadn't known existed. It went deeper than love, encompassing every emotion from admiration to lust, and, while he would never have described himself as an obsessive man, the stress of worrying about Stewart Hayes, free on bail, slowly became intolerable to him. He was prompted finally to make Hayes a surprise visit at home one day. He found him playing in the garden with his ten-year-old daughter and it was there that he made Hayes an offer Hayes couldn't refuse. A life for a life, a maiming for a maiming, should anything happen to Roz. Hayes recognized such compelling purpose in the dark eyes, perhaps because it's what he would have done himself, that he agreed to an indefinite truce. His love for his daughter, it seemed, was matched only by Hal's love for Roz.

Iris, claiming almost more credit for the book than Roz – 'if it hadn't been for me it would never have been written' – was busy selling it around the world as the latest example of British justice reeling under the body blows of its own inflexibility. A small, rather ironic footnote to the story was that the boy Crew's firm had located in Australia proved not, after all, to be Amber's lost child and the search for him was promptly abandoned. The time limit, set in Robert Martin's will, had run out and his money, swollen by Crew's investments – which were now out of his reach – continued in limbo while Olive sought leave to contest her right to it.

Epilogue

AT 5.30 ON a dark and frosty winter morning the Sculptress walked free from the gates of her prison, two hours earlier than the time announced to the press. She had sought and obtained permission to slip back into society well away from the glare of publicity that had surrounded the release of other celebrated cases of wrongful imprisonment. Roz and Sister Bridget, alerted by telephone, stood outside in the lamplight, stamping their feet and blowing on their hands. They smiled in welcome as the Judas door opened.

Only Hal, sheltering ten yards away in the warmth of the car, saw the look of gloating triumph that swept briefly over Olive's face as she put her arms around the two women and lifted them bodily into the air. He recalled some words that he'd had stencilled on his desk when he was still a policeman. '*Truth lies within a little and certain compass, but error is immense.*'

For no apparent reason, he shivered.

What follows here are the
opening pages of Minette Walters's
fourth novel, *The Dark Room*.

THE DARK ROOM

Prologue

WITH HER SHARP little face set in lines of dissatisfaction, the twelve-year-old girl sat up and searched for her knickers among the forest leaves. It had finally begun to dawn on her that sex with Bobby Franklyn wasn't all it could be. She put on her shoes and kicked him hard. 'Get up, Bobby,' she snapped. 'It's your turn to find the bloody dog.'

He rolled over on to his back. 'In a minute,' he muttered sleepily.

'No, *now*. Mum'll skin me alive if Rex goes home before me again. She's not stupid, you know.' She stood up and dug the heel of her shoe into his naked thigh, twisting it back and forth in a childish desire to hurt. 'Get up.'

'Okay, okay.' He rose sulkily to his feet, tugging at his trousers. 'But this is pissing me off, you know. It's hardly worth doing if we have to go looking for the dog every time.'

She moved away from him. 'It's not Rex that makes

it hardly worth doing.' There were tears of angry humiliation in her eyes. 'I should have listened to Mum. She always says it takes a real man to do it properly.'

'Yeah, well,' he said, zipping his fly, 'it'd be a damn sight easier if I didn't have to pretend you were Julia Roberts. What would your sodding mum know about it, anyway? It's years since anyone gave her a good shagging.' He had few feelings for these girls beyond the purely animal, but he grew to hate them very quickly when they gave him lip about his performance. The urge to smash their jeering little faces in was becoming irresistible.

The girl started to walk away. 'I *hate* you, Bobby. I really *hate* you, and I'm going to tell on you.' She tapped her watch. 'Three minutes. That's as long as you can keep it up. Three lousy minutes. Is that what you call a good shagging?' She gave a triumphant glance over her shoulder, saw something in his face that alerted her to the danger she was in, and took to her heels in sudden fear. '*Rex!*' she screamed. '*Re-ex!* He'll *kill* you if you touch me,' she sobbed out, her small wiry body darting through the trees.

But it was Bobby who was going to do the killing. His anger was out of control. He threw himself at her back and brought her crashing to the ground, breathing heavily as he tried to get astride her thrashing legs. 'Bitch!' he grunted. 'Bloody bitch!'

Fear lent her strength. She scrambled away from

him, crying for her dog, slithering and sliding in a flurry of decomposing leaves into a broad ditch that scored the forest bed. She landed on her feet, only yards away from the huge Alsatian, who stood, hackles up and growling. 'I'll set him on you, and he'll rip you to pieces. And I won't care, and I won't stop him.' She saw with satisfaction that Bobby had turned white to the gills. 'You're such a *creep*!' she yelled.

And then she saw that Rex was growling at her and not at Bobby, and that what had drained the colour from her boyfriend's face was not his fear of the dog but stunned horror at what the dog was guarding. She had a glimpse of something half-unearthed and repulsively human, before panic drove her up the slope again in sobbing, wide-eyed terror.

One

SHE CLUNG TO sleep tenaciously, wrapped in beguiling dreams. It was explained to her afterwards that they weren't dreams at all, only reality breaking through the days of confusion as she rose from deep unconsciousness to full awareness, but she found that difficult to accept. Reality was too depressing to give birth to such contentment. Her awakening was painful. They propped her on pillows and she caught glimpses of herself from time to time in the dressing-table mirror, a waxen-faced effigy with shaven head and bandaged eye *hardly recognizable* – and she had an instinctive desire to withdraw from the image and leave it to play its part alone. *It wasn't her.* A huge bear of a man with close-cropped hair and close-cropped beard leant over her and told her she'd been in a car accident. But he didn't tell her where or when. You're a lucky young woman, he said. She remembered that. Forgot everything else. She had a sense of time passing, of people talking to her, but she preferred to drowse in sleep where dreams beguiled.

She was aware. She saw. She heard. And she felt safe with the pleasant female voices that smoothed and soothed and petted. She answered them in her head but never out loud, for she clung to the spurious protection of intellectual absence. 'Are you with us today?' the nurses asked, pressing their faces up to hers. *I've been with you all along.* 'Here's your mother to see you, dear.' *I don't have a mother. I have a stepmother.* 'Come on, love, your eyes are open. We know you can hear us, so when are you going to talk to us?' *When I'm ready . . . when I'm ready . . . when I want to remember . . .*

<u>ROAD TRAFFIC ACCIDENT:</u>

Reported 21.45 approx 13.6.94 PCs Gregg and Hardy on scene at 22.04

Location: Disused airfield, Stoney Bassett, Hants

One vehicle involved. Black Rover Cabriolet automatic

Reg No: JIN 1X – vehicle written off

Driver: Miss Jane Imogen Nicola Kingsley

Unconscious and in need of emergency treatment

Driving licence gives date of birth: 26.09.59 and registered address: 12 Glenavon Gdns, Richmond, Surrey

Property Tycoon's daughter in mystery pile-up

It was reported late last night that Jane Kingsley, 34, the fashion photographer and only daughter of Adam Kingsley, 66, millionaire chairman of Franchise Holdings Ltd, was found unconscious following a mystery car crash on the disused airfield at Stoney Bassett, 15 miles south of Salisbury. Mr Andrew Wilson, 23, and his girlfriend, Miss Jenny Ragg, 19, happened upon the scene by chance at 9.45 p.m. and immediately summoned assistance for the unconscious woman.

'The car was a write-off,' said Mr Wilson. 'Miss Kingsley's very lucky to be alive. If she'd been in it when it hit the concrete pillar, she'd have been crushed to death in the wreck. I'm glad we were able to help.'

Police describe Miss Kingsley's escape as a miracle. The car, a black Rover Cabriolet automatic, had collided head-on with a solid concrete stanchion, which was once the corner support for a hangar. Police believe Miss Kingsley was thrown through the open door of her car shortly before the impact.

'That pillar is the only structure still standing on the airfield,' said PC Gavin Hardy, 'and we don't understand yet how she came to hit it. There was no one else in the car and no evidence of another vehicle being involved.'

Jane's stepmother, Mrs Betty Kingsley, 65, was shocked by the news which comes only days after the surprise cancellation of her stepdaughter's wedding. At home this morning in Hellingdon Hall, where she and Mr Kingsley have lived for the last 15 years, she wept bitterly and said she would blame Miss Kingsley's fiancé, Leo Wallader, 35, if Miss Kingsley didn't recover. 'He's treated her so badly.'

Police admitted this morning that Miss Kingsley had been drinking prior to the accident. 'She had a high level of alcohol in her blood,' said a spokesman. Miss Kingsley is unconscious in Odstock Hospital, Salisbury.

Wessex Post, 14th June

Two

JINX AWOKE ONE night with fear sucking the breath from her lungs. She opened her eyes and strained them into the blackness. She was in a dark room – *her dark room?* – and she wasn't alone. Someone – *something?* – prowled the shadows beyond her vision.

What?

Fear . . . fear . . . FEAR . . .

She sat bolt upright, water pouring down her back, screams issuing in a tumult of sound from her gaping mouth.

Light flooded the room. Comfort came in the shape of a woman's soft breasts, strong arms and sweet voice. 'There, there, Jane. It's all right. Come on, love, calm down. You had a nightmare.'

But she knew that was wrong. *Her terror was real. There was something in the dark with her.* 'My name's Jinx,' she whispered. 'I'm a photographer, and this isn't my room.' She laid her shaven head against the starched white uniform and knew the bitterness of defeat. There would be no more sweet dreams. 'Where am I?' she asked. 'Who are you? Why am I here?'

'You're in the Nightingale Clinic in Salisbury,' said the nurse, 'and I'm Sister Gordon. You were in a car accident, but you're safe now. Let's see if we can get you back to sleep again.'

Jinx allowed herself to be tucked back under the sheets by a firm pair of hands. 'You won't turn the light off, will you?' she begged. 'I can't see in the dark.'

Query prosecution of Miss J. Kingsley driving with 150 mg per 100 ml

Date: 22nd June 1994
From: Sergeant Geoff Halliwell

Miss Kingsley was thrown from her vehicle before it impacted against a concrete stanchion in one corner of the airfield. She was unconscious when she was found at 21.45 on Monday 13 June by Mr Andrew Wilson and Miss Jenny Ragg (for details see over) a courting couple who use the airfield regularly. Mr Wilson remained with Miss Kingsley while Miss Ragg drove to the nearest telephone to summon assistance. Miss Kingsley, who suffered severe concussion and bruising/laceration of her arms and face when she was thrown from the car, was taken to Odstock Hospital in Salisbury for treatment. She remained unconscious for three days and was very confused when she finally came round. She has no recollection of the accident and claims not to know why she was at the airfield. Blood samples taken at 00.23 (14.6.94) show 150 mg per 100 ml. Two empty wine bottles were recovered from the floor of the car when it was examined the following day.

PCs Gregg and Hardy had one brief interview with Miss Kingsley shortly after she regained consciousness, but she was too confused to tell them anything other than that she believed it was Saturday 4 June (i.e. some 9 days *before* the incident on 13.6.94) and that she was on her way from London to Hampshire. Since the interview (5 days) she has remained dazed and uncommunicative and visits have been suspended on the advice of her doctors. They have diagnosed post-traumatic amnesia, following concussion. Her parents report that she spent the week 4–10 June with them (though Miss Kingsley clearly has no memory of this) before returning to Richmond on the evening of Friday 10 June, following a telephone call. They describe her as being in good spirits and looking forward to her forthcoming marriage. She was expected at work on Monday 13 June, but did not show. She runs her own photographic studio in

Pimlico and her employees say they were concerned at her non-appearance. They left several messages on her answerphone on the 13th but received no reply.

Interviews by Richmond police with her neighbours in Glenavon Gdns, Colonel and Mrs Clancey (for details see over) reveal that she made an attempt on her life on Sunday 12 June. Colonel Clancey, whose garage adjoins Miss Kingsley's, heard her car engine running with the door closed. When he went to investigate, he found her garage full of fumes and Miss Kingsley half-asleep at the wheel. He dragged her outside and revived her, but did not report the incident because Miss Kingsley begged him not to. He and his wife are deeply upset that she has 'tried to do it again'.

Both Colonel & Mrs Clancey, and Mr & Mrs Adam Kingsley made reference to a Mr Leo Wallader (for details see over) who was until recently Miss Kingsley's fiancé. It appears he left 12 Glenavon Gdns on Friday 10 June, after telling Miss Kingsley he couldn't marry her (wedding scheduled for 2 July at Hellingdon Hall, Nr Fordingbridge) because he had plans to marry her closest friend, Meg Harris, instead. Mr Wallader & Ms Harris are unavailable for interview at the moment. According to Sir Anthony Wallader (father) they are currently travelling in France but plan to return some time in July.

In view of a recent MOT certificate on Miss

Kingsley's vehicle, which tends to rule out malfunction, and the fact that the chances of hitting the concrete stanchion by accident are virtually nil, it seems clear that she drove her car into it deliberately. Therefore, unless she recovers enough of her memory to give an explanation of the events leading up to the incident, Gregg and Hardy incline to the view that this was a second attempt at suicide after a drinking session in her car. Mr Adam Kingsley, her father, has offered to pay the costs of the emergency services, meanwhile Miss Kingsley has been transferred to the Nightingale Clinic where she is receiving treatment from Dr Alan Protheroe. Mr Kingsley's solicitor is pressing for a decision on whether or not we intend to proceed against Miss Kingsley. My view is to do nothing in view of her father's willingness to pick up the tab, her disturbed state of mind and the fact that she chose such a deserted location. Please advise.

Three

Wednesday 22 June, The Nightingale Clinic, Salisbury, Wiltshire – 8.30 a.m.

HOW DRAB REALITY was. Even the sun shining through her windows was less vivid than her dreams. Perhaps it had something to do with the bandage over her right eye, but she didn't think so. Consciousness itself was leaden and dull, and so restrictive that she felt only a terrible depression. The big bear of a doctor came in as she toyed with her breakfast, told her again that she'd been in an accident and said the police would like to talk to her. She shrugged. 'I'm not going anywhere.' She would have added that she despised policemen if he'd stayed to listen, but he went away again before she could put the thought into words.

She had no memory of the first police interview at the Odstock Hospital and politely denied ever having met the two uniformed constables who came to her room. She explained that she could not remember the accident, indeed could remember nothing at all since leaving her house and her fiancé in London the previous morning. They resembled each other, tall, stolid men with sandy hair and florid complexions, who showed their discomfort at her answers by turning their caps in unison between their fingers. She labelled them Tweedledum and Tweedledee and chuckled silently because they were so much more amusing than her sore head, bandaged eye and hideously bruised arms. They asked her where she had been going, and she replied that she was on her way to stay with her parents at Hellingdon Hall. 'I have to help my stepmother with wedding preparations,' she explained. 'I'm getting married on the second of July.' She heard herself announce the fact with pleasure, while the voice of cynicism murmured in her brain. *Leo will run a mile before he hitches himself to a bald, one-eyed bride.*

They thanked her and left.

Two hours later, her stepmother dissolved into tears at her bedside, blurted out that the wedding was off, it was Wednesday, the twenty-second of June, Leo had left her for Meg twelve days previously and she had, to all intents and purposes, driven her car at a concrete pillar four days later in a deliberate attempt to kill herself.

Jinx stared at her ugly, scarred hands. 'Didn't I say goodbye to Leo yesterday?'

'You were unconscious for three days and very confused afterwards. You were in hospital until Friday, and I went to see you, but you didn't know who I was. I've come here twice and you've looked at me, but you didn't want to talk to me. This is the first time you've recognized me. Daddy's that upset about it.' Her mouth wobbled rather pathetically. 'We were so afraid we'd lost you.'

'I've come to stay with you. That's why I'm here. You and I are going to confirm the arrangements for the wedding.' *If she said it slowly and clearly enough, Betty must believe her. But, no, Betty was a fool. Betty had always been a fool.* 'The week beginning the fourth of June. It's been in the diary for months.'

Mrs Kingsley's ready tears poured down her plump cheeks, scoring tiny pink rivulets in her over-powdered face. 'You've already been, my darling. You came down a fortnight and a half ago, spent the week with Daddy and me, did all the things you were supposed to do, and then went home to find Leo packing his bags. Don't you remember? He's gone to live with Meg. Oh, I could murder him, Jinx, I really could.' She wrung her hands. 'I always told you he wasn't a nice man, but you wouldn't listen. And your father was just as bad. He's a Wallader, Elizabeth . . .' She rambled on, her huge chest heaving tragically inside a woollen dress that was far too tight.

The idea that nearly three weeks had passed without her being able to recollect a single day was so far beyond Jinx's comprehension that she fixed her attention on what was real. Red carnations and white lilies in a vase on her bedside table. French windows looking out on a flagstoned terrace, with a carefully tended garden beyond. Television in the corner. Leather armchairs on either side of a coffee table – walnut, she decided, and a walnut dressing table. Bathroom to her left. Door to the corridor on her right. *Where had Adam put her this time?* Somewhere very expensive, she thought. The Nightingale Clinic, the nurse had told her. In Salisbury. *But why Salisbury when she lived in London?*

Betty's plaintive wailing broke into her thoughts. 'I wish it hadn't upset you so much, my darling. You've no idea how badly Daddy's taken it all. He sees it as an insult to him, you know. He never thought anyone could make his little girl do something so – ' she cast about for a word ' – silly.'

Little girl? What on earth was Betty talking about? She had never been Adam's little girl – *his performing puppet perhaps* – never his little girl. She felt very tired suddenly. 'I don't understand.'

'You got drunk and tried to kill yourself, my poor baby. Your car's been written off.' Mrs Kingsley fished a newspaper photograph out of her handbag and pressed it into her stepdaughter's lap. 'That's what it looked like afterwards. It's a mercy you survived, it really is.' She pointed to the date in the top right-hand corner of the clipping. 'The fourteenth of June, the day after the accident. And today's date – ' she pushed forward another newspaper – 'there, you see, the twenty-second, a whole week later.'

Jinx examined the picture curiously. The writhing mass of twisted metal, backlit by police arc lights, had the fantastic quality of surrealist art. It was a stark silhouette and, in the distortions of the chassis and the oblique angle from which the photographer had taken his shot, appeared to portray a gleaming metal gauntlet clasped about the raised sword of the pillar. It was a great picture, she thought, and wondered who had taken it.

'This isn't my car.'

Her stepmother took her hand and stroked it gently. 'Leo's not going to marry you, Jinx. Daddy and I have had to send out notices to everyone saying the wedding's been cancelled. He wants to marry Meg instead.'

Jinx watched a tear drop from the powdered chin on to her own upturned palm. 'Meg?' she echoed. 'You mean Meg *Harris?*' *Why would Leo want to marry Meg? Meg was a whore. You whore . . . you whore . . . YOU WHORE!* Some horror – *what?* – lurched through her mind, and she clamped a hand to her mouth as bile rose in her throat.

'She's been out for what she can get for as long as

you've known her, and now she's taken your husband. You always were too trusting, baby. I never liked her.'

Jinx dragged her wide-eyed stare back to her stepmother. That wasn't true. Betty had always adored Meg, largely because Meg was so uncritical in her affection. It made no difference to Meg if Betty Kingsley was drunk or sober.

'At least Meg thinks I've something sensible to say,' was her stepmother's aggressive refrain whenever she was deep in her cups and being ignored by everybody else. The irony was that Meg couldn't tolerate her own strait-laced mother for more than a couple of hours. 'You and I should swap,' she often said. 'At least Betty doesn't play the martyr all the time.'

'When was this decided?' Jinx managed at last. 'After the accident?'

'No, dear. Before. You went back to London a week ago last Friday after Leo phoned you during the afternoon. Horrible, horrible man. He called every day, pretending he still loved you, then dropped the bombshell on the Friday night. I don't suppose he was at all kind in the way he did it either.' She held the handkerchief to her eyes again. 'Then on the Sunday, Colonel Clancey from next door rescued you from your garage before you could gas yourself, but didn't have the sense to ring and tell us you needed help.' She swallowed painfully. 'But you were so cool about it all on the Saturday when you phoned home to tell Daddy the wedding was off that it never occurred to us you were going to do something silly.'

Perhaps she'd been lying . . . she always lied . . . lying was second nature to her . . . Jinx looked down at the newspaper clipping again and noticed the JIN of the personalized number-plate that her father had given her for her twenty-first birthday present staring back at her from amidst the wreckage in the photograph. J. I. N. Kingsley. *Jane Imogen Nicola – her mother's names – the most hated names in the world. JINXED!* She had to accept it was her car featured there. '*You got drunk . . . Colonel Clancey rescued you . . .*' 'There's no gas in my garage,' Jinx said, fixing on something she could understand. 'No one has gas in their garage.'

. . . Mrs Kingsley sobbed loudly. 'You were running your car engine with the doors closed. If the Colonel hadn't heard it, you'd have died on the Sunday.' She plucked at the girl's hand again, her warm fat fingers seeking the very comfort she was trying to impart. 'You promised him you wouldn't do it again and now he wishes he'd reported it to somebody. Don't be angry with me, Jinx.' The tears rolled on relentlessly in rivers of grief, and Jinx wondered, basely, how genuine they were. Betty had always reserved her affections for her own two sons and never for the self-contained little girl who was the product of Adam's dead first wife. 'Someone had to tell you, and Dr Protheroe thought it should be me. Poor

Daddy's been knocked sideways by it all, you've broken his heart. "Why did she do it, Elizabeth?" he keeps asking me.'

But Jinx had no answer for that. *For she knew Betty was lying. No one, least of all Leo, could drive her to kill herself.* Instead she dwelt on the incongruities of life. Why did she call her father Adam while his wife of twenty-seven years called him Daddy? For some reason it had never seemed significant before. She stared past her stepmother's head to her reflection in the dressing-table mirror and wondered suddenly why she felt so very little about so very much.

CRITICAL ACCLAIM FOR

Minette Walters:

The Ice House

'Terrific first novel with a high Rendellesque frisson count' *The Times*

The Sculptress

'A devastatingly effective novel' *Observer*

The Scold's Bridle

'A gothic puzzle of great intricacy and psychological power' *Sunday Times*

The Dark Room

'A marvellous, dramatically intelligent novel. It shimmers with suspense, ambiguity and a deep unholy joy' *Daily Mail*

The Echo

'It grips like steel . . . Passion, compassion, intelligence and romance is what Walters offers with no quarter for squeamish cowards' *Mail on Sunday*

The Breaker

'Stands head and shoulders above the vast majority of crime novels . . . Existing fans will love *The Breaker*, new readers will be instant converts' *Express*

The Shape of Snakes

'Breaking all the rules of popular fiction, Minette Walters asks as much of her readers as many literary novelists, and yet she offers them a book as gripping as any thriller' *Times Literary Supplement*

Acid Row

'Humane intelligence enables Walters to twist and turn her plot . . . *Acid Row* is a breathtaking achievement' *Daily Telegraph*

Fox Evil

'Fox Evil is the work of a writer at the peak of her confidence and supreme ability' *The Times*

Disordered Minds

'A powerful, acute and vivid work from a staggeringly talented writer' *Observer*

With her debut, *The Ice House*, Minette Walters won the Crime Writers' Association John Creasey Award for the best first crime novel of 1992. Rapidly establishing a reputation as one of the most exciting crime novelists writing today, her second novel, *The Sculptress*, was acclaimed by critics as one of the most compelling and powerful novels of the year and won the Edgar Allan Poe Award for the best crime novel published in America in 1993. In 1994 Minette Walters achieved a unique triple when *The Scold's Bridle* was awarded the CWA Gold Dagger for best crime novel of the year. Her following novels *The Dark Room*, *The Echo*, *The Breaker*, *The Shape of Snakes*, *Acid Row* and *Disordered Minds* were also published to further critical acclaim throughout the world and her ninth novel, *Fox Evil*, won the 2003 CWA Gold Dagger for Fiction.

Minette Walters lives in Dorset with her husband and two children. Her latest novel, *The Devil's Feather*, was published by Macmillan in September 2005.

Also by Minette Walters in Pan Books

The Sculptress
The Scold's Bridle
The Dark Room
The Echo
The Breaker
The Shape of Snakes
Acid Row
Fox Evil
Disordered Minds
The Tinder Box
The Devil's Feather

MINETTE WALTERS

THE
Ice House

PAN BOOKS

First published 1992 by Macmillan

This edition published 1993 by Pan Books
an imprint of Pan Macmillan Ltd
Pan Macmillan, 20 New Wharf Road, London N1 9RR
Basingstoke and Oxford
Associated companies throughout the world
www.panmacmillan.com

Reissued 1998

ISBN 978-0-330-45498-8

Copyright © Minette Walters 1992

The right of Minette Walters to be identified as the author of this work has been asserted by her in accordance with the Copyright, Designs and Patents Act 1988.

All rights reserved. No part of this publication may be reproduced, stored in or introduced into a retrieval system, or transmitted, in any form or by any means (electronic, mechanical, photocopying, recording or otherwise), without the prior written permission of the publisher. Any person who does any unauthorized act in relation to this publication may be liable to criminal prosecution and civil claims for damages.

1 3 5 7 9 8 6 4 2

A CIP catalogue record for this book is available from the British Library.

Typeset by CentraCet, Cambridge
Printed and bound in Great Britain by
Mackays of Chatham plc, Chatham, Kent

This book is sold subject to the condition that it shall not, by way of trade or otherwise, be lent, resold, hired out, or otherwise circulated without the publisher's prior consent in any form of binding or cover other than that in which it is published and without a similar condition including this condition being imposed on the subsequent purchaser.

Visit **www.panmacmillan.com** to read more about all our books and to buy them. You will also find features, author interviews and news of any author events, and you can sign up for e-newsletters so that you're always first to hear about our new releases.

To Alec

‘Revenge is a kind of wild justice, which the more man’s nature runs to, the more ought law to weed it out.’

FRANCIS BACON

‘O wad some Pow’r the giftie gie us
To see oursels as others see us!
It wad frae mony a blunder free us,
  And foolish notion.’

ROBERT BURNS, *‘To a Louse’*

Southern Evening Herald – 23rd March

Growing Police Anxiety

Following intensive questioning at airports, docks and ferry terminals in the search for the missing businessman, David Maybury, police have expressed concern for his welfare. 'It is now ten days since he vanished,' said Inspector Walsh, the detective in charge of the investigation, 'and we cannot rule out the possibility of foul play.' Police efforts are being concentrated on a thorough search of Streech Grange Estate and the surrounding farmland.

There have been numerous reported sightings of the missing man over the past week, but none that could be substantiated. David Maybury, 44, was wearing a charcoal-grey pinstripe suit on the night he vanished. He is 5′10″ tall, of average build, with dark hair and eyes.

Sun – 15th April

To The Manor Buried

Mrs Phoebe Maybury, 27, beautiful red-haired wife of missing businessman David Maybury, looked on in fury as police dug up her garden in their search for her husband. Mrs Maybury, an avid gardener herself, declared: 'This house has been in my family for years and the garden is the product of several generations. The police have no business to destroy it.'

Reliable sources say that David Maybury, 44, was in financial difficulties shortly before he disappeared. His wine business, funded by his wife and run from the cellars of their house, was virtually bankrupt. Friends talk of constant rows between the couple. Police are treating his disappearance as murder.

Daily Telegraph – 9th August

Police Team Disbanded

Police admitted last night to being baffled over the disappearance of Hampshire man, David Maybury. In spite of a long and thorough investigation, no trace of him has been found, and the team involved in the enquiry has been disbanded. The file will remain open, according to police sources, but there is little confidence in solving the mystery. 'The public has been very helpful,' said a police spokesman. 'We have built a clear picture of what happened the night he vanished, but until we find his body, there's little more we can do.'

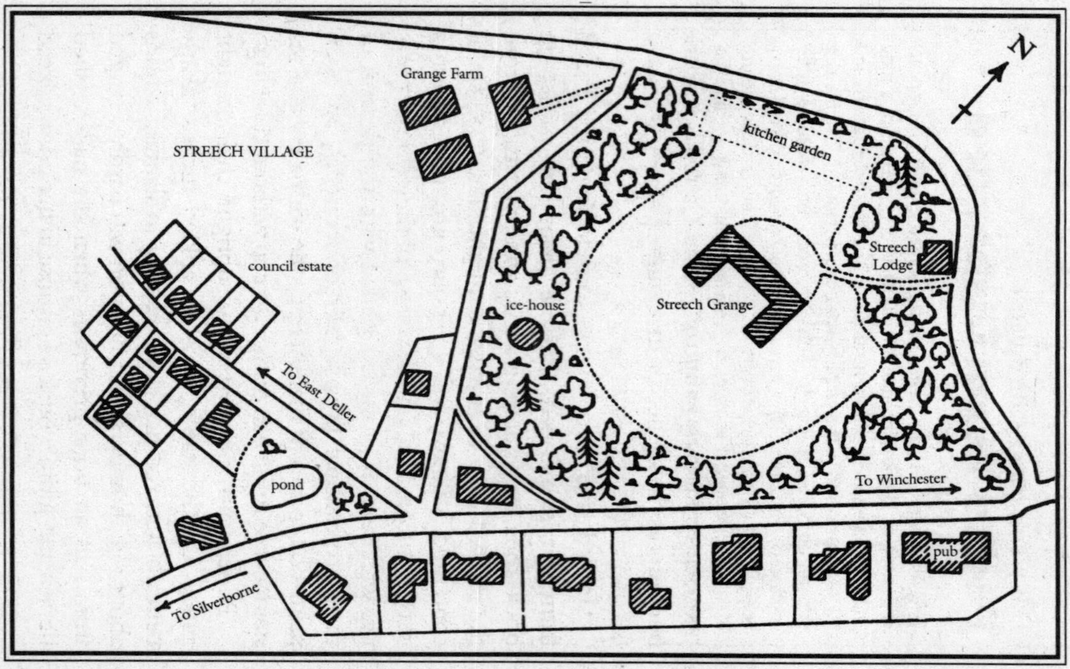
N
STREECH VILLAGE
Grange Farm
kitchen garden
council estate
Streech Lodge
ice-house
Streech Grange
To East Deller
pond
To Winchester
pub
To Silverborne

One

'FRED PHILLIPS IS *running*.' Anne Cattrell's remark burst upon the silence of that August afternoon like a fart at a vicar's tea-party.

Startled, her two companions looked up, Diana from her sketch-pad, Phoebe from her gardening book, their eyes watering at this abrupt transition from the printed page to brilliant sunlight. They had sat in contented stillness for an hour, grouped about a wrought-iron table on the terrace of their house where the wreckage of a lazy tea jostled with the flotsam of their professional lives: a pair of secateurs, an open paint-box, pages of manuscript, one with a circular tea stain where Anne had dumped a cup without thinking.

Phoebe was perched on an upright chair at right angles to the table, crossed ankles tucked neatly beneath her, red hair corkscrewing in flaming whorls about her shoulders. Her position was hardly changed from half an hour previously when she had finished her tea and guiltily buried her nose in her book instead of returning to the greenhouse to finish off a bulk order for five hundred Ivyleaf Pelargonium cuttings. Diana, unashamedly glistening with Ambre Solaire, reclined on a sun-lounger, the pleated skirt of her printed cotton dress spilling over the sides and brushing the flagstones. One elegant hand toyed with the underbelly of the Labrador lying beside her, the other drew swirling doodles in the margin of her sketch-pad which should have been filled – but was not – with commissioned designs for a cottage interior in Fowey. Anne, who had been struggling between intermittent dozes to conjure up a thousand words on 'Vaginal Orgasm – Fact or Fiction' for an obscure magazine, was drawn up tight against the table, chin on hands, dark eyes staring down the long vista of landscaped garden in front of her.

Phoebe glanced at her briefly then turned to follow her gaze, peering over her spectacles across the wide expanse of lawn. 'Good lord!' she exclaimed.

Her gardener, a man of massive proportions, was pounding across the grass, naked to the waist, his huge belly lapping at his trousers like some monstrous tidal wave. The semi-nudity was surprising enough, for Fred held strong views about his position at Streech Grange. Among other things, this required Phoebe to whistle a warning of her approach in the garden so that he might clothe himself suitably for what he referred to as a parley-vous, even in the heat of summer.

'Perhaps he's won the pools,' suggested Diana, but without conviction, as the three women watched his rapidly slowing advance.

'Highly unlikely,' countered Anne, pushing her chair away from the table. 'Fred's inertia would demand a more powerful stimulus than filthy lucre to prompt this bout of activity.'

They watched the rest of Fred's approach in silence. He was walking by the time he reached the terrace. He paused for a moment, leaning one hand heavily on the low wall bordering the flagstones, catching his breath. There was a tinge of grey to the weathered cheeks, a rasp in his throat. Concerned, Phoebe gestured to Diana to pull forward a vacant chair, then she stood up, took Fred's arm and helped him into it.

'Whatever's happened?' she asked anxiously.

'Oh, madam, something awful.' He was sweating profusely, unable to get the words out quickly. Perspiration ran in streams over his fat brown breasts, soft and round like a woman's, and the smell was all-pervading, consuming the sweet scent of the roses which nodded in beds at the edge of the terrace. Aware of this and of his nakedness, he wrung his hands in embarrassment. 'I'm so sorry, madam.'

Diana swung her legs off the lounger and sat up, twitching a rug off the back of her chair and placing it neatly across his shoulders. 'You should keep yourself warm after a run like that, Fred.'

He wrapped the rug around him, nodding his

appreciation. 'What's happened, Fred?' Phoebe asked again.

'I don't rightly know how to say it' – she thought she saw compassion in his eyes – 'but it's got to be told.'

'Then tell me,' she prompted gently. 'I'm sure it can't be that bad.' She glanced at Benson, the yellow Labrador, still lying placidly by Diana's chair. 'Has Hedges been run over?'

He reached out a rough, mud-caked hand from between the folds of the rug and with a familiarity that was quite out of character placed it on hers and squeezed gently. The gesture was as brief as it was unexpected. 'There's a body in the old ice house, madam.'

There was a moment's silence. 'A body?' echoed Phoebe. 'What sort of body?' Her voice was unemotional, steady.

Anne flicked a glance in her direction. There were times, she thought, when her friend's composure frightened her.

'To tell you the truth, madam, I didn't look too close. It was a shock, coming on it the way I did.' He stared unhappily at his feet. 'Stepped on it, like, before I saw it. There was a bit of a smell afterwards.' They all looked in fascination at his gardening boots and he, regretting his impulsive statement, shuffled them awkwardly out of sight under the rug. 'It's all right, madam,' he said, 'wiped them on the grass soon as I could.'

The cup and saucer in Phoebe's hand rattled and she put them carefully on the table beside her secateurs. 'Of course you did, Fred. How thoughtful of you. Would you like some tea? A cake perhaps?' she asked him.

'No, thank you, madam.'

Diana turned away, suppressing an awful desire to laugh. Only Phoebe, she thought, of all the women she knew would offer cake in such circumstances. In its way it was admirable, for Phoebe, more than any of them, would be affected by Fred's shocking revelation.

Anne scrabbled among the pages of her manuscript in search of her cigarettes. With an abrupt movement she flicked the box open and offered it to Fred. He glanced at Phoebe for a permission he didn't need and she nodded gravely. 'Thank you kindly, Miss Cattrell. My nerves are that shook up.'

Anne lit it for him, holding his hand steady with hers. 'Let's get this straight, Fred,' she said, her dark eyes searching his. 'It's a person's dead body. Is that right?'

'That's right, Miss Cattrell.'

'Do you know who it is?'

'I can't say I do, miss.' He spoke with reluctance. 'I can't say anyone will know who it is.' He drew deeply on his cigarette, the sweat of suppressed nausea breaking out on his forehead. 'The truth is, from the quick look I had, there's not much of it left. It must have been there a while.'

The three women looked at him aghast. 'But surely it's got clothes on, Fred?' Diana asked nervously. 'At least you know if it's a man or woman.'

'No clothes that I could see, Mrs Goode.'

'You'd better show me.' Phoebe stood up with sudden decision and Fred rose awkwardly to his feet. 'I'd rather not, madam. You shouldn't see it. I don't want to take you down there.'

'Then I'll go on my own.' She smiled suddenly and laid a hand on his arm. 'I'm sorry but I have to see it. You do understand that, don't you, Fred?'

He stubbed out his cigarette and pulled the rug tighter about his shoulders. 'If you're that intent on going, I'll come with you. It's not something you should see alone.'

'Thank you.' She turned to Diana. 'Will you phone the police for me?'

'Of course.'

Anne pushed her chair back. 'I'll come with you,' she told Phoebe. Then she called after Diana as she followed the other two across the grass. 'You might lay on some brandy, I'll be needing some, even if no one else does.'

*

They grouped themselves in a nervous huddle a few yards from the entrance to the ice house. It was an unusual structure, designed and built in the eighteenth century to resemble a small hillock. Its function as an ice-store had ceased years ago with the advent of the refrigerator, and Nature had reasserted her dominion over it so that ranks of nettles marched in their hundreds around the base, making a natural fusion between the man-made dome and the solid earth. The only entrance, a wide low doorway, was set into the ice-house wall at the end of an overgrown pathway. The doorway, too, had long since lost itself in a mass of tangled brambles which grew over it in a thorny curtain from above and below. It was revealed now only because Fred had hacked and trampled the curtain aside to reach it.

A lighted torch lay abandoned on the ground at their feet. Phoebe picked it up.'What made you go in there?' she asked Fred. 'We haven't used it for years.'

He pulled a face. 'I wish I hadn't, madam, God knows. What the eye doesn't see, the heart doesn't grieve over and that's a fact. I've been repairing the kitchen garden wall, where it collapsed a week ago. Half the bricks are unusable – I understood, when I saw the state of them, why the wall collapsed. Handful of dust, some of them. Anyway, I thought of the bricks we stored in here some years back, the ones from the outhouse we demolished. You said: "Hang on to the good ones, Fred, you never know when we might need them for repairs." '

'I remember.'

'So I wanted to use them for the wall.'

'Of course. You had to cut the brambles away?'

He nodded. 'I couldn't see the door, it was overgrown.' He pointed to a scythe lying to one side of the ice house. 'I used that and my boots to reach it.'

'Come on,' said Anne suddenly. 'Let's get it over with. Talking isn't going to make it any easier.'

'Yes,' said Phoebe quietly. 'Does the door open any wider, Fred?'

'It does, madam. I had it full open before I stepped on what's in there. Pulled it to as far as I could when I left in case anyone came by.' He pursed his lips. 'To tell you the truth, it's wider now than when I left it.'

He walked forward reluctantly and, with a sudden movement, kicked the door. It swung open on creaking hinges. Phoebe crouched and shone the torch into the interior, bathing the contents with warm golden light. It wasn't so much the blackened and eyeless corpse that caused her to vomit, as the sight of Hedges rolling quietly and purposefully in the decomposing remains of the bowels. He came out with his tail between his legs and lay on the grass watching her, head between paws, as she heaved her tea on to the grass.

Two

SILVERBORNE POLICE STATION, a modern triumph of polished chrome features and sealed tinted windows, baked in the sun amid its more traditional neighbours. Inside, the air-conditioning had broken down again and as the hours passed and the atmosphere overheated so did the policemen. They grew sticky and squabbled amongst themselves like young children. Those who could, got out; those who couldn't, jealously guarded their electric fans and prayed for a quick end to their shift. For Detective Chief Inspector Walsh, sweating profusely over some paperwork in his office, the order to take a team to Streech Grange came like a miraculous breath of air through the sealed windows. He whistled happily to himself as he made his way to the briefing room. But for Detective Sergeant McLoughlin, detailed to assist him, the knowledge that he was going to miss opening time and the cold lager he'd promised himself was the last straw.

*

Diana heard the approaching cars before the others. She finished her brandy and put the glass on the sideboard. 'Fingers out, girls. Here they come.'

Phoebe walked over to the mantelpiece, her face abnormally white against the vivid red hair. She was a tall woman who was rarely seen out of checked shirts and old Levis. But on her return from the ice house she had taken the trouble to change into a long-sleeved, high-collared silk dress. There was no doubting she looked at home in the elegant room with its pastel shades and draped velvet curtains but, to Anne at least, she had the air of a stranger. She smiled distantly at her two friends. 'I'm terribly sorry about this.'

Anne, as usual, was chain-smoking. She blew a stream of grey into the air above her where she sat on the sofa, head resting against the back. 'Don't be a fool,' she said bluntly. 'No one's going to hold you responsible because some idiot chooses to die on your property. There'll be a simple explanation: a tramp took shelter and had a heart attack.'

'My thoughts precisely,' said Diana, walking to the sofa. 'Give me a cigarette, there's a dear. My nerves are like piano wires, waiting for a Rachmaninov concerto to hit them.'

Anne chuckled and handed over the packet. 'Do you want one, Pheeb?'

She shook her head and started to polish her spectacles on her skirt hem, absent-mindedly lifting it to waist level and revealing her lack of knickers. Anne found the vagueness of the gesture reassuring.

'There won't be any glass left if you go on doing that,' she pointed out gently.

Phoebe sighed, dropped her skirt and put the spectacles back on. 'Tramps don't have heart attacks on other people's property in the nude,' she said.

The doorbell rang. They heard Molly Phillips, Fred's wife, walk to the front door and without a word, indeed quite by instinct, Anne and Diana positioned themselves on either side of the mantel-piece, flanking Phoebe. As the door opened it occurred to Diana that this might not have been a wise move. To the police mind, she feared, they would seem not so much to be supporting her – the intention – as guarding her.

Molly ushered in two men. 'Chief Inspector Walsh and Detective Sergeant McLoughlin, madam. There's a whole lot more outside. Shall I ask Fred to keep an eye on them?'

'No, that's all right, Molly. I'm sure they'll behave themselves.'

'If you say so, madam. Me, I'm not so sure. They've already scuffed their great clumsy feet over the gravel where Fred raked it so careful this morning.' She glared accusingly at the two men.

'Thank you, Molly. Perhaps you could make tea for everyone. I'm sure it will be welcome.'

'Right you are, madam.' The housekeeper closed

the door behind her and stomped off down the corridor towards the kitchen.

George Walsh listened till her footsteps died away, then he came forward and held out his hand. He was a thin stooping man who had a bizarre habit of jerking his head from side to side, like a sufferer from Parkinson's disease. It gave him an appearance of vulnerability that was deceptive.

'Good afternoon, Mrs Maybury. We've met before, if you remember.' He could recall her vividly as she had been that first time, standing where she was now. Ten years, he thought, and she had hardly changed, still the lady of the manor, remote and aloof in the security of her position. The dramas of those years might never have been. There was certainly no evidence in the calm, unlined face which smiled at him now. There was a quality of stillness about her that was unnatural. The village called her a witch, and he had always understood why.

Phoebe shook his hand. 'Yes, I do remember. It was your first big case.' Her voice was low-pitched, attractive. 'You had just been made Detective Inspector, I think. I don't believe you've met my friends, Miss Cattrell and Mrs Goode.' She gestured to Anne and Diana who shook hands solemnly in turn with the Chief Inspector. 'They live here now.'

Walsh studied the two women with interest. 'Permanently?' he asked.

'Most of the time,' said Diana, 'when our work

doesn't take us away. We're both self-employed. I'm an interior designer, Anne's a freelance journalist.'

Walsh nodded, but Anne could see that Diana had told him nothing he didn't already know. 'I envy you.' He spoke the truth. He had coveted Streech Grange since the first time he had seen it.

Phoebe put out her hand to the other man. 'Good afternoon, Sergeant McLoughlin. May I introduce Mrs Goode and Miss Cattrell.'

He was in his mid-thirties, of an age with the women, a dark, brooding man with cold eyes. In the twist of his lips, he had brought with him the irritability of the Police Station, concentrated, malignant. He regarded Phoebe and her friends with weary contempt and paid lip-service to etiquette by brushing their fingers with his in the briefest of exchanges. His dislike, uncalled-for, slapped against their unprotected cheeks.

To the consternation of her friends, who could feel the vibrations of her anger, Anne rose recklessly to the challenge. 'My, my, Sergeant, what *have* you been hearing about us?' She lifted a sardonic eyebrow then deliberately wiped her fingers down her Levis. 'You're scarcely off your mother's breast, so won't have been around the last time the Grange was the centre of police attention. Let me guess now. Our reputation – ' she indicated herself and the other two women – 'has preceded us. Which of our widely talked-about activities upsets you the most, I wonder? Child abuse, witchcraft or lesbianism?' She searched his face with scornful eyes. 'Lesbianism,' she murmured. 'Yes, you would find that the most threatening but, then, it's the only one that's true, isn't it?'

McLoughlin's temper, already fired by the heat of the day, nearly erupted. He breathed deeply. 'I've nothing against dykes, Miss Cattrell,' he said evenly. 'I just wouldn't stick my finger in one, that's all.'

Diana stubbed out her cigarette with rather more violence than was necessary. 'Don't tease the poor man, Anne,' she said dryly. 'He's going to need all his wits to sort out the mess in the ice house.'

Stiffly, Phoebe took the seat nearest her and gestured the others to sit down. Walsh sat in the chair opposite her, Anne and Diana on the sofa, leaving McLoughlin to perch on a delicate tapestry stool. His discomfort, as he folded his long legs awkwardly beneath him, was obvious to all.

'Take care you don't break that, Sergeant,' snapped Walsh. 'I don't like clumsiness any more than the housekeeper does. Well now, Mrs Maybury, perhaps you'd like to tell us why you called us out.'

'I thought Mrs Goode explained it on the telephone.'

He fished a piece of paper from his pocket. '"Body in ice house, Streech Grange. Discovered at 4.35 p.m." Not much of an explanation, is it? Tell me what happened.'

'That's it, really. Fred Phillips, my gardener, found the body about that time and came and told us. Diana phoned you while Fred took Anne and me to look at it.'

'So you've seen it?'

'Yes.'

'Who is it? Do you know?'

'The body's unrecognisable.'

With an abrupt movement, Anne lit another cigarette. 'It's putrid, Inspector, black, disgusting. *No one* would know who it was.' She spoke impatiently, her deep voice clipping the words short.

Walsh nodded. 'I see. Did your gardener suggest you look at the body?'

Phoebe shook her head. 'No, he suggested I shouldn't. I insisted on going.'

'Why?'

She shrugged. 'Natural curiosity, I suppose. Wouldn't you have gone?'

He was silent for a moment. '*Is* it your husband, Mrs Maybury?'

'I've already told you the body is unrecognisable.'

'Did you insist on going because you thought it *might* be your husband?'

'Of course. But I've realised since it couldn't possibly be.'

'Why is that?'

'It was something Fred said. He reminded me that

we stored some bricks in the ice house about six years ago when we demolished an outhouse. David had been gone four years by that time.'

'His body was never found. We never traced him,' Walsh reminded her. 'Perhaps he came back.'

Diana laughed nervously. 'He couldn't come back, Inspector. He's dead. Murdered.'

'How do you know, Mrs Goode?'

'Because he'd have been back long before this if he wasn't. David always knew which side his bread was buttered.'

Walsh crossed his legs and smiled. 'The case is still open. *We've* never been able to prove he was murdered.'

Diana's face was suddenly grim. 'Because you concentrated all your energies on trying to pin the murder on Phoebe. You gave up when you couldn't prove it. You never made any attempt to ask me for a list of suspects. I could have given you a hundred likely names; Anne could have given you another hundred. David Maybury was the most out-and-out bastard who ever lived. He deserved to die.' She wondered if she had overdone it and glanced briefly at Phoebe. 'Sorry, love, but if more people had said it ten years ago, things might have been less hard for you.'

Anne nodded agreement. 'You'll waste a lot of time if you think that thing out there is David Maybury.' She stood up and walked over to sit on the arm of Phoebe's chair. 'For the record, Inspector, both Diana and I helped clear years of accumulated rubbish out the ice house before Fred stacked the bricks in it. There were no corpses in there six years ago. Isn't that right, Di?'

Diana looked amused and inclined her head. 'It wouldn't have been the place to look for him, anyway. He's at the bottom of the sea somewhere, food for crabs and lobsters.' She looked at McLoughlin. 'Are you partial to crabs, Sergeant?'

Walsh intervened before McLoughlin could say anything. 'We followed up every known contact or associate Mr Maybury had. There was no evidence to connect any of them with his disappearance.'

Anne tossed her cigarette into the fireplace. 'Balls!' she exclaimed amiably. 'I'll tell you something, you never questioned me either and in my list of a hundred possible suspects *I* should have featured in the top ten.'

'You're quite mistaken, Miss Cattrell.' Inspector Walsh was unruffled. 'We went into your background very thoroughly. At the time of Mr Maybury's disappearance, in fact throughout most of our investigation, you were camped with your lady friends on Greenham Common under the eyes not only of the guards at the American Airforce base but also of the Newbury police and assorted television cameras. It was quite an alibi.'

'You're right. I'd forgotten. Touché, Inspector.' She chuckled. 'I was researching a feature for one of the colour supplements.' Out of the corner of her eye, she saw McLoughlin's lips thin to a disapproving line. 'But, hell, it was fun,' she went on in a dreamy voice. 'That camp is the best thing that's ever happened to me.'

Frowning, Phoebe laid a restraining hand on her arm and stood up. 'This is all irrelevant. Until you've examined the body, it seems to me quite pointless to speculate on whether or not it's David's. If you care to come with me, gentlemen, I will show you where it is.'

'Let Fred do it,' Diana protested.

'No. He's had enough shocks for one day. I'm all right. Could you make sure Molly's organising the tea?'

She opened the French windows and led the way on to the terrace. Benson and Hedges roused themselves from the warm flagstones and pushed their noses into her hand. Hedges's fur was still fluffy from his bath. She paused to stroke his head gently and pull his ears. 'There's one thing I really ought to tell you, Inspector,' she said.

Anne, watching from inside the drawing-room, gave a gurgle of laughter. 'Phoebe's confessing to Hedges's little peccadillo and the Sergeant's turned green around the gills.'

Diana pushed herself out of the sofa and walked towards her. 'Don't underestimate him, Anne,' she said. 'You're such a fool sometimes. Why do you always have to antagonise people?'

'I don't. I simply refuse to kowtow to their small-minded conventions. If they feel antagonised that's their problem. Principles should never be compromised. The minute they are, they cease to be principles.'

'Maybe, but you don't have to shove them down reluctant throats. A little common sense wouldn't come amiss at the moment. We do have a dead body on the premises. Or had you forgotten?' Her voice was more anxious than ironic.

Anne turned away from the window. 'You're probably right,' she agreed meekly.

'So you'll be careful?'

'I'll be careful.'

Diana frowned. 'I do wish I understood you. I never have, you know.'

Affection surged in Anne as she studied her friend's worried face. Poor old Di, she thought, how she hated all this. She should never have come to Streech. Her natural environment was an ivory tower where visitors were vetted and unpleasantness unheard of. 'You have no problem understanding me,' she pointed out lightly, 'you have a problem *agreeing* with me. My petty anarchies offend your sensibilities. I often wonder why you go along with them.'

Diana walked to the door. 'Which reminds me, next time you want me to lie for you, warn me first, will you? I'm not as good at controlling my facial muscles as you are.'

'Nonsense,' said Anne, dropping into an armchair. 'You're the most accomplished liar I know.'

Diana paused with her hand on the doorknob. 'Why do you say that?' she asked sharply.

'Because,' Anne teased her rigid back, 'I was there when you told Lady Weevil that her choice of colours for her drawing-room was sophisticated. Anyone who could do that with a straight face must have unlimited muscle control.'

'Lady *Keevil*,' corrected Diana, looking round with a smile. 'I should never have let you come with me. That contract was worth a fortune.'

Anne was unrepentant. 'I needed the lift and you can hardly blame me if I got her name wrong. Everything she said sounded as if it had been squeezed through a wet flannel. Anyway, I did you a favour. Cherry-red carpets and lime-green curtains, for God's sake! Think of your reputation.'

'You know her father was a fruit wholesaler.'

'You *do* surprise me,' said Anne dryly.

Three

INSIDE THE ICE house Chief Inspector Walsh firmly suppressed a slight movement in his bowels. Sergeant McLoughlin showed less control. He ran out of the building and was sick in the nettles alongside it. Unaware that she would have sympathised, he was thankful that Phoebe Maybury had returned to the Grange and was not there to see him.

'Not very nice, is it?' remarked Walsh when the Sergeant came back. 'Careful where you're stepping. There are bits all over the place. Must have been where the dog disturbed it.'

McLoughlin held a handkerchief to his mouth and retched violently. There was a strong smell of beer about him, and the Inspector eyed him with disfavour. A man of moods himself, he found inconsistency in others unendurable. He knew McLoughlin as well as any of the men he worked with, thought of him as a conscientious type, honest, intelligent, dependable. He even liked the man – he was one of the few who could cope with the notorious pendulum-swings of Walsh's temperament – but to see McLoughlin's weaknesses, disclosed like guilty secrets, irritated Walsh. 'What the hell's the matter with you?' he demanded. 'Five minutes ago you couldn't even be civil, now you're puking like a bloody baby.'

'Nothing, sir.'

'Nothing, sir,' mimicked Walsh savagely. He would have said more but there was an anger about the younger man that stilled his waspish tongue. With a sigh he took McLoughlin's arm and pushed him outside. 'Get me a photographer and some decent lights – it's impossible to see properly. And tell Dr Webster to get down here as fast as he can. I left a message for him so he should be at the Station by now.' He patted the Sergeant's arm clumsily, remembering perhaps that McLoughlin was more often his supporter than his detractor. 'If it's any consolation, Andy, I've never seen anything as nasty as this.'

As McLoughlin returned thankfully to the house, Inspector Walsh took a pipe from his pocket, filled it and lit it thoughtfully, then began a careful examination of the ground and the brambles around the door and pathway. The ground itself told him little. The summer had been an exceptional one and the last four weeks of almost perpetual sunshine had baked it hard. The only visible tracks were where feet, probably Fred's, had trampled the weeds and grass in front of the brambles. Previous tracks, if any, had long since been obliterated. The brambles might prove more interesting. It was evident, if there were no other entrance to the ice house, that the body had at some point traversed this thorny barrier, either alive on its own two legs or dead on the back of someone else's. The big question was, how long ago? How long had that nightmare been in there?

He walked slowly round the hillock. It would, of course, have been easier to satisfy himself that the door was the only entrance from inside the structure. He excused his reluctance to do this on the basis of not wishing to disturb the evidence more than was necessary but, being honest, he knew it was an excuse. The grisly tomb held no attractions for a man alone, even for a policeman intent on discovering the truth.

He spent some time investigating round the base of an untamed laurel which grew at the back of the ice house, using a discarded bamboo stake to stir up the leaf mould which had collected there. His efforts uncovered only solid brickwork, which looked strong enough to withstand another two hundred years of probing roots. In those days, he thought, they built to last.

He sat back on his heels for a moment, puffing on his pipe, then resumed his search, poking his stick at intervals into the nettles at the base of the ice-house roof but finding no other obvious points of weakness. He returned to the door and a closer examination of the brambles.

He was no gardener, he relied on his wife to tend their small patio garden where everything grew neatly in tubs, but even to his uneducated eye the brambles had a look of permanence. He spent some moments peering thoughtfully at the clods of earth and grass above the doorway, where roots had been torn free in handfuls, then, careful to avoid the grass which had been trodden on, he squatted beside the area of brambles which had been scythed and trampled flat. The broken stems were green with sap, most of the fruit was still unripe but the odd blackberry, more mature than its fellows, showed black and juicy amidst the ruins of its parent. With the end of the bamboo he carefully lifted the flattened mass of vegetation nearest to him and peered beneath it.

'Found anything, sir?' McLoughlin had returned.

'Look under here, Andy, and tell me what you see.'

McLoughlin knelt obligingly beside his superior and stared where Walsh was pointing. 'What am I looking for?'

'Stems with old breaks in them. We are safe in assuming our body didn't pole vault over this little lot.'

McLoughlin shook his head. 'We'd have to take the brambles apart for that, bit by bit, and I doubt we'd have much joy even then. Whoever flattened them did a thorough job.'

Walsh lowered the vegetation and removed the bamboo. 'The gardener, according to Mrs Maybury.'

'Looks as if he's put a steam-roller over it.'

'It's interesting, isn't it?' Walsh stood up. 'Did you get hold of Webster?'

'He's on his way, should be here in ten minutes. I've told the others to wait for him. Nick Robinson's already laid on the lights and the camera, so the gardener's showing them all down here once Webster arrives. Except young Williams. I've left him in the house to take background statements and keep his eyes open. He's a sharp lad. If there's anything to see, he'll see it.'

'Good. The mortuary van?'

'On stand-by at the station.'

Walsh moved a few yards away and sat down on the grass. 'We'll wait. There's nothing to be done until the photographs have been taken.' He blew a cloud of smoke out of the side of his mouth and squinted through it at McLoughlin. 'What is a nude corpse doing in Mrs Maybury's ice house, Sergeant? And what or, perhaps, who, has been eating it?'

With a groan, McLoughlin reached for his handkerchief.

PC Williams had taken statements from Mrs Maybury, Mrs Goode and Miss Cattrell and was now with Molly

Phillips in the kitchen. For some reason that he couldn't understand, she was being deliberately obstructive and he thought with irritation that his colleagues had a knack of landing themselves the decent jobs. With ill-disguised satisfaction they had set off down the garden with Fred Phillips and the new arrivals and their assorted paraphernalia. Williams, who had seen Andy McLoughlin's face when he came up from the ice house, was consumed with curiosity as to what was down there. McLoughlin's nerves were sprung with Scottish steel, and he had looked as sick as a dog.

Reluctantly Constable Williams returned to the job in hand. 'So the first you knew about this body was when Mrs Goode came in to telephone?'

'What if it was?'

He looked at her in exasperation. 'Do you always answer questions with questions?'

'Maybe, maybe not. That's my business.'

He was only a lad, the sort that people looked at and said: Policemen are getting younger. He tried a wheedling approach that had worked for him on a couple of occasions in the past. 'Listen, Ma – '

'Don't you "Ma" me,' she spat at him viciously. 'You're no son of mine. I don't have kids.' She turned her back on him and busied herself slicing carrots into a saucepan. 'You should be ashamed of yourself. What would your mother say? She's the only one you've a right to call Ma like that.'

Frustrated old cow, he thought. He looked at the thin, drooping shoulders and reckoned her problem was that her old man had never given her a proper working over. 'I don't even know who she is.'

She was still for a moment, knife poised in mid-air, then went on with her slicing. She said nothing.

Williams tried another tack. 'All I'm doing, Mrs Phillips, is getting some background details on the discovery of the body. Mrs Goode has told me she came into the house to make the telephone call to us. She said you were in the hall when she made it and that afterwards she went down to the cellar to get some brandy because there was none left on the sideboard. Is that right?'

'If Mrs Goode says it is, that's enough for you. There's no need to come sneaking round here behind her back trying to find out if she's telling lies.'

He looked at her sharply. '*Is* she telling lies?'

'No, she's not. The very idea.'

'Then what's all the mystery?' he asked her angry back. 'What are you being so secretive about?'

She rounded on him. 'Don't you take that tone with me. I know your sort. None better. You'll not browbeat me.' She whisked the teacup from under his nose where he sat at the table and dumped it unceremoniously in her washing-up bowl. He could have sworn there were tears in her eyes.

*

The police photographer picked his way gingerly out of the doorway and lifted the camera strap over his neck. 'Finished, sir,' he told Walsh.

The Chief Inspector placed a hand on his shoulder. 'Good man. Back to the Station with you then and get that film developed.' He turned to the pathologist. 'Shall we go in, Webster?'

Dr Webster smiled grimly. 'Do I have a choice?'

'After you,' said Walsh maliciously.

The scene was lit now with battery-run arc-lights, every detail showing with stark clarity, no shadows to soften the shocking impact. Walsh gazed dispassionately on the body. It was true, he thought, that exposure to violence desensitised a man. He could barely recall his earlier repugnance, though perhaps the lights had something to do with this. As a child the dark had held terrors for him, with nightmare creations of his imagining lurking in the corners of his bedroom. His father, in other respects a kind man but fearing the embarrassment of an effeminate son, was unsympathetic and had closed his ears to the muffled weeping inside a bedroom from which all the light bulbs had been removed.

'Good God,' said Webster, surveying the ice-house floor with marked distaste. He picked his way carefully towards the centre of it, avoiding tattered pieces of hardened entrail which lay on the flagstones. He looked at the head. 'Good God,' he said again.

The head, still tethered to the upper torso by

blackened sinew, was wedged in a gap in the top row of a neat stack of bricks. Dull grey hair, long enough to be a woman's, spilled out of the gap. Eyeless sockets, showing bone underneath, and exposed upper and lower jaw bones gleamed white against the blackened musculature of the face. The chest area, anchored by the head against the vertical face of bricks, looked as if it had been skilfully filleted. The lower half of the body lay unnaturally askew of its top half in a position that no living person, however supple, could have achieved. The abdominal region had all but disappeared though shreds of it lay about as mute witnesses that it had once existed. There were no genitals. The lower half of the left arm, propped on a smaller pile of bricks, was some four feet from the body, much of the flesh stripped away, but some sinews remaining to show it had been wrenched from its elbow. The right arm, pressed against the torso, had the same blackened quality as the head with patches of white bone showing through. Of the legs, only the calves and feet were immediately recognisable, but at a distance from each other in a grotesque parody of the splits and twisted upside down so that soles pointed at the ice-house roof. Of the thighs, only splintered bones remained.

'Well?' said Walsh after some minutes during which the pathologist took temperature readings and made a rough sketch of the lie of the body.

'What do you want to know?'

'Man or woman?'

Webster pointed to the feet. 'From the size, I'd guess a man. We can't be sure until we've done some measurements, of course, but it looks like it. If it's not a man, it was a big woman and a mannish one.'

'The hair's on the long side for a man. Unless it grew significantly after death.'

'Where have you been living, George? Even if it were down to the waist, it wouldn't tell you anything about the sex. And hair growth after death is minimal. No,' continued Webster, 'all things considered, I'd say we're dealing with a man, subject to confirmation, of course.'

'Any idea of age?'

'None, except that he's probably over twenty-one and even that's not certain. Some people go grey in their teens. I'll have to X-ray the skull for fusion between the plates.'

'How long has he been dead?'

Webster pursed his lips. 'That's going to be a bugger to decide. Old Fred out there said there was a bit of a stink when he stepped on it which would indicate a comparatively recent demise.' He sucked his teeth thoughtfully for some minutes, then shook his head and examined the floor carefully, using a spatula to loosen some dark material near the door. He sniffed the spatula. 'Excreta,' he announced, 'fairly recent, probably animal. You'd better take a cast of that to see if it's got Fred's boot prints. How long's he been dead?' He shivered suddenly. 'This is an ice house and several degrees cooler than it is outside. No obvious maggot infestation which implies the blowflies weren't attracted. If they had been, there'd be even less of it left. Frankly, George, your guess is as good as mine how long dead flesh would keep in this temperature. There is also the small matter of decomposition being hastened by consumption. We could be talking weeks, we could be talking months. I just don't know. I'll need to consult on this one.'

'Years?'

'No,' Webster said firmly. 'You'd be looking at a skeleton.'

'Supposing he was frozen when he came in. Would that make a difference?'

The pathologist snorted. 'You mean frozen as in fish fingers?' Walsh nodded. 'That's really too fantastic, George. You'd need a commercial freezer to freeze a man this size, and how would you transport him here? And why freeze him in the first place?' Webster frowned. 'It wouldn't make much difference as far as your investigation goes either. An ice house only keeps things frozen when it's full of ice. A frozen man would defrost in here just like a turkey in a larder. No, that's got to be out of the question.'

Walsh was staring thoughtfully at the severed arm. 'Has it? Odder things have happened. Perhaps he's been in cold storage for ten years and was left here recently for someone to find.'

Webster whistled. 'David Maybury?'

'It's a possibility.' He squatted down and gestured to the distorted and tattered hand. 'What do you make of this? Looks to me as if the last two fingers are missing.'

Webster joined him. 'It's difficult to say,' he said doubtfully. 'Something's had a damn good go at it.' He glanced about the floor. 'You'll have to sweep up very thoroughly, make sure you don't miss anything. It's certainly odd. Could be coincidence, I suppose.'

Walsh stood up. 'I don't believe in coincidences. Any idea what he died of?'

'A first guess, George. Massive bleeding from a wound or wounds in his abdomen.'

Walsh glanced at him in surprise. 'You're very positive.'

'A guess, I said. You'll have to find his clothes to be sure. But look at him. The area from the abdomen down has been completely devoured, except for the lower halves of the legs. Imagine him sitting up, legs out in front of him, with blood pouring out of his belly. It would be seeping over precisely those parts which have been eaten.'

Inspector Walsh felt suddenly faint. 'Are you saying whatever it was ate him while he was still alive?'

'Well, don't have nightmares about it, old chap. If he was alive, he'd have been in a coma and wouldn't have known anything about it, otherwise he'd have scared the scavengers off. Stands to reason. Of course,' he continued thoughtfully, 'if he was defrosting slowly, the blood and water would liquefy to achieve the same result.'

Walsh performed the laborious ritual of lighting his pipe again, billowing clouds of blue smoke from the side of his mouth. Webster's mention of smell had made him aware of an underlying odour which he hadn't previously noticed. For some minutes he watched the doctor making a close examination of the head and chest, at one point taking some measurements. 'What sort of scavengers are we talking about? Foxes, rats?'

'Difficult to say.' He peered closely at one of the eye sockets, before indicating the fractured thigh bones. 'Something with strong jaws, I would guess. One thing's for certain, two of them have had a fight over him. Look at the way the legs are lying and that arm, pulled apart at the elbow. I'd say there's been a tug-of-war here.' He pursed his lips again. 'Badgers possibly. More likely dogs.'

Walsh thought of the yellow Labradors lying on the warm flagstones, remembered how one of them had nuzzled the palm of his hand. With an abrupt movement, he wiped the hand down his trouser leg. He puffed smoke relentlessly into the atmosphere. 'I follow your reasoning about why the animals should have gone for the abdomen and thighs, but they seem to have done a pretty good job on the top half as well. Why is that? Is it normal?'

Webster stood up and wiped his forehead with the

sleeve of his shirt. 'God knows, George. About the only thing I'm sure of is that this whole thing is abnormal. I'll hazard a guess that the poor sod pressed his left hand to his belly to try to stop the blood running out or hold his guts in, whichever you prefer, then did what I just did – wiped the sweat off his face and smeared himself with blood. That would have attracted rats or whatever to his left hand and arm and the upper half of his body.'

'You said he'd have been in a coma.' Walsh's tone was accusing.

'Maybe he was, maybe he wasn't. How the hell should I know? Anyway, people move in comas.'

Walsh took his pipe out of his mouth and used its stem to point at the chest. 'Shall I tell you what that looks like to me?'

'Go on.'

'The bones on a breast of lamb after my wife's skinned the meat off it with a sharp knife.'

Webster looked tired. 'I know. I'm hoping it's deceptive. If it's not – well, you don't need me to spell out what it means.'

'The villagers say the women here are witches.'

Webster peeled off his gloves. 'Let's get out of here – unless there's anything else you think I can tell you. My own view is I'll find out more when I've got him on the slab.'

'Just one thing. Do you reckon he got his abdominal wound here or somewhere else?'

Webster picked up his case and led the way out. 'Don't ask me, George. The only thing I'm sure of is that he was alive when he got here. Whether he was *already* bleeding, I wouldn't know.' He paused in the doorway. 'Unless there's anything in this freezer theory, of course. Then he'd have been good and dead.'

Four

THREE HOURS LATER, after the remains had been painstakingly removed under the direction of Dr Webster, and a laborious investigation of the ice-house interior had revealed little of note beyond a pile of dead bracken in one corner, the door was sealed and Walsh and McLoughlin returned to Streech Grange. Phoebe offered them the library to work in and, with a remarkable lack of curiosity, left them to their deliberations.

A team of policemen remained behind to comb the area in expanding circles round the ice house. Privately, Walsh thought this a wasted exercise – if too much time had elapsed between the body's arrival and its discovery, the surrounding area would tell them nothing. However, routine work had produced unlikely evidence before, and now various samples from the ice house were awaiting dispatch to the forensic labs. These included brick dust, tufts of fur, some discoloured mud off the floor and what Dr

Webster asserted were the splintered remains of a lamb bone which McLoughlin had found amongst the brambles outside the door. Young Constable Williams, still ignorant of exactly what had been in the ice house, was summoned to the library.

He found Walsh and McLoughlin sitting side by side behind a mahogany desk of heroic proportions, the photographic evidence, developed at speed, spread fan-like in front of them. An ancient Anglepoise lamp with a green shade was the only lighting in the rapidly darkening room and, as Williams entered, Walsh bent the light away to soften the brightness of its glare. For the young PC, viewing the pictures upside down and in semi-darkness, it was a tantalising glimpse of the horrors he had so far only imagined. He read his small collection of statements with half an eye on McLoughlin's face, where black hollows were etched deep by the shadowy light. Jesus, but the bastard looked ill. He wondered if the whispers he'd heard were true.

'Their statements about the finding of the body are all consistent, sir. Nothing untoward in that direction.' He looked suddenly smug. 'But I reckon I've got a lead in another direction.'

'You do, do you?'

'Yes, sir. I'm betting Mr and Mrs Phillips were inside before they came to work here.' He consulted his neat and tiny script. 'Mrs Phillips was very peculiar, wouldn't answer any of my questions, kept accusing me of browbeating her, which I wasn't, and saying: "That's for me to know and you to find out." When I told her I'd have to take it up with Mrs Maybury, she damn near bit my head off. "Don't you go worrying madam," she said, "Fred and me's kept our noses clean since we've been out and that's all you need to know."' He looked up triumphantly.

Walsh made a note on a piece of paper. 'All right, Constable, we'll look into it.'

McLoughlin saw the boy's disappointment and stirred himself. 'Good work, Williams,' he murmured. 'I think we should lay on sandwiches, sir. No one's had anything to eat since midday.' He thought of the liquid lunch he'd lost into the brambles. He'd have given his right arm for a beer. 'There's a pub at the bottom of the hill. Could Gavin get something made up for the lads?'

Testily, Walsh fished two tenners out of his jacket pocket. 'Sandwiches,' he ordered. 'Nothing too expensive. Leave some with us and take the rest to the ice house. You can stay and help the search down there.' He glanced behind him out of the window. 'They've got the arc-lights. Tell them to keep going as long as they can. We'll be down later. And don't forget my change.'

'Sir.' Williams left in a hurry before the Inspector could change his mind.

'He wouldn't be so bloody keen if he'd seen what was there,' remarked Walsh acidly, poking the photographs with a skinny finger. 'I wonder if he's right about the Phillips couple. Does the name ring a bell with you?'

'No.'

'Nor with me. Let's run through what we've got.' He took out his pipe and stuffed tobacco absent-mindedly into the bowl. Aloud, he sifted fussily through what facts they had, picking at them like chicken bones.

McLoughlin listened but didn't hear. His head hurt where a blood vessel, engorged and fat, was threatening to burst. Its roaring deafened him.

He picked a pencil off the desk and balanced it between his fingers. The ends trembled violently and he let it fall with a clatter. He forced himself to concentrate.

'So where do we start, Andy?'

'The ice house and who knew it was there. It has to be the key.' He isolated an exterior shot from the photographs on the desk and held it to the lamplight with shaking fingers. 'It looks like a hill,' he muttered. 'How would a stranger know it was hollow?'

Walsh clamped the pipe between his teeth and lit it. He didn't answer but took the photograph and studied it intently, smoking for a minute or two in silence.

Unemotionally, McLoughlin gazed on the pictures of the body. 'Is it Maybury?'

'Too early to say. Webster's gone back to check the dental and medical records. The bugger is we can't compare fingerprints. We weren't able to lift any from the house at the time of his disappearance. Not that we'd get a match. Both hands out there were in ribbons.' He tamped the burning tobacco with the end of his thumb. 'David Maybury had a very distinctive characteristic,' he continued after a moment. 'The last two fingers of his left hand were missing. He lost them in a shooting accident.'

McLoughlin felt the first flutterings of awakening interest. 'So it *is* him.'

'Could be.'

'That body hasn't been there ten years, sir. Dr Webster was talking in terms of months.'

'Maybe, maybe. I'll reserve judgement till I've seen the post-mortem report.'

'What was he like? Mrs Goode called him an out-and-out bastard.'

'I'd say that's a fair assessment. You can read up about him. It's all on file. I had a psychologist go through the evidence we took from the people who knew him. His unofficial verdict, bearing in mind he never met the man, was that Maybury showed marked psychopathic tendencies, particularly when drunk. He had a habit of beating people up, women as well as men.' Walsh puffed a spurt of smoke from the side of his mouth and eyed his subordinate. 'He put himself about a bit. We turned up at least three little tarts who kept warm beds for him in London.'

'Did she know?' He nodded towards the hall.

Walsh shrugged. 'Claimed she didn't.'

'Did he beat her up?'

'Undoubtedly, I should think, except she denied it. She had a bruise the size of a football on her face when she reported him missing and we found out she was twice admitted to hospital when he was alive, once with a fractured wrist and once with cracked ribs and a broken collar-bone. She told doctors she was accident-prone.' He gave a harsh laugh. 'They didn't believe her any more than I did. He used her as his personal punch bag whenever he was drunk.'

'So why didn't she leave? Or perhaps she enjoyed the attention?'

Walsh considered him thoughtfully for a moment. He started to say something, then thought better of it. 'Streech Grange has been in her family for years. He lived here on sufferance and used her capital to run a small wine business from the house. Presumably most of the stock's still here if she hasn't drunk or sold it. No, she wouldn't leave. In fact I can't imagine any circumstances at all, not even fire, which would make her abandon her precious Streech Grange. She's a very tough lady.'

'And, I suppose, as he was in clover, he wouldn't go either.'

'That's about the size of it.'

'So she got rid of him.'

Walsh nodded.

'But you couldn't prove it.'

'No.'

McLoughlin's bleak face cracked into a semblance of a grin. 'She must have come up with one hell of a story.'

'Matter of fact, it was bloody awful. She told us he walked out one night and never returned.' Walsh wiped a dribble of tar and saliva off the end of his pipe with his sleeve. 'It was three days before she reported him missing, and she only did that because people had started to ask where he was. In that time she packed up all his clothes and sent them off to some charity whose name she couldn't remember, she burnt all his photos and went through this house with a vacuum cleaner and a cloth soaked with bleach to remove every last trace of him. In other words she behaved exactly like someone who had just murdered her husband and was trying to get rid of the evidence. We salvaged some hair that she'd missed in a brush, a current passport and photo that she'd overlooked at the back of a desk drawer, and an old blood donor card. And that was it. We turned this house and garden upside down, called in forensic to do a microscopic search and it was a waste of time. We scoured the countryside for him, showed his photo at all the ports and airports in case he'd somehow got through without a passport, alerted Interpol to look for him on the Continent, dredged lakes and rivers, released his photo to the national newspapers. Nothing. He simply vanished into thin air.'

'So how did she explain the bruise on her face?'

The Inspector chuckled. 'A door. What else? I tried to help her, suggested she killed her husband in self-defence. But no, he never touched her.' He shook his head, remembering. 'Extraordinary woman. She never made it easy for herself. She could have manufactured any number of stories to convince us he'd planned his disappearance – money troubles, for a start. He left her well-nigh penniless. But she did the reverse – she kept stolidly repeating that one night and for no reason he simply walked out and never came back. Only dead men disappear as completely as that.'

'Clever,' said McLoughlin reluctantly. 'She kept it simple, gave you nothing to pick holes in. So why didn't you charge her? Prosecutions have been brought without bodies before.'

The memories of ten years ago flooded back to try Walsh's patience. 'We couldn't put a case together,' he snapped. 'There wasn't one shred of evidence to dispute her bloody stupid story that he'd upped and left. We needed the body. We dug up half Hampshire looking for the blasted thing.' He fell silent for a moment, then tapped the photograph of the ice house which lay on the desk in front of him. 'You were right about this.'

'In what way?'

'It is the key. We searched Streech gardens from end to end ten years ago and none of us looked in here. I'd never seen an ice house in my life, never even heard of such a thing. So of course I didn't know the bloody hill was hollow. How the hell could I? No one told me. I remember standing on it at one point to get my bearings. I even remember telling one of my chaps to delve deep into those brambles. It was like a jungle.' He wiped the stem of his pipe on his sleeve again before putting it back in his mouth. Dried tar criss-crossed the tweed like black threads. 'I'll lay you any money you like, Andy, Maybury's body was in there all the time.'

There was a knock at the door and Phoebe came in carrying a tray of sandwiches. 'Constable Williams told me you were hungry, Inspector. I asked Molly to make these up for you.'

'Why thank you, Mrs Maybury. Come and sit down.' Phoebe put the tray of sandwiches on the desk, then seated herself in a leather armchair slightly to one side of it. The lamp on the desk shed a pool of light, embracing the three figures in a reluctant intimacy. The smoke from Walsh's pipe hung above them, floating in the air like curling tendrils of cirrus clouds. For one long moment there was complete silence, before the chiming mechanism of a grandfather clock whirred into action and struck the hour, nine o'clock.

Walsh, as if on cue, leant forward and addressed the

woman. 'Why didn't you tell us about the ice house ten years ago, Mrs Maybury?'

For a moment he thought she looked surprised, even a little relieved, then the expression vanished. Afterwards, he couldn't be sure it had been there at all. 'I don't understand,' she said.

Inspector Walsh gestured to McLoughlin to switch on the overhead lights. The muted lamplight disguised, deceived when he wanted to see every nuance of the extraordinarily impassive face. 'It's quite simple,' he murmured, after McLoughlin had flooded the room with brilliant white light, 'in our search for your husband, we never looked in the ice house. We didn't know it was there.' He studied her thoughtfully. 'And you didn't tell us.'

'I don't remember,' she said simply. 'If I didn't tell you, it was because I had forgotten about it. Did you not find it yourselves?'

'No.'

She gave a tiny shrug. 'Does it really matter, Inspector, after all this time?'

He ignored the question. 'Do you recall when the ice house was last used prior to your husband's disappearance?'

She leant her head tiredly against the back of her chair, her red hair splayed out around her pale face. Behind her glasses her eyes looked huge. Walsh knew her to be in her mid-thirties, yet she looked younger than his own daughter. He felt McLoughlin stir in the seat beside him as if her fragility had touched him in some way. Damn the woman, he thought with irritation, remembering the emotions she had once stirred in him. That appearance of vulnerability was a thin cloak for the sharp mind beneath.

'You'll have to let me think about it,' she said. 'At the moment, I honestly can't remember if we ever used it when David was alive. I have no recollection of it.' She paused briefly. 'I *do* recall my father using it as a darkroom one winter when I was on holiday from school. He didn't do it for very long.' She smiled. 'He said it was a confounded bore slogging all the way down there in the cold.' She gave a low ripple of laughter as if memories of her father made her happy. 'He took the films to a professional in Silverborne instead. My mother said it was because he enjoyed blaming someone else when the prints were disappointing, which they often were. He wasn't a very good photographer.' She looked steadily at the Inspector. 'I can't remember its being used after that, not until we decided to stack the bricks in there. The children might know. I suppose I could ask them.'

Walsh remembered her children, a gangling ten-year-old boy, arriving home from his boarding prep-school in the middle of the investigation, his eyes the same clear blue as his mother's, and an eight-year-old daughter with a bush of curling dark hair. They had protected her, he recalled, with the same fierce quality that her two friends had shown earlier in the drawing-room. 'Jonathan and Jane,' he said. 'Do they still live at home, Mrs Maybury?'

'Not really. Jonathan rents a flat in London. He's a medical student at Guy's. Jane is studying politics and philosophy at Oxford. They spend the odd weekend and holidays here. That's all.'

'They've done well. You must be pleased.' He thought sourly of his own daughter who had got herself pregnant at sixteen and who now, at the age of twenty-five, was divorced with four children, and had nothing to look forward to except life in a tatty council flat. He consulted his notes. 'You seem to have acquired a profession since I last saw you, Mrs Maybury. Constable Williams tells me you're a market gardener.'

Phoebe seemed puzzled by his change of direction. 'Fred's helped me build up a small Pelargonium nursery.' She spoke warily. 'We specialise in the Ivyleaf varieties.'

'Who buys them?'

'We have two main customers in this country, one's a supermarket chain and the other's a garden-supplies outlet in Devon and Cornwall. We've also had a few bulk orders from the States which we've air-freighted out.' She was intensely suspicious of him. 'Why do you want to know?'

'No particular reason,' he assured her. He sucked noisily on his pipe. 'I expect you get a lot of customers from the village.'

'None,' she said shortly. 'We don't sell direct to the

public and, anyway, they wouldn't come here if we did.'

'You're not very popular in Streech, are you, Mrs Maybury?'

'So it would seem, Inspector.'

'You worked as a receptionist in the doctor's surgery ten years ago. Didn't you like that job?'

A flicker of amusement lifted the corners of her mouth. 'I was asked to leave. The patients felt uncomfortable with a murderess.'

'Did your husband know about the ice house?' He shot the question at her suddenly, unnerving her.

'That it was there, you mean?'

He nodded.

'I'm sure he must have done, though, as I say, I don't remember him ever going in there.'

Walsh made a note. 'We'll follow that up. The children may remember something. Will they be here this weekend, Mrs Maybury?'

She felt cold. 'I suppose if they don't come down, you'll send a policeman to them.'

'It's important.'

There was a tremor in her voice. 'Is it, Inspector? You have our word there was no body in there six years ago. What possible connection can that – that thing have with David's disappearance?' She took off her glasses and pressed her fingertips against her eyelids. 'I don't want the children harassed. They suffered enough when David went missing. To have the whole ghastly trauma played out a second time and for no obvious reason would be intolerable.'

Walsh smiled indulgently. 'Routine questions, Mrs Maybury. Hardly very traumatic, surely?'

She put her glasses on again, angered by his response. 'You were extraordinarily stupid ten years ago, of course. Why I ever assumed the passage of time would make you any brighter, I can't think. You sent us to hell and you call it "hardly traumatic". Do you know what hell is? Hell is what a little girl of eight goes through when the police dig up all the flowerbeds and question her mother for hours on end in a closed room. Hell is what is in your young son's eyes when his father deserts him without a word of explanation and his mother is accused of murder. Hell is seeing your children hurting and not being able to do a damn thing to stop it. You asked me if I was pleased with their achievements.' She leaned forward, her face twisted. 'Surely even you could have come up with something a little more imaginative? They have lived through the mysterious disappearance of their father, their mother being branded a murderess, their home being turned into a tourist attraction for the ghoulish and they have survived it relatively unscathed. I think "ecstatic" might be a better description of how I feel about the way they've turned out.'

'We suggested at the time you should send the

children away, Mrs Maybury.' Walsh kept his voice carefully neutral. 'You chose to keep them here against our advice.'

Phoebe stood up. It was only the second time he had ever seen any violent emotion on that face. 'My God, I hate you.' She put her hands on the desk and he saw that the fingers trembled uncontrollably. 'Where was I to send them? My parents were dead, I had no brothers or sisters, neither Anne nor Diana was in a position to care for them. Was I supposed to entrust them to strangers when their own secure world was turning upside down?' She thought of her only relation, her father's unmarried sister, who had fallen out with the family years before. The old lady had read between every line of every newspaper with voracious delight and had penned her own small piece of poison to Phoebe on the subject of the sins of the parents. What her intentions were in writing the letter was anyone's guess but, in a strange way, her warped predictions for Jonathan and Jane had been a liberation for Phoebe. She had seen clearly then – and for the first time – that the past was dead and buried and that regrets would achieve her nothing.

'How dare you speak to me of choice! My only choice was to smile while you shat on me and never once let the children know how frightened and alone I felt.' Her fingers gripped the edge of the desk. 'I will not go through all that again. I will not allow you to stick your dirty fingers into my children's lives. You've spread your filthy muck here once. You're bloody well not going to do it again.' She turned away and walked to the door.

'I've some more questions for you, Mrs Maybury. Please don't go.'

She looked round briefly as she opened the door. 'Fuck off, Inspector.' The door slammed behind her.

McLoughlin had listened to their exchange with rapt attention. 'Bit of a sea-change from this afternoon. Is she always as volatile?'

'Quite the reverse. Ten years ago we never rattled her composure once.' He sucked thoughtfully on his filthy briar.

'It's those two dykes she's shacked up with. They've turned her against men.'

Walsh was amused. 'I should think David Maybury did that years ago. Let's talk to Mrs Goode. Will you go and find her?'

McLoughlin reached for a sandwich and crammed it into his mouth before standing up. 'What about the other one? Shall I line her up too?'

The Chief Inspector thought for a moment. 'No. She's a dark horse, that one. I'll let her stew till I've checked up on her.'

From where he was standing, McLoughlin could see pink scalp shining through Walsh's thinning hair. He felt a sudden tenderness for the older man, as if Phoebe's hostility had exorcised his own and reminded him where his loyalties lay. 'She's your most likely suspect, sir. She'd have enjoyed cutting that poor sod's balls off. The other two would have hated it.'

'You're probably right, lad, but I'm betting he was dead when she did it.'

Five

STREECH GRANGE WAS a fine old Jacobean mansion built of grey stone, with mullioned, leaded windows and steep slate roofs. Two wings, later additions, extended out at either end of the main body of the house, embracing the sides of the flagged terrace where the women had taken their tea. Stud partitions inside made each of these wings self-contained, with unlocked doors on the ground floor giving access to and from them. Sergeant McLoughlin, after a fruitless search of the drawing-room and the kitchen which were both empty, came to the communicating door with the east wing. He tapped lightly but, getting no response, turned the handle and walked down the corridor in front of him.

A door stood ajar at the end. He could hear a deep voice – unmistakably Anne Cattrell's – coming from inside the room. He listened.

'. . . stick to your guns and don't let the bastards intimidate you. God knows, I've had more experience of them than most. Whatever happens, Jane must be kept out of the way. You agree?' There was a murmur of assent. 'And, old love, if you can wipe the smirk off that Sergeant's face, you'll have my lifelong admiration.'

'I suppose it's occurred to you' – the lighter amused voice was Diana's – 'that he might have been born with that smirk. Perhaps it's a disability he's had to learn to cope with, like a withered arm. You'd be quite sympathetic if that were the case.'

Anne gave her throaty laugh. 'The only disabilities that idiot has are both in his trousers.'

'Namely?'

'He's a prick and an arsehole.'

Diana crowed with laughter and McLoughlin felt a dull flush creep up his neck. He trod softly to the communicating door, closed it behind him and knocked again, this time more loudly. When, after some moments, Anne opened the door, he was ready with his most sardonic smile.

'Yes, Sergeant?'

'I'm looking for Mrs Goode. Inspector Walsh would like a word with her.'

'This is my wing. She's not here.'

The lie was so blatant that he looked at her in astonishment. 'But – ' He paused.

'But what, Sergeant?'

'Where will I find her?'

'I've no idea. Perhaps the Inspector would like to speak to me instead?'

McLoughlin pushed past her impatiently and walked down the corridor and into the room. There was no one in there. He frowned. The room was a large one with a desk at one end and a sofa and armchairs grouped about a wide fireplace at the other. Pot plants grew in profusion everywhere, cascading like green waterfalls from the mantelpiece, climbing up lattice-work on one of the walls, dappling the light from the lamps on low occasional tables. Floor to ceiling curtains in a herring-bone pattern of pale pinks, greys and blues were drawn along the length of the two outside walls, a royal blue carpet covered the floor, bright abstract paintings laughed merrily from the picture rails. Books in bookcases stood as straight as soldiers wherever there was a space. It was a delightful room, not one that McLoughlin would ever have associated with the tiny muscular woman who had followed him in and was now leaning her cropped, dark head against the door-jamb, waiting.

'Do you make a habit of forcing your way into people's private apartments, Sergeant? I have no recollection of inviting you in.'

'We have Mrs Maybury's permission to come and go as we please,' he said dismissively.

She walked over to one of the armchairs and slumped into it, taking a cigarette from a packet on the arm. 'Of course, in her house,' she agreed, lighting the cigarette. 'But this wing is mine. You have no authority to enter here except by permission or with a warrant.'

'I'm sorry,' he said stiffly. He felt suddenly uncomfortable, towering over her, conspicuously ill-at-ease while she, by contrast, was relaxed. 'I was not aware you owned this part of the house.'

'I don't own it, I rent it, but the legal position with regard to police entry is the same.' She smiled thinly. 'As a matter of interest, what possible reason had you for thinking Mrs Goode might be in here?'

He saw one of the curtain edges lift as a gentle breeze caught it, and realised Diana must have left by a French window. He cursed himself silently for allowing this woman to make a mockery of him. 'I couldn't find her anywhere else,' he said brusquely, 'and Inspector Walsh wants to speak to her. Does she live in the other wing?'

'She rents the other wing. As to living in it – surely you've guessed we all three rather muck in together. It's what's known as a ménage à trois, though in our case, rather loosely. The average threesome includes both sexes. We, I'm afraid, are more exclusive, preferring, as we do, our peculiarly – how shall I describe it? – spicy female sex. Three makes for more exciting encounters than two, don't you think. Or have you never tried?'

His dislike of her was irrational and intense. He

jerked his head in the direction of the main part of the house. 'Have you corrupted her children the way you've corrupted her?'

She laughed softly and stood up. 'You'll find Mrs Goode in her sitting-room, I expect. I'll show you out.' She led the way along her corridor and opened the door. 'Walk straight through the main body of the house until you reach the west wing. It's a mirror image of this. You'll find a similar door to mine leading into it.' She pointed to a bell on the wall which he hadn't previously noticed. 'I should ring that if I were you. At the very least, it would be polite.' She stood watching him as he walked away, a scornful smile distorting her lips.

Andy McLoughlin had to pass the library door to reach the west wing so he looked in to tell Walsh it would be a few minutes yet before he returned with Diana Goode. To his surprise, she was in there already, sitting in the chair Phoebe had sat in. She and the Inspector turned their heads as the door opened. They were laughing together like people sharing a private joke.

'There you are, Sergeant. We've been waiting for you.'

He took his seat again and viewed Diana with suspicion. 'How did you know the Inspector wanted to talk to you?' He pictured her outside the French windows listening to Anne Cattrell making a fool of him.

'I didn't, Sergeant. I popped my head in to see if you wanted a cup of coffee.' She smiled good-humouredly and crossed one elegant leg over the other. 'What did you want to talk to me about, Inspector?'

There was an appreciative gleam in George Walsh's eye. 'How long have you known Mrs Maybury?' he asked her.

'Twenty-five years. Since we were twelve. We were at boarding school together. Anne, too.'

'A long time.'

'Yes. We've known her longer than anyone else, I suppose, longer even than her parents did. They died when she was in her early twenties.' She came to a halt. 'But you know all about that from last time,' she finished awkwardly.

'Remind us,' Walsh encouraged.

Diana lowered her eyes to hide their expression. It was all very well for Anne to say don't let the bastards intimidate you. Knowledge itself was intimidating. With one casual reference, the sort she might make to anyone, she had rekindled the sparks of an old suspicion. No smoke without fire, everyone had said when David disappeared.

'They died in a car crash, didn't they?' Walsh prompted.

She nodded. 'The brakes failed. They were dead

when they were cut out of the wreckage.' There was a long silence.

'If I remember correctly,' said Walsh to McLoughlin when Diana didn't go on, 'there were rumours of sabotage. Am I right, Mrs Goode? The village seemed to think Mrs Maybury caused the accident to get her hands prematurely on her inheritance. People have long memories. The story was resurrected at the time of Mr Maybury's disappearance.'

McLoughlin studied Diana's bent head. 'Why should they think that?' he asked.

'Because they're stupid,' she said fiercely. 'There was no truth in it. The Coroner's verdict couldn't have been clearer – the brakes failed because fluid had leaked from a corroded hose. The car was supposed to have been serviced three weeks before by a man called Casey who owned the garage in the village. He was just a bloody little crook. He took the money and didn't do the job.' She frowned. 'There was talk of a prosecution but it never came to anything. Not enough evidence, apparently. Anyway, it was Casey who started rumours that Phoebe had sabotaged the car to get her hands on Streech Grange. He didn't want to lose his customers.'

McLoughlin looked her up and down, but there was no appreciative gleam in his eyes. His indifference was complete and, to a woman like Diana who used flirtation to manipulate both sexes, it was daunting.

Charm was powerless against a stone wall. 'There must have been more to it than that,' he suggested dryly. 'People aren't usually so gullible.'

She played with the hem of her jacket. 'It was David's fault. Phoebe's parents had given them a little house in Pimlico as a wedding present which David used as collateral for a loan. He lost the lot on some stock market gamble, couldn't make the repayments and they were in the throes of foreclosure at the time of the accident, with two small children, no money and nowhere to go.' She shook her head. 'God knows how, but that became public knowledge. The locals lapped up what Casey was saying, put two and two together and made five. From the moment Phoebe took over this house, she was damned. David's disappearance a few years later simply confirmed all their prejudices.' She sighed. 'The sickening thing is, they didn't believe Casey either. He went bankrupt ten months later when all his customers deserted him. He had to sell up and move away, so there was some justice,' she said spitefully. 'Not that it did Phoebe any good. They were too damn stupid to see that if he was lying, she was innocent.'

McLoughlin leaned back in his chair, splaying strong fingers against the desk-top. He flicked her an unexpectedly boyish smile. 'It must have been awful for her.'

She responded guardedly. 'It was. She was so young and she had to cope with it alone. David either took himself off for weeks at a time or made matters worse by getting into rows with people.'

His eyes softened, as if he understood loneliness and could sympathise with it. 'And I suppose her friends here deserted her because of him?'

Diana thawed. 'She never really had any, that was half the trouble. If she had, it would have made all the difference. She went away to boarding school at the age of twelve, married at seventeen and only came back when her parents were dead. She's never had any friends in Streech.'

McLoughlin drummed his fingers softly on the mahogany. '"The worst solitude is to be destitute of sincere friendship." Francis Bacon said that four hundred years ago.'

She was quite taken aback. Anne used Francis Bacon quotes as a matter of course but they tended to be flippant, throw-away lines, tossed into a conversation for careless effect. McLoughlin's dark voice lingered over the words, rolling them on his tongue, giving them weight. She was as surprised by their aptness as by the fact that he knew them. She regarded him thoughtfully.

'But he also said, "The mould of a man's fortune is in his own hands."' His lips twisted cruelly. 'It's odd, isn't it, how Mrs Maybury brings out the worst in people? What's her secret, I wonder?' He stirred the photographs of crude death with the end of his pencil, turning them slowly so that Diana could see them.

'Why didn't she sell the Grange and move away, once she'd got rid of her husband?'

For all her surface sophistication, Diana was naive. Brutality shocked her because she never saw it coming. 'She couldn't,' she snapped angrily. 'It's not Phoebe's to sell. After a year of marriage to that bastard, she persuaded her father to change his Will and leave the house to her children. We three rent it from them.'

'Then why haven't her children sold it? Have they no sympathy for their mother?' He caught her eye. 'Or perhaps they don't like her? It seems to be a common problem for Mrs Maybury.'

Anger threatened to overwhelm Diana. She forced herself to stay calm. 'The idea, Sergeant, was to prevent David turning the house into ready cash and leaving Phoebe and the children homeless the minute the Gallaghers died. He'd have done it, too, given half a chance. He went through the money she inherited in record time. Colonel Gallagher, Phoebe's father, left instructions that the house could not be sold or mortgaged except under the most exceptional circumstances before Jane's twenty-first birthday. The responsibility for deciding whether those circumstances – principally financial distress on the part of Phoebe and her children – ever materialise was left to two trustees. In the view of the trustees, things have never got so bad that the sale of the Grange was the only option.'

'Was no other distress taken into account?'

'Of course not,' she said with heavy sarcasm. 'How could it have been? Colonel Gallagher wasn't clairvoyant. He did give discretion to the trustees but they have chosen to stick to the precise terms of the Will. In view of the uncertainty over David, whether he's dead or alive, it seemed the safest thing to do, even if Phoebe did suffer.' She glanced at Walsh to draw him back into the discussion. McLoughlin frightened her. 'The trustees have always put the children first, as they were instructed to do under the terms of the Will.'

McLoughlin's amusement was genuine. 'I'm beginning to feel quite sorry for Mrs Maybury. Does she dislike these trustees as much as they seem to dislike her?'

'I wouldn't know, Sergeant. I've never asked her.'

'Who are they?'

Chief Inspector Walsh chuckled. The lad had just hanged himself. 'Miss Anne Cattrell and Mrs Diana Goode. It was some Will, gave you two ladies a deal of responsibility when you were barely in your twenties. We've a copy on file,' he told the Sergeant. 'Colonel Gallagher must have thought very highly of you both to entrust you with his grandchildren's future.'

Diana smiled. She must remember to tell Anne how she'd wiped the smirk off McLoughlin's face. 'He did,' she said. 'Why should that surprise you?'

Walsh pursed his lips. 'I found it surprising ten years ago, but then I had never met you and Miss

Cattrell. You were abroad at that time, I think, Mrs Goode.' He smiled and dropped one eyelid in what looked remarkably like a wink. 'I do not find it surprising now.'

She inclined her head. 'Thank you. My ex-husband is American. I was with him in the States when David vanished. I returned a year later after my divorce.'

She continued to look at Walsh but the hairs on her neck bristled under the weight of McLoughlin's gaze. She didn't want to catch his eye again. 'Did Colonel Gallagher know about the relationship you and Miss Cattrell had with his daughter?' he asked softly.

'That we were friends, you mean?' She kept her eyes on the Inspector.

'I was thinking more in terms of the bedroom, Mrs Goode, and the effect your fun and games might have on his grandchildren. Or didn't he know about that?'

Diana stared at her hands. She found people's contempt so difficult to handle and she wished she had one half of Anne's indifference to it. 'Not that it's any of your business, Sergeant,' she said at last, 'but Gerald Gallagher knew everything there was to know about us. He was not a man you had to hide things from.'

Walsh had been busily replenishing his pipe with tobacco. He put it into his mouth and lit it, belching more smoke into the already fuggy atmosphere. 'After they came back to the house, did either Mrs Maybury or Miss Cattrell suggest that they thought the body in the ice house was David Maybury's?'

'No.'

'Did either of them say who they thought it might be?'

'Anne said it was probably a tramp who had had a heart attack.'

'Mrs Maybury?'

Diana thought for a moment. 'Her only comment was that tramps don't die of heart attacks in the nude.'

'What's your view, Mrs Goode?'

'I don't have a view, Inspector, except that it isn't David. You've already had my reasons for that.'

'Why do you and Miss Cattrell want Jane Maybury kept out of the way?' McLoughlin asked suddenly.

There was no hesitation in her answer though she glanced at him curiously as she spoke. 'Jane was anorexic until eighteen months ago. She took a place at Oxford last September with her consultant's blessing, but he warned her not to put herself under unnecessary pressure. As trustees, we endorse Phoebe's view that Jane should be protected from this. She's still painfully thin. Undue anxiety would use up her reserves of energy. Do you consider that unreasonable, Sergeant?'

'Not at all,' he answered mildly.

'I wonder why Mrs Maybury didn't explain her daughter's condition to us,' asked Walsh. 'Has she a particular reason for keeping quiet about it?'

'None that I know of, but perhaps experience has taught her to be circumspect where the police are concerned.'

'How so?' He was affable.

'It's in your nature to go for the weak link. We all know that Jane can tell you nothing about that body, but Phoebe's probably afraid you'll question her until she cracks. And only when you've broken her will you be satisfied that she knew nothing in the first place.'

'You've a very twisted view of us, Mrs Goode.'

Diana forced a light laugh. 'Surely not, Inspector. Of the three of us, I'm the only one who retains some confidence in you. It is I, after all, who is giving you information.' She uncrossed her legs and drew them up on to the chair, covering them entirely with her knitted jacket. Her eyes rested briefly on the photographs. 'Is it a man's body? Anne and Phoebe couldn't tell.'

'At the moment we think so.'

'Murdered?'

'Probably.'

'Then take my advice and look in this village or the surrounding ones for your victim and your murderer. Phoebe is such an obvious scapegoat for someone else's crime. Shove the body on to her property and leave her to carry the can, that will have been the thinking behind this.'

Walsh nodded appreciatively as he pencilled a note

on his pad. 'It's a possibility, Mrs Goode, a definite possibility. You're interested in psychology?'

He's quite a poppet after all, thought Diana, unleashing one of the calculatedly charming smiles she reserved for her more biddable customers. 'I use it all the time in my work,' she told him, 'though I don't suppose a clinician would call what I use psychology.'

He beamed back at her. 'So what would *he* call it?'

'Hidden persuasion, I should think.' She thought of Lady Keevil and her lime-green curtains. Lies, Anne would call it.

'Do your clients come here to consult you?'

She shook her head. 'No. It's their interiors they want designing, not mine. I go to them.'

'But you're an attractive woman, Mrs Goode.' His admiration for her was blatant. 'You must have a lot of friends who come visiting, people from the village, people you've met over the years.'

She wondered if he guessed how tender this particular nerve was, how deeply she felt the isolation of their lives. At first, bruised and battered from the break-up of her marriage, it had hardly mattered. She had withdrawn inside the walls of Streech Grange to lick her wounds in peace, grateful for the absence of well-meaning friends and their embarrassing commiserations. The shock of discovery, as her scars healed and she tendered for one or two small design contracts, that Phoebe's exclusion had been imposed and not chosen had been a real one. She had learnt what it was to be a pariah; she had watched Phoebe nurture her hate; she had watched Anne's tolerance turn to cynical indifference; she had heard her own voice grow brittle. 'No,' she corrected him. 'We have very few visitors, certainly never from the village.'

His eyes were encouraging. 'Then tell me, assuming you're right and our victim and murderer are local, how could they know about the ice house and, if they did know about it, how did they find it? I think you'll agree it's well disguised.'

'Anyone could know about it,' she said dismissively. 'Fred may have mentioned it in the pub after he stacked the bricks in there. Phoebe's parents may have told people about it. I don't see that as a mystery.'

'All right. Now tell me how you find it if you haven't been shown where it is? Presumably none of you has noticed an intruder searching the grounds or you'd have mentioned it. And another thing, why was it necessary to put the body in there at all?'

She shrugged. 'It's a good hiding place.'

'How did the murderer know that? How did he or she know the ice house wasn't in regular use? And what was the point of hiding the body if the idea was to make Phoebe Maybury the scapegoat? You see, Mrs Goode, the picture is rather unclear.'

She thought for a moment. 'You can't rule out pure chance. Someone committed a murder, decided to get rid of the body in the Grange grounds in the hopes that, if it was discovered, the police would concentrate their efforts on Phoebe, and stumbled on the ice house by accident while looking for somewhere to put the body.'

'But the ice house is half a mile from the gates,' Walsh objected. 'Do you seriously believe that a murderer staggered past the Lodge House and all the way down your drive and across your lawn in pitch darkness with a body on his shoulders? We can assume, I think, that no one would have been mad enough to do it during the daytime. Why didn't he simply bury the body in the wood near the gates?'

She looked uncomfortable. 'Perhaps he came over the wall at the back and approached the ice house from that direction.'

'Wouldn't that have meant negotiating his way through Grange Farm, which if I remember correctly adjoins the Grange at the back?' She nodded reluctantly. 'Why run that danger? And why, having run it, not bury the body quickly, in the woodland there? Why was it so important to put him in the ice house?'

Diana shivered suddenly. She understood perfectly that he was trying to box her in, force her on to the defensive and admit that knowledge of the ice house and its whereabouts was a crucial element. 'It seems to me, Inspector,' she continued coolly, 'that you have made a number of assumptions which – correct me if I'm wrong – have yet to be substantiated. First, you are assuming the body was taken there. Perhaps whoever it was went under his – or her – own steam and met the murderer there.'

'Of course we've considered that possibility, Mrs Goode. It doesn't alter our thinking at all. We must still ask: Why the ice house and how did they know where to find it unless they had been there before?'

'Well, then,' she said, 'work on the assumption that people have been there and find out who they are. Off the top of my head, I could make several suggestions. Friends of Colonel Gallagher and his wife, for example.'

'Who would be in their seventies or eighties by now. Of course it's possible that an elderly person was responsible but statistically unlikely.'

'People to whom Phoebe or David pointed it out.'

McLoughlin moved on his chair. 'Mrs Maybury has already told us she'd forgotten all about it, so much so that she omitted to tell the police it was there when they were searching the grounds for her husband. It seems unlikely, if she had forgotten it to that extent, that she would have remembered to point it out to casual visitors who, from what you yourself have said, don't come here anyway.'

'David then.'

'Now you have it, Mrs Goode,' said the Inspector. 'David Maybury may well have shown the ice house to someone, to several people even, but Mrs Maybury has no recollection of it. Indeed, she cannot recall *him* ever using it though she did agree that he was probably aware of its existence. Frankly, Mrs Goode, at the moment I don't see how we can proceed in that direction unless Mrs Maybury or the children can remember occasions or names that might give us a lead.'

'The children,' said Diana, leaning forward. 'I should have thought of it before. They will have taken their friends there when they were younger. You know how inquisitive children are, there can't be an inch of this estate they won't have explored with their gang.' She sank back with sudden relief. 'That's it, of course. It'll be one of the village children who grew up with them, hardly a child now, though – someone in his early twenties.' She noticed the smirk was back on McLoughlin's face.

Walsh spoke gently. 'I agree entirely that that is a possibility. Which is why it's so important for us to question Jonathan *and* Jane. It can't be avoided, you know, however much you and her mother may dislike the idea. Jane may be the only one who can lead us to a murderer.' He reached for another sandwich. 'The police are not barbarians, Mrs Goode. I can assure you we will be sympathetic and tactful in our dealings with her. I hope you will persuade Mrs Maybury of that.'

Diana uncurled her legs and stood up. Quite unaware of it, she leant on the desk in just the way Phoebe had done, as if close proximity had taught the women to adopt each other's mannerisms. 'I can't promise anything, Inspector. Phoebe has a mind of her own.'

'She has no choice in the matter,' he said flatly, 'except to influence her daughter over whether we question her here or in Oxford. Under the circumstances, I imagine Mrs Maybury would prefer it to be here.'

Diana straightened. 'Is there anything else you want to ask me?'

'Only two more things tonight. Tomorrow Sergeant McLoughlin will question you in more detail.' He looked up at her. 'How did Mrs Maybury come to employ the Phillipses? Did she advertise or did she apply to an agency?'

Diana's hands were fluttering. She thrust them into the pockets of her jacket. 'I believe Anne arranged it,' she said. 'You'll have to ask her.'

'Thank you. Now, just one more thing. When you helped clear the rubbish from the ice house what exactly was in there and what did you do with it?'

'It was ages ago,' she said uncomfortably. 'I can't remember. Nothing out of the way, just rubbish.'

Walsh looked at her thoughtfully. 'Describe the inside of the ice house to me, Mrs Goode.' He watched her eyes search rapidly amongst the photographs on the desk, but he had turned over all the general shots when she first came in. 'How big is it? What shape is the doorway? What's the floor made of?'

'I can't remember.'

He smiled a slow, satisfied smile and she was reminded of a stuffed timber wolf she had once seen with bared teeth and staring glass eyes. 'Thank you,' he said. She was dismissed.

Six

DIANA FOUND PHOEBE watching the ten o'clock news in the television room. The flickering colours from the set provided the only light and they played across Phoebe's glasses, hiding her eyes and giving her the look of a blind woman. Diana snapped on the table lamp.

'You'll get a headache,' she said, flopping into the seat beside Phoebe, reaching out to stroke the softly tanned forearm.

Phoebe muted the sound of the television with the remote control on her lap, but left the picture running. 'I've got one already,' she admitted tiredly. She took off her glasses and held a handkerchief to her red-rimmed eyes. 'Sorry,' she said.

'What about?'

'Blubbing. I thought I'd grown out of it.'

Diana pulled a footstool forward with her toes and settled her feet on it comfortably. 'A good blub is one of my few remaining pleasures.'

Phoebe smiled. 'But not very helpful.' She tucked the handkerchief into her sleeve and replaced her glasses.

'Have you had anything to eat?'

'I'm not hungry. Molly left a casserole in the Aga if you are.'

'Mm, she told me before she left. I'm not hungry either.'

They lapsed into silence.

'It's a bloody mess, isn't it?' said Phoebe after a while.

'I'm afraid so.' Diana pushed her sandals off her feet and let them drop to the floor. 'The Inspector's no fool.' She kept her voice deliberately light.

Phoebe spoke harshly. 'I hate him. How old would you say he is?'

'Late fifties.'

'He hasn't aged much. He looked like a genial professor ten years ago.' She considered for a moment. 'But that's not his character. He's anything but genial. He's dangerous, Di. For God's sake don't forget it.'

The other woman nodded. 'And his incubus, Jock-the-Ripper? What did you make of him?'

Phoebe looked surprised as if the other woman had mentioned an irrelevance. 'The Sergeant? He didn't say much. Why do you ask?'

With rhythmical movements, as if she were stroking a cat, Diana smoothed the woollen pile on the front of her jacket. 'Anne's spoiling for a fight with him and

I'm not sure why.' She glanced speculatively at Phoebe, who shrugged. 'She's making a mistake. She took one look at him in the drawing-room, labelled him "Pig-ignorant" and made up her mind to walk all over him. Damn!' she said with feeling. 'Why can't she learn to compromise occasionally? She'll have us up to our necks in shit if she's not careful.'

'Have they spoken to her yet?'

'No, they've told her they'll talk to her tomorrow. They seem very relaxed about it all. We have their official permission to go to bed.'

Phoebe closed her eyes and pressed long fingers against her temples. 'What did they ask you?'

Diana twisted in her chair to look at her friend. 'From what they implied, exactly what they asked you.'

'Except that I walked out and refused to answer their questions.' She opened her eyes and looked ruefully at the other woman. 'I know,' she said. 'It was very silly of me but they made me so angry. Strange, isn't it? I stood up to hours of interrogation when David went. This time, I lasted five minutes. I found myself hating that man so much, I wanted to claw his eyes out. I could have done it, too.'

Diana reached out again and briefly touched her arm. 'I don't think it's strange – any psychiatrist would tell you that anger is a normal reaction to stress – but it's probably unwise.' She pulled a face. 'Anne will say I've bottled out, of course, but my view is we should give them all the co-operation we can. The sooner they sort it out and leave us alone, the better.'

'They want to question the children.'

'I know and I don't think we can prevent it.'

'I could ask Jane's psychiatrist to write a report advising against it. Would that stop them?'

'For a day or two perhaps before they secured an order for a second opinion. That would declare her competent to answer questions. You know yourself, her own psychiatrist pronounced her fit eighteen months ago.'

'Not for this.' Phoebe massaged her temples vigorously. 'I'm frightened, Di. I really think she's managed to blot it all out. If they make her remember now, God knows what will happen.'

'Talk to Anne,' Diana said. 'She can be more objective than you. You may find that you're underestimating Jane's strengths. She is your daughter, after all.'

'Meaning that I am less able to be objective?'

Go easy, Diana told herself. 'Meaning that she will have inherited the rigid Gallagher backbone, you oaf.'

'You're forgetting her father. However much I might like to pretend otherwise, there is some of David in each of them.'

'He wasn't all bad, Pheeb.'

Tears welled uncontrollably in Phoebe's eyes. She blinked them away angrily. 'But he was, and you know it as well as I do. You told the Inspector so this afternoon and you were right. He was rotten to the core. In time, if we hadn't got shot of him, he'd have turned me and the children rotten too. He had a damn good try in all conscience.' She was silent for a moment. 'It's the only thing I hold against my parents. If they hadn't been so conventional I need never have married him. I could have had Jonny and brought him up on my own.'

'It was difficult for them.' But I agree with her, thought Diana. There was no excuse for what her parents did, so why am I defending them? 'They did what they thought was right.'

'I was seventeen, for Christ's sake – ' Phoebe's nails bit deep into her palms – 'younger than Jane is now. I allowed myself to be married off to a bastard twice my age simply because he'd seduced me, and then I just stood by and watched him rewarded for it. Christ,' she spat, 'it makes me sick to think of the money he bled from my father.'

Then don't think about it, Diana wanted to say. You've tried to forget them, but there *were* good times, times at the beginning when Anne and I envied you because you were a woman and we were still gangling schoolgirls. One weekend in particular, it was still vivid in her memory, when David on some mad whim had taken the three of them on a business trip to Paris. She forgot which company he was working for, there had been so many, but the weekend she would never forget. David, so assured, so deft in his choice of where to go and what to do, so unaffected by the foreignness of it all; Phoebe, four months pregnant, lovely face framed in a glorious picture hat, so delighted with herself and with David; and Anne and Diana, out for half-term, in a fantasy of beautiful people in beautiful places. And it was fantasy, of course, for the reality of David Maybury was brutish, ugly – Diana had discovered that for herself – yet once, in Paris, they had known enchantment.

Phoebe stood abruptly, walked over to the television set and switched it off. She spoke with her back to Diana. 'Do you know what kept me going through all those hours of police questioning last time? How it was I managed to stay so calm in spite of what they were accusing me of?' She turned round and Diana saw that the tears had stopped as suddenly as they had started. 'It was relief, sheer bloody relief that I had got rid of the bastard so easily.'

Diana glanced at the curtains. It was cold for a night in August, she thought, and Phoebe must have left the window open. 'You're talking rubbish,' she said firmly. 'The last ten years have addled your brain. There was nothing easy about getting rid of David. Good God, woman, he'd been an albatross round your neck since the day you married him, still is.' She pulled her jacket tighter about her. 'If only they'd found a body somewhere that you could have identified.'

'If pigs could fly,' reflected Phoebe as she tidied the

room and punched the cushions ferociously into airy plumpness.

Diana picked up an empty coffee cup and walked through into the kitchen. 'They're concentrating their efforts on the ice house,' she announced over her shoulder. She ran the tap and washed the cup. 'They're working on the assumption that no one knows where it is.' She heard the sound of the window being closed in the televison room. 'If I were you, I'd make a list of anyone you, David or the children have ever shown it to. I'm sure there'll be a lot of names.'

Phoebe laughed bitterly and drew a scrap of paper from her pocket. 'I've been racking my brains ever since I left the library. Result: Peter and Emma Barnes, and I can't swear to them.'

'You mean the awful Dilys's children?'

'Yes. They used to roam about the garden during one school holidays, looking for Jonathan and Jane. I'm sure Dilys put them up to it as a way of getting in with us.'

'But there must have been other children, Pheeb, in the early days.'

'No, not even schoolfriends. Jon was boarding, remember, and never wanted friends to stay, and Jane never wanted friends full stop. It was my fault. I should have encouraged them but things were just so difficult that I was really glad they were antisocial.'

'So what happened with Peter and Emma?'

'It all became rather unpleasant. Emma kept taking

her knickers down in front of Jonathan.' She shook her head. 'I drew the line when he started taking his down, too. He was nine.' She sighed. 'Anyway, like a fool, I told David. So he promptly phoned Dilys and gave her an earful. He called her a vulgar bitch and said "like mother, like daughter". After that, they never came up here again, but I suppose Jon might have shown them the ice house before they were banned.'

Diana gave a guilty giggle. 'For once David was probably right. Emma hasn't improved much with the passing years, let's face it.'

'He had no business to speak to anyone like that,' said Phoebe coldly. 'God knows, I can't stand the woman, but Jon was behaving as badly as Emma. David never even told him off for it. He thought it was a great joke, talking about Jon becoming a man. I could have killed him for that. If anyone was vulgar, David was.'

Diana was disturbed by Phoebe's mood. She had known her to be bitter before but never with such a depth of feeling over something so petty. It was as if the events of the afternoon had caused a breach in her long-held defences, releasing the pent-up emotions of years. She saw the dangers of it only too clearly. She and Anne had thought of Jane as the weak link. Were they wrong? Was it not Phoebe, after all, who was the more vulnerable?

'You're tired, old thing,' she said calmly, putting

her arm through the other woman's. 'Let's go to bed and sleep on it.'

Phoebe's head drooped wearily. 'I've got such a bloody awful headache.'

'Hardly surprising in the circumstances. Take some aspirin. You'll be a new woman in the morning.'

They walked arm in arm down the corridor. 'Did they ask you about Fred and Molly?' queried Phoebe suddenly.

'A bit.'

'Oh, lord.'

'Don't worry about it.' They had reached the stairs. Diana gave her a kiss and released her. 'Walsh also asked me to describe the ice house,' she said with reluctance.

'I told you he was dangerous,' said Phoebe, walking up the stairs.

Diana's footsteps were loud in the silence. The phrase 'quiet as the grave' came to haunt her as she took off her shoes and tip-toed along the corridor. She eased Anne's door open and looked round it. Anne was at the desk, working at her word-processor. Diana whistled quietly to attract her attention, then pointed at the ceiling. Together they crept up the stairs to Anne's bedroom.

Anne followed her in, eyes alight with mischief and laughter. 'My God, Di, this is so unlike you. You're always such a stickler for appearances. You do realise the place is still crawling with filth?'

'Don't be an idiot. It's not a game this time, so just shut up and listen.'

She pushed Anne on to the bed and perched, cross-legged, beside her. As she spoke, her hands worked nervously, kneading and pummelling the softness of the duvet.

Seven

THE CURTAIN WAS drawn aside and Phoebe Maybury appeared at the window. She stared out for a moment, her hair a fiery red where the lamplight caught it from behind, her eyes huge in her strained white face. Looking at her, George Walsh wondered what emotions had stirred her. Fear? Guilt? Madness even? There was something amiss in those staring eyes. She was so close he could have touched her. He held his breath. She reached out, caught the handle and pulled the window to. The curtain fell back into place and moments later the light was switched off. The murmur of Phoebe's and Diana's voices continued in the kitchen, but their words were no longer audible.

Walsh beckoned to McLoughlin, whom he could dimly see, and led the way on soft feet across the terrace and on to the grass. He had been keeping a wary eye on the lighted windows of Anne's wing where her silhouette, seated at her desk, showed up strongly against the curtains. She had changed position frequently in the last half hour, but had not moved from her seat. Walsh was as sure as he could be that his and McLoughlin's short spell of eavesdropping had been unobserved.

They set off silently in the direction of the ice house, McLoughlin lighting their way with a torch which he kept shaded with one hand. When Walsh judged them far enough away from the house to be unheard, he stopped and turned to his colleague.

'What did you make of that, Andy?'

'I'd say we just heard the clearest admission of guilt we're ever likely to hear,' the other threw out.

'Hm.' Walsh chewed thoughtfully on his lower lip. 'I wonder. What was it she said?'

'She admitted to relief at having got rid of her husband so easily.' He shrugged. 'Seems clear enough to me.'

Walsh started to walk again. 'It wouldn't stand up in a court of law for a minute,' he mused. 'But it's interesting, definitely interesting.' He came to an abrupt halt. 'I think she's cracking at long last. I got the impression that Mrs Goode certainly thinks so. What's her part in this? She can't have been involved in Maybury's disappearance. We had her thoroughly checked and there's no doubt she was in America at the time.'

'Accessory after the fact? She and the Cattrell woman have known Mrs Maybury did it but have kept quiet for the sake of the children.' He shrugged again.

'Bar that, she seems straight enough. She doesn't know much about the ice house, that's for sure.'

'Unless she's bluffing.' He pondered for a few minutes. 'Doesn't it seem odd to you that she can have lived here for eight years and not have seen inside that place?'

The moon came out from behind a cloud and lit their way with a cold grey lustre. McLoughlin switched off the torch. 'Perhaps she didn't fancy it,' he observed with grim humour. 'Perhaps she knew what was in there.'

This remark brought Walsh up short again. 'Well, well,' he murmured, 'I wonder if that's it. It makes sense. No one's going to poke around in a place where they know there's a dead body. They're a hard-bitten trio. I can't see any of them going out of her way to do what's morally right. They'd harbour a corpse quite happily, provided it was out of sight. What do you think?'

His Sergeant scowled. 'Women are a closed book to me, sir. I wouldn't even pretend to understand them.'

Walsh chuckled. 'Kelly been playing you up again?'

The laugh pierced McLoughlin's brain, scintillating and sharp as a needle. He turned away and thrust his hands and the torch deep into the pockets of his bomber jacket. Tempt me, he thought, just tempt me. 'We've had a row. Nothing serious.'

Walsh, who knew enough of McLoughlin's prolonged marital problems to be sympathetic, grunted. 'Funnily enough, I saw her a couple of days ago with Jack Booth. She was swinging along without a care in the world, never seen her so cheerful. She's not pregnant, I suppose? She had a real bloom on her.'

The bastard should have hit him. It would have hurt less. 'That's probably because she's gone to live with Jack,' he said casually. 'She left last week.' Now laugh, you sod, laugh, laugh, laugh, and give me an excuse to smash your face in.

Walsh, at a loss, gave McLoughlin's arm an awkward pat. He understood now why the lad had been so touchy the last few days. To lose your wife was bad enough, to lose her to your closest friend was a belter. My God! Jack Booth, of all people! He'd been best man at their wedding. Well, well. It explained a good deal. Why McLoughlin walked alone these days. Why Jack had suddenly decided to leave the force to work for a security firm in Southampton. 'I had no idea. I'm sorry.'

'It's no big deal, sir. It was all very amicable. No hard feelings on either side.'

He was very cool about it. 'Perhaps it's a temporary infatuation,' Walsh suggested lamely. 'Perhaps she'll come back when she's got over it.'

McLoughlin's teeth gleamed white inside his grin, but the night hid the black rage in his eyes. 'Do me a favour, sir, that's about the last thing I want to hear. God knows we never had much to say to each other before she went. What the hell would we talk about if she came back?' Jesus, he wanted to hit someone. Did they all know? Were they all laughing? He would kill the first person who laughed.

He quickened his pace. 'Thank God we didn't have children. This way, no one loses.'

Walsh, following a few steps behind, pondered the capriciousness of human nature. He could recall a conversation he had had with McLoughlin only months before when the younger man had blamed his marital problems on the fact that he and Kelly had no children. She was bored, he claimed, found her job as a secretary unsatisfying, needed a baby to keep her occupied. Walsh had wisely kept silent, knowing from experience with his daughter that advice on domestic disputes was rarely appreciated, but he had hoped quite fervently that Fate would intervene to prevent some wretched baby being born to keep this ill-matched couple occupied. His own daughter's first pregnancy at the age of sixteen when she was still at school and unmarried had been a shock to him, but the greater shock was to discover that his wife and daughter had never really liked each other. His daughter blamed two disastrous marriages and four children on her restless seeking after love; while his wife blamed their daughter for her wasted opportunities and lack of self-esteem. George tried to make up for past failings by taking an interest in his grandchildren, but he found it difficult. His interest tended to be critical.

He thought them wild and undisciplined and blamed this on his daughter's leniency and their lack of a father-figure.

Walsh's recurring nightmare was that with the careless conception of his daughter he had sown seeds of unhappiness which would grow and mature with every succeeding generation.

He caught up with McLoughlin. 'Life's a puzzle, Andy. You'll look back at the end and see where all the pieces fitted, even if you can't see it now. Things will work out for the best. They always do.'

'Of course they will, sir. "All is for the best in the best of all possible worlds." You believe that crap, do you?'

Walsh was crushed. 'Yes, as a matter of fact.'

They were approaching the ice house which stood silhouetted against the arc-lights on the far side. McLoughlin jerked his head at the open doorway and the blackness inside. 'I can guess where he would have told you to stick your little aphorism. He wouldn't agree with it.'

'But his murderer might.' And so might your wife, Walsh thought acidly, tucked up in bed with a little warm and jovial humanity in the shape of Jack Booth. He raised a hand in greeting to DC Jones as they rounded the building. 'Found anything?'

Jones pointed to a piece of canvas on the ground. 'That's it, sir. We've worked a fifty-metre radius round the ice house. I've told the lads to leave the woodland along the back wall until tomorrow. The lights throw too many shadows to see properly.'

Walsh squatted on his haunches and used a pencil to sort and turn the collection of empty crisp packets, sweet wrappers, two thread-bare tennis balls and other odds and ends. He isolated three used condoms, a pair of faded bikini underpants and several spent cartridges. 'We'll follow these up. I don't think the rest is going to tell us anything.' He pushed himself to his feet. 'Right, I think we'll call it a day. Jones, I want you to continue searching the grounds tomorrow. Concentrate on the areas of woodland, along the back wall and up by the front gates. Get a team together to help you. Andy, you carry on with the questioning until I join you. Ask Fred Phillips if he's used a shotgun recently. We'll check at the station to see whether he or anyone else here is licensed to use one. Sergeant Robinson and the PCs can go door to door in the village.' He indicated the condoms and the knickers. 'They seem unlikely objects for anyone in the Grange to have abandoned in the garden though you' – he looked at McLoughlin – 'might ask tactfully.' He turned to Jones. 'Were they together in the same place?'

'Scattered about, sir. We marked the positions.'

'Good man. It looks as if a local Lothario is in the habit of bringing his girlfriends up here. If so, he may be able to give us some information. I'll have Nick Robinson concentrate on that.'

There was a sour look on McLoughlin's face. He didn't relish the prospect of discussing used condoms with the women at the Grange. 'And you, sir?' he asked.

'Me? I'm going to check back through one or two files, particularly our friend Ms Cattrell's. That's a tough nut. I don't fancy it, not one little bit.' He pursed his lips and tugged at them with a finger and thumb.

'There's a Special Branch file on her as long as your arm, dating back to when she was a student. I had access to bits of it when Maybury went missing. It's how I knew she was at Greenham Common. She's thrown a few spanners in the works over the years. Do you remember the furore a couple of years ago over creative accounting in the Defence Ministry? Someone added a nought to a three million pound tender and the Ministry paid out ten times what the contract was worth. That was an Anne Cattrell scoop. Heads rolled. She's a dab hand at getting heads to roll.' He fingered his jaw thoughtfully. 'I suggest you remember that, Andy.'

'You're coming it a bit strong, aren't you, sir? If she's that good what the hell's she doing stuck out here in the wilds of Hampshire? She should be in London on one of the big nationals.' Walsh's tones of amused admiration had needled him.

'Oh, she's good,' said Walsh waspishly, 'and she did work on a London national before she chucked it all up to come down here and turn freelance. Don't make the mistake of underestimating her. I've seen some of the comments on her file. She's a gutsy little bitch, not the sort to cross swords with lightly. She has a history of left-wing involvement and she knows everything there is to know about civil rights and police powers. She's been a press officer with CND, she's an outspoken feminist, active trade unionist, she's been linked with the Militant Tendency and at one time she was a member of the British Communist Party – '

'Jesus Christ!' McLoughlin broke in angrily. 'What the hell's she doing living in a bloody mansion? Damn it all, sir, they've got a couple of servants working for them.'

'Fascinating, isn't it? What made her jack in her job *and* her principles? I suggest you ask her tomorrow. It's the first damn chance we've had to find out.'

The old man reeked of whisky. He sat like a lumpy Guy Fawkes in the doorway of a tobacconist in Southampton, his legs encased in incongruously bright pink trousers, his ancient hat awry on his bald head, a jolly song on his lips. It was nearly midnight. As drunks will, he called out to passers-by between snatches of song; they, with sidelong glances, crossed the road or scurried by with quickened pace.

A policeman approached and stood in front of him,

wondering what to do with the silly old fool. 'You're a pain in the flaming arse,' he said amiably.

The tramp glared at him. 'A blooming bluebottle,' he said, showing his age, before a gleam of recognition crept into the rheumy eyes. 'Gawd love me, it's Sergeant Jordan,' he cackled. He fished a brown-paper-covered bottle from the recesses of his coat, pulled the cork out with brown teeth and offered it to the bobby. 'Have a drink, me old mate.'

Sergeant Jordan shook his head. 'Not tonight, Josephine.'

The old man tipped up the bottle and emptied the contents into his mouth. His hat fell off and rolled across the doorstep. The Sergeant bent down and retrieved it, clapping it firmly on the tramp's head. 'Come on, you old fool.' He put his hand under an unsavoury arm and heaved the filthy object to its feet.

'You nicking me?'

'Is that what you want?'

'Wouldn't mind, son,' he whined. 'I'm tired. Could just do wiv a decent kip.'

'And I can just do without fumigating the cell after you've been in it,' the policeman muttered, pulling a card out of his pocket and reading the address on it. 'I'm going to do you a favour, probably the first one you've had in years that didn't involve free booze. Come on, you're going to sleep in the Hilton tonight.'

*

George Walsh dropped Sergeants Robinson and McLoughlin at the Lamb and Flag in Winchester Road for a quick pint before closing time, then drove to Silverborne Police Station. His route took him along the High Street past the war memorial and the old cornmarket, now a bank, and between the two rows of darkened shops. Beyond its rapid expansion, Silverborne's only claim to fame in the last ten years had been its physical proximity to Streech Grange and the mystery surrounding David Maybury's disappearance. That Streech should again be the centre of police attention was no coincidence in Walsh's view. There was an inexorability about murder investigations, he believed, with comparatively few remaining unsolved. Certainly lightning like this never struck twice. He was whistling tunelessly as he pushed through the front doors.

Bob Rogers was on duty behind the desk. He looked up as Walsh came in. 'Evening, sir.'

'Bob.'

'The word is you've found Maybury.'

Walsh leant an arm on the desk. 'I'm not taking anything for granted,' he growled. 'The bastard's eluded me for ten years. I can wait another twenty-four hours before I pop the champagne. Any word from Webster?'

Rogers shook his head.

'Busy tonight?'

'Not so you'd notice.'

'Do me a favour then. Get me a list of all persons, men and women, reported missing in our area in, say, the last six months. I'll be in my office.'

Walsh went upstairs, his feet echoing loudly in the deserted corridor. He liked the place at night, empty, silent, with no ringing telephones and no inane chatter outside his door to intrude on his thoughts. He went into his office and snapped on the light. His wife had bought him a painting two Christmases ago to lend a personal touch to his bleak white walls. It hung on the wall opposite the door and greeted him every time he entered the room. He loathed it. It was a symbol of her taste, not his, a herd of glossy black horses with flowing manes galloping through an autumnal forest. He would have preferred some Van Gogh prints for the same price but his wife had laughed at the suggestion. Darling, she had said, anyone can have a print; surely you'd rather have an original? He glared at the pretty picture and wondered, not for the first time, why he found it so hard to say no to his wife.

He went to his filing cabinet and sorted through the C's. 'Cairns', 'Callaghan', 'Calvert', 'Cambridge', 'Cattrell'. He gave an exclamation of satisfaction, withdrew the file from the drawer and took it over to his desk. He opened it and settled into his chair, loosening his tie and kicking off his shoes.

The information was set out in the form of a CV, giving details of Anne Cattrell's history as far as it was known to the Silverborne police at the time of Maybury's disappearance. Additional, more recent information had been added from time to time on the last page. Walsh fingered his lips thoughtfully as he read. It was disappointing on the whole. He had hoped to find a chink in her armour, some small point of leverage he could use to his advantage. But there was nothing. Unless the fact that the last nine years of her life was contained on one page, while the previous ten years covered several, was worth consideration. Why *had* she given up a promising career? If she'd stayed in London she'd have been a top name by now. But in nine years her biggest success had been the Defence Ministry scoop and that, published in a monthly magazine, had been hijacked by staff reporters on the nationals. She had got little credit for it. Indeed, Walsh had only known it was her story because the name had registered in connection with Maybury. If she'd got hitched, her sudden drop in profile would have made sense, but – his face creased into a deep scowl. Was it that simple? Had she and those women entered into some sort of perverted marriage the minute they were all free? He found the idea oddly reassuring. If Mrs Maybury had always been a lesbian, it explained so much. He was gathering the file together when Bob Rogers came in.

'I've got those names for you, sir, and a cup of tea.'

'Good man.' He took the cup gratefully. 'How many?'

Sergeant Rogers consulted his list. 'Five. Two women and three men. The women are pretty obvious runaways – both adolescent or late adolescent, both left home after rows with parents and haven't been seen since. The youngest was fourteen, Mary Lucinda Phelps, known as Lucy. We mounted quite a search for her, if you remember, but never found anything.'

'Yes, I do remember. Looked about twenty-five from her photograph.'

'That's the one. Parents swore she was a virgin, but it turned out she'd had an abortion at the age of thirteen. Poor kid's probably on the streets in London by now. The other one's Suzie Miller, aged eighteen, last seen in early May hitching on the A31 with an older man. We have a witness to that who said she was all over him. Her parents wanted us to treat it as a murder, but there was nothing to suggest anything untoward had happened and we've certainly never found a body. Of the three men, one's a probable suicide, though again we've not found a body, one's semi-senile and gone walkabout, and the other's bolted. That's a young Asian lad of twenty-one, with a history of depression, Mohammed Mirahmadi, five previous suicide attempts, all attempted drownings. Left home three months ago. We dragged some nearby quarry pits but without success. The second on the list's an old man, Keith Chapel, who wandered out of sheltered accommodation in the middle of March, that's nearly five months, and hasn't come back. Mind you, it's odd no one's spotted him. It says here he was wearing bright pink trousers. And finally, a Daniel Clive Thompson, fifty-two, reported missing by his wife nine, ten weeks ago. Inspector Staley looked into that one quite thoroughly. The man's business had gone bust and left a lot of people hopping mad, including most of the employees. The Inspector's view is that he's done a bunk to London. He was last seen getting off a train on Waterloo station.' He looked up.

'Any of them live near Streech?'

'One of the men, Daniel Thompson. Address: Larkfield, East Deller. That's the neighbouring village, isn't it?'

'What's the description?'

'Five feet eleven, grey hair, hazel eyes, well-built, wearing a brown suit, forty-four-inch chest and brown shoes, size eight. Other information: blood group O, appendectomy scar, full set of dentures, tattoos on both forearms. Last sighting, May 25th, at Waterloo. Last seen by his wife on same day when she dropped him at Winchester station. That's all I've got here, but Inspector Staley's got quite a file on him. Shall I look it out for you?'

'No,' Walsh growled angrily. 'It's Maybury.' He watched Bob Rogers walk to the door. 'Damn and blast it! It's like leaving your umbrella behind on a fine day. It always rains. Leave me the list. If I hang on to it, it's bound to be Maybury.' He waited till the door closed, then stared glumly at the description of Daniel Thompson. His face looked ten years older.

Eight

WHEN ANNE ENTERED the library the following morning she found McLoughlin standing by the window, gazing broodingly out over the gravel drive. He turned as she came in and she noticed the black rings of a sleepless night round his eyes and the tell-tale nicks of a clumsy shave on his neck and chin. He smelled of anger and frustration and yesterday's beer. He gestured for her to sit down, waited until she had done so, then settled himself in the chair behind the desk. Particles of dust shimmered and danced in the sunlight that shafted between them. They eyed each other with open dislike.

'I won't keep you long, Miss Cattrell. Chief Inspector Walsh will be here later and I know he has some questions to ask you. For the moment, I'd like to concentrate on the finding of the body and one or two related matters. Perhaps you could start by running through the events of yesterday afternoon, beginning with the arrival of the gardener.'

Anne did as she was asked, knowing it would be a waste of time to point out that she had already done this the previous afternoon for PC Williams. From time to time she glanced at McLoughlin but looked away again when he refused to drop his gaze. There was a new awareness in his eyes which meant he was better informed about her. And how tiresome that was, she thought. Yesterday, he had despised her; today, he saw her as a challenge. With an inward sigh she began to prepare her defences.

'You don't know who he was, how he got there, or when. Had you seen inside the ice house before yesterday?'

'No.'

'Then why did you tell us that you and Mrs Goode had cleared the rubbish out of it six years ago?'

Anne had been well prepared for this by Diana. 'Because it seemed like a good idea at the time.' She fished a cigarette out of her pocket and lit it. 'I wanted to save you time and trouble. You should be looking outside the Grange for your victim and your suspects. It's nothing to do with anyone here.'

He was unimpressed. 'It's never a good idea to tell lies to the police. With your experience you should know that.'

'My experience?' she queried silkily.

'If you don't mind, we'll dispense with the word games, Miss Cattrell. It'll save a lot of time.'

'You're quite right, of course,' she agreed mildly. What a prig the man was!

His eyes narrowed. 'Did you lie because you understood the significance of the ice house and the importance of knowing where it was?'

She was silent for a moment. 'I certainly understood that *you* would consider it significant. You have yet to persuade me that it is. I share Mrs Goode's view that its location is probably known to a number of people, or that chance played a part in the body's being there.'

'We have found some used condoms in the area round the ice house,' McLoughlin said, abruptly changing the subject. 'Have you any idea who would have left them there?'

Anne grinned. 'Well, it isn't me, Sergeant. I don't use them.'

He showed his irritation. 'Have you had intercourse there with someone who does, Miss Cattrell?'

'What, with a *man*?' She gave her throaty chuckle. 'Is that a very sensible question to ask a lesbian?'

He gripped his knees tightly with trembling fingers as a sudden black rage hammered in his head. He felt terrible, his eyes smarting from lack of sleep, his mouth tasting foul. What a loathsome bloody bitch she was, he thought. He took a few shallow breaths and eased his hands on to the desk. They shook with a life of their own. 'Have you?' he asked again.

She watched him closely. 'No, I haven't,' she

answered calmly. 'Nor, as far as I know, has anyone else in the house.' She leaned forward and tapped the end of her cigarette against the side of an ashtray. He moved his hands to his lap.

'Perhaps you could clear up something that puzzles both Chief Inspector Walsh and myself,' he continued. 'We understand you and Mrs Goode have been living here for several years. How is it neither of you has seen inside the ice house?'

'In the same way that most Londoners have never seen inside the Tower. One doesn't tend to explore things on one's own doorstep.'

'Did you know of its existence?'

'I suppose so.' She thought for a moment. 'I must have done. I don't remember being surprised at Fred mentioning it.'

'Did you know where it was?'

'No.'

'What did you think the hillock was?'

'I can only recall walking right round these gardens once and that was when I first came here. I expect I thought the hillock was a hillock.'

McLoughlin didn't believe her. 'Don't you go for walks? With the dogs, with your friends?'

She turned her cigarette in her fingers. 'Do I look like someone who takes exercise, Sergeant?'

He studied her briefly. 'As a matter of fact you do. You're very slim.'

'I eat very little, drink only neat spirits and smoke like a chimney. It does wonders for the figure but leaves me gasping for breath halfway up the stairs.'

'Don't you help with the gardening?'

She raised an eyebrow. 'I'd be a liability. I couldn't tell the difference between a rose-bay willow-herb and a Michaelmas daisy. In any case, when would I find the time? I'm a professional woman. I work all day. We leave the gardening arrangements to Phoebe, that's her province.'

He thought of the pot plants in her room. Was she lying again? But why lie about gardening, for Christ's sake? His hand wandered to the uneven stubble on his jaw, touching, testing, fingering. Without warning, a shutter of panic snapped shut in his brain, blanking his memory. Had he shaved? Where had he slept? Had he had breakfast? His eyes glazed and he looked straight through Anne into a darkness beyond her, as if she was in a dimension outside his narrow line of vision.

Her voice was remote. 'Are you all right?'

The shutter opened again and left him with the nausea of relief. 'Why are you living here, Miss Cattrell?'

'Probably for exactly the same reason you're living in your house. It's as nice a roof over my head as I could find.'

'That's hardly an answer. How do you square Streech Grange and its two servants with your conscience? Isn't it rather too – privileged for your taste?' His voice grated with derision.

Anne stubbed out her cigarette. 'I simply can't answer that question. It's based on so many false premisses that it's entirely hypothetical. Nor, frankly, do I see its relevance.'

'Who suggested you come here? Mrs Maybury?'

'No one. It was my suggestion.'

'Why?'

'Because,' she repeated patiently, 'I thought it would be a nice place to live.'

'That's crap,' he said angrily.

She smiled. 'You're forgetting the sort of woman I am, Sergeant. I have to take my pleasures where I find them. Phoebe wouldn't – couldn't – leave this house to come to London, so I had to come here. It's very simple really.'

There was a long silence. 'Pleasures don't last,' he said softly. The shutter flickered horribly in his brain. '"Pleasures are like poppies spread, You seize the flower, its bloom is shed; Or like the snow falls in the river, A moment white – then melts for ever."' He spoke the words to himself. There was another silence. 'In your case, Miss Cattrell, the price of pleasure would seem to be hypocrisy. That's a high price to pay. Was Mrs Maybury worth it?'

If he'd turned a knife in her gut, he couldn't have hurt her more. She took refuge in anger. 'Let me give you a brief résumé of what led up to this line of questioning. Someone, probably Walsh, told you: she's a feminist, a lefty, a member of CND, an ex-Commie, and God knows what other rubbish besides. And you, exulting in your superiority because you're male and heterosexual, leapt at the chance of having a go at me on matters of principle. You're not interested in truth, McLoughlin. The only issue here is whether you and your inflated ego can make a dent in mine and, Jesus,' she spat at him, 'you're hardly original in that.'

He, too, leant forward so that they were facing each other across the desk. 'Who are Fred and Molly Phillips?'

She was unprepared, as he had known she would be, and she couldn't hide the flash of concern in her eyes. She sat back in her chair and reached for another cigarette.

'They work for Phoebe as housekeeper and gardener.'

'Mrs Goode told us you arranged their employment here. How did you find them?'

'I was introduced to them.'

'Through your work, through your political contacts? Perhaps penal reform is one of your interests?'

Damn him to hell and back, she thought, he wasn't a complete clod after all. 'I'm on the committee of a London-based group for the rehabilitation of ex-prisoners. I met them through that.'

She expected triumph and gave him reluctant credit when he didn't show it. 'Have they always been called Phillips?'

'No.'

'What was their surname?'

'I think you should ask them that.'

He passed a weary hand across his face. 'Well, of course, I can, Miss Cattrell, and that will simply drag out the agony for everybody. We will find out one way or the other.'

She looked out of the window, over his shoulder, to where Phoebe was pinching the dead-heads off the roses bordering the drive. She had lost her tension of the previous evening and squatted contentedly in the sun, tongues of flame curling in her shining hair, nimble fingers snapping through the flower stems. Benson sat hotly beside her, Hedges lay panting in the shade of a dwarf rhododendron. The sun's heat, still far from its peak, shimmered above the warm gravel.

'Jefferson,' said Anne.

The Sergeant made the connection immediately. 'Five years each for the murder of their lodger, Ian Donaghue.'

Anne nodded. 'Do you know why the sentences were so lenient?'

'Yes, I do. Donaghue buggered and killed their twelve-year-old son. They found him before the police did and hanged him.'

She nodded.

'Do you approve of personal vengeance, Miss Cattrell?'

'I sympathise with it.'

He smiled suddenly and for a brief moment she thought he looked quite human. 'Then at last we've found something we can agree on.' He tapped his pencil on the desk. 'How well do the Phillipses get on with Mrs Maybury?'

'Extremely well.' Surprisingly, she giggled. 'Fred treats her like royalty and Molly treats her like muck. It's a stunning combination.'

'I expect they're grateful to her.'

'The reverse. I'd say Phoebe is more grateful to them.'

'Why? She's given them a new home and employment.'

'You see the Grange as it is now but when I moved in nine years ago, Phoebe had been managing on her own for a year. She was shunned by everybody. No one from the village or even Silverborne would work for her. She had to do the gardening, the housework and house maintenance herself and the place was like a tip.' A stone lurched sickeningly in her mind as memories struggled to get out. It was the stench of urine, she thought. Everywhere. On the walls, the carpets, the curtains. She would never forget the terrible stench of urine. 'Fred and Molly's arrival a couple of months after us changed her life.'

McLoughlin stared about the library. There was a

good deal that was original, the carved oak bookcases, moulded plaster cornices, the panelled fireplace, but there were other things that were new, the paintwork, a radiator under the window, secondary glazing in white stove-enamel frames, all certainly under ten years old.

'Have the local people changed their attitude to Mrs Maybury now?'

She followed his gaze. 'Not at all. They still won't do any work for her.' She flicked ash from her cigarette. 'She tries from time to time without success. Silverborne's a dead duck. She's been as far as Winchester and Southampton with the same result. Streech Grange is notorious, Sergeant, but then you already know that, don't you?' She smiled cynically. 'They all seem to think they're going to be murdered the minute they set foot in the place. With some justification, it would seem, after yesterday's little discovery.'

He jerked his head at the window. 'Then who put in the central heating and the double glazing? Fred?'

'Phoebe.'

He laughed with genuine amusement. 'Oh, for God's sake! Look, I know you're on some personal crusade to prove that women are the be-all and end-all, but you can't expect me to swallow *that*.' He got up and strode across to the window. 'Have you any idea how much glass like this weighs?' He tapped a pane of the double-glazing and drew the unwelcome attention of Phoebe outside. She looked at him curiously for a moment then, seeing him turn away, resumed her gardening. He came back to his chair. 'She couldn't begin to lift it, let alone set it professionally in its frame. It would need at least two men, if not three.'

'Or three women,' said Anne, unmoved by his outburst. 'We all lend a hand with the lifting. There are five of us after all, eight on the week-ends when the children come home.'

'Eight?' he queried sharply. 'I thought there were only two children.'

'Three. There's Elizabeth, Diana's daughter, as well.'

McLoughlin ruffled his fingers through his hair, leaving a dark crest pointing towards the ceiling. 'She never mentioned a daughter,' he said sourly, wondering what other surprises lay in store.

'You probably didn't ask her.'

He ignored this. 'You said Mrs Maybury also did the central heating. How?'

'The same way plumbers do it, presumably. I remember she favoured capillary joints so there was a lot of wire wool involved and flux and soldering equipment. There were also numerous lengths of fifteen- and twenty-two-millimetre copper piping lying around. She hired a pipe-bending machine for several weeks with different sized pre-formers to make S-bends and right angles. I got a damned good article on women and DIY out of it.'

He shook his head. 'Who showed her how to do it? Who connected up the boiler?'

'She did.' She was amused by his expression. 'She got a book from the library. It told her exactly what to do.'

Andy McLoughlin was intensely sceptical. In his experience, a woman who could connect a central-heating boiler simply didn't exist. His mother, who held unenlightened ideas about a woman's place in the home, rooted herself firmly in the kitchen, scrubbed and cleaned, washed and cooked and refused adamantly even to learn how to change an electric plug, maintaining it was man's work. His wife, who by contrast had claimed enlightened ideas, had enrolled as a temporary secretary and called herself a career woman. In reality she had idled her days away, painting her nails, playing with her hair, complaining constantly of boredom but doing nothing about it. She had reserved her energies for when her husband came home, unleashing them in a fury of recriminations over his long hours of work, his neglect of her, his failure to notice her appearance, his inability to be the admiring prop her insecure personality demanded. The irony was that he had been attracted to her in the first place because his mother's kitchen mentality appalled him and yet, of the two of them, his mother had the brightest intellect. He had come away from both relationships with a sense, not of his own inadequacy, but of theirs. He had looked for equality and found only an irritating dependence.

'What else has she done?' he demanded curtly, eyeing the professional finish on the rag-rolled emulsion. 'The decorating?'

'No, that's mostly Diana's work, though we've all lent a hand. Di's also done the upholstery and curtaining. What else has Phoebe done?' She thought for a moment. 'She's rewired the house, made two extra bathrooms and put up the stud partitions between our wings and the main body. At the moment, she and Fred are working out how best to tackle a complete overhaul of the roof.' She felt the weight of his scepticism and shrugged. 'She's not trying to prove anything, Sergeant, nor am I by telling you. Phoebe's done what everyone else does and has adapted herself to the situation she finds herself in. She's a fighter. She's not the type to throw in her hand when the cards go against her.'

He thought of his own circumstances. Loneliness frightened him.

'Were you and Mrs Goode worried about Mrs Maybury's mental condition after twelve months alone in this house? Was that your real reason for moving here?'

Could reality be quantified, Anne wondered, any more than truth? To say yes to such a question from such a man would be a betrayal. His capacity for understanding was confined by his prejudices. 'No, Sergeant,' she lied. 'Diana and I have never had a moment's concern over Phoebe's mental condition, as you put it. She's a good deal more stable than you are, for example.'

His eyes narrowed angrily. 'You're a psychiatrist, are you, Miss Cattrell?'

'Put it this way,' she said, leaning forward and studying him coolly. 'I can always recognise a chronic drink problem when I see one.'

The speed with which his hand shot out and gripped her throat was staggering. He pulled her relentlessly towards him across the desk, his fingers biting into her flesh, a tumult of confused emotions governing his actions. The kiss, if the brutal penetration of another's mouth can be called a kiss, was as unplanned as the assault. He released her abruptly and stared at the red weals on her neck. A cold sweat drenched his back as he realised how vulnerable he had made himself. 'I don't know why I did that,' he said. 'I'm sorry.' But he knew that under the same circumstances he would do it again. At last he felt revenged.

She wiped his saliva from her mouth and pulled her shirt collar up round her neck. 'Did you want to ask me anything else?' She spoke as if nothing had happened.

He shook his head. 'Not at the present.' He

watched her stand up. 'You can report me for that, Miss Cattrell.'

'Of course.'

'I don't know why I did it,' he said again.

'I do,' she said. 'Because you're an inadequate little shit.'

Nine

SERGEANT NICK ROBINSON looked up and saw with relief that he had only two more houses to do before he reached the pub. Off to his right rose the hill which passed Streech Grange gates; behind him, some miles distant, lay Winchester; ahead of him, the brick wall which surrounded the southern flank of the Grange Estate hugged the road to East Deller. He checked his watch. It was ten minutes to opening time and he could murder a pint. If there was one thing he loathed, it was door-to-door questioning. With a lighter step he walked up the short drive to Clementine Cottage and – he checked his list – Mrs Amy Ledbetter. He rang the bell.

After some minutes and the laborious rattle of an anti-burglar chain, the door opened six inches. A pair of bright eyes examined him. 'Yes?'

He held out his identification. 'Police, Mrs Ledbetter.'

The card was taken by an arthritically deformed

hand and disappeared inside. 'Wait there, please,' said her voice. 'I intend to phone the Police Station and make sure you are who you say you are.'

'Very well.' He leaned against the side of her porch and lit a cigarette. This was the third telephoned check on him in two hours. He wondered if the uniformed constables were having as much trouble as he was.

Three minutes later the door opened wide and Mrs Ledbetter gestured him into the living-room. She was well into her seventies with a leathery skin and a no-nonsense look about her. She returned his warrant and told him to take a seat. 'There's an ashtray on the table. Well, Sergeant, what can I do for you?'

No need to beat about the bush with this old bat, he thought. Not like her twee little neighbour who claimed that to hear about murder on the television gave her palpitations. 'The remains of a murdered man were discovered in the garden of the Grange yesterday afternoon,' he said baldly. 'We're making enquiries to see if anyone in the village knows anything about it.'

'Oh, no,' said Amy Ledbetter. 'Poor Phoebe.'

DS Robinson looked at her with interest. This was a reaction he hadn't met with before. The mood of the other villagers he had spoken to had been one of vituperative satisfaction.

'Would it surprise you,' he asked the old lady, 'if I said you're the only person so far who's expressed any sympathy for Mrs Maybury?'

She wrinkled her lips into a moue of disgust. 'Of course it wouldn't. The lack of intelligence in this community is staggering. I'd have moved away years ago if I wasn't so fond of my garden. I suppose it's David's body?'

'We don't know yet.'

'I see.' She considered him thoughtfully. 'Well, fire away. What do you want to ask me?'

'Do you know Mrs Maybury well?'

'I've known her all her life. Gerald Gallagher, Phoebe's father, and my husband were old friends. I used to see a lot of her when she was younger and my husband was still alive.'

'And now?'

She frowned. 'No, I see very little of her now. My fault.' She raised one of her gnarled hands. 'Arthritis is the devil. It's more comfortable to stay at home and potter than go out paying calls and it makes you irritable. I was very short with her last time she came to see me and she hasn't been back since. That was about twelve months ago. My fault,' she said again.

Game old bird, he thought, and probably more reliable than the others he'd talked to who had dealt in innuendo and gossip. 'Do you know anything about her two friends, Mrs Goode and Miss Cattrell?'

'I've met them, knew them quite well at one time. Phoebe used to bring them home from school. Nice girls, interesting, full of character.'

Robinson consulted his notebook. 'One of the villagers told me – ' he looked up briefly – 'and I quote: "Those women are dangerous. They have made several attempts to seduce girls in the village, they even tried to get my daughter to join one of their lesbian orgies."' He looked up again. 'Do you know anything about that?'

She brushed a stray hair from her forehead with the back of her curled hand. 'Dilys Barnes, I suppose. She won't thank you for describing her as a villager. She's a shocking snob, likes to think she's one of us.'

He was intrigued. 'How did you know?'

'That it was Dilys? Because she's a very silly woman who tells lies. It's lack of breeding, of course. That type will do anything to avoid being laughed at. They've ruined their children with all their snobbish ideas. They sent the boy off to public school, and he's come back with a chip on his shoulder the size of a mountain. And the daughter, Emma,' she pulled a wry face. 'I'm afraid poor little Emma has become very loose. I think it's her way of getting back at her mother.'

'I see,' he said, completely lost.

She chuckled at his expression. 'She copulates in the woods at Streech Grange,' she explained. 'It's a favourite spot for it.' She chuckled again as the Sergeant's mouth dropped open. 'Emma was seen sneaking out of the grounds late one night and the story her mother put about the next day was that absurd one she's repeated to you.' She shook her head. 'It's nonsense, of course, and no one really believes it, but they pay lip-service to it because they don't like Phoebe. And she's her own worst enemy. She will let them see how much she despises them. That's always a mistake. Anyway, ask Emma. She's not a bad girl. If you keep what she says confidential, she'll tell you the truth I expect.'

He made a note. 'Thank you, I will. You say the woods are a favourite spot for – er – copulation.'

'Very much so,' she said firmly. 'Reggie and I used them a lot before we were married. They're particularly nice in the spring. Bluebell woods, you know. Very pretty.'

He boggled at her.

'Well, well,' she said calmly, 'that surprises you, I see, but the young are really very ignorant about sex. People were no more able to control their desire for it in my day than they are now and, thanks to Marie Stopes, we were not unprotected.' She smiled. 'When you're as old as I am, young man, you'll know that where human nature is concerned, very little changes. Life, for most of us, is the pursuit of pleasure.'

Well, that's true, he thought, thinking of his pint. He abandoned his inhibitions. 'We've found some used condoms on the Grange Estate which ties in with what you've been saying, Mrs Ledbetter. Apart from Emma Barnes, do you know of anyone else who might have been making love up there?'

'Precise knowledge, no. Guesses, yes. If you promise to be tactful in approaching the people concerned, I'll give you two more names.'

He nodded. 'I promise.'

'Paddy Clarke, the landlord at the pub. He's married to a harridan who has no idea how highly sexed he is. She thinks he takes the dog for a walk after closing time while she clears up inside, but I've seen the dog running loose in the moonlight too often to believe that. I don't sleep well,' she added, by way of explanation.

'And the other?'

'Eddie Staines, one of the farmhands up at Bywater Farm. A good-looking young devil, out with a different girlfriend every month. I've seen him set off up that hill a few times.' She nodded in the direction of the Grange.

'That's very helpful,' he said.

'Anything else?'

'Yes.' He looked a little sheepish. 'Have you noticed any strangers about? In the last six months, say?' This question had been greeted with universal amusement.

Mrs Ledbetter cackled. 'Twenty-five years ago I might have been able to give you a sensible answer to a question like that. Nowadays, impossible.' She shrugged. 'There are always strangers about, especially in the summer. Tourists, people driving through and stopping at the pub for lunch, campers from the site at East Deller. We've had a few caravans get stuck in the ditch on the corner, usually French ones, such bad drivers they are. Ask Paddy. He pulls them out with his jeep. No, I can't help you there, I'm afraid.'

'Sure?' he prompted. 'Someone on foot perhaps, someone you remember from years ago?'

She gave an amused snort. 'David Maybury, you mean? I certainly haven't seen him in the last few months. I'd have reported that. The last time I saw David was a week before he disappeared. It was in Winchester in the days when I could still drive and I came across him in Woolworths buying a teddy-bear for Jane. He was a strange character. Vile one day, charming the next, what my husband would have called a cad, the sort of man that women are invariably attracted to.' She lapsed into silence for a moment. 'There was the tramp, of course,' she said.

'What tramp?'

'He came through the village some weeks back. Funny old man with a brown trilby hanging off the back of his head. He was singing "Molly Malone", I remember. Quite beautifully. Ask Paddy. I'm sure he went into the pub.' Her head sank wearily against the back of her chair. 'I'm tired. I can't help you any more. Show yourself out, young man, and don't forget to shut the gate.' She closed her eyes.

DS Robinson rose smartly to his feet. 'Thank you for giving me so much of your time, Mrs Ledbetter.'

She was snoring quietly as he tip-toed out.

Inspector Walsh replaced the telephone receiver and stared thoughtfully into the middle distance. Dr Webster had been irritatingly unhelpful.

'Can't prove it is Maybury, can't prove it isn't,' he had said cheerfully along the wire, 'but my professional guess is it isn't.'

'Why, for God's sake?'

'Too many discrepancies. I can't make a match on the hair for a kick-off, though I'm not saying that's the end of it. I've sent samples off to a friend of mine who claims to be an expert in these things but don't get your hopes up. He warned me that the sample you got off Maybury's hairbrush may have deteriorated too far. Certainly I couldn't do anything with it.'

'What else?'

'Teeth. Did you notice our corpse was toothless? Not an incisor or molar in sight. Indications that he had dentures, but there were none with him. Looks like something or someone removed them. Now, Maybury on the other hand had all his teeth ten years ago and his records show they were in pretty good shape, only four fillings between them. That's a very different picture, George. He'd have to have suffered appalling gum disease to necessitate having all his teeth out within ten years.'

Walsh pondered for a moment. 'Let's say, for whatever reason, he wanted to lose his old identity. He could have had them taken out on purpose.'

Webster chuckled good-humouredly. 'Far-fetched though not impossible. But why would Mrs Maybury remove his dentures in that case, assuming she's our murderer? She, of all people, would know they couldn't identify him. To be honest, George, I'd say it's the other way round. Whoever murdered our chap in the ice house removed anything that would show he *wasn't* Maybury. He's had all his toes and fingertips mauled, for example, as if someone wanted to prevent us taking prints. Yet everyone at that house knows you didn't manage to lift a single workable print ten years ago.'

'God damn it,' exploded Walsh. 'I thought I had the bastard at last. Are you sure, Jim? What about the missing fingers?'

'Well, they're certainly missing, but it looks as though they've been chopped off with a meat cleaver. I've compared them with the records of Maybury's amputations and they're nothing like. Maybury had lost the top two joints of both fingers. Our corpse has had his severed at the base of each finger.'

'Doesn't prove it's not Maybury.'

'I agree, but it does look as if someone who knew

only that he'd lost his last two fingers has tried to make us think it's Maybury. To be honest, George, I'm not even positive at the moment that a human agency is involved. It is quite conceivable, if a little bizarre, that very sharp teeth have mutilated him in the way I've described. Take that filleting you pointed out. I've taken some close-ups of some furrows on the ribs and it's damned hard to say what they are. I can't rule out tooth marks.'

'Blood group?'

'Yup, you've got a match there all right. Both O positive, just like fifty per cent of the population. And, talking of blood, you must find his clothes. There's very little in that mud we scraped off the floor.'

'Great,' Walsh had growled, 'so what good news have you got for me?'

'I'm getting the report typed now, but I'll give you the gist. Male, white, five feet ten inches – give or take an inch on either side, both femurs have been well and truly smashed so I wouldn't be too dogmatic on that one – broad build probably running to fat, hair on chest and shoulder blades, indication of tattoo discolouration on right forearm, size eight shoe. No idea of hair colour but hair was probably dark brown before it went grey. Age, over fifty.'

'Oh, for God's sake, Jim. Can't you be more precise?'

'It's not a precise science as people get older, George, and a few teeth would have helped. It's all a question of fusion between the skull plates, but somewhere between fifty and sixty is my guess at the moment. I'll come back to you when I've done some more homework.'

'All right,' said Walsh grudgingly. 'When did he die?'

'I've taken some advice on this one. The consensus is, weighing the heat of the summer against the cool of the ice house – bearing in mind that the ambient temperature in the ice house may have been quite high if the door was open – and balancing that against the acceleration in decomposition after the scavengers had pulled him open and devoured him, plus possible mutilation by human agency but minus severe maggot infestation because the blowflies didn't lay in numbers, though I've sent some larvae off for further examination – '

'All right, all right, I didn't ask for a bloody biology lesson. How long's he been dead?'

'Eight to twelve weeks or two to three months, whichever you prefer.'

'I don't prefer either of them. They're too vague. There's a month's difference. Which do you favour, eight or twelve?'

'Probably somewhere in the middle, but don't quote me.'

'You'll be lucky,' was Walsh's parting shot. He slammed the phone down crossly, then buzzed his secretary on the intercom. 'Mary, love, could you get me all the details on a man who was reported missing about two months ago? Name: Daniel Thompson, address: somewhere in East Deller. I think you'll find Inspector Staley covered it. If he's free, ask him to give me five minutes, will you?'

'Sure thing,' she breezed back.

His eyes strayed to the huge file on David Maybury which he'd resurrected from the archives that morning, and which, refurbished and glossy in its pristine new folder, sat now on the edge of his desk like a promise of spring. 'You bastard!' said Chief Inspector Walsh.

Ten

SUMMONED BY URGENT telephone calls, Jonathan Maybury and Elizabeth Goode arrived early that afternoon in Jonathan's battered red Mini. As he drove it in through the gates and past the Lodge, Elizabeth turned to him with a worried frown. 'You won't tell anyone, will you?'

'Tell anyone what?'

'You know perfectly well. Promise me, Jon.'

He shrugged. 'OK, but I think you're mad. Much better to come clean now.'

'No,' she said firmly. 'I know what I'm doing.'

He glanced out of the window at the azaleas and rhododendrons, long past their best, which hedged the length of the driveway. 'I wonder if you do. From where I stand, there's very little difference between your paranoia on the subject and your mother's. You'll have to find the guts to speak out sooner or later, Lizzie.'

'Don't be an idiot,' she snapped.

He slowed as the wide sweep of gravel in front of the house opened up before them. Two cars were already parked there. 'Plain-clothes police cars,' he said with grim humour, drawing the Mini alongside one of them. 'I hope you're ready for the thumbscrews.'

'Oh, for God's sake grow up,' she exploded angrily, her worry and her uncertain temper getting the better of her. 'There are times when I could quite happily murder you, Jon.'

'We've found a pair of shoes, sir.' DC Jones placed a transparent plastic bag on the ground at Walsh's feet.

Walsh, who was sitting on a tree stump at the edge of the woodland surrounding the ice house, leaned forward to peer at the bag's contents. The shoes were good quality brown leather with irregular cloudy patches on the surface where damp had penetrated and then dried. One shoe had a brown lace, the other a black lace. Walsh turned the bag over and looked at the soles.

'Interesting,' he said. 'New heels with metal studs. There's hardly a mark on them. What size are they?'

'Eights, sir.' Jones pointed to the shoe with the brown lace. 'You can just make it out on that one.'

Walsh nodded. 'Tell one of your men to go up to the house and find out what size shoes Fred Phillips and Jonathan Maybury wear, then on down to the village to see how Robinson and his chaps are getting on. If they've finished, I want them up here.'

'Righto,' said Jones irreverently.

Walsh stood up. 'I'll be at the ice house with Sergeant McLoughlin.'

DS Robinson returned to the pub as the last customer left.

'Sorry, mate,' said the landlord amiably, recognising him from the pint he had bought earlier. 'Too late. Can't serve you now.'

Robinson proffered his identification. 'DS Robinson, Mr Clarke. I'm asking questions around the village. You're my last port of call.'

Paddy Clarke leaned his elbows on the bar and chuckled. 'The body at the Grange, I suppose. There's been talk of nothing else all lunchtime. Sod all I can tell you about it.'

Nick Robinson perched himself on a bar stool and offered Paddy a cigarette before taking one himself. 'You'd be surprised. People often know more than they think they do.'

He assessed his man rapidly and decided here was another where a straightforward approach would pay. Paddy was a big, bluff man with a ready smile and a shrewd eye. But not a person to cross, Robinson thought. His hands were the size of meat plates.

'We're interested in any strangers who may have

been through Streech in the last few months, Mr Clarke.'

Paddy guffawed with laughter. 'Give me a break. I get strangers in here every day, people taking the back roads down to the West Country, stopping off for a quick lunch. Can't help you there.'

'Fair enough, but someone mentioned seeing an old tramp a while back, thought he may have come in here. Does that ring a bell?'

Paddy squinted through the smoke from his cigarette. 'Funny. I wouldn't have remembered him myself, but now you mention it, we did have one in here, said he'd walked from Winchester. Looked like a bundle of old rags, sat in the corner over there.' He nodded to a corner by the fireplace. 'The wife wanted me to turn him away, but I'd no reason to. He had money and he behaved himself, made a couple of pints last through to closing time then shambled off along the Grange wall. You think he's involved?'

'Not necessarily. We're just looking for leads at the moment. When was this? Can you remember?'

The big man thought for a moment. 'It was pissing down outside. Reckon he came in to dry off. The wife might remember when. I'll ask her and give you a ring if you like.'

'She's not here then?'

'Gone to the Cash and Carry. She'll be back soon.'

Nick Robinson checked his notebook. 'I gather you also do a Good Samaritan act with stranded caravans.'

'About twice a year when idiots cut the corner. It's good for business, mind. They usually feel obliged to come in and eat something.' He nodded towards the window. 'It's the Council's fault. They've stuck a bloody great sign for the East Deller campsite at the top of the hill. I've complained about it but nobody takes any notice.'

'Anything strike you about the people you've rescued, anything unusual?'

'There was a one-legged German midget once with a wife like Raquel Welch. That struck me as unusual.'

Nick Robinson smiled as he made a note. 'Nothing unusual.'

'You don't have much to go on, do you?'

'That depends on you.' Unconsciously, the policeman lowered his voice. 'Is anyone else here?'

Paddy's eyes narrowed slightly. 'No one. What are you after?'

'A confidential chat, sir, preferably with no eavesdroppers,' said Robinson, eyeing the large hands.

Paddy squeezed the glowing end of his cigarette into an ashtray with fingers the size of sausages. 'Go ahead.' His tone was not inviting.

'The body was found in the ice house at the Grange. Do you know the ice house?'

'I know there is one. I couldn't lead you to it.'

'Who told you about it?'

'Probably the same person who told me there's a two-hundred-year-old oak in the woods,' said Paddy with a shrug. 'Maybe I got it from David Maybury's booklet. I couldn't say.'

'What booklet?'

'I've some copies somewhere. David had this idea of fleecing the tourists, wanted to turn the Grange into another Stourhead. He produced a map of the grounds with a short history of the house and had a hundred or so copies printed. It was a dead duck from the word go. He wouldn't spend any money on advertising and who the hell's ever heard of Streech Grange?' Paddy gave a derogatory snort. 'Stupid bastard. He was a cheapskate, always expected something for nothing.'

Robinson's eyes were alight with interest. 'Do you know who else has this booklet?'

'We're talking twelve to thirteen years, Sergeant. As far as I remember, David handed them out to anyone who would pass them on to tourists. Testing the water, he said. Whether anyone else's still got a copy I wouldn't know.'

'Can you look yours out?'

The other man was doubtful. 'Christ knows where they are, but I'll have a go. The wife might know.'

'Thanks. I gather you knew Maybury quite well.'

'As well as I wanted to.'

'What sort of man was he? What was his background?'

Paddy stared thoughtfully at the ceiling, dredging up memories. 'Upper-middle-class, I'd say. He was the son of an Army major who was killed during the war. I don't think David ever really knew his father but old Colonel Gallagher certainly did. I imagine that's why he let Phoebe's marriage go ahead, he thought the son would take after his father.' His lips twisted into a cynical smile. 'Fat chance. David was a bastard through and through. The story goes that when his mother died he had the choice of going to her funeral or going to the Derby. He chose the Derby because he had a fortune riding on the favourite.'

'You didn't like him?'

Paddy accepted another cigarette. 'He was a shit – the kind who enjoys putting people down – but he kept me supplied with fairly decent plonk, plus he was one of my best customers. Bought all his beer from me and drank in here most nights.' He took a deep inhalation of smoke. 'Nobody regretted his disappearance, except me. He left owing me over a hundred quid. I wouldn't have minded so much if I hadn't just settled my wine account with his blasted company.'

'You say "he left". You don't think he was murdered?'

'I've no view on it. Left, murdered, same result. It doubled our trade overnight. With all the media coverage, Streech became quite famous. The ghouls dropped in here for local colour before setting off up the hill to gawp through the Grange gates.' He saw a look of distaste on the Constable's face and shrugged. 'I'm a businessman. The same thing'll happen this time which is why the wife's gone to the Cash and Carry. Take my word for it, there'll be a horde of pressmen in here tonight. I pity those wretched women. They'll not be able to set foot outside their gates without being hounded.'

'How well do you know them?'

A guarded expression came over the big man's face. 'Well enough.'

'Do you know anything about their lesbian activities?'

Paddy Clarke chuckled. 'Who's been winding you up?' he asked.

'Several people have mentioned it,' said Robinson mildly. 'There's no truth in it then?'

'They've got minds like sewers,' said Paddy with disgust. 'Three women living together, keeping themselves to themselves, minding their own business and tongues start to wag.' He gave his derogatory snort again. 'Two of them have kids. That hardly ties in with lesbianism.'

'Anne Cattrell hasn't any and she admitted being a lesbian to a colleague of mine.'

Paddy gave such a shout of laughter that he choked on the smoke from his cigarette. 'For your information,' he said with watering eyes, 'Anne could give Fiona Richmond lessons on sex. 'Struth, man, she's had more lovers than you've had hot dinners. What's your colleague like? A pompous jerk, I'll bet. Anne would enjoy taking the piss out of someone like that.'

DS Robinson refused to be drawn on the subject of Andy McLoughlin. 'How come no one's mentioned this? Surely the people here would find promiscuity as titillating as lesbianism.'

'Because she's discreet, for crying out loud. Do you crap on your doorstep? Anyway, there's no one in this dump she'd give house-room to.' He spoke scathingly. 'She prefers her men with brain as well as brawn.'

'How do you know all this, Mr Clarke?'

Paddy glared at him. 'Never mind how I know. Confidential, you said, and confidential it is. I'm setting the record straight. There's enough bullshit been talked about those women to fill a midden. You'll be telling me next they run a witches' coven. That's another favourite, with poor old Fred cast in the rôle of satanic stallion because of his prison record.'

'Confidentially, sir,' said Robinson after a brief hesitation while he contemplated Fred Phillips in the rôle of satanic stallion, 'I've heard from a number of sources that you might know something about several used condoms we've found near the ice house at the Grange.'

Clarke, he thought, looked positively murderous. 'What sources?'

'A number,' said Robinson firmly, 'but I'm not going to divulge them, just as I won't divulge anything you say to me without your permission. We're in the dark, sir. We need information.'

'To hell with information,' said Paddy aggressively, thrusting his face close to Robinson's. 'I'm a publican, not a bloody policeman. You're the one who's being paid. You do your own dirty work.'

Ten years on the force had given Nick Robinson a certain wiliness. He tucked his pen into his jacket and got off the barstool. 'That's your privilege, sir, but as things stand at the moment the finger's pointing at Mrs Maybury and her friends. They seem to be the only ones with enough knowledge of the grounds to have hidden the body in the ice house. I'll guarantee that if we don't get more information, the three of them will be charged with conspiracy.'

There was a long silence while the publican stared at the policeman. Robinson felt he ought to disapprove of Clarke – if Amy Ledbetter was right, the man was a highly sexed stud – but instead he found himself liking him. Whatever his sexual morality, the man looked you in the eye when he spoke to you.

'God damn it!' said Paddy suddenly, slamming a massive fist on to the bar. 'Sit down, man. I'll get you a beer, but if you ever breathe a word of this to my wife I'll string you up by your balls.'

McLoughlin was waiting at the entrance to the ice house when Walsh arrived with the plastic bag containing the shoes. 'I was told you wanted to see me, sir.'

Walsh removed his jacket and lowered himself on to the sun-baked ground, folding the jacket neatly beside him. 'Sit down, Andy. I'm after a few quiet words away from the house. This whole damned thing's getting more complicated by the minute and I don't want any flapping ears around.' He studied the Sergeant's drawn face with sudden irritability. 'What's the matter with you?' he snapped. 'You look terrible.'

McLoughlin transferred his wallet and loose change from his rear trouser pockets and sat down at a short distance from his boss. 'Nothing,' he said, trying without success to find a comfortable position for his legs. He regarded the other man through half-closed lids. He could never decide whether he liked or disliked Walsh. The Inspector, for all his irascibility, could surprise with a kindness. But not today.

He looked across at Walsh and saw only an insignificant, skinny man, playing tough because the system allowed it. He was tempted to make the Inspector a free gift of his assault on Anne Cattrell that morning just to see his reaction. Would he bark? Or would he bite? Bark, McLoughlin thought with amused contempt. Walsh was no more able to face an unpleasantness than the next man. It would be different, of course, when she put in her written complaint. Then, the machinery of justice would roll and action would be as mechanical as it was inevitable. His certainty that this would happen lifted rather than depressed him. The cut would be clean and final, so much cleaner and so much more final than if he administered it himself. He even felt a stirring of anger against the woman that she hadn't delivered the blow already.

Walsh finished summarising the pathologist's report. 'Well?' he demanded.

The shutter clicked maddeningly in McLoughlin's brain. He stared at Walsh with vacant eyes for a moment, then shook his head. 'You say he's exploring the possibility of mutilation. He's not sure yet?'

Walsh snarled sarcastically. 'Won't commit himself. Claims he hasn't enough experience of eaten bodies. But it's a damned odd rat that chews selectively on the only two fingers Maybury had missing.'

'You'll have to tie Webster down on that,' McLoughlin pointed out thoughtfully. 'It makes a hell of a difference to the case if there was no mutilation.' Dreadful black-and-white footage of Mussolini's corpse, strung by its feet from a lamppost after an angry mob had emasculated it, floated into his mind. Violent, angry, hating faces, jeering their revenge. 'A hell of a difference,' he said quietly.

'Why?'

'It's less likely to be Maybury.'

'You're as bad as Webster,' growled Walsh. 'Jumping to bloody conclusions. Let me tell you, Andy, that body is *more* likely to be Maybury's than anyone else's. It is a statistical improbability that this house should be the centre of two unconnected police investigations in ten years, and it is a statistical *probability*, as I've said all along, that his wife murdered him.'

'Even she couldn't murder him twice, sir. If she did it ten years ago, then it wasn't him in the ice house. If it was him in the ice house, then, by God, she's had a raw deal.'

'She brought it on herself,' said Walsh coldly.

'Maybe, but you've let Maybury grow into an obsession with you, and you can't expect the rest of us to chase red herrings just to prove a point.'

Walsh poked around amongst the folds of his jacket for his pipe. He stuffed it in thoughtful silence. 'I've got this gut feeling, Andy,' he said at last, holding his lighter flame to the tobacco and puffing. 'The moment I saw that mess yesterday, I knew. Found you, you bastard, I said to myself.' He looked up and caught McLoughlin's eye. 'OK, OK, lad, I'm not a fool. I'm not about to tie you all down because of my gut feeling, but the fact remains that the blasted body is unidentifiable. And why? Because someone, somewhere, doesn't want it identified, that's why. Who took the clothes? Where are the dentures? Why no fingerprints? Oh, it's been mutilated all right, and it was as likely to be mutilated because it *was* Maybury as because it wasn't.'

'So where do we go from here? Missing persons?'

'Checked. Our area, anyway. We'll go further afield if necessary, but on the evidence so far a local connection seems probable. We've one likely candidate. A Daniel Thompson from East Deller. The description matches very closely and he went missing around the time Webster thinks our man was killed.' He nodded to the shoes in the plastic bag. 'When he disappeared, he was wearing brown lace-ups. Jones found these in the woods adjoining the farm.'

McLoughlin whistled through his teeth. 'If they're his, is there anyone who can identify them?'

'A wife.' Walsh watched McLoughlin push himself awkwardly to his feet. 'Not so fast,' he snapped petulantly. 'Let's hear how you got on. You spoke to Miss Cattrell? Learn anything?'

McLoughlin plucked at the grass beside him. 'The Phillipses' real name is Jefferson. They were sentenced to five years each for the murder of their lodger Ian Donaghue who buggered and killed their son. He was an only child, twelve years old, born when Mrs Jefferson was forty. Miss Cattrell arranged their employment here.' He looked up. 'They're a possibility, sir. What they've done once, they might do again.'

'Different MO. As far as I remember, they made no secret of Donaghue's execution, even carried out a mock trial in front of his girlfriend and hanged him when he confessed. She was a star witness in their defence, wasn't she? It doesn't square with this murder.'

'Maybe,' said McLoughlin, 'but they've proved

they're capable of murdering for revenge and they're pretty attached to Mrs Maybury. We can't ignore it.'

'Have you questioned them yet?'

McLoughlin winced. 'Up to a point. I had her in after Miss Cattrell. It was like trying to prise information out of an oyster. She's a cantankerous old biddy.' He pulled his notebook out of his shirt pocket and riffled through the pages. 'She let slip one thing which struck me as interesting. I asked her if she was happy here. She said: "The only difference between a fortress and a prison is that in a fortress the doors are locked on the inside."'

'What's interesting about that?'

'Would you describe your house as a fortress?'

'She's senile.' Walsh waved him on impatiently. 'Any more?'

'Diana Goode has a daughter, Elizabeth, who spends odd weekends here. Aged nineteen, has a flat in London which was given her by her father, works as a croupier in one of the big West End casinos. She's a bit wild, or that's the impression her mother gave.'

Walsh grunted.

'Phoebe Maybury has a licensed shotgun,' McLoughlin continued, reading down his notes. 'She's responsible for the spent cartridges. According to Fred, there's a colony of feral cats in and around Grange Farm which use his kitchen garden as their private bog. Mrs Maybury scares them off with a blast from the shotgun but Fred claims she's rather lost interest lately, says it's like trying to hold back the tide.'

'Anyone know anything about the condoms?'

McLoughlin raised a sardonic eyebrow. 'No,' he said with feeling. 'But they all found it very amusing, at my expense. Fred said he's raked up quite a few in the past. I questioned him again about finding the body. His story's the same, no discrepancies.' He ran through the sequence for Walsh's benefit.

When Fred arrived at the ice house, the door was completely obscured by the brambles. He returned to his shed to fetch a torch and a scythe, and trampled the brambles so thoroughly because he had intended to take a wheelbarrow in to remove the bricks and had wanted a clear path. The door had been half-open when he finally came to it. There had been no indication that anyone had been that way recently. After he had found the body, he had paused long enough to swing the door to as far as it would go, then he had taken to his heels.

'Did you press him hard?' Walsh asked.

'I went over it with him three or four times, but he's like his wife. He's single-minded and he doesn't volunteer information. That's the story and he's sticking to it. If he did flatten the brambles after he found the body, he's not going to admit to it.'

'What's your guess, Andy?'

'I'm with you, sir. I'd say it's odds on he found plenty of evidence to show there'd been traffic that way and did his utmost to obliterate it after he found the body.' McLoughlin glanced at the mass of torn vegetation on either side of the doorway. 'He did a good job, too. There's no way of knowing now how many people went in there or when.'

Elizabeth and Jonathan found their mothers and Anne drinking coffee in the drawing-room. Benson and Hedges roused themselves from the carpet to greet the newcomers, sniffing hands, rubbing delightedly against legs, rolling over in an ecstasy of joyful welcome. By contrast the three women were positively diffident. Phoebe held out a hand to her son. Diana patted the seat beside her in tentative invitation. Anne nodded.

Phoebe spoke first. 'Hello, darling. Journey down all right?'

Jonathan perched on the arm of her chair and bent down to peck her cheek. 'Fine. Lizzie persuaded her boss to give her the night off and met me at the hospital. I've skipped an afternoon's lectures. We were on the M3 by midday. We haven't eaten yet,' he added as an afterthought.

Diana stood up. 'I'll get you something.'

'Not yet,' said Elizabeth, catching her hand and pulling her on to the sofa again. 'A few minutes won't make any difference. Tell us what's been happening. We had a quick word with Molly in the kitchen but she didn't exactly lavish us with detail. Do the police know whose body it is? Have they said anything about how it was done?' She blurted the questions, insensitive to feelings, eyes overbright.

Her questions were greeted with surprised silence. In twenty-four hours, the women had unconsciously adjusted themselves to a climate of suspicion. A question must be thought about; answers carefully considered.

Predictably, it was Anne who broke the silence. 'It's really quite frightening, isn't it? Your judgement becomes impaired.' She flicked ash into the fireplace. 'Imagine what it must be like in a police state. You wouldn't dare trust anybody.'

Diana threw her a grateful glance. 'You tell them. I'm not trained for this sort of thing. My forte is amusing anecdotes with a punchline. When this is over, I'll polish it up, exaggerate the more titillating bits and give everyone something to laugh about over dinner.' She shook her head. 'But not now. At the moment, it's not very funny.'

'Oh, I don't know,' said Phoebe surprisingly. 'I had a good laugh this morning when Molly caught Sergeant McLoughlin in the downstairs cupboard. She chased him out with a broom. The poor man looked absolutely terrified. Apparently he was trying to find the bog.'

Elizabeth giggled nervously. 'What's he like?'

'Confused,' said Anne dryly, catching the points of

her shirt collar and holding them together. 'Now, Lizzie, what was it you asked? Do they know whose body it is? No. Have they said anything about how it was done? No.' She leant forward and held up her fingers to tick off points. 'The situation, as far as we know it, is this.' Slowly and lucidly she ran through the details of the finding of the body, its removal, the police examination of the ice house and grounds and their subsequent questioning. 'The next step, I think, will be a search warrant.' She turned to Phoebe. 'It would be logical. They'll want to go through the house with a fine-tooth comb.'

'I don't understand why they didn't do it last night.'

Anne frowned. 'I've been wondering about that but I suspect they've been waiting for the results of the post-mortem. They'll want to know what they're looking for. In some ways it makes it worse.'

Jonathan turned to his mother. 'You said on the phone they wanted to question us. What about?'

Phoebe took off her glasses and polished them on her shirt hem. 'They want the names of anyone you showed the ice house to.' She looked up at him and he wondered, not for the first time, why she wore glasses. Without them she was beautiful; with them she was ordinary. Once, when he was a child, he had looked through them. It had been a kind of betrayal to discover the lenses were clear glass.

'What about Jane?' he said immediately. 'Are they going to question her too?'

'Yes.'

'You mustn't let them,' he said urgently.

She took his hand and held it between hers. 'We don't think we can stop them, darling, and if we try we may make it worse. She'll be home tomorrow. Anne says we should trust her.'

Jonathan stood up angrily. 'You're mad, Anne. She'll destroy herself and Mum.'

Anne shrugged. 'We have very little option, Jonny.' She used his childhood diminutive deliberately. 'I suggest you have more faith in your sister and keep your fingers crossed. Frankly, there's bugger all else we can do.'

Eleven

IN DRIBS AND drabs, as messages got through, Walsh's men assembled on the grass in front of the ice house to make their reports. The day was at its hottest and the company shed their jackets gratefully and sat or reclined on the ground like family men at the beach. McLoughlin, lying now on his stomach, frowned into the middle distance like an anxious father with far-off boisterous children. Sergeant Robinson, oblivious to anyone's needs but his own, guzzled happily on a packet of sandwiches and gave the whole the spurious air of an impromptu picnic.

In the background the brambles which had once flourished as a magnificent green curtain quietly leached their sap through shattered stems and turned brown in the sun.

Walsh drew out his handkerchief and wiped the sweat from his forehead. 'Let's hear what you've got then,' he snarled into the contented silence as if he had already made the suggestion once and been ignored. He was sitting with his legs stretched wide apart and a notebook on the ground between his knees. He turned to a blank page. 'Shoes,' he said, making a pencilled note then tapping the brown shoes in the bag beside him. 'Who went up to the house?'

'I did, sir,' said one of Jones's search party. 'Fred Phillips takes size ten and his feet are about as broad as they are long. He took off his boots to show me.' He chuckled at the memory. 'He's not just built like an elephant, he's got feet to match.' He caught Walsh's eye and peered hurriedly at the shoes in the bag. He shook his head. 'No chance. I doubt he'd even get those over his big toes. Jonathan Maybury takes size nine.' He looked up. 'Incidentally, he and Mrs Goode's daughter have arrived, sir. They're with their mothers now.'

Walsh murmured acknowledgement as he jotted down the sizes. 'OK, Robinson, what have you got?'

The DS crammed the last of his sandwich into his mouth and fished out his pad. 'Promotion,' he muttered under his breath to the man next to him.

'What was that?' demanded Walsh coldly.

'Sorry, sir, wind,' replied Robinson, thumbing through his pages. 'I hit upon a mine of information, sir. I'll put it all in my report, but the important bits are these: one, these woods are used regularly by local courting couples, have been for years apparently; two, David Maybury had a hundred copies of a booklet printed, showing a map of the grounds and giving a potted history of the place.' He glanced at Walsh. 'He wanted to attract tourists,' he explained, 'and gave the booklets away to anyone in the village who would pass them on.'

'Damn,' said the Chief Inspector with feeling. 'Have you got a copy?'

'Not yet. It was the landlord at the pub who told me about it and he's looking for his copies now. If he finds them, he'll give me a ring.'

'Anything else?'

'Do me a favour, sir, I've hardly started,' said Nick Robinson plaintively. 'I asked about strangers. Several people remembered seeing an old tramp hanging around the village about two, three months ago but I couldn't get a definite date on him. He had money because he bought a couple of drinks in the pub.'

'I've a date, sir,' Constable Williams interrupted eagerly. 'He knocked at two houses on the council estate asking for food and money. The first was an old lady called Mrs Hogarth who gave him a sandwich; the second was a Mrs Fowler who sent him off with a flea in his ear because he came in the middle of her son's birthday party. The twenty-seventh of May,' he finished triumphantly. 'I've got a good description, too. He shouldn't be too hard to find. Old brown trilby, green jacket and, this is the clincher, bright pink trousers.'

Walsh was doubtful. 'There's probably no connection. Tramps are two a penny round here in the summer. They follow the sun and the scenic routes just like the tourists. Any more?'

DS Robinson caught a sardonic gleam in McLoughlin's eye which told him what he'd already guessed, that the old man was in another of his moods. God rot his soul, he thought. It was like working with a yo-yo, up one minute, down the next. Any other time and all his efforts of the morning would have earned him a pat on the back. As things stood now, he'd be lucky if he got away with a kick in the pants.

He returned to his notebook. 'I followed a lead I was given and spoke to one of the condom users,' he went on. 'He comes up here with his girlfriend when it's warm enough, usually around eleven o'clock – '

'Name,' snapped Walsh.

'Sorry, sir. Promised I wouldn't reveal his name, not unless it became absolutely necessary for a prosecution and, even then, not without his permission.' In Sergeant Robinson's view, Paddy Clarke's threat to string him up by the balls had been no idle one. The big man had offered no reasons for his promiscuity but Robinson had guessed them when Mrs Clarke returned unexpectedly as he was leaving. She was big, meaty and domineering with a brittle smile and hard eyes. A Gorgon who wore the trousers. God knows, Robinson had thought, no one could blame Paddy for wanting something soft, sweet and compliant to cuddle from time to time.

'Go on,' said Walsh.

'I asked him if he'd seen anything unusual up here in the last six months. Seen, no, he said, but heard, yes. According to him it's normally pretty quiet, the odd owl or nightjar, dogs barking in the distance, that sort of thing.' He consulted his notebook. 'On two occasions in June, during the first two weeks, he reckons, he and his girlfriend were – and I'm quoting him, sir – "scared shitless by the most god-awful racket you've ever heard. Like souls crying out in hell." The first time it happened, his girlfriend was so frightened she took to her heels and ran. He followed pretty sharpish and when they reached the road, she told him she'd left her knickers behind.'

A muted snigger rippled round the seated men like a soft breeze through the grass. Even Walsh smiled. 'What was it, did they know?'

'They sussed it the second time. They came up a week later and it happened again but to a much lesser degree. This time, my man hung on to his girl and made her listen. It was cats yowling and spitting, either at each other or something else – he thought he could hear growling as well. He couldn't say where it was coming from, but it was fairly close.' He looked at Walsh. 'They've been up several times since but it's not happened again.'

McLoughlin stirred himself. 'The colony of feral cats at the farm,' he said, 'fighting over the body. If that's right and the date's accurate it gives us the beginnings of a timescale. Our victim was murdered during or before the first week in June.'

'How sure is your man of his dates?' Walsh asked Robinson.

'Pretty sure. He's going to check with the girlfriend but he remembers it being during that spell of very hot weather at the beginning of June, said the ground was dry as a bone both times so he didn't need to take anything for them to lie on.'

Walsh made some notes on his pad. 'Is that it?'

'I've had some conflicting reports about the three women up here. Almost everyone agrees they're lesbians and that they try to seduce the village girls into lesbian orgies. But two of them – in my view, sir, the two most sensible – said it was malicious rubbish. One's an old lady in her seventies or eighties who knows them pretty well, the other's my informant. He said that Anne Cattrell's had so many lovers she could give Fiona Richmond lessons on sex.' He took a cigarette out and lit it, glancing through the smoke at McLoughlin. 'If it's true, sir, it might give us another angle. *Crime passionnel*, or whatever the Frogs call it. It strikes me she's gone out of her way to make us think she's only interested in women. Why? Could be because she's done away with a jealous lover and doesn't want us to make the connection.'

'Your informant's talking crap,' McLoughlin said

bluntly. 'Everyone knows they're lesbians. Hell, I've heard more old jokes about that than I can remember.' Jack Booth had had a fund of them. 'It's hardly something new that Miss Cattrell's invented for our benefit. And if it's not true, why do they pretend it is? What on earth do they gain by it?'

Walsh was stuffing tobacco into his pipe. 'Your problem, Andy, is that you generalise too much,' he said acidly. 'The fact that everyone knows something doesn't make it true. Everyone knew my brother was a tight-fisted bastard until he died and we discovered he'd been paying out two hundred quid a year for fifteen years to educate some black kids in Africa.' He nodded approvingly at Robinson. 'You may have something, Nick. Personally, I couldn't give a monkey's what their sexual habits are and, from what I've seen of them, they couldn't give a monkey's what people say or think about them. Which is why' – he glared at McLoughlin – 'they wouldn't trouble to deny or confirm anything. But,' he continued thoughtfully, lighting his pipe, 'I *am* interested in the fact that Anne Cattrell's been shoving lesbianism down our throats since we got here. What's her motive?' He fell silent.

DS Robinson waited a moment. 'Let me have a go at her, sir. A new face, she might open up. No harm in trying.'

'I'll think about it. Has anyone else got anything?'

A constable raised a hand. 'Two people I spoke to reported hearing a woman sobbing one night, sir, but they couldn't remember how long ago.'

'Two people in the same house?'

'No, that's why I thought it worth mentioning. Different houses. There's a couple of farm cottages just off the East Deller road, belong to Grange Farm. Both sets of occupants remembered hearing the woman but said they didn't do anything about it because they thought it was a lovers' tiff. Neither cottage could remember exactly when it was.'

'Go and see them again,' said Walsh abruptly. 'You, too, Williams. Find out if they were watching telly when it happened, what programme was on, were they eating supper? Or if they were in bed, how late was it, were they awake because it was hot, because it was raining? Anything to give us an idea of time and date. If she wasn't sobbing because she'd just killed a man, she might have been sobbing because she'd just seen him killed.' He pushed himself awkwardly to his feet, gathering his notebook and jacket as he did so. 'McLoughlin, you come with me. We're going to have a chat with Mrs Thompson. Jones, you and your squad pack up here and get everything back to the Station. You can take an hour's break, then I want you all here for a search of the house. There'll be warrants on my desk,' he told Jones. 'Bring them with you.' He turned to Nick Robinson. 'OK, lad, you go and have a quiet little chat about sex with Ms Cattrell but don't go putting the wind up her. If she did chop our body up, I want to be able to prove it.'

'Leave it to me, sir,'

Walsh smiled his reptilian smile. 'Just remember one thing, Nick. In her time she's eaten Special Branch men for breakfast. You represent a small bag of peanuts.'

The door opened after some moments to reveal a drab little woman in a high-buttoned, long-sleeved black dress. She had sorrowful eyes and a pinched mouth. A gold cross on a long chain lay between her flat breasts and she needed only a coif and an open prayer book to complete the picture of devoted suffering.

Walsh proffered his identity card. 'Mrs Thompson?' he asked.

She nodded but didn't bother to look at the card.

'Chief Inspector Walsh and Sergeant McLoughlin. Could we come in? We'd like to ask you some questions about your husband's disappearance.'

She pinched her lips into an unattractive moue. 'But I've told the police all I know,' she whispered, the sorrowful eyes welling with tears. 'I don't want to think about it any more.'

Walsh groaned inwardly. His wife would be like this, he thought, if anything happened to him. Inadequate, tearful, irritating. He smiled kindly. 'We'll only keep you a minute,' he assured her.

Reluctantly, she pulled the door wide and gestured towards the living-room, though *living*-room, thought McLoughlin as he entered it, was a misnomer. It was clean to the point of obsession and bare of anything that might display character or individuality, no books, no ornaments, no pictures, not even a television. In his mind's eye, he compared it with the vivid and colourful room that Anne Cattrell lived in. If the two rooms were an outward expression of the inner person, he had no doubt who was the more interesting. Living with Mrs Thompson would be like living with an empty shell.

They sat on the sterile chairs. Mrs Thompson perched on the edge of the sofa, crumpling a lace handkerchief between her fingers, dabbing her eyes with it from time to time. Inspector Walsh took his pipe from his pocket, glanced around the room as if noticing it for the first time, then put the pipe away again.

'What size shoes does your husband take?' he asked the little woman.

Her eyes opened wide and she stared at him as if he'd made an improper suggestion. 'I don't understand,' she whispered.

Walsh felt his irritation mounting. If Thompson had done a runner, who could blame him? The woman was ridiculous. 'What size shoes does your husband take?' he asked again patiently.

'Does?' she repeated. 'Does? Have you found him

then? I've been so sure he was dead.' She became quite animated. 'He's lost his memory, hasn't he? It's the only explanation. He'd never leave me, you know.'

'No, we haven't found him, Mrs Thompson,' said the Inspector firmly, 'but you reported him missing and we are doing our best to trace him for you. It would help if we knew his shoe size. The missing person's report says size eight. Is that correct?'

'I don't know,' she said vacantly. 'He always bought his shoes himself.' She peeped at him from under her lashes and, rather shockingly, flashed him a coy smile.

McLoughlin leaned forward. 'Could you take me upstairs, Mrs Thompson, and we'll find out from the pairs he left behind?'

She shrank into the sofa. 'I couldn't possibly,' she said. 'I don't know you. It was a young policewoman who came before. Where is she? Why isn't she here?'

Inspector Walsh counted to ten and considered that Daniel Thompson must have been a saint. 'How long have you been married?' he asked curiously.

'Thirty-two years,' she whispered.

The man *was* a saint, he thought. 'Could you pop up and fetch a pair of his shoes?' he suggested. 'Sergeant McLoughlin and I will wait down here for you.'

She accepted this without demur and slipped out of the room, shutting the door behind her as if the door would somehow stop them were they really intent on raping her in her bedroom. Walsh raised his eyebrows to heaven. 'She needs her head examined.'

McLoughlin replied seriously, 'She's ill. Looks to me as if her husband's disappearance has sent her off the rails. Don't you think we ought to get her some help?'

Walsh pondered. 'There was a vicarage a few houses down, wasn't there? We'll stop off on our way back to the Grange.'

They looked up as the door opened again and Mrs Thompson reappeared with a pair of highly polished black leather shoes clasped against her chest. 'Size eight,' she said, 'and a narrow fitting. I never realised what dainty feet he had. He wasn't a short man, you know.'

Reluctantly, Walsh opened his briefcase and produced the clear plastic bag containing the brown shoes. He placed the shoes, in the bag, on the flat of one hand and held them out for the woman to examine. 'Are these your husband's shoes, Mrs Thompson? Do you remember him having a pair like this?'

There was no hesitation in her reply. 'Certainly not,' she said. 'My husband wouldn't dream of wearing co-respondent shoes.'

'The white patches are where the shoes have got damp, Mrs Thompson, not white leather. The shoes were uniformly brown once.'

'Oh.' She moved closer, then after a few moments, shook her head. 'No, I've never seen them before. They're certainly not Daniel's. He had only one pair of brown shoes and he was wearing them the day he' – she gave a little sob – 'the day he vanished.' She used the sodden scrap of lace to dab at her eyes again. 'They were very expensive Italian shoes with pointed toes. Nothing like those. He was very conscientious about his appearance,' she finished.

Walsh put the shoes back in his briefcase. 'When you reported your husband missing, Mrs Thompson, you said he'd had some business worries recently. What exactly did you mean?'

She shied away from him as if he'd tried to touch her. 'He wouldn't leave me,' she said again.

'Of course he wouldn't, Mrs Thompson, but pressure at work does make some men act irrationally. Perhaps he couldn't cope with his problems and needed time on his own to sort them out. Is that what you meant?'

Tears poured from the sorrowful eyes in a flood. She wore her despair like a tatty cardigan, something she had grown used to and was comfortable with in spite of its ugliness. She sank on to the sofa. 'His business is bankrupt,' she explained. 'He owes money all over the place. It's all being sorted out by his assistant but people – creditors – keep ringing me. There's nothing I can do. I've told them he's dead.'

'How do you know?' asked Walsh gently.

'He wouldn't leave me,' she said, 'not if he was alive.'

Walsh looked at McLoughlin and nodded towards the door. They stood up. 'Thank you for giving us your time, Mrs Thompson. There's just one thing. Has your husband ever been to Streech Grange or had dealings with the people living there?'

Her lips thinned to an angry slit. 'Is that where those awful women live?' she spat. Walsh nodded. 'Daniel would sooner walk into the lion's den' – she fingered her cross – 'than be contaminated by their sin.' She kissed the cross and started to undo the buttons of her dress.

'Fair enough,' said Walsh with some embarrassment. 'We'll let ourselves out.'

Andy McLoughlin paused in the living-room doorway and looked back at her. 'We're going to ask the Vicar to pop round and see you, Mrs Thompson. It might do you good to have a chat with him.'

The Vicar listened to the expressions of police concern with ill-disguised panic. 'Frankly, Inspector, there's nothing I can do. Believe me, our little community has bent over backwards to assist poor Mrs Thompson. We've enlisted the aid of her doctor and a social worker, but they're powerless to act unless she herself requests psychiatric help. She's not mad, you see, nor, in the accepted sense, even depressed. In fact, outwardly, she's coping magnificently.' He had a pronounced Adam's apple which bobbed up and down as he spoke. 'It's only when people visit her, particularly men, that she acts – er – strangely. The doctor's sure it's only a matter of time before she snaps out of it.' He wrung his hands. 'The truth is neither he nor I like to go there any more. She seems to have developed sex and religious mania. I'll send my wife, though to be honest her last encounter with Mrs Thompson was less than happy, some accusation about seeing me in church with only my socks and shoes on.' The Adam's apple crowded nervously towards his chin. 'Poor woman. Such a tragedy for her. Leave it with me, Inspector. I'm sure it's only a matter of time, of coming to terms with Daniel's disappearance. There must be a text to deal with it. Leave it with me.'

Detective Sergeant Robinson rang Anne's doorbell and waited. The door was slightly ajar and a voice called: 'Come in,' from a distance. He went down the corridor to the room at the end. Anne was sitting at her desk, a pencil tucked behind her ear, one booted foot propped on an open drawer and tapping in time to 'Jumping Jack Flash' playing quietly from her stereo. She looked up and waved him to an empty chair. 'I'm Anne Cattrell,' she said, taking the pencil from behind her ear and marking a correction on a page of typed paper. 'Vaginal Orgasm – Fact or Fiction' had struggled its way towards some sort of climax on five sheets of A4.

He sat down. 'Detective Sergeant Robinson,' he introduced himself.

She smiled. 'What can I do for you?'

Hell, he thought, she's OK – more than OK. With her cap of dark hair and wide-spaced eyes, she reminded him of Audrey Hepburn. From the way McLoughlin had talked the previous evening, he'd been expecting a real dog. 'It's not much,' he said, 'just something that doesn't square.'

'Fire away. Does the music worry you?'

'No. One of my favourites,' he said truthfully. 'It's like this, Miss Cattrell, both you and the majority of people in Streech village have made out that you and your friends are lesbians.' He paused.

'Go on.'

'Yet when I mentioned it to Mr Clarke at the pub this morning, he roared with laughter and said, though not in quite these words, that you were very definitely heterosexual.'

'What were his actual words?' she asked curiously.

He noticed the full ashtray on her desk. 'Do you mind if I smoke, Miss Cattrell?'

She offered him one of hers. 'Be my guest.' She watched him light the cigarette in silence.

'He said you've had more men than I've had hot dinners,' he said in a rush.

She chuckled. 'Yes, that well-worn cliché sounds like Paddy. So, you want to know if I'm a lesbian, and if I'm not why I've given the impression that I am.' He could almost hear her mind clicking. 'Why would a woman give people reason to despise her unless it's to put them off the track of something else?' She levelled her pencil at him. 'You think I've murdered one of my lovers and left him to rot in the ice house.' Her hands were as small and delicate as a child's.

'No,' he lied gamely. 'To be honest, it's not very important one way or the other, it's just something that's puzzled us. Also,' he went on, taking a shot in the dark, 'I took to Mr Clarke more than any of the others I spoke to, and I can't really believe he's the one who's wrong.'

'Clever of you,' said Anne appreciatively. 'In matters unconnected with sex, Paddy has more sense in his little finger than the whole of Streech put together.'

'Well?' he asked.

'Was his wife there when you spoke to him?'

He shook his head. 'We spoke entirely in confidence though what he said about you was intended to be passed on. He said he was fed up with the b– er – rubbish that was spoken about the three of you.'

'Bullshit?' she supplied helpfully.

'Yes.' He grinned boyishly. 'Actually, I met his wife as I was leaving. She scared the hell out of me.'

Anne lit a cigarette. 'She was a nun once and

incredibly pretty. She met Paddy in church and he swept her off her feet and persuaded her to break her vows. She's never forgiven him for it. As she gets older, her fall from grace assumes larger and larger proportions. She thinks it's God's punishment that she hasn't any children.' She was amused by his astonishment.

'You're having me on?' He couldn't believe Mrs Clarke had ever been pretty.

Her dark eyes sparkled. 'God's truth, m'lud.' She blew a smoke ring into the air. 'Fifteen years ago she set Paddy on fire. The spark's still there. It flashes out occasionally when she forgets herself, though Paddy can't see it. He's accepted the surface image and forgotten that nine-tenths of her lies hidden.'

'You could say that about anyone,' Robinson pointed out.

'You could indeed.'

'Jumping Jack Flash' had given way to 'Mother's Little Helper'. Her foot tapped out a new rhythm.

He waited for a moment but she didn't go on. 'Was Mr Clarke's information about you correct, Miss Cattrell?'

'Hopelessly wrong on numbers unless your mother's deprived you of hot dinners, but the general drift's accurate.'

'So why did you tell Sergeant McLoughlin you were a lesbian?'

She made another pencilled note on the page. 'I

didn't,' she said, without looking up. 'He heard what he wanted to hear.'

'He's not a bad sort,' he said lamely, wondering why he felt a need to defend McLoughlin. 'He's been going through a rough patch lately.'

She raised her eyes. 'Is he a friend of yours?'

Robinson shrugged. 'I suppose so. He's done me some favours, stood by me a couple of times. We have the odd drink together.'

Anne found his answer depressing. Who listened, she wondered, when a man needed to talk? Women had friends; men, it seemed, had drinking companions. 'Whatever I said wouldn't have made any difference,' she told the Sergeant. 'It doesn't matter twopence to this case whether we bonk women every night or men every night. Or if,' she waved her pencil at her bookcase, 'we go to bed for the simple pleasure of reading ourselves to sleep. When you've solved your murder, you'll see I'm right.' She bent to her corrections once more.

Twelve

CHIEF INSPECTOR WALSH gathered his men about him on the drive in front of the Grange and divided them into four groups. Three to search the properties inside, and a fourth to comb the outhouses behind the kitchen, the garage block, the greenhouses and the cellars. Robinson had come out of the house to join them.

'What are we looking for, sir?' asked one man.

Walsh handed some typed sheets round the group. 'Read these pointers, then use your common sense. If anyone here is connected with this murder, they are not going to make you a free gift of their involvement so keep your wits about you and your eyes open. The important facts to remember are these: one, our man died approximately ten weeks ago; two, he was stabbed; three, his clothes and dentures were removed; four, and most importantly, it would help if we knew who the hell he was. David Maybury and Daniel Thompson seem the most likely contenders and there's a brief description of both of them on those sheets.' He paused to let the men read the descriptions. 'You will notice that in terms of height, colouring and shoe size, the two are not dissimilar, but bear in mind, please, that Maybury will have aged ten years since his description was written. I shall head up the search in Mrs Maybury's house, McLoughlin will take Miss Cattrell, Jones, Mrs Goode and Robinson will mastermind the outhouses. If anyone finds anything, notify me immediately.'

With a sense of reluctance, McLoughlin presented himself and his two men outside Anne's door and rang her bell. Nick Robinson's crowing account of his chat with her had set a pile-driver beating in his head. 'Got your wires crossed there, old son,' Nick had said breathily into his ear. 'Given half a chance, I'd have a shot myself. They always say the bright ones are the least inhibited.'

McLoughlin, starved of alcohol, poked stiff fingers into the fat man's beer gut and listened to the satisfying ejection of air. 'You mean they stick a knife between your ribs when the performance is lousy,' he hissed into the other man's face.

Robinson notched up a direct hit and chuckled between deep breaths. 'I wouldn't know. I never have that problem.'

McLoughlin tried to remember a time when his head hadn't hurt, when shutters stayed open in his mind, and when he hadn't felt sick. His feelings seesawed violently between intense dislike of Anne coupled with certainty that she was responsible for the mangled body in the ice house, and a hot shame that set the sweat pouring under his arms whenever he thought of his behaviour of the morning. He bunched his fist till the knuckles gleamed white. 'So why did she say she was a dyke?'

With a wary eye on the fist, Nick Robinson took a pace or two backwards. 'Claims she didn't. Face it, Andy, she reckons you're a pompous ass so she took the piss.' And it'll do you good, he thought. He liked McLoughlin, he had no reason not to, but the man fancied himself a cut above the rest of them which was why his wife's desertion had come so hard. The joke was that the Station had known about it for days, ever since Jack Booth had spilled the beans to Bob Rogers, but they had waited tactfully for McLoughlin to tell them himself. He never had. For two weeks he had come in every morning with a ferocious hangover and rambling stories about what Kelly had said or done the night before. Only his pride was hurt, they all knew it, and that not for much longer the way the WPCs were queuing up to get between his sheets. The clever money was on WPC Brownlow. And for Nick, fat, prematurely bald and with a penchant for WPC Brownlow himself, Anne's indifference to McLoughlin had been a soothing balm.

*

Anne opened the door and gestured them inside. McLoughlin removed the search warrant from his briefcase and gave it to her. She read it through carefully before handing it back with a shrug. There was no change in her manner towards him, no indication to him or his colleagues that he had overstepped that invisible mark beyond which behaviour is censured.

'Go ahead,' she said, nodding towards the small staircase leading to her upper rooms. 'I'll be in my study if you want me.' She returned to her desk in the big sunlit room. 'I Can't Get No Satisfaction' throbbed in the amplifiers.

Her spare room revealed nothing. McLoughlin doubted if it had been used for months, even years. There was a depression in the counterpane of one of the twin beds which implied that Benson or Hedges had found a comfortable retreat there, but no indication of a human presence. They moved on to her bedroom.

'Not bad,' said one of the men approvingly. 'The wife's just paid a fortune for pink frills, white melamine and mirrors. Can't get into the bloody bedroom now. Bet we could have done something like this for half the price.' He ran his hand along the front of a low oak chest.

The room gave an impression of space because it contained so little: only the chest, a delicate wicker chair, and a low double bed with a pile of pillows and a bottle-green duvet. In a recess in one corner was a built-in wardrobe. A white carpet stretched to infinity with no line to show where carpet ended and white skirting boards began. Huge colour close-ups of glorious flowers against jet-black backgrounds marched in a brilliant band round white walls. The room both challenged the eye and relaxed it.

'You two go through the chest and wardrobe,' said McLoughlin. 'I'll have a look in the bathroom.' He retreated gratefully to the normality of a pale pink bathroom but found nothing exceptional, unless two tins of shaving foam, a large packet of disposable razors and three used toothbrushes could be considered unusual possessions for a spinster. As he turned to the door, the corner of his eye caught a movement behind him. He spun sharply, heart struggling like a live thing in his mouth, and hardly recognised himself in the drawn and angry man who stared out of the mirror. He flicked the tap and splashed water over his face, dabbing it dry with a towel which smelt of roses. His head ached unbearably. He was at war with himself and the effort of trying to hold the warring parts together was destroying him. It was nothing to do with Kelly. The thought, unprompted, surprised him. It was inside him and had been inside him for a long time, a simmering rage that he could neither direct nor control, but which Kelly's departure had fired.

He went into the bedroom.

'Here's something, Sarge,' said DC Friar. He was on the bed, reclining against the pillows in a posture absurdly reminiscent of Manet's 'Olympia'. He held a small leather-bound book in one hand and was chuckling over it. 'Jesus, it's obscene.'

'Off,' said McLoughlin with a jerk of his head. He watched the man slide his feet reluctantly to the floor. 'What is it?'

'Her diary. Listen to this. "I cannot look on a penis, post-ejaculation, in a condom without laughing. I am transported immediately to my childhood and the time when my father's finger turned septic. He constructed a finger-stall out of industrial polythene – 'to keep an eye on the bugger' – and summoned my mother and me to witness the exciting climax when the finger, after much squeezing, burst. It was a jolly occasion." Jesus, that's sick!' He twitched the book out of McLoughlin's reach. 'And this one, listen to this one – ' he flicked a page – "Phoebe and Diana sunbathed nude on the terrace today. I could have watched them for hours, they were so beautiful."' Friar grinned. 'She's a dirty little bugger, isn't she? I wonder if the other two know she's a peeper.' He looked up and was surprised by the expression of distaste on McLoughlin's face. He took it for prudery. 'I was reading the entries for end of May, beginning of June,' he said. 'Take a look at June second and third.'

McLoughlin turned the pages. Her handwriting

was black and strong and not always legible. He found Saturday, June 2nd. She had written: 'I have looked into the grave and eternity frightens me. I dreamed there was awareness after death. I hung alone in a great darkness, unable to speak or move, but knowing' (this word was underscored three times) 'that I had been abandoned to exist for ever without love and without hope. I could only yearn, and the pain of my yearning was terrible. I shall keep my light on tonight. Just at the moment, the darkness frightens me.' He read on. June 3rd: 'Poor Di. "Conscience does make cowards of us all." Should I have told her?' June 4th: 'P. is a mystery. He tells me he screws fifty women a year, and I believe him, yet he remains the most considerate of lovers. Why, when he can afford to take women for granted?'

McLoughin snapped the diary shut in his palm. 'Anything else? Anything on her clothes?' The two men shook their heads. 'We'll tackle the living-room.'

Anne looked up as they went in. She saw the diary in McLoughlin's hand and a faint colour washed her cheeks. Damn, she thought. Why, of all things, had she forgotten that? 'Is that necessary?' she asked him.

'I'm afraid so, Miss Cattrell.' The Stones struck a final chord which lingered as a vibration in the air before fading into silence.

'There's nothing in it,' she said. 'Nothing that will help you, at least.'

DC Friar muttered into his colleague's ear, loud enough for McLoughlin to hear. 'Like hell there isn't! It's packed with fucking information!'

He wasn't prepared for the sudden grip of McLoughlin's fingers on the underside of his upper arm. They bit into the tender flesh like iron marlin-spikes, gouging, probing, unrelenting in their viciousness. Quite unwittingly, he had reminded McLoughlin of Jack Booth.

A head taller than Friar, McLoughlin smiled gently down on him. His voice, curling lovingly round the Scots vernacular, murmured softly and sweetly: '"Ye ugly, creepin blastit wonner, Detested, shunn'd by saunt and sinner, How daur ye set a fit upon her, sae fine a Lady! Gae somewhere else and seek your dinner, on some poor body."' There was no emotion in his dark face but his knuckles whitened. 'Recognise that, Friar?'

The DC pulled himself free with an effort and rubbed his arm. He looked thoroughly startled. 'Give over, Sarge,' he muttered uncomfortably. 'I didn't understand a bloody word.' He looked to the other constable for support but Jansen was staring at his feet. He was new to Silverborne and Andy McLoughlin scared the shit out of him.

McLoughlin placed his briefcase on the corner of Anne's desk and opened it. 'It's from a poem by Robert Burns,' he told Friar affably. 'It's called "To A Louse". Now, Miss Cattrell,' he went on, turning his attention to her, 'this is a murder investigation. Your diary will help us establish your movements during the last few months.' He removed a pad of receipts and wrote on the top one. 'It will be returned as soon as we've finished with it.' He tore off the piece of paper and held it out to her and, for a brief moment, his eyes looked into hers and saw the laughter in them. A surge of warmth lapped around the frozen heart of his solitude. She bent her head to study the receipt and his gaze was attracted to the soft curls round the base of her neck, tiny inverted question marks which posed as many problems for him as she did herself. He wanted to touch them.

'I don't record my movements in that diary,' she told him after a moment, 'only my thoughts.' She looked up and her eyes laughed still. 'It's poor fare, Sergeant, just bees in my bonnet. I fear ye'll dine but sparely on sic a place.'

He smiled. Burns had written his poem after seeing a louse on a lady's bonnet in church. 'Ye've nae got the accent, Miss Cattrell. Ye grate ma lug wi' your crabbet sound.' She laughed out loud, and he hooked his foot round a chair and drew it forward to sit on. It was such a tiny face, he thought, and so expressive. Too expressive? Did sorrow come as easily as laughter? 'You recorded some interesting thoughts in your diary on June second. You wrote' – he pictured the written page in his mind – '"I have looked into the grave and eternity frightens me."' He examined her closely.

'Why did you write that, Miss Cattrell, and why did you write it then?'

'No reason. I often write about death.'

'Had you just seen inside a grave?'

'No.'

'Does death frighten you?'

'Not in the least. It annoys me.'

'In what way?'

Her eyes were amused. They would always betray her, he thought. 'Because I'll never know what happened next. I want to read the whole book, not just the first chapter. Don't you?'

Yes, he thought, I do. 'Yet you feared it at the beginning of June. Why?'

'I don't remember.'

'"I dreamed there was awareness after death,"' he prompted her. 'You went on to say that you would keep your light on that night because the darkness frightened you.'

She thought back. 'I had a dream and my dreams are very real. That one was particularly vivid. I woke early, when it was still dark, and I couldn't think where I was. I thought the dream was true.' She shrugged. 'That's what frightened me.'

'You told Mrs Goode something on June third which troubled her conscience. What was that?'

'Did I?' He opened the diary and read the extract to her. She shook her head. 'It was probably something trivial. Di has a sensitive conscience.'

'Perhaps,' he suggested, 'you'd decided to tell her about the corpse you'd found in the ice house?'

'No, it certainly wasn't that.' Her eyes danced wickedly. 'I'd remember that.'

He was silent for a moment. 'Tell me why you don't feel sorry for that wretched man out there, Miss Cattrell.'

She turned away to look for a cigarette. 'I do feel sorry for him.'

'Do you?' He picked up her lighter and flicked the flame for her. 'You've never said so. Neither has Mrs Maybury nor Mrs Goode. It's hardly normal. Most people would have expressed some sympathy, said "Poor man" as the minimum gesture of regret. The only emotion any of you has shown so far is irritation.'

It was true, she thought. How stupid they had been. 'We save our sympathies for ourselves,' she told him coolly. 'Compassion is a frail thing. It dies at the first touch of frost. You would have to live at Streech Grange to understand that.'

'You depress me. I assumed compassion was one of your muses.' He splayed his hands on the desk, then stood up. 'You would have felt sorry for a stranger, I think. But you knew him and you didn't like him, did you?' His chair scraped back. 'Right, Friar, Jansen, let's get on with it. We'll be as quick as we can, Miss Cattrell. At the end I will ask you to go upstairs with a WPC who will search you for anything you may have concealed in your clothing. You are welcome to stay while we work in here but, if you prefer to wait outside, one of the constables will wait with you.'

She puffed a smoke ring into the air and stabbed its centre with the end of her cigarette. 'Oh, I'll stay, Sergeant,' she told him. 'Police searches are meat and drink to me. It should run to a couple of thousand words on a woman's page somewhere. I rather fancy a headline like THE PRY TRADE or LICENCE TO SNOOP. What do you think?'

Sallow-faced bitch, he thought, as he watched the smoke drift from her mouth. The room stank of her cigarettes. 'Please yourself, Miss Cattrell.' He turned away. The blood swelled and throbbed and thickened in his head till he thought only a scream would relieve its pressure.

They went through everything with a fine-tooth comb and with infinite patience. Inside books, behind pictures, beneath chairs, through drawers; they ran long needles into the earth in the plant pots, felt for lumps under the fitted carpet, upended the sofa and poked deftly into its soft cushions; and when they had finished, the room looked exactly as it had done before they started. Anne, who had been moved courteously from her place behind her desk, was duly impressed.

'Very professional,' she told them. 'I congratulate you. Is that it?'

'Not quite,' said McLoughlin. 'Would you open the safe for me, please?'

She gave him a startled look. 'What on earth makes you think I've got a safe?'

He walked over to the oak-panelled mantelpiece which was an exact replica of the one in the library. He pressed on the edge of the middle panel and slid it back, revealing the dull green metal of a wall-safe with a chromium handle and lock. He glanced at Friar and Jansen. 'I found the one in the library this morning,' he said. 'Neat, isn't it?' He couldn't look at her. Her panic, brief though it had been, had shocked him.

She walked back to her desk, collecting her thoughts. She had always believed Phoebe the better judge of character, but it was Diana who was scared of McLoughlin.

'Would you open it, please?' he asked her again.

She took an unbroached packet of cigarettes from a carton of two hundred in her top drawer and tore the seal off it. He watched her patiently, saying nothing.

'Just who do you think you are?' snapped DC Friar angrily. 'You heard the Sergeant. Open the bloody safe.'

She ignored him, flipped the lid of the packet and turned the whole thing upside down, shaking a key into the palm of her hand. 'How are you on Spenser?' she asked McLoughlin with a quirky smile. '"A man by nothing is so well betrayed as by his manners." It might have been written for your friend here.'

She's stalling, he thought, she's afraid, and I hate

her. God, how I hate her. 'The safe, please, Miss Cattrell.'

She walked over with a tiny shrug, unlocked the door and pulled it open. The safe was empty except for a carving knife with a blood-stained rag wrapped around its handle. The blade was black and crusted. McLoughlin felt sick. For all his anger, he hadn't wanted this. With a detached part of his mind, he wondered if he was ill. His head was burning as if he had a fever. He leant his shoulder against the mantelpiece to steady himself. 'Can you explain this, please?' He heard his voice from a distance, harsh and unnatural.

'What's to explain?' she asked, taking out a cigarette and lighting it.

What indeed? The shutter clicked open and shut, open and shut, behind his eyes. He glanced at the cigarette packet on the desk. 'Let's start with why you went to so much trouble to hide the key?'

'Habit.'

'That's a lie, Miss Cattrell.'

Tension had tightened the skin around his nose and mouth, giving him a curiously flat look. She thought of the steel hawser she had once seen in Shanghai, winding on to a huge capstan and drawing a crippled tanker into the docks. As the slack was taken up, it had risen from the concrete, shaking itself free of dust as it thinned and tautened, and then had come a moment of pure horror when it snapped under the strain and whipped with frightening speed through the defenceless flesh of a man's neck. He had seen it coming, she remembered, had put up his hands to protect himself. She looked at McLoughlin and felt an urge to do the same. 'I want to phone my solicitor,' she said. 'I will not answer any more questions until he gets here.'

McLoughlin stirred. 'Friar, find Inspector Walsh for me and ask him to come to Miss Cattrell's wing, will you? Tell him it's urgent, tell him she wants to make a phone call. Jensen' – he flicked his head towards the French windows – 'rustle up a WPC for a strip search. You'll find Brownlow somewhere outside.' He waited till the two men had left then turned to the mantelpiece and stood staring at the open safe. After a moment he swung the door to and put his hands on the mantelpiece, lowering his head to look into the unlit fire. It was a gas replica of a real fire and the artificial coals were peppered with cigarette ash and dog-ends. 'You should put them in a bin,' he murmured. 'They'll leave marks when they burn.'

She craned her neck to see what he was looking at. 'Oh, those. I keep meaning to hoover them up.'

'I thought Mrs Phillips did the hoovering.'

'She does, but she discriminates against certain messes, or more accurately the makers of certain messes, and won't touch them with a barge pole.'

He turned to look at her, resting his elbow on the

mantelpiece. He was shaking like a man with ague. 'I see.' He didn't, of course. What sort of discrimination did Molly go in for? Racial? Religious? Class?

'She discriminates on moral grounds,' Anne told him. Had he spoken his thoughts aloud? He couldn't remember, his head ached so much. 'She's a good old-fashioned Puritan, only truly happy when she's miserable. She can't understand why the rest of us don't feel the same way.'

'Like my mother,' he said.

She gave her throaty chuckle. 'Probably. Mine doesn't bother, thank God. I couldn't do battle with two of them.'

'Does she live near here?'

Anne shook her head. 'The last I heard of her she was in Bangkok. She remarried after my father died and set off round the world with husband mark two. I've rather lost track of them, to be honest.'

That hurt, he thought. 'When did you last see her?'

She didn't answer immediately. 'A long time ago.' She drummed her fingers impatiently on her desk. 'Give me one good reason why I should wait for the Inspector's permission to make this telephone call.'

Her voice vibrated with irritation. It made him laugh. Laughter swept over him like a kind of madness, wild, uncontrollable, joyous. He put a hand to his streaming eyes. 'I'm sorry,' he said. 'I'm so sorry. There is no good reason. Please. Be my guest.' The words, appallingly slurred, seemed to echo in his head and, even to his own ears, he sounded drunk. He clung to the mantelpiece and felt the hearth lurch beneath his feet.

'I suppose it hasn't occurred to you,' observed Anne at his shoulder, as she shoved a chair behind his legs and folded him neatly on to it with the pressure of one small hand on the nape of his neck, 'that it might be worth eating from time to time.' She abandoned him to rummage through her bottom drawer. 'Here,' she said, a moment later, pressing an unwrapped Mars bar into his hand. 'I'll get you something to drink.' She took a bottle of mineral water from a small drinks cabinet, poured a tumblerful and carried it back to him.

His hand, clasping the Mars bar, hung loosely between his knees. He made no attempt to eat it. He couldn't have moved, even if he'd wanted to.

'Oh, shit!' she said crossly, putting the glass on a table and squatting on the floor in front of him. 'Look, McLoughlin, you're a pain in the bloody arse, you really are. If you're trying to drink yourself into early retirement, fine, that's your choice – God knows why you joined the police force in the first place. You should be writing a biography of Francis Bacon or Rabbie Burns or something equally sensible. But if you're not trying for the chop, then do yourself a favour. Any minute now, that little toe-rag you sent off in search of the Inspector is going to come back through my door, and he'll wet himself when he sees you like this. Take my word for it, I know the type. And if there's anything left of you when Walsh has finished, then your friend the constable is going to piss all over it. He'll do it again and again and again, and he'll have an orgasm every time he does it. I promise you, you won't enjoy the experience.'

In her own way she was beautiful. He could drown quite happily in those soft brown eyes. He took a bite out of the Mars bar and chewed on it thoughtfully. 'You're a bloody awful liar, Cattrell.' He moved his head gently from side to side. 'You told me compassion was a frail thing, but I think you've just broken my neck.'

Thirteen

THERE WAS AN atmosphere in the room. Walsh smelled it the minute he stepped inside. McLoughlin was by the window, hands resting on the sill, looking out over the terrace and the long sweep of lawn; Miss Cattrell sat at her desk, doodling, her boots propped on her open bottom drawer, her lower lip protruding aggressively. She looked up as he approached. 'Well, thank God for small mercies!' she snapped. 'I want to phone my solicitor, Inspector, I want to do it now, and I refuse to answer any more questions until he gets here.' She looked very cross.

Anger, thought Walsh with surprise. Somehow, it hadn't smelled like anger. 'I hear you,' he said equably, 'but why would you want to do that?'

McLoughlin opened the French windows to let in Jansen and WPC Brownlow. His legs, seeping sawdust, belonged to somebody else; his stomach, reawakened by the Mars bar, was clawing at itself in a search for further nourishment; his heart was gambolling about his wilting frame like a healthy spring lamb. He felt rather pleased with himself. 'Miss Cattrell,' he said, his voice quite steady, 'would you agree to WPC Brownlow searching you now, while I explain the position to Inspector Walsh?'

'No,' she snapped again, 'I would not. I refuse to co-operate any further until my solicitor gets here.' She tapped a pencil angrily on the desk-top. 'And I'm bloody well not going to say any more in front of you, either, or those creeps you brought with you.' She glared at Walsh. 'I object to this very strongly. It's bad enough having your personal things mauled over, but to have them mauled over by men is the pits. You must have some women on your force. I refuse to talk to anyone but women.'

Walsh hid his excitement well but McLoughlin, with his new clarity of vision, could see the Inspector's scrawny tail wagging. 'Are you making a formal complaint against Sergeant McLoughlin and his team?' Walsh asked.

She glanced at Friar. 'I don't know. I'll wait until my solicitor gets here.' She reached for her telephone and started dialling. 'But my objection stands, so, if you want my co-operation, I suggest you find me some women.'

The Chief Inspector jerked his head towards the door. 'Friar, Jansen, wait in the corridor. Sergeant McLoughlin, gather together what you've found and bring it outside. Brownlow, stay here.' He stood back, eyes narrowing, as he watched McLoughlin launch himself off the wall and plough firmly across the floor. There was something wrong, something he couldn't quite put his finger on. He darted sharp glances about the room.

Anne was murmuring into the telephone. 'Hold on a moment, Bill' – she cupped her hand over the receiver – 'I'd like to remind you, Sergeant,' she said icily, 'that you haven't given me a receipt for what's in my safe. The only receipt I have is the one for my diary.'

Jesus, woman, thought McLoughlin, give me a break. I'm not Charles Atlas, I'm the puny one who gets sand kicked in his face. He bowed ironically. 'I'll make one out now, Miss Cattrell.'

She ignored him and returned to her phone call, listening for a moment. 'Dammit, Bill,' she exploded angrily into the mouthpiece, 'considering how much you charge, you might make the effort to get here a bit sooner. Hell, I may not be one of your fancy London clients, but I always pay on the nail. For God's sake, you can make it in under two hours if you pull your finger out.'

Bill Stanley, long-time friend as well as solicitor, grinned at the other end of the line. He had just told her he'd drop everything to be with her in an hour. 'I could make it three hours,' he suggested.

'That's a bit more like it,' she growled. 'OK, I'll ask him.' She turned to the Inspector. 'Are you planning to take me down to the Police Station? My solicitor wants to know where to come.'

'That's entirely up to you, Miss Cattrell. Frankly, I'm a little puzzled at the moment as to why you want your solicitor present.' McLoughlin turned round with the carving-knife and rag neatly secured in a polythene bag. 'Ah!' said Walsh with ill-concealed glee. 'Well, that does rather suggest you can help us in our enquiries. As long as you understand there is no duress involved, I think it will be simpler for everyone if we pursue our questioning at the Station.'

'Silverborne Police Station,' she told her solicitor. 'No, don't worry, I won't say anything till you get there.' She hung up and snatched the second receipt from McLoughlin. 'And there'd better be nothing of mine hidden in that briefcase,' she said spitefully. 'I've yet to meet a policeman who didn't have sticky fingers.'

'That's enough, Miss Cattrell,' said Walsh sharply, wondering how McLoughlin had managed to keep his temper with her. But perhaps he hadn't and perhaps that explained the tension in the air. 'I draw the line at unwarranted abuse against my officers. Constable Brownlow will wait with you while I have a couple of words with Sergeant McLoughlin in the corridor.' He walked stiffly from the room. 'Right,' he said, when the door had closed behind them, 'let's see what you've got.' He held out his hand for the polythene bag.

'It's like I told you, sir,' said Friar eagerly. 'She was hiding it in her safe. And then there's the diary, with talk about death and graves and God knows what else.'

'Andy?'

He supported himself against the wall. 'I'm not sure.' He shrugged.

'Not sure about what?' demanded Walsh impatiently.

'I suspect we're being had, sir.'

'Why?'

'A feeling. She's not a fool and it was very easy.'

'Friar?'

'That's balls, sir. The diary was easy, I grant you that, but the knife was well hidden. Jansen went all along that wall and missed the safe completely.' He threw a look of grudging acknowledgement in McLoughlin's direction. 'It was the Sergeant spotted it.'

Walsh thought deeply for several moments. 'Well, either way we're committed now, so if we're being had, let's find out why. Jansen, you take this back to the Station and get it fingerprinted before I bring Miss Cattrell in. Friar, cut along and give them a hand outside. Andy, I suggest you take over from me in Mrs Maybury's wing.'

'With respect, sir,' McLoughlin murmured, 'wouldn't it be a better idea if I went through her diary? Friar's right, there are some strange references in there.'

Walsh looked at him closely for a moment, then nodded. 'Perhaps you're right. Pick out anything you think relevant and have it on my desk before I talk to her.' He went back into the room, closing the door behind him.

Friar dogged McLoughlin's heels down the corridor. 'You jammy bastard!'

McLoughlin grinned evilly. 'Privilege has its perks, Friar.'

'You reckon she's going to make a complaint?'

'I doubt it.'

'Yeah.' Friar paused to light a cigarette. 'Jansen and me are clear, whichever way you look at it.' He called after McLoughlin: 'But I'd sure as hell like to know where those marks on her neck came from.'

McLoughlin drove straight to a transport café on the outskirts of Silverborne and ate and ate till he could eat no more. He kept his mind deliberately on his food and, when an errant thought popped in, he chased it out again. He was at peace with himself for the first time in months. When he'd finished, he went back to his car, reclined the seat and went to sleep.

*

Jonathan was hanging round the front door when Anne was ushered out by Walsh and WPC Brownlow. He moved aggressively into their path and Walsh had no difficulty recognising in him the gangling boy who had protected his mother so fiercely all those years ago.

'What's going on?' he demanded.

Anne laid a hand on his arm. 'I'll be back in two or three hours at the most, Jon. There's nothing to worry about, I promise. Tell your Ma I've phoned Bill Stanley and he's coming straight down.' She paused for a moment. 'And make sure she takes the phone off the hook and gets Fred to lock the front gates. The story's bound to be out by now and there'll be pressmen all over the place.' She gave him a long, straight look. 'It's a safe bet she'll be worrying, Jon, so try and take her mind off it. Play her some records or something.' She spoke over her shoulder as Walsh led her towards a car. 'Pat Boone and "Love Letters in the Sand". That's always a safe bet when you want to take Phoebe's mind off something. You know how she adores Pat Boone. And don't hang about, will you?'

He nodded. 'OK. Take care, Anne.'

He waved disconsolately as she was driven away, then retreated thoughtfully through the front door. As far as he was aware, his mother had never listened to a

Pat Boone record in her life. '*Don't hang about, will you?*' He walked towards Anne's door, took a quick look about him, then turned the handle and trod softly down her corridor. He eased her living-room door open and peered around it. The room was empty. '*Safe bet*,' she had said that twice. '*Love Letters*.' It was the work of seconds to slip the hidden catches, take a firm grasp on the chromium handle and slide the whole safe out. It weighed virtually nothing, being made of aluminium. He rested it on one hip while he plunged his hand into the dark recess in the chimney breast and retrieved a large brown envelope. He flicked it on to the nearest easy chair, then carefully repositioned the safe and thrust it back into place. As he stuffed the envelope into the front of his jacket, it occurred to him that something or someone must have frightened Anne pretty badly to make that hiding place unsafe. And why on earth should she worry over some love letters? It was odd. As he left by the French windows, he heard the door into Anne's wing open and close and the sound of footsteps in the corridor. He tip-toed across the terrace and out of sight.

He found Phoebe and Diana in the main drawing-room. They were murmuring quietly on the sofa, heads together, gold hair and red hair interwoven like threads in a tapestry. He was suddenly jealous of their intimacy. Why did his mother confide in Diana before him? Didn't she trust him? He had shouldered the guilt for ten years. Wasn't that long enough for her?

Sometimes, he felt, it was only Anne who treated him like an adult.

'They've taken Anne,' he announced laconically.

They nodded, unsurprised. 'We were watching,' said Phoebe. She gave Jonathan a comforting smile. 'Don't worry, darling. I have more sympathy for the police than I do for her. They'll find that two hours in the ring with Mike Tyson would be preferable to half an hour in Anne's company when she's fighting her corner. She's phoned Bill, I hope.'

'Yes.' He went to the window and looked out on to the terrace. 'Where's Lizzie?' he asked them.

'She's gone with Molly,' said Diana. 'They're searching the Lodge now.'

'Is Fred there, too?'

'Fred's standing guard by the gates,' said Phoebe. 'It seems the press have arrived in force. He's keeping them at bay.'

'That reminds me. Anne said to take the phone off the hook.'

Diana stood up and walked over to the mantelpiece, retrieving a dog-end from behind a clock there. She struck a match and lit the crumpled tip. 'Already done.' She squinted at the pathetic half-inch of tube and puffed inexpertly.

Phoebe exchanged a glance with Jonathan and laughed. 'I'll go and get a decent one from Anne's room,' she said, pushing herself out of the sofa. 'She's bound to have some lying around and I do hate to see you suffer.' She left the room.

Diana dropped the dog-end into the fireplace. 'She's going to bring me one and I'm going to smoke it, and it'll be my second one today. Tomorrow it'll be three and so on till I'm hooked again. I must be mad. You're a doctor, Jon. Tell me not to.'

He walked over, mollified by her sudden need of him, and put an arm round her shoulders. 'Not a doctor yet and you wouldn't take any notice of me anyway. How does it go? "A prophet is not without honour, save in his own country and in his own house." Smoke, if it helps. I'd say stress is just as bad for you as nicotine.' It was like cuddling an older Elizabeth, he thought. They were so alike: in their looks, in their constant search for reassurance, in the ironic twist they gave to everything. It explained so well why they didn't get on.

He squeezed her arm and let her go, moving back to the window. 'Have all the police gone?'

'Except for the ones at the Lodge, I think. Poor Molly. It'll take her months to get over having her long johns inspected by the fuzz. She'll probably wash them all several times before she wears them again.'

'Lizzie will calm her ruffled feathers,' he said.

She gave his back a speculative glance. 'Do you see much of Elizabeth in London?' she asked him.

He didn't turn round. 'On and off. We have lunch

together sometimes. She works pretty anti-social hours, you know. She's in the casino till nearly dawn most nights.' It was tragic, he thought, how much there was about a daughter you could never tell her mother. You couldn't describe the exquisite pleasure of waking at four in the morning to find her warm naked body rhythmically arousing yours. You couldn't explain that just to think about her made you horny or that one of the reasons you loved her was because, whenever you slipped your hand between her thighs, she was wet with longing for you. Instead, you had to say you rarely saw her, pretend indifference, and the mother would never know of the fire her daughter could kindle. 'I should think I see more of her down here,' he said, turning round.

'She doesn't tell me anything about her life in London,' said Diana with regret. 'I assume she gets taken out but I don't know and I don't ask.'

'Is that because you don't want to know or you think she wouldn't tell you?'

'Oh, because she wouldn't tell me, of course,' she said. 'She knows I don't want her to repeat my mistake and marry too young. If she is serious about someone, I'll be the last to know, and by then it'll be too late for me to urge caution. My own fault entirely,' she said. 'I quite see that.'

Phoebe came back and tossed an opened packet of cigarettes at Diana. 'Would you believe they've left that child on guard in Anne's room? PC Williams, the one Molly's taken a shine to. He's had orders to stay there until further notice. Insisted on taking every one of these fags out to have a look at it.' She crossed to the telephone and replaced the receiver. 'I must have been out of my mind,' she went on. 'Jane's due in at Winchester some time this afternoon or evening. I told her to ring when she got there. We'll just have to put up with nuisance calls until we hear from her.'

With a grimace, Jonathan opened the French windows and stepped out on to the terrace. 'I'm going to take the dogs for a walk. I think I'll try and find Lizzie. See you later.' He put his fingers to his lips and gave a piercing whistle before setting off down the garden.

Just then the telephone rang. Phoebe picked it up and listened for a moment. 'No comment,' she said, replacing the receiver. A few seconds later it began to ring again.

Benson and Hedges cavorted around him, waggling their bottoms and barking, as if a walk was a rarity. He struck out towards the woodland between the Grange and Grange Farm, flinging a stick every now and then to please the scampering dogs. His direction took him past the ice house and he watched with distaste as they made a beeline for it, only to whine and scratch with frustration outside the sealed door. He went on, pausing regularly to turn and scan the way he had come, whistling to the dogs to keep up.

When he reached the two-hundred-year-old oak, standing majestically in its clearing in the middle of the wood, he took off his jacket and sat down, relaxing his back into a natural concave in the wrinkled bark. He remained there for half an hour, listening, watching, until he was satisfied that the only witnesses to what he was about to do were dogs and wild creatures.

He stood up, removed the envelope from inside his folded jacket and popped it through a narrow slit into a hollow in the oak's great trunk where a branch had died and been discarded in infancy. Only Jane, who had swarmed with him through the leafy panoply when they were children, knew the secrets of the hidey-hole.

He whistled up the straying dogs and went back to the house.

'Can I talk to you, darling?'

Elizabeth, halfway up the stairs to her bedroom, looked reluctantly at her mother. 'I suppose so.' She had just got back from the Lodge and was tired and irritable. Molly's unspoken distress over the police search had upset her.

'We'll leave it if it's not a good time.'

Elizabeth came slowly down the stairs. 'What's the matter?'

'Everything.' Diana gave a hollow laugh. 'What isn't the matter? I could answer that more easily.'

Elizabeth followed her into their sitting-room. It was a room like Anne's, but with a very different character, less startling, more conventional, with a gold carpet and classic floral prints in tones of russet and gold at the windows and on the chairs. A dwindling sun fingered the colours with a mellow glow.

'Tell me,' said Elizabeth as she watched Jonathan cross the terrace with Benson and Hedges and disappear through Phoebe's French windows.

Diana told her and, as the shadows lengthened, Elizabeth's distress grew.

Inspector Walsh glanced at his watch and, with an inward sigh, shouldered open the door of Interview Room Number Two. It was nine fifteen. He looked sourly from Anne to her solicitor.

Bill Stanley was a great bear of a man with ungroomed ginger hair sprouting everywhere, even on his knuckles, and an air of shabbiness. From his card he was with a top London firm, no doubt earning a packet, so the black pin-striped suit, crumpled and frayed at the cuffs, was presumably some sort of statement – equality with the huddled masses, perhaps

– although why he chose to wear it over a yellowed string vest, Walsh couldn't imagine. He made a mental note to check up on him. In thirty years of rubbing shoulders with the legal profession, he had never seen the like of B. R. Stanley, LLB. The card was probably a forgery.

'You can go home now, Miss Cattrell. There's a car waiting for you.'

She gathered her bits and pieces together and stuffed them carelessly into her handbag. 'And my other things?' she asked him.

'They will be returned to you tomorrow.'

Bill unfolded himself from his chair, stretched his huge hands to the ceiling and yawned. 'I can take you home, if you'd prefer it, Anne.'

'No, it's late. You get back to Polly and the children.'

He straightened his shoulders and the snap as the bones locked into place was loud in the small room. 'This is going to cost you an arm and a leg, my girl – it's goodbye to fifty quid every time I draw breath, remember – so what do you say? Shall we sue? I'm game.' He beamed. 'We're embarrassed for choice really. Harassment, abuse of police powers, damage to your professional reputation, loss of self-esteem, loss of earnings. I always enjoy litigation cases when I've had a chance to see both teams in action.'

Her eyes gleamed. 'Would I win?'

'Good lord, yes. I've hit the opposition for six off far stickier wickets.'

Walsh, who had found Bill's wisecracks increasingly irritating, spluttered angrily. 'The law is not a joke, Mr Stanley. I regret any inconvenience Miss Cattrell may have suffered, but in the circumstances I don't see that we could have acted any differently. It was her choice to have you present while she answered questions and, frankly, had it not taken you three hours to get here, this could all have been dealt with very much more quickly.'

'Couldn't make it any sooner, old man,' said Bill, poking a finger through his string vest and scratching his bear-hairy chest. 'My day for child-minding. Can't abandon the brood to their own devices. They'd slaughter each other the minute I was out of the house. Mind you, you might have a point. Don't relish accusations of sloppiness floating around in open court.' He gave Anne's shoulder a friendly squeeze with his great paw. 'I'll give you a discount. It's less fun but probably more sensible.'

Walsh gobbled furiously. 'I've a damn good mind to charge you both with wasting police time.'

Laughter shook the solicitor's huge frame as he opened the door for Anne and ushered her out. 'No, no, Inspector. I do the charging. Indecent, isn't it? I win whichever way you look at it.' He escorted her to the front door where a police car was waiting, took her face in his hands and bent to whisper in her ear. 'That little farce is going to cost you fifty smackers to one of the AIDS charities, plus an explanation.'

She patted his cheek. 'I needed someone to hold my hand,' she told him.

He grunted his amusement. 'Bollocks! I'd have been angry if I hadn't wanted to find out what the hell was going on and if I hadn't been waiting for a chance to meet that bastard Walsh.' The smile faded from his voice. 'Give me a ring tomorrow and I'll come down and talk to the three of you. Murder is a dangerous game, Anne, even for the spectators. It's too easy to get dragged in. Phoebe knows that better than anyone.' He put his hand on her bottom and propelled her towards the car. 'Give her my love, and Diana too.' He waved goodbye, then walked to his own car and set off back to London and his weekly night-shift in a shelter for the homeless.

Andy McLoughlin lingered in his car on the other side of the road. It was parked in the twilight zone between two pools of orange lamplight and he had seen without being seen. His hands shook on the steering wheel. God, he needed a drink. Had she kissed him? It was difficult to be sure. Did it matter anyway? It was their easy understanding, the way their bodies had leant against each other in uncomplicated friendship that had rocked him. He didn't want her love.

He eased himself out of the car and went inside in search of Walsh. 'How did it go?'

The Inspector was standing at his office window, glowering into the night. 'Did you see them? They've just gone.'

'No.'

'Damned solicitor took three hours to get here, arrived sporting a filthy string vest and looking like the hairy man of Borneo. Matter of fact, I'm highly doubtful about his credentials.' He took out his pipe. 'You were quite right, Andy. It was beef blood. We were being had. Why?'

McLoughlin lowered himself into a chair. 'A diversion. To draw you away from the rest of the house.'

Walsh walked back to his desk and sat down. 'Possibly. In that case it didn't work. There wasn't a stone left unturned by the time we'd finished.' There was a long silence before he tapped his pipe on a sheaf of letters in front of him. 'Jones found this little lot in Mrs Goode's studio.' He pushed the papers towards McLoughlin and waited while the Sergeant skimmed through them. 'Interesting, don't you think?'

'Did Jonesy question her about them?'

'Tried to. She said it was none of his business, that she'd got her fingers burnt and preferred to forget it, certainly had no intention of answering questions on the matter.' He fingered tobacco into the bowl of the pipe. 'When he told her he would have to take the letters, she lost her temper and tried to snatch them back.' There was a twinkle of amusement in his eye as he lit the tobacco and sucked in warm smoke. 'Two PCs had to restrain her while he removed them to his car.'

'And I thought she was the least volatile of the three. What about Mrs Maybury?'

'Good as gold. She took herself off to the greenhouse and spent most of the afternoon rooting Pelargonium cuttings while we turned her house inside out and found nothing.' Noises of succulent contentment puttered from his mouth. 'I've detailed a couple of lads to tout those shoes round the menders. It's a long shot but someone might remember re-heeling them. I don't care what Mrs Thompson says – let's face it, she's so damn cuckoo she wouldn't recognise her own reflection if it didn't have a halo round it – those shoes are the missing Daniel's. Size eight and brown. Too much of a coincidence.'

McLoughlin forced his pricking eyes to stay open as he re-read the top letter. It was undated and very brief. 'Monday. My dear Diana, Of course I regret what's happened, but my hands are tied. If it will help I can come out on Thursday to discuss the position with you. Yours ever, Daniel.' The address was Larkfield, East Deller, and scored across the page in angry writing was: 'Meeting confirmed.' The previous letter, a carbon copy of a demand from Diana for an up-to-date statement of Daniel Thompson's business, was dated Friday, 20th May.

'So when did he go missing?'

'Thursday, twenty-fifth of May,' said Walsh with satisfaction, 'the very day he had arranged an appointment with Mrs Goode.'

'So why didn't you bring her in with Miss Cattrell?'

'I can only cope with one at a time, lad. She'll keep another twelve hours. At the moment I'm rather more interested in why Miss Cattrell went to such extraordinary lengths to get herself brought in for questioning. Any ideas?'

McLoughlin looked at the floor and shook his head.

Fourteen

ANNE WAS DOG-TIRED. Her body had been pumping adrenaline for several hours, exciting her brain, racing her heart, keeping her at a peak of almost intolerable stimulation. Her reaction when she sank into the back of the warm police car was immediate and total. She fell asleep, upright at first but ending in a flat ungainly sprawl along the length of the seat when the driver took a bend too fast. Thus, the photographers outside the unlit gates of Streech Grange missed the picture they had been waiting for: Murder Enquiry – Journalist In Questioning Drama. They had seen too many police cars come and go to be interested in one without a passenger. Fred, sitting doggedly on an old deckchair at the padlocked gates, was not so easily fooled. He let the car in, satisfied himself with a momentary flash of his torch that it contained Anne, then with a sigh of relief resumed his seat. His clutch was safely in the nest. When the police car had gone he could retire to bed.

Barely awake, Anne let herself in through the front door and staggered sleepily across the carpet. Outside, with a new passenger in the shape of PC Williams, now relieved from guard duty, the police car grated away across the gravel. Anne leaned against the wall for a moment to collect her scattered wits. Behind Phoebe's door, she heard the warning bark of the dogs. The next moment, Jane Maybury precipitated herself into the hall and flung herself on her god-mother. Together, they collapsed in a heap on the floor where Anne lay, eyes closed, and trembling.

'My God,' said Jane, turning to her mother who had appeared in the doorway behind her, 'there's something wrong with her. Jon!' she shrilled with alarm. 'Come quick. Anne's ill.'

'I'm not ill,' said the shaking body, opening its eyes. 'I'm laughing.' She sat up. 'God, I am *knackered.* Get off me, you great dollop,' she said, giving the girl a kiss, 'and get me a brandy. I'm suffering severe post-interrogation trauma.'

Phoebe hauled her to her feet and marched her into the drawing-room while Jane fetched a brandy. Anne folded happily on to the sofa and beamed about her. 'What's the matter? You all look as if you've been sucking lemons.'

Diana pulled a face. 'We've been worried sick, you idiot.'

'You should have more faith,' said Anne sternly, accepting the brandy from Jane. 'And how's my god-daughter?' She examined the girl circumspectly while she warmed her glass.

Jane smiled. 'I'm fine.' She was still too thin but Anne was pleased to see that her face had filled out and lost some of its tension.

'You look it,' she agreed.

Phoebe turned to Jonathan. 'Shall we have that celebration we promised ourselves?'

'Sure thing. I'll raid the cellar. What does anyone fancy? Château Lafite '78 or those last bottles of the '75 Champagne? Anne, you choose.'

'The Lafite. Champagne on top of brandy will make me puke.'

He looked questioningly at his mother. 'Shall I drive down and get Fred and Molly to join us? It hasn't been much fun for them either.'

Phoebe nodded. 'Good idea.' She held out a hand to Elizabeth who was sitting slightly apart on the tapestry stool. 'You go too, Lizzie darling. Molly can say no to all of us, and does regularly, but she won't refuse you.' She looked pointedly at Jonathan.

'Come on,' he said. 'You, too, Jane.' They went out.

Phoebe walked over to the mantelpiece. 'I wish David had never used the cellar for storing his wretched imports.'

Anne sniffed her brandy. 'Why? I bless his memory for it regularly.'

'Exactly,' agreed Phoebe dryly, 'so do I. It's very

upsetting.' She glanced at Diana. 'Lizzie's worried about something. Is it Molly and Fred?'

'No. I'm afraid it's me.'

'Why?'

Diana attempted a laugh which didn't work. 'Because I told her I'd be the next one in the police mincing machine.' She swung to face Anne. 'Why did they take you in?'

'They found the safe and it had some incriminating evidence in it.' Anne chuckled into her brandy. 'A bloody carving-knife, wrapped in a bloody rag.' She stirred her glass in her hands, warming it. 'It was straight out of Enid Blyton, but they all got very excited and I refused to answer any more questions till Bill arrived.'

'You're mad,' said Phoebe decidedly. 'What on earth were you up to?'

Mischief lit Anne's dark eyes. 'To tell you the truth, I didn't think they'd find the safe, and if it hadn't been for the Sergeant, they wouldn't have done.' She shrugged. 'Hell, you know me. I always put in an insurance policy, just in case.'

Diana groaned. 'You *are* mad. I do wish you'd take this whole thing a bit more seriously. God knows what they're thinking now. What was it you didn't want them to find?'

'Nothing too desperate,' said Anne easily. 'The odd document or two which probably oughtn't to be in my possession.'

'Well,' said Phoebe, 'I can't understand why you aren't still at the Police Station undergoing a grilling. That's more than Walsh ever had on me and he never let up for a minute.'

Anne sipped her brandy and looked from one to the other with laughter spilling out of her eyes. 'You didn't have my trump card. Bill did his stuff brilliantly. You should have seen him. Walsh damn nearly popped a blood vessel when he finally turned up. He was wearing his string vest.' She dabbed at her eyes and examined Diana's face through damp lashes. It was still very strained.

'It's a game with you, isn't it?' said Diana accusingly. 'I wouldn't mind so much, if I didn't think it was me they'll come down on. You are a fool, you know.'

Anne shook her head. 'What can they possibly have on you?'

Diana sighed. 'Nothing really, except that I've made a prize arsehole of myself.' She smiled unhappily at the two women. 'I hoped you'd never find out. It makes me look such an idiot.'

'It *must* be bad then,' said Anne lightly.

Phoebe squatted on her haunches with her back to the fireplace. 'It can't be worse than Anne's toy-boy, can it?' She looked at her friend and giggled. 'Do you remember him? He still had adolescent acne. You thought he was the bee's knees for about a week.'

Anne, whose earlier hysteria was still perilously close

to the surface, snorted stinging brandy through her nose. She gasped with pain and laughter. 'You mean Wayne Gibbons? A temporary aberration, I assure you. It was his whole-hearted commitment to the cause that attracted me.'

'Yes, but what cause? You looked worn out when he finally left.'

Anne mopped her running eyes. 'You know he's on a study course in Russia now? I had a letter from him not so long ago. It dwelt in extreme and tedious length on the subject of his constipation. I gather he hadn't had any green vegetables since Christmas.' She shuddered. 'God knows what it's done to his acne.' She turned to Diana with a grin. 'It can't be worse than Phoebe's wrestling match by the village pond with that ridiculous Dilys Barnes woman – the one whose daughter fornicates in our bushes. No question about that. Phoebe really looked a fool.'

In spite of herself, Diana laughed. 'Yes, that was funny.' She looked at Phoebe's smiling face. 'You should never have tackled her in a sarong.'

'How was I to know she was going to start a fight?' Phoebe protested. 'Also, it wasn't actually Mrs Barnes who pulled it off. It was Hedges. He got over-excited and did a runner with the damn thing between his teeth.'

Anne was shaking with tension-releasing laughter. 'It was the way you came stomping up the drive in your wellies, purple in the face, boobs bouncing all over the shop and with only a pair of knickers on. God, it was funny. I wish I'd seen the fight. And what were you doing wearing wellies with a sarong, anyway?'

Phoebe's eyes sparkled. 'It was hot, hence the sarong, and I wanted some pondweed from the village pond, hence the wellies. Absurd woman. She ran away screaming. I think she thought I'd taken the dress off myself in order to rape her.' She patted Diana's knee. 'If you've made a laughing-stock of yourself, it's hardly the end of the world.'

'Laughing-stock's right,' said Diana, 'Oh, hell! I'm never going to live it down. It's too bloody embarrassing. I wouldn't mind so much if I wasn't supposed to have good judgement in these things.'

Anne and Phoebe exchanged puzzled glances. 'Tell us,' prompted Phoebe.

Diana put her head between her hands. 'I was persuaded into parting with ten thousand quid,' she muttered. 'Half my savings straight down the drain, apart from anything else.'

Anne whistled sympathetically. 'That's rough. No chance of getting it back?'

'None. He's done a bunk.' She chewed her bottom lip. 'From the way they piled into my correspondence, I suspect the police think they've found him in our ice house.'

'Oh lord!' said Phoebe with feeling. 'No wonder Lizzie's worried. Who is this man?'

'Daniel Thompson. He got my name from that design consultant in Winchester, the one who helped me with the Council offices. He's an engineer, lives in East Deller. Have you come across him?'

Phoebe shook her head. 'You should have gone to the police yourself,' she said. 'It sounds to me as though you've been conned by this creep.'

'No,' said Diana tiredly, staring at her hands, 'it wasn't a con. I invested in a business he was running, all very legitimate and above board, but the bloody thing's gone bust and my money with it. Looking back, I must have been mad but it seemed like such a good idea at the time. It could have revolutionised interior design if it'd taken off.'

'Why on earth didn't you talk to us about it?'

'I would have done but it came up during that week in January when you were both away and I was holding the fort here. Another backer pulled out at the last minute and I had twenty-four hours to make up my mind. By the time you got back I'd rather forgotten about it, then things started to turn sour and I decided to keep mum. I wouldn't be telling you now if the police hadn't found out about it.'

'What business was it?'

Diana groaned. 'You'll laugh.'

'No, we won't.'

She gave them a ferocious glare. 'I'll throttle you if you do.'

'We won't.'

'See-through radiators,' she said.

The watcher in the garden was masturbating in an ecstasy of voyeuristic thrill. How many times had he spied on these cunts, preyed on them, seen them nude? Once he had creepy-crawled the house. His hand moved in mounting frenzy until, with convulsive shudders, he climaxed into his handkerchief. He held the sodden cloth to his face to muffle his giggles.

'I'm off to bed,' said Anne, putting her glass on a tray with the exaggerated care of the tipsy. 'Apart from anything else, I'm pissed. I happily volunteer to wash up in the morning, but tonight I'm off games. I'd break the lot,' she explained owlishly.

'Have you eaten anything this evening, Miss Cattrell?' scolded Molly.

'Not a thing.'

Molly muttered angrily. 'I'll have words with that Inspector in the morning. What a way to treat people.'

Anne paused on her way to the door. 'They brought me a corned beef sandwich,' she said, scrupulously fair. 'I didn't fancy it. There's something about corned beef.' She thought for a moment. 'It's the texture. Moist but crumbly. Reminds me of dog shit.' With a wave, she departed.

Diana, who was watching Molly's face, held her glass in front of her mouth to hide her smile. Even after eight years of Anne's careless bombardment, Molly's sensibilities were still so easily shocked.

Anne drank a pint of water in the kitchen, took a banana from the fruit bowl and wandered, eating it, through the hall and down the corridor. She switched on the lights in her sitting-room and collapsed gratefully into an armchair, tossing the banana skin into the waste-paper basket. She sat for some time, her weary brain in neutral, while the water slowly diluted the effects of the alcohol. After half an hour she began to feel better.

What a day! She had been shitting bricks at the Police Station, wondering if Jon had picked up her hint, and she thought now that she had probably panicked unnecessarily. Could McLoughlin be that sharp? Surely not. The room had been searched by experts – two, three years ago – when Special Branch suspected her of having a leaked MOD document in her possession. They had found the safe but not the secret cache behind it. She rubbed her eyes. Jon had whispered to her that he'd put the envelope somewhere outside where it would never be found. If that were true, she was tempted to let it stay there, wherever 'there' was. She hadn't asked for details. She ran hot and cold every time she thought of the contents of that envelope. God, she was a fool, but, at the time, a photographic record of that terrible brick tomb had made sense. She beat her fist against her head. Supposing Jon had opened it? But he hadn't, she told herself firmly. She could tell by the look in his eyes that he hadn't. But if he had? She thrust the thought away angrily.

McLoughlin held a fretful fascination for her. She kept going back to him, worrying at him, like a tongue against a loosening tooth. That business in front of the mantelpiece? Was it all a blind to cover his interest in the safe? She had looked into his face and seen only a deep, deep hurt, but an expression was only an expression, after all. She rubbed her eyes again. If only, she thought, if only, if only – There was a scream inside her, a scream that was as vast and as silent as the vast silence of space. Was her life always to be a series of *if onlys*?

There was a sharp tap on her French window.

She was so startled she flung her arm out and knocked her wrist on the occasional table beside her. She swung round, massaging the bruise, eyes straining into the night's blackness. A face was pressed against the window, eyes shielded from the bright glare of her lamps by a cupped hand. Fear flooded her mouth with sickly bile and the remembered stench of urine swamped her nostrils.

'Did I frighten you?' asked McLoughlin, easing open the unlocked window when she didn't get up.

'You gave me a shock.'

'I'm sorry.' Some shock he thought.

'Why didn't you come to the front door?' Even her lips were bloodless.

'I didn't want to disturb Mrs Maybury.' He closed the glass doors behind him. 'The light's on in her bedroom. She'd have to have come downstairs to let me in.'

'We've each got a front doorbell. If you press the one with my name on, I'm the only one who hears it.' But he knew that already, didn't he?

'Can I sit down?'

'No,' she said sharply. He shrugged and walked towards the fireplace. 'All right, yes, sit down. What are you doing here?'

He didn't sit down. 'I wanted to talk to you.'

'What about?'

'Anything. Eternity. Rabbie Burns. Safes.' He paused. 'Why are you so frightened of me?'

He wouldn't have believed she had any more blood to lose from her face. She didn't answer. He gestured towards the mantelpiece. 'May I?' He took her silence for permission and slid back the oak panelling. 'Someone's been here before me,' he said conversationally. 'You?' He looked at her. 'No, not you. Someone else.' He grasped the chrome handle and gave a strong pull. Too strong. Jonathan had forgotten to snap home the catches and the safe came out in a rush, sending McLoughlin staggering backwards. With a small laugh he lowered it to the floor and peered into the empty hole. 'Are you going to tell me what was in here?'

'No.'

'Or who removed whatever it was?'

'No.'

He ran his fingers down the side of the safe and located the spring catches. 'Very neat.' He swung it back into position and shoved it home. 'But you've been taking it in and out far more often than it was ever designed for. You're wearing away the ledge.' He pointed to the bottom of the door. 'It isn't parallel with the mantelpiece any more. It should be resting on a concrete lintel. Bricks are no good, they're too soft, too easily crumbled.' He slid the oak panelling into place and folded himself into the chair opposite her. 'One of Mrs Maybury's building efforts?' he suggested.

She ignored that. 'How did you know it wasn't the mantelpiece that was out of true?' Some of the colour had trickled back into her lips.

'I didn't, not until I opened the panel just now, but whoever's been at it in the meantime put it back even more carelessly than you did. Judging by the unsecured catches, they were presumably in a hurry. What was in there?'

'Nothing. You're imagining things.' They sat in silence looking at each other. 'Well?' demanded Anne finally.

'Well what?'

'What are you planning to do about it?'

'Oh, I don't know. Find out who cleaned it out, I suppose, and ask them a few questions. It shouldn't be too hard. The field isn't very wide, is it?'

'You'll end up with egg on your face,' she said tartly. 'The Inspector phoned through for a constable to be in here all the time I was away.' He liked her better when she fought back. 'So in that case, how could anyone have tampered with the safe? It must have dropped of its own accord.'

'That explains the hurry,' was all he said. He sank deeper into his chair and rested his chin on steepled fingers.

'I've nothing to tell you. You're wasting your time.'

He closed his eyes. 'Oh, you've got lots to tell me,' he murmured. 'Why you came to Streech. Why Mrs Phillips calls this house a fortress. Why you have nightmares about death.' He opened his eyes a fraction to look at her. 'Why you panic every time your safe is mentioned and why you like to divert interest away from it.'

'Did Fred let you in?'

'No, I climbed the wall at the bottom.'

Her eyes were deeply wary. 'Why would you do that?'

He shrugged. 'There's a barrage of photographers at your gate. I didn't particularly want to be seen coming in.'

'Did Walsh send you?'

She was as taut as piano wire. He reached out and took her hand, playing with her fingers briefly before letting them drop. 'I'm not your enemy, Cattrell.'

A smile flickered. 'I'll bet that's what Brutus said as he stuck the knife into Caesar. I'm not your enemy, Caesar, and, hell, old chap, it's nothing personal, I just happen to love Rome more.' She stood up and walked to the window. 'If you're not my enemy, McLoughlin, then drop me, drop all of us, from the enquiry and look for your murderer somewhere else.' The moon was pouring herself in a shimmering libation about the garden. Anne pressed her forehead against the cold glass and stared out at the awesome beauty of what lay beyond. Black roses with coronas of silver; the lawn glittering like an inland sea; a weeping willow, its leaves and branches wrought in sparkling tracery. 'But you can't do that, can you? You're a policeman and you love justice more.'

'How can I answer that?' he teased her. 'It's based on so many false premisses that it's entirely hypothetical. I sympathise with personal vengeance. I told you that this morning.'

She smiled cynically into the glass. 'Are you telling me you wouldn't have arrested Fred and Molly for murdering Donaghue?'

'No. I would have arrested them.'

She looked at him with surprise. 'That's a more honest answer than I expected.'

'I wouldn't have had any choice,' he said dispassionately. 'They wanted to be arrested. They sat there with the body, waiting for the police to come.'

'I see.' She smiled faintly. 'You make the arrest but you shed crocodile tears while you're doing it. That's a great way of salving your conscience, isn't it?'

He stood up and walked across to look down into her face. 'You helped me,' he said simply, putting his hands on her shoulders. 'I'd like to help you. But I can't if you won't trust me.'

He was so damn transparent, she thought, with his state-of-the-art cunning. She chuckled amiably. Two could play at this game. 'Trust *me*, McLoughlin. I don't need your help. I am as innocent of personal revenge and murder as a newborn baby.'

Abruptly, as if she were no more than a rag doll, he lifted her off her feet and twisted her towards the light, examining every inch of her face. As a face, it wasn't that special. She had laughter lines etched deeply round her eyes and mouth, frown lines on her forehead, but there was no menace lurking in her dark eyes, no shutters closed on nefandous secrets. Her skin gave off a faint scent of roses. He let go with one hand and ran the tips of his fingers along the curve of her jaw and down the soft line of her neck before, as abruptly, releasing her. 'Did you cut his balls off?'

She hadn't expected that. She straightened her sleeves. 'No.'

'You could be lying through your teeth,' he murmured, 'and I can't see it.'

'That's probably because I'm telling the truth. Why do you find that so hard to believe?'

'Because,' he growled angrily, 'my damn crotch is ruling my brain at the moment and lust is hardly an indicator of innocence.'

Anne glanced down and gave a gurgle of laughter. 'I see your problem. What do you plan to do about it?'

'You tell me. Cold showers?'

'God no. That would be Molly's choice. My advice is, when you've got an itch, scratch it.'

'I'd enjoy it a little more if you scratched it.'

Her black eyes danced. 'Did you have the sense to eat something?'

'Sausage and chips about five hours ago.'

'Well, I'm starving. I haven't eaten since lunchtime. There's an Indian take-away a couple of miles down the road. How do you fancy discussing your options over a Vindaloo?'

He lifted his hand to caress the curls round the base of her neck. The need to touch her was like an addiction. He was crazy, he didn't believe a damn word she said, but he couldn't help himself.

She saw the look in his eyes. 'I'm not your type, McLoughlin,' she warned. 'I am selfish, self-opinionated and entirely self-centred. I am independent, incapable of sustaining relationships and am often unfaithful. I dislike babies and housework and I can't cook. I am an intellectual snob with unconventional philosophies and left-wing politics. I don't conform, so I'm an embarrassment. I smoke like a chimney, am often rude, loathe getting tarted up and I fart very loudly in bed.'

He dropped his hand and grinned down at her. 'And on the plus side?'

'There isn't a plus side,' she said, suddenly serious, 'not for you. I'll get bored, I always do, and when something better comes along, as it surely will, I'll dump you just as I've dumped everyone else. We'll have a halfway decent bonk from time to time, but you'll pay heavily in emotion for what you can buy free of strings in Southampton. Is that what you want?'

He regarded her thoughtfully. 'Is this a regular turnoff, or am I privileged?'

She smiled. 'Regular. I like to be fair.'

'And what's the drop-out rate at this stage?'

'Low,' she said ruefully. 'A few sensible ones leg it. The rest plunge in thinking they're going to change me. They don't. You won't.' She watched his expression. 'Getting cold feet?'

'Well, I can't say I fancy it much,' he admitted. 'It sounds horribly like the relationship I had with my wife, dull, stifling and leading nowhere. I had no idea you were so narrow-minded. Put in "frightened to explore" after "selfish, self-opinionated and self-centred", and I guarantee the drop-out rate, pre-copulation, will astonish you.' He took her arm and steered her towards the window.

'Let's eat,' he said. 'My judgement's better on a full stomach. I'll decide then whether I want to sow my seed in sterile ground.'

She pulled away. 'Go fuck yourself, McLoughlin.'

'Getting cold feet, Cattrell?'

She laughed. 'I'll turn off the lights.' She slipped back to the door and plunged the room into darkness. He took out his torch and waited by the windows. As she approached, she neatly avoided a small table with a bronze statuette of a naked woman on it. 'Me,' she said. 'When I was a nubile seventeen-year-old. I had a bit of a thing going with the sculptor during one school holidays.'

He lit it with the torch and studied it with interest. 'Nice,' he said appreciatively.

She chuckled as she followed him out. 'The figure or the sculpture?'

'Both. Do you lock these doors?' he asked, sliding them to behind him.

'I can't, not from the outside. They'll be all right.'

He put a hand on the back of her neck and walked her across the terrace on to the lawn. An owl hooted in the distance. He looked back at the house to get his bearings and half-turned her to the left. 'This way,' he said, flashing the torch ahead of them. 'I parked the car in a lane that runs along the corner.' Beneath his fingers he could feel the tightness of her skin. They walked in silence until they entered the woodland bordering the lawn. Away to their left, something scuttered noisily through the undergrowth. Her skin leapt with fear, jolting him as violently as it jolted her. 'For God's sake, woman,' McLoughlin growled, swinging his torch beam among the trees. 'What's the matter with you?'

'Nothing.'

'Nothing?' He shone the torch into her eyes, suddenly angry. 'You've buried yourself alive, erected a mountain of barbed wire over the mound, and you call it nothing. She's not worth it. Can't you see that? What the hell can she ever have done for you that you have to sacrifice your whole life in exchange? For Christ's sake, do you enjoy dying by inches? What happened to the Anne Cattrell who seduced sculptors in her school holidays? Where's the thorn in the Establishment's flesh who stormed citadels single-handed?'

She pushed the torch away and her teeth gleamed momentarily as she smiled. 'It was fun while it lasted, McLoughlin, but I did tell you not to try and change me.'

She was gone so fast that even his torch beam couldn't follow her.

Fifteen

HE LET HER go and set off back to his car. He knew that if he went after her, her windows would be locked. He felt regret and relief in equal measure, like the suicide playing Russian roulette who hears the hammer click against an empty chamber. The Station was lousy with women wanting to console him. To hold a loaded gun to his temple by seeking his consolation with her was madness. He swiped in angry frustration at the branches of a tree and ripped the flesh on the side of his hand. He sucked the blood and swore profusely. He was in a mess, and he knew it. He needed a drink.

An owl screeched. Somewhere, far away, he thought he heard voices. He turned his head to listen but the silence only thickened about him. He shrugged and walked on, and it came again, a thread of sound, insubstantial – imagined? The skin on his scalp prickled uneasily. Damn the woman, he thought. If he went back, she would laugh at him.

He was cursing himself for a fool by the time he reached the terrace. He had seen no one, the house was in darkness and Anne was obviously already tucked up in bed. He flashed his torch across the flagstones and lit up her half-opened French window. With a frown, he walked over to it and shone his torch round the interior. He found her almost immediately. He thought she was asleep until he saw the blood glistening in her velvet cap of hair.

After the first paralysing moment of shock, he set to with such speed that time became elastic. In ten seconds he had worked up a sweat that would be rare after an hour's strenuous effort. His torch beam found a table lamp which he switched on as he sank to his knees beside the crumpled heap of clothes. He felt for a pulse in her neck, couldn't find one; laid his head on her chest, no heartbeat. With one fluid movement he rolled the tiny body over, shoved a hand under her neck, pinched her nostrils closed and began mouth-to-mouth respiration. He needed help. The part of his brain that wasn't directly concerned with the resuscitation directed him backwards, drawing the lifeless body with him, feeling with his feet for the table with the bronze statuette. He found it. While he continued the regular in-flows of air, he gave a vicious backward kick and sent the heavy bronze smashing through the plate-glass window. The glass exploded outwards on to the terrace, shattering the silence of the night and sending Benson and Hedges into a frenzy of alarm in another part of the house. He realised with a sense of desperation that he was getting no response. Her face was grey, her lips blue. He placed the heel of his right hand over her breast bone and with the heel of his left hand pressed down, rocking forward, arms straight. While his mouth was free, he shouted for help. After five compressions, he gave her another mouth-to-mouth respiration, before returning to the heart massage. As he rocked forward on the third compression, he saw Jonathan press his fingers against the colourless neck and feel for the pulse.

'Give her another breath,' said Jonathan. 'There's a very faint pulse. My bag, Mum. It's in the hall.'

McLoughlin breathed again into her lungs and, this time, when he turned his head to look at her chest it fluttered weakly. 'Keep going,' said Jonathan, 'one breath every five seconds until she's breathing normally. You're doing great.' He took his bag from a white-faced Phoebe. 'Get some blankets,' he told her. 'Hot-water bottles, anything to keep her warm. And get an ambulance.' He took out his stethoscope, pulled open Anne's shirt and listened for the heartbeat. 'Brilliant,' he said warmly. 'It's weak, but there.' He pinched her cheek and watched with relief as the sluggish blood tinged it faintly pink. Her breathing began to take on a regular rhythm. Gently, he pushed McLoughlin off. 'OK,' he said. 'I think she's under her own steam now. We'll put her in the recovery position.' With the Sergeant's help he pulled her arm across her midriff, then rolled her on to her front, turning her face gently to one side and bending her nearest arm and leg at the elbow and knee. Her breathing was slow but even. She muttered something into the carpet and opened her eyes.

'Hey, McLoughlin,' she said distinctly before giving a huge yawn and falling asleep.

McLoughlin's face was running with sweat. He sat back and wiped it with his shirt sleeve. 'Can't you give her something?'

'Nothing to give. I'm not qualified yet. Don't worry. She's doing all right.'

McLoughlin pointed to the bloody hair. 'She may have a fractured skull.'

Phoebe had come in quietly with a pile of blankets which she spread over the prone figure. She popped her own hot-water bottle at the feet. 'Diana's on the phone for an ambulance. Jane's run down to wake Fred and get the gates open.' She squatted by Anne's head. 'Is she going to be all right?'

'I don't – ' Jonathan began.

'Your daughter's outside?' McLoughlin interrupted, staggering to his feet.

Phoebe stared at him. 'She's gone to the Lodge. They're not on the phone.'

'Is anyone with her?'

Phoebe's face turned pale. 'No.'

'Jesus!' swore McLoughlin, thrusting past her. 'Ring the police for God's sake, get some cars up here.

I don't want to tackle a bloody maniac on my own.' He shouted back to them as he ran down Anne's corridor: 'Tell them someone's tried to murder your friend and may have a go at your daughter. Tell them to get a fucking move on.'

He ran past Diana and burst out of the front door, his sweat turning ice-cold in the night air. It was four hundred yards to the gates and he reckoned Jane was a couple of minutes ahead of him. He set off at a blistering pace. Two minutes was an eternity to kill a woman, he thought, when a second was all it needed to smash an unsuspecting skull. The drive was in pitch darkness with the overhanging trees and bushes blocking out even the weak light of a shrouded moon. He swore at himself for not bringing his torch as he blundered unseeingly into the stinging branches at the edge of the way. He set off again, this time using the crown of the road for his guide, eyes straining to adjust themselves to the night. It was several seconds before he realised that the bobbing yellow pin-point in the distance ahead of him was a torch beam. The drive had straightened out.

'Jane!' he yelled. 'Stop! Wait there.' He pounded on.

The torch swung round to point in his direction. The beam wobbled as if the hand that held it was unsteady.

'I'm a police officer,' he called, his lungs straining. 'Stay there.'

He slowed to a walk as he approached her, hands held placatingly in front of him, chest heaving. The torchlight, wavering frantically now, danced across his face and dazzled him. He fished for his warrant card in his trouser pocket, holding it in front of him like a talisman. With a groan he put his hands on his knees, bent forward and whooped for breath.

'What's the m-matter?' she stammered in a shrill, frightened voice.

'Nothing,' he said, straightening. 'I didn't think you should come alone, that's all. Could you shine the torch on the ground? You're blinding me.'

'Sorry,' She dropped her hand to her side and he saw she was wearing a dressing-gown and carpet slippers.

'Let's go,' he suggested. 'It can't be far now. Shall I take the torch?'

She passed it to him and he caught a brief glimpse of her in its gleam as he turned to light the way ahead. She was like a bloodless ghost, white-faced and insubstantial with a cloud of dark hair. She looked absolutely terrified.

'Please don't be frightened. Your mother knows me,' he said inadequately as they went on. 'She agreed I should come after you.' They could see the black mass of the Lodge in the distance.

She tried to speak but it was a second or two before the sound came. 'I could hear b-breathing,' she wobbled out.

'That was my lungs gasping,' he said, attempting a joke.

'No,' she whispered, 'it wasn't you.' Her step faltered and he swung the beam towards her. She plucked pathetically at her dressing-gown. 'I've got my nightie on.' Her lips were trembling uncontrollably. 'I thought it was my father.'

McLoughlin caught her as she slumped in a dead faint. In the distance, carried on the wind, came the faint sough of a siren.

'What did she mean, Mrs Maybury?' McLoughlin was leaning wearily against the Aga, watching Phoebe make tea.

Anne had been rushed to hospital with Jonathan and Diana in attendance. Jane was asleep in bed with Elizabeth watching over her. Police were swarming all over the garden in search of a suspect. Phoebe, under pressure from McLoughlin, was answering questions in the kitchen.

She had her back to him. 'She was frightened. I don't suppose she meant anything by it.'

'She wasn't frightened, Mrs Maybury, she was terrified, and not of me. She said: "I've got my nightie on. I thought it was my father."' He moved round so that he was facing her. 'Forgetting for the moment that she hasn't seen her father for ten years, why should she associate him with the fact that she was wearing a nightie? And why should it terrify her? She said she heard breathing.'

Phoebe refused to meet his eyes. 'She was upset,' she said.

'Are you going to make me ask Jane when she wakes up?' he demanded brutally.

She raised her lovely face. 'You'd do that, I suppose.' She made as if to push her spectacles up her nose, then realised she hadn't got them on and dropped her hand to the table.

'Yes,' he said firmly.

With a sigh, she poured two cups of tea. 'Sit down, Sergeant. You may not know it but you look dreadful. Your face is covered in scratches and your shirt's torn.'

'I couldn't see where I was going,' he explained, taking a chair and straddling it.

'I gathered that.' She was silent for a moment. 'I don't want you asking Jane questions,' she said quietly, taking the other chair, 'even less so after tonight. She couldn't cope. You'll understand that because I think you've guessed already what she meant by her remark.' She looked at him enquiringly.

'Your husband abused her sexually,' he said.

She nodded. 'I blame myself because I had no idea what he was doing. I found out one night when I came home early from work. I was the evening receptionist at the doctor's surgery,' she explained. 'We needed the money. David had sent Johnny to a boarding prep-school. That day I had flu and Dr

Penny sent me home and told me to go to bed. I walked in on my poor little Jane's rape.' Her face was quite impassive as if, long ago, she had realised the futility of nurtured anger. 'His violence had always been directed at me,' she went on, 'and in a way I asked for it. While he was beating me, I could be certain he wasn't touching the children. Or I thought I could.' She gave a mirthless laugh. 'He took full advantage of my naivety and Jane's terror of him. He had been raping her systematically since she was seven years old and he kept her quiet by telling her he would kill me if she ever said anything. She believed him.' She fell silent.

'Did you kill him?'

'No.' She raised her eyes to his. 'I could have done quite easily. I would have, if I'd had anything to kill him with. A child's bedroom doesn't lend itself to murder weapons.'

'What happened?'

'He ran away,' she said unemotionally. 'We never saw him again. I reported him missing three days later after several people had phoned to say he hadn't kept appointments. I thought it might look odd if I didn't.'

'Why didn't you tell the police the truth about him?'

'Would you, Sergeant, with a severely disturbed child your only witness? I wasn't going to let her be questioned, nor was I going to give the police a motive for a murder I didn't commit. She was under a psychiatrist for years because of what happened. When she became anorexic, we thought she was going to die. I'm only telling you now to protect her from further distress.'

'Have you any idea what happened to your husband?'

'None. I've always hoped he killed himself but, frankly, I doubt he had the guts. He loved inflicting pain on others but couldn't take it himself.'

'Why did he run away?'

She didn't answer immediately. 'I honestly don't know,' she said at last. 'I've thought about it often. I think, perhaps, for the first time in his life he was afraid.'

'Of what? The police? Prosecution?'

She smiled grimly, but didn't answer.

McLoughlin toyed with his teacup. 'Someone tried to murder Miss Cattrell,' he said. 'Your daughter thought she heard her father. Could he have come back?'

She shook her head. 'No, Sergeant, David would never come back.' She looked him straight in the eye as she brushed a strand of red hair from her forehead. 'He knows if he did, I'd kill him. I'm the one he's afraid of.'

A very irritable Walsh sat in Anne's armchair and watched a policeman photographing prints on the outside of what was left of the French windows. It was a job that couldn't be put off till the morning in case it rained. The broken slivers of glass on the flagstones had been covered with weighted-down polythene. 'There are going to be dozens of prints,' he muttered to McLoughlin. 'Apart from anything else, half the Hampshire police force have left their grubby paw marks round the shop.' McLoughlin was examining the carpet by the French windows, looking for blood spots. He moved across to the desk. 'Anything?' Walsh demanded.

'Nothing.' His eyes were red-rimmed with exhaustion.

'So what happened here, Andy?' Walsh cast a speculative eye over his Sergeant, before glancing at his watch. 'You say you found her at eleven forty or thereabouts. It is now one thirty and we have come up with some vague sounds in the distance and a woman with a fractured skull. What's your guess?'

McLoughlin shook his head. 'I haven't got one, sir. I wouldn't even know where to start. We'd better pray she comes round soon and can tell us something.'

Walsh levered himself out of the chair and shuffled over to the window. 'Haven't you finished yet?' he demanded of the man outside.

'Just about, sir.' He took a last photograph and lowered his camera.

'I'll leave someone here overnight and you can do the inside tomorrow.' Walsh watched while the man packed up his equipment and left, carefully skirting the broken glass, then he shuffled back to the chair, playing up his age. He took out his pipe and began the process of filling it, watching McLoughlin closely from beneath the angry jut of his brows. 'All right, Sergeant,' he snapped, 'now you can tell me just what the hell you've been up to. I don't like the smell of this one little bit. If I find you've been getting your priorities mixed, by God you'll be for the high jump.'

Exhaustion and jangling nerves combined in a prolonged yawn. 'I was trying to steal a bit of a march, sir. I thought there might be promotion in it.' Bold, bare-faced lies, he thought, nothing too concrete, not even a half-truth that Walsh could check up on. If Phoebe could get away with it, then so could he.

Walsh's frown deepened. 'Go on.'

'I came over the wall at the bottom to see what happened when she came back from the Station. I must have got here by about ten forty-five. The others had all gone to bed but Miss Cattrell was sitting in that chair you're sitting in. She finally switched off her downstairs light at about eleven fifteen. I hung around for another ten minutes then set off for the car. I hadn't gone far when I thought I heard voices, so I came back to investigate. Her window was slightly open. I shone my torch round inside and found her there.' He jerked his head towards the middle of the room.

Walsh champed thoughtfully on the stem of the

pipe. 'It was lucky you did. Mrs Maybury said you were giving her heart massage when she came in. You probably saved her life.' He lit the pipe and studied the Sergeant through the smoke. 'Is this the truth?'

McLoughlin gave another huge yawn. He couldn't control them. 'It's the truth, sir,' he said wearily. Why was he trying to protect himself? This morning he would have welcomed an excuse to go. Perhaps he just wanted to know the end of the story, or perhaps he wanted vengeance.

Walsh was deeply suspicious. 'If I find there's something been going on between the two of you, you'll be up on a discipline charge so damned fast you'll wonder what happened. She's a suspect in a murder enquiry.'

The dark face cracked into a grin. 'Do me a favour, sir, she's been treating me like Vlad the Impaler since I called her a dyke.' He yawned again. 'But I appreciate the compliment. In view of the bashing it's taken in the past couple of weeks, it does my ego good that you think I can pull a reluctant bird after twenty-four hours. Kelly wouldn't agree with you,' he finished bitterly.

Walsh grunted, 'Was it you who hit her?'

McLoughlin didn't have to feign surprise. 'Me? Why would *I* want to hit her?'

'To get even. You're in the mood for it.'

He stared at Walsh for a moment, then shook his head. 'That's not the way I'd choose,' he said. 'But if

Jack Booth ever turns up with a hole in his head, that might be down to me.'

The Inspector nodded. 'So what was Miss Cattrell doing for the half hour you watched her?'

'She sat in that armchair, sir.'

'And did what?'

'Nothing. I presume she was thinking.'

'You say the Maybury woman made no bones about wanting to kill her husband. Would she kill her friend too?'

'Possibly. If she was angry enough. But what was her motive?'

'Revenge? Perhaps she thought Miss Cattrell had talked to us.'

McLoughlin shook his head slowly. 'I imagine she knows Miss Cattrell better than that.'

'Mrs Goode? The Phillipses? The children?'

'Same question, sir. What was the motive?'

Walsh stood up. 'I suggest we start looking,' he said acidly, 'before we all end up on point-duty. A weapon would be helpful. I want this entire house turned upside down, Sergeant. You can lead the search till Nick Robinson gets here. He'll be my number two in this investigation.' He looked at his watch. 'You'll be concentrating on the Maybury file. Be in my office at ten tomorrow morning. There's a pattern to all of this and I want it found.'

'With respect, sir, I believe I can make a more valuable contribution here.'

'You'll do as you're told in future, Sergeant,' the older man snapped angrily. 'I'm not sure what your game is, but I don't like people who try to steal a march over me.'

McLoughlin shrugged. 'Then I urge you not to get too sold on a pattern, sir. Mrs Maybury has told you what she thinks happened and, as I pointed out this morning, Mrs Phillips describes this house as a fortress. Why?'

Walsh eyed him thoughtfully for a moment then walked to the door. 'You're being conned by some very professional liars, lad. If you don't sharpen up, you're going to look very foolish indeed.'

Sixteen

THERE WAS A new sense of urgency about police activities. They moved into top gear with alacrity, demonstrating all too clearly that there was another gear to move into. It was as if the attempted murder of a known woman was on a different scale from the murder of an anonymous male stiff in the garden. Anne would have found it disquieting, except that she was in a coma in Intensive Care and knew nothing about it. Walsh would have denied it vigorously, but his irascible temper flayed his men instead when, after a thorough search of the house and grounds, they failed to come up with anything.

In the press, Streech Grange was likened, quite inappropriately, to 10 Rillington Place, as a setting for mass murder and decomposing remains. To Anne's friends, the burden of their association with it was heavy. In retrospect, their previous interrogations had the relaxed air of a social gathering. After the assault on Anne, the gloves came off and they were grilled dry. Walsh was looking for a pattern. Logic told him there was one. The odds against three unconnected mysteries in one house were so incalculable as to be beyond consideration.

For the children, it was a new experience altogether. As yet none of them had been questioned and it came like a baptism of fire. Jonathan hated his sense of impotence, of being involved in something over which he had no control. He was surly and uncooperative and treated the police with a sort of weary disdain. Walsh wanted nothing so much as to kick him up the backside, but after two hours of questioning he was satisfied there was nothing more he could get out of him. Jonathan had vindicated the three youngsters of the assault on Anne. According to him, they had changed into their nightclothes after the impromptu Lafite party, wrapped themselves in duvets and curled up in Jane's room to watch the late film on her television. The shattering glass, followed by McLoughlin's shouts for help, had startled them. No, they had heard nothing before that, but then the television had been quite loud. Walsh questioned Elizabeth. She was nervous but helpful. When asked for her movements on the previous evening, her account tallied exactly with Jonathan's down to the most trivial detail. Jane, after a day's respite, gave a similar story. Unless they were in some fantastic and well-organised conspiracy, they had had nothing to do with the attempt on Anne's life.

For Phoebe it was a case of déjà vu. The only difference this time was that her interrogators now had information she had withheld from them ten years previously. She answered them with the same stolid patience she had shown before, annoyed them with her unshakeable composure and refused to be drawn when they needled her on the subject of her husband's perversions.

'You say you blame yourself for not knowing what he was doing to your daughter,' said Walsh on more than one occasion.

'Yes, I do,' she answered. 'If I had known earlier, perhaps I could have minimised the damage.'

He got into the habit of leaning forward for the next question, waiting for the tell-tale flicker of weakening resolve. 'Weren't you jealous, Mrs Maybury? Didn't it madden you that your husband preferred sex with your daughter? Didn't you feel degraded?'

She always paused before she answered, as if she were about to agree with him. 'No, Inspector,' she would say. 'I had no such feelings.'

'But you've said you could easily have murdered him.'

'Yes.'

'Why did you want to murder him?'

She smiled faintly at this. 'I should have thought it was obvious, Inspector. If I had to, I'd kill any animal I found savaging my children.'

'Yet you say you didn't kill your husband.'

'I didn't have to. He ran away.'

'Did he come back?'

She laughed. 'No, he didn't come back.'

'Did you kill him and leave him to rot in the ice house?'

'No.'

'It would have been a sort of justice, wouldn't it?'

'It certainly would.'

'The Phillipses, or should I say Jeffersons, believe in that kind of justice, don't they? Did they do it for you, Mrs Maybury? Are they your avenging arm?'

It was always at this point that Phoebe's anger threatened to spill over. The first time he put the question it had come like a blow to the solar plexus. Afterwards, she was better prepared, though it still required iron self-control to keep from tearing and gouging at his hated face. 'I suggest you ask Mr and Mrs Phillips that,' she always said. 'I wouldn't be so presumptuous as to answer anything on their behalf.'

'I'm asking you for an opinion, Mrs Maybury. Are they capable of exacting vengeance for you and your daughter?'

A pitying smile would curl her lips. 'No, Inspector.'

'Was it you who struck down Miss Cattrell? You say you were in bed, but we only have your word for it. Was she going to reveal something you didn't want revealed?'

'Who was she going to reveal it to? The police?'

'Perhaps.'

'You're such a fool, Inspector.' She smiled humourlessly. 'I've told you what I think happened to Anne.'

'Guesswork, Mrs Maybury.'

'Perhaps, but in view of what happened to me nine years ago, not unlikely.'

'You never reported it.'

'You wouldn't have believed me if I had. You'd have accused me of doing it to myself. In any case, nothing would have induced me to have you back in the house, not once I'd got rid of you. In some ways I was luckier than Anne. My scars were all internal.'

'It's too convenient. You must think me very gullible.'

'No,' she said honestly, 'narrow-minded and vindictive.'

'Because I don't share your taste for melodrama? Your daughter is very vague about what frightened her. Even Sergeant McLoughlin only *thinks* he heard someone. I'm a realist. I prefer to deal in fact, not female neurosis.'

She studied him with a new awareness. 'I never realised how much you dislike women. Or is it just me, Inspector? The idea that I might be getting my just deserts really appeals to you, doesn't it? Would I have saved myself all this misery if I'd said "yes" ten years ago?'

Invariably it was Walsh who became angry. Invariably, after a bout of questioning, Phoebe would get in her car and drive to the hospital to sit at Anne's bedside, massaging her hands and talking to her, willing her back to consciousness.

Diana's interrogations probed and prodded her connection with Daniel Thompson. She couldn't control her anger against Walsh in the way that Phoebe did and she frequently lost her temper. Even so, after two days, he could still detect no flaws in her story.

He tapped the pile of correspondence. 'It's perfectly clear from your letters that you were furious with him.'

'Of course I was furious,' she snapped. 'He had squandered ten thousand pounds of my money.'

'Squandered?' he repeated. 'But he was doing his best, wasn't he?'

'Not in my view.'

'Didn't you have the business checked before you agreed to invest in it?'

'We've already been through all this, for God's sake. Don't you listen to anything?'

'Answer the question, please, Mrs Goode.'

She sighed. 'I wasn't given much time. I spent a day going through the company books. They seemed in order, so I made over the cheque for ten thousand. Satisfied?'

'So why do you say he squandered your money?'

'Because as I got to know him, I realised he was supremely incompetent, may even have been an out-

and-out rogue. The figures I saw had been heavily massaged. For example, I now think he inflated the company's assets by overvaluing his stock and I have discovered he was also using his employees' National Insurance contributions to keep the business afloat. The order books I saw were full, yet after three months he had sold virtually nothing and the little stock he had at his factory apparently had nowhere to go. His PR was a joke. He kept saying that word-of-mouth would spread and the thing would take off.'

'And that made you angry?'

'God give me strength,' she said, raising her hands to heaven. 'Do you need it spelled out? It made me livid. I was conned.'

'Do you know anything about Mr Thompson's disappearance?'

'For the last time, no. N-O, no.'

'But you knew he'd disappeared before we told you.'

'Yes, Inspector, I knew. He was supposed to come here to explain what was going on.' She leaned forward and banged her fist on the letters. 'You've got the date and the time in front of you. He never turned up. I rang his office and was told he wasn't there. I rang his home and was given a flea in my ear by his wife. I rang his offices again a couple of days later and was told Mrs Thompson had reported him missing. I went to the office the next day to find some very angry employees who had not been paid for three weeks and had just discovered that their insurance contributions had not been paid for nearly a year. There has been no sign of Daniel Thompson since. The business is bankrupt and a lot of people, not just me, are owed a considerable amount of money.'

'Frankly, Mrs Goode, anyone who invests money in see-through radiators should expect to lose it.'

Ice-blue eyes, he thought, had a capacity for murderous dislike that the greens and browns lacked. The epithets she now applied to him were unprintable.

'It's your pride that's hurt, isn't it?' he said with interest. 'Your amour-propre. I can easily imagine you killing someone who made a fool of you.'

'Can you?' she snapped. 'Then you've an overactive imagination. No wonder the police have such a poor detection record.'

'I think Mr Thompson did come here, Mrs Goode, and I think you got as angry with him as you are with me, and you hit out at him.'

She laughed. 'Have you ever seen him? No? Well, take it from me, he's built like a tank. Ask his silly wife if you don't believe me. If I'd hit him, he'd have hit me back and I'd still be sporting the bruises.'

'Were you sleeping with him?'

'I'll make a confession,' she conceded. 'I found Daniel even less fanciable than I find you. He had wet lips, very like yours. I don't like wet lips. Does that answer your question?'

'His wife denied any connection between him and the Grange.'

'That doesn't surprise me. I've only met her once. She didn't approve of me.'

'Did Fred and Molly know about this investment of yours?'

'No one here knew.'

'Why not?'

'You know bloody well.'

'You didn't want to look a fool.'

She didn't bother to answer.

'Perhaps Fred and Molly did your dirty work for you, Mrs Goode?'

She massaged the beginnings of a headache. 'What a nasty manipulative man you are.'

'Did they, Mrs Goode?'

She studied him thoughtfully. 'No,' she said. 'And if you ever dare ask me that question again, I'll hit you.'

'And be arrested for assault?'

'It would be worth it,' she said.

'You're a very aggressive woman, aren't you? Did you take out your aggressions on Miss Cattrell?'

She punched him on the nose.

Jonathan tapped his mother on the shoulder, then bent forward and looked at Anne. 'How is she?' She was off the critical list and had been removed from

Intensive Care to a side room on a surgical ward. She was attached via a catheter and a plastic tube to an intravenous drip.

'I don't know. She's very restless. She's opened her eyes once or twice, but she's not seeing anything.'

He squatted on the floor beside her. 'You're going to have to leave her for a bit, I'm afraid. Diana needs you.'

'Surely not.' Phoebe frowned.

''Fraid so. She's been arrested.'

She was visibly surprised. 'Diana? Whatever for?'

'Assault on a police officer. She punched Inspector Walsh and gave him a nose bleed. She's been carted off to the nick.'

Phoebe's mouth dropped open. 'Oh, lord, how funny,' she said, beginning to laugh. 'Is he all right?'

'Bloody but unbowed.'

'I'll come. We'd better get hold of poor Bill again.' She looked down at Anne. 'Nothing I can do for you at the moment, old girl. Keep fighting. We're all rooting for you.'

'I'll bring Jane in later,' said Jonathan. 'She wants to come.'

They walked into the corridor. 'Is she up to it?'

'I'd say so. She's coped fantastically since it happened. We had a long chat this afternoon. She was more objective than I've ever known her. Ironically, the whole thing may have done her some good, silver linings and all that, made her realise she's tougher than she thought she was. She likes the Sergeant, by the way. If they want to question her again, we should press for him to do it.'

'Yes,' said Phoebe. 'Apart from anything else, he saved Anne's life. That would always commend him to Jane. She dotes on her godma.'

Jonathan linked his arm through his mother's. 'She dotes on you, too. We all do.'

Phoebe gave her rich laugh. 'Only because you haven't discovered my clay feet yet.'

'No,' he said seriously. 'It's because you've never pretended they were anything else.'

They walked on and disappeared round a bend in the corridor. Behind them, Andy McLoughlin inched with the embarrassment of the eavesdropper from where he had been hiding in a recessed doorway.

Damn Walsh and his bloody pattern, he thought. Logic was fallible. It had to be.

He showed his warrant card to the Sister. 'Miss Cattrell?' he asked. 'Any change?'

'Not really. She's getting restless and opening her eyes which is a good sign but, as I told the Inspector, you'll be wasting your time if you want to interview her. She could come out of it any moment or she could be like this for a day or two. We'll let you know as soon as she's up to talking.'

'I'll stay for a few minutes, if that's all right. You never know.'

'She's in side ward two. Chat to her,' the Sister

encouraged. 'Might as well make yourself useful while you're here.'

He hadn't seen her since she had been taken away in the ambulance and he was shocked. She was even smaller than he remembered, a tiny, shrunken thing with bandaged head and ugly, sallow skin. But, even unconscious, she seemed to be smiling at some private joke of her own. He felt no lust – how could he? – but his heart warmed with a sense of recognition as if he had known her a long time. He pulled the chair close to her pillows and started to speak. There was no hesitation for he knew, without thinking, just what would give her pleasure. After half an hour he ran dry and looked at his watch. She had moved once or twice, like a child in her sleep, but her eyes had stayed firmly closed. He pushed his chair back. 'That's it, Cattrell. Time's up, I'm afraid. I'll see if I can get you alone again tomorrow.' He touched her cheek with his fingertips.

'You're a mean sod,' she mumbled. 'Give me "Tam o' Shanter".' She opened one eye and glared at him. 'I'm dying.'

'You've been awake all the time,' he accused her.

She opened the other eye and there was a twinkle amidst the confusion. 'Was Phoebe here?'

He nodded.

'I remember Phoebe being here. Am I at home?'

'You're in hospital,' he told her.

'Oh, shit. I hate hospitals. What day is it?'

'Friday. You've had a two-day snooze.'

That worried her. 'What happened?'

'I'll find a nurse.' He started to get up.

'You bloody well won't,' she growled. 'I hate nurses too. What happened?'

'Someone hit you. Tell me what you remember.'

She knit her brows into a deep furrow. 'Curry,' she said experimentally.

He gripped her hand tightly. 'Can we forget the curry, Cattrell?' he asked her. 'It'll be easier all round if you never saw me that evening.'

She wrinkled her forehead. 'But what happened? Who found me?'

He rubbed her fingers. 'I found you, but I've had the devil's own job explaining to Walsh what I was doing there. I can hardly admit to carnal designs on a suspect.' He searched her face. 'Do you understand what I'm saying? I want to stay on the case, Anne. I want justice.'

'Of course I bloody understand.' Humour danced in the dark eyes and he wanted to hug her. 'I can chew gum and walk at the same time, you know.' She thought deeply. 'I remember now. You were telling me how to live my life.' She looked at him accusingly. 'You had no right, McLoughlin. As long as I can live with myself, that's all that matters.'

He raised her fingertips and brushed them softly across his lips. 'I'm learning. Give me time. Tell me what else you remember?'

'I ran all the way back,' she said with an effort of concentration. 'I opened the window, I remember that. And then' – she frowned – 'I heard something, I think.'

'Where?'

'I don't remember.' She looked worried. 'What happened then?'

'Someone hit you on the back of the head.'

She looked dazed. 'I don't remember.'

'I found you inside your room.'

A heavy hand descended on his shoulder and made him jump. 'You've no business to be asking her questions, Sergeant,' said the Sister angrily. 'Get me Dr Renfrew,' she called to a nurse in the corridor. 'Out,' she told McLoughlin.

Anne looked at her with unalloyed horror and clung to his hand. 'Don't you dare go,' she whispered. 'I've seen her picture on *World at War* and she wasn't fighting for the Allies.'

He turned and raised his hands in helpless resignation.

'Is there anything I should remember?' she asked him. 'I wouldn't want to confuse the Inspector.'

His eyes softened. 'No, Miss Cattrell. You just concentrate on getting better and leave the remembering to me.'

She winked sleepily. 'I'll do that.'

*

DS Robinson was after promotion. He had gone diligently door-to-door again, looking for leads to Anne's assailant, but he had come up against the proverbial brick wall. No one had seen or heard anything on that night, except the ambulance, and they'd all heard that. He had had another pint with Paddy Clarke, this time under the beady eye of Mrs Clarke. He had found her immensely intimidating, more so since Anne's revelation that she had once been a nun. Paddy assured him they had looked for the map of the grounds but hadn't found it and, with Mrs Clarke breathing over his shoulder, he expressed complete ignorance of Streech Grange and its inhabitants. In particular, he knew nothing at all about Anne Cattrell. Nick Robinson didn't press him. Frankly, he didn't rate his chances if he got caught up between Mr and Mrs Clarke and he was unashamedly attached to his balls.

There was nothing to stop him going home now. By rights, he was off-duty. Instead, he turned his car in the direction of Bywater Farm and one Eddie Staines. So far, Mrs Ledbetter's information had paid dividends. No harm in giving her another whirl.

The farmer pointed him to the cow-sheds where Eddie was cleaning up after the evening's milking. He found Eddie leaning on a rake and carelessly chatting up an apple-cheeked girl who giggled inanely at everything he said. They fell silent as Nick Robinson approached and looked at him curiously.

'Mr Staines?' he asked, producing his warrant card. 'Can I have a word?'

Eddie winked at the girl. 'Sure,' he said. 'Would bollocks do?'

The girl shrieked her mirth. 'Ooh, Eddie! You are funny!'

'Preferably in private,' continued Robinson, making a mental note of Eddie's riposte for his own future use.

'Buzz off, Suzie. I'll see you later in the pub.'

She went reluctantly, scuffing her boots through the muck in the yard, looking over her shoulder in the hopes of being invited back. For Eddie, it was clearly a case of out of sight out of mind. 'What do you want?' he asked, raking soiled straw into a heap while he spoke. He was wearing a sleeveless tee-shirt which gave full expression to the muscles of his shoulders.

'You've heard about the murder at the Grange?'

'Who hasn't?' said Staines, uninterestedly.

'I'd like to ask you a few questions about it.'

Staines leant on his rake and eyed the detective. 'Listen, mate, I've already told your lot all I know and that's nothing. I'm a farmhand, a salt-of-the-earth prole. The likes of me don't mix with the people at the Grange.'

'No one said you did.'

'Then what's the point of asking me questions?'

'We're interested in anyone who's been into the grounds in the last couple of months.'

Staines resumed his raking. 'Not guilty.'

'That's not what I've heard.'

The young man's eyes narrowed. 'Oh, yeah? Who's been blabbing?'

'It's common knowledge you take your girlfriends up there.'

'You trying to pin something on me?'

'No, but there's a chance you may have seen or heard something that could help us.' He offered the man a cigarette.

Eddie accepted a light. He appeared to be thinking deeply for several minutes. 'Happen I did then,' he said surprisingly.

'Go on.'

'Seems you've been asking my sister questions about a woman crying one night. Seems you've been back a couple of times.'

'The farm cottages on the East Deller road?'

'That's right. Maggie Trewin's my sister, lives in number two. Her man works up at Grange Farm. She tells me you want to know which night this – woman' – he put a derisory emphasis on the word – 'was crying.'

Robinson nodded.

'Well, now,' said Staines, blowing perfect smoke rings into the air above his head, 'I can probably tell you, but I'd want a guarantee my brother-in-law'll never know where you got it from. No court appearances, nothing like that. He'd skin me alive if he knew I'd been up there and he'd not give up till he found out who I was with.' He shook his head morosely. 'It's more'n my life's worth.' His brother-in-law's young sister was the apple of his eye.

'I can't guarantee no court appearances,' said Robinson. 'If the prosecution serves a writ on you, you'll have to attend. But it may never happen. The woman may have no bearing on the case.'

'You reckon?' Staines snorted. 'More'n I do.'

'I could take you in for questioning,' said Robinson mildly.

'Wouldn't get you nowhere. I won't say nothing till I'm certain Bob Trewin won't find out. He'd kill me, no mistake.' He flexed his muscles and returned to his raking.

Nick Robinson wrote his name and the address of the Police Station on a page of his notebook. He tore it out and handed it to Staines. 'Write down what happened and when, and send it to me unsigned,' he suggested. 'I'll treat it as an anonymous tip-off. That way no one will know where it came from.'

'You'll know.'

'If you don't,' Robinson warned, 'I'll come back and next time I'll bring the Inspector. He won't take no for an answer.'

'I'll think on it.'

'You do that.' He started to leave. 'I suppose you weren't up there three nights ago?'

Staines hefted a lump of dung to the top of his straw pile. 'You suppose right.'

'One of the women was attacked.'

'Oh, yeah?'

'You hadn't heard?'

Staines shrugged. 'Maybe.' He cast a sideways glance at the detective. 'One of her girlfriends did it, bound to be. Bitches fight like the devil when they're roused.'

'So you didn't hear or see anything that night?'

Eddie turned his back to attack the farthest corner of the shed. 'Like I just said, I wasn't there.'

Now, why don't I believe you, Robinson wondered, as he picked his way with distaste through the cow dung in the yard. The apple-cheeked girl giggled as he passed her by the gate then, like a moth to the flame, she dashed back to the cow-sheds and the arms of her philanderer.

Seventeen

WALSH WAS STILL nursing a bloody nose when McLoughlin got back to the Station. It had long since stopped bleeding but he persisted in holding his blood-stained handkerchief to it. McLoughlin, who hadn't overheard that part of Phoebe's and Jonathan's conversation, looked at him in surprise.

'What happened?' he asked.

'Mrs Goode hit me, so I arrested her for assault,' said Walsh maliciously. 'That soon wiped the smile off her face.'

McLoughlin sat down. 'Is she still here?'

'No, dammit. Mrs Maybury persuaded her to apologise and I let her go with a caution. Bloody women,' he said. He stuffed the handkerchief into his pocket. 'We've had a result on the shoes. Young Gavin Williams turned up an old cobbler in East Deller who does it for pin money.'

McLoughlin whistled. 'And?'

'Daniel Thompson's for sure. The old boy keeps

records, bless him. Writes a description of the shoes – in this case, made a special note of the different coloured laces – what needs to be done, name of owner and the dates they come in and go out. Thompson collected them a week before he went missing.' Walsh fingered his nose tenderly. 'The time-scale's perfect. It's not looking good for Mrs Goode.' He chuckled at his witticism. 'If we can find just one person who saw him going into the Grange – ' He let the thought hang in the air while he took out his pipe and started to clean it with cheerful industry. 'How do you fancy Miss Cattrell for that part? She went through the little pantomime with her solicitor to steer us away from her friend, then panicked her friend by letting on how much she knew.' He tapped the pipe against his head. 'Goodbye Miss Cattrell.'

'No chance,' said McLoughlin decidedly, watching the pipe-cleaner turn black with tar. 'I dropped into the hospital on my way here. She's come round. I've sent Brownlow down to sit with her.'

'Has she now? Did you speak to her?'

'Briefly, before I was booted out by the Sister. She needs a good sleep, apparently, before she can answer questions.'

'Well?' demanded Walsh sharply. 'What did she say?'

'Nothing much. The whole thing's a complete blank to her.' He examined his nails. 'She did say she thought she heard something outside.'

Walsh grunted suspiciously. 'Suits your case rather neatly, doesn't it?'

McLoughlin shrugged. 'You're barking up the wrong tree, sir, and if you hadn't tied my hands I'd have proved it by now.'

There was malice in the older man's voice. 'Jones has taken his team over the ground twice and they haven't found anything.'

'Then let me have a look. I'm wasting my time on the Maybury file. No one I've spoken to so far knew anything about his penchant for little girls. Jane appears to be the only one. It's a dead end, sir.'

Walsh dropped the fouled pipe-cleaner into his waste-paper basket and glared at his Sergeant with open dislike. McLoughlin's admission that he had been trying to steal a march rankled with him, all the more because his own grip on the case was so tenuous. He was deeply suspicious of the man in front of him. What did McLoughlin know that *he* didn't? Had he found the pattern? 'You'll stick with that file till you've talked to everyone who knew Maybury,' he said angrily. 'It's a whole new line of enquiry and I want it thoroughly explored.'

'Why?'

Walsh's brows snapped together. 'What do you mean, why?'

'Where will it lead us?'

'To Maybury's murderer.'

McLoughlin looked at him with amusement. 'She's

got the better of you, sir, and there's damned all you can do about it. Raking over dead ashes isn't going to produce a prosecution. He terrorised one child and that was his own daughter, and now he's dead. My guess is he's buried in that garden somewhere, possibly in one of the flowerbeds at the front. She does those herself. Fred is never allowed near them. I think you were right and she hid the body in the ice house till the coast was clear and I doubt very much if, after ten years, there's anything left for us to find. Those dogs of hers are rather partial to human remains.'

Walsh plucked at his lips. 'I'm keeping an open mind. Webster still hasn't proved to my satisfaction that it wasn't Maybury in the ice house.'

McLoughlin gave a derisive snort. 'A minute ago you were convinced it was Daniel Thompson. For God's sake, sir, face up to the fact that you've got a *closed* mind on this whole thing. Result, we're all working with one hand behind our backs.' He leaned forward. 'There is no pattern, or not the sort you're looking for. You're trying to force unrelated facts to fit and you're making a mess of it.'

A panic of indecision gripped Walsh's belly. It was true, he thought. There was too much pressure. Pressure from within him to close the Maybury case once and for all, pressure from the media for eye-catching headlines, pressure from above to find quick solutions. And, always, the unrelenting pressure from below as the new bloods challenged for his job. He eyed McLoughlin covertly as he fingered tobacco into his pipe bowl. He had liked and trusted this devil once, he reminded himself, when the devil was shackled to a tiresome wife and troubled by his inadequacies. 'What do you suggest?'

McLoughlin, who had been up for three nights in a row, rubbed his tired eyes vigorously. 'A constant watch on Streech Grange. I'd suggest a minimum of two in each shift. Another thorough search of the grounds, but concentrated up near the Lodge. And, finally, let's be done with Maybury and put our energies into pursuing the Thompson angle.'

'With Mrs Goode as chief suspect?'

McLoughlin pondered for a moment or two. 'We can't ignore her certainly, but it doesn't feel right.'

Walsh touched his sore nose tenderly. 'It feels very right to me, lad.'

Mrs Thompson greeted them with her look of long-suffering martyrdom and showed them into the pristine but characterless room. McLoughlin had a sense of going back in time, as if the intervening days hadn't happened and they were about to explore the same conversation in the same way and with the same results. Walsh produced the shoes, no longer in their polythene bag, but with the odd meagre dusting of powder where an attempt had been made to bring up fingerprints and had failed. He put them on a low coffee table for her to look at.

'You said these weren't your husband's shoes, Mrs Thompson,' he accused her mildly.

Her hands fluttered to the cross on her bosom. 'Did I? But of course they're Daniel's.'

Walsh sighed. 'Why did you tell us they weren't?'

The awful tears swam into her eyes and drizzled over her cheeks. 'The devil whispers in my ear.' Her fingers fumbled at her shirt buttons.

'Give me strength,' muttered Walsh.

McLoughlin stood up abruptly and walked to a telephone in one corner. 'Pull yourself together, Mrs Thompson,' he ordered sharply. 'If you don't, I shall call for an ambulance and have you taken into hospital.'

She shrank into her chair as if he had slapped her.

Walsh frowned angrily at his Sergeant. 'Are these the shoes Mr Thompson was wearing when he disappeared?' he asked the woman gently.

She examined them closely. 'No,' she said.

'Are you sure? You told us the other day he had only one pair of brown shoes and he was wearing them the day he went.'

Her eyelids fluttered uncontrollably. 'Did I?' she gasped. 'How very odd. I don't believe I was feeling quite well the last time you came. Daniel loved brown shoes. You can have a look in his cupboard if you like.

He had pairs and pairs.' She waved her hand at the table. 'No, these are the ones Daniel gave to the tramp.'

Walsh closed his eyes. His threadbare case against Diana was disintegrating. 'What tramp?' he demanded.

'We didn't ask his name,' she said. 'He came to the door, begging. The shoes were on the stairs to go up and Daniel said he could have them.'

'When was this?'

She produced the lace handkerchief and touched it to her eyes. 'The day before he left. I remember it very clearly. Daniel was a saint, you know. In spite of all his troubles he had time for a poor beggarman.'

Walsh took some papers from his briefcase and flicked through them. 'You reported your husband missing on the night of the twenty-fifth of May,' he said. 'So this tramp came on the twenty-fourth.'

'He must have done,' she said through her tears.

'What time was it?'

She looked helpless. 'Oh, I couldn't remember that. Some time during the day.'

'Why was your husband at home during the day, Mrs Thompson?' asked McLoughlin, looking at his diary. 'The twenty-fourth was a Wednesday. Shouldn't he have been at work?'

She pouted. 'His beastly business,' she said viciously. 'All his worries came from that. It wasn't his fault, you know. People expected too much of him. He stopped going in towards the end,' she admitted lamely.

'Can you give me a description of this tramp?' asked Walsh.

'Oh, yes,' she said. 'He'll be able to help you, I'm sure. He was wearing a pair of pink trousers and an old brown hat.' She thought back. 'He was about sixty, I suppose, not much hair and he smelled terribly. He was very drunk.' She paused, a thought suddenly occurring to her. 'But you must have found him already,' she said, 'or why would you have the shoes?'

Walsh picked them up and turned them over. 'You said your husband had no connection with the women at Streech Grange, yet one of them, Mrs Goode, invested money in his business.'

A shadow crossed her face. 'I didn't know.'

'Mrs Goode claims to have met you,' Walsh went on.

There was a long silence. 'Possibly, I do recall talking to someone of that name three or four months ago in the street. Daniel told me she was a client.' A glint sharpened in her eye. 'Brassy blonde woman, over-dressed, with a come-hither look.'

'Yes,' said Walsh who found the description inept but entertaining.

'She rang me,' said Mrs Thompson, pursing her lips in disapproval, 'wanting to know where Daniel was. I told her to mind her own business.' She pinioned the Inspector with a basilisk's glare. 'Did she have something to do with Daniel's disappearance?'

'We've been going through your husband's books,' said McLoughlin glibly from his corner. 'We noted the discrepancy. It puzzled us.'

'I didn't know she was one of them.' She held her handkerchief to dry eyes. 'Now you tell me she invested money in his company?' The floodgates opened and this time her tears were of real distress. 'How could he?' she sobbed. 'How could he? Such terrible women.'

Walsh looked at McLoughlin and stood up. 'We'll be off now, Mrs Thompson. Thank you for your help.'

She tried without success to stem the flood.

'Have you thought about going away at all?' the younger man asked.

She gave a long shuddering sigh. 'The Vicar's arranged a holiday,' she said. 'I'm going to a hotel by the seaside at the end of the week, just for a few days' rest. It won't do any good though, not without Daniel.'

McLoughlin looked very thoughtful as he closed the door behind him.

Chief Inspector Walsh ground his teeth with fury as he jerked the clutch on his brand new Rover and promptly stalled. 'What are you looking so damned cheerful about? We've just lost our only promising lead.'

McLoughlin waited until the car was moving. 'Who was in charge of the case at the beginning?'

'If you mean Thompson's disappearance, it was Staley.'

'Did he do a thorough job? Did he check Mrs Thompson?'

'Checked everything. I've been through the file.'

'Does he know about our body?'

'He does.'

'And it hasn't made him suspicious?'

'No. Her alibi's too good. She took Mr T. to Winchester station where he boarded a train to London. Various people remember seeing him during the journey and one remembers seeing him on the platform at Waterloo. After dropping him off, Mrs T. went straight to East Deller Church where she took part in a twenty-four-hour fast with other members of the congregation. The saintly Daniel was due to join her there at six o'clock on his return from London where, incidentally, he was supposed to be raising a loan to keep the business afloat. He never came back. At ten o'clock, the Vicar's wife took Mrs T. home to Larkfield and waited with her while she telephoned office, friends and acquaintances. At nearly midnight, Mrs Vicar rang the police and stayed with Mrs T., who was by then quite hysterical, through the night and most of the following day. Daniel has not been seen since he got off the train in London.'

'But her alibi's only good for the twenty-fifth and twenty-sixth. Supposing he came back later?'

Walsh manoeuvred his way into the traffic on a roundabout. 'Why would he, if he'd gone to the lengths of doing the bunk in the first place? Staley reckons he planned to kill two birds with one stone – get shot of the awful wife and duck out of the bankruptcy. He hopped into the bog at Waterloo, reversed his mac, stuck on a false moustache and went to ground with whatever he'd managed to stash away from the business. For what it's worth, Thompson's number two at the radiator firm said he wasn't in the least surprised Thompson legged it, he only wondered why it had taken him so long. According to him, Thompson had no balls and less bottle and from the moment things began to get dicey, he looked like running.'

McLoughlin picked at a fingernail. 'You must have thought he had a good reason for coming back, sir. Otherwise, how could Mrs Goode have killed him?'

'Yes, well, Mrs Goode's a damn sight more attractive than that silly bitch back there. I felt there was a good chance he staged his disappearance in order to throw in his lot with a blonde bombshell.'

'But when he turned up on her doorstep, Mrs Goode, who was down by ten thousand, found she didn't fancy him as much as she thought she did and stuck a knife into him?'

'Something like that.'

McLoughlin laughed out loud. 'Sorry, sir.' He thought for a moment. 'The Thompsons don't have any children, do they?'

'No.'

'OK, let's say you've been married to a man for thirty-odd years. He's been the be-all and end-all of your existence and he suddenly deserts you.' He paused for further thought.

'Go on.'

'I'll need to think it through properly but something along these lines. Daniel does a runner because the business has gone down the chute and he can't cope. He hangs around in London for a bit but finds that living off his wits there is worse than facing the music at home, so he comes back. Meanwhile, Mrs Thompson has discovered, because Mrs Goode telephones and tells her that Daniel was supposed to have gone to Streech Grange, that her husband has been seeing another woman, worse, a woman steeped in sin. She's very near the edge already and this sends her right over. Bear in mind she's a religious fanatic, her marriage has been a sham and she's had several days to sit and brood. What's she going to do when Daniel comes home unexpectedly?'

'Yes,' agreed Walsh thoughtfully. 'That works quite nicely. But how did she get the body to the ice house?'

'I don't know. Perhaps she persuaded him to go there when he was alive. But it's entirely logical for her to leave the body somewhere in Streech Grange, the site of Daniel's sin, and it's logical for her to have stripped him and chopped him about a bit so that we'd think it was David Maybury. She'd see that as retribution against the evil women – she probably thought they were all in it – who'd ruined her life. Do we have a follow-up on that report of someone crying near the Grange Farm cottages?'

'We do, but it's not very helpful. Both sets of occupants agreed it was after midnight because they were in bed, and they both agreed it was during the spell of hot weather that spanned the last week in May and the first two weeks in June. One lot said it was May, the other lot said it was the second week in June. Yer pays yer money and takes yer choice.'

'It's all too nebulous. We need a fix on some dates. Did Staley search the Thompsons' house?'

'Twice, once on the night of his disappearance and again about two weeks later.'

McLoughlin frowned. 'Why the second time?'

'Well, it's interesting that. He had an anonymous tip-off that Mrs T. had lost her marbles, butchered Daniel and hidden him under the floorboards. He turned up out of the blue one day, a couple of weeks into June, and went through the house with a magnifying glass. He found nothing except one sex-starved little woman who kept following him from room to room and making advances. He's convinced it was Mrs Thompson who made the tip-off.'

'Why?'

Walsh chuckled. 'He reckons she fancied him.'

'Perhaps her conscience was troubling her.'

Walsh pulled into the kerb outside the Police Station. 'It's all very well, Andy, but where do those blasted shoes fit in? If Daniel was wearing them, why did she leave them in the grounds? And if he wasn't, how did they get there?'

'Yes,' mused McLoughlin. 'I've been wondering about that. I can't help feeling she's telling the truth about the shoes. There must have been a tramp, you know. The description was too fluent and it matches the one Nick Robinson came up with. I remember the pink trousers.' He raised an enquiring eyebrow. 'I could try and trace him.'

'Waste of time,' muttered Walsh. 'Even if you found him, what could he tell you?'

'Whether or not Mrs Thompson's telling lies.'

'Hmm.' He hunched his shoulders over the steering wheel. 'I've had an awful thought.' He looked sick.

McLoughlin glanced at him.

'You don't suppose those damn women have been right all along, do you? You don't suppose this miserable tramp went into the ice house and had a heart attack?'

'What happened to his pink trousers?'

Walsh's face cleared. 'Yes, yes, of course. All right, then, see if you can find him.'

'I'll have to give up on the Maybury file.'

'Temporarily,' growled Walsh.

'And I want to take a team to search Streech grounds again.' He saw thunder clouds gathering across the Inspector's face. 'With a view to linking Mrs Thompson with the ice house,' he finished dispassionately.

Elizabeth stood in her favourite position, by the long window in her mother's room, watching the shadows lengthen on the terrace. She wondered how many times she had stood just so in just that place, watching. 'I shall have to go back,' she said at last. 'They won't keep the job open indefinitely.'

'You haven't any holiday owing?' asked Diana, glad that the silence was finally broken.

'Not spare. I'm going to the States for two weeks at the end of September. It leaves me with nothing to play with.' She turned round. 'I'm sorry, Mum.'

Diana shook her head. 'No need to be. Will you be staying with your father?'

Elizabeth nodded. 'It's three years since I've seen him,' she excused herself, 'and the flight's booked.'

What a gulf of misunderstanding lay between them,

Diana thought, and all because they found each other so hard to talk to. When she thought back over the years, she realised their conversations had been polite but safe, never touching on anything that might lead to embarrassment. In one way, Phoebe had been lucky. There had been no division of loyalties for her children, no lingering love for their father, no need for her to justify why he had deserted them.

'Would you like a drink?' She walked over to a mahogany cabinet.

'Are you having one?'

'Yes.'

'OK. I'll have a gin and tonic.'

Diana poured the drinks and took the glasses over to the window. 'Cheers.' She perched on the back of a chair and joined her daughter's contemplation of the terrace. It was easier, on the whole, not to look at her. 'For years I couldn't think about your father without getting angry. When his letters arrived for you and I saw his handwriting, I used to get so tensed up my jaw would ache for hours. I kept wondering what Miranda had that I hadn't.' She gave a short laugh. 'That's when I first understood what "grinding your teeth" meant.' She paused. 'It took me a while but I've got over it. Now I try to remember the good times. Is she nice? I never met her, you know.'

Elizabeth's attention was riveted on the antics of a sparrow on the flagstones outside, as if in its small person it was about to provide an answer to the mysteries of the universe. 'It wasn't all his fault,' she said defensively.

'No, it wasn't. Actually, in many ways it was more my fault. I took him for granted. I assumed he was the sort of man who could cope with a working wife, and he wasn't. He particularly disliked competing with me as a business partner. I don't blame him. He couldn't help that, any more than I could help wanting a career after you were born. The truth is, we should never have married. We were far too young and neither of us knew what we were doing. Phoebe feels the same. She married David because she was pregnant with Jonathan, and propriety amongst the middle classes twenty years ago dictated marriage. I married your father for virtually the same reasons. I wanted to go to the States with him and my parents wouldn't hear of my going as his mistress.' She sighed. 'God knows, Lizzie, we've all lived to regret it. We made a mess of each other's lives because we didn't have the courage to raise two fingers to convention.'

The girl stared at the sparrow. 'If you regret the marriage, do you also regret its consequence?'

'Do you mean, do I regret you?'

'Of course,' she snapped angrily. 'The two are rather closely linked, wouldn't you say?' The hurt ran deep.

Diana sought carefully for the right words. 'When you were born, I used to be driven mad by people asking: Who does she take after? Is she like you or Steven? My answer was always the same: Neither. I couldn't understand why they needed to tie you to one or other of us. To me, from the moment you drew breath, you were an individual with your own character, your own looks, your own way of doing things. I love you because you're my daughter and we've grown up together, but much more than that I actually like you. I like Elizabeth Goode.' She brushed a speck of dust from the girl's sleeve where it rested on the chair beside her. 'You exist in your own right. You're not a consequence of a marriage.'

'But I *am*,' the girl cried. 'Don't you see that? I am what you and Dad have made me.'

Diana looked at her. 'No, you were bolshy as a baby. I had to put you on solids when you were about eight weeks old because you wouldn't stop yelling for food. Steven always called you "The Despotic Diaper" because you had us both so well trained. Whatever makes you think now that you were born without personality and had to be fashioned by two untrained people? God knows, you've a horrible shock coming if you think babies don't have minds of their own.'

Elizabeth smiled. 'You know what I mean.'

'Yes,' her mother conceded, 'I know what you mean.' She was silent for a moment. 'The truth is, I should have thought this one out before. On the one hand, I've been patting myself on the back for having a strong-minded, independent daughter even if she is a bit wilful; on the other, I've been nagging at you not to make my mistakes.' She smiled ruefully. 'Sorry, darling. Hardly a consistent position.'

'Phoebe's just the same,' said Elizabeth. 'It must be a common maternal weakness.'

Diana laughed. 'What does Phoebe do?'

'Haven't you noticed? Whenever Jonathan takes a drink she quietly marks the level in the bottle with a felt-tip pen. She thinks he's never noticed.'

'Well, I haven't,' said Diana in some surprise. 'How extraordinary. Why does she do it?'

'Because his father drank too much. She's watching like a hawk to make sure Jonathan doesn't do the same.'

God, and I can't blame her, thought Diana, yet how foolish her actions seemed when looked at objectively. 'Does Jonathan understand?' she asked curiously.

'I think so.'

'Do you understand?'

'Yes, but that's not to say you or Phoebe are right. My own view is you're both getting your knickers in a twist over something that may never happen.'

'I'll drink to that,' said Diana, clinking her glass against her daughter's, but if she hoped this new fragile accord would lead to confidences, she was disappointed. Elizabeth had kept her own counsel too long to give it free expression on such tenuous beginnings.

'She *is* nice,' said Elizabeth unexpectedly. 'Very different from you. She's short and rather dumpy and she wears pinafore dresses all the time. She cooks very well. Dad's put on about two stone since he married her.' She smiled. 'None of his shirts do up any more, or they didn't three years ago.'

Good lord, thought Diana, so that's what he wanted. She thought of the slim young man she had married with the cadaverous good looks and the designer clothes, and she chuckled. 'Poor old Steven.'

'He's very happy,' her daughter protested, quick to see a criticism.

Diana held up her hands in mock surrender. 'I'm sure he is and I'm glad. Very glad,' she said, and she was.

'I suppose I'll have to ask the police if it's all right for me to go back to London,' Elizabeth hazarded after a moment.

'When do you want to go?'

'Straight after lunch tomorrow. Jon said he'd drive me to the station.'

'We'll ask Walsh in the morning,' said Diana. 'He's sure to be up here bright and early to rap me over the knuckles for this afternoon's little naughtiness.'

'Oh, Mum,' scolded Elizabeth as if she were speaking to a child, 'you will be careful, won't you? You've got such a temper when you're angry. Frankly, I think you're damn lucky to have got off as lightly as you did.'

'Yes,' agreed Diana meekly, marvelling at how rapidly roles reversed.

Elizabeth pursed her lips. 'Jon got into a fight today,' she announced surprisingly, 'but don't tell Phoebe. She'll have a fit.'

'Where?'

'Silverborne. Some yobbos recognised him from that photo in the local newspaper, the one taken outside the hospital the night Anne was attacked. They called him a lessies' pimp, so he bopped one of them in the eye and took to his heels.' She smiled. 'I was rather impressed when he told me. I didn't think he had it in him.'

Diana thought of David Maybury. Jonathan had it in him all right.

Eighteen

WITHIN TWENTY-FOUR hours Anne had made such a rapid recovery that she was suffering severe nicotine withdrawal symptoms and announced her intention of discharging herself. Jonathan told her not to be such a fool. 'You nearly died. If it hadn't been for the Sergeant, you probably would have done. Your body needs time to recover and get over the shock.'

'Damn,' she said roundly, 'and I can't remember a thing about it. No near-death experiences, no free-floating on the ceiling, no tunnels with shining lights at the end. What an absolute bugger. I could have written it all up. That's what comes of being an atheist.'

Jonathan, who for various reasons had come to view McLoughlin as a bit of a hero, certainly not all to do with coming to Anne's rescue, took her to task. 'Have you thanked him?'

She scowled from him to the WPC beside the bed. 'What for? He was only doing his job.'

'Saving your life.'

She glowered. 'Frankly, the way I feel at the moment, it wasn't worth saving. Life should be effortless, painless and fun. None of those apply here. It's a gulag, run by sadists.' She nodded in the direction of the ward. 'That Sister should be locked up. She laughs every time she sticks the needles into me and trills that she's doing it for my own good. God, I need a fag. Smuggle some in for me, Jonny. I'll puff away under the sheets. No one will know.'

He grinned. 'Until the bed goes up in flames.'

'There you are, you're laughing,' she accused. 'What's the matter with everyone? Why do you all find it so hilarious?'

WPC Brownlow, on duty on the other side of the bed, sniggered.

Anne cast a baleful eye upon her. 'I don't even know what you're doing here,' she snapped. 'I've told you all I can remember, which is absolutely zero.' She had been unable to talk freely to anyone, which was undoubtedly why the bloody woman had been stationed there, and it was driving her mad.

'Orders,' said the WPC calmly. 'The Inspector wants someone on hand when your memory comes back.'

Anne closed her eyes and thought of all the ways she could murder McLoughlin the minute she got her hands on him again.

He for his part had collated the information on the

tramp and relayed his description through the county. He rang a colleague in Southampton and asked him, for a favour, to check round the hostels there.

'What makes you think he came here?'

'Logic,' said McLoughlin. 'He was heading your way and your Council's more sympathetic to the homeless than most in this area.'

'But two months, Andy. He'll have been on his way weeks ago.'

'I know. It's a good description though. Someone might remember him. If we had a name, it'd make things easier. See what you can do.'

'I'm pretty busy at the moment.'

'Aren't we all. Cheers.' He put an end to the grumbles by the simple expedient of replacing the receiver, abandoned a cup of congealing plastic coffee and left in a hurry before his friend could ring back with a string of excuses. With a light conscience, he set off for the Grange and a chat with Jane Maybury who had announced herself ready to answer questions.

He asked her if she would prefer to have her mother present, but she shook her head and said no, it wasn't necessary. Phoebe, with a faintly troubled smile, showed them into her drawing-room and closed the door. They sat by the French windows. The girl was very pale, with a skin like creamy alabaster, but McLoughlin guessed this was her natural colouring. She was wearing a pair of faded jeans and a baggy tee-shirt with BRISTOL CITY emblazoned across the chest. He thought how incongruous it looked on the waif-like body.

She read his mind. 'It's the triumph of hope over experience,' she said. 'I go in for a lot of that.'

He smiled. 'I suppose everyone does, one way or another. If at first you don't succeed and all that.'

She settled herself a little nervously. 'What do you want to ask me?'

'Just a few things but, first, I want you to understand that I have no desire to distress you. If you find my questions upsetting, please say so and we'll stop. If at any point you decide you'd rather talk to a policewoman, again just tell me and I'll arrange it.'

She nodded. 'I understand.'

He took her back to the night of the assault and quickly ran through her account of watching television and hearing the sound of the breaking glass. 'Your brother was the first to go downstairs, I think you said.'

'Yes. He decided it was a burglar and told Lizzie and me to stay where we were until he called for us.'

'But did you stay?'

'No. Lizzie insisted on going downstairs after him to get through to Diana's wing. We didn't know at that stage which window had been broken. I said I'd check Mum's rooms and Jon ran through to where you were.'

'What happened then?'

'Mum and Diana arrived in the hall at the same

time as us. Mum followed Jonathan. I checked this room, Diana checked the library and Lizzie the kitchen. When I got back to the hall, Mum was running downstairs with some blankets and a hot-water bottle and yelling at Diana to call an ambulance. I said, someone ought to warn Fred to open the gate and Mum said, of course, she hadn't thought of that.' She spread her hands in her lap. 'So I took the torch from the hall table and left.'

'Why you? Why didn't Mrs Goode's daughter go?'

She shrugged. 'It was my idea. Anyway, Lizzie hadn't come back from the kitchen.'

'You weren't frightened? You didn't think of waiting for her to go with you?'

'No,' she said, 'it never occurred to me.' She was surprised now that it hadn't. She thought about it. 'To be honest, there was nothing to be frightened of. Mum just said Anne was ill. I suppose I thought she'd got an appendix or something. I just kept thinking what a nuisance it was that we had to keep the reporters at bay by locking the gates.' Her voice rose. 'And it's not as if I've never been up the drive before on my own. I've done it hundreds of times, and in the dark. I sometimes go and chat to Molly when Fred goes to the pub.'

'Fine,' he said unemotionally. 'That's all very logical.' He smiled encouragement. 'You're a fast runner. I had the devil's own job to catch you and I was going like a train.'

She unknit her fingers from the tangled bottom of her tee-shirt. 'I was worried about Anne,' she admitted. 'I keep telling her she's going to drop dead of cancer any minute. I had this ghastly thought that that was exactly what she'd done. So I put a spurt on.'

'You're fond of her, aren't you?'

'Anne's good news,' she said. 'Live and let live, that's her motto. She never interferes or criticises, but I suppose it's easier for her. She doesn't have children to worry about.'

'My mother's a worrier,' lied McLoughlin, thinking the only thing Mrs McLoughlin Snr ever worried about was whether she was going to be late for Bingo.

Jane put her chin in her hands. 'Mum's an absolute darling,' she confided naively, 'but she still thinks I need protection. Anne keeps telling her to let me fight my own battles.' She twisted a lock of the long dark hair round her finger.

He crossed his legs and pushed himself down into the chair, deliberately relaxed. 'Battles?' he teased gently. 'What battles do you have?'

'Silly things,' she assured him. 'Molehills to you, mountains to me. They'd make you laugh.'

'I shouldn't think so. You're just as likely to laugh at some of my battles.'

'Tell me,' she demanded.

'All right.' He looked at her smiling, trusting face and he thought, pray God there is nothing you can tell me or that smile will never come again. 'The worst battle I ever had was with my mother when I was about your age,' he told her. 'I'd sneaked my girlfriend into my bedroom for a night of passion. Ma walked in on us in the middle.'

'Golly,' she breathed. 'Why didn't you lock the door?'

'No key.'

'How embarrassing,' said Jane with feeling.

'Yes, it was,' he said reminiscently. 'My girlfriend hopped it and I had to do battle with the old dragon in the nuddy. She gave me two choices: if I swore on oath I'd never do it again, I'd be allowed to stay; if I refused to swear, then she'd boot me out just as I was.'

'What did you do?'

'Guess,' he invited.

'You left, starkers.'

He pointed his finger at her with thumb cocked. 'Got it in one.'

She was like a wide-eyed child. 'But where did you get clothes from? What did you do?'

He grinned. 'I hid in the bushes until all the lights went out, then I took a ladder from the shed and climbed up to my bedroom. The window was open. It was very easy. I crept back into bed, had a decent night's kip and scarpered with a suitcase before she got up in the morning.'

'Do you still see her?'

'Oh, yes,' he said, 'I do my duty Sunday lunches.

To tell you the truth, I think she regretted it afterwards. The house became very quiet when I left.' He was silent for a moment. 'Your turn now,' he said.

She giggled. 'That's not fair. Your battle was funny, mine are all pathetic. Things like: Will I or will I not eat my mashed potato? Am I working too hard? Shouldn't I go out and enjoy myself?'

'And do you?'

'Go out and enjoy myself?' He nodded. 'Not much.' Her lips twisted cynically and made her look older. 'Mum's idea of my enjoying myself is to go out with boys. I don't find that enjoyable.' Her eyes narrowed. 'I don't like men touching me. Mum hates that.'

'It's not surprising,' he said. 'She must feel it's her fault.'

'Well, it's not,' she said dismissively, 'and I wish she'd realise it. The hardest thing in the world is to cope with someone else's guilt.'

'What do you think happened to your father, Jane?'

The question hung in the air between them like a bad smell. She turned away and looked out of the window and he wondered if he had pushed too fast and lost her. He hoped not, as much for her own sake as for the sake of the enquiry.

'I'll tell you what happened the night he left,' she said at last, speaking to the window. 'I remember it very clearly but even my psychiatrist doesn't know all of it. There are bits I kept back, bits that at the time didn't fit the pattern and which I left out.' She paused for a moment. 'I hadn't thought about it for ages until the other night. Since then I've thought of nothing else, and I think now that what I left out may be important.'

She spoke slowly and clearly as though, having geared herself to tell the story, she saw no point in making it garbled. She told him how, after her mother had left for work, her father had run her bath. That was the signal, she said, that he intended to have sex with her. It was a routine he had established and which she had learned to accept. She described the entire process without a flicker of emotion and McLoughlin guessed she had rehearsed it many times on the psychiatrist's couch. She spoke of her father's approaches and her removal to her bedroom as if she were commentating on a chess game.

'But he did something different that night,' she said, turning her dark gaze on the Sergeant.

He found his voice. 'What was it?'

'He told me he loved me. He'd never done that before.'

McLoughlin was shocked. So much pain and without a word of love. Yet, after all, what good would kind words have done except make the man a hypocrite? 'Why do you think that's important?' he asked dispassionately.

'Let me finish the story,' she suggested, 'and perhaps it will strike you, too.' Before raping her this time, he had given her a present, carefully wrapped in tissue paper. 'He'd never done that before either.'

'What was it?'

'A little teddy-bear. I used to collect them. When he had finished,' she said, dismissing the entire incident in four words, 'he stroked my hair and said he was sorry. I asked him why because he'd never apologised before, but my mother came in and he never answered.' She fell silent and stared at her hands.

He waited but she didn't go on. 'What happened then?' he asked after several minutes.

She gave a mirthless laugh. 'Nothing really. They just looked at each other for what seemed like hours. In the end, he got off the bed and pulled up his trousers.' Her voice was brittle. 'It was like one of those awful Whitehall farces. I do remember my mother's face. It was frozen, like a statue's. She was very pale except for the bruise on her face where he hit her the day before. She only moved after he'd left the room, then she lay beside me on the bed and hugged me. We stayed like that all night and in the morning he'd gone.' She shrugged. 'We've never seen him again.'

'Did she say anything to him?' he asked.

'No. She didn't need to.'

'Why not?'

'You know that expression "if looks could kill".' He nodded. 'That was what was frozen on her face.' She bit her lip. 'What do you think?'

She caught him off guard. He so nearly said, I think your mother killed him. 'About what?' he asked her.

She showed her disappointment. 'It seems so obvious to me. I hoped it would strike you, too.' There was a hunger in the thin face, a yearning for something that he didn't understand.

'Hang on,' he said firmly. 'Give me a minute to think about it. You know the story backwards. This is the first time I've heard it, remember.' He looked at the notes he had been taking and cudgelled his brain to find what she wanted him to find. He had ringed the three things she said her father had never done before: love, present, apology. What was their significance? Why did she think he had done them? Why *had* he done them? Why would any father tell his daughter he loved her, give her a present and regret his unkindnesses? He looked up and laughed. It was stunningly obvious, after all. 'He was planning to leave anyway. He was saying goodbye. That's why he disappeared without trace. He'd arranged it all beforehand.'

She let out a long sigh. 'Yes, I think so.'

He leaned forward excitedly. 'But do you know why he would want to disappear?'

'No. I don't.' She sat up straight and pushed the hair back off her face. 'All I do know, Sergeant, is that it wasn't my fault.' A slow smile curved her lips. 'You can't imagine how good that makes me feel.'

'But surely no one's ever suggested it was?' The idea appalled him.

'When I was eight years old, my mother caught me in bed with my father. My father ran away because of it and my mother was labelled a murderess. At the age of ten, my brother's personality changed. He stopped being a child and took his father's place. He was sworn to secrecy about what had happened and has never mentioned his father again.' She played with her fingers. 'My mother's guilt has been an irrelevancy beside mine.' She raised her eyes. 'What happened the other night was a blessing in disguise. For years I've sat with a psychiatrist who has done his level best to intellectualise me out of my feelings of guilt. To a certain extent he succeeded and I pushed it all to the back of my mind. I was the victim, not the culprit. I was manipulated by someone I had been taught to respect. I played the role that was demanded of me because I was too young to understand I had a choice.' She paused briefly. 'But the other night, perhaps because I was so frightened, it all came back to me with amazing clarity. For the first time, I realised how the pattern had changed the night he left. For the first time, I didn't need to consciously justify my innocence, because I saw that the misery and uncertainty of the last ten years would have happened anyway, whether my mother had found us or not.'

'Have you told her all this?'

'Not yet. I will after you've gone. I wanted someone else to reach the same conclusion I had.'

'Tell me what happened when you were going to the Lodge,' he encouraged. 'You said you heard breathing.'

She compressed her lips in thought. 'It's a bit of a blur now,' she admitted. 'I was fine till I came to the beginning of the long straight bit leading to the gates. I slowed down as I came round the bend because I was getting a stitch and I heard what sounded like someone letting out a long breath, the sort of sound you make when you've been holding your breath for hiccups. It seemed to be very close. I was so frightened, I started to run again. Then I heard running footsteps and someone shouting.' She looked at him sheepishly. 'That was you. You scared me out of my wits. Now I'm not sure I heard breathing at all.'

'OK,' he said. 'It's not important. And when you said you thought it was your father, that was just because you were frightened? There wasn't anything about the breathing that reminded you of him?'

'No,' she said. 'I can't even remember what he looked like. It was so long ago and Mum's burnt all his photos. I couldn't possibly recognise his breathing.' She watched him gather his bits and pieces together. 'Have I been any good?'

'Good?' On impulse, he reached forward and gave her hands a quick impersonal squeeze. 'I'd say your godma's going to be pretty pleased with you, young lady. Forget about fighting battles, you've just scaled your own Mount Everest. And it's all downhill from now on.'

Phoebe was sitting on a garden seat beside the front door, chin in hands, staring unseeingly at the flower-beds which bordered the gravel drive. 'May I join you?' he asked her.

She nodded.

They sat in silence for some minutes. 'The dividing line between a fortress and a prison is a fine one,' he remarked softly. 'And ten years is a long time. Do you not think, Mrs Maybury, that you've served your sentence?'

She sat up straight and gestured bitterly in the direction of Streech Village and beyond. 'Ask them,' she said. 'It was they who put up the barbed wire.'

'Was it?'

Instinctively, defensively, she pressed her glasses up her nose. 'Of course. It was never my choice to live like this. But what do you do when people turn against you? Beg them to be kind?' She gave a harsh laugh. 'I wouldn't do it.'

He stared at his hands. 'It wasn't your fault,' he said quietly. 'Jane understands that. He was what he was. Nothing you did or didn't do would have made any difference.'

She withdrew into herself and let the silence lengthen. Above them swallows and house martins dipped and darted and a lark swelled its little throat and sang. At long last she took a handkerchief from her sleeve and held it to her eyes. 'I don't think I like you very much,' she said.

He looked at her. 'We all carry our burden of guilt – it's human nature. Listen to anyone newly bereaved or divorced and you'll hear the same story – if only I had done this . . . if only I hadn't done that . . . if only I had been kinder . . . if only I had realised. Our capacity for self-punishment is enormous. The trick is to know when to stop.' He rested a light hand on her shoulder. 'You've been punishing yourself for far too long. Can you not see that?'

She turned her face away from him. 'I should have known,' she said into her handkerchief. 'He was hurting her and I should have known.'

'How could you have known? You're no different from the rest of us,' he told her brutally. 'Jane loved you, she wanted to protect you. If you blame yourself, you take away everything she tried to do for you.'

There was another long silence while she fought to control her tears. 'I'm her mother. There was only me to save her, but when she needed me I never came. I can't bear to think about it.' A convulsive tremor rocked the shoulder beneath his hand.

He didn't stop to consider whether it was a good idea but reacted instinctively, drawing her into the fold of his arm and letting her weep. They were not the first tears she had shed, he guessed, but they were the first she had shed for her lost self, that self who had come into an enchanted world, wide-eyed and sure that she could do anything. The triumph of the human condition was to face one small defeat after another and to survive them relatively intact. The tragedy, as for Phoebe, was to face the worst defeat too soon and never to recover. His heart, still bruised and battered, ached for her.

He stopped his car on the bend before the straight stretch of drive and got out. Close, Jane had said, which meant in all probability crouched among the rhododendron bushes along the edge of the way. His searches so far had been disappointing. While he had set a team to scour the ice house for a link with Mrs Thompson, he himself had gone on hands and knees about the terrace for signs of Anne's attacker. If what he believed had happened, there would have been ample evidence of it. But Walsh was right. Bar some dislodged bricks and a cigarette end which was a brand that neither Fred nor Anne smoked, there was nothing. No weapon – he'd examined every brick and stone minutely for bloodstains; no footprints – the lawn was too hard from lack of rain and the flagstones too clean from Molly's regular sweepings; no blood, not even the tiniest speck, to prove that Anne had been hit outside and not inside. He had begun to wonder if he'd put too much faith in Phoebe's certainty – ten years was a long time and people changed – and she admitted herself it had only happened the once. But if she were wrong or if she were lying? He couldn't bring himself to explore either alternative. Not yet.

He sank to hands and knees again and began to inch along the drive. If there *was* anything, it wouldn't be easy to find. A team had been over here once without success but then he had told them to concentrate further down, near where he had caught her and where, for one brief moment, he had had the feeling that he and Jane were being watched. He crawled along the left-hand side, knees aching, eyes constantly alert, but after half an hour he had found nothing.

He sat back wearily on his heels and swore at the injustice of it. Just once, he thought, let me be lucky. Just once, let something come my way that I haven't had to work my bloody butt off for.

He moved to the right-hand side of the drive and inched back towards the bend. Predictably, he was almost at the car before he found it. He took a deep breath and thumped his fist on the tarmac, growling and shaking his head from side to side like a mad dog. Had he only started on the right-hand side, he would have found the damn thing over an hour ago and saved himself a lot of trouble.

'You all right, son?' asked a voice.

McLoughlin looked over his shoulder to find Fred staring at him. He grinned self-consciously and stood up. 'Fine,' he assured him. 'I've just found the bastard who did for Miss Cattrell.'

'I don't see him,' muttered Fred, eyeing McLoughlin doubtfully.

McLoughlin crouched down and parted the bushes, sweeping leaves away from something on the ground. 'Look at that. The forensic boys are going to have a field day.'

With much panting and heaving Fred squatted beside him. 'Well, I'll be blowed,' he said, 'it's a Paddy Clarke Special.'

Nestling in the débris under the rhododendron, beautifully camouflaged, was an old-fashioned stone beer bottle with a dark brown crust clinging to its bottom. McLoughlin, who had been thinking only in terms of some decent fingerprints and what looked like the imprint of a trainer in the soft damp earth beneath the dense bushes, flicked him a curious glance. 'What on earth is a Paddy Clarke Special?'

Fred lumbered unhappily to his feet. 'There's no harm in it, not really. It's more of a hobby than a business, though I don't s'pose the tax man would agree. He's got a room at the back of his garage where he makes it. Uses only traditional materials and leaves it to mature till it has the kick of a horse and tastes like nectar. There's not a beer to touch Paddy's Special.' He stared glumly at the rhododendron. 'You have to drink it on the premises. He sets great store by those bottles, says they breathe flavour in a way glass never does.' He looked immensely troubled. 'I've never known him let one out of the pub.'

'What's he like? The type to beat up women?'

The old man shuffled his feet. 'No, never that. He's a good sort. Mind you, the wife's got little time for him on account of he's married and not too particular about his vows, but – hit Miss Cattrell?' He shook his head. 'No, he'd not do that. He and she are' – he looked away – 'friends, as you might say.'

An entry in Anne's diary swam before his eyes. '*P. is a mystery. He tells me he screws fifty women a year, and I believe him, yet he remains the most considerate of lovers.*' 'Does he smoke?'

Fred, who had supplied Paddy with many a cigarette over the years, thought the question odd. 'Other people's,' he said warily. 'His wife's a bit of a tyrant, doesn't approve of smoking.'

McLoughlin pictured her fireplace awash with cigarette ends. 'Don't tell me,' he said gloomily, 'let me guess. He looks like Rudolph Valentino, Paul Newman and Laurence Olivier, all rolled into one.' He opened his car door and reached for his radio.

'Tut, tut, tut,' clicked Fred impatiently. 'He's a big man, dark, full of life, clever in his way. Always reminds me of the one who plays *Magnum*.'

Tom Selleck! I hate him, thought McLoughlin.

*

Sergeant Jones was leaving the Station as McLoughlin came in. 'You know that tramp you're after, Andy?'

'Mm.'

'Got a sighting from your friend the Vicar in East Deller. Wife claims she gave him a cup of tea.'

'Any idea of a date?'

'No, but the Vicar remembers he was writing a sermon at the time and was annoyed by the disturbance, found himself praying to the Good Lord for deliverance from tramps, then had to reprimand himself for his lack of charity.'

McLoughlin chuckled. 'That sounds like the Vicar all right.'

'Apparently he always writes his sermons on a Saturday while he's watching the sport on telly. Any good?'

'Could be, Nick, could be.'

Nineteen

THE PHONE RANG on McLoughlin's desk the following morning. 'You're a jammy bastard, Andy. I've got a lead on that tramp of yours,' said his mate in Southampton. 'One of the uniformed sergeants recognised the description. Seems he picked up the old boy about a week ago and took him to a new hostel out Shirley way. No guarantee he's still there but I'll give you the address. You can check it out for yourself. He's called Wally Ferris and he's a regular down here during the summer. Sergeant Jordan's known him for years.' McLoughlin wrote down the address, Heaven's Gate Hostel, and thanked him. 'You owe me one,' said the other cheerfully and hung up.

Heaven's Gate was a large detached Victorian house, probably much sought after in the days before motor cars, but its appeal was diminished now by the busy thoroughfare which mewled and milled about its front door.

Wally Ferris bore no resemblance to the description

McLoughlin had circulated, except in age and height. He was clean. Scrubbed rosy cheeks and gleaming pate with frill of washed hair dazzled above a white shirt, black slacks and highly polished shoes. He looked, for all the world, like an elderly schoolboy on his first day in class. They met in the sitting-room and Wally gestured to a chair.

'Take a pew,' he invited.

McLoughlin showed his disappointment. 'No point,' he said. 'To be honest, I don't think you're the person I'm looking for.'

Wally did a rapid about-turn and beetled for the door. 'Suits me, son. I'm not comfortable wiv bluebottles and that's a fact.'

'Hold on,' said McLoughlin. 'At least, let's establish it.'

Wally turned and glowered at him. 'Make yer bleeding mind up. I'm only 'ere because the lady of the 'ouse arst me. She's scratched my back, in a manner o' speaking, so I'm scratching 'ers. What you after?'

McLoughlin sat down. 'Take a pew,' he said, echoing Wally.

'Gawd, you're a shilly-shallyer and no mistake. Can't make yer mind up, can yer.' He perched on a distant chair.

'What were you wearing when you came here?' asked McLoughlin.

'None of your effing business.'

'I can ask the lady of the house,' said McLoughlin.

'What's it to you, anyway?'

'Just answer. The sooner you do, the sooner I'll leave you in peace.'

Wally sucked his teeth noisily. 'Green jacket, brown 'at, black shoes, blue jumper and pink trews,' he reeled off.

'Did you have them long?'

'Long enough.'

'How long?'

'All different. 'Ad the 'at and jacket near on five years, I'd say.'

'The trousers?'

'Twelve monfs or so. Bit on the bright side but a good fit. 'Ere, you're not finking I nicked 'em, are you? I was give 'em.' He looked thoroughly indignant.

'No, no,' said McLoughlin soothingly. 'Nothing like that. The truth is, Wally, we're trying to trace a man who's disappeared and we think you may be able to help us.'

Wally planted his feet firmly on the ground, one in front of the other beneath his chair, poised to take flight. 'I don't know nuffink about nuffink,' he said with absolute conviction.

McLoughlin raised his hands in a conciliatory gesture. 'Don't panic, Wally. As far as we know, there's no crime involved. The man's wife asked us to find him. She says you came to the house the day before he disappeared. All we're wondering is if you remember going there, and if you saw or heard anything that might help us find out why he went.'

Wally's rheumy eyes looked his suspicion. 'I go to a lot of 'ouses.'

'These two gave you a pair of brown shoes.'

Something like relief flickered across the wizened features. 'If the wife was there, why can't she tell you why 'er old man went?' he asked reasonably.

'She's become very ill since her husband went,' said McLoughlin, stretching the truth like a rubber band. 'She hasn't been able to tell us much at all.'

'What's this chap done?'

'Nothing, except lose all his money and run away.'

That struck a chord with Wally, 'Poor bastard. Does 'e want to be found?'

'I don't know. What do you think? His wife certainly wants him back.'

Wally considered for several minutes. 'No one bovvered to come looking for me,' he said in the end. 'Sometimes I wished they 'ad 'ave done. They was glad to see the back of me, and that's the trufe. Go on then. Arst yer questions.'

It took over an hour, but in the end McLoughlin had a clear picture of Wally's movements during the last week in May, or as clear as the old man could make it, bearing in mind he had been tight most of the time. 'I was give a fiver,' he explained. 'Some old geezer in the middle of Winchester popped it in me 'and. Put the lot on a gee-gee called Vagrant, didn't

I. Came up eleven to one. Ain't 'ad so much cash for years. Kept me plastered for free weeks 'fore it ran out.'

He had hung around Winchester for most of the three weeks, then, when he was down to his last few quid, he'd made his way along the back roads to Southampton in search of new pickings. 'I like the villages,' he said. 'Reminds me of cycling holidays in my youf.' He remembered stopping at the pub in Streech. 'It was pissing down,' he explained. 'Landlord was a decent sort, gave me no bovver.' Paddy's wife, by contrast, was a fat old cow whom, for unspecified reasons, Wally didn't take to, but he winked ferociously a couple of times as he mentioned her. At three o'clock, they turned him out into the rain. 'Ain't no fun when it's wet,' he said lugubriously, 'so I took meself off to a little shelter I know of and spent the afternoon and night there.'

'Where?' asked McLoughlin when the old man fell silent.

'Never did no 'arm,' said Wally defensively. 'No call for anyone to complain.'

'There haven't been any complaints,' said McLoughlin encouragingly. 'I won't rat on you, Wally. As far as I'm concerned, if you behave yourself, you can use it as often as you like.'

Wally pursed his lips into a pink rosette. 'There's a big 'ouse there. Easy as winking to pop over the wall. Been in the garden a few times, never seen no one.'

He gave McLoughlin a speculative look to see if he was interested. He was. 'There's a sort of man-made cave near the woods,' he went on. 'Can't fink what it's for but it's got some bricks stacked in it. The door's 'idden by a big bramble but it's a doddle to creep in be'ind it. I always take bracken in wiv me to give me a good kip. 'Ere, why you looking like that?'

McLoughlin shook his head. 'No reason. I'm just interested. Have you any idea what day this was, Wally?'

'Gawd knows, son.'

'And you didn't see anyone when you were in the garden?'

'Not a soul.'

'Was this cave in darkness?'

'Well, there ain't no electricity, if that's what you mean, but while it's light you can see. If the door's ajar, of course,' he added.

McLoughlin wondered how to put the next question. 'And the place was empty except for this stack of bricks you mentioned?'

'What you getting at?'

'Nothing. I'm just trying to get a clear picture.'

'Then yes. It was empty.'

'And what happened the next morning?'

'Hung around till lunchtime, didn't I?'

'In the cave?'

'No. In the woods. Nice and peaceful, it was. Then I got to feeling peckish, so I 'opped over the wall and looked about for somefing to eat.' He had knocked on several doors, without much success.

'Why didn't you buy something with your winnings?' asked McLoughlin, fascinated.

Wally was intensely scornful. 'Do me a favour,' he admonished. 'Why pay for somefink you can get free? It's booze they won't give away. Anyway, I 'adn't much winnings left and that's a fact.'

He had found a group of houses on the outskirts of Streech where 'an old bat' had given him a sandwich. The council houses, McLoughlin thought. 'Did you try anyone else?' he asked.

'Young lass told me to push off. Gawd knows, I sympathised wiv 'er. There was a dozen nippers yelling their 'eads off in 'er front room.' He abandoned Streech as a dead duck at that point and set off down the road. After about an hour, he came to another village. 'Don't recall the name, son, but there was a vicarage. Always good for a touch, they are.' He had roused the Vicar's wife and persuaded her out of a cup of tea and some cake. 'Nice little woman, but she came over sanctimonious. That's the trouble wiv vicarages. You can always get a bite but you has to take the lecture wiv it. I scarpered sharpish.' It had begun to rain again. 'Strange wevver, I can tell yer. 'Ot as blazes most of the time, but every now and then there was a funder storm. You know the sort. Fat rain, I calls it. Flashes of lightning and great claps of funder.' He had looked around for shelter. 'Not a blooming fing. Nice little boxes wiv neat garages. No help to me. Then I comes to this bigger house, set back a bit. I fought I'd explore the back, see if there was a shed. I sneaks down the side and lo and be'old there's just what I'm looking for, nice little shed wiv no one in sight. I opens the door and pops inside.' He stopped.

'And?' prompted McLoughlin.

A cunning gleam had appeared in the old man's eyes. 'Seems like I'm giving you a lot of information for nuffink, son. What's in it for me?'

'A fiver,' said McLoughlin, 'if what you tell me's worth it.'

'Ten,' said Wally. He glanced behind him at the closed door then leaned forward confidentially. 'To tell you the trufe, son, it's a bit claustrophobic this place. The lady of the 'ouse does 'er best but there's no fun. Know what I mean. A tenner'd give me a day out. I've been 'ere a week for Gawd's sake. I've 'ad more fun in prison.'

McLoughlin considered the morality of giving Wally the wherewithal to turn his back on Heaven's Gate and concluded that Wally was on the point of scarpering whatever happened. You can't teach an old dog new tricks. Ten pounds would give him a start at least. 'Done,' he said. 'What happened when you went into this shed?'

'Looked around for somefink to sit on, didn't I,

make meself comfortable while I was there. Found this feller 'iding at the back be'ind some boxes. When 'e realised I'd seen 'im, 'e came over all 'oity-toity and ordered me off 'is property. I arst, reasonable like, why I should imagine 'e was the owner when 'e was skulking in the shed same as me. 'E got properly riled and called me a few names. In the middle of it, this woman comes out of the kitchen door to see what the noise is. I explains the situation and she tells me the geezer's 'er 'usband and 'e's in the shed looking for a paintbrush.' Wally pulled a wry face. 'They must've fought I was born yesterday. The paintbrushes was all laid out neat and tidy on a workbench at the side. The geezer was 'iding, no mistake. Anyway, I sees my opportunity. They wants rid of me and they'd pay up to see me go. I got a bottle of whisky, a decent pair of shoes and twenty quid out of it. Tried for more but they turned nasty and I reckoned it was time to skedaddle. This the feller you're looking for?'

McLoughlin nodded. 'Sounds like it. Can you describe him?'

Wally's brow wrinkled. 'Five tennish, fat, grey 'air. 'E 'ad nancy feet for a man. The shoes they gave me didn't 'alf pinch.'

'What did the woman look like?'

'Mousey little fing, sorrowful eyes, but Gawd she 'ad a temper. Lammed into me and 'er old man somefink rotten for making a noise.' He looked suddenly thoughtful. 'Not that we was, mind you. Froughout the 'ole fing, we spoke in whispers.' He shook his head. 'Bats the pair of 'em.'

McLoughlin was jubilant. Got you, Mrs T., he thought. 'Where did you go then?'

A thoughtful expression crossed Wally's face. 'There's a saying, son. A bird in the 'and is worf two in the bush. It had stopped raining but I 'ad this feeling we was in for anover funder storm. I fought to meself I've a bottle o' whisky and nowhere cosy to drink it. If I push on, 'oo's to say if I'll find a dry place for the night. So I 'ightailed it back to the cave at the big 'ouse and passed a 'alfway decent night.' He considered McLoughlin out of the corner of his eyes. 'The next day, I finks to myself, I've a few quid in me pocket and I've 'ad nuffink decent to eat for days, so I 'eaded off towards Silverborne. There's a nice café on the road – '

'Did you leave anything behind?' McLoughlin cut in.

'Like what?' asked the old man sharply.

'Like the shoes?'

'Dumped 'em in the woods,' said Wally scornfully. 'Damn fings gave me corns a right drubbing. That's where experience comes in. A young bloke would've chucked the old pair out before 'e'd properly tried the new. Then 'e'd've been in agony till 'e found some more.'

McLoughlin tucked his notebook into his pocket. 'You've been a great help, Wally.'

'That it?'

McLoughlin nodded.

'Where's my tenner?'

McLoughlin took a ten-pound note out of his wallet and stretched it between his fingers. 'Listen to me, Wally. I'm going to give you ten pounds now as a token of good faith, but I want you to stay here another night because I may want to talk to you again. If you do, I'll come back tomorrow morning with another ten, making twenty in all.' He held out the tenner. 'Is it a deal?'

Wally got up and pounced on the note, secreting it in the depths of his shirt. 'Are you on the level, son?'

'I'll give you an IOU if you like.'

Wally made as if to spit on the carpet, then thought better of it. 'Be about as much use to me as a mug of water,' he said. 'OK, son, it's a deal. But if you don't come back first fing, I'm off.' His eyes narrowed. 'Don't you go telling the lady of the 'ouse, mind. I've 'ad my fill of good works this week. They don't know when to leave a bloke alone in this place.'

McLoughlin chuckled. 'Your secret's safe with me, Wally.'

'I spotted the *pattern*,' said McLoughlin to Walsh, with a tinge of irony which brought a glitter to the older man's eyes, 'when I marked the houses which reported seeing the tramp.' He pointed to small red crosses on the map in front of them. 'If you remember, Nick Robinson had two reports. One from a woman in Clementine Cottage who said the tramp passed her house and went into the pub, which meant he was coming from the direction of Winchester. The next from the landlord at the pub who said he stayed until closing time then ambled off in the lee of the wall round the Grange estate, in other words heading towards East Deller.' He traced his finger along the printed road. 'The next reports we had of him were PC Williams's. He said an elderly woman had given the tramp a sandwich and a young woman had turned him away because it was her son's birthday. They both live on the council estate which is to the west of Streech and on the East Deller road. The date the young woman gave was May twenty-seventh. But when we spoke to Mrs Thompson she told us he'd visited them in East Deller on the twenty-fourth. That would have meant he had doubled back on himself for some reason to come through Streech three days later from the direction of Winchester.'

Walsh gathered together the remnants of his authority and buttoned them about himself with as much dignity as he could muster. 'I went into all this myself,' he lied. 'The fact that we found the shoes at the Grange implies he did just that.'

'I agree, so we needed another sighting in East

Deller, with a date, if possible. Jonesy went out there to see what he could dig up. He had a chat with our friend the Vicar who told Jonesy he was writing a sermon when the tramp called at the vicarage. The Vicar couldn't give a date but he always writes his sermons on a Saturday. OK, now only two people have offered a definite date, May twenty-fourth, supplied by Mrs Thompson, a Wednesday, and May twenty-seventh, the day of the birthday party, a Saturday. Wally is adamant he went from the council estate in Streech to the vicarage and the Thompsons at East Deller which puts him there on Saturday, May twenty-seventh. So why did Mrs T. lie about the date?'

'Get on with it,' ordered Walsh impatiently.

'Because, in face of her blatant lie, we had proved the shoes were her husband's and she had to explain why they were no longer in her possession. She opted for the truth this time, or as near the truth as damn it, and invited us to corroborate the story by giving us a description of the tramp. Remember, we never told her where we found the shoes. For all she knew we got them from the tramp himself.' He collected his thoughts. 'Now she could be sure, if we had the tramp, that he would say he'd seen her husband. So to give us the actual day of his visit would be tantamount to telling us her husband was alive and well and living in East Deller after she'd reported him missing. Bang would go her alibi. So she advanced the tramp's visit by three days. It was a gamble but it damn nearly paid off. Wally hasn't a clue when he went through, and if it wasn't for the child's birthday, neither would we. No one else can remember the date.' He paused for a moment. 'It's going to come as a nasty shock when we tell her where Wally dumped the shoes. In her wildest nightmares she couldn't believe it would be at the scene of her proposed crime.'

Walsh stood up. 'Poetic justice, I say. But I'd like to know how she persuaded him to lie low and how she got him to the ice house.'

'Use your charm and she'll probably tell us,' said McLoughlin.

Twenty

MRS THOMPSON OPENED the door with a smile of welcome. She was dressed to go out in a neat blue suit and white gloves but there was a sad, rather dated air about her as if her fashion sense had expired with the '50s. Two suitcases stood behind her in the hall. Splashes of rouge on her cheeks and a touch of lipstick gave her face a bogus gaiety but when she saw the gathered policemen her mouth drooped tragically.

'O-oh.' She breathed her disappointment. 'I thought it was the Vicar.'

'May we come in?' asked Walsh. Her inadequacies repulsed as effectively as cheap perfume.

'So many of you,' she whispered. 'Has the devil sent you?'

Walsh took her arm and eased her backwards, allowing his men in behind. 'Shall we go into the sitting-room, Mrs Thompson? No point in standing around on the doorstep.'

She put up a feeble resistance. 'What is this?' she

beseeched, eyes welling, little heels digging into the hall carpet. 'Please don't touch me.'

McLoughlin slipped his hand under her other arm and, together, they whisked her through the sitting-room door and into a chair. While McLoughlin kept her seated with a firm hand on her shoulder, Walsh directed his men to a thorough search of the house and garden. He flashed the warrant under her eyes before tucking it back into his jacket pocket and sitting in the chair opposite her.

'Well, now, Mrs Thompson,' he said genially. 'Off for your little rest by the sea?'

She shook McLoughlin's hand from her shoulder but remained seated. 'I'm expecting the Vicar at any moment to take me to the station,' she announced with dignity. McLoughlin noticed a thinning patch in her hair. He found it oddly embarrassing as if she had taken off part of her clothing and revealed something best kept hidden.

'Then I suggest we don't beat around the bush,' announced Walsh. 'We wouldn't want to keep him waiting.'

'Why are you here? Why are your men searching my house?'

Walsh steepled his fingers in his lap. 'You remember that tramp you told us about, Mrs Thompson?' She gave a brief nod. 'We've found him.'

'Good. Then you'll know I was telling you the truth about dear Daniel's generosity.'

'Indeed, yes. He also happened to mentioned that Mr Thompson gave him a bottle of whisky and twenty pounds.'

The sad eyes lit with pleasure. 'I told you Daniel was a saint. He would have given the shirt off his back if the man had asked for it.'

McLoughlin took the chair next to Walsh and leaned forward aggressively. 'The tramp's name is Wally Ferris. I've had a long talk with him. He says you and Mr Thompson wanted rid of him, that's why you were so generous.'

'The ingratitude,' she gasped, her lips parting on a tremor. 'What did our Lord say? "Give to the poor and you shall have treasure in Heaven." My poor Daniel has earned his place there by his kindness. The same cannot be said of this tramp.'

'He also said,' continued McLoughlin doggedly, 'that he found your husband hiding in the shed outside.'

She tittered behind her hand like a teenager. 'Actually,' she said, looking directly at him, 'it was the other way round. Daniel found the tramp hiding in the shed. He went out to look for a paintbrush and tripped over a bundle of old clothes behind some boxes at the back. Imagine his surprise when the bundle spoke.'

Her words carried conviction and McLoughlin knew a sudden doubt. Had he relied too heavily on an old man who, by his own admission, lived in an alcoholic haze? 'Wally claims it was raining while he was in your shed. I've checked with the local meteorological office and they have no record of any rainfall on Wednesday, twenty-fourth May. The storms began two days later and lasted on and off for the next three days.'

'Poor man,' she murmured. 'I told Daniel at the time we should have tried to get him to a doctor. He was drunk and very confused. You know, he asked me if I was his sister. He thought I'd come looking for him at last.'

'But, Mrs Thompson,' said Walsh, allowing surprise into his voice, 'if he was as drunk as you say, why did you give him a bottle of whisky? Were you not compounding his already severe problems?'

She cast her eyes to the ceiling. 'He begged us in tears, Inspector. Who were we to refuse? Judge not and you shall not be judged. If the poor man chooses to kill himself with demon alcohol, I have no right to condemn him.'

'But you do have the right to speed up the process, I suppose,' said McLoughlin sarcastically.

'He's a sad little man whose only comfort lies in a whisky bottle,' she said quietly. 'It would have been cruel to deny him his comfort. We gave him money to spend on food, shoes for his feet and we urged him to seek help for his addiction. There was not much more we could do. My conscience is clear, Sergeant.'

'Wally claims he came here on Saturday, May twenty-seventh.' Walsh spoke casually.

She wrinkled her forehead and thought for a moment. 'But it can't have been,' she said with genuine puzzlement. 'Daniel was here. Didn't we decide it was the twenty-fourth?'

McLoughlin was fascinated by her performance. It occurred to him that she had expunged the memory of murder from her mind and had convinced herself that the story she told was the real one. If that was so, they were going to have the devil's own job bringing a prosecution. With only Wally's testimony, backed by the woman in the council house, they wouldn't stand a chance. They needed a confession.

'The date is corroborated by an independent witness,' he told her.

'Really?' she breathed. 'How extraordinary. I don't remember seeing anyone with him and we are so secluded here.' She fingered her cross and gazed at him with reproachful eyes. 'Who could it be, I wonder?'

Walsh cleared his throat noisily. 'Would it interest you to know where we found your husband's shoes, Mrs Thompson?'

'Not really,' she assured him. 'I assume from the things you've said that the tramp – Wally – discarded them as useless. I find that hurtful to my dear Daniel's memory.'

'You're very sure he's dead, aren't you?' said McLoughlin.

She produced her lace hankie like a magician and dabbed at the inevitable tears. 'He would never leave me,' came the refrain.

'We found the shoes in the woods at Streech Grange, not far from the ice house,' said Walsh, watching her closely.

'Did you?' she asked politely.

'Wally spent the night of the twenty-seventh of May in the ice house and abandoned the shoes in the woods the next morning as he left.'

She lowered the handkerchief and looked with curiosity from one to the other. 'Really,' she commented. Her expression was one of bafflement. 'Is that significant?'

'You do know we've found a corpse in Streech Grange ice house, don't you?' McLoughlin remarked brutally. 'It is male, aged between fifty and sixty, broad build, grey hair and five feet ten inches tall. He was murdered two months ago, around the time your husband went missing.'

Her amazement was utter. For several seconds a kaleidoscope of emotions transformed her face. The two men watched closely, but if guilt was there, it was impossible to isolate. To the forefront was surprise. 'I had no idea,' she said, 'no idea at all. No one's said anything to me. Whose corpse is it?'

McLoughlin turned to Walsh and raised a despairing eyebrow. 'It's been in all the newspapers, Mrs Thompson,' said the Inspector, 'and on the local television news. You could hardly have missed it. The body has decomposed to such an extent that we have not yet been able to identify it. We have our suspicions, however.' He studied her pointedly.

She was taking deep breaths as though breathing were difficult. The rouge stood out on her cheeks in bright spots. 'I don't have a television,' she told them. 'Daniel used to get a paper at work and tell me all the news when he came home.' She struggled for air. 'God,' she said surprisingly, holding a hand to her chest, 'they've all been keeping it from me, protecting me. I had no idea. No one's said a word.'

'No idea we'd found the body, or no idea there was a body to find?' asked McLoughlin.

She digested the implications of this for a moment. 'No idea there was one, of course,' she snapped, eyeing him with dislike. She calmed her breathing with a conscious effort and tightened her lips into their customary thin lines. She addressed herself to Walsh. 'I now understand your interest in Daniel's shoes,' she told him. A small tic had started above her lip. 'You are assuming they are connected in some way with this body you've found.'

'Perhaps,' he said guardedly.

A gleam of triumph showed in her eyes. 'Yet this

tramp you've found has proved they can't be. You say he spent the night of the twenty-seventh in the – what did you call it?'

'Ice house.'

'In the ice house. I assume he wouldn't have stayed if the dead body had been there, too, so he must have abandoned the shoes before the body ever got there.' She seemed to relax slightly. 'I cannot see a connection, merely a bizarre coincidence.'

'You're absolutely right,' agreed Walsh. 'In that sense, there is no connection.'

'Then why have you been asking me questions?'

'The bizarre coincidence led us to the tramp, Mrs Thompson, and to some interesting facts about you and your husband. We can prove he was alive in this house two days after you reported him missing and well outside the time for which you'd provided yourself with an alibi. Mr Thompson has not been seen since, and a week ago we were presented with an unidentifiable body, corresponding to his description and less than four miles away. Frankly, we can make out an excellent case against you for the murder of your husband on or after the twenty-eighth of May.'

The tic came faster. 'It can't be Daniel's body.'

'Why not?' demanded McLoughlin.

She was silent, gathering her thoughts.

'Why not?' he pressed.

'Because I had a letter from him about two weeks ago.' Her shoulders slumped and she started to weep again. 'It was a beastly letter, telling me how much he hated me and what a bad wife I'd – '

McLoughlin cut her short. 'Will you show us the letter, please?'

'I can't,' she sobbed. 'I burnt it. He'd written such vile things.'

There was a knock on the door and one of the uniformed policemen came in. 'We've been through the house and garden, sir.' He shook his head at Walsh's questioning look. 'Nothing yet. There's still this room to do and Mrs Thompson's cases. They're locked. We'll need the keys.'

The little woman grabbed her handbag and held it to her middle. 'I will not give you the keys. You will not search my cases. They contain my underwear.'

'Fetch me a WPC,' instructed the Inspector. He leaned towards Mrs Thompson. 'I'm sorry, but you've no choice in the matter. If you prefer it, I will ask the WPC to bring the cases in here and you may watch while she examines the contents.' He held out his hand. 'The keys, please.'

'Oh, very well,' she said crossly, delving into her handbag and producing two small keys tied together with a white ribbon. 'Personally, I think the whole thing's outrageous. I intend to make a strong complaint to the Chief Constable.'

Walsh wasn't surprised she objected to having her underwear scrutinised. Pieces of filmy black lacework, more at home in a brothel, he would have thought, than in the luggage of this drab, boring woman, were held up for inspection. But a truth he had discovered during his career was that some of the unlikeliest women possessed attractive lingerie. His own wife was a case in point. She had come to bed every night of their married lives in silks or soft satins, with only him to appreciate the effect. And for a long time he *had* appreciated it and done his best to show it, before years of indignant rejection had taught him that Mrs Walsh did not don her lingerie for his benefit but for some private delight of her own. And he had long since given up trying to discover what that was.

The WPC shook her head as she re-locked the cases. 'Nothing there, sir.'

'I did tell you,' said Mrs Thompson. 'Heaven knows what you think you're looking for.'

'Your handbag, please.'

She relinquished it with a moue of disgust. The constable emptied the contents carefully on to the coffee table, felt the soft leather bag for anything hidden in the lining, then sorted through the various objects. She glanced enquiringly at Walsh. 'Seems OK, sir.'

He gestured to her to return everything to the bag. 'Would you rather wait outside while we search this room?' he asked Mrs Thompson.

She settled herself deeply into her chair, gripping the cushion beneath her as if she expected to be wrestled from it. 'I would not, Inspector.'

As the search got under way, Walsh returned to the questioning. 'You say you've had a letter from your husband. Why haven't you mentioned this before?'

She cringed away from him, tucking herself sideways into a tight ball in the chair. 'Because I have only my pride left. I didn't want anyone to know how shamefully he's treated me.' She dabbed at her dry eyes.

'What was the postmark?' asked McLoughlin.

'London, I think.'

'Presumably the letter was handwritten,' he mused. 'He wouldn't have access to a typewriter.'

She nodded. 'It was.'

'What sort of envelope?'

She thought for a moment. 'White,' she told him.

McLoughlin laughed. 'It won't wash, you know. You can't just keep pulling lies out of the hat and expect us to applaud your ingenuity. We'll check with your postman. In a place like this you'll have had the same postman for years, it's probably the chap who runs the little shop-cum-post-office near the church. Your letters will have been a source of great interest to him in the last couple of months. He's probably scrutinised every one carefully in the hopes of being first with news of the errant Daniel. You won't persuade us your husband's still alive by dreaming up letters, Mrs Thompson.'

She glanced beyond him to where the woman constable was going through the sideboard. 'Ask the postman, Sergeant. You'll find I'm telling you the truth.' She spoke with sincerity, but the look in her eyes was as level and calculating as any he'd seen. 'If only I'd known what was in your mind, I'd have told you about the letter the first time you came.'

McLoughlin stood up and leaned over her, resting his hands on the arms of her chair. 'Why were you so shocked to hear about the body at the ice house? If you know your husband's alive, it couldn't mean anything to you.'

'This man's threatening me,' she snapped at Walsh. 'I don't like it.' She cringed deep into the chair.

'Back off, Andy.'

'With pleasure.' Without warning, he hooked his hand under her arm and stepped back sharply. She popped out of the chair like a champagne cork, then wriggled and spat with ferocity. He clung on to a flailing arm, dodged a swipe from the other and felt warm spittle smear his cheek. 'The chair, sir,' he called. 'She's hiding something.'

'Got it.'

McLoughlin took a grip on both her arms, arching his body away to avoid the kicking points of her shoes. 'Come on, you sods,' he shouted angrily at the two constables. 'She's pulverising me. Who's got the handcuffs, for God's sake?'

'Bastard!' she screamed. 'Bloody fucking bastard!' She rolled another ball of spittle into her mouth and launched it at him. To his immense disgust, it caught his lip and dribbled inside.

The constables, galvanised out of frozen inactivity, snapped on the handcuffs and pushed the woman on to the sofa. She looked at McLoughlin's vain attempts to get rid of the venom and laughed. 'Serves you bloody right. I hope you catch something.'

'Looks like I've caught you,' he said grimly. He turned to Walsh. 'What is it?'

Walsh handed him a thin envelope. 'She must have slipped it out of her bag when we were gawping at her blasted knickers.' He chuckled good-humouredly. 'Waste of time, dear lady. We'd have found it eventually.'

McLoughlin opened the envelope. Inside were two aeroplane tickets, made out to Mr and Mrs Thompson, for a flight to Marbella that evening. 'Where's he been hiding all this time?' he asked her.

'Go to hell!'

'Mrs Thompson! Mrs Thompson!' exclaimed a shocked voice from the doorway. 'Some control, I beg you.'

She laughed. 'Go and play with yourself, you silly little man.'

'Is she mad?' asked the horrified Vicar.

'In a manner of speaking,' said Inspector Walsh cheerfully.

Twenty-One

ANNE LAUGHED AS McLoughlin told the story. Colour had returned to her face and lively enjoyment sparkled in her eyes. The only visible reminder that she'd been attacked was the brilliant red and white spotted scarf that she had tied, bandit-style, over her bandage. Against medical advice, she had discharged herself the day before, maintaining that five days in hospital was the absolute maximum that a sentient drug addict could tolerate. Bowing to the inevitable, Phoebe had brought her home after extracting a promise that she would do precisely as she was told. Anne gave the promise readily. 'Just lead me to a cigarette,' she said, 'and I'll do anything you say.'

What she didn't know was that Phoebe had also assumed responsibility for her safety. 'If she leaves hospital, Mrs Maybury, we won't be able to protect her,' Walsh had pointed out, 'any more than we can protect you. We simply haven't enough men to patrol

Streech Grange. I shall be advising her to stay put in hospital, just as I've advised you to move out.'

'Don't waste your breath, Inspector,' Phoebe told him contemptuously. 'Streech is our home. If we had to rely on you to protect us it wouldn't be worth living in.'

Walsh shrugged. 'You're a very foolish woman, Mrs Maybury.'

Diana, who was in the room with them, was incensed. 'My God, you really are the pits,' she snapped. 'Two days ago you didn't believe a word Phoebe told you. Now, because Sergeant McLoughlin took the trouble to find some evidence, you tell her she's a fool for not running away on your bloody say-so. Well, let me tell you this, the only thing that's changed in the last two days is your mind.' She stamped her foot in exasperation. 'Why the hell should we run away today when we didn't run away yesterday or the day before that? The danger's the same for God's sake. And who do you imagine has been protecting us all this time?'

'Who, Mrs Goode?'

She turned her back on him.

'We've been protecting ourselves of course,' said Phoebe coolly, 'and we'll go on doing it. The dogs are the best safeguard we've got.'

Anne was propped on pillows in her favourite armchair, her feet resting on Phoebe's tapestry stool, an old donkey jacket which passed for a dressing-gown round her shoulders, a pencil stuck behind one ear. She was, McLoughlin thought, completely careless of other people's opinions. The message was simple: I am what you see; take it or leave it. He wondered if it came from supreme self-confidence or total indifference. Whatever it was, he wished he shared it. For his own part, he still felt the need of others' approval.

'So where was Mr Thompson hiding?' she asked him.

'She wouldn't tell us, but it wasn't very difficult to find him. He turned up like a lamb, for the seven-thirty flight to Marbella.'

'Skedaddling with the loot?'

McLoughlin nodded. Once caught and identified by Wally as the man in the shed, Daniel Thompson had offered to co-operate. The idea had come to them, he said, when they had found a book in the library describing the life of luxury enjoyed by British embezzlers on the Spanish riviera. Thompson's engineering business was on the decline and he had complained to his wife about the injustice of having to work his balls off to keep it alive when other men, faced with the same problem, simply absconded with the capital and lived it up in the sun. The answer was simple, announced Mrs T., they too would follow the sun. They had no dependants, she had never liked England, positively loathed East Deller where the community was worthy and stultifying, and she had no intention of spending the next ten years scrimping and saving to keep Daniel's business from going broke. 'The most extraordinary thing,' said Thompson reminiscently, 'was how easy it was to persuade people to invest in transparent radiators. It just proved to me how much money and how little sense there is floating around in the South.' He reminded McLoughlin of Arthur Daley.

'What do you make transparent radiators from?' he'd asked him curiously.

'Toughened, heatproof glass,' said Thompson, 'the same sort of stuff they use for those saucepans. The idea was to add dyes to the water in the expansion tank and watch them flow through the system.'

'Mrs Goode said it could have revolutionised interior design.'

The saintly Daniel sighed. 'That was the terrible irony of it all. I think she may have been right. I opted for the idea because while it was feasible to make the things, it was also absurd enough to make bankruptcy a likely possibility. Imagine my surprise when, without any publicity, it started to take off. By that time, of course, it was too late. To turn the business into a success then would have presented enormous difficulties. On top of which, Maisie – the wife' – he explained helpfully – 'had set her heart on the Costa del Sol. Sad, really,' he mused with a faraway look in his eyes. 'They might well have made my fortune and we could have retired to the sun anyway.'

'Why did you bother with the disappearing act? Why not simply pack up, both of you, and go?'

Mr Thompson beamed. 'Moonlight flits worry people,' he said, 'make them suspicious, and we didn't want the Spanish to take against us. They're not as easy-going as they used to be. While Maisie remained, everyone merely felt sorry for her for having married so weak and inept a man.'

'So where have you been for the last two months?'

'East Deller,' he said, as if surprised by the question, 'until two nights ago when I went to a B & B so Maisie could pack up. Your visits were becoming a little too frequent for comfort.'

'You were hiding in your own house?'

He nodded. 'It was quite safe. Maisie phoned me at my hotel in London after the police had searched the house and garden the first time. I came home during the night of the twenty-sixth and lay low in the attic. We reckoned that was safer than my being on the loose with my description floating about.'

'Wally saw you in the shed,' McLoughlin pointed out.

'That was a mistake,' he admitted. 'We thought the shed would be the best hiding place because it would be easier to escape from if the police turned up unexpectedly. Of course it was also the easiest place for someone to walk into. Not that any normal person walking in would have mattered,' he said without rancour. 'Maisie had hidden me behind a stack of old boxes, no way I'd have been seen by a casual visitor.' He tapped two pudgy forefingers together. 'But the silly old fool was looking for a place to hide himself. I don't know who got the worse shock when he pulled the boxes aside, him or me.'

'The police made two searches,' McLoughlin said. 'How did they miss you the second time?'

'Because we were expecting it. We worked out if the police made a surprise search and found nothing, they'd conclude I really had run away because of my business problems and abandoned Maisie to fend for herself. So Maisie made an anonymous phone call to stimulate another search. It was a nerve-racking two days waiting for it, but we were ready when it came. I simply hopped over the fence at the bottom of the garden and crouched in a bush in our neighbours' orchard until Maisie gave me the all-clear.' He smiled amiably. He was, as Diana had described him, built like a tank. The smile split his chubby face into two half moons, the lower half pendulous with double chins. 'After that we had no more trouble till you turned up with those shoes. Until then my disappearance had been a nine-day wonder.'

McLoughlin acknowledged he was right. 'You were taking a gamble, though. Neighbours must have been popping in all the time.'

'Not after Maisie developed her wonderfully outrageous sex mania,' said Thompson. 'The women kept coming for a few days out of kindness, but it's amazing how rapidly embarrassment alienates people. Maisie should have gone on the stage, I've always said it. We got the idea of the attic from Anne Frank's diary,' he volunteered.

'And she really didn't know about the body in the ice house? I find that extraordinary.'

'It was a damn nuisance,' said Thompson, showing annoyance for the first time. 'She couldn't be seen to change her habits. If she had rented a telly or started buying papers, people might have thought she was taking an interest again. Wrong image, do you see?'

McLoughlin nodded. 'And no one told her because they were afraid the body was yours.'

Daniel sighed. 'Hoist with our own petard.'

'Why did you leave it so long to fly out? You could have gone weeks ago.'

'We were greedy,' confessed Thompson. 'We wanted the money from selling the house. You're talking over a quarter of a million pounds for a property like that. It was the icing on the gingerbread. The plan was for Maisie to become more and more depressed until the obvious solution was to sell the house and move somewhere smaller which had no memories for her. No one would have questioned it. If the truth be told, they'd have been relieved to see the back of her. Then, with the money safely under our belts, we were off on a ferry to France and from there to sunny Spain.'

'And you were intending to use your own passports?'

The other man nodded.

'You'd been reported missing, Mr Thompson. You'd have been stopped.'

'Oh, I don't think so, Sergeant,' he said comfortably. 'Six months on, brouhaha died down, hundreds of people on day trips, a middle-aged couple with a common name. What would they have against me anyway? My wife could testify I was no longer missing. And it's not as though there's a warrant out for my arrest, is there?' He cocked his head on one side and considered the Sergeant with amusement.

'No,' McLoughlin admitted.

'I was incompetent,' said Thompson. 'I admit it freely. But no one person lost very much money through my failure.' He folded his hands across his plump stomach. 'My employees have all found other jobs and the Inland Revenue has agreed to honour their National Insurance contributions which I so rashly – how shall I put it? – "borrowed" to keep the business afloat.' He winked outrageously. 'I give credit to my number two for that. He's done all the negotiations on their behalf, or so Maisie tells me. Splendid chap, great organisational flair, full of integrity. He's sorted out the mess I made and wound up the business. Mind you, he's said some harsh words to Maisie on the phone, called me an amateurish bungler, but I don't hold it against him.' He flicked a speck of dust from his jumper. 'My investors took a gamble on me which was sadly misplaced, but they have cheerfully cut their losses and moved on to more lucrative ventures. I'm delighted. It saddened me to have failed them.'

'Hang on,' said McLoughlin sharply. 'You didn't fail them, Mr Thompson. You embezzled their money.'

'Who says so?'

'You admitted it yourself.'

'When?'

McLoughlin turned to WPC Brownlow who had been taking shorthand notes. 'Find that bit where he said he got the idea from British embezzlers living in Spain.'

She flicked back through her notebook. 'He didn't actually say *he* was an embezzler,' she admitted after a couple of minutes, 'only that his business was in decline.'

'Skip on a few pages,' said McLoughlin. 'He said it was ridiculously easy to get people to invest in the radiator idea.'

'It was,' said Thompson. 'It was a good idea.'

'Dammit all,' exploded McLoughlin. 'You said it was absurd enough to make bankruptcy likely.'

'And I was proved right. That's just what happened.'

'You didn't go bankrupt because it wouldn't work. You salted the money away. You said yourself it could have been a great success.'

Thompson sighed. 'I'm sure it would have been, too, if I'd had more business sense. My problem, as I've tried to explain to you, is incompetence. Are you going to arrest us, Sergeant?'

'Yes, Mr Thompson, I bloody well am.'

'On what charge?'

'Wasting police time, for a kick-off, while I find someone who's willing to press a more serious charge.'

'Who?'

'One of your creditors, Mrs Goode.'

'I'll get my solicitor to discuss an out-of-court settlement with her,' he said comfortably. 'Much more satisfactory than pursuing me through the courts.'

'I'll get your wife on an assault charge.'

'Poor Maisie. She's demented, you know.' He winked with enormous enjoyment. 'Doesn't know what she's doing half the time. A short spell of treatment with a sympathetic doctor will do her far more good than a police prosecution. The Vicar will agree with me on that.'

'You're a pair of rogues.'

'Harsh words, Sergeant. The truth is I'm a coward who couldn't face the disappointment of those who'd put their trust in me. I ran away and hid. Contemptible, I agree, but hardly criminal.' His gaze was level and sincere, but his double chins wobbled. Whether from mirth or contrition, McLoughlin couldn't say.

By the end of his account, Anne was laughing so much it hurt. 'Did you let them go?'

He grinned sheepishly. 'It was like trying to hold on to a couple of eels. Every time you thought you'd got a grip, they wriggled out of it. They're back home now, but due to answer a charge of obstruction in a couple of weeks' time. Meanwhile, I've got on to his number two, who's hopping mad at being taken for a ride, and told him to go through the books with an accountant and look for straightforward embezzlement.'

'He won't find it,' said Anne, mopping her eyes. 'Mr Thompson sounds like a real pro. It'll all be neatly tied up in a villa in Spain by now.'

'Perhaps.' McLoughlin stretched his arms above his head, then subsided comfortably into his chair. He had been up all night again and he was tired.

Jane had told Anne that McLoughlin was in the wrong job. Why? Anne had asked. Because he was over-sensitive to other people's problems. Anne watched him through the smoke from her cigarette. She had none of her god-daughter's naivety so her appraisal was untinged by sentiment. Lust after him she might, but it in no way affected her objectivity. He was not troubled by over-sensitivity towards others, she concluded, but by over-sensitivity towards himself, a trap, in Anne's view, that far too many men fell into. To burden oneself with a socially acceptable image was to put oneself in a strait-jacket. She wondered when McLoughlin had last had a good laugh at himself – if ever. Life for him, she thought, was a series of hurdles which had to be taken cleanly. To touch one would represent failure.

'What are you thinking?' he asked.

'I was wondering why men take themselves so seriously.'

'I didn't know they did.'

'I'm trying to think if I've ever met one who doesn't. Your Mr Thompson sounds a likely candidate.' She waggled her toes on the tapestry stool. 'A woman's problems centre round her biological programming. Without her willingness to reproduce and nurture a new generation, the species would die out. Her frustrations come from the species' unwillingness to recognise the sacrifices she makes for the general good. You don't get paid by a grateful government for being on duty twenty-four hours a day to raise a family; you don't get an MBE for training your children to be good citizens; nine times out of ten even your children don't thank you for your efforts, but chuck in your face that they didn't ask to be born anyway.' She tapped the end of her cigarette against the ashtray and chuckled. 'It's a dog's life being a mother. There's no management structure to speak of, no independent arbitrator, no dismissal procedure for repeated offences and no promotion prospects. Emotional blackmail and sexual harassment are rampant and backhanders commonplace.' Her eyes gleamed as she leant forward. 'No man would tolerate it. His self-esteem would suffer.'

McLoughlin cursed himself silently for being a fool. He should have trusted his first impressions and steered clear. She would have to be very special in bed to make it worth his while to sit through feminist claptrap to get her there. After all, he thought, was there really so much difference between her and his absent wife? The complaints were the same, merely more fluent and better articulated from Anne. He vowed to become celibate. He had neither the inclination nor the energy to wage war every time he felt randy. If the price of pleasure was capitulation, he could do without it. He'd had to grovel past his wife's headaches and stay awake through low-budget late films for Saturday night sex. He was damned if he'd do it for a woman he wasn't tied to.

He stood up abruptly and unleashed his pent-up rage and disappointment. 'Let me tell you something, *Ms* Cattrell. I'm sick to death of hearing women complain about their lot. You're all so bloody strident about what a grand time men have and how badly we treat you.' He walked to the fireplace and leaned both hands on the mantelpiece, staring into the unlit fire. 'Do you think yours is the only sex to suffer from biological programming? The burden on men to perform is infinitely greater. If we weren't programmed to sow our seed, female disinclination would have wiped out the human race centuries ago. You try persuading a woman to have sex. It costs money, effort, emotional commitment and the trauma of regular rejection. If a man wants to do his bit by society, he has to spend a lifetime in chains flogging his guts out to keep his woman content and well fed so that she first agrees to have his offspring and then looks after them properly when she's got them.' He turned to look at her. 'It's humiliating and degrading,' he said with bitterness. 'My procreative chemistry is no different from a dog's. Nature compels us both to eject sperm into a fertile female, the difference is that he doesn't have to justify why he wants to do it whereas I do. Think about that next time you feel like sneering at male self-esteem. It's fragile in the extreme. You're damn right I take myself seriously. I bloody well have to. I've only my office left where rules of behaviour still apply and where I don't have to tie myself in knots to achieve the goals set for me.'

She took an apple from the bowl beside her and tossed it to him. 'You're doing great, McLoughlin. In a minute you'll be telling me you'd rather be a woman.'

He looked at her, saw the amused lift of her lips and laughed. 'I damn nearly did. You're winding me up.'

'No,' she said with a smile, 'I'm winding you down. Life is pure farce from beginning to end, with a little black comedy thrown in for shade. If it was anything else, mankind would have stuck his collective head in the gas oven years ago. No one could tolerate seventy years of tragedy. When I die – probably of cancer – Jane has promised to put on my tombstone: "Here lies Anne Cattrell who laughed her way through it. The joke was on her but at least she knew it."' She tossed another apple into the air and caught it. 'In a couple of weeks, if you last the pace, you could be as cynical as I am, McLoughlin. You'll be a happy man, my son.'

He sat down with the apple clenched between his teeth and drew his briefcase towards him. 'You're not all cynic,' he said, speaking round the apple.

She smiled. 'What makes you say that?'

'I've read your diary.' He snapped the locks on the briefcase, half-opened it and withdrew the slim volume.

She watched him curiously. 'Did you enjoy it?'

'Was I supposed to?'

'No,' she said tartly. 'I didn't write it for publication.'

'Good thing too,' he said frankly. 'It needs editing to make it readable.'

She glared at him. 'You would know, I suppose?' She was incredibly hurt. Her writing, even the writing she did for herself, mattered to her.

'I can read.'

'I can hold a paintbrush. That doesn't make me an expert on art.' She looked pointedly at her watch. 'Shouldn't you be trying to solve a murder? As far as I can see you're still no nearer finding out who the body belongs to or, for that matter, who hit me on the head.' She couldn't give a damn what he thought, he was only a policeman, so why did her stomach feel as if it had just bounced off the floor?

He munched on his apple. 'P. needs editing out,' he told her. 'P. ruins it.' He flicked the diary into her lap. 'The carving-knife is still at the Station, awaiting your signature. I rescued this early on to prevent Friar sneaking it out to photocopy the rude bits.' He was sitting with his back to the windows and his eyes, shadowed, gave nothing away. She couldn't tell if he was joking.

'Pity. Friar might have appreciated it.'

'Tell me about P., Anne.'

She eyed him cautiously. 'What do you want to know?'

'Would he have attacked you?'

'No.'

'Sure? Perhaps he's the jealous type. It was one of his Special Brew bottles that was used to hit you, and I'm told he never lets them out of the pub.'

She could deny that P. and Paddy were one – the prospect of McLoughlin meeting the P. he had read about rather appalled her – but that would be coy, and Anne was never coy. 'I'm positive,' she said. 'Have you spoken to him?'

'Not yet. We only got confirmation of the forensic results this morning.' The match on Anne's blood and hair proved the bottle was the weapon, but the other results were disappointing. A smudged set of fingerprints round the neck and an incomplete footprint built up from barely seen depressions in the ground. It wasn't enough to take them any further.

Anne wished she knew what he was thinking. Was he a harsh judge? Would he ever understand how Paddy, just because he always came back, however irregularly, made Streech bearable? Somehow she doubted it, for, in spite of his strange attraction to her, McLoughlin was a conventional man. The attraction wouldn't last, she knew that. Sooner or later he would snap back into character and then she would be remembered only as a brief madness. And for Anne, there would be just Paddy, once again, to remind her that the walls of Streech Grange were not totally impenetrable. Tired tears pricked at the back of her eyes. 'He's a kind man,' she said, 'and he understands everything.'

If McLoughlin understood, he didn't show it. He left without saying goodbye.

Paddy was hefting empty beer barrels at the rear of the pub. He eyed McLoughlin thoughtfully as he swung another barrel effortlessly atop the pile. 'Can I help you?'

'Detective Sergeant McLoughlin, Silverborne Police.' Imagination had created in McLoughlin's mind a huge, muscular Adonis with the magnetic attraction of the North Pole and the brain of Einstein. The reality was a big, rather overweight, hairy man in a tatty jumper and seated trousers. The jealous fire dimmed perceptibly in McLoughlin's belly. He showed Paddy a photograph of the stone beer bottle, taken after its removal from the undergrowth. 'Do you recognise it?'

Paddy squinted briefly at the picture. 'Maybe.'

'I'm told you bottle your Special in it.'

For a moment they scented the air suspiciously like two powerful mongrels poised to defend their territory. Then Paddy chose to back off. He shrugged good-humouredly. 'OK, yes, it looks like one of mine,' he said, 'but it's a hobby. I'm writing a book on traditional beer-making methods to make damn sure the old ways aren't forgotten.' His gaze was level and without guile. 'I host the odd tasting session where I give it away to the locals to get their opinions.' He studied the other's dark face, looking for a reaction. 'All right, so I may have asked for a donation from time to time towards my costs. That's not unreasonable, it's an expensive hobby.' He found the other's silence irritating. 'Dammit, man, haven't your lot got more important things to exercise your minds at the moment? Who gave it to you anyway? I'll skin the bastard.'

'Is it true you never let these bottles out of the pub, Mr Clarke?' McLoughlin asked coldly.

'Yes, it's true, and I'd bloody well like to get my hands on the bugger who took it. Who was it?'

McLoughlin tapped the black stain round the bottom of the monochrome bottle. 'That's blood, Mr Clarke, Miss Cattrell's blood.'

The big man became very still. 'What the hell is this?'

'It's the weapon that was used to beat a woman's skull in. I thought you might know how it found its way into her garden.'

Paddy opened his mouth to say something, then sank abruptly on to the nearest barrel. 'Jesus Christ! Those bottles weigh a ton. I heard she was all right, but Jesus!'

'How did the bottle get into her garden, Mr Clarke?'

Paddy took no notice. 'Robinson said she'd had a knock on the head. I thought it was concussion. Those bloody wankers keep calling it concussion.'

'What wankers?'

'Journalists.'

'Someone fractured her skull.'

Paddy stared at the ground. 'Is she all right?'

'They used one of your bottles to do it.'

'Goddammit, man, I asked you a question.' He

surged to his feet and stared angrily into McLoughlin's face. 'Is she all right?'

'Yes. But why are you so interested? Did you hit her harder than you meant to?'

Anger flared briefly in Paddy's face. He glanced towards the kitchen door to make sure it was closed. He lowered his voice. 'You're on the wrong track. Anne's a friend of mine. We go back a long way. She'll tell you I wouldn't hurt her.'

'It was dark. Perhaps you thought it was Mrs Goode or Mrs Maybury.'

'Don't be a fool, man. I go back a long way with them, too. Hell, they're all friends of mine.'

McLoughlin's mouth dropped open. 'All three of them?'

'Yes.'

'You're telling me you sleep with all three of them?'

Paddy made damping gestures with his hands. 'Keep your voice down for God's sake. Who said anything about sleeping with anybody? It's damn lonely up there. I keep each one company from time to time, that's all.'

McLoughlin shook with laughter as the jealous flame spluttered and died. 'Do they know?'

Paddy sensed the lack of hostility and grinned. 'I don't know. It's not the sort of thing you ask, is it?' He made a snap judgement. 'Will your conscience allow you a bottle of Special? We might as well drink it before Customs and Excise get their miserable paws on it. And while we're enjoying it, I'll give you a list of all my Special customers. I never let strangers near it, so I know each customer personally. The bastard you're looking for has to be one of them, and I rather think I know who it is. There's only one person in this village who's stupid enough and vindictive enough.' He led McLoughlin across the yard and into the room behind the garage where the rich smell of fermenting malt tingled in the nose. 'To tell you the truth, I've often toyed with the idea of doing the thing properly and going into full legal production. Maybe this is the push I needed. The wife can take over the pub licence, she's a far better landlord than I am.' He took two unopened bottles, removed the clamped rubber stoppers and with immense care poured a deep amber liquid with a foaming white head into two straight-sided glasses. He handed one to McLoughlin. 'Be advised by me, Sergeant.' There was a twinkle in his eye. 'You have all the time in the world, so approach it the way you approach your women. Slowly, lovingly, patiently, and with infinite respect. Because if you don't, you'll be flat on the floor within three mouthfuls, wondering what hit you.'

'Is that your secret?'

'It is.'

McLoughlin raised his glass. 'Cheers.'

*

The letter was waiting on Detective Sergeant Robinson's desk when he arrived that morning. The handwriting on the envelope was childish and unformed, the postmark local. He ripped it open eagerly and spread the lined paper flat on the desk in front of him. The lines were covered in the same unformed script, a rambling, hard-to-read account of a bizarre happening one night in the middle of May. Eddie Staines, anonymously, had come up trumps.

> You been asking about a woman when and so forth. It were a Sunday. Know that becos my girls relijus and took some purswading becos she'd been to comunion. Must of been May 14 as May 12 is my birthday and it was by way of a late pressent. We did it in Grange woods as per normal. We left after 12 and wolked along the wall by the farm. We heard this waleing and weeping on the other side. My girl wanted to beet it but I hopped up for a look. Well you got it rong see. It was a man not a woman and he was rocking about and banging his head. Mad as a hatter if you ask me. I shone the torch on him and said was he all write. He said fuck off so I did. I seen the descripshun of the dead bloke. Sounds write to me. He had long grey hair anyways. Forgot about it till reesently. Thing is I knew him. Couldn't put a name to him mind just knew his face from sumwere. But it weren't no one

reglar if you follow. Reckon now it was Mayberry. Thats all.

With promotion signs flickering in his eyes, Sergeant Robinson rang through to Walsh. He had a momentary qualm about his promise of anonymity – there was no way he could keep Eddie's identity secret now – but it was only momentary. When all was said and done, Eddie had not threatened to string him up by his balls.

Twenty-Two

MCLOUGHLIN THREW OPEN the glass doors of the Police Station and let the heat from outside billow in behind him like a swelling spinnaker. Paddy's Special, taken slowly, lovingly and with immense respect, was swirling nicely in his brain. '"Now's the day and now's the hour,"' he roared. '"See the front of battle lour." Where's Monty? I need troops.'

The Desk Sergeant gave a grunt of amusement. There *was* a certain skinny similarity between Walsh and Montgomery. 'On manoeuvres.'

'Hell!'

'Someone's identified the body.'

'And?'

'David Maybury. The Inspector's wetting himself.'

Shock waves drove the alcohol from McLoughlin's brain. Goddammit, he thought, it couldn't be. He'd come to love those women. The pain of loving them gnawed at his insides like a half-starved rat. 'Where's he gone?'

The other shook his head. 'No idea. Presumably questioning the witness. He and Nick took off like scalded cats about two hours ago.'

'Well, he's wrong.' His voice was harsh. 'It's not Maybury. Tell him that if he gets back before I do, will you?'

Not bloody likely, thought the Desk Sergeant, watching the angry young man shoulder open the doors and surge out on to the pavement. If McLoughlin was intent on self-destruction, he had no plans to go with him. He glanced at his watch and saw with relief that his shift was nearly over.

McLoughlin pulled Anne bodily out of her chair and shook her till her teeth rattled. 'Was it David Maybury?' he shouted at her. 'Was it?' he spat.

She didn't say anything and, with a groan, he pushed her from him. The donkey jacket slipped from her shoulders, leaving her clad only in a pair of men's pyjamas that were far too big for her. She looked oddly pathetic, like a child playing at being an adult. 'I don't know,' she said with dignity. 'The body was unrecognisable, but I shouldn't think it was David. He's not likely to have come back here after ten years, assuming he was still alive.'

'Don't play games, Anne,' he said angrily. 'You saw the body before it rotted. Who was it?'

She shook her head.

'Someone's ID'd it. They say it's David Maybury.'

She licked her lips but didn't answer.

'Help me.'

'I can't.'

'Can't or won't?'

'Does it matter?'

'Yes,' he said bitterly, 'it matters to me. I believed in you. I believed in all of you.'

Her face twisted. 'I'm sorry.'

He gave a savage laugh. 'You're sorry? Jesus Christ!' He gripped her arms again, his long fingers curling into the flesh. 'Don't you understand, you little bitch? I trusted you. I've put my head on the line for you. Dammit, you owe me.'

There was a long silence. When she spoke, her voice was brittle. 'Well, hey, McLoughlin, never let it be said that Cattrell doesn't pay her debts.' She pulled the cord on her pyjama trousers and let them slither to the floor. 'Go ahead. Screw me. That's all you were ever interested in, wasn't it? A good fuck. Just like your precious boss ten years ago.'

The sands shifted under his feet. He raised his hands to her throat and stroked the soft white flesh of her neck.

'You didn't know?' Her eyes glittered as she put her hands between his wrists and thrust them apart to break his grip. 'The horny little bastard made Phoebe a proposition – a nice clean line drawn under the investigation in return for a weekly screw. Oh, he wasn't quite so vulgar. He dressed it up a bit.' She mimicked Walsh's voice. 'She was alone and vulnerable. He wanted to protect her. Her beauty had touched him. She deserved something better after her husband's brutal treatment.' Her lip curled in derision. 'She turned him down and told him where to stick his protection.' A strident note made her voice unattractive. 'My God, but she was naive. She never considered for one moment that the man held her future in his hands.'

'I don't believe this.'

She walked across to her armchair and took a cigarette from the packet on the arm. 'Why not?' she asked coolly, flicking her lighter. 'What makes you think you have a monopoly on wanting to ball murder suspects?' Her eyes mocked him. 'God knows what it is, but there's something very attractive about us. Perhaps it's the uncertainty.'

He shook his head. 'What did you mean when you said he held her future in his hands? You said she was naive.'

'Oh, for pity's sake,' she countered scornfully. 'Who told the world and his wife that Phoebe killed her husband? Who briefed the press, McLoughlin?'

He looked very thoughtful. 'She could have sued.'

'Who?'

'The newspapers.'

'She was never libelled. They weren't so crude as to call her a murderess. They referred to her as "an avid gardener" in one sentence, then in the next revealed that the police were digging up the flowerbeds. And all neatly sign-posted for them by your boss.'

'Why didn't she put in a complaint?' He saw the expression on her face and held up his hands. 'Don't say it. Her word against his and he was a Detective Inspector.' He lapsed into silence. 'So what happened?'

She drew on her cigarette and raked him with angry eyes. 'Walsh couldn't produce the goods because of course David had never been murdered, so the investigation was eventually stopped. It was then the fun started. She found herself on the wrong end of a malicious smear campaign and there wasn't a soul in this bloody place who would give her the time of day. She was on the verge of a nervous breakdown by the time I moved in. Jonny, at the age of eleven, had started to wet his bed and Jane – ' She searched his face. 'It's going to happen again. That bastard is going to throw Phoebe to the wolves a second time.' She looked pale beneath the scarlet bandanna.

'Why didn't you tell me all this at the beginning?'

'Would you have believed me?'

'No.'

'And now?'

'Maybe.' He eyed her for a long time, rubbing his jaw in thoughtful silence. 'You're a good journalist, Anne. Couldn't you have written Phoebe's side of it and got her off the hook?'

'You tell me how I can do that without giving Jane as her alibi and I'll write it. Phoebe would burn at the stake before she let her daughter become a sideshow for ghouls. Me, too, if it comes to that.' She inhaled deeply. 'It's not an alibi anyway. Jane might have fallen asleep.'

He nodded. 'In that case, why are you so sure he left this house alive?'

She turned away to stub out her cigarette. 'Why are *you* so sure?' She looked back at him. 'You are, aren't you?'

'Yes.'

'Because someone claims now it was David in the ice house?'

'No.'

'Why then?'

He looked at her for a long moment. 'Because you chose to bury yourself in Streech Grange. That's how I know he walked out of here alive.'

'I don't know what you're talking about.'

'You're a bloody awful liar, Cattrell.'

'I wish you wouldn't keep saying that,' she said crossly, stamping her foot, 'and I'm freezing.'

'So, stop waggling your fanny at me and put some clothes on,' he said reasonably, reaching down for her pyjama trousers and tossing them across to her. He watched while she put them on. 'It's a nice fanny, Cattrell,' he murmured, 'but I only came for the truth. I got rather more than I bargained for.'

*

He drove to the forensic laboratories and searched out Dr Webster in his office. 'I was passing,' he said. 'I wondered if you'd had any new ideas on that corpse of ours.'

If Dr Webster found this approach a little unorthodox, he didn't remark on it. 'I've the full report here,' he said, tapping a folder on the desk beside him. 'The typist finished this morning. You can take a copy back with you if you like.' He chuckled. 'Mind you, I don't think it's going to please George much, but there we are, he will push for instant opinions and they're not always accurate. Made any progress?'

McLoughlin made a see-saw motion with his hand. 'Not much. Our most promising lead turned up alive. Now we're in the dark again.'

'In that case I doubt that anything I've managed to piece together is going to help you much. Give me a description, better still a photograph, and I'll say yea or nay to whether he's on my slab. But I can't tell you who he is. George is on the phone every day, yelling for results, but miracles take time. Fresh bodies are one thing, bits of old shoe leather need patience to sort out.'

'What about Maybury?'

The pathologist grunted impatiently. 'You're all obsessed with that wretched man. Of course it's not Maybury. And you can tell George I've taken a second opinion and it agrees with mine. Facts are facts,' he grumbled, 'and in this case they are not open to interpretation.'

McLoughlin breathed deeply through his nose. 'How do you know?'

'Too old. I've done a lot of work on the X-rays and the fusion's more advanced than I thought. I'm sure now we're looking at a sixty-five to seventy-year-old. The bottom line's sixty. Maybury would be what? Fifty-four, fifty-five?'

'Fifty-four.'

Webster reached for the folder and removed some photographs. 'In the report, I've come down against mutilation but it's only an opinion and I'm prepared to be proved wrong. There *are* some scratches on the bone that might have been made with a sharp knife, but my own view is it wasn't.' He pointed to one of the photographs. 'Clearly rat droppings.'

McLoughlin nodded. 'Anything else?'

'I'm in two minds about how he died. It really depends on whether he was wearing any clothes at the time of his death. Have you sorted that one out yet?'

'No.'

'I scraped up a lot of earth from the floor round the body. We've analysed it but, frankly, there's a negligible amount of blood in it.'

McLoughlin frowned. 'Go on.'

'Well, that makes it very difficult for me to say with any certainty how he died. If he was nude and he was stabbed, the ground would have been saturated with blood. If he was fully clothed and stabbed, then the clothes would have soaked up most of the blood. You'll have to find his clothes.'

'Hang on a minute, Doctor. You're saying that if he was nude he couldn't have been stabbed, but if he was clothed he might have been?'

'In essence, that's right. There's an outside chance animals might have licked the floor but you'll never get a prosecution on that.'

'Does Chief Inspector Walsh know this?'

Webster peered at him over his glasses. 'Why do you ask that?'

McLoughlin rumpled his hair. 'He hasn't mentioned it.' Or had he? McLoughlin could remember very little of what Walsh had said that first night. 'OK. Supposing he was nude. How did he die?'

Webster pursed his lips. 'Old age. Cold. From the little that's left, it's impossible to say. I couldn't find any traces of barbiturates or asphyxia, but – ' He shrugged, and tapped the photographs. 'Shoe leather. Find the clothes. They'll tell you more than I can.'

McLoughlin put his hands on the desk and hunched his shoulders. 'We've been conducting a murder enquiry on the basis that he was stabbed in the belly. Now you're telling me he could have died of natural causes. Have you any idea how many hours I've worked in the last week?'

The pathologist chuckled. 'About half as many as

I have, at a rough guess. I've pulled out the stops on this one. Good grief, man, we don't get cases like this every day. Most bodies have at least ninety per cent of their constituent parts. In any case, until you produce some intact and unstained clothes to prove me wrong, stabbing still looks the most likely. Old men, wandering around nude in search of an ice house to freeze to death in, are quite outside my experience.'

McLoughlin straightened. 'Touché. Any more surprises?'

'Just a little bit of fun which I've tacked on to the end of the report, so I don't want you coming back and accusing me of putting ideas into your head.' He chuckled. 'I had another look in the ice house yesterday. It's been sealed for over a week now and the temperature's dropped considerably. The door's as old as the hills but it still fits perfectly. I was impressed. Obviously an extraordinarily efficient method of storing ice. Very cold and very sterile. Must have kept for months.'

'And?'

The doctor turned his attention to some letters in front of him. 'I've speculated on what sort of condition he would have been in if the door had remained closed until the gardener found him.' He scratched his name in spidery writing on the top letter. 'Surprisingly good, I think. I'd like to have seen it. Purely out of scientific interest, of course.'

He raised his head. McLoughlin and the report had gone.

Sergeant Bob Rogers, who had switched to the afternoon shift after a two-day break and was now on duty at the desk, looked up as McLoughlin came in through the front doors. 'Ah, Andy. The very man.' He held up the description of Wally Ferris that had circulated round the county. 'This tramp you're looking for.'

'Found him. Matter of fact, as soon as I've seen the Inspector, I'm off after him again.'

'Good, then you can bring him in. He's on our missing persons' list.'

McLoughlin walked slowly across the floor. 'You've got Wally Ferris down as a missing person? But he's been on the road for years.'

Rogers frowned and turned the list for McLoughlin to look at. 'See for yourself. The description here fits the one you put out to a T.'

McLoughlin looked at what was written. 'Did Walsh see this?'

'Left it with him the first night.'

McLoughlin reached for the telephone. 'Do me a favour, Bob. The next time you see me too hung over to double-check what that bastard does' – he pointed to his chin – 'hit me here.'

*

He slouched in a chair in the Chief Inspector's office and watched the thin, bloodless lips dribble smoke. Imperceptibly, the face had changed. Where respect had once fleshed it with a genial wisdom, contempt had uncovered its malice. Phrases registered here and there – 'definitely Maybury' . . . 'young man recognised him' . . . 'in the ice house two weeks' . . . 'tramp must have seen him there' . . . 'you missed it completely' . . . 'writing a report' . . . 'domestic problems can't excuse your negligence' – but the bulk of what was said passed over McLoughlin's head. He stared unblinkingly at Walsh's face and thought about the teeth behind the smile.

Walsh jabbed his pipe stem angrily at his Sergeant. 'DS Robinson is out rounding up Wally Ferris now and by God, there are going to be no mistakes this time.'

The younger man stirred. 'What will you do? Show him a photograph of Maybury and suggest he was the dead man? Wally will agree with you just to get out of here.'

'Staines has already made the identification. If Wally confirms it, we're on safe ground.'

'How old is Staines?'

'Twenty-fiveish.'

'So he was fifteen when he last saw Maybury? And he claims to have recognised him in the dark? You'll never get a prosecution on that.'

'It's a good case,' said Walsh calmly. 'We've motive, means and opportunity, plus a wealth of circumstantial evidence. Mutilation to obscure identity, lamb bones to tempt scavengers to the ice house, the removal of the clothes to hinder investigation, Fred's obliteration of tracks and evidence. With all that and the positive IDs, she'll confess this time, I think.'

McLoughlin rubbed his unshaven jaw and yawned. 'You're forgetting the forensic evidence. That's not so easy to fabricate. Webster won't lie for you.'

Walsh's ferocious brows snapped together. 'What's that supposed to mean?'

'You know damn well – *sir*. The dead man was too old to be Maybury. And what happened to all the blood?'

Walsh eyed him with intense dislike. 'Get out of here!' he growled.

There was humour in the dark face. 'Are you going to tell her defence barrister to bugger off every time he asks a reasonable question?'

'The blood was on the clothes, presumably destroyed with them,' said Walsh tightly. 'As to Webster's interpretation of his skull X-rays, it is just that, an interpretation. The discrepancy between his position and mine is six years. I say fifty-four. He says sixty. He's wrong. Now get out.'

McLoughlin shrugged and stood up, reaching into his pocket and removing a piece of folded paper. 'The missing persons' list,' he said, dropping it on to the desk. 'I took a photocopy. It's yours. Keep it as a memento.'

'I've seen it.'

McLoughlin studied the pink scalp through the thinning hair. He remembered liking this man once. But that was before Anne's revelations. 'So I gather. Bob Rogers showed it to you the night the body was discovered. The case, for all it ever was a case, should have been over by the morning.'

Walsh stared at him for a moment, then took the paper and unfolded it. There were the same five names and descriptions, but with 'Since Traced' scrawled across Daniel Thompson's box. The two young women were of no consequence because of their sex, which left the Asian lad, Mohammed Mirahmadi, who was too young, and the semi-senile Keith Chapel, sixty-eight, who had walked out of his warden-run hostel five months before, wearing a green jacket, blue jumper and bright pink slacks. A tight, cold fist gripped at Walsh's insides. He laid the paper on the desk. 'The tramp didn't come into it until the next day,' he muttered. 'And how could this old man know about Streech Grange or the ice house?'

McLoughlin stabbed at the box with his finger. 'Look at his initials,' he said. 'Keith Chapel. K.C. I rang the warden of his hostel. The old boy used to ramble on endlessly about a garage he'd owned and what a success it was until a woman spread lies about him and he was forced to sell up. You knew all about it. Dammit, it was you who prompted Mrs Goode to tell the story.'

'Only by hearsay,' Walsh muttered. 'I never met the man. He was gone by the time Maybury disappeared. I thought Casey was a name. Everyone called him Casey. It's in the file as Casey.'

'You're damn right it's in the file. For a bit of hearsay, you gave it a hell of an airing. Great story, shame about the facts. Was that about the size of it?'

'It's not my fault if people thought she killed her parents. We just recorded what they told us.'

'Like hell you did! You fed it to them first. Jesus, you even hoicked it out for my benefit the other evening. And I believed it.' He shook his head. 'What did she do, for pity's sake? Laugh? Call you a dirty old man? Threaten to tell your wife?' He waited for a moment. 'Or couldn't she hide her revulsion?'

'You're suspended,' Walsh whispered. His hands quivered with a life of their own.

'What for? Uncovering the truth?' He slammed his palm on to the missing persons' list. 'You bastard! You had the bloody nerve to accuse me of negligence. Those trousers should have registered with you. You heard them described twice in twelve hours. How many men wear pink slacks, for Christ's sake? You knew a man had been reported missing wearing pink trousers. And it wasn't difficult to find Wally. If I'd had that information when I spoke to him – ' He shook his head angrily and reached for his briefcase. 'There's Dr Webster's final report.' He flung it on to the desk. 'Judging by the fact that Wally felt K.C.'s clothes were fit to wear, I think we can safely assume they were neither ripped with a knife nor blood-soaked. The poor old chap probably died of cold.'

'He went missing five months ago,' muttered the Inspector. 'Where was he for the first two months?'

'In a cardboard box in a subway, I should think, just like all the other poor sods this bloody awful society rejects.'

Walsh moved restlessly. 'And Maybury? You know all the answers. So where's Maybury?'

'I don't know. Living it up in France, I expect. He seems to have had enough contacts out there through his wine business.'

'She killed him.'

McLoughlin's eyes narrowed. 'The bastard ran away when the money dried up and left her and his two small children to carry the can. It was planned, for God's sake.' He was silent for a moment. 'I can't think of one good reason why he would have wanted to punish them but, if he did, he must have been praying for a shit like you to turn up.' He walked to the door.

'What are you going to do?' The words were barely above a whisper.

McLoughlin didn't answer.

*

On his way down the corridor, he bumped into Nick Robinson and Wally Ferris. He gave the old man a friendly punch on the shoulder. 'You might have left him his underpants, you old rogue.'

Wally shuffled his feet and cast sideways glances at both policemen. 'You lot gonna charge me then?'

'What with?'

'Didn't do no 'arm, not really. Wet frough I was wiv all that flamin' rain and 'im sittin' there quiet as a mouse. To tell you the trufe I didn't click to 'im bein' dead, not for a while. Put 'im down as one of my sort, but wiv a screw loose. There's a lot like that who've 'ad too much mefs and too little whisky. 'Ad quite a chat wiv 'im one way and anuvver.' He pulled a lugubrious face. ''E didn't 'ave no underpants, son, didn't 'ave nuffink 'cept the 'fings 'e'd folded up and put on the floor beside 'im.' He gave McLoughlin a sly peep. 'Didn't see no 'arm in taking 'em, not when 'e didn't need 'em and I did. Bloody parky, it was. I put 'em on over me own cloves.'

Nick Robinson, who had had no success in getting Wally to talk, snorted. 'You're saying he was sitting there stark naked, dead as a dodo, and you had a chat with him?'

'It was company,' muttered Wally defensively, 'an' it was a while before I got used to the gloom in the cave. You see some funny fings in my line of business.'

'Pink elephants mostly, I should think.' Robinson

looked enquiringly at McLoughlin. 'What's all this about the clothes?'

'You'll find out. What do you reckon he died of, Wally?'

'Gawd knows. Cold, I should fink. That place is freezin' wiv ve door closed, an' 'e'd wedged a brick against it. I 'ad to push pretty 'ard to get it open. It weren't nuffink nasty. 'E 'ad a smile on 'is face.'

There was a sharp indrawn breath from Robinson. 'But there was blood, wasn't there?'

Wally's old eyes looked shocked. 'Course there weren't no blood. I wouldn't 'ave stayed if there was blood. 'E was in lovely shape. On the white side per'aps but that was natural. It was dark wiv all the rain outside.' He wrinkled his nose. 'Whiffed a bit, but I didn't 'old it against 'im. Dare say I didn't smell too good meself.'

It was like something out of a Samuel Beckett play, thought McLoughlin. Two old men sitting in semi-darkness, chatting – one nude and dead, the other sodden, and in more ways than one. He didn't doubt for a minute that Wally had spent the night with K.C., rambling happily about this and that. Wally loved to talk. Was it a horrible shock, he wondered, to find in the sober morning light that he'd been chatting with a corpse? Probably not. Wally, he was sure, had seen many worse things. 'So did you shut the door again when you left?'

The old man pulled thoughtfully at his lower lip.

'Sort of.' He seemed to be weighing the problem in his mind. 'That's to say, I did the first time. The first time I shut it. Seemed to me 'e wanted to be left in peace or 'e wouldn't 'ave wedged a brick against it. Then that geezer in the shed gave me the whisky, an' I 'ad a few mouffuls, an' I got to finking about proper burials an' such. Seemed wrong some'ow to leave 'im wivout a chance of a few good words bein' said for 'im, wouldn't want it personally, so I nips back and opens the door. Reckoned 'e'd 'ave more chance of bein' found wiv ve door open.'

It would be cruel, McLoughlin thought, to tell him that by opening the door he had let in the heat, the dogs, the rats and putrefaction. He hoped Walsh wouldn't do it.

'And that,' Wally finished firmly, 'is all I knows. Can I go now?'

'Not likely,' said Nick Robinson, 'the Inspector wants a word with you.' He took a firm grip on Wally's arm and looked enquiringly at McLoughlin. 'How about filling me in?'

McLoughlin grinned evilly. 'Let's just say, you got your wires crossed, old son.'

Twenty-Three

HE FOLDED HIMSELF wearily into his car and sat for some time staring blankly through the windscreen. Some words of Francis Bacon kept repeating themselves in his mind like a memory-jerk mnemonic. 'Revenge is a kind of wild justice. The more man's nature runs to it, the more ought law to weed it out.' He rubbed his gaunt face. He had told Anne he sympathised with personal vengeance but he knew now that wasn't true. The end result of an 'eye for an eye' was a world gone blind. With a sigh, he fired the motor and drew out into the traffic.

He lived in a modern box on a large estate to the north-west of Silverborne where every house was depressingly similar and where individuality expressed itself only in what colour you chose to paint your front door. It had satisfied him once. Before he had seen Streech Grange.

'Hello, Andy,' said Kelly. She was standing irresolutely by the kitchen sink, mop in hand, washing the dirty dishes he had left untouched for ten days. He had forgotten how stunning she was and how easily that fabulous body had once been able to turn him on.

'Hello.'

'Pleased to see me?'

He shrugged. 'Sure. Look, you don't need to do those. I was planning to tackle them over the weekend. I haven't been around much this week.'

'I know. I've been trying to phone you.'

He went to the fridge and took out a piece of cheese from among the opened tins of furred tomatoes and sliced cling peaches. He held it out to her. 'Want some?' She shook her head, so he ate the whole lump before looking at his watch. 'I've a phone call to make, then I'll grab a quick shower before I go out.' He waved his arm to encompass the whole house. 'Take your time and take what you like.' He smiled without hostility. 'Except my books and my two boat paintings. You won't quibble over those, will you? You always said they were only good for gathering dust.' So much so that they had been relegated, along with him, to the spare room.

He was on his way to the stairs when his conscience smote and he turned round. 'Look, really, don't do the washing-up. It's not necessary. I'd have done it myself if I'd had the time.' He smiled again. 'You'll ruin your nail varnish.'

Her mouth trembled. 'Jack and me, it didn't work.'

She flung herself after him and burrowed her sweet-smelling head into his chest. 'Oh, Andy, I've missed you. I want to come home. I want to come home so much.'

An awful lethargy stole over him then, like the lethargy a drowning man must feel in the moment before he gives up. His eyes looked into the middle distance above her head, seeking straws. There were none. He held her for a second or two, then gently disentangled himself. 'Come home,' he said. 'It's yours as much as mine.'

'You're not angry?'

'Not at all. I'm glad.'

Her wonderful eyes shone like stars. 'Your mother said you would be.'

Straws, he thought, were useless to drowning men. It was the unquenchable longing for life that kept heads above water. 'I'll have that shower, then I'll be off,' he said. 'I'll fetch the books and the paintings tomorrow, and maybe the records I bought before we were married.' He glanced through the sitting-room door at the chromium coffee table, the oatmeal carpet, the net curtains, the white formica wall units and the dainty pastel three-piece suite, and he thought, no one has ever lived here. He shook his head. 'There's nothing else I want.'

She caught him by the arm. 'You *are* angry.'

His dark face cracked into a grin. 'No. I'm glad. I needed a push. I hate this place. I always have done.

It's so' – he sought for a word – 'sterile.' He looked at her with compassion. 'Like our marriage.'

She dug her fingers into his arm. 'I knew you'd bring that up, you bastard. But it's not my fault. You never wanted kids any more than I did.'

He removed her hands. 'That wasn't quite the sterility I was referring to.'

She was bitter. 'You've found someone else.'

He moved to the telephone, took a piece of paper from his pocket and dialled the number written on it. 'McLoughlin,' he said into the mouthpiece. 'We've identified the body. That's it, all over the newspapers tomorrow, so if he's any sense he'll lie low. Yes, it'll have to be tonight. Damn right, I want him. Let's just say I take what he did personally. So can you swing it?' He listened for a moment. 'Just make the point that they've got away with murder again. I'll be with you by ten.' He looked up and caught Kelly's eye.

Water had gathered in great droplets round the mascaraed lashes. 'Where will you go?'

'I don't know yet. Maybe Glasgow.'

Tears turned to anger, and her anger lashed out at him as it always had done. 'You've left that bloody job, haven't you? After all the begging I did for you to leave, you've left it because someone else asked you.'

'No one's asked me, Kelly, and I haven't left it, not yet.'

'But you will.'

'Maybe.'

'Who is she?'

He found he wanted to hurt her, so there must be some feeling left. Perhaps there always would be. Seven years, however sterile, had left their mark. 'She's my rose,' he said, 'my red, red rose.' And Kelly, who had heard enough of hated Rabbie Burns to last a lifetime, felt a knot of panic tighten round her heart.

Phoebe rocked Diana's shoulder and prodded her into wakefulness. 'We've got visitors,' she whispered. 'I need help.' Somewhere in the darkness behind her came the low growls of the dogs.

Diana squinted at her out of one eye. 'Turn the light on,' she said sleepily.

'No, I don't want them to know we're awake.' She bundled Diana's dressing-gown on to her chest. 'Come on, old girl, get a move on.'

'Have you called the police?' Diana sat up and shrugged her arms into the dressing-gown.

'No point. It'll be over one way or another long before the police get here.' Phoebe switched on a small torch and pointed it at the floor. 'Come on,' she urged, 'we haven't much time.'

Diana pulled on her slippers and padded after her. 'Why are the dogs here? Why aren't they outside? And where's McLoughlin?'

'He didn't come tonight.' She sighed. 'The one night we needed him, he didn't turn up.'

'So what are you planning to do?'

Phoebe lifted her shotgun from where she had propped it outside Diana's bedroom door. 'I'm going to use this,' she said, leading the way downstairs, 'and I don't want to shoot the dogs by mistake. It'll be their turn to have a go if the bastards manage to break in.'

'Lord, woman,' muttered Diana, 'you're not intending to kill anyone, are you?'

'Don't be a fool.' She crept across the hall and into her drawing-room. 'I'm going to scare the shit out of the creeps. They didn't get rid of me last time. They won't get rid of me now.' She gestured Diana to one side of the curtains and, switching off the torch, took up a position on the other side. 'Keep your eyes peeled. If you see anyone on the far side of the terrace, let me know.'

'I'm going to regret this,' Diana groaned, twitching the curtain aside and peering into the darkness. 'I can't see a bloody thing. How do you know they're out there?'

'Benson came in through the cellar window and woke me. I trained him to do it after the first time these yobs had a go at me.' She patted the old dog's head. 'You're such a good boy, aren't you. It's years since I've had you patrolling the grounds and you haven't forgotten.' The sound of the dog's tail swishing backwards and forwards across the carpet was loud in the quiet room. Hedges, unborn at the time of David Maybury's disappearance, crouched by his mistress's feet, muscles tensed for when his turn came. Phoebe scanned the wide terrace for signs of movement. 'Your eyes will soon adjust.'

'There *is* someone,' said Diana suddenly. 'By the right-hand wall. Do you see him?'

'Yes. There's another coming round Anne's wing.' She gripped her shotgun firmly. 'Can you unlock the windows without making a noise?'

For a brief moment Diana hesitated, then she shrugged and applied herself carefully to the key. Phoebe, she argued, knew all there was to know about hell. She had been there. She wouldn't willingly go back a second time. In any case, the adrenaline was racing in her as strongly as it was racing in Phoebe. It was backs-against-the-wall time, she thought, when everyone, even rabbits, showed their teeth. 'OK,' she whispered, as the lock clicked quietly open. She peeped past the edge of the curtain again. 'Oh, lord,' she breathed, 'there are dozens of them.'

Black figures crouched along the edge of the terrace like a troop of apes, but to think of them as such was to demean the animals. It is only man, with his single evolutionary advancement of reason, who takes pleasure in other people's pain. Diana's mouth went dry. There was something unbelievably chilling in mob hysteria where individual accountability was subordinate to the group.

'Hardly dozens; five, six at the most. When I say, "Now," open the door wide.' Phoebe gave a wild laugh. 'We'll put the old adage to the test and wait till we see the whites of their eyes. I've always wanted to try it.'

There was confusion in the huddled mass as they seemed to crowd together about the terrace wall, then separate again. 'What are they doing?' asked Diana.

'Pulling bricks off the top by the look of it. Keep your head down if they start throwing them.'

One of the crouching group seemed to be the leader. He used his arms to direct his troop, half to go down one side of the terrace, half to take the other side. 'Now,' muttered Phoebe urgently. 'I don't want them splitting up.'

Diana twisted the handle and thrust the door open. Phoebe was through it in a second, her tall figure melting into the shadows. She had raised the heavy stock to her shoulder and was about to sight down the barrel when one large hand clamped itself over her mouth and another plucked the gun from her grasp.

'I wouldn't if I were you, madam,' whispered Fred's soft voice in her ear. He kept his hand firmly over her mouth and used his forearm on her shoulder to force her to her knees. Bent double, he laid the shotgun noiselessly on the flagstones then, urging her upright again, he caught her round the waist as if she were no more than a piece of thistledown, and lifted her through the drawing-room windows. He felt Diana's presence, rather than saw it. 'Not a sound,' he cautioned her in a tight whisper, 'and close the window, if you please.'

'But, Fred – ' she began.

'Do as I say, Mrs Goode. Do you want madam hurt?'

Thoroughly shaken, Diana did as he said.

Ignoring Phoebe's biting teeth, Fred hauled her unceremoniously across the room and bundled her into the hall. Diana pursued him. 'What are you doing?' she demanded fiercely, buffeting him around his shoulders with bunched fists. 'Put Phoebe down this minute.' Benson and Hedges, alarmed by Diana's tone, threw themselves against Fred's legs.

'This door, too, Mrs Goode, if you please.'

She caught a handful of his sparse hair and tugged hard. 'Let her go,' she grunted.

With a sigh of pain, he swung round, carrying both women with him, and kicked the door to with his foot. Seconds later the French windows shattered inwards into a thousand pieces. 'There,' he said amiably, setting Phoebe carefully on the floor and removing his hand from her mouth. 'We're all right now, I think. If you wouldn't mind, Mrs Goode, that *is* a little painful. Thank you.' He fished a handkerchief from his pocket and wrapped it round his bleeding fingers. 'Good boys,' he murmured, fondling the dogs' muzzles, 'that's the ticket. I don't say I'm not annoyed about another window needing new glass, but this time we'll make sure it's paid for.' He opened the door. 'Would you excuse me, madam? I'd hate to miss the fun.'

Speechlessly, the two women watched his great bulk pad lightly across the broken glass and step out on to the terrace. Beyond, lit by brilliant moonlight, was a scene from Hieronymus Bosch. A grotesque tangle of misshapen figures writhed in hideous and noisy confusion upon the lawn. As Fred, with a blood-curdling roar, charged across the terrace and launched himself atop the mêlée, Phoebe took in the situation at a glance, whistled up Hedges and pointed to one flying fugitive who had managed to pull himself free. 'Off you go, boy.' Hedges, barking his excitement, bounded across the grass, bowled his man over and pranced about him, howling his achievement to the moon. Benson, not to be outdone, waddled on to the terrace, sat comfortably on his haunches and raised his old muzzle in joyous unison.

The row from dogs and flailing bodies was deafening.

'Men!' exclaimed Diana in Phoebe's ear and Phoebe, with adrenaline still running rampant in her bloodstream, burst into tears of laughter.

Twenty-Four

THE CONFUSION WAS short-lived. By the time Diana thought of switching on the drawing-room lights, the half dozen vandals had thrown in the towel and were being herded across the terrace by a panting semicircle of McLoughlin, young PC Gavin Williams, out of uniform, Jonathan, Fred and Paddy Clarke.

'Inside,' ordered McLoughlin curtly. 'You're all nicked.'

Stripped of their menace by the glare of the overhead lamps, they were an unprepossessing bunch of shuffling, sweaty youths with surly faces and evasive eyes. Diana knew them all by sight as lads from the village, but she could put a name to only two of them, Eddie Staines and nineteen-year-old Peter Barnes, son of Dilys and brother to Emma. She looked them over in amazement. 'What have we ever done to you? I don't even know who most of you are.'

Barnes was a good-looking young man, tall, athletic, an ex-public school boy, now working in his father's print business in Silverborne. He sneered at her but didn't answer. Eddie Staines and the remaining four stared fixedly at the floor.

'It's a reasonable enough question,' said McLoughlin evenly. 'What have these ladies ever done to you?'

Barnes shifted his gaze. 'Which ladies?' he asked insolently. 'Do you mean the dykes?'

Barnes's voice, unaccented, interested McLoughlin. The shouts on the lawn had all carried the strangled vowels of the working class. A slight shake of his head kept Diana quiet. 'I was referring to Mrs Maybury and her friends,' he said in the same even tone. 'What have they ever done to you?' He searched the line of unresponsive faces. 'All right, for the moment you will be charged with aggravated assault on the owner of Streech Grange.'

'We never touched her,' complained Eddie Staines.

'Shut up,' said Barnes.

'Never touched who?'

'Her. Mrs Maybury.'

'I didn't say you did.'

'What was all that aggravated assault crap?'

'She's not the owner of Streech Grange,' McLoughlin pointed out. 'Mr Jonathan Maybury and his sister own this property.'

'Oh.' Eddie frowned. 'We thought it was the dyke's.'

McLoughlin arched an eyebrow. 'Do you mean Mrs Maybury?'

'You soft in the head, or what?'

'That,' murmured McLoughlin mildly, 'would appear to be your privilege. Eddie Staines, is it?'

'Yeah.'

'Keep your big mouth shut, you ignorant turd,' Barnes grated through clenched teeth.

A cold gleam lit McLoughlin's eyes. 'Well, well, Paddy, you were right. It's the jumped-up little oik who calls the shots. So what's his problem?'

'His mother,' was Paddy's laconic reply.

The boy threw him a murderous glance.

Paddy gave an indifferent shrug. 'I'm sorry for you, lad. If you'd had half your sister's sense, you'd have got by. You'd have raised two fingers to that stupid bitch with her twisted ambitions, and you'd have kept your sanity. Try asking yourself who Emma's really screwing when she comes up here and spreads her legs.' He glanced at McLoughlin. 'Ever heard the expression, a beggar on horseback? A beggar comes into a bit of money, buys a horse to raise himself up, only to find he can't ride the damn thing. That's Dilys Barnes. She came a cropper when she set her sights too high and moved the family into Streech. No harm in that, of course. It's a free country. But you don't, if you've any sense, treat one end of the village like muck because you think they're beneath you, while you lick the backsides of the other end and brandish your painfully transparent family tree under their noses. That way, you alienate everybody.'

Peter's face worked unpleasantly. 'Bastard!' he hissed.

Paddy let it pass. 'People laughed at her, of course. They would. Social climbing's a spectator sport in a place like this, and Dilys was never any good at it.' He stroked his chin. 'She's a very unintelligent woman. She couldn't grasp the first rule, that class is in inverse proportion to its relevance.' His eyes flickered over Peter. 'You'll need a translation, lad. The classier you are the less you have to talk about it.'

Barnes bunched his fists. 'Fuck you, Paddy. Cheap Irish trash, that's all you are.' Fleetingly, McLoughlin had the odd impression that the boy was enjoying himself.

A deep laugh rumbled in Paddy's throat. 'I'll take it as a compliment, lad. It's a long time since anyone's recognised the Irish in me.' He dodged a flying fist. 'Jesus Christ!' he said crossly. 'You're even more stupid than your mother, despite your fancy education and the puffed-up ideas she's given you.' He wagged a finger at Phoebe. 'It's your fault, woman. You made a laughing-stock of her and, believe me, you don't do that to the Dilys Barneses of this world. She has a poisoned callus on her soul for every slight, true or imagined, that she's suffered, and the biggest and the most venomous is the one you gave her. She's fed her venom to this little creep by the bucket-load.'

Phoebe looked at him in astonishment. 'I hardly

know her. She made a scene by the village pond once but I was far too angry to laugh.'

'Before David went missing,' he prompted. 'He did the real damage. He repeated the story in the pub and it was all round the village before you could say Jack Robinson.'

Phoebe stared at him blankly and shook her head.

He reached down to scratch the ears of the old Labrador lying at his feet. 'When Benson was little more than a puppy, Dilys caught him humping her Pekinese.' His eyes twinkled encouragingly. 'Harangued you over the telephone for not keeping him under better control.'

'Oh, good God!' Phoebe clapped her hands to her face. 'Not my Barnes pun. But it was a joke,' she protested. 'You're not going to tell me she took it personally. I was referring to her Peke. The damn thing was on heat and she let it out, reeking of pheromones.'

Paddy's great chuckle boomed about the room, stirring the heightened adrenalin into a responsive froth.

Phoebe's voice shook. 'It was all her fault anyway. She would keep calling Benson a dirty dog.' Quite unconsciously, she took on the refined tones of Dilys Barnes. '"Your dirty dog should be ashamed of himself, Mrs Maybury." God, it was funny. She couldn't bring herself to say that Benson had rogered her ghastly bitch.' She wiped her eyes on her sleeve. 'So I said, I was very sorry but, as she knew better than I, you couldn't stop dirty dogs poking into smelly barns.' She looked up, caught Diana's eye and laughed out loud. The room quivered.

Eddie Staines, not too bright but with a well-developed sense of humour, grinned broadly. 'That's good. Never heard it before. That why they call old man Barnes "the dirty dog" then? God, struth!' He doubled up as Peter Barnes, without any warning, swung a booted foot and kicked him in the groin. 'Ah, Jesus!' He backed away, clutching his balls.

McLoughlin watched this little sally with amused detachment. 'And presumably Dilys got lumbered with Smelly?' he said to Paddy.

The big man grinned. 'For a month or two, maybe. Far as I recall, Dirty Dog stuck to Tony longer than Smelly Barnes stuck to Dilys, but the damage was done. Takes herself too seriously, you see. When you're eaten up with frustrated ambition, there's no room for humour.' His eyes rested on the bitter young face of the boy. 'Respectability,' he said with heavy irony, 'it's a sickness with her. With this one, too. They won't be laughed at.'

And that, McLoughlin knew, was as far as Paddy could take him. He had been suspicious enough of Peter Barnes to set him up, but he had no proof that the lad had struck Anne any more than he had proof that Dilys initiated all the slander against Phoebe. 'She's far too cunning,' he had said that morning.

'She's a type. Pathologically jealous. You come across them now and then. They're usually women, invariably inadequate and their spite is always directed against their own sex because that's the sex they're jealous of. They are completely vicious. As often as not, the target is their own daughter.'

'So why single out Mrs Maybury?' McLoughlin had asked.

'Because she was the first lady of Streech and you buggers dropped her in the shit. For ten years, Dilys has been wetting herself because she can look down on Mrs Maybury of Streech Grange. God knows, she was never going to do it any other way.'

'What did she do?'

'Piled shit on shit, of course. People were ready to believe anything after you lot left, and murder was the least of the garbage Dilys fed them.'

'What a sewer you live in, Paddy.' McLoughlin spoke quietly, his voice level.

The big man surprised him. 'If it is, it's Phoebe's fault,' he had observed. 'She's the focus for it all. Whatever the rights and wrongs, any normal woman would have sold up and moved on. The Grange isn't worth the price she's had to pay for it.'

No, McLoughlin thought, Paddy was wrong about that. The Grange was worth whatever Phoebe had to pay, and she would go on paying because it was cheap at the price. The real cost was being borne by the people who loved her. He glanced across at her with a sudden irritation. God damn the woman! People loved her or hated her. The one thing no one seemed to feel was indifference.

'OK,' he said abruptly into the silence, 'you' – he jerked a finger at Eddie Staines – 'are going to listen to a few home truths. You're not the brightest thing on two legs but you have to be brighter than this dickhead here.' He scowled at Barnes, then held up a finger. 'Number one, Eddie. Mrs Maybury did not murder her parents. Colonel and Mrs Gallagher died because their brakes didn't work, and their brakes didn't work because K.C. hadn't serviced the car properly. Had he done so, he would have found the corroded brake hose. Got that?'

'Yeah, but who corroded it?' asked Eddie triumphantly. 'That's the question.'

'Read the coroner's report,' said McLoughlin wearily. 'Colonel Gallagher took the car to K.C. *because* the brakes felt soft. He wrote a note to that effect and the note, in his handwriting, is in the file. K.C. ignored it.' He held up a second finger. 'Number two. Mr David Maybury walked out of this house alive ten years ago. No one murdered him. He legged it because he had finally run through all of Mrs Maybury's money and he didn't fancy working for his living.'

'So who's arguing? Saw the bugger myself three months ago. Mind you, he's dead now.' Eddie glared at Phoebe. 'Hell of a way to get your own back, lady.'

McLoughlin held up a third finger. 'Number three, Eddie. That man wasn't David Maybury.'

He looked sceptical. 'Oh, yeah?'

'Oh, yeah. It was K.C. And it's not a matter for debate. It is a matter of proven fact.'

There was a long silence. Very slowly, recognition dawned. 'Hell, happen it was, too. Knew I knew him. But that Inspector of yours was damn sure it was Maybury.'

Paddy snorted. 'The only people who are ever damn sure of anything are idiots and politicians. Same difference, some would say.'

They could almost follow Eddie's thought processes in the contortions of his face. 'Still, I don't see it makes much difference. We're back to square one. If it was K.C. she did in this time, then stands to reason she did her old man in ten years ago. The only proof you thought she didn't was that I thought the old guy was him. You follow me?'

'I follow you,' McLoughlin told him. 'But the whole thing stinks. Didn't it occur to you that if it was Maybury this time, then you've been beating up on an innocent woman for ten years?'

'There was her parents – ' He broke off as his brain caught up with his mouth. 'Yeah, well, as I say, we're back to square one now.'

'Anything but. Mrs Maybury didn't kill K.C., Eddie. You did.'

'Cobblers!'

'He wasn't murdered. He died of cold, starvation and self-neglect. You were the last person to see him alive. If you'd offered him a hand he wouldn't be dead now. He needed help, and you didn't give it to him.'

'Now listen here, mister. You trying to set me up or something? The Inspector said he was stabbed in the gut.'

Between the Scylla of Barnes and the Charybdis of Walsh, was it any wonder, thought McLoughlin, that Phoebe had retreated into her fortress? Without a twinge of regret, he rode rough-shod over Walsh's thirty years on the Force. 'The Inspector greased a few palms and was over-promoted,' he said bluntly. 'It happens in the police just as it happens everywhere else. They'll give him early retirement as a result of this cock-up and get shot of him.'

'Jesus!' said Eddie, impressed by so much honesty from a policeman.

'You cretin,' muttered Peter Barnes. 'He's running bloody rings round you.'

McLoughlin ignored him. 'Number four, Eddie,' he went on. 'When you and the scum you associate with come up here for a spot of queer-bashing, you miss the mark. There are no queers living in Streech Grange. Who told you there were?'

'It's common knowledge.' Eddie looked uncomfortable. 'The three dykes. The three witches.

They're always called one or the other.' He darted a quick glance at Peter Barnes. 'Me, I'm not into queer-bashing.'

'I see.' McLoughlin transferred his attention to Barnes. 'So it's you who's not keen on queers.' He yawned suddenly and rubbed his eyes. 'What happened? Someone try it on at that school you went to?' He saw the sudden pinching round the boy's nostrils and his brooding face cracked into a grin. 'Don't tell me you enjoyed it, and now you're busting a gut to prove you didn't.'

'Fucking perverts,' the boy blurted out. 'They make me sick.' He spat at Phoebe. 'Fucking perverts. They should be locked up.' A well of loathing seemed to overflow. 'I hate them.'

Something malignant stirred in the depths of McLoughlin's dark eyes. He took a lightning step forward and clamped his hand across Barnes's mouth, digging his fingers and thumb into the soft flesh of the cheeks and forcing the boy up on to the balls of his feet. 'I find you extremely offensive,' he said softly. 'You're a moronic little psychopath and in my book it's the likes of you who should be locked up, not the likes of Oscar Wilde. The only contribution you will ever make to society will be a negative one when you pass your prejudices and your miserably inadequate IQ to a succeeding generation.' He levered Barnes up another inch. 'In addition it makes me very angry to hear these women referred to as perverts. Do you understand me?'

Barnes tried to speak but the words stuck in his throat. McLoughlin dug his fingers deeper and Barnes nodded vigorously.

'Good.' McLoughlin unlocked his fingers and pushed him away with the heel of his hand. He favoured Staines with a friendly smile. 'I hope you can see where all this is leading, Eddie. You do realise I am giving you the benefit of the doubt. I am assuming you genuinely believed these people were guilty of something.'

Eddie's good-humoured face puckered in worried concentration. 'Listen, mister, I just came along to see justice done. I swear to God that's all I came for.' He waved a hand at the other youths. 'That's all any of us came for. We got the call you were letting her off again. This queer-bashing stuff, that's Peter's kick.' He flicked a shy look at Phoebe and Diana. 'Jesus, it doesn't make sense anyway. If you're not queer, why do you go along with it?'

Diana rolled her eyes to Heaven. 'Do you know, I've often wondered that myself.' She turned to Phoebe. 'I've forgotten, old thing, why do we go along with it?'

Phoebe's rich laugh tumbled from her mouth. 'Don't be such a fool.' She looked at Eddie and raised her hands helplessly. 'We've never had a choice.

Hardly anyone ever speaks to us. Those who do, know all about us. Those who don't, assume whatever they want to assume. You have assumed we're gay.' Her eyes laughed softly. 'Bar copulating naked by the village pond with a series of men, I don't see how we could ever prove we weren't. In any case, would you have thought any better of us if you'd known we preferred men?'

'Yeah,' said Eddie with an appreciative wink. 'I bloody well would. Mind you,' he continued thoughtfully, 'none of this explains what happened to your old man. If the only reason he legged it was because the money'd dried up why didn't he get you off the hook when he read what was happening to you? It only needed a phone call to the police.'

There was an awkward silence.

'You talk as if the man had a clear conscience,' said McLoughlin at last. Out of the corner of his eye he saw the colour drain from Jonathan's set face. Dammit, he thought. Whichever way you turned, you were always caught between the rock and the hard place. 'It's sub judice, Eddie, which is why we've never released details. But I can tell you this, the minute the man re-surfaces he will be prosecuted.' He shrugged. 'For the moment you'll just have to take my word that it suits his book if everyone thinks he's dead. He was a villain. We'll find him one day.'

Even Paddy looked impressed.

'Jesus!' said Eddie again. 'Je – sus!' He scrunched

his foot on some broken glass. 'Listen, lady,' he offered, 'about these windows.' He gestured to the youths behind him. 'We'll clear up and put some new ones in. It's only fair.'

'You can do better than that, Eddie,' said McLoughlin pleasantly. 'It's names we want. Let's start with who attacked Miss Cattrell?'

Eddie shook his head with genuine regret. 'I can guess, same as you can, but if it's proof you need, then I can't help you. Like I said, queer-bashing doesn't turn me on.' He indicated one of his mates. 'Me and Bob took a couple of birds to the flicks that night. I don't know about the rest of them.'

A chorus of denials greeted this statement.

'Not me. I was watching telly with my folks.'

'Jesus, Eddie, I was round your sister's place. You bloody know that.'

'Fuck that. I only heard about it the next morning, same as you.'

Above their heads, McLoughlin caught Paddy's eye and saw his own disappointment mirrored there. The truth had an unmistakable ring about it. 'And what about you?' he asked Peter Barnes, knowing the little bastard would get away with it. 'Where were you?'

Barnes grinned. 'I was with my mother all evening until half-past midnight. Then I went to bed. She'll sign a statement if you ask her nicely.' He raised his middle finger and jabbed it in the air at Paddy. 'That's to you and your beggar crap, shithead.' He giggled and crooked his arm over his other fist, thrusting the finger skyward. 'And that's to your pathetic little set-up. What a joke. It was so fucking transparent, a blind man could have seen through it. You think I haven't creepy-crawled this place, seen the tame fuzz they've got watching over them?' He giggled again.

Alarm bells rang in McLoughlin's head. What the hell sort of psychopath was this boy? A Charles Manson freak? Je – sus! 'Creepy-crawled', he knew, was an expression the Charles Manson Family had used to describe the way they had entered Sharon Tate's house before they murdered her. 'So what brought you up here?' he asked, loosing some handcuffs from his jacket pocket. 'Gives you a buzz, does it, being arrested?'

'It sure as hell gives me a buzz to see you cretins screw up. That's got to be worth a slapped wrist and a fine any day. Hell, it was a bit of high spirits. Dad'll ante-up for the damage.'

There was a moment of silence before Jonathan's cool voice spoke from the shattered window. 'That seems reasonable,' he said. 'In return, I'll ante-up for the damage I'm going to do to you.'

It was the element of surprise that held everyone frozen. Like a slow motion sequence they watched him cross the room, release the safety catch on his mother's shotgun, shove the barrel between Barnes's legs and pull the trigger. The explosion left them deaf. Through a dense cloud of dust they saw, rather than heard, the screams that issued from the boy's writhing mouth. They watched the pool of liquid collect on the floor at his feet.

McLoughlin, stunned, tried to intervene, only to find a pair of thick arms clamped around his chest, holding him back. 'Jon!' he yelled, his voice muffled by the ringing echoes in his ears. 'For God's sake! He's not worth it!'

'Leave him be, sir.' It was Fred's voice. 'He's waited a long time for this.'

Shocked beyond belief, McLoughlin watched Jonathan Maybury drive Peter Barnes against the wall and ram the shotgun into the boy's screaming mouth.

Twenty-Five

GAP-TOOTHED WHERE the windows yawned, its finery ruffled by birdshot, the old house slumbered on, a silent witness to many worse things in its four-hundred-year history. Within half an hour, three patrol cars had arrived to ferry the culprits to the Station with PC Gavin Williams in firm but reluctant charge. 'It's down to you, Sarge,' he protested. 'You should be taking them in.'

'*Nn-nn*. They're all yours. I've some unfinished business here.'

'What do I do about Maybury, Sarge?'

McLoughlin folded his arms and didn't say anything.

'Barnes is bound to mention it.'

'Let him.'

'Shouldn't we charge Maybury?'

'What with? Accidental discharge of a licensed firearm?'

'You'll never get away with that. Eddie, for one, knows it wasn't an accident.'

McLoughlin was amused. 'I think you'll find Eddie's somewhat disenchanted with Peter Barnes. Apart from anything else, he doesn't take kindly to being set up as a fall-guy for Barnes's warped sense of humour. He tells me he and his mates were looking the other way when the accident happened.'

Williams looked worried. 'What do I say?'

'That's up to you, Gavin. I can't help you I'm afraid. When the gun went off, I had my back turned, taking down the names and addresses of the intruders. After that I couldn't see anything for dust.'

'Hell, Sarge!'

'I thought you were taking down the names and addresses of all the witnesses to the vandalism. It's standard police procedure in incidents of this sort.'

The constable pulled a wry face. 'And how do you explain Barnes's confession? I mean if it was just an accident why would he want to stitch himself up? Jesus, Sarge, he was so bloody terrified, he was pissing all over the floor.'

McLoughlin clapped him amiably on the shoulder. 'Is that right, Gavin? I couldn't see a damn thing because of the dust in my eyes. So don't ask me what loosened his tongue, because I couldn't tell you, unless it was the shock of the gun going off. Explosions react on people in different ways. Left me temporarily blinded but with my ears working overtime. Some sort of compensation effect, I imagine.

Couldn't see worth a damn, but I heard every word the little weasel said.'

Williams shook his head. 'I was in a blue funk. I thought the doctor shot his balls off.'

So did I, thought McLoughlin. So did I. And so it seemed had Peter Barnes. Swept back by the violence of Jonathan's assault and numbed by the blast of the shotgun between his legs which had discharged itself harmlessly into Phoebe's drawing-room wall, he had burst into tears of self-pity as Jonathan rammed the barrel against his teeth and threatened to pull the second trigger. 'I didn't mean to do it,' he babbled. 'I was creepy-crawling the house. I didn't mean to do it. I didn't mean to do it,' he screamed. 'She came back. The silly bitch came back. I had to hit her.'

Jonathan's finger whitened on the trigger. 'Now tell me about nine years ago.'

'Oh, God, help me! Somebody help me!' The front of his trousers was saturated with urine.

'TELL ME!' roared Jonathan, his face white and drawn with rage. 'Someone ransacked this house. WHO WAS IT?'

'It was my dad,' the boy screamed, sobbing convulsively. 'He got drunk with some friends.' His eyes widened alarmingly as Jonathan started to squeeze the trigger. 'It's not my fault. Mum's always giggling about it. It's not my fault. It was my dad.' His eyes rolled into the back of his head and he collapsed on the floor.

Jonathan lowered the gun and looked across at McLoughlin. 'We never knew who it was. Mum, Jane and I locked ourselves in the cellar and waited till they'd gone. I have never been so frightened in my life. We could hear them shouting and breaking all the furniture. I thought they were going to kill us.' He shook his head and looked down at the twitching boy. 'I swore I'd make them pay if I ever found out who they were. They used the house as a toilet and wrote "Murdering Bitch" all over the walls in tomato ketchup. I was only eleven. I thought it was blood.' His jaw tightened.

McLoughlin shook off Fred's bear hug and started to slap the dust out of his clothes. 'That was a hell of a close shave, Jon. What happened, for God's sake? Did you trip on some broken glass or something?'

'That's it, Sergeant,' said Fred impassively. 'I was watching. Could have been quite nasty if young Jon hadn't kept his wits about him.'

'Yes, well, do something with the flaming thing before it goes off again.' He watched Fred take the gun, break it open and remove the second cartridge. 'Oh, for Christ's sake, Barnes, get up and stop belly-aching. You're damn lucky Dr Maybury had the good sense to keep the barrel down.' He hauled him to his feet and snapped on the handcuffs. 'You're under arrest. Constable Williams will read you your rights.'

The boy was still sobbing. 'He tried to kill me.'

'There's gratitude for you,' said Paddy, shaking

plaster from his hair. 'Jon nearly blows his own foot off to protect the little scum and all he can do is accuse him.' He looked at Jonathan's stricken face, saw the obvious danger signals, and glanced across at Fred with a Gary Lineker finger to eye gesture.

Calmly Fred took the boy's arm and steered him towards the door into the hall. 'I suggest we check on the rest of the house, sir. I don't like the idea of Miss Cattrell alone upstairs.' He closed the door firmly behind them.

Half an hour, thought McLoughlin, and it seemed more like a year. He smoothed the stubble on his jaw and stared thoughtfully at the young constable. 'I can't help you, Gavin. You're a good copper and it's not my place to tell you what to do. You must make your own decision.'

The young man glanced through the drawing-room door where Fred was helping Phoebe restore order. 'I agreed to do the patrols with you because of him and the old lady really. They're decent folks. Seemed wrong to abandon them to yobbos.'

'I agree,' said McLoughlin dryly.

He frowned. 'If you want my opinion, the Chief Inspector's got some explaining to do on this one. You should hear what Molly has to say about when she and Fred first came here. The house had been totally vandalised. Mrs Maybury and the two kids were living in one bedroom which Miss Cattrell and the lad, Jonathan, had managed to clean up. According to Molly, Mrs Maybury and Jane were so shell-shocked by the whole thing they didn't know if they were coming or going. Molly says you could still smell the piss even after three months, and the mould on the tomato ketchup had started to grow inwards, into the walls. It took them weeks to scrub the place clean. What's the Chief got against them, Sarge? Why wouldn't he believe them?'

Because, thought McLoughlin, he couldn't afford to. It was Walsh himself who, all those years ago, had created the climate of hate in which this woman and her two young children could be terrorised. For him, and for whatever reason, Phoebe had always been guilty, and his prolonged and hostile hounding of her had led inevitably to others meting out justice when he failed to prove it himself. 'He's a small man, Gavin,' was all he said.

'Well, I don't like it and I'm going to say something. It's not what I joined the Force for. I asked Molly why they didn't call the police in when it happened, and do you know what she said? "Because madam knew better than to ask help from the enemy."' He scuffed his foot shyly against the floor. 'I'm planning to take Molly and Fred around and about a bit, no fuss, nothing like that, but I'd like them to know we're not all enemies.'

McLoughlin smiled down on the bent head. If

Williams wanted to wrap up his affection in the guise of community policing, that was fine with him. 'I'm told she makes a damn good lardy cake.'

'Bloody brilliant!' The young eyes sparkled. 'You should try some.'

'I will.' He pushed the lad towards the front door and the waiting cars. 'It won't do Eddie and his mates any harm to spend the night in a police cell, so book 'em and lock 'em up. If Mrs Maybury wants to press charges in the morning, then we'll fill out all the sheets then. But I don't think she will. She laid the first stone of a bridge this evening.'

'And Barnes?'

'Keep him on ice for me. I'll be in first thing tomorrow morning. I'll take his statement myself. And Gavin?'

'Yes?'

'He would have talked anyway. He couldn't have resisted it. He's too arrogant to keep quiet for long. You'll see. Tomorrow, without any pressure from me, he'll give us the whole works.'

A weight seemed to drop from the lad's shoulders. 'Yeah. Anything else I should do?'

'Bell his parents in a couple of hours, three o'clock, say, tell them we're holding their son, and get them down to the Station. But, whatever you do, don't let them talk to him. Keep them waiting through the dark hours till I get there. Just tell them he's confessed to ten years of persecution. I want them softened up.'

Williams looked doubtful. 'You'll never get a prosecution after ten years, will you?'

'No.' McLoughlin grinned. 'But for a few hours, I can sure as hell make them think I will.'

Paddy was another who took his leave reluctantly. 'You'll have to come out of retreat now,' he told Phoebe and Diana. 'One way and another the door's been forced. It's a damn good thing too. It's time you made a bit of an effort. Come down to the pub tomorrow. It's as good a place as any to start.' He shook hands with McLoughlin. 'Jack in the job, Andy, and join me in starting a brewery. It'll need a strong hand at the helm.'

'I don't know the first thing about brewing.'

'I wouldn't want you for your brewing skills. That's my province. Organise the business, find me customers, get the whole thing rolling. You'd be good at that. I need someone I can trust.'

McLoughlin grinned. 'You mean someone Customs and Excise trusts? You're too anarchic for me, Paddy. I'd be a nervous wreck in three months, trying to remember what I was supposed to be hiding.'

Paddy gave a roar of laughter and punched him on the shoulder. 'Think about it, old son. I enjoy your company.' He left.

Jonathan had retreated to an armchair where he sat in embarrassed silence, studiously avoiding everyone's gaze. His anger had long since abated and he was desperately trying to come to terms with what he had done to Peter Barnes. He could find no excuses for his violence. Fred coughed politely. 'If there's nothing more I can do, madam,' he said to Phoebe, 'I'll be heading back to the Lodge. The wife and young Jane will be wondering how we got on.' Jane had been sleeping at the Lodge with Molly for the past few nights while Fred patrolled the grounds with McLoughlin and PC Williams.

'Oh, Fred,' said Phoebe with genuine contrition, 'I'm so sorry. I am so sorry. I never really thought you were one of them. It was the shock. You do believe that, don't you? I'll take you down for your tetanus tomorrow.'

Fred looked at his bandaged hand, washed, disinfected, cried over and dressed by Phoebe and Diana amidst a welter of apology. 'I think, madam,' he said severely, 'that if one more word is said on this matter I shall be forced to give in my notice. I can stand a lot of things, but I can't stand fuss. Is that understood? Good. Now, if you will excuse me?'

'I'll drive you,' said Phoebe immediately.

'I'd rather the young doctor drove me, if that's all right. There's something I'd like his opinion on.'

The door closed behind them.

Phoebe turned away to hide the dampness in her eyes. 'God broke the mould after He made Fred and Molly,' she said gruffly. 'They never deserved any of this and yet they've stuck with us through thick and thin. I've made up my mind, Di,' she went on fiercely,

'I will brave that wretched pub tomorrow. Someone's got to make the first move and it might as well be me. Fred's been going there for years and no one, apart from Paddy, ever talks to him. I'm damn well going to do something about it.'

Diana looked at her friend's furious face. 'What, for instance? Hold your shotgun on them till they agree to talk?'

Phoebe laughed. 'No. I am going to let bygones be bygones.'

'Well, in that case, I'll come with you.' She looked at McLoughlin. 'Can we do that? It's all over now, isn't it? The Inspector was very curt over the phone but he seems to have absolved us.'

He nodded. 'Yes, you're absolved.'

'Was it suicide?' asked Phoebe.

'I doubt it. He was a confused old man whose memories of Streech survived all his other memories. I think he made his way back here, looking for somewhere to die.'

'But how could he possibly have known where the ice house was?'

'From the pamphlets your husband had printed. If you're touting for tourists, a garage is the obvious place to leave them. On paper, K.C. probably knew this garden better than you did.'

'Still. To remember it after all this time.'

'But the memory is like that,' said Diana. 'Old people remember every detail of their childhood but can't remember what they had for breakfast.' She shook her head. 'I never knew the man but I've always felt very bitter about what happened to Phoebe's parents and the lies he told afterwards. Still' – she shrugged – 'to die like that, alone and with nothing. It's very sad. It may sound silly, but I wish he hadn't taken his clothes off. It makes it worse, somehow, as if he were pointing out the futility of living. Naked we're born and naked we die. I have this awful feeling that, for him, everything that happened in between was worthless.'

McLoughlin stretched. 'I wouldn't get too sentimental about that, if I were you, Mrs Goode. We've only Wally's word for it that the corpse was nude. I think he's probably a little ashamed of himself. There's a world of difference between taking some unwanted, folded clothes and undressing a corpse to rob it.' He looked at his watch. 'Anything else?'

'We'd like to thank you,' said Phoebe.

'What for?'

'Everything. Jane. Jonathan. Anne. Us.'

He nodded and made for the door into the hall. The two women looked at each other.

'You will be coming back, won't you?' said Diana in a rush.

He laughed quietly. 'If I have to, I will.'

'What's that supposed to mean?'

Phoebe chuckled. 'I think it means that he wasn't

planning on leaving. He can't come back if he's never gone, can he?'

The gun-shot and shouting had dragged Anne from a deep barbiturate-induced sleep to a lighter sleep where dreams enacted themselves in glorious Technicolor. There were no nightmares, just an endless parade of places and faces, some only half-remembered, which fluttered across the screen of her sleeping mind in surrealistic juxtaposition. And, somewhere, irritatingly, McLoughlin was tapping the double-glazing in the windows of a huge citadel and telling her it needed two people to lift it if they weren't to be buried alive.

She sat up with a start and looked at him. Her bedside light was on. 'I dreamt that Jon and Lizzie were getting married,' she said, isolating the one memory from the cloud of others which vanished for ever.

He pulled up the wicker chair and sat on it. 'Given time and room to breathe, perhaps they will.'

She thought about that. 'You don't miss much, do you?'

'That depends. We've caught your assailant.' He stretched out his long legs and gave her all the details. 'Paddy wants me to join him in starting a brewery.'

She smiled. 'Do you like him?'

'He's a bastard.'

'But do you like him?'

He nodded. 'He's his own man. I like him very much.'

'Will you join him?'

'I shouldn't think so. It would be too easy to get addicted to that Special of his.' He looked at her through half-closed lids. 'Jon's going back to London tomorrow. He asked me to find out if you wanted your love letters returned. He says he can try and fish them out before he goes.'

She looked at her hands. 'Do you know where he's put them?'

'I gather they're in a fissure in the old oak tree behind the ice house. He's a little worried about whether or not he can retrieve them. He asked me to give him a hand.' He studied her face. 'Should I, Cattrell?'

'No. Let them stay there.' She raised her head to look at him. 'When I'm firing on all cylinders again I'll take some cement and stick it into every crack in the oak tree so the damn things never see the light of day again. I had to ask Jon to hide them – he was the only one there when Walsh took me away – but he's the last person in the world I want looking at them. Oh God, I wish they *were* love letters.' She fell silent.

'What are they?'

'Photographs.'

'Of David Maybury?' She nodded. 'After Phoebe

had killed him?' She nodded again. 'One of your famous insurance policies, I suppose.'

She sighed. 'I never thought we'd get away with it. I kept a record in case the body was found and Phoebe needed a defence.' Her face clouded. 'I developed them myself. Awful, awful pictures, showing David two weeks after Phoebe killed him, showing Phoebe herself, looking so damn mad you wouldn't believe it was the same woman, showing what the vandals did to the house, showing the tomb I built in the cellar. I never want to see them again.'

'Tell me, Anne.'

She took a deep breath. 'David came back the night after the house had been ransacked. It was inevitable he would turn up some time, but to choose that night – ' She shook her head. 'Not that he knew, of course. He wouldn't have come back if he'd known. The doors were barred with stacked-up furniture, so he came in through the cellar window. Phoebe was in the kitchen and she heard him stumbling around in the dark downstairs.' Her eyes searched his. 'You must understand how frightened she was. She thought the drunks had come back to kill her and the children.'

'I do understand.'

'She picked up the heaviest thing she could find, the wood-chopping axe by the Aga, and when he came through the cellar door she split his head in two.'

'Did she recognise him?'

'You mean, did she know it was David when she killed him? I shouldn't think so. It all happened too fast. She certainly recognised him afterwards.'

There was a long silence. 'You could have brought the police in then,' he said at last. 'With the evidence of what had happened the night before, she could have pleaded self-defence. She would have got off with no trouble at all.'

She stared at her hands. 'I would have done if I'd known about it. But Jon didn't phone me for a fortnight.' She raised her hands to her eyes to block out the nightmare pictures. 'Phoebe has absolutely no recollection of that two-week period. The only thing she had the sense to do before she went into shock was to shove David's body back down the cellar steps and bolt the door. The children have never known about it. Jon only phoned me because for two weeks she had kept them all locked in her bedroom, living on a diet of tinned food that she'd rescued from the larder. He took the key while she was asleep, let himself out of the bedroom and kept ringing my number till I answered.' Tears welled in her eyes, spilling over her tired lids, as she remembered. 'He was only eleven, hardly more than a baby really, and he said he was doing his best but he thought Jane and Mummy needed a proper person to look after them.' She dashed the tears from her eyes. 'Oh God, I'm sorry. It just makes me cry every time I think of it. He must have been so frightened. I came straight down.'

She looked suddenly very tired. 'I couldn't possibly go to the police, McLoughlin. She was completely off her head and Jon and Jane would hardly speak. I thought Phoebe had vandalised the house herself *after* killing David. There was no way of proving which came first. And if I thought that, what the hell conclusion would Walsh have come to? It was a nightmare. All I could think of doing was to put the children before everything else, because that is what Phoebe's father had asked me to do when he set up the trust. And putting them first, I decided, meant keeping their mother out of a prison hospital.' She sighed. 'So, over a period of days, I bought small quantities of grey stone from DIY shops all over South Hampshire. I had to be able to fit it in Phoebe's car. I didn't dare get anyone to deliver. Then I locked myself in the cellar and bricked that revolting, stinking mess that had once been David behind a fake wall.' She gagged on bile. 'He's still there. The wall has never been disturbed. Diana went down and checked after Fred found that thing in the ice house. We were so afraid he had somehow got out.'

'Does Fred know?'

'No. Only Diana, Phoebe and I.'

'And Phoebe knows what she did?'

'Oh, yes. It took a while, but she remembered it all

in the end. She wanted to confess about four years ago, but we persuaded her out of it. Jane at fourteen was down to four and a half stone. Diana and I said her peace of mind was more important than Phoebe's.' She took another deep breath. 'It meant we've never been able to sell the Grange, of course. Sod's Law predicts that whoever buys it will want to rip the guts out of the cellar to put in a jacuzzi.' She smiled faintly. 'At times it has been quite unbearable. But when I look at the three of them now, I know it was all worth it.' Her damp eyes pleaded for a reassurance she would never put into words.

He took one of her hands. 'What can I say, woman? Except that next time I tell you how to run your life, remind me that you know best.' He played with her fingers, pulling at them. 'I could use your photographs of the house to smash Walsh and Barnes for what they've done to Phoebe.'

'No,' she said immediately. 'No one knows they exist, except you and me. Phoebe and Diana don't know. Let's leave them where they are. I see death too often in my nightmares as it is. Phoebe wouldn't want it, anyway. Walsh was right. She did kill David.'

He nodded and looked away. It was a while before he spoke. 'My wife came back to me tonight.'

She forced herself to smile. 'Are you glad?'

'As a matter of fact I am.' She tried to extract her hand tactfully from his, but he wouldn't let her.

'Then I'm pleased for you. Will it work this time, do you think?'

'Oh, yes. I'm toying with the idea of leaving the police force. What do you think?'

'It'll make things easier at home. The divorce rate amongst policemen is phenomenal.'

'Forget the practicalities. Advise me, for myself.'

'I can't,' she said. 'It's something you will have to decide for yourself. All I can say is that, whatever decision you come to, make sure it's one you can live with.' She looked at him shyly. 'I was mistaken before, you know. I think you were probably right to go into the police, and I think the police would be the poorer without you.'

He nodded. 'And you? What will you do now?'

She smiled brightly. 'Oh, the usual. Storm a few citadels, seduce a sculptor or two.'

He grinned. 'Well, before you do that, will you give me a hand in the cellar one night? I think it's time that wall came down, and David Maybury left this house for good. Don't worry. It won't be unpleasant. After nine years there will be very little left and this time we'll get rid of him properly.'

'Wouldn't it be better to leave well alone?'

'No.'

'Why not?'

'Because, Cattrell, if Phoebe isn't freed of him, you and Diana will be tied to this house for ever.'

She looked into a private darkness beyond him. How little he understood. They would always be tied now. It had been too long. They had lost the confidence to start again.

He gave her fingers a last squeeze and stood up. 'I'd better make tracks for bed then.'

She nodded, her eyes over-bright. 'Goodbye, McLoughlin. I wish you luck, I really do.'

He scratched the side of his face. 'I suppose you couldn't lend me a pillow? And maybe a toothbrush from the bathroom?'

'What for?'

'I've got nowhere to sleep, woman. I told you, my wife came back. I'm damned if I'm spending another seven years with someone whose favourite colour is beige. I walked out.' He watched her smile. 'I thought I'd shack up with a friend this time.'

'What sort of friend?'

'Oh, I don't know. How about a cynical, selfish intellectual snob, who can't sustain relationships, doesn't conform and embarrasses people?'

She laughed quietly. 'It's all true.'

'Of course it is. We've a lot in common. It's not a bad description of me either.'

'You'd hate living here.'

'About as much as you do, probably. How does Glasgow sound?'

'What would we do there?'

'Explore, Cattrell, explore.'

Her eyes danced. 'Are you going to take no for an answer, McLoughlin?'

'No.'

'Well what the hell are you waiting for then?'

THE ECHO

Minette Walters

'It was the smell that Mrs Powell noticed first. Slightly sweet. Slightly unpleasant . . . It shocked her badly to find a dead man in the corner, his head slumped on his knees.'

Who was Billy Blake, other than a homeless alcoholic who wandered the streets? Why was he found dead from starvation in one of the richest areas of one of the richest capitals in the world? And why did he die in the garage of wealthy architect Amanda Powell, without once calling for her help?

Having thwarted press interest at the time, six months on from the bizarre tragedy Amanda is suddenly eager to talk to journalist Michael Deacon. She seems to have developed a strange obsession with her dead visitor, and Deacon's curiosity – both about her and her motives in trying to establish Billy's true identity – is intense.

But Deacon's interest in Billy Blake has more to do with forgotten echoes in his own life than in the moralistic stance taken by Amanda Powell – a woman whose wealth can only be explained if her husband is dead . . .

The Echo is available in Pan Books
paperback priced £6.99

What follows here is an early scene from the novel.

MRS POWELL was certainly immaculately groomed but she was twenty years short of late fifties. She was also far too controlled ever to display the sorts of emotion that Lisa was hoping for. She greeted them with a brisk, professional courtesy before showing them into an impeccable sitting-room which smelt of rose-petal pot-pourri and had the clean, spare look of designer minimalism. She clearly liked space, and Deacon rather approved of the cream leather and chrome chairs and sofa that formed an island about a low glass coffee table in the middle of a russet-coloured carpet. Beyond them an expanse of window, framed by draped but undrawn curtains, looked across the Thames to the lights on the other side. There was very little else in the room: only a series of glass shelves above tinted glass cabinets which clearly contained a stereo system; and three canvases – one white, one grey and one black – which adorned the wall opposite the shelves.

He nodded towards them. 'What are they called?'

'The title's in French. *Gravure à la manière noire.*' It means mezzotint in English. They're by Henri Benoit.'

'Interesting,' he said, glancing at her, although it

wasn't clear if he was referring to the canvases or to the woman herself.

In fact he was thinking that her taste in interior design sat rather oddly with her choice of house. It was an uninteresting brick box on a new estate in the Isle of Dogs which would probably be billed in estate agents' jargon as 'an exclusive development of detached executive homes with views of the river'. He guessed the house to be about five years old, with three bedrooms and two reception rooms, and put its value at well outside an average price range. But why, he wondered, would an obviously wealthy woman with interesting taste choose something so characterless when, for the equivalent money, she could have had a spacious flat anywhere in the heart of London? Perhaps she liked detached houses, he thought rather cynically. Or views of the river. Or perhaps *Mr* Powell had chosen it.

'Do sit down,' she said gesturing towards the sofa. 'Can I get you something to drink?'

'Thank you,' said Lisa, who'd taken an instant dislike to her. 'Black coffee would be nice.' In the scheme of feminine competition, Mrs Powell oozed success. She appeared to have everything – even femininity – and Lisa looked around for something to criticize.

'Mr Deacon?'

'Do you have anything stronger?'

'Of course. Whisky, brandy, beer?'

'Red wine?' he suggested hopefully.

'I've a 1984 Rioja open. Would that do?'

'It would. Thank you very much.'

Mrs Powell disappeared down the corridor and they heard her filling the kettle in the kitchen.

'What's with black coffee, Smith,' murmured Deacon, 'when there's alcohol on offer?'

'I thought we were supposed to be behaving ourselves,' she whispered. 'And, for Christ's sake, don't start smoking. There are no ashtrays. I've already looked. I don't want you putting her back up before she agrees to the photographs.'

He watched her critical appraisal of the room. 'What's the verdict?'

'JP was right about everything except her age and her husband. *She*'s the stockbroker. I'll bet the Mrs is a courtesy title to give her some status in a male-dominated world. There's no sign of a man living here. It's all too uncomfortable and it doesn't half stink of roses. She probably sprayed the room before we arrived.' She turned her mouth down. 'I hate women who do that. It's a kind of one-upmanship. They want to prove their house is cleaner than yours.'

He lifted an amused eyebrow. 'Are you jealous?'

'What's to be jealous of?' she hissed.

'Success,' he murmured, holding a finger to his lips as they heard Mrs Powell returning.

'If you want to smoke,' she said, passing a coffee cup to Lisa and a glass of red wine to Deacon, 'I'll find you an ashtray.' She put her own wine glass on the table near an armchair and looked at them both.

'No, thank you,' said Lisa, thinking of JP's instruction.

'Yes, please,' said Deacon, doubting he could stand the scent of rose petals for an hour. He wished Lisa hadn't mentioned them. Once noticed, the smell was cloying, and he was reminded of the second Mrs Deacon who had plundered his very mediocre fortune in order to dowse herself in Chanel No. 5. It had been the shorter of his two marriages, lasting a mere three years before Clara had cleared off with a twenty-year-old toyboy and rather too much of her husband's capital. He took the china saucer Mrs Powell handed him, then placed a cigarette between his lips and lit it. The smell of burning tobacco immediately swamped the roses, and Deacon felt guilt and satisfaction in equal measures. He left the cigarette jutting from his mouth as he took a tape recorder and a notebook from his pocket and placed them on the table in front of him. 'Do you mind if I record what you say?'

'No.'

He set the tape in motion and reluctantly broached the subject of photographs. 'We'd like a small visual to accompany the piece, Mrs Powell, so have you any objections to Lisa photographing you?'

She stared at him as she sat down. 'Why would you want photographs of me if you're planning to write about Billy Blake, Mr Deacon?'

Why indeed? 'Because in the absence of pictures of Billy, which we've established don't exist,' he lied, transferring the cigarette to the ashtray, 'I'm afraid you're the next best thing. Is that a problem for you?'

'Yes,' she said flatly. 'I'm afraid it is. I've already told you I have no intention of being used by your magazine.'

'And, as I told you, Mrs Powell, I don't make a habit of using people.'

She had ice-blue eyes which reminded him of his mother's, and that was a shame, he thought, because in other respects she was quite attractive. 'Then surely you agree that it's absurd to illustrate an article on poverty and the homeless with a picture of a woman who lives in an expensive house in an expensive part of London.' She paused for a moment, inviting him to speak. When he didn't she went on: 'In fact, there *are* pictures of Billy Blake. I have two which I'm prepared to lend you. One is a mugshot from when he was first arrested and the other was taken in the mortuary. Either would illustrate poverty better than a photograph of me.'

Deacon shrugged but didn't say anything.

'You said you were interested in Billy.'

She sounded put out, he thought, and that made him curious, for he'd been a journalist long enough to recognize that Mrs Powell was keener to tell her story than he was to hear it. *But why now, when she had refused to talk to the press at the time?* That question intrigued him. 'No pictures of you, no story, I'm afraid,' he said, reaching forward to switch off the tape. 'Editor's instructions. I'm sorry to have wasted your time, Mrs Powell.' He looked with regret at his untouched wine. 'And your Rioja.'

She watched him as he began to gather his bits and pieces together, clearly weighing something in her mind. 'All right,' she said abruptly, 'you can take your photographs. Billy's story needs to be told.'

'Why?' He shot the word at her as he depressed the record button a second time.

It was a question she had prepared for. The words came out so fluently that he was sure she'd rehearsed the answer in advance. 'Because we're in terrible trouble as a society if we assume that any man's life is so worthless that the manner of his death is the only interesting thing about him.'

'That's a fine sentiment,' he said mildly, 'but hardly very newsworthy. People die in obscurity all the time.'

'But why starve to death? Why here? Why does nobody know anything about him? Why had he told the police he was twenty years older than he actually was?' She searched his face intently. 'Aren't you at all curious about him?'

Of course! Curiosity wormed like a maggot in his brain, but he was far more interested in her than he was in the man who had died in her garage. *Why, for example, did she take Billy's death so personally that she was prepared to be exploited in order to have his story publicized?* 'Are you sure you didn't know him?' he suggested with apparent indifference.

Her surprise was genuine. 'No. Why would I need answers if I'd known him?'

He opened his notebook on his lap, and wrote: *Why does anyone need answers about a complete stranger six months after his death?* 'Which would you prefer,' he asked, 'that Lisa takes her photograph before we talk or while we're talking?'

'While.'

He waited as Lisa unzipped her bag and removed her camera. 'Do you have a Christian name, Mrs Powell?'

'Amanda.'

'Do you prefer Amanda Powell or Mrs Powell?'

'I don't mind.' She frowned into the camera lens.

'A smile would be better,' said Lisa. She snapped the shutter. Click. 'That's great.' Click. 'Could you look at the floor? Good.' Click. 'Keep your eyes cast down. That's really touching.' Click, click.

'Go on, Mr Deacon,' said the woman curtly. 'I'm sure you don't want me to be sick over my own carpet.'

He grinned. 'I prefer Deacon or Mike. How old are you?'

'Thirty-six.'

'What do you do for a job?'

She glanced at him as Lisa took another photograph. 'I'm an architect.'

'On your own or with a firm?'

'I'm with W. F. Meredith.' Click.

Not bad, he thought. Meredith was about as good as you could get. 'What are your political affiliations, Amanda?'

'None.'

'How about off the record?'

She gave a faint smile which Lisa caught. 'The same.'

'Do you vote?' She caught him watching her, and he looked away.

'Of course. Women fought long and hard to give me that right.'

'Are you going to tell me which party you usually vote for?'

'Whichever I think will do the least damage.'

'You seem to have little time for politicians. Is there a particular reason for that or is it just *fin-de-siècle* depression?'

The faint smile again as she reached for her wine glass. 'Personally, I'd hesitate to qualify a huge abstract concept like *fin-de-siècle* depression with "just", but for the purpose of your article it's as truthful as anything else.'

He wondered what it would be like to kiss her. 'Are you married at the moment, Amanda?'

'Yes.'

'What does your husband do?'

She raised the glass to her lips, momentarily forgetting the camera lens pointing at her, then lowered it with a frown as Lisa took another photograph. 'My husband wasn't here when I found the body,' she said, 'so what he does is irrelevant.'

Deacon caught the look of amused cynicism on Lisa's face. 'It's human interest,' he countered lightly. 'People will want to know what sort of man a successful architect is married to.'

Perhaps she realized that his curiosity was personal, or perhaps, as Lisa had guessed, there *was* no Mr Powell. In either case, she refused to expand on the matter. 'It was I who found the body,' she repeated, 'and you have my details already. Shall we continue?'

The pale eyes, so like his mother's, rested on Deacon's craggy face too long for comfort, and his mild fantasy about kissing her shifted from harmless fun to sadistic revenge. He could imagine what JP's reaction was going to be to the paucity of information that he'd managed to drag out of her so far. *Name, rank and number*. And he had little optimism that the photographs would be any better. Her features were so controlled that she might as well be a poker-faced prisoner of war backed against a wall. He wondered if fires had ever burned in her cool little face, or if her life had been entirely passionless. Predictably, the idea excited him.

'All right,' he agreed, 'let's talk about finding the

body. You said you were shocked. Can you describe the experience for me? What sort of thoughts went through your mind when you saw him?'

'Disgust,' she said, careful to keep her voice neutral. 'He was behind a stack of empty boxes in the corner and he'd covered himself in an old blanket. The smell was really quite awful once I'd pulled it away from him. Also, his body fluids had seeped out all over the floor.' Her mouth tightened in sudden distaste and she blinked as the flash of the camera stung her eyes. 'Afterwards, when the police told me that he'd died of self-neglect and malnutrition, I kept wondering why he'd made no attempt to save himself. It wasn't just that I found him beside my chest freezer' – she gestured unhappily towards the window – 'everyone's so affluent on this estate that even the dustbins have perfectly edible food in them.'

'Any ideas?'

'Only that he was so weak by the time he found my garage that he hadn't the energy to do more than crawl into the corner and hide himself.'

'Why would he want to hide?'

She studied him for a moment. 'I don't know. But if he wasn't hiding, why didn't he try to attract my attention? The police think he must have entered the garage on the Saturday, because his only opportunity to get inside when I went to the shops that afternoon and left the doors unlocked for half an hour.' In so far as she was capable of showing emotion, she did. Her hand flicked nervously towards her mouth before she remembered the camera and dropped it abruptly. 'I found his body on the following Friday and the pathologist estimated he'd been dead five days. That means he was alive on the Sunday. I could have helped him if he'd called out and let me know he was there. So why didn't he?'

'Perhaps he was afraid.'

'Of what?'

'Being turned over to the police for trespass.'

She shook her head. 'Certainly not that. He had no fear of the police or of prison. I understand he was arrested quite regularly. Why should this time have been any different?'

Deacon made shorthand notes on his pad to remind himself of the nuances of expression that crossed her face as she talked about Billy. *Anxiety. Concern. Bewilderment even.* Curiouser and curiouser. *What was Billy Blake to her that he could inspire emotion where her husband couldn't?* 'Maybe he was just too weak to attract your attention. Presumably the pathologist can't say if he was conscious on the Sunday?'

'No,' she said slowly, 'but I can. There was a bag of ice-cubes in the freezer. Someone had opened it, and it certainly wasn't me, so I presume it must have been Billy. And one corner of the garage had been urinated in. If he was strong enough to move around the garage, then he was strong enough to bang on the connecting door between the garage and my hall. He must have known I was here that weekend because he could have heard me. The door's not thick enough to block out sound.'

'What did the police make of that?'

'Nothing,' she said. 'It made no difference to the pathologist's verdict. Billy still died of malnutrition whether through wilful self-neglect or involuntary self-neglect.'

He lit another cigarette and eyed her through the smoke. 'How much did the cremation cost you?'

'Does the amount matter?'

'It depends how cynical you believe the average reader to be. He might think you're being coy about the figure because you want everyone to assume you spent more.'

'Five hundred pounds.'

'Which is a great deal more than you would have given him alive?'

She nodded. Click. 'If I'd met him as a beggar in the street, I'd have thought I was being generous if I gave him five pounds.' Click. Click. She glanced with irritation at Lisa, looked as if she were about to say something, then thought better of it. Her face took on its closed expression again.

'You said yesterday that you felt you owed him something. What exactly?'

'Respect, I suppose.'

'Because you felt he hadn't been shown any in life?'

'Something like that,' she admitted. 'But it sounds ridiculously sentimental when it's put into words.'

He wrote for a moment. 'Do you have a religion?'

She turned away as another flash exploded in her eyes. 'Surely she's taken enough by now?'

Lisa kept the camera lens on her face. 'Just a couple more shots with the eyes cast down, Amanda.' Click. 'Yes, that's really nice, Amanda.' Click. 'More compassion maybe.' Click. 'Great, Amanda.' Click, click, click.

Deacon watched increasing irritatioin gather in the woman's eyes. 'All right, Smith. Let's call a halt, shall we?'

'How about a few more in the garage?' suggested the girl, reluctant to waste the end of film. 'It won't take a minute.'

Mrs Powell stared into the blood-red depths of her glass before taking a sip. 'Be my guest,' she said without raising her head. 'The keys are on the table in the hall, and the light comes on automatically when the garage door is lifted. I don't use the connecting door any more.'

'I meant a few more of you,' said Lisa. 'I'll need you to come with me. If it's cold and damp out there, a few atmospheric shots could be really good. More in tune with a wino dying of starvation.'

The woman's stillness following this remark persuaded Lisa she hadn't been listening. She tried again.

'Five minutes, Amanda, that's all we'll need. You might like to stand near where you found him, look a bit upset, that sort of thing.'

The only sound in the room was the ticking of a clock on the mantelpiece, and it grew louder as Mrs Powell's silence lengthened. She seemed to Deacon to be waiting for something, and he held his breath and waited with her. It startled him to hear her speak. 'I'm sorry,' she said to the girl, 'but you and I are very different animals. I could no more pose weepy-eyed over where Billy died than I could wear your fuck-me clothes or your fuck-me make-up. You see, I'm neither so vulgar nor so desperate to be noticed.'

There were too many sibilants in the last sentence, and her careful diction abandoned her. With a slight shock, Deacon realized she was drunk.

CRITICAL ACCLAIM FOR

Minette Walters

The Ice House

'Terrific first novel with a high Rendellesque frisson count'
The Times

The Sculptress

'A devastatingly effective novel' *Observer*

The Scold's Bridle

'A gothic puzzle of great intricacy and psychological power'
Sunday Times

The Dark Room

'A marvellous, dramatically intelligent novel. It shimmers with suspense, ambiguity and a deep unholy joy' *Daily Mail*

The Echo

'It grips like steel . . . Passion, compassion, intelligence and romance is what Walters offers with no quarter for squeamish cowards' *Mail on Sunday*

The Breaker

'Stands head and shoulders above the vast majority of crime novels . . . Existing fans will love *The Breaker*, new readers will be instant converts' *Express*

The Shape of Snakes

'Breaking all the rules of popular fiction, Minette Walters asks as much of her readers as many literary novelists, and yet she offers them a book as gripping as any thriller' *Times Literary Supplement*

Acid Row

'Humane intelligence enables Walters to twist and turn her plot . . . *Acid Row* is a breathtaking achievement' *Daily Telegraph*

Fox Evil

'*Fox Evil* is the work of a writer at the peak of her confidence and supreme ability' *The Times*

Disordered Minds

'A powerful, acute and vivid work from a staggeringly talented writer' *Observer*

With her debut, *The Ice House*, Minette Walters won the Crime Writers' Association John Creasey Award for the best first crime novel of 1992. Rapidly establishing a reputation as one of the most exciting crime novelists writing today, her second novel, *The Sculptress*, was acclaimed by critics as one of the most compelling and powerful novels of the year and won the Edgar Allan Poe Award for the best crime novel published in America in 1993. In 1994 Minette Walters achieved a unique triple when *The Scold's Bridle* was awarded the CWA Gold Dagger for best crime novel of the year. Her following five novels, *The Dark Room*, *The Echo*, *The Breaker*, *The Shape of Snakes* and *Acid Row* were also published to further critical acclaim throughout the world and her ninth novel, *Fox Evil*, won the 2003 CWA Gold Dagger for Fiction.

Minette Walters lives in Dorset with her husband and two children. Her tenth novel, *Disordered Minds*, was published in 2003, and her latest novel, *The Devil's Feather*, is out now in Macmillan hardcover.

Also by Minette Walters in Pan Books

The Ice House
The Sculptress
The Dark Room
The Echo
The Breaker
The Shape of Snakes
Acid Row
Fox Evil
Disordered Minds
The Tinder Box
The Devil's Feather

MINETTE WALTERS

THE
Scold's Bridle

PAN BOOKS

For Jane, Lisanne, Maria and Hope

First published 1994 by Macmillan

This edition published 1995 by Pan Books
an imprint of Pan Macmillan Ltd
Pan Macmillan, 20 New Wharf Road, London N1 9RR
Basingstoke and Oxford
Associated companies throughout the world
www.panmacmillan.com

Reissued 1998

ISBN 978-0-330-45501-5

Copyright © Minette Walters 1994

The right of Minette Walters to be identified as the author of this work has been asserted by her in accordance with the Copyright, Designs and Patents Act 1988.

All rights reserved. No part of this publication may be reproduced, stored in or introduced into a retrieval system, or transmitted, in any form or by any means (electronic, mechanical, photocopying, recording or otherwise), without the prior written permission of the publisher. Any person who does any unauthorized act in relation to this publication may be liable to criminal prosecution and civil claims for damages.

1 3 5 7 9 8 6 4 2

A CIP catalogue record for this book is available from the British Library.

Typeset by Set Systems Ltd, Saffron Walden, Essex
Printed and bound in Great Britain by
Mackays of Chatham plc, Chatham, Kent

This book is sold subject to the condition that it shall not, by way of trade or otherwise, be lent, resold, hired out, or otherwise circulated without the publisher's prior consent in any form of binding or cover other than that in which it is published and without a similar condition including this condition being imposed on the subsequent purchaser.

Visit **www.panmacmillan.com** to read more about all our books and to buy them. You will also find features, author interviews and news of any author events, and you can sign up for e-newsletters so that you're always first to hear about our new releases.

‘**Scold** *skold*, n. a rude clamorous woman or other’

Chambers English Dictionary

‘**Branks** *brangks*, (Scot.) n.pl., rarely in sing., a scold’s bridle; an instrument of punishment used in the case of scolds, etc., consisting of a kind of iron framework to enclose the head, having a sharp metal gag or bit which entered the mouth and restrained the tongue.’

Oxford English Dictionary

'Create her child of spleen, that it may live
And be a thwart disnatur'd torment to her!
Let it stamp wrinkles in her brow of youth;
With cadent tears fret channels in her cheeks;
Turn all her mother's pains and benefits
To laughter and contempt; that she may feel
How sharper than a serpent's tooth it is
To have a thankless child!'

Shakespeare, *King Lear*

'Forty-two!' yelled Loonquawl. 'Is that all you've got to show for seven and a half million years' work?'

'I checked it very thoroughly,' said the computer, 'and that quite definitely is the answer. I think the problem, to be quite honest with you, is that you've never really known what the question is . . . Once you know what the question is, you'll know what the answer means.'

Douglas Adams, *The Hitch Hiker's Guide to the Galaxy*

The police Sergeant gestured at the pitiful grey head. 'What in God's name is *that* thing?' His voice grated with repugnance.

Sarah waited a moment until she felt her own voice was under control. 'It's a scold's bridle,' she told him, 'a primitive instrument of repression. They were used in the Middle Ages to curb the tongues of nagging women. It's been in Mathilda's family for years. I know it looks awful like that, but she kept it downstairs in the hall over a pot of geraniums. As a decoration it was rather effective.' She raised a hand to her mouth in distress and the policeman patted her shoulder awkwardly. 'They were white geraniums and they poked their heads through the iron framework. Her coronet weeds, she always called them.' She cleared her throat. 'She was rather fine, you know. Very proud, very snobbish, very intolerant and not overly friendly, but she had a brilliant mind for someone who had never been trained to do anything more than keep house and she had a wonderful sense of humour. Dry and incisive.'

'Coronet weeds,' echoed the pathologist thoughtfully. 'As in:

"There with fantastic garlands did she come,
Of crowflowers, nettles, daisies, and long purples,
That liberal shepherds give a grosser name,
But our cold maids do dead men's fingers call them:
There, on the pendent boughs her coronet weeds – "'

'*Hamlet*,' he explained apologetically to the policeman. 'Ophelia's end. I had to learn it for O level. Amazing what you remember as you get older.' He stared at the bath. 'Did Mrs Gillespie know *Hamlet*?'

Sarah nodded unhappily. 'She told me once that her entire education was based on learning chunks of Shakespeare by heart.'

'Well, we're not going to learn much by standing staring at the poor woman,' said the policeman abruptly. 'Unless Ophelia was murdered.'

Dr Cameron shook his head. 'Death by drowning,' he said thoughtfully, 'while of unsound mind.' He glanced at Sarah. 'Was Mrs Gillespie depressed at all?'

'If she was, she never gave any indication of it.'

The policeman, decidedly more uncomfortable in the presence of death than either of the two doctors, ushered Sarah on to the landing. 'Many thanks for your time, Dr Blakeney. I'm sorry we had to subject you to that but as her GP you probably knew her better than most.' It was his turn to sigh. 'They're always the worst. Old people, living alone. Society's rejects. Sometimes it's weeks before they're found.' His mouth turned down in a curve of distaste. 'Very unpleasant. I suppose we're lucky she was found so quickly. Less than forty hours according to Dr Cameron. Midnight Saturday, he estimates.'

Sarah leant her back against the wall and stared across the landing towards Mathilda's bedroom where the open door showed the old oak bed piled high with pillows. There was a strange sense of ownership still, as if her possessions retained the presence that her flesh had lost. 'She wasn't that old,' she protested mildly. 'Sixty-five, no more. These days that's nothing.'

'She looks older,' he said matter-of-factly, 'but then she would, I suppose, with all the blood drained out of her.' He consulted his notebook. 'A daughter, you say, living in

London, and you think a granddaughter at boarding school.'

'Don't Mr and Mrs Spede know?' She had caught a glimpse of them in the library as she came in, grey faces curiously blank from shock, hands clasped tightly together like petrified children. 'They've been coming in twice a week for years. He looks after the garden and she cleans. They must know more about her than anyone.'

He nodded. 'Unfortunately we've had nothing but hysterics out of them since Mrs Spede found the body. We'll be asking round the village, anyway.' He looked towards the bedroom. 'There's an empty bottle of barbiturates on her bedside table beside the remains of a glass of whisky. It looks like a belt and braces job. Whisky for courage, sleeping pills, then the Stanley knife in the bath. Do you still say you wouldn't have expected her to kill herself?'

'Oh, lord, I don't know.' Sarah ran a worried hand through her short dark hair. 'I wouldn't have prescribed barbiturates if I thought there was a chance she'd abuse them, but one can never be certain about these things. And anyway, Mathilda had been taking them for years, they were commonly prescribed once. So yes, I would rule out suicide from what I knew of her, but we had a doctor–patient relationship. She had severe pain with her arthritis and there were nights when she couldn't sleep.' She frowned. 'In any case, there can't have been many of the sleeping pills left. She was due for another prescription this week.'

'Perhaps she was hoarding them,' he said unemotionally. 'Did she ever open her heart to you?'

'I doubt she opened her heart to anyone. She wasn't the type. She was a very private person.' She shrugged. 'And I've only known her – what? – twelve months. I live in Long Upton, not here in Fontwell, so I haven't come across her socially either.' She shook her head. 'There's nothing in her records to suggest a depressive personality. But the trouble is—' She fell silent.

'The trouble is what, Dr Blakeney?'

'The trouble is we talked about freedom the last time I saw her, and she said freedom is an illusion. There's no such thing in modern society. She quoted Rousseau at me, the famous rebel-cry of students in the sixties: "Man was born free, and everywhere he is in chains." There was only one freedom left, according to Mathilda, and that was the freedom to choose how and when to die.' Her face looked bleak. 'But we had conversations like that every time I saw her. There was no reason to assume that one was any different.'

'When was this conversation?'

Sarah sighed heavily. 'Three weeks ago during my last monthly visit. And the awful thing is, I laughed. Even that wasn't a freedom any more, I said, because doctors are so damn scared of prosecution they wouldn't dream of giving a patient the choice.'

The policeman, a large detective nearing retirement, placed a comforting hand on her arm. 'There now, it's nothing to fret about. It was slitting her wrists that killed her, not barbiturates. And the chances are we're looking at murder anyway.' He shook his head. 'I've seen a few suicides one way and another, but I've yet to see an old

woman turn herself into a flower arrangement in her bath. It'll be money that's behind it. We all live too long and the young get desperate.' He spoke with feeling, Sarah thought.

An hour later, Dr Cameron was more sceptical. 'If she didn't do it herself,' he said, 'you'll have the devil's own job proving it.' They had removed the body from the bath and lain it, still with the scold's bridle in place, on plastic sheeting on the floor. 'Apart from the incisions in her wrists there's not a mark on her, bar what one would expect, of course.' He pointed to the lividity above and around the wrinkled buttocks. 'Some post mortem hypostasis where the blood has settled but no bruising. Poor old thing. She didn't put up any sort of a fight.'

Sergeant Cooper leaned against the bathroom doorjamb, drawn to look at the poor grey body, but deeply repulsed by it. 'She couldn't if she was drugged,' he murmured.

Cameron peeled off his gloves. 'I'll see what I can find out for you back at the lab, but my advice is, don't hold your breath. I can't see your Chief Super wasting too much time and resources on this one. It's about as neat as anything I've seen. Frankly, unless something pretty unusual shows up in the post mortem, I'll be recommending a suicide verdict.'

'But what does your gut tell you, Doctor? The nettles are telling mine it was murder. Why would she deliberately sting herself before she died?'

'Self-reproach, probably. Good God, man, there's no logic to this kind of thing. Suicides are hardly in their right mind when they top themselves. Still,' he said thoughtfully,

'I am surprised she didn't leave a note. There's so much of the theatre about this headdress that I'd have expected something by way of explanation.' He began to tuck the plastic sheet about the body. 'Read *Hamlet*,' he suggested. 'The answer's in there, I expect.'

Mr and Mrs Spede hovered in the library like two squat spectres, so unprepossessing and shifty in their appearance that Cooper wondered if they were quite normal. Neither seemed able to meet his gaze and every question required unspoken consultation between them before one would offer an answer. 'Dr Blakeney tells me Mrs Gillespie has a daughter living in London and a granddaughter at boarding school,' he said. 'Can you give me their names and tell me where I can contact them?'

'She kept her papers very neat,' said Mrs Spede eventually, after receiving some sort of permission to speak from her husband. 'It'll all be in the papers.' She nodded towards the desk and an oak filing cabinet. 'In there some place. Very neat. Always very neat.'

'Don't you know her daughter's name?'

'Mrs Lascelles,' said the man after a moment. 'Joanna.' He tugged at his lower lip which drooped oddly as if it had been tugged many times before. With a petulant frown his wife smacked him on the wrist and he tucked the offending hand into his pocket. They were very childlike, thought Cooper, and wondered if Mrs Gillespie had employed them out of compassion.

'And the granddaughter's name?'

'Miss Lascelles,' said Mrs Spede.

'Do you know her Christian name?'

'Ruth.' She consulted with her husband behind lowered lids. 'They're not nice, either of them. The Mrs is rude to Mr Spede about his gardening and the Miss is rude to Jenny about her cleaning.'

'Jenny?' he queried. 'Who's Jenny?'

'Jenny is Mrs Spede.'

'I see,' said Cooper kindly. 'It must have been a terrible shock for you, Jenny, to find Mrs Gillespie in her bath.'

'Oh, it was that,' she howled, grabbing her husband's arm. 'A terrible, terrible shock.' Her voice rose on a wail.

With some reluctance, because he feared an even louder outburst, Cooper took the polythene bag containing the Stanley knife from his pocket and laid it across his broad palm. 'I don't want to upset you any more, but do you recognize this? Is it a knife you've seen before?'

Her lips puckered tragically but she stopped the wailing to nudge her husband into speech. 'The kitchen drawer,' he said. 'It's the one from the kitchen drawer.' He touched the handle through the bag. 'I scratched an h'aitch on it for "house". The one I keep in the shed has a gee on it for "garden".'

Cooper examined the crude 'h' and nodded as he tucked the bag back out of sight into his pocket. 'Thank you. I'll need the one from the garden for comparison. I'll ask an officer to go out with you when we've finished.' He smiled in a friendly way. 'Now, you presumably have keys to the house. May I see them?'

Mrs Spede drew a string from around her neck, revealing a key that had lain within the cleft of her bosom. 'Only me,' she said. 'Jenny had the key. Mr Spede didn't need one for

the garden.' She gave it to Cooper and he felt the warmth of her body seeping into his hand. It repelled him because it was damp and oily with sweat, and this made him feel guilty because he found them both deeply unattractive and knew that, unlike Mrs Gillespie, he could not have tolerated them about his house for even half an hour.

Mathilda Gillespie's nearest neighbours lived alongside her in a wing adjoining the house. At some stage Cedar House must have been one residence, but now a discreet sign indicated the door to Wing Cottage at the western end of the building. Before Cooper knocked on it, he walked along a gravel path to the rear corner and surveyed the patio at the back, neatly bordered by tubs of everlasting pansies, beyond which a clipped box hedge separated this garden from the expanse of lawn and distant trees that belonged to Cedar House. He felt a sudden envy for the occupants. How drear his own small box was by comparison, but then it was his wife who had chosen to live on a modern estate and not he. He would have been happy with crumbling plaster and a view; she was happy with all mod. cons and neighbours so close they rubbed shoulders every day. It was a policeman's lot to give in to a wife he was fond of. His hours were too unpredictable to allow him to impose his own yearning for isolation on a woman who had tolerated his absences with stoical good humour for thirty years.

He heard the door open behind him and turned, producing his warrant card from his breast pocket, to greet the fat elderly man who approached. 'DS Cooper, sir, Dorset police.'

'Orloff, Duncan Orloff.' He ran a worried hand across his wide, rather pleasant face. 'We've been expecting you. Dear me, dear me. I don't mind admitting Jenny Spede's howling is a little difficult to take after a while. Poor woman. She's a good soul as long as nothing upsets her. I can't tell you what it was like when she found Mathilda. She came rushing out of the house screaming like a banshee and set her wretched husband off in sympathy. I realized something dreadful must have happened which is why I phoned your people and an ambulance. Thank God they came quickly and had the sense to bring a woman with them. She was really quite excellent, calmed the Spedes down in record time. Dear me, dear me,' he said again, 'we live such a quiet life. Not used to this sort of thing at all.'

'No one is,' said Cooper. 'You've been told what's happened, I suppose.'

He wrung his hands in distress. 'Only that Mathilda's dead. I kept the Spedes here until the police car arrived – thought it best, really, what with them collapsing in heaps about me – mind you, I wasn't going to let my wife downstairs till it was safe – one can't be certain about things – anyway the uniformed chaps told me to wait until someone came to ask questions. Look, you'd better come in. Violet's in the drawing-room now, not feeling too well in the circumstances, and who can blame her? Frankly, not feeling a hundred per cent myself.' He stood aside to let Cooper enter. 'First door on the right,' he said. He followed the policeman into a cosy, over-furnished room with a television on low volume in the corner, and bent over the prostrate figure of his wife on the sofa. 'There's a Sergeant to see us,' he said, raising her gently to a sitting position

with one hand and using the other to swing her legs to the floor. He lowered his large bulk on to the sofa beside her and gestured Cooper towards an armchair. 'Jenny kept screaming about blood,' he confided unhappily. 'Red water and blood. That's all she said.'

Violet shivered. 'And Jesus,' she whispered. 'I heard her. She said Mathilda was "like Jesus".' She raised a hand to her own bloodless lips. 'Dead like Jesus in blood red water.' Her eyes filled. 'What's happened to her? Is she *really* dead?'

'I'm afraid she is, Mrs Orloff. It's only approximate, but the pathologist estimates the time of death between nine o'clock and midnight on Saturday.' He looked from one to the other. 'Were you here during those three hours?'

'We were here all night,' said Duncan. He was clearly drawn between his own perceived good taste of not asking questions and an overwhelming need to satisfy a very natural curiosity. 'You haven't told us what's happened,' he blurted out. 'It's much, much worse if you don't know what's happened. We've been imagining terrible things.'

'She hasn't been *crucified*, has she?' asked Violet tremulously. 'I said she's probably been crucified, otherwise why would Jenny have said she looked like Jesus?'

'I said someone had tried to clean up afterwards,' said Duncan, 'which is why there's red water everywhere. You hear about it every day, old people being murdered for their money. They do terrible things to them, too, before they kill them.'

'Oh, I do hope she wasn't *raped*,' said Violet. 'I couldn't bear it if they'd raped her.'

Cooper had time to feel regret for this elderly couple who, like so many of their peers, lived the end of their lives

in terror because the media persuaded them they were at risk. He knew better than anyone that statistics proved it was young men aged between fifteen and twenty-five who were the group most vulnerable to violent death. He had sorted out too many drunken brawls and picked too many stabbed and bludgeoned bodies from gutters outside pubs to be in any doubt of that. 'She died in her bath,' he said unemotionally. 'Her wrists were slit. At the moment the pathologist is inclining towards suicide and we are only asking questions to satisfy ourselves that she did in fact take her own life.'

'But Jesus didn't die in his bath,' said Violet in bewilderment.

'She was wearing a scold's bridle on her head with flowers in it. I think perhaps Mrs Spede thought it was a crown of thorns.' It made no sense otherwise, he thought.

'I *hated* that thing. Mathilda was always *very* peculiar about it.' Violet had a habit, Cooper noticed, of emphasizing words she thought important. 'It must have been suicide, then. She wore it when her arthritis was bad. It took her mind off the *pain*, you know. She always said she'd kill herself if it got so bad she couldn't stand it.' She turned tear-filled eyes to her husband. 'Why didn't she call out to us? I'm sure there's *something* we could have done to help.'

'Would you have heard her?' asked Cooper.

'Oh, yes, especially if she was in the bathroom. She could have rattled the pipes. We'd certainly have heard *that*.'

Cooper transferred his attention to Mr Orloff. 'Did you hear anything at all that night?'

Duncan gave the question long and thoughtful consider-

ation. 'Our days are very uneventful,' he said apologetically. 'All I can say is that if we had heard something, we'd have acted' – he spread his hands in a gesture of surrender – 'like this morning when Jenny started screaming. There was nothing like that on Saturday.'

'Yet you both assumed she'd been murdered by a gang. You mentioned "they".'

'It's difficult to think straight when people are screaming,' he said, reproaching himself with a shake of the head. 'And to be perfectly honest, I wasn't at all sure the Spedes themselves hadn't done something. They're not the brightest couple as you've probably discovered for yourself. Mind you, it wouldn't have been intentional. They're foolish, not dangerous. I assumed there'd been some sort of accident,' he spread his palms on his fat knees, 'I've been worrying that I should have gone in to do something, saved her perhaps, but if she died on Saturday . . . ?' His voice tailed off on a query.

Cooper shook his head. 'You couldn't have done anything for her. What about during the daytime? Did you hear anything then?'

'On Saturday, you mean?' He shook his head. 'Nothing that leaps to mind. Certainly nothing unsettling.' He looked at Violet as if seeking inspiration. 'We notice if the bell rings in Cedar House, because it's very rare for Mathilda to have visitors, but otherwise' – he shrugged helplessly – 'so little happens here, Sergeant, and we do watch a lot of television.'

'And you didn't wonder where she was on Sunday?'

Violet dabbed at her eyes. 'Oh, dear,' she whispered, 'could we have saved her then? How *awful*, Duncan.'

'No,' said Cooper firmly, 'she was certainly dead by three o'clock on Sunday morning.'

'We were friends, you know,' said Violet. 'Duncan and I have known her for fifty years. She sold us this cottage when Duncan retired five years ago. That's not to say she was the *easiest* person in the world to get on with. She could be very cruel to people she didn't like, but the trick with Mathilda was not to *impose*. We never did, of course, but there were those who did.'

Cooper licked the point of his pencil. 'Who for example?'

Violet lowered her voice. 'Joanna and Ruth, her daughter and granddaughter. They *never* left her alone, always complaining, always demanding money. And the vicar was shocking.' She cast a guilty glance at her husband. 'I know Duncan doesn't approve of tittle-tattle but the vicar was always pricking her conscience about the less well off. She was an *atheist*, you know, and very rude to Mr Matthews every time he came. She called him a Welsh leech. To his face, too.'

'Did he mind?'

Duncan gave a rumble of laughter. 'It was a game,' he said. 'She was quite generous sometimes when he caught her in a good mood. She gave him a hundred pounds once towards a centre for alcoholics, saying there but for the grace of her metabolism went she. She drank to deaden the pain of her arthritis, or so she said.'

'Not to excess, though,' said Violet. 'She was never *drunk*. She was too much of a lady ever to get drunk.' She blew her nose loudly.

'Is there anyone else you can think of who imposed on her?' asked Cooper after a moment.

Duncan shrugged. 'There was the doctor's husband, Jack Blakeney. He was always round there, but it wasn't an imposition. She liked him. I used to hear her laughing with him sometimes in the garden.' He paused to reflect. 'She had very few friends, Sergeant. As Violet said, she wasn't an easy woman. People either liked Mathilda or loathed her. You'll find that out soon enough if you're planning to ask questions of anyone else.'

'And you liked her?'

His eyes grew suddenly wet. 'I did,' he said gruffly. 'She was beautiful once, you know, quite beautiful.' He patted his wife's hand. 'We all were, a long, long time ago. Age has very few compensations, Sergeant, except perhaps the wisdom to recognize contentment.' He pondered for a moment. 'They do say slitting the wrists is a very peaceful way to die, although how anyone knows I can't imagine. Did she suffer, do you think?'

'I'm afraid I can't answer that, Mr Orloff,' said Cooper honestly.

The damp eyes held his for a moment and he saw a deep and haggard sadness in them. They spoke of a love that Cooper somehow suspected Duncan had never shown or felt for his wife. He wanted to say something by way of consolation, but what could he say that wouldn't make matters worse? He doubted that Violet knew, and he wondered, not for the first time, why love was more often cruel than it was kind.

I watched Duncan clipping his hedge this afternoon and could barely remember the handsome man he was. If I had been a charitable woman, I would have married him forty years ago and saved him from himself and Violet. She has turned my Romeo into a sad-eyed Billy Bunter who blinks his passion quietly when no one's looking. Oh, that his too, too solid flesh should melt. At twenty, he had the body of Michelangelo's David, now he resembles an entire family group by Henry Moore.

Jack continues to delight me. What a tragedy I didn't meet him or someone like him when I was 'green in judgement'. I learnt only how to survive, when Jack would, I think, have taught me how to love. I asked him why he and Sarah have no children, and he answered: 'Because I've never had the urge to play God.' I told him there was nothing godlike about procreation – doglike perhaps – and it's a monumental conceit that allows him to dictate Sarah's suitability as a mother. 'The vicar would say you're playing the devil, Jack. The species won't survive unless people like you reproduce themselves.'

But he is not an amenable man. If he were, I would enjoy him less. 'You've played God for years, Mathilda. Has it given you any pleasure or made you more content?'

No, and I can say that honestly. I shall die as naked as I was born . . .

Two

A WEEK LATER the receptionist buzzed through to Dr Blakeney's office. 'There's a Detective Sergeant Cooper on the line. I've told him you have a patient with you but he's very insistent. Can you speak to him?' It was a Monday and Sarah was covering afternoon surgery in Fontwell.

She smiled apologetically at the pregnant mother, laid out like a sacrificial offering on her couch. She put her hand over the receiver. 'Do you mind if I take this call, Mrs Graham? It's rather important. I'll be as quick as I can.'

'Get on with you. I'm enjoying the rest. You don't get many opportunities when it's your third.'

Sarah smiled at her. 'Put him through, Jane. Yes, Sergeant, what can I do for you?'

'We've had the results of Mrs Gillespie's post mortem. I'd be interested in your reactions.'

'Go on.'

He shuffled some papers at the other end of the line. 'Direct cause of death: loss of blood. Traces of barbiturates were discovered in her system, but not enough to prove fatal. Traces also discovered in the whisky glass, implying she dissolved the barbiturates before she drank them. Some

alcohol absorbed. No bruising. Lacerations on the tongue where the rusted bit of the scold's bridle caused the surface to bleed. Nothing under her fingernails. Slight nettle rash on her temples and cheeks, and minor chafing of the skin beneath the bridle's framework, both consistent with her donning the contraption herself and then arranging it with the nettles and daisies. No indications at all that she put up any sort of struggle. The scold's bridle was not attached to her head in any way and could have been removed, had she wished to do so. The wounds to the wrists correspond precisely with the Stanley knife blade discovered on the bathroom floor, the one on the left wrist made with a downward right-handed stroke, the one on the right with a downward left-handed stroke. The knife had been submerged in water, probably dropped after one of the incisions, but there was an index fingerprint, belonging to Mrs Gillespie, one-point-three centimetres from the blade on the shaft. Conclusion: suicide.' He paused. 'Are you still there?' he demanded after a moment.

'Yes.'

'So what do you think?'

'That I was wrong last week.'

'But surely the barbiturates in the whisky glass trouble you?'

'Mathilda hated swallowing anything whole,' she said apologetically. 'She crushed or dissolved everything in liquid first. She had a morbid fear of choking.'

'But your immediate reaction when you saw her was that she was the last person you'd expect to kill herself. And now you've changed your mind.' It sounded like an accusation.

'What do you want me to say, Sergeant? My gut feeling remains the same.' Sarah glanced towards her patient who was becoming restless. 'I would not have expected her to take her own life, but gut feelings are a poor substitute for scientific evidence.'

'Not always.'

She waited, but he didn't go on. 'Was there anything else, Sergeant? I do have a patient with me.'

'No,' he said, sounding dispirited, 'nothing else. It was a courtesy call. You may be required to give evidence at the inquest, but it'll be a formality. We've asked for an adjournment while we check one or two small details but, at the moment, we aren't looking for anyone else in connection with Mrs Gillespie's death.'

Sarah smiled encouragingly at Mrs Graham. *Be with you in a minute*, she mouthed. 'But you think you should be.'

'I learnt my trade in a simpler world, Dr Blakeney, where we paid attention to gut feelings. But in those days we called them hunches.' He gave a hollow laugh. 'Now, hunches are frowned on and forensic evidence is God. But forensic evidence is only as reliable as the man who interprets it and what I want to know is why there are no nettle stings on Mrs Gillespie's hands and fingers. Dr Cameron began by saying she must have worn gloves but there are no gloves in that house with sap on them, so now he thinks the water must have nullified the reaction. I don't like that kind of uncertainty. My hunch is Mrs Gillespie was murdered but I'm an Indian and the Chief says, drop it. I hoped you'd give me some ammunition.'

'I'm sorry,' said Sarah helplessly. She murmured a good-

bye and replaced the receiver with a thoughtful expression in her dark eyes.

'It'll be old Mrs Gillespie, I suppose,' said Mrs Graham prosaically. She was a farmer's wife, for whom birth and death held little mystery. Both happened, not always conveniently, and the whys and wherefores were largely irrelevant. The trick was coping afterwards. 'There's talk of nothing else in the village. Awful way to do it, don't you think?' She shivered theatrically. 'Slitting your wrists and then watching your blood seep into the water. I couldn't do that.'

'No,' agreed Sarah, rubbing her hands to warm them. 'You say you think the baby's head has engaged already?'

'Mm, won't be long now.' But Mrs Graham wasn't to be side-tracked so easily and she'd heard enough of the doctor's end of the conversation to whet her appetite. 'Is it true she had a cage on her head? Jenny Spede's been hysterical about it ever since. A cage with brambles and roses in it, she said. She keeps calling it Mrs Gillespie's crown of thorns.'

Sarah could see no harm in telling her. Most of the details were out already, and the truth was probably less damaging than the horror stories being put about by Mathilda's cleaner. 'It was a family heirloom, a thing called a scold's bridle.' She placed her hands on the woman's abdomen and felt for the baby's head. 'And there were no brambles or roses, nothing with thorns at all. Just a few wild flowers.' She omitted the nettles deliberately. The nettles, she thought, *were* disturbing. 'It was more pathetic than frightening.' Her probing fingers relaxed. 'You're right. It won't be long now. You must have got your dates wrong.'

'I always do, Doctor,' said the woman comfortably. 'I can tell you to the minute when a cow's due but when it's my turn,' she laughed, 'I haven't time to mark calendars.' Sarah linked arms with her to pull her into a sitting position. 'Scold's bridle,' she went on thoughtfully. 'Scold, as in a woman with a vicious tongue?'

Sarah nodded. 'They were used up until two or three centuries ago to shut women up, and not just women with vicious tongues either. Any women. Women who challenged male authority, inside the home *and* outside.'

'So why do you reckon she did it?'

'I don't know. Tired of living perhaps.' Sarah smiled. 'She didn't have your energy, Mrs Graham.'

'Oh, the dying I can understand. I've never seen much sense in struggling for life if the life isn't worth the struggle.' She buttoned her shirt. 'I meant why did she do it with this scold's bridle on her head?'

But Sarah shook her head. 'I don't know that either.'

'She was a nasty old woman,' said Mrs Graham bluntly. 'She lived here virtually all her life, knew me and my parents from our cradles, but she never acknowledged us once. We were too common. Tenant farmers with muck on our shoes. Oh, she spoke to old Wittingham, the lazy sod who owns Dad's farm, all right. The fact he's never done a hand's turn since the day he was born, but lives on his rents and his investments, made him acceptable. But the workers, rough trade like us – ' she shook her head – 'we were beneath contempt.' She chuckled at Sarah's expression. 'There, I'm shocking you. But I've a big mouth and I use it. You don't want to take Mrs Gillespie's death to heart. She wasn't liked, and not through want of trying, believe me. We're

not a bad lot here, but there's only so much that ordinary folk can take, and when a woman brushes her coat after you've bumped into her by accident, well, that's when you say enough's enough.' She swung her legs to the floor and stood up. 'I'm not much of a church-goer, me, but some things I do believe in, and one of them's repentance. Be it God or just old age, I reckon everyone repents in the end. There's few of us die without recognizing our faults which is why death's so peaceful. And it doesn't really matter who you say sorry to – a priest, God, your family – you've said it, and you feel better.' She slipped her feet into her shoes. 'I'd guess Mrs Gillespie was apologizing for her vicious tongue. That's why she wore her scold's bridle to meet her Maker.'

Mathilda Gillespie was buried three days later beside her father, Sir William Cavendish MP, in Fontwell village churchyard. The coroner's inquest had still to be held but it was common knowledge by then that a verdict of suicide was a foregone conclusion, if not from Polly Graham, then from a simple putting two and two together when the Dorset police removed their seals from Cedar House and returned to headquarters in the nearby coastal resort of Learmouth.

The congregation was a small one. Polly Graham had told the truth when she said Mathilda Gillespie wasn't liked, and few could be bothered to find time in their busy lives to say goodbye to an old woman who had been known only for her unkindness. The vicar did his best in difficult circumstances but it was with a feeling of relief that the

mourners turned from the open grave and picked their way across the grass towards the gate.

Jack Blakeney, a reluctant attendant on a wife who had felt duty-bound to put in an appearance, muttered into Sarah's ear: 'What a bunch of whited sepulchres, and I am not referring to the tombstones either, just we hypocrites doing our middle-class duty. Did you see their faces when the Rev referred to her as "our much loved friend and neighbour"? They all hated her.'

She hushed him with a warning hand. 'They'll hear you.'

'Who cares?' They were bringing up the rear and his artist's gaze roamed restlessly across the bowed heads in front of them. 'Presumably the blonde is the daughter, Joanna.'

Sarah heard the deliberate note of careless interest in his voice and smiled cynically. 'Presumably,' she agreed, 'and presumably the younger one is the granddaughter.'

Joanna stood now beside the vicar, her soft grey eyes huge in a finely drawn face, her silver-gold hair a shining cap in the sunlight. A beautiful woman, thought Sarah, but as usual she could admire her with complete detachment. She rarely directed her resentment towards the objects of her husband's thinly disguised lust, for she saw them as just that, objects. Lust, like everything in Jack's life apart from his painting, was ephemeral. A brief enthusiasm to be discarded as rapidly as it was espoused. The days when she had been confident that, for all his appreciation of another woman's looks, he wouldn't jeopardize their marriage were long past and she had few illusions left about her own role. She provided the affluence whereby Jack Blakeney, struggling artist, could live and slake his very mundane cravings,

but as Polly Graham had said – *there was only so much that ordinary folk could take.*

They shook hands with the vicar. 'It was kind of you both to come. Have you met Mathilda's daughter?' The Reverend Matthews turned to the woman. 'Joanna Lascelles, Dr Sarah Blakeney and Jack Blakeney. Sarah was your mother's GP, Joanna. She joined the practice last year when Dr Hendry retired. She and Jack live at The Mill in Long Upton, Geoffrey Freeling's old house.'

Joanna shook hands with them and turned to the girl beside her. 'This is my daughter Ruth. We're both very grateful to you, Dr Blakeney, for all you did to help my mother.'

The girl was about seventeen or eighteen, as dark as her mother was fair, and she looked anything but grateful. Sarah had only an impression of intense and bitter grief. 'Do you know why Granny killed herself?' she asked softly. 'Nobody else seems to.' Her face was set in a scowl.

'Ruth, please,' sighed her mother. 'Aren't things difficult enough already?' It was a conversation they had clearly had before.

Joanna must be approaching forty, thought Sarah, if the daughter was anything to go by, but against the black of her coat, she looked only very young and very vulnerable. Beside her, Sarah felt Jack's interest quicken and she had an angry impulse to turn on him and berate him publicly once and for all. How far did he think her patience would stretch? How long did he expect her to tolerate his contemptuous and contemptible indifference to her beleaguered pride? She quelled the impulse, of course. She was too trammelled by her upbringing and the behavioural demands of her

profession to do anything else. *But, oh God, one day* . . . she promised herself. Instead she turned to the girl. 'I wish I could give you an answer, Ruth, but I can't. The last time I saw your grandmother she was fine. In some pain from her arthritis, of course, but nothing she wasn't used to or couldn't cope with.'

The girl cast a spiteful glance at her mother. 'Then something must have happened to upset her. People don't kill themselves for no reason.'

'Was she easily upset?' asked Sarah. 'She never gave me that impression.' She smiled slightly. 'She was tough as old boots, your grandmother. I admired her for it.'

'Then why did she kill herself?'

'Because she wasn't afraid of death perhaps. Suicide isn't always a negative, you know. In some cases it's a positive statement of choice. I will die now and in this manner. "To be or not to be." For Mathilda "not to be" would have been a considered decision.'

Ruth's eyes filled. '*Hamlet* was her favourite play.' She was tall like her mother but her face, pinched with cold and distress, lacked the other's startling looks. Ruth's tears made her ugly where her mother's, a mere glistening of the lashes, enhanced a fragile beauty.

Joanna stirred herself, glancing from Sarah to Jack. 'Will you come back to the house for tea? There'll be so few of us.'

Sarah excused herself. 'I'm afraid I can't. I have a surgery in Mapleton at four thirty.'

Jack did not. 'Thank you, that's very kind.'

There was a small silence. 'How will you get home?' asked Sarah, fishing in her pocket for her car keys.

'I'll beg a lift,' he said. 'Someone's bound to be going my way.'

One of Sarah's colleagues dropped in as evening surgery was finishing. There were three partners in a practice serving several square miles of Dorset coast and countryside, including sizeable villages, scattered hamlets and farmhouses. Most of the villages had small self-contained surgeries, either attached to the doctors' houses or leased from patients and, between them, the partners covered the whole area, boxing and coxing in neat rotation. Mapleton was Robin Hewitt's home village but, like Sarah, he spent as much time out of it as he did in. They had so far resisted the logic of pooling their resources in one modern clinic in the most central of the villages, but it was doubtful if they could resist for much longer. The argument, a true one, that most of their patients were elderly or lacked transport, was far outweighed by the commercial pressures now existing inside the health service.

'You look tired,' said Robin, folding himself into the armchair beside her desk.

'I am.'

'Trouble?'

'Only the usual.'

'Domestic, eh? Get rid of him.'

She laughed. 'And supposing I told you, as casually, to get rid of Mary?'

'There's a small difference, my darling. Mary is an angel and Jack is not.' But the idea was not without a certain appeal. After eighteen years, Mary's complacent self-

assurance was so much less attractive than Sarah's troubled seeking after truths.

'I can't argue with that.' She finished writing some notes and pushed them wearily to one side.

'What's he done this time?'

'Nothing, as far as I know.'

Which sounded about right, thought Robin. Jack Blakeney made a virtue of doing nothing while his wife made a virtue of supporting him in idleness. Their continuing marriage was a complete mystery to him. There were no children, no ties, nothing binding them, Sarah was an independent woman with independent means, and she paid the mortgage on their house. It only required the services of a locksmith to shut the bastard out for ever.

She studied him with amusement. 'Why are you smiling like that?'

He switched neatly away from his mild fantasy of Sarah alone in her house. 'I saw Bob Hughes today. He was very put out to find me on duty and not you.' He fell into a fair imitation of the old man's Dorset burr. '"Where's the pretty one?" he said. "I want the pretty one to do it."'

'Do what?'

Robin grinned. 'Examine the boil on his bum. Dirty old brute. If it *had* been you, he'd have come up with another one, presumably, lurking under his scrotum and you'd have had the fun of probing for it and he'd have had the thrills while you did it.'

Her eyes danced. 'And it's completely free, don't forget. Relief massage comes expensive.'

'That's revolting. You're not telling me he's tried it on before.'

She chuckled. 'No, of course not. He only comes in for a chat. I expect he felt he had to show you something. Poor old soul. I bet you sent him away with a flea in his ear.'

'I did. You're far too amenable.'

'But they're so lonely some of them. We live in a terrible world, Robin. No one has time to listen any more.' She toyed with her pen. 'I went to Mathilda Gillespie's funeral today and her granddaughter asked me why she killed herself. I said I didn't know, and I've been thinking about that ever since. I *should* know. She was one of my patients. If I'd taken a little more trouble with her, I *would* know.' She flicked him a sideways glance. 'Wouldn't I?'

He shook his head. 'Don't start down that route, Sarah. It's a dead end. Look, you were one person among many whom she knew and talked to, me included. The responsibility for that old woman wasn't yours alone. I'd argue that it wasn't yours at all, except in a strict medical sense, and nothing you prescribed for her contributed to her death. She died of blood loss.'

'But where do you draw the line between profession and friendship? We laughed a lot. I think I was one of the few people who appreciated her sense of humour, probably because it was so like Jack's. Bitchy, often cruel, but witty. She was a latterday Dorothy Parker.'

'You're being ridiculously sentimental. Mathilda Gillespie was a bitch of the first water, and don't imagine she viewed you as an equal. For years, until she sold off Wing Cottage to raise money, doctors, lawyers and accountants were required to enter by the tradesman's entrance. It used to drive Hugh Hendry mad. He said she was the rudest woman he'd ever met. He couldn't stand her.'

Sarah gave a snort of laughter. 'Probably because she called him Doctor Dolittle. To his face, too. I asked her once if it was by way of a job description and she said: "Not entirely. He had a closer affinity with animals than he had with people. He was an ass."'

Robin grinned. 'Hugh was the laziest and the least able doctor I've ever met. I suggested once that we check his medical qualifications because I didn't think he had any, but it's a bit difficult when the bloke in question is the senior partner. We just had to bite the bullet and hang on for his retirement.' He cocked his head on one side. 'So what did she call you, if she called him Dr Dolittle?'

She held the pen to her lips for a moment and stared past him. There was a haunting disquiet in her dark eyes. 'She was obsessed with that wretched scold's bridle. It was rather unhealthy really, thinking about it. She wanted me to try it on once to see what it felt like.'

'And did you?'

'No.' She fell silent for a moment, then seemed to make up her mind to something. 'She called her arthritis her "Resident Scold" because it caused her so much nagging pain' – she tapped the pen against her teeth – 'and in order to take her mind off it, she used to don the bridle as a sort of counter-irritant. That's what I mean about her unhealthy obsession with it. She wore it as a sort of penance, like a hair shirt. Anyway, when I took her off that rubbish Hendry had been prescribing and got the pain under some sort of manageable control, she took to calling me her little scold's bridle by way of a joke.' She saw his incomprehension. 'Because I'd succeeded in harnessing the Resident Scold,' she explained.

'So what are you saying?'

'I think she was trying to tell me something.'

Robin shook his head. 'Why? Because she was wearing it when she died? It was a symbol, that's all.'

'Of what?'

'Life's illusion. We're all prisoners. Perhaps it was her final joke. My tongue is curbed for ever, something like that.' He shrugged. 'Have you told the police?'

'No. I was so shocked when I saw her that I didn't think about it.' She raised her hands in a gesture of helplessness. 'And the pathologist and the policeman latched on to what I said she always called the geraniums inside the beastly thing. Her coronet weeds. It comes from the speech about Ophelia's death and, what with the bath and the nettles, I thought they were probably right. But now I'm not so sure.' Her voice tailed off and she sat staring at her desk.

Robin watched her for several seconds. 'Supposing she *was* trying to say that her tongue was curbed for ever. You realize it has a double meaning?'

'Yes,' said Sarah unhappily, 'that someone else curbed it. But that doesn't make sense. I mean, if Mathilda knew she was going to be murdered she wouldn't have wasted time donning the scold's bridle in the hall when all she had to do was run to the front door and scream her head off. The whole village would have heard her. And the murderer would have taken it off anyway.'

'Perhaps it was the murderer who was saying, "Her tongue is curbed for ever".'

'But that doesn't make sense either. Why would a murderer advertise that it's murder when he's gone to so much trouble to make it look like suicide?' She rubbed her

tired eyes. 'Without the scold's bridle, it would have looked straightforward. With it, it looks anything *but*. And why the flowers, for God's sake? What were they supposed to tell us?'

'You'll have to talk to the police,' said Robin with sudden decision, reaching for the telephone. 'Dammit, Sarah, who else knew she called you her scold's bridle? Surely it's occurred to you that the message is directed at you.'

'What message?'

'I don't know. A threat, perhaps. You next, Dr Blakeney.'

She gave a hollow laugh. 'I see it more in terms of a signature.' She traced a line on the desk with her fingertip. 'Like the mark of Zorro on his victims.'

'Oh, Jesus!' said Robin, putting the receiver back. 'Maybe it's wiser not to say anything. Look, it was obviously suicide – you said yourself she was unhealthily obsessed with the damn thing.'

'But I was fond of her.'

'You're fond of everyone, Sarah. It's nothing to be proud of.'

'You sound like Jack.' She retrieved the telephone, dialled Learmouth Police Station and asked for Detective Sergeant Cooper.

Robin watched with gloomy resignation – she had no idea how the tongues would wag if they ever got wind of Mathilda's nickname for her – and wondered disloyally why she had chosen to tell him before anyone else. He had the strangest impression that she had been using him. As a yardstick by which to measure other people's reactions? As a confessor?

DS Cooper had already left for home and the bored

voice at the other end of the wire merely agreed to pass on Sarah's request to speak to him when he arrived the next morning. There was no urgency, after all. The case was closed.

How I detest my arthritis and the cruel inactivity it imposes. I saw a ghost today but could do nothing about it. I should have struck it down and sent it back to Hell whence it came, instead I could only lash it with my tongue. Has Joanna brought him back to haunt me? It makes sense. She has been plotting something since she found that wretched letter. 'Ingratitude, thou marble-hearted fiend, more hideous when thou show'st thee in a child than the sea monster.'

But to use James of all people. That I shall never forgive. Or is it he who is using her? Forty years haven't changed him. What loathsome fun he must have had in Hong Kong where I've read the boys dress up as girls and give paederasts the thrill of pretended normality as they parade themselves and their disgusting perversion before a naïve public. He looks ill. Well, well, what a charming solution his death would be.

I made a 'most filthy bargain' there. They talk glibly about cycles of abuse these days but, oh, how much more complex those cycles are than the simple brutality visited by parent on child. Everything comes to him who mates . . .

Three

JACK WAS WORKING in his studio when Sarah's key finally grated in the lock at around eleven o'clock. He looked up as she passed his open door. 'Where have you been?'

She was very tired. 'At the Hewitts'. They gave me supper. Have you eaten?' She didn't come in, but stood in the doorway watching him.

He nodded absent-mindedly. Food was a low priority in Jack's life. He jerked his head at the canvas on the easel. 'What do you think?'

How much simpler it would be, she thought, if she were obtuse, and genuinely misunderstood what he was trying to achieve in his work. How much simpler if she could just accept what one or two critics had said, that it was pretentious rubbish and bad art.

'Joanna Lascelles presumably.'

But not a Joanna Lascelles that anyone would recognize, except perhaps in the black of her funeral weeds and the silver gold of her hair, for Jack used shape and colour to paint emotions, and there was an extraordinary turbulence about this painting, even in its earliest stage. He would go

on now for weeks, working layer on layer, attempting through the medium of oils to build and depict the complexity of the human personality. Sarah, who understood his colour-coding almost as well as he did, could interpret much of what he had already blocked in. Grief (for her mother?), disdain (for her daughter?), and, all too predictably, sensuality (for him?).

Jack watched her face. 'She's interesting,' he said.

'Obviously.'

His eyes narrowed angrily. 'Don't start,' he murmured. 'I'm not in the mood.'

She shrugged. 'Neither am I. I'm going to bed.'

'I'll work on the jacket tomorrow,' he promised grudgingly. He made a living of sorts by designing book jackets, but the commissions were few and far between because he rarely met deadlines. The disciplines imposed by the profit motive infuriated him.

'I'm not your mother, Jack,' she said coolly. 'What you do tomorrow is your own affair.'

But he was in the mood for a row, probably, thought Sarah, because Joanna had flattered him. 'You just can't leave it alone, can you? No, you're not my mother, but by God you're beginning to sound like her.'

'How odd,' she said with heavy irony, 'and I always thought you didn't get on with her because she kept telling you what to do. Now I'm tarred with the same brush, yet I've done the exact opposite, left you to work things out for yourself. You're a child, Jack. You need a woman in your life to blame for every little thing that goes wrong for you.'

'Is this babies again?' he snarled. 'Dammit, Sarah, you knew the score before you married me, and it was your

choice to go through with it. The career was everything, remember? Nothing's changed. Not for me, anyway. It's not my fault if your bloody hormones are screaming that time's running out. We had a deal. No children.'

She eyed him curiously. After all, she thought, Joanna must have been less accommodating than he had hoped. Well, well! 'The deal, Jack, for what it's worth, was that I would support you until you established yourself. After that, all options were open. What we never considered, and for that I blame myself because I relied on my own artistic judgement, was that you might *never* establish yourself. In which circumstance, I suspect, the deal is null and void. So far, I have kept you for six years, two years before marriage and four afterwards, and the choice to marry was as much yours as mine. As far as I remember we were celebrating your first major sale. Your only major sale,' she added. 'I think that's fair, don't you? I can't recall your selling a canvas since.'

'Spite doesn't suit you, Sarah.'

'No,' she agreed, 'any more than behaving like a spoilt brat suits you. You say nothing's changed, but you're wrong, everything's changed. I used to admire you. Now I despise you. I used to find you amusing. Now you bore me. I used to love you. Now I just feel sorry for you.' She smiled apologetically. 'I also used to think you'd make it. Now I don't. And that's not because I think any less of your painting, but because I think less of you. You have neither the commitment nor the discipline to be great, Jack, because you always forget that genius is only one per cent inspiration and ninety-nine per cent sheer, bloody graft. I'm a good doctor, not because I have an especial talent for

diagnosis, but because I work my fingers to the bone. You're a rotten artist, not because you lack talent, but because you're too damn lazy and too damn snobbish to get down on your hands and knees with the rest of us and earn your reputation.'

The dark face split into a sardonic grin. 'Hewitt's doing, I suppose? A cosy little supper with Cock Robin and his wife, and then it's dump on Jack. Jesus, he's a greasy little toad. He'd be in your bed quicker than winking if sweet little Mary and the kiddiwinkles weren't guarding his door.'

'Don't be absurd,' she said coldly. 'It's your doing entirely. I ceased having any feelings for you whatsoever the day I had to refer Sally Bennedict for an abortion. I draw the line at being asked to approve the murder of your bastards, Jack, particularly by a selfish bitch like Sally Bennedict. She enjoyed the irony of it all, believe me.'

He stared at her with something like shock, and she saw that for once she had scored a direct hit. He hadn't known, she thought, which was something in his favour at least. 'You should have told me,' he said inadequately.

She laughed with genuine amusement. 'Why? You weren't my patient, Sally was. And, sure as eggs is eggs, she wasn't going to go to term with your little bundle of joy and lose her chance with the RSC. You can't play Juliet six months pregnant, Jack, which is what she would have been when the run started. Oh, I did my bit, suggested she talk it through with you, suggested she talk it through with a counsellor, but I might have been pissing in the wind for all the good it did. She'd have preferred cancer, I think, to an unwanted pregnancy.' Her smile was twisted. 'And let's face it, we both knew what your reaction would be. It's the only

time I've felt confident that the wretched foetus, were it born, would be rejected by both parties. I passed the buck on to the hospital and they had *her* in and *it* out within two weeks.'

He swirled his brush aimlessly around the colours on his palette. 'Was that the reason for the sudden move down here?'

'Partly. I had a nasty feeling Sally would be the first of many.'

'And the other part?'

'I didn't think the wilds of Dorset would appeal to you. I hoped you'd stay in London.'

'You should have told me,' he said again. 'I never was very good at taking hints.'

'No.'

He put the palette and the brush on a stool and started to wipe his hands with a kitchen towel dipped in turpentine. 'So how come the year's grace? Charity? Or malice? Did you think it would be more fun to cast me adrift down here than in London where I'd be assured of a bed?'

'Neither,' she said. 'Hope. Misplaced, as usual.' She glanced at the canvas.

He followed her gaze. 'I had tea with her. Nothing more.'

'I believe you.'

'Why so angry then? I'm not making a scene because you had supper with Robin.'

'I'm not angry, Jack. I'm bored. Bored with being the necessary audience that your ridiculous ego requires. I sometimes think that was the real reason you married me, not for security but because you needed somebody else's

emotion to stimulate your creativity.' She gave a hollow laugh. 'In that case you should never have married a doctor. We see too much of it at work to play it all out again at home.'

He studied her closely. 'That's it then, is it? My marching orders? Pack your bags, Jack, and never darken my door again.'

She smiled the Mona Lisa smile that had first bewitched him. He thought he could predict exactly what she was going to say. *It's your life, make your own decisions.* For Sarah's strength and her weakness was her belief that everyone was as confident and single-minded as she was.

'Yes,' she said, 'that's it. I made up my mind that if you ever went near Sally again I'd call it quits. I want a divorce.'

His eyes narrowed. 'If this was about Sally, you'd have given me an ultimatum two weeks ago. I made no secret of where I was going.'

'I know,' she said wearily, staring at the painting again. 'Even your betrayals demand an audience now.'

He was gone when she came downstairs the next morning. There was a note on the kitchen table:

> Send the divorce papers c/o Keith Smollett. You can find yourself another solicitor. I'll be going for a fifty-fifty split so don't get too attached to the house. I'll clear the studio as soon as I've found somewhere else. If you don't want to see me, then don't change the locks. I'll leave my key behind when I've retrieved my stuff.

Sarah read it through twice then dropped it in the rubbish bin.

Jane Marriott, the receptionist at the Fontwell surgery, looked up as Sarah pushed open the door of the empty waiting-room. Sarah covered Fontwell on Monday afternoons and Friday mornings and, because she was more sympathetic than her male colleagues, her sessions were usually busy ones. 'There's a couple of messages for you, dear,' said Jane. 'I've left them on your desk.'

'Thanks.' She paused by the desk. 'Who's first?'

'Mr Drew at eight forty-five and then it's hectic until eleven thirty. After that, two home visits, I'm afraid, but I've told them not to expect you before midday.'

'Okay.'

Jane, a retired teacher in her sixties, eyed Sarah with motherly concern. 'No breakfast again, I suppose?'

Sarah smiled. 'I haven't eaten breakfast since I left school.'

'Hm, well, you look washed out. You work too hard, dear. Doctoring's like any other job. You should learn to pace yourself better.'

Sarah put her elbows on the desk and propped her chin on her hands. 'Tell me something, Jane. If heaven exists, where exactly is it?' She looked for all the world like one of the eight-year-olds Jane had once taught, puzzled, a little hesitant, but confident that Mrs Marriott would know the answer.

'Goodness! No one's asked me a question like that since I stopped teaching.' She plugged in the kettle and spooned

coffee into two cups. 'I always told the children it was in the hearts you left behind. The more people there were who loved you, the more hearts would hold your memory. It was a devious way of encouraging them to be nice to each other.' She chuckled. 'But I thought you were a non-believer, Sarah. Why the sudden interest in the afterlife?'

'I went to Mrs Gillespie's funeral yesterday. It was depressing. I keep wondering what the point of it all is.'

'Oh dear. Eternal truths at eight thirty in the morning.' She put a cup of steaming black coffee in front of Sarah. 'The point to Mathilda Gillespie's life might not emerge for another five generations. She's part of a line. Who's to say how important that line might be in years to come?'

'That's even more depressing,' said Sarah gloomily. 'That means you have to have children to give meaning to your life.'

'Nonsense. I haven't any children but I don't feel it makes me any less valuable. Our lives are what we make them.' She didn't look at Sarah as she spoke, and Sarah had the feeling that the words were just words, without meaning. 'Sadly,' Jane went on, 'Mathilda made very little of hers. She never got over her husband running out on her and it made her bitter. I think she thought people were laughing at her behind her back. Which, of course, a lot of us were,' she admitted honestly.

'I thought she was a widow.' How little she really knew about the woman.

Jane shook her head. 'Assuming he's still alive, then James is her widower. As far as I know they never bothered with a divorce.'

'What happened to him?'

'He went out to Hong Kong to work in a bank.'

'How do you know?'

'Paul and I took a holiday in the Far East about ten years after he and Mathilda separated, and we bumped into him by accident in a hotel in Hong Kong. We'd known him very well in the early days because he and Paul went through the war together.' She gave a quirky little smile. 'He was happy as Larry, living amongst the other expatriates, and quite unconcerned about his wife and daughter back home.'

'Who was supporting them?'

'Mathilda was. Her father left her very well provided for, which was a shame, I sometimes thought. She'd have been a different woman if she'd had to use that brain of hers to keep the wolf from the door.' She tut-tutted. 'It's bad for the character to have everything handed to you on a platter.'

Well, that was certainly true, thought Sarah, if Jack was anything to go by. Fifty-bloody-fifty, she thought wrathfully. She'd see him in hell first. 'So when did he leave her? Recently?'

'Good heavens, no. It was about eighteen months after they married. Well over thirty years ago, anyway. For a year or two we had letters from him, then we lost touch. To be honest, we found him rather tiresome. When we met in Hong Kong he'd taken to the bottle in a big way and he became very aggressive when he got drunk. We were both rather relieved when the letters dried up. We've never heard from him again.'

'Did Mathilda know he'd written to you?' Sarah asked curiously.

'I really couldn't say. We'd moved to Southampton by then and had very little to do with her. Mutual friends

mentioned her from time to time, but other than that we lost touch completely. We only came back here five years ago when my poor old chap's health broke down and I took a decision that fresh Dorset air had to be better for him than the polluted city rubbish in Southampton.'

Paul Marriott suffered from chronic emphysema and his wretched wife agonized over his condition. 'It was the best thing you could have done,' said Sarah firmly. 'He tells me he's been much better since he came home to his roots.' She knew from past experience that Jane wouldn't be able to let the subject drop once she'd embarked upon it and contrived to steer her off it. 'Did you know Mathilda well?'

Jane thought about that. 'We grew up together – my father was the doctor here for many years and Paul was her father's political agent for a time – Sir William was the local MP – but I honestly don't think I knew Mathilda at all. The trouble was I never liked her.' She looked apologetic. 'It's awful to say that about someone who's dead but I refuse to be hypocritical about it. She was quite the nastiest woman I've ever met. I never blamed James for deserting her. The only mystery was why he married her in the first place.'

'Money,' said Sarah with feeling.

'Yes, I think it must have been,' Jane agreed. 'He was very much poor gentry, heir to nothing but a name, and Mathilda was beautiful, of course, just like Joanna. The whole thing was a disaster. James learnt PDQ that there were some things worse than poverty. And being dictated to by a virago who held the purse strings was one of them. He *hated* her.'

*

One of the messages on Sarah's desk was from Ruth Lascelles, a short note, presumably put through the surgery door the previous evening. She had surprisingly childish writing for a girl of seventeen or eighteen. 'Dear Dr Blakeney, Please can you come and see me at Granny's house tomorrow (Friday). I'm not ill but I'd like to talk to you. I have to be back at school by Sunday night. Thanking you in anticipation. Yours sincerely, Ruth Lascelles.'

The other was a telephoned message from Detective Sergeant Cooper. 'Dr Blakeney's call drawn to DS Cooper's attention this morning. He will contact her later in the day.'

It was nearly three o'clock before Sarah found time to call in at Cedar House. She drove up the short gravel drive and parked in front of the dining-room windows which faced out towards the road on the left-hand side of the house. It was a Georgian building in yellowy-grey stone, with deep windows and high-ceilinged rooms. Far too big for Mathilda, Sarah had always thought, and very inconvenient for a woman who, on bad days, was little better than an invalid. Her one concession to poor health had been the introduction of a stair-lift which had allowed her continued access to the upper floor. Sarah had once suggested that she sell up and move into a bungalow, to which Mathilda had replied that she wouldn't dream of any such thing. 'My dear Sarah, only the lower classes live in bungalows which is why they are always called Mon Repos or Dunroamin. Whatever else you do in life, *never* drop your standards.'

Ruth came out as she was opening her car door. 'Let's

talk in the summer-house,' she said jerkily. She didn't wait for an answer but set off round the corner of the house, her thin body, dressed only in tee-shirt and leggings, hunched against the biting north wind that was swirling the autumn leaves across the path.

Sarah, older and more susceptible to the cold, retrieved her Barbour from the back seat and followed. Out of the corner of her eye, she caught a glimpse of Joanna watching her from the dark depths of the dining-room. Had Ruth told her mother she'd asked Sarah to call, Sarah wondered, as she tramped across the lawn in the girl's wake. And why so much secrecy? The summer-house was a good two hundred yards from Joanna's listening ears.

Ruth was lighting a cigarette when Sarah joined her amongst the litter of art deco cane chairs and tables, relics from an earlier – happier? – age. 'I suppose you're going to lecture me,' she said with a scowl, pulling the doors to and flopping on to a chair.

'What about?' Sarah took another chair and folded the Barbour across her chest. It was bitterly cold, even with the doors closed.

'Smoking.'

Sarah shrugged. 'I'm not in the habit of lecturing.'

Ruth stared at her with moody eyes. 'Your husband said Granny called you her scold's bridle. Why would she do that if you didn't tick her off for nagging?'

Sarah looked out of the windows to where the huge cedar of Lebanon, after which the house was named, cast a long shadow on the grass. As she watched, the blustery wind drove a cloud across the sun and wiped the shadow away. 'We didn't have that sort of relationship,' she said,

turning back to the girl. 'I enjoyed your grandmother's company. I don't recall any occasion when a ticking-off would have been appropriate.'

'*I* wouldn't have liked being called a scold's bridle.'

Sarah smiled. 'I found it rather flattering. I believe she meant it as a compliment.'

'I doubt it,' said the girl bluntly. 'I suppose you know she used the bridle on my mother when my mother was a child?' She smoked the cigarette nervously, taking short, rapid drags and expelling the smoke through her nose. She saw Sarah's disbelief. 'It's true. Granny told me about it once. She hated people crying, so whenever Mum cried she used to lock her in a cupboard with that thing strapped to her head. Granny's father did it to her. That's why she thought it was all right.'

Sarah waited but she didn't go on. 'That was cruel,' she murmured.

'Yes. But Granny was tougher than Mum and, anyway, it didn't matter much what you did to children when Granny was young, so being punished by wearing a bridle was probably no different from being thrashed with a belt. But it was awful for my mother.' She crushed the cigarette under her foot. 'There was no one to stand up for her and take her side. Granny could do what she liked whenever she liked.'

Sarah wondered what the girl was trying to tell her. 'It's an increasingly common problem, I'm afraid. Men, under stress, take their problems out on their wives. Women, under stress, take theirs out on their children, and there's nothing more stressful for a woman than to be left holding the baby.'

'Do you condone what Granny did?' There was a wary look in her eyes.

'Not at all. I suppose I'm trying to understand it. Most children in your mother's position suffer constant verbal abuse, and that is often as damaging as the physical abuse, simply because the scars don't show and nobody outside the family knows about it.' She shrugged. 'But the results are the same. The child is just as repressed and just as flawed. Few personalities can survive the constant battering of criticism from a person they depend on. You either crawl or fight. There's no middle way.'

Ruth looked angry. 'My mother had both, verbal and physical. You've no idea how vicious my grandmother was to her.'

'I'm sorry,' said Sarah helplessly. 'But if it's true that Mathilda was also punished brutally as a child, then she was as much a victim as your mother. But I don't suppose that's any consolation to you.'

Ruth lit another cigarette. 'Oh, don't get me wrong,' she said with an ironic twist to her mouth, 'I loved my grandmother. At least she had some character. My mother has none. Sometimes I hate her. Most of the time I just despise her.' She frowned at the floor, stirring the dust with the toe of one shoe. 'I think she killed Granny and I don't know what to do about it. Half of me blames her and the other half doesn't.'

Sarah let the remark hang in the air for a moment while she cast around for something to say. What sort of accusation was this? A genuine accusation of murder? Or a spiteful sideswipe by a spoilt child against a parent she disliked? 'The police are convinced it was suicide, Ruth.

They've closed the case. As I understand it, there's no question of anyone else being involved in your grandmother's death.'

'I don't mean Mum actually did it,' she said, 'you know, took the knife and did it. I mean that she drove Granny to killing herself. That's just as bad.' She raised suspiciously bright eyes. 'Don't you think so, Doctor?'

'Perhaps. If such a thing is possible. But from what you've told me of your mother's relationship with Mathilda, it sounds unlikely. It would be more plausible if it had happened the other way round and Mathilda had driven your mother to suicide.' She smiled apologetically. 'Even then, that sort of thing doesn't happen very often, and there would be a history of mental instability behind the person who saw suicide as their only escape from a difficult relationship.'

But Ruth wasn't to be persuaded so easily. 'You don't understand,' she said. 'They could be as unpleasant as they liked to each other and it didn't matter a damn. Mum was just as bad as Granny, but in a different way. Granny said what she thought while Mum just went on chipping away with snide little remarks. I hated being with them when they were together.' Her lips thinned unattractively. 'That was the only good thing about being sent to boarding school. Mum moved out then and went to London, and I could choose whether to come here for my holidays or go to Mum's. I didn't have to be a football any more.'

How little Sarah knew about these three women. Where was Mr Lascelles, for example? Had he, like James Gillespie, run away? Or was Lascelles some kind of courtesy title that

Joanna had adopted to give her daughter legitimacy? 'How long did you and your mother live here, then, before you went away to school?'

'From when I was a baby to when I was eleven. My father died and left us without a bean. Mum had to come crawling home or we'd have starved. That's her story at least. But personally I think she was just too snobbish and too lazy to take a menial job. She preferred Granny's insults to getting her hands dirty.' She wrapped her arms about her waist and leaned forward, rocking herself. 'My father was a Jew.' She spoke the word with contempt.

Sarah was taken aback. 'Why do you say it like that?'

'It's how my grandmother always referred to him. *That Jew*. She was an anti-Semite. Didn't you know?'

Sarah shook her head.

'Then you didn't know her very well.' Ruth sighed. 'He was a professional musician, a bass guitarist, attached to one of the studios. He did the backing tracks when the groups weren't good enough to do them themselves, and he had a band of his own which did gigs occasionally. He died of a heroin overdose in 1978. I don't remember him at all, but Granny took great delight in telling me what a worthless person he was. His name was Steven, Steven Lascelles.' She lapsed into silence.

'How did your mother meet him?'

'At a party in London. She was supposed to get off with a deb's delight but got off with the guitarist instead. Granny didn't know anything about it until Mum told her she was pregnant, and then the shit hit the fan. I mean, can you imagine it? Mum up the spout by a Jewish rock guitarist with a heroin habit.' She gave a hollow laugh. 'It was a hell

of a revenge.' Her arms were turning blue with cold but she didn't seem to notice it. 'So, anyway, they got married and she moved in with him. They had me and then six months later he was dead after spending all their money on heroin. He hadn't paid the rent for months. Mum was a widow – before she was twenty-three – on the dole with a baby and no roof over her head.'

'Then coming back here was probably her only option.'

Ruth pulled a sour face. 'You wouldn't have done it though, not if you knew you'd never be allowed to forget your mistake.'

Probably not, thought Sarah. She wondered if Joanna had loved Steven Lascelles or if, as Ruth had implied, she had taken up with him simply to spite Mathilda. 'It's easy to be wise after the event,' was all she said.

The girl went on as if she hadn't heard. 'Granny tried to change my name to something more WASP – you know, White Anglo-Saxon Protestant – to erase the Hebrew in me. She called me Elizabeth for a while but Mum threatened to take me away, so Granny gave in. Other than that and her refusal to let Granny put the bridle on me when I cried, Mum let Granny dictate terms on everything.' Her eyes flashed scornfully. 'She was so wet. But it was easy to stand up to my grandmother. I did it all the time and we got on like a house on fire.'

Sarah had no desire to be drawn into a domestic squabble between a mother and daughter she barely knew. She watched the long shadow creep across the lawn again as the sun emerged from behind a cloud. 'Why did you ask me to come here, Ruth?'

'I don't know what to do. I thought you'd tell me.'

Sarah studied the thin, rather malicious face and wondered if Joanna had any idea how much her daughter disliked her. 'Don't do anything. Frankly, I can't imagine what your mother could have said or done that would have driven Mathilda to kill herself and, even if there were something, it would hardly be a chargeable offence.'

'Then it should be,' said Ruth harshly. 'She found a letter in the house last time she was down here. She told Granny she'd publish it if Granny didn't change her will immediately and move out of the house. So Granny killed herself. She's left everything to me, you see. She *wanted* to leave everything to me.' Now there was definite malice in the immature features.

Oh God, thought Sarah. *What were you trying to tell me, Mathilda?* 'Have you seen this letter?'

'No, but Granny wrote and told me what was in it. She said she didn't want me to find out from my mother. So, you see, Mum did drive her to it. Granny would have done anything to avoid having her dirty linen washed in public.' Her voice grated.

'Do you still have the letter she wrote to you?'

Ruth scowled. 'I tore it up. But that one wasn't important, it's the one Mum found that's important. She'll use it to try and overturn Granny's will.'

'Then I think you should find yourself a solicitor,' said Sarah firmly, drawing her legs together under her chair preparatory to getting up. 'I was your grandmother's doctor, that's all. I can't get involved between you and your mother, Ruth, and I'm quite sure Mathilda wouldn't have wanted me to.'

'But she would,' the girl cried. 'She said in her letter that

if anything happened to her I was to talk to you. She said you would know what to do for the best.'

'Surely not? Your grandmother didn't confide in me. All I know about your family is what you've told me today.'

A thin hand reached out and gripped hers. It was icy cold. 'The letter was from Granny's uncle, Gerald Cavendish, to his solicitor. It was a will, saying he wanted everything he had to go to his daughter.'

Sarah could feel the hand on hers trembling, but whether from cold or nerves she didn't know. 'Go on,' she prompted.

'This house and all the money was his. He was the elder brother.'

Sarah frowned again. 'So what are you saying? That Mathilda never had any rights to it? Well, I'm sorry, Ruth, but this is way beyond me. You really must find a solicitor and talk it through with him. I haven't a clue what your legal position is, truly I haven't.' Her subconscious caught up with her. 'Still, it's very odd, isn't it? If his daughter was his heir, shouldn't she have inherited automatically?'

'No one knew she was his daughter,' said Ruth bleakly, 'except Granny, and she told everyone James Gillespie was the father. It's my mother, Dr Blakeney. Granny was being fucked by her uncle. It's really sick, isn't it?'

Joanna came to visit me today. She fixed me with that peculiarly unpleasant stare of hers through most of lunch – I was reminded of a terrier Father once had which turned vicious after a beating and had to be put down; there was the same malicious gleam in his eyes just before he sank his teeth into Father's palm and ripped the flesh from the bone – then spent most of the afternoon searching about in the library. She said she was looking for my mother's book on flower arranging, but she was lying, of course. I remember giving that to her when she moved back to London. I did not interfere.

She looked very tarty, I thought – far too much make-up for a trip to the country and in a ridiculously short skirt for a woman of her age. I suspect some man brought her down and was abandoned to forage for himself at the pub. Sex, to Joanna, is a currency to be used quite shamelessly in return for services rendered.

Oh, Mathilda, Mathilda! Such hypocrisy!

Do these men realize, I wonder, how little she cares for and about them? Not through contempt, I think, but through sheer indifference to anyone's feelings but

her own. I should have taken Hugh Hendry's advice and insisted on a psychiatrist. She's quite mad, but then, so, of course, was Gerald. 'The wheel is come full circle.'

She came out of the library with his idiotic will held in front of her like some holy relic and cursed me in the most childish and absurd way for stealing her inheritance. I wonder who told her about it . . .

Four

WHEN SARAH ARRIVED home that evening, she made a bee-line for Jack's studio. To her relief, nothing had been moved. She passed the canvas on the easel without so much as a glance, and started rummaging feverishly through the portraits stacked against the far wall. Those she recognized, she left; those she didn't, she lined up side by side, facing into the room. In all, there were three paintings she had no recollection of ever having seen before. She stood back and gazed at them, trying to decipher who they were. More accurately, she was trying to isolate one that might strike a chord.

She hoped quite earnestly that she wouldn't find it. But she did, of course. It screamed at her, a violent and vivid portrayal of bitterness, savage wit and repression, and the whole personality was encaged in a rusted iron framework that was all too clearly the scold's bridle. Sarah's shock was enormous, driving the breath from her body in a surge of panic. She collapsed on to Jack's painting stool and closed her eyes against the jeering anger of Mathilda's image. *What had he done?*

The doorbell rang, jerking her to her feet like a mari-

onette. She stood for a moment, wide-eyed with shock, then, without consciously rationalizing why she was doing it, she seized the picture, turned it round and thrust it amongst the others against the wall.

It crossed DS Cooper's mind that Dr Blakeney wasn't well. She looked very pale when she opened the door, but she smiled a welcome and stepped back to let him in, and by the time they were settled on chairs in the kitchen some of the colour had returned to her cheeks. 'You telephoned last night,' he reminded her, 'left a message saying you had more information about Mrs Gillespie.'

'Yes.' Her mind raced. *She said you would know what to do for the best.* But I don't! I DON'T! 'I've been worrying about why she wore the bridle,' she said slowly. 'I've come to the conclusion that she was trying to tell me something, although I must emphasize that I don't know what that something could have been.' As clearly as she could, she repeated what she had told Robin Hewitt the night before about Mathilda's nickname for her. 'It's probably just me being fanciful,' she finished lamely.

The Sergeant frowned deeply. 'She must have known you'd make a connection. Could she have been accusing you, perhaps?'

Sarah showed an unexpected relief. 'I hadn't thought of that,' she admitted. 'You mean a slap over the knuckles to bring me down a peg or two. Doctors can't cure unhappiness, Sarah. Something along those lines?'

He found her relief puzzling. 'It's possible,' he agreed. 'Who else knew that she called you her scold's bridle, Dr Blakeney?'

She folded her hands in her lap. 'I don't know. Whoever she mentioned it to, presumably.'

'You didn't tell anyone?'

She shook her head. 'No.'

'No one at all? Not even your partners or your husband?'

'No.' She forced a light chuckle. 'I wasn't altogether sure that she meant it as a compliment. I always took it as such because it would have strained our relationship if I hadn't, but she might have been implying that I was as repressive and tormenting as the instrument itself.'

He nodded thoughtfully. 'If she killed herself, then you and I will be puzzling over the significance of this for the rest of our lives.' His eyes watched Sarah's face. 'If, however, somebody else killed her, and that person knew she called you her scold's bridle, then it does seem to me that the message is very direct. Namely, I have done this *for* you, Dr Blakeney, or *because of* you. Would you agree with that?'

'No,' she said with a spark of anger. 'Of course I wouldn't. You can't possibly make assumptions like that. In any case I was under the impression that the inquest verdict was a foregone conclusion. The only reason I felt I should tell you all this was because it's been worrying me, but at the end of the day I'm probably reading far more into it than Mathilda intended. I suspect the pathologist was right, and that she simply wanted to deck herself out like Ophelia.'

He smiled pleasantly. 'And, of course, you may not have been the only person she used the nickname on.'

'Well, exactly.' She plucked a hair from the front of her jacket. 'May I ask you something?'

'By all means.'

'Does the pathologist's report come down firmly in favour of suicide or is there any room for doubt?'

'Not much,' the policeman admitted. 'He's unhappy about the absence of a letter of explanation, particularly in view of the rather dramatic way she killed herself, and he's unhappy about the flower arrangement.'

'Because the nettles stung her?'

'No. If she was set on killing herself the way she did, a few nettle stings wouldn't have worried her.' He tapped his pencil on the table top. 'I persuaded him to do some experiments. He's been unable to reproduce the arrangement she came up with without assistance.' He drew a quick diagram in his notebook. 'If you remember, the Michaelmas daisies were set upright in the forehead band, which incidentally is so rusted it can't be tightened, and the nettles hung down like a veil over her hair and cheeks. The stems were alternate, a nettle down, a daisy up, completely symmetrical all the way round. Now that is impossible to achieve without help. You can hold half the arrangement in place with one hand but the minute you get beyond the stretch of the fingers, the flowers start to drop out. It's only when three-quarters of the arrangement is in place that the gap between the frame and the head has reduced enough to retain the other quarter without dropping them, assuming the same circumference head as Mrs Gillespie. Do you follow?'

She frowned. 'I think so. But couldn't she have used cotton wool or tissues to pad the gap while she put in the flowers?'

'Yes. But if she had, then something in that house would have had rust marks on it. We searched it from top to

bottom. There was nothing. So what happened to the padding?'

Sarah closed her eyes and pictured the bathroom. 'There was a sponge on the bathrack,' she said, remembering. 'Perhaps she used that and then washed it in the bath.'

'It does have particles of rust on it,' he admitted, 'but then the bath was full of them. The sponge could have picked them up when it was soaked by the water.' He pursed his lips in frustration. 'Or, as you say, it could have been used as padding. We don't know, but what worries me is this: if she did it herself, then she must have sat at her dressing-table to do it. It's the only surface where we've discovered any sap.' He made a vague gesture with his hand. 'We picture it something like this. She placed the flowers on the dressing-table, sat down in front of the mirror and then set about arranging them in the framework on her head, but she wouldn't have discovered she needed padding until she was half-way round, at which point the natural thing to do would have been to reach for some Kleenex or some cotton wool, both of which were there in front of her. So why go to the bathroom for the sponge?' He fell silent for a moment or two. 'If, however, someone else killed her and arranged the flowers after she was in the bath, then the sponge would have been the obvious thing to use. It's a far more logical scenario and would explain the absence of nettle rash on Mrs Gillespie's hands and fingers.'

'You said the pathologist's report mentioned nettle rash on her cheeks and temples,' said Sarah apologetically. 'But she'd have to have been alive for her skin to react to the stings.'

'It was only slight,' he amended. 'The way I see it, her killer didn't wait till she was dead – you don't hang about when you're murdering someone – he or she shoved the nettles in while she was dying.'

Sarah nodded. 'It sounds plausible,' she agreed, 'except—' She didn't finish the sentence.

'Except what, Dr Blakeney?'

'Why would anyone want to murder her?'

He shrugged. 'Her daughter and her granddaughter had strong enough motives. According to the will, the estate is to be divided equally between the two of them. Mrs Lascelles gets the money and Miss Lascelles gets Cedar House.'

'Did they know?'

He nodded. 'Mrs Lascelles certainly did because she showed us where to find the will – Mrs Gillespie was very methodical, kept all her papers and correspondence in neat files in a cabinet in the library – but whether *Miss* Lascelles knew the precise terms, I don't know. She claims her grandmother intended her to have everything and is very put out to discover she is only going to get the house.' His face assumed a somewhat ironic expression. 'She's a greedy young woman. There's not many seventeen-year-olds would turn their noses up at a windfall like that.'

Sarah smiled slightly. 'Presumably you've checked to find out where they were the night she died?'

He nodded again. 'Mrs Lascelles was at a concert in London with a friend; Miss Lascelles was thirty miles away under the watchful eye of a housemistress at school.'

She forced another smile. 'Which puts them out of the picture.'

'Maybe, maybe not. I never set much store by alibis and someone had to get into Cedar House.' He frowned. 'Apart from Mrs Spede and Mrs Gillespie herself, the Lascelles women were the only other ones with keys.'

'You're determined to make it murder,' protested Sarah mildly.

He went on as if she hadn't spoken. 'We've questioned everyone in the village. Mrs Spede was at the pub with her husband and, as far as friends are concerned, we can't find anyone who was on calling terms with Mrs Gillespie, let alone at around nine o'clock on a Saturday night in November.' He shrugged. 'In any case, her neighbours, Mr and Mrs Orloff, say they would have heard the bell ringing if someone had come to her door. When Mrs Gillespie sold them their part of the house, she simply had the bell moved from the kitchen, which is now theirs, to the corridor outside which remained hers. I tested it. They couldn't have missed it if it was rung that night.'

Sarah caught his eye. 'Then it seems fairly obvious that it must have been suicide.'

'Not to me, Dr Blakeney. In the first place, I intend to put those two alibis under a microscope and, in the second place, if Mrs Gillespie's murderer was someone she knew, they could have tapped on the windows or the back door without the Orloffs hearing them.' He closed his notebook and tucked it into his pocket. 'We'll get them eventually. Probably through their fingerprints.'

'You're going on with it then? I thought your boss had decided to drop it.'

'We raised a number of fingerprints in that house which don't belong to Mrs Gillespie or the three women who had

keys. We'll be asking everyone in the village and outsiders like you, who knew her, to let us take prints for comparison purposes. I've persuaded the Chief to find out who else went in there before he draws a line under this one.'

'You seem to be taking Mrs Gillespie's death very personally.'

'Policing's no different from any other job, Doctor. The higher up the ladder you are the better the pension at the end.' His amiable face grew suddenly cynical. 'But promotion has more to do with empire-building than ability, and to date my light has always been hidden under some other sod's bushel. I do take Mrs Gillespie's death personally. It's my case.'

Sarah found this bleakly amusing. She wondered how Mathilda would feel about a policeman benefiting from her death, assuming, of course, he could prove it was murder and then convict the murderer. She might have felt happier if she wasn't so convinced that he was going to score on both counts.

'Keith? It's Sarah. Sarah Blakeney. Has Jack been in touch with you, by any chance?' She toyed with the telephone wire while she listened to the sound of Cooper's car fading into the distance. There were too many shadows in this hall, she thought.

'Not recently,' said Keith Smollett's pleasant voice. 'Should he have been?'

There was no point beating about the bush. 'We had a row. I told him I wanted a divorce and he's gone off in a

huff. He left a note saying I could contact him through you.'

'Oh, good God, Sarah! Well, I can't act for both of you. Jack will have to find himself another solicitor.'

'He's opted for you. I'm the one who has to find someone else.'

'Bugger that,' said Keith cheerfully. '*You're* my client, sweetheart. The only reason I've ever done anything for that lazy good-for-nothing is because you married him.' He and Sarah had been friends from university days and there had been a time, before Jack entered the frame, when Keith had had designs on Sarah himself. Now, he was happily married with three strapping young sons, and only thought about her on the rare occasions when she telephoned.

'Yes, well, that's a side issue at the moment. The main issue is that I need to talk to him rather urgently. He's bound to contact you so will you let me know where he is as soon as he does. It's desperately important.' She glanced towards the stairs, her face a pale glimmer in the reflected light from the kitchen. Far too many shadows.

'Will do.'

'There's something else. What's my legal position with regard to a police investigation into a possible murder?' She heard his indrawn breath. 'I don't mean I'm involved or anything but I think I've been given some information that I really ought to pass on. The police don't seem to know about it, but it's incredibly sensitive stuff and very second-hand, and if it doesn't have any bearing then I shall be betraying a confidence that's going to affect quite a few lives really badly.' She drew to a halt. *Why had Ruth told*

her about the letter and not Cooper? Or had she told Cooper as well? 'Does any of that make any sense?'

'Not much. My advice, for what it's worth, is don't withhold anything from the police unless it's confidential medical information on a patient. Force them to go through the proper channels for that. They'll do it, of course, but you'll be squeaky-clean.'

'The person who told me isn't even a patient.'

'Then you don't have a problem.'

'But I could ruin lives by speaking out of turn,' she said doubtfully. 'We're talking ethics here, Keith.'

'No, we're not. Ethics don't exist outside church and ivory towers. We're talking big, bad world, where even doctors go to prison if they obstruct the police in their enquiries. You won't have a leg to stand on, my girl, if it turns out you withheld information that could have resulted in a conviction for murder.'

'But I'm not sure it *is* murder. It looks like suicide.'

'Then why is your voice quivering about two pitches higher than normal? You sound like Maria Callas on a bad night. It's only a snap judgement, of course, but I'd say you're one hundred per cent certain that you're looking at murder and ninety-nine per cent certain that you know who did it. Talk to the police.'

She was silent for so long that he began to wonder if the line had been cut. 'You're wrong about the ninety-nine per cent,' she said at last. 'Actually, I haven't a clue who might have done it.' With a muted goodbye, she hung up.

The telephone started to ring before she had removed her hand from the receiver, but her nerves were so shot to

pieces that it was several moments before she could find the courage to pick it up.

The following morning, Saturday, a solicitor drove from Poole to Fontwell with Mathilda's will in his briefcase. He had telephoned Cedar House the previous evening to introduce himself and to unleash his bombshell, namely that all Mathilda's previous wills were rendered null and void by the one she had signed in his office two days before she died. He had been instructed by Mrs Gillespie to break the news to her daughter and granddaughter in person as soon as convenient after her funeral, and to do it in the presence of Dr Sarah Blakeney of Mill House, Long Upton. Dr Blakeney was free tomorrow. Would eleven o'clock be convenient for Mrs and Miss Lascelles?

The atmosphere in Mathilda's drawing-room was icy. Joanna stood by the french windows, staring out over the garden, her back to both Sarah and her daughter. Ruth smoked continuously, darting malicious glances between the rigid back of the one woman and the obvious discomfort of the other. No one spoke. To Sarah, who had always loved this room with its mish-mash of beautiful antiques: Georgian corner cabinets, old and faded chintz covers on the Victorian sofa and chairs, nineteenth-century Dutch watercolours and the Louis XVI Lyre clock on the mantelpiece, this unwelcome and unwelcomed return was depressing.

The sound of car tyres on the gravel outside broke the tension. 'I'll go,' said Ruth, jumping up.

'I can't even remember what he said his name was,' declared Joanna, turning back into the room. 'Dougall, Douglas?'

'Duggan,' said Sarah.

Joanna frowned. 'You know him, then.'

'No. I wrote his name down when he phoned last night.' She fished a piece of paper from her pocket. 'Paul Duggan of Duggan, Smith and Drew, Hills Road, Poole.'

Joanna listened to her daughter greeting someone at the door. 'My mother seems to have had considerable faith in you, Dr Blakeney. Why was that, do you suppose? You can only have known her – what? – a year?' Her face was impassive – schooled that way, thought Sarah, to preserve her youthfulness – but her eyes were deeply suspicious.

Sarah smiled without hostility. She had been placed in a very invidious position, and she wasn't enjoying the experience. She had considerable sympathy for Joanna, one way and another, and she was becoming increasingly troubled by Mathilda's memory. Their relationship, a light-hearted one at best, was turning oppressive in retrospect, and she resented the old woman's assumption that she could manipulate her doctor after her death and without prior permission. It was neither Sarah's business nor her wish to act as mediator in an acrimonious legal battle between Joanna and her daughter. 'I'm as much in the dark as you are, Mrs Lascelles, and probably just as annoyed,' she said frankly. 'I've a week's shopping to do, a house to clean and a garden to take care of. I'm only here because Mr Duggan said if I didn't come then he would have to postpone this meeting until I could. I thought that would be even more upsetting for you and Ruth' – she shrugged – 'so I agreed to it.'

Joanna was on the point of answering when the door swung open and Ruth walked in, followed by a smiling middle-aged man carrying a video recorder with a briefcase balanced on top of it. 'Mr Duggan,' she said curtly, flopping into her chair again. 'He wants to use the television. Would you believe, Granny's made a frigging video-will?'

'Not strictly true, Miss Lascelles,' said the man, bending down to place the recorder on the floor beside the television. He straightened and held out a hand to Joanna, guessing correctly that she was Mathilda's daughter. 'How do you do, Mrs Lascelles.' He moved across to Sarah, who had stood up, and shook her hand also. 'Dr Blakeney.' He gestured to the chairs. 'Please sit down. I'm very aware that all our time is precious, so I don't intend to take up more of it than I need to. I am here as one of the joint executors of the last written will and testament of Mrs Mathilda Beryl Gillespie, copies of which I will give you in a few minutes, and from which you may satisfy yourselves that it does in fact supersede any previous will or wills made by Mrs Gillespie. The other joint executor is Mr John Hapgood, currently manager of Barclays Bank, Hills Road, Poole. In both instances, of course, we hold our responsibilities as executors on behalf of our firms so should either of us cease employment with the said firms, then another executor will be appointed in our place.' He paused briefly. 'Is all that quite clear?' He glanced from one to the other. 'Good. Now, if you'll bear with me for a moment, I'll just connect the video to the television.' He produced a coil of coaxial cable like a magician from his pocket and plugged one end into the television and the other into the video recorder. 'And now a power socket,' he murmured, unrolling a wire

and a plug from the back of the video. 'If I remember correctly, it's above the skirting board to the right of the fireplace. Ah, yes, here we are. Splendid. And just in case you're wondering how I knew, then let me explain that Mrs Gillespie invited me here to make an inventory of all her possessions.' He beamed at them. 'Purely to avoid acrimonious arguments between the relative parties after the will has been read.'

Sarah was aware that her mouth had been hanging open since he entered the room. She shut it with a conscious effort and watched him deftly tune the television to receive the signal from the recorder, then open his briefcase and remove a video cassette which he inserted into the recorder before standing back to let Mathilda speak for herself. You could have heard a pin drop, she thought, as Mathilda's face materialized on the screen. Even Ruth sat as if carved in stone, her cigarette temporarily forgotten between her fingers.

The well-remembered voice, with its strident upper-class vowels, spoke confidently from the amplifier.

'Well, my dears,' Mathilda's lips thinned scornfully, 'I'm sure you're wondering why I insisted on bringing you together like this. Joanna, I have no doubt, is cursing me quietly under her breath, Ruth is nursing yet another grievance and Sarah, I suspect, is beginning to wish she had never met me.' The old woman gave a dry laugh. 'I am, by now, impervious to your curses, Joanna, so if there is awareness after death, which I doubt, they won't be troubling me. And, Ruth, your grievances have become so tiresome recently that, frankly, I'm bored with them. They

won't be troubling me either.' Her voice softened a little. 'The irritation, however, that I am sure Sarah is feeling at my unilateral decision to involve her in my family's affairs *does* concern me. All I can say is that I have valued your friendship and your strength of character, Sarah, during the time I've known you, and I cannot think of anyone else who could even begin to support the burden that I am about to place on your shoulders.'

There was a brief pause while she consulted some notes on her lap. To Sarah, whose uncritical affection now appeared naïve in the face of the universal dislike which Mathilda had inspired in those who knew her, the old woman's eyes were uncharacteristically cruel. Where, she wondered, had her humour gone?

'I wish to make it absolutely clear that Joanna is not James Gillespie's daughter, but the daughter of my uncle, Gerald Cavendish. He was my father's elder brother and . . .' she sought for the right words to express herself, 'the liaison between us began some four years after he invited me and my father to live with him in Cedar House following the death of my mother. My father had no money of his own because the estate had been settled on the elder son, Gerald. My mother's money reverted to her family when she died, apart from a small inheritance which was left in trust for me. Without Gerald's invitation to live with him in Cedar House, my father and I would have been homeless. To that extent I was grateful. In every other respect I despised and loathed the man.' She smiled coldly. 'I was a child of thirteen when he first raped me.'

Sarah was shocked – not just by what Mathilda was

saying, but by the way she was saying it. This was not a Mathilda *she* recognized. Why was she being so brutal, so coldly calculating?

'He was a drunken monster, like my father, and I hated them both. Between them, they destroyed any chance I might ever have had of forming a lasting and successful relationship. I have never known if my father knew what Gerald was doing but, even if he did, I am in no doubt whatsoever that he would have let it continue for fear of Gerald evicting us from Cedar House. My father was an intensely lazy man who scrounged off his wife's family until she died, and then scrounged off his brother. The only time I ever knew him to work was later, when he stood for election to the House of Commons, and then only because he saw membership as an easy route to a knighthood. Once elected, of course, he reverted to what he truly was – a contemptible man.' She paused again, her mouth turned down in bitter remembrance.

'Gerald's abuse of me continued on and off for twelve years when, in desperation, I told my father about it. I cannot adequately explain why it took me so long, except to say that I lived in constant terror of both of them. I was a prisoner, financially and socially, and I was brought up to believe, as many of my generation were, that men held natural authority within a family. I thank God those times are passing because I see now that natural authority belongs only to those who earn the respect to exercise it, be they male or female.' She paused for a moment. 'My father, of course, blamed me for what had happened, calling me a disgusting slut, and was disinclined to do anything. He preferred, as I knew he would, to maintain the status quo at

my expense. But he was vulnerable. He was now a Member of Parliament, and in desperation I threatened to write to the Conservative Party and the newspapers in order to expose what sort of family the Cavendishes really were. As a result of this, a compromise was reached. I was allowed to marry James Gillespie who had declared an interest in me, and in return I agreed to say nothing. Under these conditions, we made some attempt to resume our lives although my father, fearing perhaps that I would go back on my word, insisted that my marriage to James take place immediately. He secured James a position at the Treasury, and packed us off to a flat in London.'

There was a longer silence this time while she turned to another page of her notes, adjusting her glasses as she did so. 'Unfortunately, I was already pregnant, and when Joanna was born less than five months after our marriage, even James, by no means the brightest of men, realized the baby couldn't possibly be his. Life became very difficult after that. Not unreasonably, he resented us both, and this led to bouts of violence whenever he had too much to drink. We continued in this unhappy vein for another eighteen months until, mercifully, James announced that he had secured a job abroad and would be sailing the next day without us. I have never regretted his departure or cared one iota what happened to him. He was a very unpleasant piece of work.' The old eyes stared straight out of the screen, arrogant and disdainful, but for Sarah at least there was a sense of something withheld. Mathilda, she thought, was not being quite honest.

'It is tedious now to recall the difficulties of those months after his departure. Suffice it to say that money was short.

Joanna experienced similar problems herself when Steven died. The difference was that my father refused to help me – he had by now received his knighthood and enough water had passed under the bridge to mitigate my threats of exposure – while *I* did help *you*, Joanna, although you have never thanked me for it. In the end, when it was clear that eviction was becoming a real possibility, I wrote in desperation to Gerald and asked him to support his daughter. This, I gather, was the first he knew of Joanna's existence,' she smiled cynically, 'and my letter prompted him into the one honourable act of his life. He killed himself with an overdose of barbiturates. The pity is he didn't have the decency to do it sooner.' Her voice was brittle with dislike. 'A verdict of accidental death was recorded, but I cannot believe the two things were unrelated, particularly in view of the letter he sent to his solicitor, making Joanna heir to all his property.'

She turned to what was obviously the last page of her notes. 'I now come to what has prompted me to make this film. Joanna first. You threatened me with exposure if I refused to leave Cedar House immediately and make the property over to you. I have no idea who suggested you look for your father's letter, although,' she smiled grimly, 'I have my suspicions. But you were very misinformed about your rights. Gerald's absurd will could not break the trust whereby his father granted him a life interest in the property after which it passed to the nearest male relative, namely my father. By dying, Gerald merely conferred on his brother and his brother's heirs a permanent interest in the Cavendish wealth. He knew it, too. Please don't imagine that his pathetic codicil was anything more than a weak man's

atonement for sins of commission and omission. Perhaps he was naïve enough to believe that my father would honour the obligation, perhaps he just thought that God would be less harsh if he showed willing to make amends. Either way he was a fool. He did, however, have the sense to send me a copy of the codicil and, by threatening to go to court with it in order to challenge the trust, I was able to use it to influence my father. He agreed to finance you and me in London while he remained alive and to make the property over to me on his death which he was entitled to do. As you know, he was dead within two years, and you and I moved back to Cedar House.' Her eyes, staring fixedly into the lens, picked out her daughter. 'You should never have threatened me, Joanna. You had no reason to, whereas I had every reason to threaten my father. I have made some very handsome settlements on you, one way and another, and feel that I have discharged all my obligations towards you. If you haven't already taken me to court when you see this, then I urge you not to waste your money after I'm gone. Believe me, I have given you more than the law ever entitled you to.

'Now, Ruth.' She cleared her throat. 'Your behaviour since your seventeenth birthday has appalled me. I can find no way to account for it or excuse it. I have always told you that the property would be yours when I died. I was referring to Cedar House but you assumed, without any prompting from me, that the contents and the money would be yours, too. That was a false assumption. My intention was always to leave the more valuable contents and the money to Joanna, and the house to you. Joanna, I assumed, would not wish to move from London, and you

would have had the choice either to sell up or stay but you would have sold, I'm sure, because the house would have lost its charms once the estate was approved. What little remained to the property would never have satisfied you because you're as greedy as your mother. In conclusion, I can only repeat what I said to Joanna: I have made some very handsome settlements on you and feel that I have more than discharged my obligations to you. It may be the fault of inbreeding, of course, but I have come to realize that neither of you is capable of a decent or a generous thought.' Her eyes narrowed behind her glasses. 'I therefore intend to leave everything I own to Dr Sarah Blakeney of Mill House, Long Upton, Dorset, who will, I am confident, use her windfall wisely. In so far as I have ever been capable of feeling fondness for anyone I have felt it for her.' She gave a sudden chuckle. 'Don't be angry with me, Sarah. I must have died without changing my mind, or you wouldn't be watching this. So remember me for our friendship and not for this burden I have laid on you. Joanna and Ruth will hate you, as they have hated me, and they will accuse you of all manner of beastliness, just as they have accused me. But "what's done cannot be undone", so take it all with my blessing and use it to promote something worthwhile in my memory. Goodbye, my dear.'

'When sorrows come, they come not as single spies but in battalions.' I am afraid that Ruth's behaviour is becoming compulsive but am reluctant to tackle her about it for fear of what she might do to me. She is not above taking a stick to an old woman who annoys or frustrates her. I see it in her eyes, an awareness that I am more valuable to her dead than alive.

It was truly said: 'He that dies pays all debts.'

If I knew where she was going every day, it would help, but she lies about that as she lies about everything. Could it be schizophrenia? She is certainly the right age for it. I trust the school will do something about it next term. I am not strong enough for any more scenes nor will I be blamed for what was never my fault. God knows, there was only one victim in all this, and that was little Mathilda Cavendish. I wish I could remember her, that loving lovely child, but she is as insubstantial to me now as memories of my mother. Forgotten wraiths, both of them, unloved, abused, neglected.

Thank God for Sarah. She convinces me that like Shakespeare's sad old man 'I am more sinned against than sinning . . .'

Five

PAUL DUGGAN switched off the television set and spoke into the silence. 'The video recording, of course, has no legal standing which is why I referred to Mrs Gillespie's last *written* will and testament.' He reached into his briefcase and produced some sheaves of paper. 'These are photocopies only but the original is available for inspection at my office in Hills Street.' He handed a copy to each of the women. 'Mrs Gillespie felt you might try to contest this document, Mrs Lascelles. I can only advise you to consult a solicitor before you do so. As far as Dr Blakeney is concerned' – he turned to Sarah – 'Mr Hapgood and I will need to discuss details with you as soon as possible. We can offer you three mornings next week. Tuesday, Wednesday or Thursday. In my office for preference, although we will come to Long Upton if necessary. You understand, however, that executors are entitled to charge for expenses.' He beamed encouragingly at Sarah, waiting for an answer. He appeared to be completely unaware of the brewing hostility in the room.

Sarah gathered her scattered wits together. 'Do I have any say in this at all?'

'In what, Dr Blakeney?'

'In the will.'

'You mean, are you free to reject Mrs Gillespie's bequest?'

'Yes.'

'There's an alternative provision which you will find on the last page of the document.' Joanna and Ruth rustled through their copies. 'If for any reason you are unable to take up the bequest, Mrs Gillespie instructed us to sell her entire estate and donate the proceeds to the Seton Retirement Home for donkeys. She said, if you couldn't or wouldn't have her money, then it might as well go to deserving asses.' He was watching Sarah closely and she thought that, after all, he wasn't quite so complacent as he seemed. He was expecting that remark to strike a chord. 'Tuesday, Wednesday or Thursday, Dr Blakeney? I should point out that an early meeting is essential. There is the future of Mrs Lascelles and her daughter to be considered, for example. Mrs Gillespie recognized that they would be in residence at Cedar House when the will was read and had no wish that we as executors should demand their immediate vacation of the property. It was for this reason, and without any offence intended,' he smiled amiably at the two women, 'that a full inventory of the contents was made. I'm sure the last thing any of us wants is a battle royal over just what was in the house at the time of Mrs Gillespie's death.'

'Oh, bloody fabulous,' said Ruth scathingly, 'now you're accusing us of theft.'

'Not at all, Miss Lascelles. It's standard procedure, I assure you.'

Her lip curled unattractively. 'What's our future got to

do with anything, anyway? I thought we'd ceased to exist.' She dropped her cigarette butt deliberately on to the Persian carpet and ground it out under her heel.

'As I understand it, Miss Lascelles, you have another two terms at boarding school before you take your A levels. To date, your grandmother paid your fees but there is no provision in the will for further expenditure on your education so, in the circumstances, whether you remain at Southcliffe may well depend on Dr Blakeney.'

Joanna raised her head. 'Or on me,' she said coolly. 'I am her mother, after all.'

There was a short silence before Ruth gave a harsh laugh. 'God, you're a fool. No wonder Granny didn't want to leave her money to you. What are you planning to pay with, Mother dear? No one's going to give you an allowance any more, you know, and you don't imagine your sweet little flower arrangements are going to produce four thousand a term, do you?'

Joanna smiled faintly. 'If I contest this will then, presumably, things will continue as normal in the meantime.' She looked enquiringly at Paul Duggan. 'Do you have the authority to give the money to Dr Blakeney if I, too, am laying claim to it?'

'No,' he admitted, 'but, by the same token, you will receive nothing either. You are putting me in a difficult position, Mrs Lascelles. I was your mother's lawyer, not yours. All I will say is there are time limits involved and I urge you to seek independent legal advice without delay. Things will not, as you put it, continue as normal.'

'So in the short term Ruth and I lose either way?'

'Not necessarily.'

She frowned. 'I'm afraid I don't understand.'

Ruth flung herself out of the sofa and stormed across to the window. 'God, why do you have to be so obtuse? If you behave nicely, Mother, Dr Blakeney may feel guilty enough about inheriting a fortune to keep subsidizing us. That's it, isn't it?' She glared at Duggan. 'Granny's passed the buck of trying to create something decent out of the Cavendishes to her doctor.' Her mouth twisted. 'What a frigging awful joke! She warned me about it, too. Talk to Dr Blakeney. She'll know what to do for the best. It's so unfair.' She stamped her foot. 'It's so bloody unfair.'

Joanna's face was thoughtful. 'Is that right, Mr Duggan?'

'Not strictly, no. I will admit that Mrs Gillespie's reading of Dr Blakeney's character was that she would honour some of the undertakings Mrs Gillespie made to you and your daughter, but I must stress that Dr Blakeney is not obliged to do so. There is nothing in the will to that effect. She is free to interpret your mother's wishes any way she chooses, and if she believes that she can promote something worthwhile in Mrs Gillespie's memory by ignoring you and building a clinic in this village instead, then she is entitled to do so.'

There was another silence. Sarah looked up from a prolonged study of the carpet to discover all their eyes upon her. She found herself echoing Ruth's words. *What a frigging awful joke.* 'Thursday,' she said with a sigh. 'I'll come to your office on Thursday and I shall probably bring my own solicitor with me. I'm not happy about this, Mr Duggan.'

'Poor Dr Blakeney,' said Joanna with a tight smile. 'I do believe you're finally beginning to realize what a ruthless

bitch my mother was. From the moment she seduced Gerald, she had her hands on the Cavendish purse strings and she kept them there, through threats and blackmail, upwards of fifty years.' A look of compassion crossed her curiously impassive face. 'And now she's appointed you to carry on her tyranny. The dictator is dead.' She gave a small, ironic bow. 'Long live the dictator.'

Sarah stood by Paul Duggan's car as he packed the video recorder into the boot. 'Have the police seen that film?' she asked him as he straightened up.

'Not yet. I've an appointment with a Sergeant Cooper in half an hour or so. I'll give him a copy then.'

'Shouldn't you have shown it to them straight away? Mathilda didn't sound to me like a woman who was about to commit suicide. *I must have died without changing my mind* . . . She wouldn't have said that if she was planning to kill herself two days later.'

'I agree.'

His moon face beamed at her and she frowned her irritation. 'You're very relaxed about it,' she said tartly. 'I hope, for your sake, DS Cooper understands why you've delayed producing it. I certainly don't. Mathilda's been dead two weeks and the police have been tying themselves in knots trying to find evidence of murder.'

'Not my fault, Dr Blakeney,' he said amiably. 'It's been with the film company who made it for the last two weeks, waiting to have titles and music added. Mrs Gillespie wanted Verdi playing in the background.' He chuckled. 'She chose *Dies Irae* – The Day of Wrath. Rather appropriate, don't

you think?' He paused briefly, waiting for a reaction, but she was in no mood to oblige. 'Anyway, she wanted to vet it afterwards and they told her to come back in a month for a viewing. These things can't be hurried, I gather. They were very put out to hear from me that she was already dead. All of which lends weight to your argument, that she wasn't planning to kill herself.' He shrugged. 'I wasn't there when she made it, so I didn't know what was in it. As far as I was concerned it was a message to her family. I saw it for the first time last night, at which point I rang for an appointment with the boys in blue.' He glanced at his watch. 'And I'm going to be late. I'll see you on Thursday, then.'

Sarah watched him drive away with a horrible feeling of insecurity chewing at the pit of her stomach. She should have guessed, prepared herself a little. *Talk to Dr Blakeney. She will know what to do for the best.* And what about Jack? Had *he* known?

She felt suddenly very lonely.

Sarah was raking up leaves when DS Cooper arrived that afternoon. He picked his way across the grass and stood watching her. 'Hard work,' he murmured sympathetically.

'Yes.' She propped the rake against a tree and thrust her hands into her Barbour pockets. 'We'd better go in. It's warmer inside.'

'Don't worry on my account,' he said. 'I'd just as soon stay out and have a smoke.' He fished a crumpled pack of Silk Cut from inside his coat and lit up with obvious

enjoyment. 'Disgusting habit,' he murmured, eyeing her warily. 'I'll give it up one day.'

Sarah lifted an amused eyebrow. 'Why are smokers always so consumed with guilt?'

'Cigarettes reveal the weakness of our character,' he said morosely. 'Other people give up, but we can't. To tell you the truth I've never understood why society treats us like pariahs. I've yet to meet the smoker who's beaten his wife after one too many fags or killed a child while in charge of a car, but I could show you a hundred drunks who've done it. I'd say drink is a far more dangerous drug than nicotine.'

She led him to a bench seat beside the path. 'The moral majority will get round to condemning the drinkers, too, eventually,' she said. 'And then the whole world will be jogging around in its vest and pants, bristling with good health, eating vegetables, drinking carrot juice and never doing anything remotely detrimental to its health.'

He chuckled. 'Shouldn't you applaud that, as a doctor?'

'I'll be out of a job.' She leant her head against the back of the seat. 'Anyway, I have a problem with the moral majority. I don't like it. I'd rather have free-thinking individuals any day than politically correct mobs who behave the way they're told to because somebody else has decided what's socially acceptable.'

'Is that why you liked Mrs Gillespie?'

'Probably.'

'Tell me about her.'

'I can't really add anything to what I've told you already. She was quite the most extraordinary person I've ever met. Completely cynical. She had no respect for anyone or

anything. She didn't believe in God or retribution. She loathed mankind in general and the people of Fontwell in particular, and she considered everybody, past and present, beneath her. The only exception to that was Shakespeare. She thought Shakespeare was a towering genius.' She fell silent.

'And you *liked* her?'

Sarah laughed. 'I suppose I enjoyed the anarchy of it all. She put into words what most of us only think. I can't explain it any better than that. I always looked forward to seeing her.'

'It must have been mutual or she wouldn't have left you her money.'

Sarah didn't answer immediately. 'I had no idea what she was planning,' she said after a moment or two. She thrust a hand into her hair, fluffing it skyward. 'It's come as a nasty shock. I feel I'm being manipulated and I don't like that.'

He nodded. 'According to Duggan, Mrs Gillespie instructed the two executors to keep the whole thing secret.' He examined the glowing tip of his cigarette. 'The trouble is, we can't be sure that she herself didn't tell someone.'

'If she had,' said Sarah, 'she would probably still be alive. Assuming she was murdered, of course.'

'Meaning whoever killed her didn't know you were the beneficiary but thought they were?'

She nodded. 'Something like that.'

'Then it must have been the daughter or the granddaughter.'

'It depends what was in the previous will. She may have made other bequests. People have been murdered for far tinier amounts than Joanna or Ruth were expecting to get.'

'But that's assuming she was murdered for her money. It's also assuming that neither you nor anyone dependent on you murdered her.'

'True,' she said unemotionally.

'Did you murder her, Dr Blakeney?'

'I wouldn't have done it that way, Sergeant. I would have taken my time.' She gave a light chuckle. A little forced, he thought. 'There was no hurry, after all. I've no outstanding debts and I certainly wouldn't want to link her death so closely to a will changed in my favour.' She bent forward, clasping her hands between her knees. 'And it would have looked very natural, too. Doctors have a built-in advantage when it comes to committing the perfect murder. A period of illness, followed by a gentle death. Nothing so dramatic or traumatic as slitting the wrists while wearing an instrument of torture.'

'It might be a magnificent bluff,' he said mildly. 'As you say, who would suspect a doctor of doing something so crass within hours of an old lady making over three-quarters of a million pounds?'

Sarah stared at him with undisguised horror. 'Three-quarters of a million?' she echoed slowly. 'Is that what she was worth?'

'More or less. Probably more. It's a conservative estimate. Duggan's valued the house and its contents at around four hundred thousand, but the clocks alone were insured for well over a hundred thousand and that was based on a ten-year-old valuation. I'd hate to guess what they're worth now. Then there's the antique furniture, her jewellery and, of course, Mrs Lascelles's flat in London, plus innumerable stocks and shares. You're a rich woman, Dr Blakeney.'

Sarah put her head in her hands. 'Oh, my God!' she groaned. 'You mean, Joanna doesn't even own her own flat?'

'No. It's part of Mrs Gillespie's estate. If the old woman had had any sense she'd have made it over to her daughter in annual dollops to avoid anyone having to pay inheritance tax on it. As it is, the Treasury's going to have almost as big a windfall as you're getting.' He sounded sympathetic. 'And it'll be your job to decide what has to be sold off to pay the bill. You're not going to be very popular with the Lascelles women, I suspect.'

'That must be the understatement of the year,' said Sarah bleakly. 'What on earth was Mathilda thinking of?'

'Most people would see it as manna from heaven.'

'Including you?'

'Of course, but then I live in a very ordinary house, I've three grown-up children who touch me for money whenever they can, and I dream about retiring early and taking the wife on an extended cruise round the world.' He glanced about the garden. 'In your shoes, I'd probably react as you are reacting. You're not exactly short of a bob or two, and your conscience will stop you spending it on yourself. She was right when she said she was laying a burden on your shoulders.'

Sarah digested this for a moment or two in silence. 'Does that mean you don't think I murdered her?'

He looked amused. 'Probably.'

'Well, thank God for small mercies,' she said dryly. 'It's been worrying me.'

'Your dependants, however, are a different matter. They stand to benefit just as much as you do from Mrs Gillespie's death.'

She looked surprised. 'I don't have any dependants.'

'You have a husband, Dr Blakeney. I'm told he's dependent on you.'

She stirred some leaves with the toe of her wellington boot. 'Not any more. We're separated. I don't even know where he is at the moment.'

He took out his notebook and consulted it. 'That must be fairly recent then. According to Mrs Lascelles, he attended the funeral two days ago, went on to Cedar House afterwards for tea and then asked her to drive him back here at around six o'clock, which she did.' He paused to look at her. 'So when exactly did the separation begin?'

'He left some time that night. I found a note from him in the morning.'

'Was it his idea or yours?'

'Mine. I told him I wanted a divorce.'

'I see.' He regarded her thoughtfully. 'Was there a reason for choosing that night to do it?'

She sighed. 'I was depressed by Mathilda's funeral. I found myself exploring that old chestnut, the meaning of life, and I wondered what the point of *her* life was. I suddenly realized that my own life was almost as pointless.' She turned her head to look at him. 'You probably think that sounds absurd. I'm a doctor, after all, and you don't enter medicine without some sort of vocation. It's like police work. We're in it because we believe we can make a difference.' She gave a hollow laugh. 'There's an awful arrogance in a statement like that. The presumption is that we know what we're doing when, frankly, I'm not sure that we do. Doctors strive officiously to keep people alive, because the law says we must, and we talk grandly about

quality of life. But what *is* quality of life? I kept Mathilda's pain under control with some sophisticated drugs but the quality of her life was appalling, not because of pain, but because she was lonely, bitter, intensely frustrated and very unhappy.' She shrugged. 'I took a long hard look at myself and my husband during the funeral, and I realized that the same adjectives could be applied to the two of us. We were both lonely, both bitter, both frustrated and both unhappy. So I suggested a divorce, and he left.' She smiled cynically. 'It was as simple as that.'

He felt sorry for her. Nothing was ever that simple, and it sounded to him as if she had tried to bluff a hand at poker, and lost. 'Had he met Mrs Lascelles before the funeral?'

'Not as far as I know. *I* hadn't, so I can't imagine how he could have done.'

'But he knew Mrs Gillespie?'

She looked out across the garden, playing for time. 'If he did, then it wasn't through me. He never mentioned meeting her.'

DS Cooper's already lively interest in the absent Jack Blakeney was growing. 'Why did he go to the funeral?'

'Because I asked him to.' She straightened. 'I hate funerals but I always feel I have to go to them. It seems so churlish to turn your back on a patient the minute they're dead. Jack was very good about lending support.' Unexpectedly, she laughed. 'To tell you the truth, I think he rather fancies himself in his black overcoat. He enjoys looking satanic.'

Satanic. The Sergeant pondered over the word. Duncan Orloff had said Mathilda liked Blakeney. Mrs Lascelles had

described him as 'a peculiar man who said very little and then demanded to be taken home'. Ruth had found him 'intimidating'. The vicar, on the other hand, had had a great deal to say when Cooper had approached him about the various members of the funeral congregation. 'Jack Blakeney? He's an artist though not a very successful one, poor chap. If it wasn't for Sarah, he'd be starving. Matter of fact, I like his work. I'd buy a canvas if only he'd lower his sights a little, but he knows his worth, or says he does, and refuses to sell himself cheap. Did he know Mathilda? Yes, he must have done. I saw him leaving her house one day with his sketchpad under his arm. She'd have been a wonderful subject for his type of work. He couldn't have resisted her.'

He took the bull by the horns. 'The Reverend Matthews tells me your husband was painting a portrait of Mrs Gillespie. He must have known her quite well to do that.' He lit another cigarette and watched Sarah through the smoke.

She sat for a long time in silence, contemplating a distant cow in a far field. 'I feel inclined to say I won't answer any more questions until my solicitor's present,' she murmured at last, 'except that I have a nasty feeling you'd regard that as suspicious.' He didn't say anything, so she glanced at him. There was no sympathy in the pleasant face, only a patient confidence that she would answer in the affirmative, with or without a solicitor. She sighed. 'I could deny a portrait quite easily. They're all in the studio, and there isn't a chance in a million you'd recognize Mathilda's. Jack doesn't paint faces. He paints personalities. And you have to understand his colour-coding and the way he uses

dynamics in shape, depth and perspective to interpret what he's done.'

'But you're not going to deny it?' he suggested.

'Only because Jack won't, and I'm not particularly keen to perjure myself.' She smiled and her eyes lit with enthusiasm. 'Actually, it's brilliant. I think it's probably the best thing he's ever done. I found it yesterday just before you came.' She pulled a wry face. 'I knew it would be there because of something Ruth said. According to her, Jack mentioned that Mathilda called me her scold's bridle.' She sighed again. 'And he couldn't have known that unless Mathilda had told him, because I never did.'

'May I see this painting?'

She ignored the question. 'He wouldn't have murdered her, Sergeant, not for money, anyway. Jack despises materialism. The only use he has for money is as a guide to the value of his genius. Which is why he never sells anything. His own valuation of his art is rather higher than everybody else's.' She smiled at his frown of disbelief. 'Actually, it makes sense in a funny sort of way, but it's irritating because it's so conceited. The argument goes something like this: your average prole is incapable of recognizing genius so he won't be interested in buying your picture whatever price you put on it. While a Renaissance man, on the other hand, will recognize genius and will pay handsomely for it. Ergo, if you're a genius, you put a high price on yourself and wait for the right person to come and discover you.'

'If you'll pardon the language, Dr Blakeney, that is bullshit.' He felt quite angry. 'The man's conceit must be colossal. Has anyone else said he's a genius?'

'No one said Van Gogh was a genius either until after he was dead.' Why, she wondered, did Jack's single-minded view of himself always put people's backs up? Was it because, in an uncertain world, his certainty was threatening? 'It really doesn't matter,' she said calmly, 'what sort of an artist Jack is. Good, bad, indifferent. I happen to think he's good, but that's a personal opinion. The point is he would never have killed Mathilda for her money, assuming he knew she'd made the will in my favour, which I doubt. Why should she have told him when she never told me?'

'Except that he thought you were going to divorce him and push him into the cold.'

'Hardly. That would leave me enjoying the loot all by myself, wouldn't it? How could he get his hands on the inheritance if he and I were divorced?' *I'll be going for a fifty-fifty split* . . . She pushed that thought away. 'And in any case, two weeks ago when Mathilda died, he didn't know I wanted to divorce him. How could he? I didn't know myself.'

Cooper took that with a pinch of salt. 'These things don't happen out of the blue, Dr Blakeney. He must have had an inkling that the marriage was in difficulties.'

'You're underestimating Jack's egotism,' she answered with a somewhat bitter irony. 'He's far too self-centred to notice anyone else's unhappiness unless he's painting them. Believe me, my decision *did* come out of the blue. For him, anyway.'

He puffed thoughtfully on his cigarette. 'Do you expect him to come back at all?'

'Oh, yes. He'll want to collect his paintings if nothing else.'

'Good. Some of the fingerprints we lifted may well be his. It will help if we can eliminate them. Yours, too, of course. There'll be a team taking prints in Fontwell on Wednesday morning. I assume you've no objections to giving yours? They'll be destroyed afterwards.' He took her silence for assent. 'You say you don't know where your husband is, but can you think of anyone who might be in contact with him?'

'Only my solicitor. He's promised to let me know the minute he hears anything.'

The Sergeant dropped his cigarette end on to the damp grass and stood up, drawing his mackintosh about him. 'No friends he might have gone to?'

'I've tried everyone I can think of. He's not been in touch with any of them.'

'Then perhaps you'll be so kind as to write out your solicitor's name and phone number while I take a look at this painting.' He grinned. 'In view of what you've said, I'm fascinated to see if I can make anything of it.'

Sarah found his careful appraisal of the picture rather impressive. He stood for a long time without saying anything, then asked her if Jack had done a portrait of her. She fetched hers from the drawing-room and placed it alongside the one of Mathilda. He resumed his silent study.

'Well,' he said at last, 'you're quite right. I would never have guessed that this was a portrait of Mrs Gillespie, any more than I would have guessed that that was a portrait of you. I can see why no one else considers him a genius.'

Sarah's disappointment surprised her. But what had she

expected? He was a country policeman, not a Renaissance man. She forced the polite smile to her lips that was her customary response to other people's often rude comments on Jack's paintings and wondered, not for the first time, why she was the only person who seemed able to appreciate them. It wasn't as if she were blinded by love – rather the reverse in fact – and yet, to her, the portrait of Mathilda was extraordinary and brilliant. Jack had worked layer on layer to bring a deep golden translucence into the heart of the painting – Mathilda's wit, she thought, shining through the complex blues and greys of cruelty and cynicism. And round it all the browns of despair and repression, and the rusted red of iron, shorthand in Jack's work for backbone and character, but moulded here into the shape of the scold's bridle.

She shrugged. After all, perhaps it was a mercy the Sergeant couldn't see it. 'As I said, he paints personalities and not faces.'

'When did he paint the one of you?'

'Six years ago.'

'And has your personality changed in six years?'

'I shouldn't think so. Personalities change very little, Sergeant, which is why Jack likes to paint them. You are what you are. A generous person remains generous. A bully remains a bully. You can smooth the rough edges but you can't transform the core. Once painted, the personality should be recognizable for ever.'

He rubbed his hands together in anticipation of a challenge. 'Then let's see if I can work out his system. There's a lot of green in yours and your most obvious characteristics are sympathy – no – ' he contradicted himself

immediately, 'empathy – you enter into other people's feelings, you don't make a judgement on them. So, empathy, honour – you're an honourable woman or you wouldn't feel so racked with guilt about this bequest – truthful – most people would have lied about this painting – nice.' He turned to look at her. 'Does niceness count as a personality trait or is it too flabby?'

She laughed. 'Far too flabby, and you're ignoring the unpleasant aspects. Jack sees two sides to everybody.'

'All right.' He stared at her portrait. 'You're a very opinionated woman who is confident enough to fly in the face of established fact, otherwise you wouldn't have liked Mrs Gillespie. A corollary to that is that you are also naïve or your views wouldn't be so divergent from everyone else's. You're inclined to be rash or you wouldn't be regretting your husband's departure, and that implies a depth of affection for hopeless causes which is probably why you became a doctor and probably, too, why you were so fond of the old bitch in this amazing painting next to you. How am I doing for a prole?'

She gave a surprised chuckle. 'Well, I don't think you are a prole,' she said. 'Jack would adore you. Renaissance man in all his glory. They are good, aren't they?'

'How much does he charge for them?'

'He's only ever sold one. It was a portrait of one of his lovers. He got ten thousand pounds for it. The man who bought it was a Bond Street dealer, who said Jack was the most exciting artist he'd ever come across. We thought our ship had come in, then three months later the poor soul was dead, and no one's expressed an interest since.'

'That's not true. The Reverend Matthews told me he'd

buy a canvas like a shot if they were cheaper. Come to that, so would I. Has he ever done a man and wife? I'd go to two thousand for me and the old girl over the mantelpiece.' He studied Mathilda closely. 'I take it the gold is her one redeeming feature of humour. My old lady's a laugh a minute. She'd be gold through and through. I'd love to see it.'

There was a sound behind them. 'And what colour would you be?' asked Jack's amused voice.

Sarah's heart leapt, but Sergeant Cooper only eyed him thoughtfully for a moment or two. 'Assuming I've interpreted these pictures correctly, sir, I'd say a blend of blues and purples, for hard-headed cynicism-cum-realism, common to your wife and Mrs Gillespie, some greens which I think must represent the decency and honour of Dr Blakeney because they are markedly absent from Mrs Gillespie's portrait,' he smiled, 'and a great deal of black.'

'Why black?'

'Because I'm in the dark,' he said with ponderous humour, fishing his warrant card from his inside pocket. 'Detective Sergeant Cooper, sir, Learmouth Police. I'm enquiring into the death of Mrs Mathilda Gillespie of Cedar House, Fontwell. Perhaps you'd like to tell me why she sat for you with the scold's bridle on her head? In view of the way she died, I find that fascinating.'

Arthritis is a brute. It makes one so vulnerable. If I were a less cynical woman, I would say Sarah has the gift of healing, though, frankly, I'm inclined to think anyone would have been an improvement on that old fool, Hendry. He was lazy, of course, and didn't bother to keep up his reading. Sarah tells me there have been huge advances in the field which he obviously knew nothing about. I am rather inclined to sue, if not on my own behalf, then on Joanna's. Clearly, it was he who set her on the path to addiction.

Sarah asked me today how I was, and I answered with a line from King Lear*: 'I grow; I prosper. Now, gods, stand up for bastards.' She quite naturally assumed I was referring to myself, laughed good-naturedly and said: 'A bitch, possibly, Mathilda, but never a bastard. There's only one bastard I know, and that's Jack.' I asked her what he had done to deserve such an appellation. 'He takes my love for granted,' she said, 'and offers his to anyone who's foolish enough to flatter him.'*

How very flawed are human relationships. This is

not a Jack I recognize. He guards his love as jealously as he guards his art. The truth, I think, is that Sarah perceives both herself and him 'through a glass darkly'. She believes he strays, but only, I suspect, because she insists on using his effect on women as a criterion by which to judge him. His passions frighten her because they exist outside her control, and she is less adept than she thinks she is at seeing where he directs them.

I adore the man. He encourages me to 'dare damnation', for what is life if it is not a rebellion against death . . .

Six

VIOLET ORLOFF stood motionless in the kitchen of Wing Cottage, listening to the row that had broken out in the hall of Cedar House. She had the guilty look of an eavesdropper, torn between going and staying, but, unlike most eavesdroppers, she was free of the fear of discovery, and curiosity won out. She took a glass from the dishwasher, placed the rim against the wall, then pressed her ear to the base. The voices drew closer immediately. Perhaps it was a mercy she couldn't see herself. There was something indecent and furtive about the way she bent to listen, and her face wore the same expression that a Peeping Tom might wear as he peers through a window to see a woman in the nude. Excited. Leering. Expectant.

'. . . think I don't know what you do in London? You're a fucking whore, and Granny knew it, too. It's your bloody fault all this, and now you're planning to whore him, I suppose, to cut me out.'

'Don't you dare speak to me like that. I've a damn good mind to wash my hands of you. Do you think I care tuppence whether you get to university or not?'

'That's you every time. Jealousy, jealousy, fucking

JEALOUSY! You can't stand me doing anything you didn't do.'

'I'm warning you, Ruth, I won't listen to this.'

'Why not? Because it's true, and the truth hurts?' The girl's voice was tearful. 'Why can't you behave like a mother sometimes? Granny was more of a mother than you are. All you've ever done is hate me. I didn't ask to be born, did I?'

'That's childish.'

'You hate me because my father loved me.'

'Don't be absurd.'

'It's true. Granny told me. She said Steven used to moon over me, calling me his angel, and you used to fly into a temper. She said if you and Steven had got a divorce, then Steven wouldn't be dead.'

Joanna's voice was icy. 'And you believed her, of course, because it's what you wanted to hear. You're your grandmother all over again, Ruth. I thought there'd be an end of it once she was dead but I couldn't have been more wrong, could I? You've inherited every drop of poison that was in her.'

'Oh, that's great! Walk away, just like you always do. When are you going to face up to a problem, Mother, instead of pretending it doesn't exist? Granny always said that was your one true accomplishment, to brush every unpleasantness under the carpet, and then carry on as if nothing had happened. For Christ's SAKE' – her voice rose to a shout – 'YOU HEARD THE DETECTIVE.' She must have caught her mother's attention because her tone dropped again. 'The police think Granny was murdered. So what am I supposed to tell them?'

'The truth.'

Ruth gave a wild laugh. 'Fine. So I tell them what you spend your money on, do I? I tell them Granny and Dr Hendry thought you were so bloody mad they were thinking of having you committed? Jesus' – her voice broke – 'I suppose I might just as well be really honest and tell them how you tried to kill me. Or do I keep quiet because if I don't we won't have a hope in hell's chance of putting in a counter-claim for the money? You're not allowed to benefit from the murder of your mother, you know.'

The silence went on for so long that Violet Orloff began to wonder if they had moved to another part of the house.

'It's entirely up to you, Ruth. I've no compunction at all about saying you were here the day your grandmother died. You shouldn't have stolen her earrings, you stupid little bitch. Or, for that matter, every other damn thing your sticky little fingers couldn't resist. You knew her as well as I did. Did you really think she wouldn't notice?' Joanna's voice grated with sarcasm. 'She made a list and left it in her bedside drawer. If I hadn't destroyed it you'd be under arrest by now. You're making no secret of your panic over this idiotic will, so the police will have no trouble believing that if you were desperate enough to steal from your grandmother, you were probably desperate enough to murder her as well. So I suggest we both keep our mouths shut, don't you?'

A door was slammed so forcefully that Violet felt the vibrations in her kitchen.

Jack perched on his stool and rubbed his unshaven jaw, squinting at the policeman through half-closed lids. Satanic,

thought DS Cooper, suited him well. He was very dark with glittering eyes in a hawklike face, but there were too many laughter-lines for a Dracula. If this man was a devil, he was a merry one. He reminded Cooper of an unrepentant Irish recidivist he had arrested on innumerable occasions over a period of twenty years. There was the same 'take-me-as-I-am' expression, a look of such startling challenge that people who had it were impossible to ignore. He wondered with sudden curiosity if the same expression had looked out of Mathilda Gillespie's eyes. He hadn't noticed it on the video, but then the camera invariably lied. If it didn't, no one would tolerate having their picture taken.

'I'll do it,' said Jack abruptly.

The policeman frowned. 'Do what, Mr Blakeney?'

'Paint you and your wife for two thousand pounds, but I'll string you up from a lamp-post if you tell anyone what you're paying.' He stretched his arms towards the ceiling, easing the muscles of his back. 'I'd say two thousand from you is worth ten thousand any day from the likes of Mathilda. Perhaps a sliding scale isn't such a bad idea, after all. It should be the dent in the sitter's pocket that sets the value on the painting, not my arbitrary pricing of my worth.' He raised sardonic eyebrows. 'What right have I to deprive impoverished vicars and policemen of things of beauty? You'd agree with that, wouldn't you, Sarah?'

She shook her head at him. 'Why do you always have to be so offensive?'

'The man likes my work, so I'm offering him a subsidized portrait of himself and the wife in blues, purples, greens and golds. What's offensive about that? I'd call it a compliment.'

He eyed Cooper with amusement. 'Purples represent your libido, by the way. The deeper they are, the randier you are, but it's how I see you, remember, not how you see yourself. Your wife might have her illusions shattered if I paint you in deep purple and her in pale lilac.'

Sergeant Cooper chuckled. 'Or vice versa.'

Jack's eyes gleamed. 'Precisely. I don't set out to flatter anyone. As long as you understand that, we can probably do business.'

'And presumably, sir, you need the money at the moment. Would your terms be cash in advance, by any chance?'

Jack bared his teeth in a grin. 'Of course. At that price you could hardly expect anything else.'

'And what guarantee would I have that the portrait would ever be finished?'

'My word. As a man of honour.'

'I'm a policeman, Mr Blakeney. I never take anyone's word for anything.' He turned to Sarah. 'You're a truthful woman, Doctor. Is your husband a man of honour?'

She looked at Jack. 'That's a very unfair question.'

'Sounds fair to me,' said Jack. 'We're talking two thousand pounds here. The Sergeant's entitled to cover himself. Give him an answer.'

Sarah shrugged. 'All right. If you're asking me: will he take your money and run? Then, no, he won't. He'll paint your picture for you, and he'll do it well.'

'But?' prompted Jack.

'You're not a man of honour. You're far too thoughtless and inconsiderate. You respect no one's opinion but your

own, you're disloyal, and you're insensitive. In fact,' she gave him a twisted smile, 'you're a shit about everything but your art.'

Jack tipped a finger to the policeman. 'So, do I have a commission, Sergeant, or were you simply working on my wife's susceptibilities to get her to spill the beans about me?'

Cooper pulled forward a chair and offered it to Sarah. She shook her head so he sat in it himself with a faint sigh of relief. He was getting too old to stand when there was a seat available. 'I'll be honest with you, sir, I can't commission anything from you at the moment.'

'I knew it,' said Jack contemptuously. 'You're just like that slime-ball Matthews.' He aped the vicar's sing-song Welsh accent. 'I do love your work, Jack, and no mistake, but I'm a poor man as you know.' He slammed his fist into his palm. 'So I offered him one of my early ones for a couple of thousand, and the bastard tried to negotiate me down to three miserable hundred. Jesus wept!' he growled. 'He gets paid more than that for a few lousy sermons.' He glared at the Sergeant. 'Why do you all expect something for nothing? I don't see you taking a pay cut,' he flicked a glance at Sarah, 'or my wife either for that matter. But then the state pays you while I have to graft for myself.'

It was on the tip of Cooper's tongue to point out that Blakeney had chosen the path he was following, and had not been forced down it. But he refrained. He had had too many bruising arguments with his children on the very same subject to want to repeat them with a stranger. In any case, the man had misunderstood him. Deliberately, he suspected. 'I am not in a position to commission anything

from you *at the moment*, sir,' he said with careful emphasis, 'because you were closely connected with a woman who may or may not have been murdered. Were I to give you money, for whatever reason, it would be extremely prejudicial to your chances in court if you were unfortunate enough to appear there. It will be a different matter entirely when our investigations are concluded.'

Jack eyed him with sudden fondness. 'If *I* paid *you* two thousand, you might have a point, but not the other way round. It's your position you're safeguarding, not mine.'

Cooper chuckled again. 'Do you blame me? It's probably empty optimism, but I haven't quite given up on promotion, and back-handers to murder suspects would go down like a lead balloon with my governor. The future looks a lot brighter if you make Inspector.'

Jack studied him intently for several seconds, then crossed his arms over his tatty jumper. He found himself warming to this rotund, rather untypical detective with his jolly smile. 'So what was your question? Why did Mathilda sit for me with the scold's bridle on her head?' He looked at the portrait. 'Because she said it represented the essence of her personality. She was right, too.' His eyes narrowed in recollection. 'I suppose the easy way to describe her is to say she was repressed, but the repression worked both ways.' He smiled faintly. 'Perhaps it always does. She was abused as a child and grew up incapable of feeling or expressing love, so became an abuser herself. And the symbol of her abuse, both active and passive, was the bridle. It was strapped to her and she strapped it to her daughter.' His eyes flickered towards his wife. 'The irony is that it was also a symbol of her love, I think, or those cessations from

hostility that passed for love in Mathilda's life. She called Sarah her scold's bridle and she meant it as a compliment. She said Sarah was the only person she had ever met who came to her without prejudice and took her as she was.' He grinned amiably. 'I tried to explain that that was hardly something to applaud – Sarah has many weaknesses, but the worst in my view is her naïve willingness to accept everyone at his or her own valuation – but Mathilda wouldn't have a word spoken against her. And that's all I know,' he finished ingenuously.

DS Cooper decided privately that Jack Blakeney was probably one of the least ingenuous men he had ever met, but he played along with him for disingenuous reasons of his own. 'That's very helpful, sir. I never knew Mrs Gillespie myself, and it's important for me to understand her character. Would you say she was the type to commit suicide?'

'Without a doubt. And she'd do it with a Stanley knife, too. She found as much enjoyment in making an exit as she did in making an entrance. Possibly more. If she's looking at the three of us now, picking over the bones of her demise, she'll be hugging herself with delight. She was talked about in life because she was a bitch, but that's nothing to the way she's being talked about in death. She'd love every cliff-hanging moment of it.'

Cooper frowned at Sarah. 'Do you agree, Dr Blakeney?'

'It has an absurd sort of logic, you know. She *was* like that.' She thought for a moment or two. 'But she didn't believe in an afterlife, or only the maggot variety which means we're all cannibals.' She smiled at Cooper's expression of distaste. 'A man dies and is eaten by maggots,

the maggots are eaten by birds, the birds are eaten by cats, the cats defecate on the vegetables and we eat the vegetables. Or any permutation you like.' She smiled again. 'I'm sorry, but that was Mathilda's view of death. Why would she waste her last, great exit? I honestly believe she would have prolonged it for all it was worth and, in the process, made as many people wriggle as she could. Take that video, for example. Why did she want music and credits added if it was only to be shown after she was dead? She was going to watch it herself, and if someone walked in while she was doing it, then so much the better. She meant to use it as a stick to beat Joanna and Ruth with. I'm right, aren't I, Jack?'

'Probably. You usually are.' He spoke without irony. 'Which video are we talking about?'

She had forgotten he hadn't seen it. 'Mathilda's posthumous message to her family,' she said, with a shake of her head. 'You'd have loved it, by the way. She looked rather like Cruella De Vil out of *The Hundred and One Dalmatians*. Dyed black wings on either side of a white streak, nose like a beak, and mouth a thin line. Very paintable.' She frowned. 'Why didn't you tell me you knew her?'

'You'd have interfered.'

'How?'

'You'd have found a way,' he said. 'I can't paint them when you bleat your interpretations of them into my ear.' He spoke in a mocking falsetto. 'But I like her, Jack. She's really very nice. She's not half as bad as everyone says. She's a softy at heart.'

'I never talk like that,' said Sarah dismissively.

'You should listen to yourself once in a while. The dark side of people scares you, so you close your eyes to it.'

'Is that a bad thing?'

He shrugged. 'Not if you want existence without passion.'

She studied him thoughtfully for a moment. 'If passion means confrontation, then yes, I prefer existence without passion. I lived through the disintegration of my parents' marriage, remember. I'd go a long way to avoid repeating that experience.'

His eyes sparkled in his tired face. 'Then perhaps it's your own dark side that scares you. Is there a fire in there waiting to blaze out of control? A scream of frustration that will topple your precarious house of cards? You'd better pray for gentle breezes and no strong winds, my angel, or you'll find you've been living in a fool's paradise.'

She didn't respond and the room fell silent, its three occupants curiously abstracted like the portraits round the walls. It occurred to DS Cooper, fixed in fascinated immobility upon his chair, that Jack Blakeney was a terrible man. Did he devour everyone in the way he was devouring his wife? *A scream of frustration that will topple your precarious house of cards.* Cooper had held his own scream in check for years, the scream of a man caught in the toils of rectitude and responsibility. Why couldn't Jack Blakeney do the same?

He cleared his throat. 'Did Mrs Gillespie ever tell you, sir, what her intentions were with regard to her will?'

Jack had been watching Sarah intently. He glanced now

towards the policeman. 'Not in so many words. She asked me once what I would do if I had her money.'

'What did you say?'

'I said I'd spend it.'

'Your wife told me you despise materialism.'

'Quite right, so I'd use it to enhance my spirituality.'

'How?'

'I'd blow the lot on drugs, alcohol and sex.'

'Sounds very materialistic to me, sir. There's nothing spiritual about surrendering to the senses.'

'It depends who you follow. If you're a Stoic like Sarah, your spiritual development comes through duty and responsibility. If you're an Epicurean like me, though I hasten to say poor old Epicurus probably wouldn't recognize me as an adherent, it comes through the gratification of desire.' He arched an amused eyebrow. 'Unfortunately, we modern Epicureans are frowned upon. There's something infinitely despicable about a man who refuses to acknowledge his responsibilities but prefers to fill his cup at the fountain of pleasure.' He was watching Cooper closely. 'But that's only because society is composed of sheep and sheep are easily brainwashed by advertisers' propaganda. They may not believe that the whiteness of a woman's wash is a symbol of her success, but they sure as hell believe that their kitchens should be as germ-free, their smiles as white, their children as well-mannered, their husbands as hard-working, and their moral decency as obvious. With men it's lager. It's supposed to persuade them they have balls, but all it really persuades them to do is wear a clean jumper, shave regularly, have at least three friends, never get drunk

and talk amusingly in the pub.' His grim face cracked into a smile. 'My problem is, I'd rather be stoned out of my mind and rogering a sixteen-year-old virgin any day, particularly if I have to take off her gym slip slowly to do it.'

Christ, thought Cooper in alarm, feeling the weight of the other's gaze upon his bent head. Could the bastard read minds as well? He made a pretence of writing something on his notepad. 'Did you explain all that as graphically to Mrs Gillespie or did you just stick with the spending of her money if you had it?'

Jack glanced at Sarah, but she was staring at Mathilda's portrait and didn't look up. 'She had great skin for her age. I expect I said I'd rather be stoned and rogering a granny.'

Cooper, who was far more respectable than he realized, was shocked into looking up. 'What did she say?'

Jack was enjoying himself. 'She asked me if I'd like to paint her in the nude. I said I would, so she took her clothes off. If it's of any interest to you, the only thing Mathilda was wearing when I made my sketches of her was the scold's bridle.' He smiled, his perceptive eyes searching the policeman's. 'Does that excite you, Sergeant?'

'It does as a matter of fact,' said Cooper evenly. 'Would she also have been in the bath by any chance?'

'No. She was very much alive and lying on her bed in all her glory.' He stood up and went to a chest in the corner. 'And she looked bloody fantastic.' He took a sketchpad from the bottom drawer. 'There.' He flung the pad across the room and it fluttered to the floor at the policeman's feet. 'Be my guest. They're all of Mathilda. One of life's great individuals.'

Cooper retrieved the pad and turned the pages. They did

indeed show Mrs Gillespie, nude upon her bed, but a very different Mrs Gillespie from the tragic cadaver in the bath or the bitter harridan with the cruel mouth on the television set. He laid the pad on the floor beside him. 'Did you sleep with her, Mr Blakeney?'

'No. She never asked me to.'

'Would you have done if she *had* asked you?' The question was out before Cooper had time to consider its wisdom.

Jack's expression was unreadable. 'Does that have a bearing on your case?'

'I'm interested in your character, Mr Blakeney.'

'I see. And what would my accepting an elderly woman's invitation to sleep with her tell you? That I was a pervert? Or that I was infinitely compassionate?'

Cooper gave a small laugh. 'I'd say it was an indication that you needed your eyes testing. Even in the dark, Mrs Gillespie could hardly have passed for a sixteen-year-old virgin.' He fished his cigarettes from his pocket. 'Do you mind?'

'Be my guest.' He kicked the wastepaper basket across the floor.

Cooper flicked his lighter to the cigarette. 'Mrs Gillespie has left your wife three-quarters of a million pounds, Mr Blakeney. Did you know?'

'Yes.'

The Sergeant hadn't expected that. 'So Mrs Gillespie *did* tell you what her intentions were?'

'No,' said Jack, resuming his seat on the stool. 'I've just spent a delightful two hours at Cedar House.' He stared impassively at Sarah. 'Joanna and Ruth are labouring under

the misapprehension that I have some influence over my wife so they put themselves out to be charming.'

Cooper scratched his jaw and wondered why Dr Blakeney put up with it. The man was toying with her in the way a sleek cat playfully inserts its claws into a half-mangled mouse. The mystery was not why she had decided to divorce him so suddenly, but why she had tolerated him for so long. Yet there was a sense of a challenge unmet, for a cat only remains interested while the mouse plays the game, and Cooper had the distinct impression that Jack felt Sarah was letting him down. 'Did you know before that?'

'No.'

'Are you surprised?'

'No.'

'Do your wife's patients often leave her money then?'

'Not as far as I know.' He grinned at the Sergeant. 'If they have, she's never told me.'

'Then why aren't you surprised?'

'Give me a good reason why I should be. If you'd told me Mathilda had left her money to the Police Benevolent Fund or New Age Travellers, that wouldn't have surprised me either. It was hers to do with as she liked, and good luck to her. Mind you, I'm glad it's the *wife*,' he put an offensive emphasis on the word, 'who hit the jackpot. It'll make things considerably easier for me. I don't mind admitting I'm a bit short at the moment.'

Sarah raked him from head to toe with angry eyes. 'My God, Jack, if you knew how close I am to sinking my fist into your self-satisfied gut.'

'Ah,' he murmured, 'passion at last.' He stood up and

approached her, spreading his hands wide in an invitation to do it. 'Feel free. It's all yours.'

She took him by surprise and kneed him in the groin instead. 'Next time,' she said through gritted teeth, 'I'll break Mathilda's canvas over your head. And that would be a shame because it's probably the best thing you've ever done.'

'GODDAMMIT, WOMAN, THAT HURT!' he roared, clutching his balls and collapsing back on to the stool. 'I asked for passion not fucking castration.'

Sarah's eyes narrowed. 'It was supposed to hurt, you cretin. Don't even think about getting your hands on Mathilda's money. You're certainly not getting any of mine if I can help it. Fifty–fifty? Fat – bloody – chance. I'll sell up and give it to a cats' home before I see you living the life of Riley on the back of my hard work.'

He poked his fingers into his Levi's pocket and removed a folded piece of paper. 'My contract with Mathilda,' he said, holding it out to her with one hand while he fondled himself gingerly with the other. 'The silly old sod snuffed it before she paid me, so I reckon her executors owe me ten thousand and her heir gets the painting. Jesus, Sarah, I feel really sick. I think you've done me some severe damage.'

She ignored him to read what was on the paper. 'This looks kosher,' she said.

'It *is* kosher. Keith drew it up.'

'He never told me.'

'Why should he? It was none of your business. I just hope I've got a claim on the estate. The way my luck's running, the contract's probably invalid because she's dead.'

Sarah passed the paper to DS Cooper. 'What do you think? It would be a shame if Jack's right. It's his second major sale.'

She was genuinely pleased for the bastard, Cooper thought in surprise. What a peculiar couple they were. He shrugged. 'I'm no expert but I've always understood that debts have to be met out of an estate. If you'd supplied her with new carpeting, which she hadn't paid for, the bill would presumably be honoured. I don't see why a painting should be any different, particularly one where the subject is the deceased. It's not as though you can sell it to anyone else, is it?' He glanced at the canvas. 'Bearing in mind, of course, you might have a problem proving it's Mrs Gillespie.'

'Where would I have to prove it? In court?'

'Possibly.'

His eyes gleamed as he clicked his fingers for the contract. 'I'm relying on you, Sarah,' he said, tucking the paper back into his pocket.

'To do what?'

'Tell the executors not to pay, of course. Say you don't think it's Mathilda. I need the publicity of a court battle.'

'Don't be stupid. I *know* it's Mathilda. If the contract's legally binding on her estate, they'll have to pay.'

But he wasn't listening. He tossed his paints, brushes and bottles of turpentine and linseed oil into a hold-all, then released the canvas of Joanna Lascelles from the easel. 'I've got to go. Look, I can't take the rest of this stuff because I haven't found a studio yet, but I'll try and get back for it during the week. Is that okay? I only came for some clothes. I've been sleeping in the car and this lot's a bit rank.' He

padded towards the door, slinging the hold-all over his shoulder and carrying the painting in his hand.

'One moment, Mr Blakeney.' Cooper stood up to block his path. 'I haven't finished with you yet. Where were you on the night Mrs Gillespie died?'

Jack glanced at Sarah. 'I was in Stratford,' he said coolly, 'with an actress called Sally Bennedict.'

Cooper didn't look up, merely licked the point of his pencil and jotted the name on his pad. 'And how can I contact her?'

'Through the RSC. She's playing Juliet in one of their productions.'

'Thank you. Now, as someone with material evidence, I must warn you that if you intend to go on sleeping in your car then you will be required to present yourself at a police station every day, because if you don't I shall be forced to apply for a warrant. We also need your fingerprints so that we can isolate yours from the others we lifted in Cedar House. There will be a fingerprinting team in Fontwell Parish Hall on Wednesday morning but if you can't attend, I shall have to make arrangements for you to come to the station.'

'I'll be there.'

'And your whereabouts in the meantime, sir?'

'Care of Mrs Joanna Lascelles, Cedar House, Fontwell.' He booted open the door into the hall and eased through the gap. It was clearly something he had done many times before to judge by the dents and scratches on the paintwork.

'Jack!' Sarah called.

He turned to look at her. His eyebrows lifted enquiringly.

She nodded to the portrait of Mathilda. ‘Congratulations.’

He flashed her an oddly intimate smile before letting the door slam behind him.

The two, left behind in the studio, listened to his footsteps on the stairs as he went in search of clothes. ‘He’s a law unto himself, isn’t he?’ said Cooper, drawing thoughtfully on his cigarette.

‘One of life’s great individuals,’ Sarah said, consciously echoing Jack’s description of Mathilda, ‘and very difficult to live with.’

‘I can see that.’ He bent down to stub the butt against the rim of the wastepaper basket. ‘But equally difficult to live *without*, I should imagine. He leaves something of a vacuum in his wake.’

Sarah turned away from him to look out of the window. She couldn’t see anything, of course – it was now very dark outside – but the policeman could see her reflection in the glass as clearly as if it were a mirror. He would have done better, he thought, to keep his mouth shut but there was an openness about the Blakeneys that was catching.

‘He’s not always like that,’ said Sarah. ‘It’s rare for him to be quite so forthcoming, but I’m not sure if that was for your benefit or mine.’ She fell silent, aware that she was speaking her thoughts aloud.

‘Yours, of course.’

They heard the front door open and close. ‘Why “of course”?’

‘I haven’t hurt him.’

Their reflected eyes met in the window pane.

‘Life’s a bugger, isn’t it, Sergeant?’

Joanna's demands on my purse are becoming insatiable. She says it's my fault that she's incapable of finding a job, my fault that her life's so empty, my fault that she had to marry Steven and my fault, too, that she was saddled with a baby she didn't want. I forbore to point out that she couldn't get into the Jew's bed quick enough or that the pill had been available for years before she allowed herself to get pregnant. I was tempted to catalogue the hells I went through – the rape of my innocence, marriage to a drunken pervert, a second pregnancy when I'd barely got over the first, the courage it took to climb out of an abyss of despair that she couldn't begin to imagine. I didn't, of course. She alarms me enough, as it is, with her frigid dislike of me and Ruth. I dread to think how she would react if she ever found out that Gerald was her father.

She says I'm a miser. Well, perhaps I am. Money has been a good friend to me and I guard it as jealously as others guard their secrets. God knows, I've had to use every ounce of cunning I possess to acquire it. If shrouds had pockets, I'd take it with me and 'to hell, allegiance!'

It is not we who owe our children but they who owe us. The only regret I have about dying is that I won't see Sarah's face when she learns what I've left her. That would, I think, be amusing.

Old Howard quoted Hamlet at me today: 'We go to gain a little patch of ground that hath no profit but the name.' I laughed – he is a most entertaining old brute at times – and answered from The Merchant*: 'He is well paid who is well satisfied . . .'*

Seven

VIOLET ORLOFF sought out her husband in the sitting-room, where he was watching the early evening news on the television. She turned down the volume and placed her angular body in front of the screen.

'I was watching that,' he said in mild reproof.

She took no notice. 'Those awful women next door have been screaming at each other like a couple of fishwives, and I could hear every word. We should have taken the surveyor's advice and *insisted* on a double skin with soundproofing. What's going to happen if it's sold to hippies or people with young children? We'll be driven *mad* with their row.'

'Wait and see,' Duncan said, folding his plump hands in his ample lap. He could never understand how it was that old age, which had brought him serenity, had brought Violet only an aggressive frustration. He felt guilty about it. He knew he should never have brought her back to live in such close proximity with Mathilda. It was like placing a daisy beside an orchid and inviting comparisons.

She scowled at him. 'You can be so infuriating at times. If we wait and see, it'll be too late to do anything. I think we should demand that something be done *before* it's sold.'

'Have you forgotten,' he reminded her gently, 'that we were only able to afford this house in the first place precisely because there was no soundproofing and Mathilda agreed to a five thousand pound discount when the surveyor pointed out the deficiency? We're hardly in a position to demand anything.'

But Violet hadn't come in to discuss demands. 'Fish-wives,' she said again, 'screaming at each other. The police now think Mathilda was *murdered*, apparently. And do you know what Ruth called her mother? A whore. She said she knew her mother was a whore in London. Rather *worse*, in fact. She said Joanna was,' her voice dropped to a whisper while her lips, in exaggerated movement, mouthed the words, 'a *fucking* whore.'

'Good lord,' said Duncan Orloff, startled out of his serenity.

'Quite. And Mathilda thought Joanna was mad, and she tried to murder Ruth, and she's spending her money on something she shouldn't and, worst of all, Ruth was in the house the night Mathilda died and she took Mathilda's earrings. *And*,' she said with particular emphasis, as if she hadn't already said 'and' several times, 'Ruth has stolen other things as well. They obviously haven't told the police any of it. I think we should report it.'

He looked slightly alarmed. 'Is it really any of our business, dear? We do have to go on living here, after all. I should hate any more unpleasantness.' What Duncan called serenity, others called apathy, and the hornets' nest stirred up two weeks ago by Jenny Spede's screams had been extremely unsettling.

She stared at him with shrewd little eyes. 'You've known

it was murder all along, haven't you? *And* you know who did it.'

'Don't be absurd,' he said, an edge of anger in his voice.

She stamped her foot angrily on the floor. 'Why do you insist on treating me like a child? Do you think I didn't *know*? I've known for forty years, you silly man. Poor Violet. Only second best. Always second best. What did she tell you, Duncan?' Her eyes narrowed to slits. 'She told you *something*. I know she did.'

'You've been drinking again,' he said coldly.

'You never accused Mathilda of drinking, but then *she* was perfect. Even drunk, Mathilda was perfect.' She tottered very slightly. '*Are* you going to report what I heard? Or will I have to do it? If Joanna or Ruth murdered her they don't deserve to get away with it. You're not going to tell me you don't care, I hope. I *know* you do.'

Of course he cared – it was only Violet for whom he felt a numbing indifference – but had she no sense of self-preservation? 'I don't imagine Mathilda was killed for fun,' he said, holding her gaze for a moment, 'so I do urge you to be very cautious in what you say and how you say it. On the whole I think it would be better if you left it to me.' He reached past her to switch up the volume on the television set. 'It's the weather forecast,' he pointed out, gesturing her gravely to one side, as if tomorrow's atmospheric pressures across the United Kingdom were of any interest to a fat, flabby old man who never stirred out of his armchair if he could possibly avoid it.

*

Ruth opened the door to Jack with a sullen expression in her dark eyes. 'I hoped you wouldn't come back,' she said bluntly. 'She always gets what she wants.'

He grinned at her. 'So do I.'

'Does your wife know you're here?'

He pushed past her into the hall, propping the canvas of Joanna against a wall and lowering the hold-all to the floor. 'Is that any of your business?'

She shrugged. 'She's the one with the money. We'll all lose out if you and Mum put her nose out of joint. You must be mad.'

He was amused. 'Are you expecting me to lick Sarah's arse so that you can live in clover for the rest of your life? Forget it, sweetheart. The only person I lick arse for is myself.'

'Don't call me sweetheart,' she snapped.

His eyes narrowed. 'Then don't judge me by your own standards. My best advice to you, Ruth, is to learn a little subtlety. There is no bigger turn-off than a blatant woman.'

For all her outward maturity, she was still a child. Her eyes filled. 'I hate you.'

He studied her curiously for a moment, then moved off in search of Joanna.

No one could accuse Joanna of being unsubtle. She was a woman of understatement, in words, dress and action. She sat now in the dimly lit drawing-room, a book open on her lap, face impassive, hair a silver halo in the light from the table lamp. Her eyes flickered in Jack's direction as he entered the room, but she didn't say anything, only gestured

towards the sofa for him to sit down. He chose to stand by the mantelpiece and watch her. He thought of her in terms of ice. Glacial. Dazzling. Static.

'What are you thinking?' she asked after several moments of silence.

'That Mathilda was right about you.'

There was no expression in her grey eyes. 'In which particular respect?'

'She said you were a mystery.'

She gave a faint smile but didn't say anything.

'I liked her, you know,' Jack went on after a moment.

'You would. She despised women but looked up to men.'

There was a lot of truth in that, thought Jack. 'She liked Sarah well enough.'

'Do you think so?'

'She left her three-quarters of a million pounds. I'd say that was a pretty good indication she liked her.'

Joanna leant her head against the back of the sofa and stared at him with a disconcertingly penetrating gaze. 'I assumed you knew Mother better than that. She didn't *like* anyone. And why ascribe such a mundane motive to her? She would have viewed a bequest of three-quarters of a million pounds in terms of the power it could buy her, not as a sentimental hand-out to someone who had done her a small kindness. Mother never intended that will to be her last. It was a piece of theatre, made for Ruth and me to find. Money buys power just as effectively if you threaten to withhold it.'

Thoughtfully, Jack rubbed his jaw. Sarah had said something very similar. 'But why Sarah? Why not leave it to a dogs' home? It would have achieved the same purpose.'

'I've wondered about that,' she murmured, her eyes straying towards the window. 'I think perhaps she disliked your wife even more than she disliked me. Do you imagine Ruth and I would have kept quiet if we'd seen that video while Mother was alive?' She stroked her hand rhythmically up and down her arm as she spoke. It was an extraordinarily sensuous action but she seemed unaware that she was doing it. She brought her head round to look at Jack again. Her eyes were strangely glassy. 'Your wife's position would have become untenable.'

'What would you have done?' asked Jack curiously.

Joanna smiled. 'Nothing very much. Your wife would have lost all her patients within six months once it got out that she had persuaded a rich patient to make over her entire estate. She'll lose them anyway.'

'Why?'

'Mother died in suspicious circumstances and your wife is the only person to benefit from her death.'

'Sarah didn't kill Mathilda.'

Joanna smiled to herself. 'Tell that to the people of Fontwell.' She stood up and smoothed her black dress over her flat stomach. 'I'm ready,' she said.

He frowned. 'What for?'

'Sex,' she said matter-of-factly. 'It's what you came for, isn't it? We'll use Mother's room. I want you to make love to me the way you made love to her.' Her strange eyes rested on him. 'You'll enjoy it far more with me, you know. Mother didn't like sex, but then I presume you discovered that for yourself. She never did it for pleasure, only for gain. A man's humping disgusted her. She said it reminded her of dogs.'

Jack found the remark fascinating. 'I thought you said she looked up to men?'

Joanna smiled. 'Only because she knew how to manipulate them.'

The news that Mathilda Gillespie had left Dr Blakeney three-quarters of a million pounds spread through the village like wildfire. The information surfaced after matins on Sunday, but precisely who started the fire remained a mystery. There was no doubt, however, that it was Violet Orloff who let slip the interesting snippet that Jack Blakeney had taken up residence at Cedar House. His car had remained on the gravel drive all Saturday night and looked like remaining there indefinitely. Tongues began to wag.

Jane Marriott was careful to keep her expression neutral when Sarah put in a surprise appearance at lunchtime on Wednesday. 'I wasn't expecting you,' she said. 'Shouldn't you be on your way to Beeding?'

'I had to give my fingerprints in the parish hall.'

'Coffee?'

'I suppose you've heard. Everyone else has.'

Jane switched on the kettle. 'About the money or about Jack?'

Sarah gave a humourless laugh. 'That makes life a lot easier. I've just spent an hour in a queue outside the hall, listening to heavy-handed hints from people who should have been diagnosed brain-dead years ago. Shall I tell you what the current thinking seems to be? Jack has left me to

live with Joanna because he is as shocked as everyone else that I used my position as Mathilda's GP to persuade her to forget her duty to her family in favour of me. This being the same Jack Blakeney who, only last week, everyone loved to hate because he was living off his wretched wife.'

'Oh dear,' said Jane.

'They'll be saying next that I killed the old witch before she could change the will back.'

'You'd better believe it,' said Jane dispassionately. 'There's no point burying your head in the sand.'

'You're joking.'

Jane handed her a cup of black coffee. 'I'm serious, dear. There were two of them discussing it here in the waiting-room this morning. It goes something like this: none of the locals had reason to hate Mathilda more than usual in the last twelve months so none of them is likely to have murdered her. Therefore it has to be a newcomer, and you're the only newcomer with a motive who had access to her. Your husband, afraid for himself and Mrs Lascelles, has moved in to protect her. Ruth is safe because she's at school. And last, but by no means least, why did Victor Sturgis die in such peculiar circumstances?'

Sarah stared at her. 'You *are* serious, aren't you?'

''Fraid so.'

'Do I gather I'm supposed to have killed Victor as well?'

Jane nodded.

'How? By suffocating him with his own false teeth?'

'That seems to be the general view.' Jane's eyes brimmed with laughter suddenly. 'Oh dear, I shouldn't laugh, really I shouldn't. Poor old soul, it was bad enough that he

swallowed them himself, but the idea of you wrestling with a ninety-three-year-old in order to ram his dentures down his throat' – she broke off to mop her eyes – 'it doesn't bear thinking about. The world is full of very foolish and very envious people, Sarah. They resent your good fortune.'

Sarah mulled this over. 'Do you think I'm fortunate?'

'Good lord, yes. It's like winning the pools.'

'What would you do with the money if Mathilda had left it to you?'

'Go on a cruise. See the world before it sinks under the weight of its own pollution.'

'That seems to be the most popular choice. It must be something to do with the fact that we're an island. Everyone wants to get off it.' She stirred her coffee then licked the spoon absent-mindedly.

Jane was dying of curiosity. 'What are you going to do with it?'

Sarah sighed. 'Use it to pay for a decent barrister, I should think.'

DS Cooper stopped at Mill House on his way home that evening. Sarah offered him a glass of wine which he accepted. 'We've had a letter about you,' he told her while she was pouring it.

She handed him the glass. 'Who from?'

'Unsigned.'

'What does it say?'

'That you murdered an old man called Victor Sturgis for his walnut desk.'

Sarah pulled a wry face. 'Actually, he did leave me a desk

and it's rather a nice one, too. The matron at the nursing home gave it to me after he died. She said he wanted me to have it. I was very touched.' She lifted weary eyebrows. 'Did it say how I murdered him?'

'You were seen suffocating him.'

'It makes a weird sort of sense. I was trying to prise his dentures out of his throat. The poor old boy swallowed them when he dozed off in his chair.' She sighed. 'But he was dead before I even started. I had a vague idea of trying mouth-to-mouth if I could unblock his airway. I suppose, from a distance, it might have looked as if I were suffocating him.'

Cooper nodded. He had checked the story already. 'We've had a few letters, one way and another, and they're not all about you.' He took an envelope from his pocket and handed it to her. 'This is the most interesting. See what you make of it.'

'Should I touch the letter?' she asked doubtfully. 'What about fingerprints?'

'Well, that's interesting in itself. Whoever wrote it wore gloves.'

She took the letter from the envelope and spread it on the table. It was printed in block capitals:

RUTH LASCELLES WAS IN CEDAR HOUSE THE DAY MRS GILLESPIE DIED. SHE STOLE SOME EARRINGS. JOANNA KNOWS SHE TOOK THEM. JOANNA LASCELLES IS A PROSTITUTE IN LONDON. ASK HER WHAT SHE SPENDS HER MONEY ON. ASK HER WHY SHE TRIED TO KILL HER DAUGHTER. ASK HER WHY MRS GILLESPIE THOUGHT SHE WAS MAD.

Sarah turned the envelope over to look at the frank mark. It had been posted in Learmouth. 'And you've no idea who wrote it?'

'None at all.'

'It can't be true. You told me yourself that Ruth was under the watchful eye of her housemistress at school.'

He looked amused. 'As I told you, I never set much store by alibis. If that young lady wanted to sneak out I can't see her housemistress stopping her.'

'But Southcliffe's thirty miles away,' Sarah protested. 'She couldn't have got here without a car.'

He changed tack. 'What about this reference to madness? Did Mrs Gillespie ever mention to you that her daughter was mad?'

She considered this for a moment. 'Madness is a relative term, quite meaningless out of context.'

He was unruffled. 'So Mrs Gillespie did mention something of the sort?'

Sarah didn't answer.

'Come on, Dr Blakeney. Joanna's not your patient so you're not giving away any confidences. And let me tell you something else, she's not doing you any favours at the moment. Her view is that you had to kill the old lady PDQ before she had time to change her will back, and she isn't keeping those suspicions to herself.'

Sarah fingered her wine glass. 'The only thing Mathilda ever said on the subject was that her daughter was unstable. She said it wasn't Joanna's fault but was due to incompatibility between Mathilda's genes and Joanna's father's genes. I told her she was talking rubbish but, at the time, I didn't know that Joanna's father was Mathilda's uncle. I

imagine she was concerned about the problems of recessive genes but, as we didn't pursue it any further, I can't say for sure.'

'Inbreeding, in other words?'

Sarah gave a small shrug of acquiescence. 'Presumably.'

'Do you like Mrs Lascelles?'

'I hardly know her.'

'Your husband seems to get on with her well enough.'

'That's below the belt, Sergeant.'

'I don't understand why you're bothering to defend her. She's got her knife into you right up to the hilt.'

'Do you blame her?' She leaned her chin on her hand. 'How would you feel if in a few short weeks, you discovered that you were the product of an incestuous relationship, that your father killed himself with an overdose, that your mother died violently either by her own hand or someone else's and that, to cap it all, the security you were used to was about to be snatched away and given to a stranger? She seems remarkably sane to me in the circumstances.'

He took a drink from his glass. 'Do you know anything about her being a prostitute?'

'No.'

'Or what she spends her money on?'

'No.'

'Any ideas?'

'It's nothing to do with me. Why don't you ask her?'

'I have. She told me to mind my own business.'

Sarah chuckled. 'I'd have done the same.'

He stared at her. 'Has anyone ever told you you're too good to be true, Dr Blakeney?' He spoke with a touch of sarcasm.

She held his gaze, but didn't say anything.

'Women in your position drive their husband's car through their rival's front door, or take a chainsaw to the rival's furniture. At the very least, they feel acute bitterness. Why don't you?'

'I'm busy shoring up my house of cards,' she said cryptically. 'Have some more wine.' She filled her own glass, then his. 'It's not bad, this one. Australian Shiraz and fairly inexpensive.'

He was left with the impression that, of the two women, Joanna Lascelles was the less puzzling. 'Would you have described yourself and Mrs Gillespie as friends?' he asked.

'Of course.'

'Why "of course"?'

'I describe everyone I know well as a friend.'

'Including Mrs Lascelles.'

'No. I've only met her twice.'

'You wouldn't think it to listen to you.'

She grinned. 'I have a fellow-feeling with her, Sergeant, just as I have with Ruth and Jack. You don't feel comfortable with any of us. Joanna or Ruth might have done it if they didn't know the will had been changed, Jack or I might have done it if we did. On the face of it, Joanna appears the most likely which is why you keep asking me questions about her. I imagine you've quizzed her pretty thoroughly about when she first learnt who her father was, so you'll know that she threatened her mother with exposure?' She looked at him enquiringly, and he nodded. 'At which point, you're thinking, Mathilda turned round and said, any more threats like this and I'll cut you out altogether. So, in desperation, Joanna dosed her mother

with barbiturates and slit the old lady's wrists, unaware that Mathilda had altered the will already.'

'What makes you think I don't feel comfortable with that scenario?'

'You told me Joanna was in London that night.'

He shrugged. 'Her alibi is very shaky. The concert ended at nine thirty which meant she had plenty of time to drive down here and kill her mother. The pathologist puts the time of death somewhere between nine p.m. on the Saturday night and three a.m. the following morning.'

'Which does he favour?'

'Before midnight,' Cooper admitted.

'Then her defence barrister will tear your case to shreds. In any case, Mathilda wouldn't have bothered with pretence. She'd have told Joanna straight out she'd changed the will.'

'Perhaps Mrs Lascelles didn't believe her.'

Sarah dismissed this with a smile. 'Mathilda always told the truth. That's why everyone loathed her.'

'Perhaps Mrs Lascelles just suspected that her mother might change the will.'

'It wouldn't have made any difference as far as Joanna was concerned. She was preparing to use her father's codicil to fight her mother in court. At that stage, it didn't matter a twopenny damn who Mathilda left the money to, not if Joanna could prove she had no right to it in the first place.'

'Perhaps it wasn't done for money. You keep wondering about the significance of the scold's bridle. Perhaps Mrs Lascelles was revenging herself.'

But Sarah shook her head. 'She hardly ever saw her

mother. I think Mathilda mentioned that she came down once in the last twelve months. It would be a remarkable anger that could sustain itself at fever pitch over such a lengthy cooling period.'

'Not if Mrs Lascelles is unstable,' murmured Cooper.

'Mathilda wasn't killed in a mad frenzy,' said Sarah slowly. 'It was all done with such meticulous care, even down to the flowers. You said yourself the arrangement was difficult to reproduce without help.'

The Sergeant drained his glass and stood up. 'Mrs Lascelles works freelance for a London florist. She specializes in bridal bouquets and wreaths. I can't see her finding a few nettles and daisies a problem.' He walked to the door. 'Good night, Dr Blakeney. I'll see myself out.'

Sarah stared into her wine glass as she listened to his footsteps echoing down the hall. She felt like screaming, but was too afraid to do it. Her house of cards had never seemed so fragile.

There was a conscious eroticism to every movement Joanna made and Jack guessed she had posed before, probably for photographs. For money or for self-gratification? The latter, he thought. Her vanity was huge.

She was obsessed with Mathilda's bed and Mathilda's bedroom, aping her mother's posture against the piled pillows. Yet the contrast between the two women could not have been greater. Mathilda's sexuality had been a gentle, understated thing, largely because she had no interest in it; Joanna's was mechanical and obtrusive, as if the same visual stimuli could arouse all men in the same way on every

occasion. Jack found it impossible to decide whether she was acting out of contempt for him or out of contempt for men in general.

'Is your wife a prude?' she demanded abruptly after a long period of silent sketching.

'Why do you ask?'

'Because what I'm doing shocks you.'

He was amused. 'Sarah has a very open and healthy libido and far from shocking me, what you're doing offends me. I resent being categorized as the sort of man who can be turned on by cheap pornographic posturing.'

She looked away from him towards the window and sat in strange self-absorption, her pale eyes unfocused. 'Then tell me what Sarah does to excite you,' she said finally.

He studied her for a moment, his expression unreadable. 'She's interested in what I'm trying to achieve in my work. That excites me.'

'I'm not talking about that, I'm talking about sex.'

'Ah,' he said apologetically, 'we're at cross purposes then. *I* was talking about love.'

'How very twee.' She gave a small laugh. 'You ought to hate her, Jack. She must have found someone else or she wouldn't have kicked you out.'

'Hate is too pervasive,' he said mildly. 'It leaves no room for anything else.' With an idle flick of his fingers he tossed a torn page of his sketchpad towards her and watched it flutter to the bed beside her. 'Read that,' he invited. 'If you're interested, it's my assessment of your character after three sittings. I jot down my impressions as I go along.'

With a remarkable lack of curiosity – most women, he thought, would have seized on it with alacrity – she

retrieved it and gave a cursory glance to both sides of the paper. 'There's nothing on it.'

'Exactly.'

'That's cheap.'

'Yes,' he agreed, 'but you've given me nothing to paint.' He passed her the sketchpad. 'I don't do glossy nudes and so far that's all you've offered me, bar a dreary and unremitting display of Electra complex, or more accurately demi-Electra complex. There's no attachment to a father, only a compulsive hostility towards a mother. You've talked about nothing else since I've been here.' He shrugged. 'Even your daughter doesn't feature. You haven't mentioned the poor kid once since she went back to school.'

Joanna got off the bed, wrapped herself in her dressing-gown and walked to the window. 'You don't understand,' she said.

'Oh, I understand,' he murmured. 'You can't con a conman, Joanna.'

She frowned. 'What are you talking about?'

'One of the most colossal egos I've ever come across, and God knows I should recognize one when I see it. You may persuade the rest of the world that Mathilda wronged you, but not me. You've been screwing her all your life,' he tipped a finger at her, 'although you probably didn't know until recently just why you were so damn good at it.'

She didn't say anything.

'I'll hazard a guess that your childhood was one endless tantrum, which Mathilda attempted to control with the scold's bridle. Am I right?' He paused. 'And then what? Presumably you were bright enough to work out a way to stop her using it.'

Her tone was frigid. 'I was terrified of the beastly thing. I used to convulse every time she produced it.'

'Easily done,' he said with amusement. 'I did it myself as a child when it suited me. So how old were you when you worked that one out?'

Her peculiarly fixed gaze lingered on him, but he could feel the growing agitation underneath. 'The only time she ever showed me any affection was when she put the scold's bridle over my head. She'd put her arms about me and rub her cheek against the framework. "Poor darling," she'd say, "Mummy's doing this for Joanna."' She turned back to the window. 'I hated that. It made me feel she could only love me when I was at my ugliest.' She was silent for a moment. 'You're right about one thing. It wasn't until I found out that Gerald was my father that I understood why my mother was afraid of me. She thought I was mad. I'd never realized it before.'

'Didn't you ever ask her why she was afraid?'

'You wouldn't even put that question if you'd really known my mother.' Her breath misted the glass. 'There were so many secrets in her life that I learnt very rapidly never to ask her anything. I had to make up a fantasy background for myself when I went to boarding school because I knew so little about my own.' She dashed the mist away with an impatient hand and turned back into the room. 'Have you finished? I've things to do.'

He wondered how long he could stall her this time before the demands of her addiction sent her scurrying for the bathroom. She was always infinitely more interesting under the stress of abstinence than she ever was drugged. 'Southcliffe?' he asked. 'The same school Ruth's at now?'

She gave a hollow laugh. 'Hardly. Mother wasn't so free with her money in those days. I was sent to a cheap finishing school which made no attempt to educate, merely groomed cattle for the cattle market. Mother had ambitions to marry me off to a title. Probably,' she went on cynically, 'because she hoped a chinless wonder would be so inbred himself he wouldn't notice the lunacy in me.' She glanced towards the door. 'Ruth has had far more spent on her than I ever had, and not because Mother was fond of her, believe me.' Her mouth twisted. 'It was all done to stamp out the Jew in her after my little faux pas with Steven.'

'Did you love him?'

'I've never loved anyone.'

'You love yourself,' he said.

But Joanna had already gone. He could hear her scrabbling feverishly through the vanity case in the bathroom. For what? he wondered. Tranquillizers? Cocaine? Whatever it was, she wasn't injecting it. Her skin was flawless and beautiful like her face.

Sarah Blakeney tells me her husband is an artist. A painter of personalities. I guessed he would be something in that line. It's what I would have chosen myself. The arts or literature.

'I have heard of your paintings too, well enough. God hath given you one face and you make yourselves another.' Funnily enough, that might have been written for Sarah. She projects herself as a frank and open person, with strong, decided views and no hidden contradictions, but in many ways she is very insecure. She positively loathes confrontation, preferring agreement to disagreement, and will placate if she can. I asked her what she was afraid of, and she said: 'I was taught to be accommodating. It's the curse of being a woman. Parents don't want to be left with spinsters on their hands so they teach their daughters to say "yes" to everything except sex.'

Times haven't changed then . . .

Eight

SARAH WAS WAITING outside the doorway of Barclays Bank in Hills Street when Keith Smollett arrived. She had her coat collar pulled up around her ears and looked pale and washed out in the grey November light. He gave her a warm hug and kissed her cold cheek. 'You're not much of an advertisement for a woman who's just scooped the jackpot,' he remarked, holding her at arm's length and examining her face. 'What's the problem?'

'There isn't one,' she said shortly. 'I just happen to think there's more to life than money.'

He smiled, his thin face irritatingly sympathetic. 'Would we be talking Jack by any chance?'

'No, we would not,' she snapped. 'Why does everyone assume that my equanimity depends on a shallow, two-faced skunk whose one ambition in life is to impregnate every female he meets?'

'Ah!'

'What's that supposed to mean?' she demanded.

'Just, ah!' He tucked her hand into his arm. 'Things are pretty bad at the moment, then?' He gestured towards the road. 'Which way to Duggan's office?'

'Up the hill. And, no, things are not pretty bad at the moment. At the moment things are pretty good. I haven't felt so calm and so in control for years.' Her bleak expression belied her words. She allowed herself to be drawn out on to the pavement.

'Or so lonely, perhaps?'

'Jack's a bastard.'

Keith chuckled. 'Tell me something I don't know.'

'He's living with Mathilda Gillespie's daughter.'

Keith slowed down and eyed her thoughtfully. 'Mathilda Gillespie as in the old dear who's left you her loot?'

Sarah nodded.

'Why would he want to live with her daughter?'

'It depends who you listen to. Either because he feels guilty that I, his greedy wife, have deprived poor Joanna of her birthright, or he is protecting her and himself from my murderous slashes with a Stanley knife. No one appears to give any credence to the most obvious reason.'

'Which is?'

'Common-or-garden lust. Joanna Lascelles is very beautiful.' She pointed to a door ten yards ahead. 'That's Duggan's office.'

He stopped and drew her to one side. 'Let me get this straight. Are people saying you murdered the old woman for her money?'

'It's one of the theories going the rounds,' she said dryly. 'My patients are abandoning me in droves.' Dampness sparkled along her lashes. 'It's the absolute pits if you want to know. Some of them are even crossing the road to avoid me.' She blew her nose aggressively. 'And my partners

aren't happy about it either. Their surgeries are overflowing while mine are empty. If it goes on, I'll be out of a job.'

'That's absurd,' he said angrily.

'No more absurd than an old woman leaving everything she had to a virtual stranger.'

'I talked with Duggan on the phone yesterday. He said Mrs Gillespie was clearly very fond of you.'

'I'm very fond of you, Keith, but I don't intend to leave you all my money.' She shrugged. 'I probably wouldn't have been surprised if she'd left me a hundred quid or even her scold's bridle, but leaving me the whole caboodle just doesn't make sense. I didn't do anything to deserve it, except laugh at her jokes from time to time and prescribe a few pain-killers.'

He shrugged in his turn. 'Perhaps that was enough.'

She shook her head. 'People don't dispossess their families in favour of a slight acquaintance who turns up once a month for half an hour. It's completely crazy. Old men besotted with young girls might be foolish enough to do it, but not tough old boots like Mathilda. And, if she was that way inclined, then why didn't she leave it to Jack? According to him, he knew her so well she was happy to let him paint her in the nude.'

Keith felt unreasonably irritated as he pushed open the door of Duggan, Smith and Drew and ushered Sarah inside. There was, he thought, something deeply offensive about Jack Blakeney persuading a wretched old woman to strip for him. And why would she want to anyway? He couldn't get to grips with that at all. But then Blakeney's attraction, if it existed at all, was entirely lost on Keith. He preferred

conventional types who told amusing anecdotes, bought their own drinks and didn't rock the boat by speaking or acting out of turn. He consoled himself with the idea that the story wasn't true. But in his heart of hearts he knew it must be. The real crippler about Jack Blakeney was that women *did* take their clothes off for him.

The meeting dragged on interminably, bogged down in technical details about the 1975 family provision legislation, which, as Duggan had warned Mathilda, might entitle Joanna, as a dependent, to claim reasonable provision for maintenance. 'She ignored my advice,' he said, 'and instructed me to draw up the will leaving all her assets at the time of her death to you. However, it is my considered opinion that in view of the allowance she was paying her daughter and the fact that Mrs Lascelles does not own her own flat, Mrs Lascelles has a good case in law for claiming maintenance. In which case a capital sum now, without prejudice, is worth consideration. I suggest we take counsel's opinion on it.'

Sarah lifted her head. 'You're jumping the gun a little. I haven't yet said that I'm prepared to accept the bequest.'

He could be very direct when he chose. 'Why wouldn't you?'

'Self-preservation.'

'I don't follow.'

'Probably because you haven't had a policeman parked on your doorstep for the last three weeks. Mathilda died in very mysterious circumstances and I'm the only person who

stands to gain by her death. I'd say that makes me rather vulnerable, wouldn't you?'

'Not if you didn't know about the bequest.'

'And how do I prove *that*, Mr Duggan?'

He smiled in his amiable way. 'Let me put it to you another way, Dr Blakeney, how will refusing the bequest prove that you didn't murder her? Won't everyone just say you've taken fright because your attempt to make it look like suicide didn't work?' He paused for a moment, but went on when she didn't say anything. 'And no one will applaud you for your magnanimity, you know, because the money won't go to Mrs Lascelles or her daughter but to a handful of donkeys. At least if you accept the bequest, they've a chance of a capital sum.'

Sarah stared past him towards the window. 'Why did she do it?'

'She said she was fond of you.'

'Didn't you question that at all? I mean, do you normally have rich old ladies turning up out of the blue, saying that they want to make new, secret wills which they don't wish their families to know about? Shouldn't you have tried to persuade her out of it? It might have been a spur-of-the-moment whim which we're all saddled with because she died on us. People are saying I used undue influence.'

He turned his pencil in his fingers. 'It wasn't spur-of-the-moment. She first approached me about three months ago and, yes, as a matter of fact I did try to persuade her out of it. I pointed out that, as a general rule, family money is best left with families however much one individual may dislike his or her children. I argued, with no success at all, that she

should not regard the Cavendish wealth as hers but as a sort of inherited trust to be passed on to succeeding generations.' He shrugged. 'She wouldn't have it. So I tried to persuade her to discuss it with you first, but I'm afraid she wouldn't have that either. She was quite adamant that you were to inherit but weren't to know about it in advance. For the record, and as I told the police, I was satisfied there was no question of undue influence.'

Sarah was appalled. '*Three months*,' she echoed slowly. 'Have you told the police that?'

He nodded. 'They were also working on the theory that it was a sudden whim.'

She put unsteady fingers to her lips. 'I could just about prove I couldn't have known about it if she made the will two days before she died. There is no way I can prove ignorance if she'd been planning it for three months.'

John Hapgood, the bank manager, cleared his throat. 'It does seem to me, Dr Blakeney, that you are concentrating on entirely the wrong issue. The night Mrs Gillespie died was a Saturday if I remember correctly. Where were you that night, and what were you doing? Let's establish whether you *need* to prove your ignorance of the bequest.'

'I was at home on call. I checked when I learnt about the will.'

'And did you receive any calls?'

'Only one, shortly before eight o'clock. It was nothing serious so I dealt with it over the phone.'

'Was your husband with you?'

'No, he was in Stratford that weekend. No one was with me.' She smiled faintly. 'I'm not a complete moron, Mr Hapgood. If I had an alibi I'd have produced it by now.'

'Then I think you must have more faith in the police, Dr Blakeney. Despite what you read in the papers, they are probably still the best in the world.'

She studied him with amusement. 'You may be right, Mr Hapgood, but, personally, I have no faith at all in my ability to prove I didn't kill Mathilda for her money, and I have a nasty feeling the police know it.' She held up her fingers and ticked off point after point. 'I had motive, I had opportunity and I provided at least half the means.' Her eyes glittered. 'In case you didn't know, she was drugged with the barbiturates I prescribed for her before the incisions were made in her wrists. On top of that, I did twelve months in a pathology department because I was considering a career in forensic medicine before I became a GP, so if anyone would know how to fake a suicide it would be me. Now give me one good argument that I can quote in my defence when the police decide to arrest me.'

He steepled his fingers under his chin. 'It's an interesting problem, isn't it?' He beetled his white eyebrows into a ferocious scowl. 'What were you doing that Saturday?'

'The usual. Gardening, housework. I think I used most of that Saturday to prune the roses.'

'Did anyone see you?'

'What difference does it make whether anyone saw me or not?' She spoke with considerable irritation. 'Mathilda was killed some time during the night, and I certainly wasn't gardening in the dark.'

'What *were* you doing?'

Cursing Jack. Feeling sorry for myself. 'I was painting one of the bedrooms.'

'After doing the garden all day?'

'Someone had to do it,' she said curtly.

There was a short silence.

'You're obviously a workaholic,' said Mr Hapgood lamely. She reminded him of his wife, always on the move, always restless, never pausing long enough to work out where she was going.

Sarah gave a slight smile. 'Most women are. We can't shrug off the responsibility of the home just because we want a career. We got the worst of both worlds when we set out to storm the male bastions.' She pressed her thumb and forefinger to her tired eyes. 'Look, none of this is relevant to why we're here. As far as I can see Mathilda has put me in an impossible position. Whatever I do, I shall be saddled with guilt over her daughter and granddaughter. Is there no way I can simply side-step the issue and leave them to fight it out between themselves?'

'There's nothing to stop you giving it back to them in the form of a gift,' said Duggan, 'once it's yours. But it would be a very inefficient use of the money. The tax liability would be colossal.' He smiled apologetically. 'It would also be flying in the face of Mrs Gillespie's wishes. Whatever the rights and wrongs of it, she did not want Mrs Lascelles or Miss Lascelles to inherit her estate.'

Keith reached for his briefcase. 'Is there any hurry for Dr Blakeney to make her decision,' he asked reasonably, 'or can I suggest we put the whole thing on a back burner for another week or two until the police resolve this one way or another? I can't help feeling Dr Blakeney will find it easier to make her decision once the inquest has been held.'

And so it was agreed, although for Sarah it was simply the postponement of a choice already made.

Keith and Sarah had lunch in a small restaurant at the bottom of the hill. Keith watched her over the rim of his wine glass. 'Was that an act or are you genuinely afraid of being arrested?'

She shrugged. 'Does it matter?' He thought how deeply Jack's departure had affected her. He had never encountered Sarah's bitterness before.

'Of course it matters,' he said bluntly. 'If you're worried, then I suggest I come with you now to sort it out with the police. Where's the sense in tearing yourself apart over something that may never happen?'

She smiled faintly. 'It was an act,' she said. 'I got very tired of them discussing me as if I wasn't there. I might have been as dead as Mathilda. It's the money that excites them.'

Unfair, he thought. Both men had gone out of their way to sympathize with the difficult situation in which Sarah found herself but she was determined to see everyone as an enemy. *Including himself*? Impossible to judge. He turned his glass, letting the sober wall-lights gleam through the red wine. 'Do you want Jack back? Is that why you're so angry? Or are you just jealous because he's found someone else?'

'Can you be *just* jealous?'

'You know what I mean.'

She smiled again, a bitter smile that twisted her mouth. 'But I don't, Keith. I've been jealous for years. Jealous of

his art, jealous of his women, jealous of his talent, jealous of him and his ability to bedazzle every damn person he meets. What I feel now is nothing like the jealousy I've felt before. Perhaps it's there but, if it is, it's overlaid with so many other emotions that it's difficult to isolate.'

Keith frowned. 'What do you mean, his ability to bedazzle everyone he meets? I can't stand the man, never have been able to.'

'But you think about him. Mostly with irritation and anger, I expect, but you do think about him. How many other men do you dwell on with the compulsion with which you dwell on Jack? The policeman who's dogging my tracks put it rather well: he said: "He leaves something of a vacuum in his wake."' She held Keith's gaze. 'That's one of the best descriptions I've ever heard of him, because it's true. At the moment I'm living in a vacuum and I'm not enjoying it. For the first time in my life I do not know what to do and it frightens me.'

'Then cut your losses and formalize the separation. Make the decision to start again. Uncertainty is frightening. Certainty never is.'

With a sigh she pushed her plate to one side. 'You sound like my mother. She has a homily for every situation and it drives me mad. Try telling a condemned man that certainty isn't frightening. I doubt he'd agree with you.'

Keith beckoned for the bill. 'At the risk of blotting my copybook again I suggest you go for a long walk by the sea and blow the cobwebs out of your head. You're allowing sentiment to cloud your judgement. There are only two things to remember at a time like this: one, *you* told Jack to leave, not he you; and two, you had good reasons for doing

so. It doesn't matter how lonely, how rejected or how jealous you feel now, it cannot affect the central issue, namely that you and Jack do not get on as man and wife. My advice is to get yourself a decent husband who'll stand by you when you need him.'

She laughed suddenly. 'There's not much hope of that. The decent ones are all spoken for.'

'And whose fault's that? You had your chance, but you chose not to take it.' He handed a credit card to the waitress, watched her walk away to the counter, then transferred his gaze to Sarah. 'I don't suppose you'll ever know how much you hurt me, not unless what you're feeling now is something like the hurt that I felt then.'

She didn't answer immediately. 'Now who's being sentimental?' she said at last, but he thought he saw dampness in her eyes again. 'You've forgotten that you only found me truly desirable after you lost me, and by then it was too late.'

And the tragedy was, he knew she was right.

The door of Cedar House opened six inches in answer to Keith's ring. He smiled pleasantly. 'Mrs Lascelles?'

A tiny frown creased her forehead. 'Yes.'

'I'm Jack Blakeney's solicitor. I'm told he's staying here.'

She didn't answer.

'May I come in and talk to him? I've driven all the way from London.'

'He's not here at the moment.'

'Do you know where I can find him? It is important.'

She gave an indifferent shrug. 'What's your name? I'll tell him you called.'

'Keith Smollett.'

She closed the door.

Violet Orloff, sheltering by the corner of the house, beckoned to him as he walked back to his car. 'I do hope you won't think I'm *interfering*,' she said breathily, 'but I couldn't help overhearing what you said. She's in a funny mood at the moment, won't talk to anyone, and if you've come all the way from London . . .' She left the rest of the sentence unsaid.

Keith nodded. 'I have, so if you can tell me where Jack is I'd be very grateful.'

She cast a nervous sideways glance towards Joanna's door, then gestured rapidly to the path running round the far corner of the house. 'In the garden,' she whispered. 'In the summer-house. He's using it as a studio.' She shook her head. 'But don't tell *her* I told you. I thought Mathilda's tongue was wicked, but *Joanna's* – ' she cast her eyes to heaven, 'she calls Mr Blakeney a homosexual.' She shooed at him. 'Quickly now, or she'll see you talking to me and Duncan would be *furious*. He's so afraid, you know.'

Somewhat bewildered by this eccentric behaviour, Keith nodded his thanks and followed the same route that Sarah had taken with Ruth. Despite the cold, the doors to the summer-house stood open and he could hear a woman singing a Cole Porter song as he approached across the lawn. The voice was unmistakable, rich and haunting, backed by a simple piano accompaniment.

Every time we say goodbye, I die a little,
Every time we say goodbye, I wonder why a little,
Why the gods above me, who must be in the know,
Think so little of me they allow you to go . . .

Keith paused in the entrance. 'Since when were you a Cleo Laine fan, Jack? I thought Sarah was the aficionado.' He pressed the eject button on the recorder and removed the tape to read the handwritten label on the front. 'Well, well. Unless I'm very much mistaken, this is the one I made for her before you married. Does she know you've got it?'

Jack surveyed him through half-closed lids. He was on the point of telling him to put his hackles down, his customary response to Smollett's invariably critical opening remarks, when he thought better of it. For once, he was pleased to see the pompous bastard. In fact, he admitted to himself, he was so damn pleased he could be persuaded to change the habits of the last six years and greet him as a friend instead of a marriage-breaking incubus. He stuck his paintbrush in a jar of turpentine and wiped his hands down the front of his jumper, producing a huge paint-smeared palm as a peace-offering. 'I suppose Sarah's sent you.'

Keith pretended not to see the hand, instead eyed the sleeping-bag, abandoned in a dishevelled heap in a corner, then pulled forward a chair. 'No,' he said, folding himself into it. 'I left her in Poole. She doesn't know I'm here. I've come to try and talk some sense into you.' He studied the portrait. 'Mrs Lascelles presumably.'

Jack crossed his arms. 'What do you think?'

'Of her or the portrait?'

'Either.'

'I only saw six inches of her through the gap in the door.' He cocked his head on one side to examine the painting. 'You've been pretty heavy-handed with the purples. What is she, a nymphomaniac? Or is that just wishful thinking on your part?'

Jack lowered himself gingerly into the chair opposite – the cold and the floorboards were wreaking havoc on the muscles of his back – and wondered if the gentlemanly thing was to bop Keith on the nose now or wait till the man was on guard. 'Not all the time,' he said, answering the question seriously, 'only when she's stoned.'

Keith digested this in silence for a moment or two. 'Have you told the police?'

'What?'

'That she's a user.'

'No.'

'Then I think it's better all round if you never told me and I never heard it.'

'Why?'

'Because I'm on the side of law and order and I don't have your freedom to behave as I like.'

'Don't blame your profession for your lack of freedom, Smollett,' Jack growled, 'blame yourself for selling out to it.' He nodded towards the house. 'She needs help and the best person to give it to her is the one she won't see. Sarah, in other words. What good would a policeman be to her?'

'He could prevent her murdering someone else.'

Thoughtfully, Jack rubbed his unshaven jaw. 'Meaning that because she's degenerate enough to use drugs, she's ipso facto degenerate enough to kill her mother. That's crap, and you know it.'

'It gives her a damn sight better motive than the one Sarah's been saddled with. It's expensive to feed a habit, not to mention the effect it has on the personality. If she didn't kill the old woman for money, then she's probably unpredictable enough to have done it out of sudden fury.'

'You'd have no qualms about briefing a barrister with that codswallop either, would you?' murmured Jack.

'No qualms at all, particularly if it's Sarah's neck that ends up on the line.' Keith turned the cassette in his fingers, then reached out to put it beside the recorder. 'You do know she's worried sick about losing her patients and being arrested for murder, I suppose, while you're here mooning over a drug-addicted nymphomaniac? Where's your loyalty, man?'

Was this Sarah talking? Jack wondered. He hoped not. 'Mooning' was not a word he recognized as part of her vocabulary. She had too much self-respect. He gave a prodigious yawn. 'Does Sarah want me back. Is that why you're here? I don't mind admitting I'm pretty fed up with freezing my balls off in this miserable dump.'

Keith breathed deeply through his nose. 'I don't *know* what she wants,' he said, bunching his fists in his lap. 'I came because I had an absurd idea that you and I could discuss this mess in an adult way without either of us needling the other. I should have known it was impossible.'

Jack squinted at the bunched fists, while doubting that Keith could ever be provoked into using them. 'Did she tell you why she wanted a divorce?'

'Not precisely.'

He linked his hands behind his head and stared at the

ceiling. 'She took against me when she had to arrange an abortion for my lover. It's been downhill ever since.'

Keith was genuinely shocked. *That* explained Sarah's bitterness all right. With a shake of his head, he pushed himself out of his chair and stood by the door, gazing out across the garden. 'If I wasn't so sure I'd lose, I'd invite you out there for a thrashing. You're a shit, Jack. JE-SUS!' he said, as the full import of what the man had said slowly dawned. 'You had the bloody nerve to make Sarah murder *your* baby. That is so damn sick I can hardly believe it. She's your wife, for God's sake, not some sleazy back-street abortionist slaughtering wholesale for money. No wonder she wants a divorce. Don't you have any sensibilities at all?'

'Clearly not,' said Jack impassively.

'I warned her not to marry you.' He turned back bludgeoning the air with his finger because he hadn't the courage to bludgeon Jack with a fist. 'I knew it wouldn't last, told her exactly what to expect, what sort of a man you were, how many women you'd used and discarded. But not this. Never this. How could you *do* such a thing?' He was almost in tears. 'Dammit, I wouldn't even turn my back on the baby, but to make your own wife responsible for its murder. You're sick! Do you know that? You're a sick man.'

'Put like that, I rather agree with you.'

'If I have my way you won't get a penny out of this divorce,' he said ferociously. 'You do realize I'm going to report this back to her, and make sure she uses it in court?'

'I'm relying on you.'

Keith's eyes narrowed suspiciously. 'What's that supposed to mean?'

'It means, Smollett, that I expect you to repeat every word of this conversation verbatim.' His expression was unreadable. 'Now do me a favour and take yourself off before I do something I might regret. Sarah's friendships are entirely her concern, of course, but I admit I've never understood why she always attracts domineering little men who think she's vulnerable.' He flipped the tape, pushed it back into the recorder and pressed the 'play' button. This time it was Richard Rodney Bennett's 'I never went away' that drifted in melancholy splendour upon the air.

> No matter where I travelled to,
> I never went away from you . . .
> I never went away . . .

Jack closed his eyes. 'Now bugger off,' he murmured, 'before I rip your arms off. And don't forget to mention the sleeping-bag, there's a good chap.'

Duncan and Violet Orloff are the most absurd couple. They spent the entire afternoon on the lawn with Duncan fast asleep and Violet twittering non-stop drivel at him. She's like a manic little bird, constantly twitching her head from side to side for fear of predators. As a result she never once looked at Duncan and was quite oblivious to the fact that he wasn't listening to a word she said. I can't say I blame him. She was empty-headed as a child and age has not improved her. I still can't decide whether it was a good or a bad idea to offer them Wing Cottage when Violet wrote and said they'd set their hearts on spending their retirement in Fontwell. 'We do so want to come home,' was her appallingly sentimental way of putting it. The money was very useful, of course – Joanna's flat was a shocking expense, as is Ruth's education – but, on balance, neighbours should be eschewed. It's a relationship that can all too easily descend into forced intimacy. Violet forgot herself and called me 'love' last week, then went into paroxysms of hysteria when I pointed it out, beating her chest with her hands and ululating like some peasant

woman. A most revolting display, frankly. I'm inclined to think she's going senile.

Duncan, of course, is a very different kettle of fish. The wit is still there, if somewhat slower through lack of practice. Hardly surprising when it has been blunted for forty years on Violet's plank of a brain. I wonder sometimes how much they remember of the past. I worry that Violet will twitter away to Joanna or Ruth one day and let cats out of bags that are better confined. We all share too many secrets.

I read back through my early diaries recently and discovered, somewhat to my chagrin, that I told Violet the week before her wedding that her marriage would never last. If the poor creature had a sense of humour, she could reasonably claim the last laugh . . .

Nine

JOANNA SHOWED little surprise at finding Sarah on her doorstep at noon the next day. She gave the faintest of smiles and stepped back into the hall, inviting the other woman inside. 'I was reading the newspaper,' she said, as if Sarah had asked her a specific question. She led the way into the drawing-room. 'Do sit down. If you've come to see Jack, he's outside.'

This was a very different reception from the one Keith described having the previous evening, and Sarah wondered about Joanna's motives. She doubted that it had anything to do with the drug addiction Keith had harped on about, and thought it more likely that curiosity had got the better of her. It made sense. She was Mathilda's daughter and Mathilda had been insatiably curious.

She shook her head. 'No, it's you I've come to see.'

Joanna resumed her own seat but made no comment.

'I always liked this room,' said Sarah slowly. 'I thought how comfortable it was. Your mother used to sit over there,' she pointed to a high-backed chair in front of the french windows, 'and when the sun shone it turned her hair into a

silver halo. You're very like her to look at but I expect you know that.'

Joanna fixed her with her curiously inexpressive eyes.

'Would it help, do you think, if you and I talked about her?'

Again Joanna didn't answer and to Sarah, who had rehearsed everything on the assumption that the other woman would be a willing party to their conversation, the silence was as effective as a brick wall. 'I hoped,' she said, 'that we could try to establish some sort of common ground.' She paused briefly but there was no response. 'Because, frankly, I'm not happy about leaving everything in the hands of solicitors. If we do, we might just as well burn the money now and be done with it.' She gave a tentative smile. 'They'll pick the bones clean and leave us with a worthless carcase. Is that what you want?'

Joanna turned her face to the window and contemplated the garden. 'Doesn't it make you angry that your husband's here with me, Dr Blakeney?'

Relieved that the ice was broken, though not in a way she would have chosen herself, Sarah followed her gaze. 'Whether it does or doesn't isn't terribly relevant. If we bring Jack into it, we'll get nowhere. He has a maddening habit of hi-jacking almost every conversation I'm involved in, and I really would prefer, if possible, to keep him out of this one.'

'Do you think he slept with my mother?'

Sarah sighed inwardly. 'Does it matter to you?'

'Yes.'

'Then, no, I don't think he did. For all his sins, he never takes advantage of people.'

'She might have asked him to.'

'I doubt it. Mathilda had far too much dignity.'

Joanna turned back to her with a frown. 'I suppose you know she posed in the nude for him. I found one of his sketches in her desk. It left nothing to the imagination, I can assure you. Do you call that dignified? She was old enough to be his mother.'

'It depends on your point of view. If you regard the female nude as intrinsically demeaning or deliberately provocative, then, yes, I suppose you could say it was undignified of Mathilda.' She shrugged. 'But that's a dangerous philosophy which belongs to the dark ages and the more intolerant religions. If, on the other hand, you see the nude figure, be it male or female, as one of nature's creations, and therefore as beautiful and as extraordinary as anything else on this planet, then I see no shame involved in allowing a painter to paint it.'

'She did it because she knew it would excite him.' She spoke the words with conviction and Sarah wondered about the wisdom of continuing – Joanna's prejudice against her mother was too ingrained for reasoned argument. But the offensiveness of the statement irritated her enough to defend Jack, if only because she had encountered the same sort of blinkered stupidity herself.

'Jack's seen far too many naked women to find nakedness itself a turn-on,' she said dismissively. 'Nudity is only erotic if you want it to be. You might just as well say that I get a thrill every time a male patient undresses for me.'

'That's different. You're a doctor.'

Sarah shook her head. 'It's not, but I'm not going to argue the toss with you. It would be a waste of both our

times.' She ran her fingers through her hair. 'In any case your mother was too incapacitated by her arthritis, and in too much pain from it, to want to have intercourse with a virile man thirty years her junior. It's important to keep a sense of proportion, Mrs Lascelles. It might have been different if she had been sexually active all her life or even liked men very much, but neither was true of your mother. She once told me that the reason there were so many divorces these days was because relationships based on sex were doomed to fail. The pleasures of orgasm were too fleeting to make the remaining hours of boredom and disappointment worth while.'

Joanna resumed her study of the garden. 'Then why did she take her clothes off?' It was, it seemed, very important to her. Because she was jealous, Sarah wondered, or because she needed to go on despising Mathilda?

'I imagine it was no big deal, one way or the other, and she was interested enough in art for art's sake to help Jack explore the unconventional side of her nature. I can't see her doing it for any other reason.'

There was a brief silence while Joanna considered this. 'Do you still like her now that she's dead?'

Sarah clasped her hands between her knees and stared at the carpet. 'I don't know,' she said honestly. 'I'm so angry about the will that I can't view her objectively at the moment.'

'Then say you don't want the bequest. Let me and Ruth have it.'

'I wish it was that easy, believe me, but if I turn it down then you'll have to fight the donkeys' charity for it, and I honestly can't see how that will improve your chances

unless, presumably, you can show that Mathilda never intended that will to be her last.' She looked up to find Joanna's pale eyes studying her intently.

'You're a very peculiar woman, Dr Blakeney,' she said slowly. 'You must realize that the easiest way for me to do that is to prove that my mother was murdered and that you were the one who did it. It fits so neatly, after all. You knew the will was just a threat to make me and Ruth toe the line, so you killed Mother quickly before she could change it. Once you're convicted, no court on earth will rule in favour of the donkeys.'

Sarah nodded. 'And if you can cajole my husband into testifying that I knew about the will in advance, then you're home and dry.' She raised an eyebrow in enquiry. 'But, as I suspect you're beginning to discover, Jack is neither so amenable nor so dishonest. And it wouldn't make any difference, you know, if you did manage to persuade him into bed with you. I've known him for six years and the one thing I can say about him is that he cannot be bought. He values himself far too highly to tell lies for anyone, no matter how much of an obligation they may put him under.'

Joanna gave a small laugh. 'You're very confident that I haven't slept with him.'

Sarah felt compassion for her. 'My solicitor phoned last night to say that Jack's camped out in your summer-house, but I was sure anyway. You're very vulnerable at the moment, and I do know my husband well enough to know he wouldn't exploit that.'

'You sound as though you admire him.'

'I could never admire him as much as he admires himself,'

she said dryly. 'I hope he's extremely cold out there. I've suffered for his art for years.'

'I gave him a paraffin heater,' said Joanna with a frown. The memory obviously annoyed her.

Sarah's eyes brimmed with sudden laughter. 'Was he grateful?'

'No. He told me to leave it outside the door.' She gazed through the window. 'He's an uncomfortable person.'

'I'm afraid he is,' Sarah agreed. 'It never occurs to him that other people have fragile egos which need stroking from time to time. It means you have to take his love on faith if you want a relationship with him.' She gave a throaty chuckle. 'And faith has a nasty habit of deserting you just when you most need it.'

There was a long silence. 'Did you talk to my mother like this?' Joanna asked at last.

'Like what?'

Joanna sought for the right words. 'So – easily.'

'Do you mean did I find her easy to talk to?'

'No.' There was a haunted look in the grey eyes. 'I meant, weren't you afraid of her?'

Sarah stared at her hands. 'I didn't need to be, Mrs Lascelles. She couldn't hurt me, you see, because she wasn't my mother. There were no emotional strings to be arbitrarily plucked when she felt like it; no shared family secrets that would lay me open to her vituperative tongue; no weaknesses from my childhood that she could exploit into adulthood whenever she felt like belittling me. If she'd tried, of course, I'd have walked away, because I've had all that from my own mother for years and there is no way I would put up with it from a stranger.'

'I didn't kill her. Is that what you came to find out?'

'I came to find out if bridges could be built.'

'For your benefit or mine?'

'Both, I hoped.'

Joanna's smile was apologetic. 'But I've got nothing to gain by being friendly with you, Dr Blakeney. It would be tantamount to admitting Mother was right and I can't do that, not if I want to contest the will in court.'

'I hoped to persuade you there were other options.'

'Every one of which is dependent on your charity.'

Sarah sighed. 'Is that so terrible?'

'Of course. I served forty years for my inheritance. You served one. Why should I have to beg from you?'

Why indeed? There was no justice in it that Sarah could see. 'Is there any point in my coming here again?'

'No.' Joanna stood up and smoothed the creases from her skirt. 'It can only make matters worse.'

Sarah smiled wryly. 'Can they *be* any worse?'

'Oh, yes,' she said with a twisted little smile. 'I might start to like you.' She waved dismissively towards the door. 'You know your way out, I think.'

DS Cooper was gazing thoughtfully at Sarah's car when she emerged from the front door. 'Was that wise, Dr Blakeney?' he asked as she approached.

'Was what wise?'

'Bearding the lioness in her den.'

'Do lionesses have beards?' she murmured.

'It was a figure of speech.'

'I gathered that.' She observed him with fond amuse-

ment. 'Wise or not, Sergeant, it was instructive. I've had my anxieties laid to rest and, as any doctor will tell you, that's the best panacea there is.'

He looked pleased for her. 'You've sorted things out with your husband?'

She shook her head. 'Jack's a life sentence not an anxiety.' Her dark eyes gleamed with mischief. 'Perhaps I should have paid a little more attention when my mother was making her predictions for our future.'

'Marry in haste, repent at leisure?' he suggested.

'More along the lines of "She who sups with the devil needs a long spoon". Which I, of course, countered with "The devil has all the best tunes".' She made a wry face. 'But try forgetting "Hey, Jude" or "Twenty-four hours from Tulsa". Like Jack they have a nasty habit of lingering in the memory.'

He chuckled. 'I'm more of a "White Christmas" man myself, but I know what you mean.' He glanced towards the house. 'So, if it's not your husband who's set your mind at rest it must be Mrs Lascelles. Does that mean she's decided to accept the terms of the will?'

Again Sarah shook her head. 'No. She's convinced me she didn't kill her mother.'

'And how did she manage to do that?' He looked very sceptical.

'Feminine intuition, Sergeant. You'd probably call it naïvety.'

'I would.' He patted her arm in an avuncular way. 'You really must learn not to be so patronizing, Doctor. You'll see things in a different light if you do.'

'Patronizing?' echoed Sarah in surprise.

'We can always call it something else. Intellectual snobbery or self-righteousness, perhaps. They cloak themselves just as happily under the guise of naïvety but, of course, naïvety sounds so much less threatening. You're a very decided woman, Dr Blakeney, and you rush in where angels fear to tread, not out of foolishness but out of an overweening confidence that you know best. I am investigating a murder here.' He smiled grimly. 'I don't pretend that I would ever have liked Mrs Gillespie because I'm rather inclined to accept the established view that she was an evil-minded old bitch who got her kicks out of hurting people. However, that did not give anyone the right to strike her down prematurely. But the point I want to stress to you is that whoever killed her was clever. Mrs Gillespie made enemies right, left and centre, and knew it; she was a bully; she was cruel; and she trod rough-shod over other people's sensibilities. Yet, someone got so close to her that they were able to deck her out in a diabolical headdress and then take her semi-conscious to the bath where they slit her wrists. Whoever this person was is not going to make you a free gift of their involvement. To the contrary, in fact, they will make you a free gift of their non-involvement, and your absurd assumption that you can tell intuitively who is or who is not guilty from a simple conversation is intellectual arrogance of the worst kind. If it was so damned easy – forgive my French – to tell murderers from the rest of society, do you not think by now that we'd have locked them up and confined unlawful killing to the oddities page of the history textbooks?'

'Oh dear,' she said. 'I seem to have exposed a nerve. I'm sorry.'

He sighed with frustration. 'You're still patronizing me.'

She opened her car door. 'Perhaps it would be better if I left, otherwise I might be tempted to return the insult.'

He looked amused. 'Water off a duck's back,' he said amiably. 'I've been insulted by professionals.'

'I'm not surprised,' she said, slipping in behind the wheel. 'I can't be the only person who gets pissed off when you decide to throw your weight about. You don't even know for sure that Mathilda was murdered, but we're all supposed to wave our arms in the air and panic. What possible difference can it make to anyone if I choose to satisfy myself that Mrs Lascelles hasn't disqualified herself from a cut of the will by topping the old lady who made it?'

'It could make a lot of difference to you,' he said mildly. 'You could end up dead.'

She was intensely scornful. 'Why?'

'Have you made a will, Dr Blakeney?'

'Yes.'

'In favour of your husband?'

She nodded.

'So, if you die tomorrow, he gets everything, including, presumably, what Mrs Gillespie has left you.'

She started the car. 'Are you suggesting Jack is planning to murder me?'

'Not necessarily.' He looked thoughtful. 'I'm rather more interested in the fact that he is – potentially – a very eligible husband. Assuming, of course, you die before you can change your will. It's worth considering, don't you think?'

Sarah glared at him through the window. 'And you say

Mathilda was evil-minded?' Furiously, she ground into gear. 'Compared with you she was a novice. Juliet to your Iago. And if you don't understand the analogy, then I suggest you bone up on some Shakespeare.' She released the clutch with a jerk and showered his legs with gravel as she drove away.

'Are you busy, Mr Blakeney, or can you spare me a few minutes?' Cooper propped himself against the doorjamb of the summer-house and lit a cigarette.

Jack eyed him for a moment, then went back to his painting. 'If I said I was busy would you go away?'

'No.'

With a shrug, Jack clamped the brush between his teeth and took a coarser one from the jar on the easel, using it to create texture in the soft paint he had just applied. Cooper smoked in silence, watching him. 'Okay,' said Jack at last, flipping the brushes into turpentine and swinging round to face the Sergeant. 'What's up?'

'Who was Iago?'

Jack grinned. 'You didn't come here to ask me that.'

'You're quite right, but I'd still like to know.'

'He's a character from *Othello*. A Machiavelli who manipulated people's emotions in order to destroy them.'

'Was Othello the black bloke?'

Jack nodded. 'Iago drove him into such a frenzy of jealousy that Othello murdered his wife Desdemona and then killed himself when he learnt that everything Iago had said about her was a lie. It's a story of obsessive passion and trusts betrayed. You should read it.'

'Maybe I will. What did Iago do to make Othello jealous?'

'He exploited Othello's emotional insecurity by telling him Desdemona was having an affair with a younger, more attractive man. Othello believed him because it was what he was most afraid of.' He stretched his long legs in front of him. 'Before Othello fell on his sword he described himself as "one that lov'd not wisely but too well". It gets misused these days by people who know the quote but don't know the story. They interpret "lov'd not wisely" as referring to a poor choice of companion, but Othello was actually acknowledging his own foolishness in not trusting the woman he adored. He just couldn't believe the adoration was mutual.'

Cooper ground his cigarette under the heel of his shoe. 'Topical stuff then,' he murmured, glancing towards the sleeping-bag. 'Your wife's not loving too wisely at the moment, but then you're hardly encouraging her to do anything else. You're being a little cruel, aren't you, sir?'

Jack's liking for the man grew. 'Not half as cruel as I ought to be. Why did you want to know about Iago?'

'Your wife mentioned him, said I was Iago to Mrs Gillespie's Juliet.' He smiled his amiable smile. 'Mind, I'd just suggested that if she were to die an untimely death you would make an eligible catch for someone else.' He took out another cigarette, examined it then put it back again. 'But I don't see Mrs Gillespie as Juliet. King Lear, perhaps, assuming I'm right and King Lear was the one whose daughter turned on him.'

'Daughters,' Jack corrected him. 'There were two of them, or two who turned on him, at least. The third tried

to save him.' He rubbed his unshaven jaw. 'So you've got your knife into Joanna, have you? Assuming I've followed your reasoning correctly, then Joanna killed her mother to inherit the funds, found to her horror that Mathilda had changed her will in the meantime, so immediately made eyes at me to get me away from Sarah with a view to topping Sarah at the first opportune moment and then hitching herself to me.' He chuckled. 'Or perhaps you think we're in it together. That's one hell of a conspiracy theory.'

'Stranger things have happened, sir.'

He eased his stiff shoulders. 'On the whole I prefer Joanna's interpretation. It's more rational.'

'She's accusing your wife.'

'I know. It's a neat little package, too. The only flaw in it is that Sarah would never have done it, but I can't blame Joanna for getting that wrong. She can't see past her own jealousy.'

Cooper frowned. 'Jealousy over you?'

'God no.' Jack gave a rumble of laughter. 'She doesn't even like me very much. She thinks I'm a homosexual because she can't account for my irreverence in any other way.' His eyes gleamed at Cooper's expression, but he didn't elaborate. 'Jealousy over her mother, of course. She was quite happy loathing and being loathed by Mathilda until she discovered she had a rival. Jealousy has far more to do with ownership than it has with love.'

'Are you saying she knew about your wife's relationship with her mother before her mother died?'

'No. If she had, she would probably have done something about it.' He scraped his stubble again, his eyes narrowing thoughtfully. 'But it's too late now, and that can

only make the jealousy worse. She'll start to forget her mother's faults, fantasize about the relationship she imagines Sarah had with Mathilda and torment herself over her own missed opportunities. Let's face it, we all want to believe that our mothers love us. It's supposed to be the one relationship we can depend on.'

Cooper lit another cigarette and stared thoughtfully at the glowing tip. 'You say Mrs Lascelles is jealous of your wife's intimacy with Mrs Gillespie. Why isn't she jealous of her daughter? According to the young lady herself she got on with her grandmother like a house on fire.'

'Do you believe her?'

'There's no evidence to the contrary. The housemistress at her boarding school says Mrs Gillespie wrote regularly and always seemed very affectionate whenever she went there. Far more affectionate and interested, apparently, than Mrs Lascelles who puts in infrequent appearances and shows little or no interest in how her daughter's doing.'

'All that says to me is that Mathilda was a magnificent hypocrite. You can't ignore her snobbery, you know, not without distorting the picture. Southcliffe is an expensive girls' boarding school. Mathilda would never have let the side down in a place like that. She always talked about "people of her sort" and regretted the lack of them in Fontwell.'

The Sergeant shook his head in disbelief. 'That doesn't square with what you told me before. You called her one of life's great individuals. Now you're saying she was pandering to the upper classes in order to make herself socially acceptable.'

'Hardly. She was a Cavendish and inordinately proud of

the fact. They were bigwigs round here for years. Her father, Sir William Cavendish, bought his knighthood by doing a stint as the local MP. She was already socially acceptable, as you put it, and didn't need to pander to anyone.' He frowned in recollection. 'No, what made her extraordinary, despite all the trappings of class and respectability which she played up to and tossed about in public to keep the proles in their place, was that privately she seethed with contradictions. Perhaps her uncle's sexual abuse had something to do with it, but I think the truth is she was born into the wrong generation and lived the wrong life. She had the intellectual capacity to do anything she wanted, but her social conditioning was such that she allowed herself to be confined in the one role she wasn't suited for, namely marriage and motherhood. It's tragic really. She spent most of her life at war with herself and crippled her daughter and granddaughter in the process. She couldn't bear to see their rebellions succeed where hers hadn't.'

'Did she tell you all this?'

'Not in so many words. I gleaned it from things she said and then put it into the portrait. But it's all true. She wanted a complete explanation of that painting, down to the last colour nuance and the last brush stroke, so' – he shrugged – 'I gave her one, much along the lines of what I've just told you, and at the end she said there was only one thing wrong, and it was wrong because it was missing. But she wouldn't tell me what it was.' He paused in reflection. 'Presumably it had something to do with her uncle's abuse of her. I didn't know about that. I only knew of her father's abuse with the scold's bridle.'

But Cooper was more interested in something he had

said before. 'You can't call Mrs Lascelles's rebellion a success. She lumbered herself with a worthless heroin addict who then died and left her penniless.' His gaze lingered on the portrait.

Jack's dark face split into another grin. 'You've led a very sheltered life if you think rebellion is about achieving happiness. It's about anger and resistance and inflicting maximum damage on a hated authority.' He lifted a sardonic eyebrow. 'On that basis, I'd say Joanna scored a spectacular success. If you're calling her husband worthless now, what on earth do you imagine Mathilda's peers said about him at the time? Don't forget she was a very proud woman.'

Cooper drew heavily on his cigarette and looked up towards the house. 'Your wife's just been to see Mrs Lascelles. Did you know?'

Jack shook his head.

'I met her as she was leaving. She told me she's convinced Mrs Lascelles didn't kill her mother. Would you agree with that?'

'Probably.'

'Yet you just told me that Mrs Lascelles's rebellion was to inflict maximum damage on the object of her hatred. Isn't death the ultimate damage?'

'I was talking about twenty-odd years ago. You're talking about now. Rebellion belongs to the young, Sergeant, not to the middle-aged. It's the middle-aged who're rebelled against because they're the ones who compromise their principles.'

'So how is Ruth rebelling?'

Jack studied him lazily from beneath his hooded eyelids. 'Why don't you ask her?'

'Because she's not here,' said Cooper reasonably, 'and you are.'

'Ask her mother then. You're being paid to meddle,' he cocked his irritating eyebrow again, 'and I'm not.'

Cooper beamed at him. 'I like you, Mr Blakeney, though God alone knows why. I like your wife, too, if it's of any interest. You're straightforward types who look me in the eye when you talk to me and, believe it or not, that warms my heart because I'm trying to do a job that the people have asked me to do but for which, most of the time, I get called a pig. Now, for all I know, one or other, or both of you together, killed that poor old woman up there, and if I have to arrest you I'll do it, and I shan't let my liking get in the way because I'm an old-fashioned sod who believes that society only works if it's bolstered by rules and regulations which give more freedom than they take away. By the same token, I don't like Mrs Lascelles or her daughter, and if I was the sort to arrest people I didn't like, I'd have banged them up a couple of weeks ago. They're equally malicious. The one directs her malice against your wife, the other directs hers against her mother, but neither of them has said anything worth listening to. Their accusations are vague and without substance. Ruth says her mother's a whore without principles, and Mrs Lascelles says your wife's a murderess but when I ask them to prove it, they can't.' He tossed his dog-end on to the grass. 'The odd thing is that you and Dr Blakeney, between you, appear to know more about these two women and their relationship with Mrs

Gillespie than they do themselves, but out of some kind of misguided altruism you don't want to talk about it. Perhaps it's not politically correct amongst gilded intellectuals to dabble their fingers in the seamy side of life, but make no mistake, without something more to go on, Mrs Gillespie's death will remain an unsolved mystery and the only person who will suffer will be Dr Blakeney because she is the only person who had a known motive. If she is innocent of the murder of her patient, her innocence can only be proved if someone else is charged. Now, tell me honestly, do you think so little of your wife that you'd let her reputation be trampled in the mud for the sake of not wanting to assist the police?'

'My God!' said Jack with genuine enthusiasm. 'You're going to have to let me do this portrait of you. Two thousand. Is that what we agreed?'

'You haven't answered my question,' said the policeman patiently.

Jack reached for his sketchpad and flicked through to a clean page. 'Just stand there for a moment,' he murmured, taking a piece of charcoal and making swift lines on the paper. 'That was some speech. Is your wife as decent and honourable as you are?'

'You're taking the mickey.'

'Actually, I'm not.' Jack squinted at him briefly before returning to his drawing. 'I happen to think the relationship between the police and society is drifting out of balance. The police have forgotten that they are there only by invitation; while society has forgotten that, because it chooses the laws which regulate it, it has a responsibility to uphold them. The relationship should be a mutually sup-

portive one; instead, it is mutually suspicious and mutually antagonistic.' He threw Cooper a disarmingly sweet smile. 'I am thoroughly enchanted to meet a policeman who seems to share my point of view. And, no, of course I don't think so little of Sarah that I'd allow her reputation to suffer. Is that really likely?'

'You've not been out and about much since you moved in here.'

'I never do when I'm working.'

'Then perhaps it's time you left. There's a kangaroo court operating in Fontwell and your wife is their favourite target. She's the newcomer, after all, and you've done her no favours by shacking up with the opposition. She's lost a goodly number of patients already.'

Jack held the sketchpad at arm's length to look at it. 'Yes,' he said, 'I'm going to enjoy doing you.' He started to pack his hold-all. 'It's too damn cold here anyway, and I've got enough on Joanna to finish her at home. Will Sarah have me back?'

'I suggest you ask her. I'm not paid to meddle in domestic disputes.'

Jack tipped a finger in acknowledgement. 'Okay,' he said, 'the only thing I know about Ruth is what Mathilda told me. I can't vouch for its accuracy, so you'll have to check that for yourself. Mathilda kept a float of fifty pounds locked in a cash-box in her bedside table and opened it up one day because she wanted me to go to the shop and buy some groceries for her. It was empty. I said, perhaps she'd already spent the money and forgotten. She said, no, it's what came of having a thief for a granddaughter.' He shrugged. 'For all I know she may have been excusing her

own memory lapse by slandering Ruth, but she didn't elaborate and I didn't ask. More than that I can't tell you.'

'What a disappointing family,' said the Sergeant. 'No wonder she chose to leave her money elsewhere.'

'That's where we part company,' said Jack, standing up and stretching towards the ceiling. 'They are Mathilda's creations. She had no business passing the buck to Sarah.'

I had an appalling shock today. I walked into the surgery, completely unprepared, and found Jane Marriott behind the counter. Why did nobody tell me they were back? Forewarned would have meant forearmed. Jane, of course, knowing our paths must cross, was as cool as ever. 'Good morning, Mathilda,' she said. 'You're looking well.' I couldn't speak. It was left to Doctor Dolittle, asinine man, to bray the good news that Jane and Paul have decided to move back to Rossett House following the death of their tenant. I gather Paul is an invalid – chronic emphysema – and will benefit from the peace and quiet of Fontwell after the rigours of Southampton. But what am I to do about Jane? Will she talk? Worse, will she betray me?

'Is there no pity sitting in the clouds, that sees into the bottom of my grief?'

I would feel less desperate if Ruth had not gone back to school. The house is empty without her. There are too many ghosts here and most of them unlaid. Gerald and my father haunt me mercilessly. There are times, not many, when I regret their deaths. But I have high hopes

of Ruth. She is bright for her age. Something good will come of the Cavendishes, I'm sure of it. If not, everything I have done is wasted.

'Hush! Hush! Whisper who dares! Mathilda Gillespie is saying her prayers.' I have such terrible headaches these days. Perhaps it was never Joanna who was mad, but only I . . .

Ten

RUTH, SUMMONED OUT of a chemistry lesson, sidled into the room set aside for Sergeant Cooper by her housemistress and stood with her back to the door. 'Why did you have to come back?' she asked him. 'It's embarrassing. I've told you everything I know.' She was dressed in mufti and, with her hair swept back into a tight bun, she looked more than her seventeen years.

Cooper could appreciate her embarrassment. Any school was a goldfish bowl but a boarding school peculiarly so. 'Police investigations are rarely tidy things,' he said apologetically. 'Too many loose ends for tidiness.' He gestured towards a chair. 'Sit down, Miss Lascelles.'

With a bad grace, she did so, and he caught a brief glimpse of the gawky adolescent beneath the pseudo-sophistication of the outer shell. He lowered his stocky body on to the chair in front of her and studied her gravely but not unkindly.

'Two days ago we received a letter about you,' he said. 'It was anonymous. It claimed you were in Cedar House the day your grandmother died and that you stole some earrings. Are either of those facts true, Miss Lascelles?'

Her eyes widened but she didn't say anything.

'Since which time,' he went on gently, 'I have been told on good authority that your grandmother knew you were a thief. She accused you of stealing money from her. Is that also true?'

The colour drained from her face. 'I want a solicitor.'

'Why?'

'It's my right.'

He stood up with a nod. 'Very well. Do you have a solicitor of your own? If you do, you may give your housemistress the number and ask her to telephone him. If not, I'm sure she will be happy to call the one the school uses. Presumably they will charge it to the fees.' He walked to the door. 'She may even offer to sit in herself to safeguard your interests. I have no objection to either course.'

'No,' she said sharply, 'I want the duty solicitor.'

'Which duty solicitor?' He found her transparency oddly pathetic.

'The one the police provide.'

He considered this during a prolonged and thoughtful silence. 'Would you be referring to duty solicitors at police stations who act on behalf of persons who have no legal representation of their own?'

She nodded.

He sounded genuinely sympathetic. 'With the best will in the world, Miss Lascelles, that is out of the question. These are harsh recessionary times, and you're a privileged young woman, surrounded by people only too willing to watch out for your rights. We'll ask your housemistress to contact a lawyer. She won't hesitate, I'm sure. Apart from anything else, she will want to keep the unpleasantness

under wraps so to speak. After all, she does have the school's reputation to think of.'

'Bastard!' she snapped. 'I just won't answer your questions then.'

He manufactured a look of surprise. 'Do I gather you don't want a solicitor after all?'

'No. Yes.' She hugged herself. 'But I'm not saying anything.'

Cooper returned to his seat. 'That's your privilege. But if I don't get any answers from you, then I shall have to ask my questions elsewhere. In my experience, thieves do not confine themselves to stealing from just one person. I wonder what will happen if I call the rest of your house together and ask them en masse if any of their possessions have gone missing in the last year or so. The inference, surely, will be obvious because they know my only connection with the school is you.'

'That's blackmail.'

'Standard police procedure, Miss Lascelles. If a copper can't get his information one way, then he's duty-bound to try another.'

She scowled ferociously. 'I didn't kill her.'

'Have I said you did?'

She couldn't resist answering, it seemed. 'It's what you're thinking. If I was there I must have killed her.'

'She probably died during the early half of the night, between nine o'clock and midnight, say. Were you there then?'

She looked relieved. 'No. I left at five. I had to be back in time for a physics lecture. It's one of my A level subjects and I gave the vote of thanks at the end.'

He took out his pad. 'What time did the lecture start?'

'Seven thirty.'

'And you were there for the start?'

'Yes.'

'How did you manage to do that? You clearly didn't walk thirty miles in two and a half hours.'

'I borrowed a bicycle.'

He looked deeply sceptical. 'What time did you arrive at your grandmother's, Miss Lascelles?'

'I don't know. About three thirty, I suppose.'

'And what time did you leave the school?'

'After lunch.'

'I see,' he said ponderously, 'so you rode thirty miles in one direction in two hours, rested for an hour and a half with your grandmother and then rode thirty miles back again. You must be a very fit young woman. May I have the name of the person whose bicycle you borrowed?' He licked the point of his pencil and held it poised above the page.

'I don't know whose it was. I borrowed it without asking.'

He made a note. 'Shall we call a spade a spade and be done with the pretence? You mean you stole it. Like the earrings and the fifty pounds.'

'I put it back. That's not stealing.'

'Back where?'

'In the bike shed.'

'Good, then you'll be able to identify it for me.'

'I'm not sure. I just took the best one I could find. What difference does it make which bicycle it was?'

'Because you're going to hop on board again and I'm

going to follow closely behind you all the way to Fontwell.' He looked amused. 'You see, I don't believe you're capable of riding thirty miles in two hours, Miss Lascelles, but I'm quite happy for you to prove me wrong. Then you can have an hour and a half's rest before you ride back again.'

'You can't do that. That's just fucking – ' she cast about for a word ' – harassment.'

'Of course I can do it. It's called a reconstruction. You've just put yourself at the scene of a crime on the day the crime was committed, you're a member of the victim's family with easy access to her house and you thought you were going to inherit money from her. All of which puts you high on the list of probable suspects. Either you prove to my satisfaction that you did go by bicycle, or you tell me now how you really got there. Someone drove you, didn't they?'

She sat in a sullen silence, scraping her toe back and forth across the carpet. 'I hitched,' she said suddenly. 'I didn't want to tell you because the school would throw a fit if they knew.'

'Was your grandmother alive when you left Cedar House at five o'clock?'

She looked put out by the sudden switch of direction. 'She must have been, mustn't she, as I didn't kill her.'

'So you spoke to her?'

Ruth eyed him warily. 'Yes,' she muttered. 'I left my key at school and had to ring the doorbell.'

'Then she'll have asked you how you got there. If you had to hitch, she won't have been expecting you.'

'I said I had a lift from a friend.'

'But that wasn't true, was it, and, as you knew you were going to have to hitch back to school again on a dark

November evening, why didn't you ask your grandmother to drive you? She had a car and, according to you, she was fond of you. She'd have done it without a murmur, wouldn't she? Why would you do something so dangerous as hitching in the dark?'

'I didn't think about it.'

He sighed. 'Where did you hitch from, Miss Lascelles? Fontwell itself, or did you walk the three miles along Gazing Lane to the main road? If it was Fontwell, then we'll be able to find the person who picked you up.'

'I walked along Gazing Lane,' she said obligingly.

'And what sort of shoes were you wearing?'

'Trainers.'

'Then they'll have mud from the lane squeezed into every seam and crevice. It was raining most of that afternoon. The boys at forensic will have a field day. Your shoes will vindicate you if you're telling the truth. And if you're not . . .' he smiled grimly, 'I will make your life a misery, Miss Lascelles. I will interview every girl in the school, if necessary, to ask them who you consort with, who's had to cover for you when you've gone AWOL, what you steal and why you're stealing it. And if at the end of it you have an ounce of credibility left, then I'll start all over again. Is that clear? Now, who drove you to your grandmother's?'

There were tears in her eyes. 'It's got nothing to do with Granny's death.'

'Then what can you lose by telling me?'

'I'll be expelled.'

'You'll be expelled far quicker if I have to explain why I'm carting your clothing off for forensic examination.'

She buried her face in her hands. 'My boyfriend,' she muttered.

'Name?' he demanded relentlessly.

'Dave – Dave Hughes.'

'Address?'

She shook her head. 'I can't tell you. He'd kill me.'

Cooper frowned at the bent head. 'How did you meet him?'

She raised her tear-stained face. 'He did the tarmac on the school drive.' She read censure in his eyes and leapt to defend herself. 'It's not like that.'

'Like what?'

'I'm not a slut. We love each other.'

Her sexual morality had been the last thing on his mind but it was clearly at the forefront of hers. He felt sorry for her. She was accusing herself, he thought, when she called her mother a whore. 'Does he own the house?'

She shook her head. 'It's a squat.'

'But he must have a telephone or you wouldn't be able to contact him.'

'It's a mobile.'

'May I have the number?'

She looked alarmed. 'He'd be furious.'

You bet your life he would, thought Cooper. He wondered what Hughes was involved in. Drugs? Under-age sex? Pornography? Expulsion was the least of Ruth's problems if any of these were true. He showed no impatience for the address or phone number. 'Tell me about him,' he invited instead. 'How long have you known him? How old is he?'

He had to prise the information from her with patient cajoling and, as she spoke and listened to herself, he saw the dawning confirmation of her worst fears: that this was not a story of Montagues and Capulets thwarting innocent love but, rather, a seedy log of sweaty half-hours in the back of a white Ford transit. Told baldly, of course, it lacked even the saving attraction of eroticism and Cooper, like Ruth, found the telling uncomfortable. He did his best to make it easy for her but her embarrassment was contagious and they looked away from each other more often than their eyes met.

It had been going on for six months since the tarmac crew had relaid the drive, and the details of how it began were commonplace. A school full of girls; Dave with an eye for the most likely; she flattered by his obvious admiration, more so when the other girls noticed he only had eyes for her; a wistful regret when the tarmac was done and the crew departed; followed by an apparently chance meeting when she was walking alone; he, streetwise and twenty-eight; she, a lonely seventeen-year-old with dreams of romance. He respected her, he loved her, he'd wait for ever for her, but (how big a word 'but' was in people's lives, thought Cooper) he had her in the back of his transit within a week. If she could forget the squalor of a blanket on a tarpaulin, then she could remember the fun and the excitement. She had crept out of a downstairs window at two o'clock in the morning to be enveloped in her lover's arms. They had smoked and drunk and talked by candlelight in the privacy of the parked van and, yes, all right, he wasn't particularly well educated or even very articulate, but that didn't matter. And if what happened afterwards had not been part of her

gameplan, then that didn't matter either because, when it came to it (her eyes belied the words) she had wanted sex as much as he had.

Cooper longed to ask her, why? Why she valued herself so cheaply? Why she was the only girl in the school who fell for it? Why she would want a relationship with an illiterate labourer? Why, ultimately, she was so gullible as to imagine that he wanted anything more than free sex with a clean virgin? He didn't ask, of course. He wasn't so cruel.

The affair might have ended there had she not met him by sheer mischance (Cooper's interpretation, not hers) one day during the holidays. She had heard nothing from him since the night in the van, and hope had given way to depression. She was spending Easter with her grandmother at Fontwell (she usually went to Fontwell, she told Cooper, because she got on better with her grandmother), and caught the bus to Bournemouth to go shopping. And suddenly there was Dave, and he was so pleased to see her, but angry, too, because she hadn't answered his letter. (Sourly, Cooper imagined the touching scene. What letter? Why, the one that had got lost in the post, of course.) After which they had fallen into each other's arms in the back of the Ford, before Dave had driven her home and realized (Cooper reading between the lines again) that Ruth might be good for a little more than a quick tumble on a blanket when he felt horny.

'He took me everywhere that holidays. It was wonderful. The best time I've ever had.' But she spoke the words flatly, as if even the memory lacked sparkle.

She was too canny to tell her grandmother what she was doing – even in her wildest dreams she didn't think

Mathilda would approve of Dave – so, instead, like a two-timing spouse, she invented excuses for her absences.

'And your grandmother believed you?'

'I think her arthritis was really bad about then. I used to say I was going somewhere, but in the evening she'd have forgotten where.'

'Did Dave take you to his home?'

'Once. I didn't like it much.'

'Did he suggest you steal from your grandmother? Or was that your idea?'

'It wasn't like that,' she said unhappily. 'We ran out of money, so I borrowed some from her bag one day.'

'And couldn't pay it back?'

'No.' She fell silent.

'What did you do?'

'There was so much stuff there. Jewellery. Ornaments. Bits of silver. She didn't even like most of it. And she was so mean. She could have given me a better allowance, but she never did.'

'So you stole her things and Dave sold them.'

She didn't answer.

'What happened to Dave's job with the tarmac crew?'

'No work.' She shrugged. 'It's not his fault. He'd work if he could.'

Did she really believe that? 'So you went on stealing from your grandmother through the summer term and the summer holidays?'

'It wasn't stealing. I was going to get it anyway.'

Dave had indoctrinated her well – or was this Ruth herself speaking? 'Except that you didn't.'

'The doctor's no right to it. She's not even related.'

'Dave's address, please, Miss Lascelles.'

'I can't,' she said with genuine fear. 'He'll kill me.'

He was out of patience with her. 'Well, let's face it, it won't be much of a loss whichever way you look at it. Your mother won't grieve for you, and to the rest of society you'll be a statistic. Just another young girl who allowed a man to use and abuse her.' He shook his head contemptuously. 'I think the most depressing aspect of it all is how much money has been wasted on your education.' He looked around the room. 'My kids would have given their eye-teeth to have had your opportunities, but then they're a good deal brighter than you, of course.' He waited for a moment then shut his notebook and stood up with a sigh. 'You're forcing me to do it the hard way, through your headmistress.'

Ruth hugged herself again. 'She doesn't know anything. How could she?'

'She'll know the name of the firm that was employed to do the drive. I'll track him down that way.'

She wiped her damp nose on her sleeve. 'But, you don't understand, I have to get to university.'

'Why?' he demanded. 'So that you and your boyfriend can have a field day with gullible students? What does he deal in? Drugs?'

Tears flowed freely down her cheeks. 'I don't know how else to get away from him. I've told him I'm going to Exeter, but I'm not, I'm trying for universities in the north because they're the farthest away.'

Cooper was strangely moved. It occurred to him that this was very likely true. She did see running away as the only option open to her. He wondered what Dave had

done to make her so afraid of him. Grown impatient, perhaps, and killed Mrs Gillespie to hasten Ruth's inheritance? He resumed his seat. 'You never knew your father, of course. I suppose it's natural you should have looked for someone to take his place. But university isn't going to solve anything, Miss Lascelles. You may have a term or two of peace before Dave finds you, but no more. How did you plan to keep it a secret? Were you going to tell the school that they were never to reveal which university you'd gone to? Were you going to tell your mother and your friends the same thing? Sooner or later there'd be a plausible telephone call and someone would oblige with the information.'

She seemed to shrink in front of his eyes. 'Then there's nothing I can do.'

He frowned. 'You can start by telling me where to find him.'

'Are you going to arrest him?'

'For what?'

'Stealing from Granny. You'll have to arrest me, too.'

He shrugged. 'I'll need to talk to your grandmother's executors about that. They may decide to let sleeping dogs lie.'

'Then you're just going to ask him questions about the day Granny died?'

'Yes,' he agreed, assuming it was what she wanted to hear.

She shook her head. 'He does terrible things to me when he's angry.' Her eyes flooded again. 'If you don't put him in prison then I can't tell you where to find him. You just don't understand what he's like. He'll punish me.'

'How?'

But she shook her head again, more violently. 'I can't tell you that.'

'You're protected here.'

'He said he'd come and make a scene in the middle of the school if I ever did anything he didn't like. They'll expel me.'

Cooper was perplexed. 'If you're so worried about expulsion, why did you ever go out and meet him in the first place? You'd have been expelled on the spot if you'd been caught doing that.'

She twisted her fingers in the hem of her jumper. 'I didn't know then how much I wanted to go to university,' she whispered.

He nodded. 'There's an old saying about that. You never miss the water till the well runs dry.' He smiled without hostility. 'But all of us take things for granted so you're not alone in that. Try this one: desperate diseases call for desperate remedies. I suggest you make a clean breast of all this to your headmistress, throw yourself on her mercy, so to speak, before she finds out from me or Hughes. She might be sympathetic. You never know.'

'She'll go mad.'

'Do you have a choice?'

'I could kill myself,' she said in a tight little voice.

'It's a very weak spirit,' he said gently, 'that sees cutting off the head as the only solution to a headache.' He slapped his hands against his knees. 'Find a bit of courage, girl. Give me Dave's address and then sort things out with your headmistress.'

Her lip wobbled. 'Will you come with me if I do?'

Oh, good grief, he thought, hadn't he had to hold his own children's hands often enough? 'All right,' he agreed, 'but if she asks me to leave I shall have to. I've no authority here as your guardian, remember.'

'Twenty-three, Palace Road, Bournemouth,' she whispered. 'It was my mother who told you I was a thief, wasn't it?' She sounded desperately forlorn, as if she realized that, for her, there was no one left.

'No,' said Cooper compassionately. 'More's the pity, but your mother hasn't told me anything.'

When Sarah pulled into her driveway later that Friday afternoon, she was greeted by the unexpected sight of Jack's car and Cooper's car nestling side by side against the wall in cosy intimacy. Her first inclination was to turn round and drive away again. She hadn't the stomach for a confrontation with either of them, even less for another baring of her soul in front of Cooper while her husband severed his remaining ties. But second thoughts prevailed. Dammit all – she banged her fist angrily against the steering wheel – it was *her* house. She was buggered if she was going to drive around for hours just to avoid her scumbag of a husband and a pompous policeman.

Quietly, she let herself in through the front door, half-thinking that if she tiptoed past the studio, she could possess herself of the kitchen before they knew she was there. As her mother had once said, slamming the kitchen door on Sarah's father: 'An Englishman's home may be his castle, but an Englishwoman's kitchen is where he eats his humble pie.' The sound of voices drifted down the corridor,

however, and she knew they had possessed it before her. With a sigh, she fastened her dignity about her like armour plating, and advanced.

Jack, DS Cooper and Ruth Lascelles looked up from their glasses of wine with differing shades of alarm and embarrassment colouring their faces.

'Hi,' said Sarah into the silence. 'You found the '83 Cheval Blanc with no trouble then.'

'Have some,' said Jack, reaching for a clean glass off the draining board. 'It's good.'

'It should be,' she said. 'It's a St Emilion, Premier Grand Cru Classé, and it cost me a small fortune when I laid it down.'

'Don't be so stuffy, woman. You've got to try them from time to time, otherwise you'll end up with a collector's item that's totally undrinkable.' He filled the glass and pushed it across the table, his eyes bright with mischief. She felt a surge of affection for the randy bastard – love, she thought, was the most stubborn of all the diseases – but hid it under a ferocious glare. 'The consensus view amongst the three of us,' he went on cheerfully, 'is dark ruby colour, brilliant legs, and a very exotic nose – curranty fruit, cigar box and hints of herbs and spices.'

'It's a vintage wine, you moron. It's supposed to be savoured and appreciated, not drunk at five o'clock in the afternoon round the kitchen table. I bet you didn't let it breathe. I bet you just poured it out like Lucozade.'

Cooper cleared his throat. 'I'm sorry, Dr Blakeney. We did say we'd be happier with tea.'

'You pusillanimous rat,' said Jack with imperturbable good humour. 'You drooled when I waved the bottle under

your nose. Well, come on, old thing, you might as well try it. We're all dying for second helpings but we thought it would be tactful to wait till you arrived before we opened another one.'

'Your life expectancy would be nil if you had,' she said, dropping her handbag and shrugging her coat to the floor. 'All right. Give it here, but I can tell you now it won't be drinkable. It needs another three years at least.' She sat in the vacant chair and drew the glass towards her, covering it with one hand and swirling it gently to release the bouquet. She sniffed appreciatively. 'Who smelt cigar boxes?'

'I did,' said Cooper nervously.

'That's good. The book says the bouquet should be smoky oak and cedar. Curranty fruit?'

Cooper indicated himself again. 'Me.'

'Have you done this before?' He shook his head. 'You should take it up. You've obviously got a nose for it.'

'Ruth and I sussed the herbs and spices,' said Jack. 'What's the verdict?'

Sarah took a sip and let the flavours play across her tongue. 'Spectacular,' she said finally, 'but you're bloody well not opening another bottle. The book says another three years, and I'm going by the book. You can use the wine box for refills. What are you all doing here anyway?' Her eyes rested on Ruth. 'Shouldn't you be at school?'

There was an uncomfortable silence.

'Ruth's been expelled,' said Jack. 'We're all wondering if she can live here with you and me until something more permanent is sorted out.'

Sarah took another sip of her wine and eyed him

thoughtfully. 'You and me?' she queried silkily. 'Does that mean you intend to inflict your company on me again?'

The dark face softened. 'That rather depends, my angel.'

'On whether or not I'm prepared to have you back?'

'No. On whether I come back on my terms or your terms.'

'My terms,' she said bluntly, 'or not at all.'

He gave a ghost of a smile. 'Shame,' he murmured.

Sarah held his gaze for a moment, then transferred her attention to Ruth. 'So why were you expelled?'

Ruth, who had been staring at her hands since Sarah came in, flicked a sideways glance at Cooper. 'The Sergeant knows. He can tell you.'

'I'd rather hear it from you.'

'I broke the school rules.' She resumed her study of her hands.

'All of them or one in particular?'

'Leaving school without permission.'

'Times haven't changed then. A friend of mine was expelled for sneaking down the fire escape and talking to some boys at the bottom of it. She was only caught because the rest of us were hanging out of the windows giggling. We were making such a row the housemistress heard us and expelled her on the spot. She's a barrister now. Rather a good one, too.'

'I've been sleeping with someone,' Ruth whispered, 'and the headmistress said I was a bad influence on the others. She said I was immoral.'

Sarah raised enquiring eyebrows at Cooper, who nodded. 'Ah, well, perhaps times have changed, after all,' she said

matter-of-factly. 'I can't imagine any of us having the courage to do anything so daring, not after we'd had it firmly dinned into us that a prospective husband could always tell if a girl wasn't a virgin.' She gave a throaty chuckle. 'We knew a great deal about love bites and the bruising effects of frantic French kissing, and absolutely nothing about anything else. We were convinced we'd turn green or break out in pustules if we let a man loose below the neckline. It came as something of a shock to discover we'd been sold a lie.' She took another sip of her wine. 'Was it worth getting expelled for?'

'No.' A tear ran down the girl's face and on to the table. 'I don't know what to do. I want to go to university.'

'Surely the most sensible thing would be to go back to Cedar House and your mother. She'll have to find you another school.' Why had Cooper brought her here anyway? *Or was it Jack who'd brought her?*

Cooper rumbled into life. 'Her boyfriend's liable to cut up rough, once I've had a word with him, and Cedar House will be the first place he goes looking. It's an imposition, I know, but off-hand I couldn't think of anywhere else, not after the way the school dealt with her.' He looked quite put out. 'She was told to pack a suitcase while they ordered a taxi to take her home, so I said, forget the taxi, I'll take her. I've never seen the like of it. You'd think she'd committed a hanging offence the way they carried on. And the worst of it was, they wouldn't have known anything about it if I hadn't persuaded her to tell them herself. I feel responsible, I really do, but then I thought they'd give her some credit for being honest and let her off with a caution. It's what I would have done.'

'Does your mother know?' Sarah asked Ruth.

'Jack let me phone.'

'Is she happy about you staying here?'

'I don't know. All she said was she'd heard from Miss Harris and then hung up. She sounded furious.' Ruth kept her head down and dabbed at her eyes with a handkerchief.

Sarah made a wry face at Jack. 'You'll have to be the one to tell her then. I'm not exactly flavour of the month at the moment, and I can't see her being very pleased about it.'

'I've already tried. She hung up on me, too.'

It was on the tip of Sarah's tongue to ask why, before she thought better of it. Knowing Jack, the answer would be as teasingly illusive as the answer to life itself. What puzzled her more was the speed with which events, like the ball in a pinball machine, had taken such an unpredictable course. This morning she'd had only another solitary weekend to look forward to – *and now*? 'Well, someone's got to tell her,' she said irritably, isolating the one fact she could get to grips with. She looked at the Sergeant. 'You'll have to do it. I'm quite happy for Ruth to stay but only if her mother knows where she is.'

Cooper looked wretched. 'Perhaps it would be better if we involved social services,' he suggested, 'asked a third party to intercede, as it were.'

Sarah's eyes narrowed. 'I'm an extremely amenable woman on the whole but I do resent my good nature being taken advantage of. There is no such thing as a free lunch, Sergeant, and I'd like to remind you that you have just drunk some very expensive St Emilion of mine which, at a conservative estimate and allowing for inflation, costs well over seven pounds per glass. In other words, you owe me

one, so you will not shuffle your responsibility and this child's future on to some overworked and underpaid social worker whose only solution to the problem will be to place her in a hostel full of disturbed adolescents.'

Cooper's wretchedness grew.

'You have also, by underestimating the old-fashioned ethics that still exist within girls' boarding schools, caused a young woman approaching the most important exams of her life to be expelled. Now, in a world where the renting out of a woman's womb is still the only reliable method that men have discovered to replicate themselves, the very least they can do in return is to allow their women enough education to make the life sentence of child-rearing endurable. To sit and stare at an empty wall is one thing; to have the inner resources, the knowledge and the confidence to turn that wall into a source of endless stimulation is another. And that's ignoring the positive influence that educated and intelligent women have on succeeding generations. Ruth wants to go to university. To do so, she must pass her A levels. It is imperative that Joanna finds another school to accept her PDQ. Which means someone' – she cocked her finger at him – 'namely *you*, must explain to her that Ruth is here, that she is here for a good reason, and that Joanna must come and talk it through before Ruth loses her opportunity to take her education as far as it can go.' She turned her gaze on the girl. 'And if you dare tell me now, Ruth, that you've given up on your future, then I'll put you through the first mangle I can find and, I promise you, the experience will not be a pleasant one.'

There was a long silence.

Finally, Jack stirred. 'Now you begin to see what Sarah's

terms consist of. There's no allowing for human frailty. I grant you, there are pages of subtext and small print dealing with the awful imperfections that most of us suffer from – namely, inadequacy, lack of confidence, seeing both sides and sitting on fences – but they are grey areas which she treats with insufferable patience. And, take it from me, you allow her to do that at your peril. It undermines what little self-respect you have left.' He beamed fondly at Cooper. 'I sympathize with you, old son, but Sarah's right as usual. Someone's got to talk to Joanna and you're the one who's run up the most debts. After all, you *did* get Ruth expelled and you *did* drink a glass of wine that cost over seven quid.'

Cooper shook his head. 'I hope Miss Lascelles can put up with the pair of you. I know I couldn't. You'd have me climbing the walls before you could say knife.'

The 'pair' wasn't lost on Sarah. 'How come you know so much more about my domestic arrangements than I do, Sergeant?' she asked casually.

He chuckled amiably, pushing himself to his feet. 'Because I never say never, Doctor.' He winked at her. 'As someone once told me, life's a bugger. It creeps up behind you and gets you where you least expect it every time.'

Sarah felt the girl start to tremble as she pushed open the door of the spare room and switched on the light. 'What's the matter?' she asked.

'It's downstairs,' she blurted out. 'If Dave comes, he could get in.'

'Not my choice. Geoffrey Freeling's. He turned the house upside down so that the reception rooms would have

the best views. We're slowly turning it back again, but it takes time.' She pushed open a communicating door. 'It has its own bathroom.' She glanced back at the girl, saw the pinched look to her face. 'You're frightened, aren't you? Would you rather sleep upstairs in my room?'

Ruth burst into tears. 'I'm so sorry,' she wept. 'I don't know what to do. Dave will kill me. I was all right at school. He couldn't have got in there.'

Sarah put her arms about the other's thin shoulders and clasped them tightly. 'Come upstairs,' she said gently. 'You'll be safe with me. Jack can sleep in here.'

And serve the bastard right, she thought. *Ho, ho! For once, sod's law was on the side of the angels.* She had been toying with the ethics of medical castration but was prepared to compromise on a cold bed and a grovelling apology. It was a very partial compromise. She was so damn glad to have him back she felt like doing handsprings.

Joanna moved to the flat in London last week and for the first time since her abortive attempt at marriage I am in sole possession of Cedar House. It is a victory of sorts, but I have a sense of anticlimax. The game, I fear, was not worth the candle. I am lonely.

It occurs to me that in some strange way Joanna and I are necessary to each other. There is no denying the understanding that exists between us. We do not get along, of course, but that is largely irrelevant in view of the fact that we don't get along with anyone else either. There was some comfort in treading the mill of clichéed insults that trundled us quite happily through our lives, so worn and over-used that what we said to each other passed largely unnoticed. I miss the little things. The way she pursued Spede about the garden, taking the wretched man to task if he missed a weed. Her waspish remarks about my cooking. And oddly enough, as they always used to irritate me at the time, her long, long silences. After all, perhaps companionship is less to do with conversation than with the comfort of another human presence, however self-centred that presence might be.

I have a terrible fear that, by pushing her out to fend for herself, I have diminished us both. At least, while we were together, we checked each other's worst excesses. And now? The road to hell is paved with good intentions . . .

Eleven

IT WASN'T UNTIL late the following afternoon, a Saturday, that Sergeant Cooper felt he had enough information on Dave Hughes to make an approach viable. He was pessimistic about bringing charges of theft, but in respect of Mathilda's death there was some room for optimism. Ruth's mention of a white Ford transit had rung bells in his memory and a careful sifting of the statements taken in and around Fontwell in the days after the body was found had produced a gem. When asked if he'd seen anything unusual the previous Saturday, the landlord of the Three Pigeons, Mr Henry Peel, had said:

> I can't swear it had anything to do with Mrs Gillespie, but there was a white Ford transit parked on my forecourt that Saturday afternoon and evening. Had a young lad in it, as far as I could judge. Stayed ten minutes the first time then drove off towards the church and picked someone up. I saw it again that evening. I pointed it out to my wife and said some wretch was using our forecourt but not using the pub. I can't give you the registration number.

Underneath in a PC's handwriting was a short note:

Mrs Peel disagrees. She says her husband is confusing this with another occasion when white vans were there twice in one day, but her recollection is that the vans were different. Three of our regulars drive white vans, she said.

Cooper talked the problem through with his Detective Chief Inspector. 'I need to question Hughes, Charlie, so do I take a team with me, or what? According to the girl, he's living in a squat, so he won't be alone, and I don't fancy trying to winkle him out from under a mob of squatters. Assuming they let me in at all. It's bloody rich, isn't it?' he grumbled. 'Somebody else's property and they can take it over lock, stock and barrel. The only way the poor sod who owns it can get it back is to pay through the nose for an eviction order, by which time he finds they've turned the place into a cess-pit.'

Charlie Jones's squashed face wore a permanently lugubrious expression which always reminded Cooper of a sad-eyed Pekinese. He was more of a terrier, however, who, once he got his teeth into something, rarely let go. 'Can we charge him with theft on what Miss Lascelles has told you?'

'We could, but he'd be out again in a couple of hours. Bournemouth have him on file. He's been brought in three times and he's walked on each occasion. All similar offences to this one, i.e. persuading youngsters to steal for him. It's a clever scam.' He sounded frustrated. 'The children only prey off their families and, so far, the parents have refused to co-operate when they discover that Hughes's prosecution will involve their daughters in a prosecution, too.'

'So how come he was brought in in the first place?'

'Because three indignant fathers have independently

accused him of forcing their daughters to steal and demanded that charges be brought. But when the girls were questioned, they told a different story, denied the coercion and insisted that the thieving was their own idea. It's a real honey, this one. You can't do him without the daughters, and the fathers won't have the daughters done.' He smiled cynically. 'Too much unpleasant publicity.'

'What sort of backgrounds?'

'Middle class, wealthy. The girls are all over sixteen, so no question of under-age sex. Mind, I'm sure these three and Miss Lascelles are only the tip of a very large iceberg. It sounds to me as if he's got the whole thing down to a very fine art.'

'*Does* he coerce them?'

Cooper shrugged. 'All Miss Lascelles said was, he does terrible things when he's angry. He threatened to make a scene at the school if she did anything he didn't like, but when I asked her about it in the car on the way to Dr Blakeney's, in other words after that particular threat had lost its sting because she'd already been expelled, she clammed up and burst into tears.' He tugged his nose thoughtfully. 'He must be using some form of coercion because she's terrified he's going to find her. I wondered if he makes videos of them but when I asked Bournemouth if they've found any equipment on him, they said no. Your guess is as good as mine, Charlie. He's got some hold on these girls, and it must be fear because they're desperate to get shot of him the minute they're found out. But precisely what's involved, I don't know.'

The Inspector frowned. 'Why aren't they afraid to name him?'

'Presumably because he's given them permission to shop him if they're caught. Look, he must know how easy it would be for us to track him down. If Miss Lascelles hadn't proffered the information, all I had to do was ask the headmistress for the tarmac firm and take it from there. I think his MO goes something like this: target a girl who's young enough and cosseted enough to warrant her parents' protection, win her over, then use some sort of threat to make sure she accuses herself along with him when she's caught. That way he's as sure as he can be that charges won't be brought and, if they are, he'll take her down with him. Perhaps his threat is as simple as that.'

The Inspector was doubtful. 'He can't make much out of it. How long before the parents notice what's going on?'

'You'd be amazed. One of the girls was borrowing her mother's credit card for months before the father queried the amount his wife was spending. It was a jointly held card, the balance was paid off automatically out of the current account, and neither of them noticed that it had increased by upwards of five hundred pounds a month. Or if they did, they assumed the other partner's expenditure was behind it. It's a different world, Charlie. Both parents working and earning a good screw, and enough money sloshing around in the coffers to obscure their daughter's thieving. Once they started looking into it, of course, they discovered she'd sold bits of silver, jewellery that her mother never wore, some valuable first editions of her father's and a five-hundred-pound camera that her father thought he'd left on a train. I'd say Hughes is doing very nicely out of it, particularly if he's running more than one of them at the same time.'

'Good grief! How much has Ruth Lascelles stolen then?'

Cooper took a piece of paper from his pocket. 'She made a list of what she could remember. That's it.' He put it on the desk. 'Same pattern as the other girl. Jewellery that her grandmother had forgotten about. Silver-backed hairbrushes from the spare room that were never used. China ornaments and bowls that were kept in cupboards because Mrs Gillespie didn't like them, and some first editions out of the library. She said Hughes told her the sort of thing to look for. Valuable bits and pieces that wouldn't be missed.'

'What about money?'

'Twenty pounds from her grandmother's handbag, fifty pounds from the bedside table and, a few weeks later, five hundred out of the old lady's account. Went to the bank as cool as cucumber with a forged cheque and a letter purporting to come from Mathilda, instructing them to hand over the loot. According to her, Mrs Gillespie never even noticed. But she did, of course, because she mentioned the fifty-pound theft to Jack Blakeney and, when I tackled her bank this morning, they told me she had queried the five-hundred-pound withdrawal on her statement, and they advised her that Ruth had drawn it out on her instructions.' He scratched his jaw. 'According to them, she agreed that it was her mistake and took no further action.'

'What date was that?'

Cooper consulted his notes again. 'The cheque was cashed during the last week in October, Ruth's half-term in other words, and Mrs Gillespie rang the bank as soon as she got the statement, which was the first week in November.'

'Not long before she died then, and *after* she'd made up her mind to change the will. It's a bugger that one. I can't

get the hang of it at all.' He thought for a moment. 'When did Ruth steal the fifty pounds?'

'At the beginning of September before she went back to school. She had some idea apparently of buying Hughes off. She said: "I thought he'd leave me alone if I gave him some money."'

'Dear God!' said Charlie dismally. 'There's one born every minute. Did you ask her if Hughes put pressure on her to cash the five hundred at half-term?'

'I did. Her answer was: "No, no, no. I stole it because I wanted to," and then she turned the waterworks on again.' He looked very rueful. 'I've left the ball in Dr Blakeney's court. I had a word with her on the phone this morning, gave her the gist of what Hughes has been up to and asked her to try and find out why none of the girls will turn QE against him. She may get somewhere but I'm not counting on it.'

'What about the mother? Would Ruth talk to her?'

Cooper shook his head. 'First, you'd have to get *her* to talk to Ruth. It's unnatural, if you ask me. I stopped off last night to tell her the Blakeneys had taken her daughter in and she looked at me as if I'd just climbed out of a sewer. The only thing she was interested in was whether I thought Ruth's expulsion meant she'd killed her grandmother. I said, no, that as far as I knew there were no statistics linking truancy and promiscuous sex to murder, but there were a great number linking them to poor parenting. So she told me to eff off.' He chuckled happily at the memory.

Charlie Jones grunted his amusement. 'I'm more interested in friend Hughes at the moment, so let's break this down into manageable proportions. Have Bourne-

mouth tried getting the three families together so that the girls gain strength from numbers?'

'Twice. No go either time. The parents have taken legal advice and no one's talking.'

Charlie pursed his lips in thought. 'It's been done before, you know. George Joseph Smith did it a hundred years ago. Wrote glowing references for pretty servant girls, then found them placements in wealthy households. Within weeks of starting work they would steal valuables from their employers and take them faithfully to George to convert into ready cash. He was another one with an extraordinary pulling-power over women.'

'George Smith?' said Cooper in surprise. 'I thought he did *away* with women. Wasn't he the brides-in-the-bath murderer?'

'That's him. Started drowning wives when he discovered how easy it was to get them to make wills in his favour upon marriage. Interesting, isn't it, in view of the way Mrs Gillespie died.' He was silent for a moment. 'I read a book about Smith not so long ago. The author described him as a professional and a literal lady-killer. I wonder if the same thing applies to Hughes.' He rapped a tattoo on his desk-top with his knuckles. 'Let's pull him in for questioning.'

'How? Do I take an arrest warrant?'

Charlie reached for his phone. 'No. I'll get Bournemouth to pick him up tomorrow morning and hold him on ice till you and I get there.'

'Tomorrow's Sunday, Charlie.'

'Then with any luck he'll have a hangover. I want to see his expression when I tell him we have reason to believe he murdered Mrs Gillespie.'

Cooper was sceptical. 'Have we? The landlord's statement won't stand close scrutiny, not if his wife's claiming he was confused.'

A wolfish grin spread across the Inspector's features, and the sad Pekinese became a Dobermann. 'But we know he was there that afternoon because Ruth told us he was, and I'm inclined to be a little creative with the rest. He was using Mrs Gillespie's granddaughter to extort money. He has a history of ruthless exploitation of women, and he's probably feeding a habit because his outgoings far exceed his income. If they didn't, he wouldn't have to live in squats. I'd say his psychological profile runs something like this: a dangerously unstable, psychopathic addict, whose hatred of women has undergone a dramatic change recently and taken him from their brutal manipulation to their destruction. He will be the product of a broken home and inadequate education, and boyhood fear of his father will govern most of his actions.'

Cooper looked even more sceptical. 'You've been reading too many books, Charlie.'

Jones allowed himself a laugh. 'But Hughes doesn't know that, does he? So let's try and dent his charisma a little and see if we can't stop him using other people's little girls to do his dirty work.'

'I'm trying to solve a murder,' said Cooper in protest. 'That's what I want answers on.'

'But you've still to convince me it *was* a murder, old son.'

Ruth crept stealthily down the stairs and stood to one side of the studio doorway, watching Jack's reflection in her tiny

hand mirror. Not that she could see him very well. He was sitting with his back to the window, working on a portrait but, because the easel was placed directly between him and the door, the canvas obscured all but his legs. From the bedroom window she had watched Sarah leave the house two hours ago, so she knew they were alone. *Would Jack notice when she slipped past the doorway*? She waited for ten minutes in panicky indecision, too afraid to take a step.

'If you want something to eat,' he murmured finally into the silence, 'then I suggest you try the kitchen. If you want someone to talk to, then I suggest you come in here, and if you're looking for something to steal, then I suggest you take Sarah's engagement ring which belonged to my grandmother and was valued at two thousand pounds four years ago. You'll find it in the left-hand drawer of her dressing-table.' He leaned to one side so that she could see his face in her mirror. 'You might as well show yourself. I'm not going to eat you.' He nodded curtly as she came round the doorjamb. 'Sarah gave me strict instructions to be sympathetic, patient and helpful. I'll do my best, but I warn you in advance I can't stand people who sniff into handkerchiefs and creep about on tiptoe.'

Ruth's cheeks lost what little colour they had left. 'Do you think it would be all right if I made myself a cup of coffee?' She looked very unattractive, damp hair clinging to her scalp, face puffy and blotched with crying. 'I don't want to be a nuisance.'

Jack returned to his painting so that she wouldn't see the flash of irritation in his eyes. Self-pity in others invariably brought out the worst in him. 'As long as you make me one, too. Black and no sugar, please. The coffee's by the

kettle, sugar's in the tin marked "sugar", milk's in the fridge and lunch is in the oven. It will be ready in half an hour so, unless you're starving, my advice is to skip breakfast and wait for that.'

'Will Dr Blakeney be here for lunch?'

'I doubt it. Polly Graham's gone into labour and as Sarah agreed to a home-birth, she could be there for hours.'

Ruth hovered for a moment, then turned to go to the kitchen, only to change her mind again. 'Has my mother phoned?' she blurted out.

'Did you expect her to?'

'I thought—' She fell silent.

'Well, try thinking about making me a cup of coffee instead. If you hadn't mentioned it, I probably wouldn't have wanted one, but as you have, I do. So get your skates on, woman. This is not a hotel and I'm not in the best of moods after being relegated to the spare room.'

She fled down the corridor to the kitchen and, when she returned five minutes later with a tray and two cups, her hands were shaking so much that the cups chattered against each other like terrified teeth. Jack appeared not to notice but took the tray and placed it on a table in the window. 'Sit,' he instructed, pointing to a hard-backed chair and swinging his stool round to face her. 'Now, is it me you're frightened of, the boyfriend, men in general, Sarah not coming home for lunch, the police, or are you worried about what's going to happen to you?'

She shrank away from him as if he'd struck her.

'Me then.' He moved the stool back a yard to give her more room. 'Why are you afraid of me, Ruth?'

Her hands fluttered in her lap. 'I'm – you—' Her eyes widened in terror. 'I'm not.'

'You feel completely secure and at ease in my presence?'

'Yes,' she whispered.

'You have an odd way of showing it.' He reached for his coffee cup. 'How old were you when your father died?'

'I was a baby.'

'Since which time you've lived with your mother and your grandmother and, latterly, a bevy of women at boarding school.' He took a sip of coffee. 'Am I right that this Hughes character is the first boyfriend you've ever had?'

She nodded.

'So he's your only experience of men?'

She stared at her hands.

'Yes or no?' he demanded, the words whipping out impatiently.

'Yes,' she whispered again.

'Then you obviously require lessons on the male of the species. There are only three things to remember. One: most men need to be told what to do by women. Even sex improves when women take the trouble to point the man in the right direction. Two: compared with women, most men are inadequate. They are less perceptive, have little or no intuition, are poorer judges of character and, therefore, more vulnerable to criticism. They find aggression immensely intimidating because they're not supposed to and, in short, are by far the more sensitive of the two sexes. Three: any man who does not conform to this pattern should be avoided. He will be a swaggering, uneducated brute whose intellect will be so small that the only way he

can give himself a modicum of authority is by demeaning anyone who's foolish enough to put up with him, and, finally, he will lack the one thing that all decent men have in abundance, namely a deep and abiding admiration for women.' He picked up her coffee cup and held it under her nose so that she had to take it. 'Now I don't pretend to be a paragon, but I'm certainly not a brute, and between you, me and the gatepost, I am extremely fond of my irascible wife. I accept that what I did was open to interpretation, but you can take it from me that I went to Cedar House for one reason only and that was simply to paint your mother. The temptation to capture two generations of one family was irresistible.' He eyed her speculatively. Almost as irresistible, he was thinking, as the temptation to capture the third generation. 'And if my much-put-upon wife hadn't chosen that precise moment to expel me, well,' he shrugged, 'I wouldn't have had to freeze on your mother's summer-house floor. Does all that set your mind at rest or are you going to go on quaking like a great jelly every time you see me?'

She stared at him with stricken eyes. She was beautiful after all, he thought, but it was a tragic beauty. Like her mother's. Like Mathilda's.

'I'm pregnant,' she said finally, exhausted tears seeping on to her cheeks.

There was a moment of silence.

'I thought – I hoped – my mother—' She dashed at her eyes with a sodden tissue. 'I don't know what – I ought to go – I shouldn't have told you.'

Somewhere in the recesses of his heart, Jack blushed for himself. Was the self-pity of a child under intolerable stress

so despicable that he had to savage it? He reached across and took her hand, drawing her off the chair and into his arms, holding her tight and stroking her hair as her father would have done had he lived. He let her weep for a long time before he spoke. 'Your grandmother once said to me that mankind was doomed unless he learnt to communicate. She was a wise old lady. We talk a lot but we rarely communicate.' He eased her off his chest and held her at arm's length so that he could look at her. 'I'm glad you told me. I feel rather privileged that you felt you could. Most people would have waited until Sarah came home.'

'I was going—'

He stopped her with a chuckle and released her back on to her chair. 'Let me hang on to my illusions. Let me believe just once that someone thought I could be as easy to confide in as Sarah. It's not true, of course. There is no one in the world who can listen as well as my wife, or who can impart such sound advice. She'll look after you, I promise.'

Ruth blew her nose. 'She'll be angry with me.'

'Do you think so?'

'You said she's irascible.'

'She is. It's not so frightening. You just keep your head down till the saucepans stop flying.'

She dabbed frantically at her eyes. 'Saucepans? Does she—'

'No,' he said firmly. 'It was a figure of speech. Sarah's a nice person. She brings home wounded pigeons, splints their wings, and watches them die in slow and terrible agony with an expression of enormous sympathy on her face. It's one of the things they teach them at medical school.'

She looked alarmed. 'That's awful.'

'It was a joke,' he said ruefully. 'Sarah is the most sensible doctor I know. She will help you reach a decision about what you want to do and then take it from there. She won't force you to have the baby, and she won't force you not to have it.'

The tears welled again. 'I don't want it.' She clenched her hands in her lap. 'Is that wrong, do you think?'

'No,' he said honestly. 'If I were in your shoes, I wouldn't want it either.'

'But I made it. It was my fault.'

'It takes two to make babies, Ruth, and I can't see your boyfriend showing much enthusiasm when it's fully-fledged and bawling its head off. It's your choice, not his. Sperm comes two-a-penny and most of it gets washed down the sink. Wombs and their foetuses come extremely expensive. Sarah's right when she says it's a life sentence.'

'But isn't it alive? Won't I be murdering it?'

He was a man. How could he begin to understand the agony that women suffered because a biological accident has given them power over life and death? He could only be honest with her. 'I don't know, but I'd say it's only alive at the moment because you're alive. It has no existence as an individual in its own right.'

'But it could have – if I let it.'

'Of course. But on that basis every egg that any woman produces and every sperm that any man produces has the potential for life, and no one accuses young men of being murderers every time they spill their seed on the ground behind the bike sheds. I think for each of us our own life has priority over the potential life that exists inside us. I

don't for a moment pretend that it's an easy decision, or even a black and white one, but I do believe that you are more important at this moment than a life that can only come into being if you are prepared to pay for it, emotionally, physically, socially and financially. And you'll bear that cost alone, Ruth, because the likelihood of Hughes paying anything is virtually nil.'

'He'll say it isn't his anyway.'

Jack nodded. 'Some men do, I'm afraid. It's so easy for them. It's not their body that's been caught.'

She hid her face in her hands. 'You don't understand.' She wrapped her arms around her head. *To protect herself? To hide herself?* 'It might be one of the others'. You see I had to – he made me – Oh, God – I wish—' She didn't go on, only curled herself into a tight ball and sobbed.

Jack felt completely helpless. Her anguish was so strong that it washed over him in swamping waves. He could think only in platitudes – *there's nothing so bad that it might not be worse . . . it's always darkest before the dawn* – but what use were platitudes to a girl whose life lay in tatters before her? He put out an awkward hand and placed it on her head. It was an instinctive gesture of comfort, an echo of a priestly benediction. 'Tell me what happened,' he said. 'Perhaps it's not as bad as you think.'

But it was. What she told him in tones of abject terror rocked the foundations of his own humanity. So shocked was he that he felt physically sick.

Sarah found him in the garden when she came home at three-thirty after helping to deliver Polly Graham of a

healthy baby daughter. He was forking industriously round some roses and scattering handfuls of fertilizer about the roots. 'It's almost December,' she said. 'Everything's dormant. You're wasting your time.'

'I know.' He looked up and she thought she saw traces of tears in his eyes. 'I just needed to do something active.'

'Where's Ruth?'

'Asleep. She had a headache so I gave her some codeine and packed her off to bed.' He brushed the hair from his forehead with the back of a muddy hand. 'Have you finished for the day?'

She nodded. 'What's happened?'

He leant on the fork and stared across the fields. The slowly fading light gave a misty quality to a landscape in which cows grazed and trees, shorn of their leaves, fingered the sky with dark filigree lacework. 'That's the England men and women die for,' he said gruffly.

She followed his gaze with a small frown creasing her forehead.

Tears glistened on his lashes. 'Do you know that poem by Rupert Brooke? "The Soldier". The one that goes:

"If I should die, think only this of me:
That there's some corner of a foreign field
That is for ever England. There shall be
In that rich earth a richer dust concealed;
A dust whom England bore, shaped, made aware . . ."'

He fell silent. When he spoke again, his voice shook. 'It's beautiful, isn't it, Sarah? England *is* beautiful.'

She wiped the tears from his face. 'You're crying,' she

said, her heart aching for him. 'I've never seen you cry before. What's happened, Jack?'

He didn't seem to hear her. 'Rupert Brooke died in 1915. A sacrifice of war. He was only twenty-eight, younger than you and me, and he gave his life with all the other millions, whatever country they came from, for the sake of other people's children. And do you know what breaks my heart?' His dark gaze slid away from her, looking into a private hell that only he could see. 'That a man who could write one of the most perfect pieces of poetry about his homeland that has ever been written should have sacrificed himself for the filth that England spawns today.'

'No one's all bad, Jack, and no one's all good. We're just human. The poor kid only wanted to be loved.'

He wiped a weary hand around his jaw. 'I'm not talking about Ruth, Sarah. I'm talking about the men who attacked her. I'm talking about the animal who taught her obedience by shutting her in a van with a group of low-grade scum who raped her one after the other for five hours to break her spirit.' He stared over the fields again. 'Apparently she objected when Hughes told her to start stealing from Mathilda, said she didn't want to do it. So he locked her in the van with his mates who gave her a graphic demonstration of what was going to happen every time she refused. I've had to give my word that I'm not going to repeat this to anyone except you. She is absolutely terrified they're going to find her and do it again, and when I said we should report it to the police I thought she was going to die on me. Hughes told her that if she was ever caught, all she had to do was say the stealing was her idea. As long as she does that and doesn't mention the rape, he'll leave her alone in

the future.' His lips thinned. 'But if she talks, he'll send his goons after her to punish her, and he doesn't care how long he has to wait to do it. Police protection won't save her, marriage won't save her. He'll wait for years if he has to, but for every year her punishment is delayed, he'll add another hour to the final ordeal. She'd have to be a quite extraordinary person to talk to the police with a threat like that hanging over her.'

Sarah was too shocked to respond. 'No wonder she was frightened to sleep downstairs,' she said at last.

'She's hardly slept at all for weeks, as far as I can gather. The only way I could get her to take the codeine was to promise again and again that I wouldn't leave the house. She's paranoid about being caught unawares and she's paranoid about the police asking any more questions.'

'But the Sergeant knows there's something,' Sarah warned him. 'He phoned this morning and asked me to try and find out what it was. His word for it was coercion. Hughes must be using coercion, he said, but we can't do much unless we know what sort of coercion it is. Ruth's not the only one it's happened to. They know of at least three others and they think it's only the tip of the iceberg. None of them talk.'

'She's pregnant,' said Jack flatly. 'I said you'd know what to do. JE-SUS!' He threw the fork like a lance into the middle of the lawn, his bellow of rage roaring into the air. 'I-COULD-KILL-THE-FUCKING-BASTARD!'

Sarah put a hand on his arm to calm him. 'How many weeks is she?'

'I don't know,' he said, rubbing his eyes. 'I didn't ask. I wish to God you'd been here. I did my best but I was so

damn useless. She needed a woman to talk to, not a clumsy sod who started out by telling her what nice people men are. I gave her a lecture, for Christ's sake, on male decency.'

She hushed him as his voice started to rise again. 'She wouldn't have talked to you if she hadn't felt comfortable with you. How long's she been asleep?'

He looked at his watch. 'A couple of hours.'

'Okay, we'll leave her a little bit longer, then I'll go and see her.' She linked her arm with his. 'I don't suppose you've eaten.'

'No.'

She drew him towards the house. 'Come on then. Things always look worse on an empty stomach.'

'What are we going to do, Sarah?'

'Whatever's best for Ruth.'

'And to hell with all the other wretched girls who get broken in the future?'

'We can only take one step at a time, Jack.' She looked desperately worried.

'O vile, intolerable, not to be endur'd!' Ruth is crying again and it is driving me mad. I simply cannot bear it. I want to take the wretched child and shake her till her teeth rattle, smack her, hit her, anything to stop this petulant whining. My anger never goes away. Even when she's silent, I find myself waiting for her to begin.

It is so unjust when I went through the same thing with Joanna. If she would only show some interest in her daughter, it wouldn't be so bad, but she does everything she can to avoid her. In desperation this morning, I tried to put the scold's bridle on Ruth's head, but Joanna convulsed at the sight of it. I called Hugh Hendry out again and this time he had the sense to prescribe tranquillizers. He said she was overwrought.

Would to God they had had Valium in my day. As always, I had to cope alone . . .

Twelve

DS COOPER'S CAR had barely drawn to a halt in Mill House driveway later that evening when Jack wrenched open the passenger door and folded himself on to the seat. 'Do me a favour, old son, reverse out slowly with as little noise as possible and drive me a mile or two down the road.' He nodded approval as Cooper eased into gear. 'And next time, phone first, there's a good chap.'

Cooper, apparently unconcerned by this somewhat disrespectful behaviour towards an officer of the law, manoeuvred backwards through the gate, pulling the wheel gently to avoid crunching the gravel. 'Doesn't she trust me?' he asked, changing to first gear and driving off in the direction of Fontwell.

'Not you personally. The police. There's a lay-by about half a mile ahead on the right. Pull in there and I'll walk back.'

'Has she said anything?'

Jack didn't answer and Cooper flicked him a sideways glance. His face looked drawn in the reflected light from the headlamps, but it was too dark to read his expression.

'You're obliged by law to assist the police in their enquiries, Mr Blakeney.'

'It's Jack,' he said. 'What's your name, Sergeant?'

'Just what you'd expect,' said Cooper dryly. 'Thomas. Good old Tommy Cooper.'

Jack's teeth gleamed in a smile. 'Rough.'

'Rough is right. People expect me to be a comedian. Where's this lay-by of yours?'

'A hundred yards or so.' He peered through the windscreen. 'Coming up on your right now.'

Cooper drew across the road and brought the car to a halt, placing a restraining hand on Jack's arm as he switched off the engine and killed the lights. 'Five minutes,' he said. 'I really do need to ask you some questions.'

Jack let go of the door handle. 'All right, but I warn you there is very little I can tell you except that Ruth is scared out of her wits and extremely reluctant to have anything more to do with the police.'

'She may not be given a choice. We may decide to prosecute.'

'For what? Stealing from a member of her family who didn't even bother to report the few trinkets that were taken? You can't prosecute Ruth for that, Tommy. And anyway, Sarah as legatee would insist on any charges being dropped. Her position's delicate enough without forcing a criminal record on the child she's effectively disinherited.'

Cooper sighed. 'Call me Cooper,' he said. 'Most people do. Tommy's more of an embarrassment than a name.' He took out a cigarette. 'Why do you call Miss Lascelles a child? She's a young woman, Jack. Seventeen years old and

legally responsible for her actions. If she's prosecuted she will be dealt with in an adult court. You really shouldn't allow sentiment to cloud your judgement. We're not talking just trinkets here. She took her grandmother for five hundred pounds a month ago and didn't bat an eyelid while she was doing it. And on the day of the murder she stole some earrings worth two thousand pounds.'

'Did Mathilda report the money stolen?'

'No,' Cooper admitted.

'Then Sarah certainly won't.'

Cooper sighed again. 'I guess you've been talking to a lawyer, told you to keep your mouths shut, I suppose, and never mind what Hughes does to anyone else.' He struck a match and held it to the tip of his cigarette, watching Jack in the flaring light. Anger showed itself in every line of the other man's face, in the aggressive jut of his jaw, in the compressed lips and the narrowed eyes. He seemed to be exercising enormous self-control just to hold himself in. With a flick of his thumbnail Cooper extinguished the match and plunged the car into darkness again. Only the glow of burning tobacco remained. 'Hughes is working to a pattern,' he said. 'I explained as much of it as we have been able to find out to your wife this morning. In essence—'

'She told me,' Jack cut in. 'I know what he's doing.'

'Okay,' said Cooper easily, 'then you'll know how important it is to stop him. There'll be other Ruths, make no mistake about that, and whatever he's doing to these girls to force them to work for him will get more extreme as time goes by. That's the nature of the beast.' He drew on his cigarette. 'He does force them, doesn't he?'

'You're the policeman, Cooper. Arrest the sod and ask him.'

'That's exactly what we're planning to do. Tomorrow. But we'll have a much stronger hand if we know what to ask him *about*. We're stumbling around in the dark at the moment.'

Jack didn't say anything.

'I could get a warrant for Miss Lascelles's arrest and take her down to the station. How would she stand up to the psychological thumbscrews, do you think? You might not have realized it but she's different from the other girls Hughes has used. She doesn't have parents she can rely on to protect her.'

'Sarah and I will do it,' Jack said curtly. 'We're in loco parentis at the moment.'

'But you've no legal standing. We could insist that her mother was present during questioning and if it's of any interest to you the only thing Mrs Lascelles was concerned about last night was whether her daughter's expulsion had anything to do with Mrs Gillespie's murder. She'd break Ruth for us if she thought it would help her get her hands on the old lady's money.'

Jack gave a faint laugh. 'You're all piss and wind, Cooper. You're too damn nice to do anything like that, and we both know it. Take it from me, you'd have it on your conscience for life if you added to the damage that's already been done to that poor kid.'

'It's bad then.'

'I'd say that was a fair assumption, yes.'

'You must tell me, Jack. We won't get anywhere with Hughes if you don't tell me.'

'I can't. I've given my word to Ruth.'

'Break it.'

Jack shook his head. 'No. In my book a word, once given, cannot be taken back.' He thought for a moment. 'There's one thing I could do, though. You deliver him to me and I'll deliver him to you. How does that grab you as an idea?'

Cooper sounded genuinely regretful. 'It's known as aiding and abetting. I'd be kissing goodbye to my pension.'

Jack gave a low laugh. 'Think about it,' he said, reaching for the handle and thrusting open the door. 'It's my best offer.' The smoke from Cooper's cigarette eddied after him as he got out. 'All I need is an address, Tommy. When you're ready, phone it through.' He slammed the door and loped off into the darkness.

Violet Orloff tiptoed into her husband's bedroom and frowned anxiously at him. He was swathed in yards of Paisley dressing-gown and reclined like a fat old Buddha against his pillows, a mug of cocoa in one hand, a cheese sandwich in the other, the *Daily Telegraph* crossword on his knees. 'She's crying again.'

Duncan peered at her over his bifocals. 'It's not our business, dear,' he said firmly.

'But I can *hear* her. She's sobbing her heart out.'

'It's not our business.'

'Except I keep thinking, suppose we'd *done* something when we heard Mathilda crying, would she be dead now? I feel very badly about that, Duncan.'

He sighed. 'I refuse to feel guilty because Mathilda's

cruelties to her family, imagined or real, provoked one of them into killing her. There was nothing we could have done to prevent it then, and as you keep reminding me, there is nothing we can do now to bring her back. We have alerted the police to possible motive. I think we should leave it there.'

'But, Duncan,' Violet wailed, 'if we *know* it was Joanna or Ruth, then we must tell the police.'

He frowned. 'Don't be silly, Violet. We don't know who did it, nor, frankly, are we interested. Logic says it had to be someone with a key or someone she trusted enough to let into the house, and the police don't need me to tell them that.' The frown deepened. 'Why do you keep pushing me into meddling, anyway? It's almost as if you want Joanna and Ruth to be arrested.'

'Not *both* of them. They didn't do it together, did they?' She grimaced horribly, screwing her face into an absurd caricature. 'But Joanna *is* crying again, and I think we should do something. Mathilda always said the house was full of ghosts. Perhaps she's come back.'

Duncan stared at her with open alarm. 'You're not ill, are you?'

'Of course I'm not ill,' she said crossly. 'I think I'll pop round, see if she's all right, talk to her. You never know, she might decide to *confide* in me.' With an arch wave she tiptoed off again, and moments later he heard the sound of the front door opening.

Duncan shook his head in perplexity as he returned to his crossword. *Was* this the beginnings of senility? Violet was either very brave or very foolish to interfere with an emotionally disturbed woman who had, quite clearly,

loathed her mother enough to murder her. He could only imagine what Joanna's reaction would be to his wife's naïve assertions that she knew more than she'd told the police. The thought worried him enough to force him out of his warm bed and into his slippers, before padding downstairs in her wake.

But whatever had upset Joanna Lascelles was destined to remain a mystery to the Orloffs that night. She refused to open the door to Violet's ringing and it wasn't until the Sunday at church that they heard rumours about Jack Blakeney returning to his wife and Ruth being so afraid to go home to Cedar House and her mother that she had chosen to live with the Blakeneys. Southcliffe, it was said, had asked her to leave because of the scandal that was about to break around the Lascelles family. This time the furiously wagging tongues centred their suspicion on Joanna.

If Cooper was honest with himself, he could see Dave Hughes's attraction for young middle-class girls. He was a personable 'bit of rough', handsome, tall, with the clean, muscular looks of a Chippendale, dark shoulder-length hair, bright blue eyes and an engaging smile. Unthreatening was the word that leapt immediately to mind, and it was only gradually in the confined atmosphere of a Bournemouth police interview room that the teeth began to show behind the smile. What you saw, Cooper realized, was very professional packaging. What lay beneath the surface was anyone's guess.

Detective Chief Inspector Charlie Jones was another where the packaging obscured the real man. It amused Cooper to see how seriously Hughes underestimated the sad Pekinese face that regarded him with such mild-mannered apology. Charlie took the chair on the other side of the table from Hughes and sifted rather helplessly through his briefcase. 'It was good of you to come in,' he said. 'I realize time's precious. We're grateful for your co-operation, Mr Hughes.'

Hughes shrugged amiably. 'If I'd known I had a choice, I probably wouldn't've come. What's this about then?'

Charlie isolated a piece of crumpled paper and spread it out on the table. 'Miss Ruth Lascelles. She says you're her lover.'

Hughes shrugged again. 'Sure. I know Ruth. She's seventeen. Since when was sex with a seventeen-year-old a crime?'

'It's not.'

'What's the hassle then?'

'Theft. She's been stealing.'

Hughes looked suitably surprised but didn't say anything.

'Did you know she was stealing?'

He shook his head. 'She always told me her granny gave her money. I believed her. The old bitch was rolling in it.'

'Was? You know she's dead then.'

'Sure. Ruth told me she killed herself.'

Charlie ran his finger down the page. 'Ruth says you told her to steal silver-backed hair brushes, jewellery and valuable first editions from Mrs Gillespie's library. Similar items, in

fact, to what Miss Julia Sefton claims you told her to steal from her parents. Small bits and pieces that wouldn't be missed but could be disposed of very easily for ready cash. Who sold them, Mr Hughes? You or Ruth?'

'Do me a favour, Inspector. Do I look the sort of mug who'd act as a fence for an over-privileged, middle-class tart who'd drop me in it quick as winking the minute she was rumbled? Jesus,' he said with disgust, 'give me some credit for common sense. They only take up with me because they're bored out of their tiny minds with the jerks their parents approve of. And that should tell you something about the sort of girls they are. They call them slags where I come from, and thieving's in their blood along with the whoring. If Ruth says I set her up to it, then she's lying to get herself off the hook. It's so bloody easy, isn't it? I'm just scum from a frigging squat and she's Miss Lascelles from Southcliffe girls' school. Who's going to believe me?'

Charlie smiled his lugubrious smile. 'Ah, well,' he murmured, 'belief isn't really the issue, is it? We both know you're lying and that Ruth is telling the truth, but the question is can we persuade her to stand up in court and tell the *whole* truth? You made a bad choice there, Mr Hughes. She doesn't have a father, you see, only a mother, and you probably know as well as I do that women are far harder on their daughters than men ever could be. Mrs Lascelles won't protect Ruth the way Julia's father protected *her*. Apart from anything else, she positively loathes the girl. It would have been different, I suspect, if Mrs Gillespie were still alive, she would probably have hushed it up for the sake of the family's reputation, but as she isn't I can't see anybody championing Ruth.'

Hughes grinned. 'Well, go ahead then. Prosecute the thieving little bitch. It's no skin off my nose.'

It was Charlie's turn to look surprised. 'You don't like her?'

'She was okay for the odd screw, no great shakes but okay. Look, I told you, they only make out with me because they want to get back at their folks. So what am I supposed to do? Tug my forelock in gratitude for the use of their very ordinary bodies? I can get as good if not better down the nightclub of a Saturday.' He grinned again, a captivatingly wicked grin, guaranteed to melt female hearts but totally lost on Jones and Cooper. 'I do the business for them, give them their thrills, and I only complain when they try and lay their fucking thieving on me. It really gets up my nose, if you want the truth. You're such bloody suckers, you lot. A pretty face, a posh accent, a sob story, and, bingo, get Dave Hughes down here and give him the works. You just won't accept that they're slags, same as the prozzies on the streets in the red light district.'

Charlie looked thoughtful. 'That's the second time you've called Miss Lascelles a slag. What's your definition of a slag, Mr Hughes?'

'The same as yours, I guess.'

'A vulgar, coarse woman who sells her body for money. I wouldn't say that was a description of Miss Lascelles.'

Hughes looked amused. 'A slag's an easy lay. Ruth was so bloody easy, it was pathetic.'

'You said she was no great shakes as a screw,' Charlie carried on imperturbably. 'That's a very revealing admission, don't you think?'

'Why?'

'It says more about you than it does about her. Didn't she fancy you? Did you have to force her? What is it you like doing that she didn't like you enough to go along with? I find that fascinating.'

'I've had better, that's all I meant.'

'Better what, Mr Hughes?'

'Lovers, for Christ's sake. Women who know what they're doing. Women who handle themselves and me with more fucking finesse. Screwing Ruth was like screwing blancmange. It was me had to do all the work while she just lay there telling me how much she loved me. It pisses me off, that, it really does.'

Charlie frowned. 'Why did you bother with her then?'

Hughes smiled cynically at the all-too-patent trap. 'Why not? She was free, she was available, and I get horny like the next man. Are you going to charge me with doing what comes naturally?'

Charlie thought for a moment or two. 'Did you ever go into Cedar House?'

'The old biddy's place?' He shook his head. 'No way. She'd have done her nut if she'd got wind of who Ruth had hitched herself to. I don't go looking for trouble though you'd be amazed at the girls. Half of them think their parents are going to welcome me with open arms.' He mimicked the clipped diction of the upper classes. 'Mummy, Daddy, I'd like you to meet my new boyfriend, Dave.' The boyish grin again. 'They're so bloody thick, you wouldn't believe.'

'There've been a lot of these girls then. We thought there might have been.'

Hughes tilted his chair back, relaxed, complacent, unbe-

lievably confident. 'I appeal to them, Inspector. It's a talent I have. Don't ask me where it comes from, though, because I couldn't tell you. Perhaps it's the Irish in me.'

'On your mother's side, presumably.'

'How did you guess?'

'You're a type, Mr Hughes. Probably the illegitimate son of a whore who screwed anything for money, if your extreme prejudice against prostitutes is anything to go by. You wouldn't have a clue who your father was because he might have been any one of fifty who shafted her during the week you were conceived. Hence your contempt and hatred for women and your inability to conduct an adult relationship. You had no male role model to learn from or emulate. Tell me,' he murmured, 'does getting it free make you feel superior to the sad, anonymous little man who paid to father you? Is that why it's so important?'

The blue eyes narrowed angrily. 'I don't have to listen to this.'

'I'm afraid you do. You see, I'm very interested in your pathological dislike of women. You can't speak about them without being offensive. That isn't normal, Mr Hughes, and as Sergeant Cooper and I are investigating an extraordinarily abnormal crime, your attitude alarms me. Let me give you a definition of psychopathic personality disorder.' He consulted the piece of paper again. 'It manifests itself in poor or non-existent job performance, persistent criminality, sexual promiscuity and aggressive sexual behaviour. People with this disorder are irresponsible and extremely callous; they feel no guilt over their antisocial acts and find it difficult to make lasting relationships.' He looked up.

'Rather a good description of you, don't you think? Have you ever been treated for this type of disorder?'

'No, I fucking well haven't,' he said furiously. 'Jesus, what is this garbage, anyway? Since when was thieving an abnormal crime?'

'We're not talking about thieving.'

Hughes looked suddenly wary. 'What are we talking about then?'

'The things you do to the girls.'

'I don't get you.'

Charlie leaned forward aggressively, his eyes like flints. 'Oh, yes, you do, you filthy little nonce. You're a pervert, Hughes, and when you go down and the rest of the prisoners find out what you've been banged up for, you'll learn what it's like to be on the receiving end of aggressive behaviour. They'll beat the shit out of you, urinate on your food and use a razor on you if they can get you in the shower alone. It's one of the oddities of prison life. Ordinary prisoners hate sex offenders, particularly sex offenders who can only get a hard-on with children. Whatever they've done themselves pales into insignificance beside what you and people like you do to defenceless kids.'

'Jesus! I don't do kids. I hate bloody kids.'

'Julia Sefton had just turned sixteen when you did her. She could almost have been your daughter.'

'That's not a crime. I'm not the first man who's slept with someone young enough to be his daughter. Get real, Inspector.'

'But you always pick young girls. What is it about young girls that gets you so excited?'

'I don't pick them. They pick me.'

'Do older women frighten you? That's the usual pattern with nonces. They have to make out with children because mature women terrify them.'

'How many times do I have to tell you? I don't make out with children.'

Abruptly Jones switched tack. 'Ruth stole some diamond earrings from her grandmother on Saturday, November the sixth, the same day that Mrs Gillespie killed herself. Did you take Ruth there that day?'

Hughes looked as if he was about to deny it, then shrugged. 'She asked me to.'

'Why?'

'Why what?'

'Why did she ask you to take her? What did she want to do there?'

Hughes looked vague. 'She never said. But I never went in the frigging place and I didn't know she planned to steal any frigging earrings.'

'So she rang you at your squat, asked you to drive all the way out to Southcliffe to pick her up, take her from there to Fontwell and then back to Southcliffe, without ever explaining why.'

'Yeah.'

'And that's all you did? Acted as her chauffeur to and fro and waited outside Cedar House while she went in?'

'Yeah.'

'But you've admitted you didn't like her. In fact you despised her. Why go to so much trouble for someone you didn't like?'

'It was worth it for a screw.'

'With blancmange?'

Hughes grinned. 'I felt horny that day.'

'She told my Sergeant she was absent from school for upwards of six hours. It's thirty miles from Southcliffe to Fontwell, so let's say it took you forty minutes each way. That leaves some four and a half hours unaccounted for. Are you telling me you sat in your van in Fontwell village for four and a half hours twiddling your thumbs while Ruth was inside with her grandmother?'

'It wasn't that long. We stopped on the way back for the screw.'

'Where exactly did you park in Fontwell?'

'Can't remember now. I was always waiting for her some place or another.'

Charlie placed his finger on the crumpled page of paper. 'According to the publican at the Three Pigeons your van was parked on his forecourt that afternoon. After ten minutes you drove away, but he saw you stop beside the church to pick someone up. We must presume this was Ruth unless you are now going to tell me you took a third party to Fontwell the day Mrs Gillespie killed herself.'

The wary look was back in Hughes's eyes. 'It was Ruth.'

'Okay, then what were you and Ruth doing for four and a half hours, Mr Hughes? You certainly weren't screwing her. It doesn't take four and a half hours to screw blancmange. Or perhaps it does for someone who suffers from a psychopathic personality disorder. Perhaps it takes you that long to get it up.'

Hughes refused to be needled. 'I guess there's no reason for me to protect the silly bitch. Okay, she asked me to drive her to this backstreet jeweller somewhere in South-

ampton. I didn't ask why, I just did it. But you can't do me for that. All I did was act as a taxi. If she stole some earrings and then sold them, I knew nothing about it. I was just the patsy with the wheels.'

'According to Miss Lascelles she gave the money to you as soon as she sold the earrings. She said it was six hundred and fifty pounds in cash and that you then drove her straight back to school in time for her physics lecture.'

Hughes didn't say anything.

'You profited from a crime, Mr Hughes. That's illegal.'

'Ruth's lying. She never gave me any money and, even if she did, you'd have to prove I knew she'd thieved something in the first place. She'll tell you it was all her idea. Look, I don't deny she funded me from time to time, but she said the money was hers and I believed her. Why shouldn't I? The old granny was rolling in it. Stood to reason Ruth would be as well.' He grinned again. 'So what if she did give me cash from time to time? How was I to know the silly bitch was stealing it? She owed me something for the petrol I wasted acting as her frigging chauffeur in the holidays.'

'But she didn't fund you that day?'

'I already said no, and no's what I mean.'

'Did you have any money on you?'

'A fiver, maybe.'

'What was the name of the backstreet jeweller in Southampton?' Charlie asked abruptly.

'No idea. I never went in the place. You'll have to ask Ruth. She just told me to go to a road and stop at the end of it.'

'What was the name of the road?'

'Don't know. She had a map, told me right, left, straight on, stop. I just did what I was told. You'll have to ask Ruth.'

'She doesn't know. She says you drove her there, told her which shop to go into, who to ask for and what to say.'

'She's lying.'

'I don't think so, Mr Hughes.'

'Prove it.'

Charlie thought rapidly. He had no doubt that Hughes was telling the truth when he said he hadn't entered Cedar House or the jewellers', not in Ruth's company anyway. The beauty of his scam was that he didn't handle the stolen goods himself, merely transported the girls and the goods to someone who would. That way, the only person who could ever implicate him was the girl, and she wasn't going to because, for whatever reason, she was too frightened of him. 'I intend to prove it, Mr Hughes. Let's start with an account of your movements after you dropped Ruth back at school. Did you go to this nightclub you mentioned? It'll be expensive, they usually are, and coke and ecstasy don't come cheap, both of which I suspect you're on. People will remember you, especially if you were throwing money about.'

Hughes saw another trap and giggled. 'I already said I hadn't got any money, Inspector. I drove around a bit and then went back to the squat.'

'What time was that?'

He shrugged. 'No idea.'

'So if I find someone who says a white transit van was

parked in the vicinity of a Bournemouth nightclub that night, you'll say it couldn't have been yours because you were just driving around.'

'That's about the size of it.'

Charlie bared his teeth in a predatory smile. 'I have to inform you, Mr Hughes, that you will be transferred shortly to Learmouth Police Station where you will be questioned at length about the murder of Mrs Mathilda Gillespie.' He gathered his notes together and thrust them back into his pocket.

'Shit!' said Hughes angrily. 'What crap are you trying to lay on me now? You said she killed herself.'

'I was lying. She was murdered and I have reason to believe you were involved in that murder.'

Hughes surged aggressively to his feet. 'I told you I never went in the fucking place. Anyway, the publican's my alibi. He saw me in his car park and watched me pick up Ruth. How could I murder the old lady if I was in my van the whole time?'

'She wasn't murdered at two thirty. She was murdered later that evening.'

'I wasn't there later that evening.'

'Your van was. The publican says you returned that evening and, as you yourself have just told us, you and your van have no alibi for the night of November the sixth. You were driving around, remember?'

'I was here in Bournemouth and so was the van.'

'Prove it.' Charlie stood up. 'Until you do, I'm holding you on suspicion of murder.'

'You're really out of order on this one. I'll get my brief on you.'

'Do that. You'll be allowed your phone call at Learmouth.'

'Why would I want to kill the old cow anyway?'

Charlie lifted a shaggy eyebrow. 'Because you have a history of terrorizing women. This time you went too far.'

'I don't bloody murder them.'

'What do you do to them?'

'Shag 'em that's all. And I don't short change 'em neither. I've never had a complaint yet.'

'Which is probably what the Yorkshire Ripper said every time he came home with his hammer and his chisel in the boot of his car.'

'You're way out of order,' said Hughes again, stamping his foot. 'I didn't even know the old bitch. I didn't *want* to know her. Jesus, you bastard, how could I kill someone I didn't even know?'

'You got born, didn't you?'

'What the hell's that supposed to mean?'

'Birth and death, Hughes. They happen at random. Your mother didn't know your father but you still got born. The not-knowing is irrelevant. You were there that day, you were using her granddaughter to steal from her and Mrs Gillespie knew it. You had to shut her up before she talked to us.'

'I don't work it that way.'

'How do you work it then?'

But Hughes refused to say another word.

I have brought Joanna and her baby home to live with me. I could not believe the squalor I found them in when I arrived in London. Joanna has given up all attempts at caring for the child or even practising elementary hygiene. She is clearly not fit to live alone and, while I abhorred that wretched Jew she married, at least while he was alive she had some pretensions to normality.

I am very afraid that the shock of Steven's death has sent her over the edge. She was in the baby's room this morning, holding a pillow over the cot. I asked her what she was doing, and she said: 'Nothing,' but I have no doubt at all that, had I entered the room a few minutes later, the pillow would have been across the baby's face. The awful part is that I saw myself standing there, like some ghastly reflection in a distorted mirror. The shock was tremendous. Does Joanna suspect? Does anyone, other than Jane, suspect?

There is no cure for inbred insanity. 'Unnatural deeds do breed unnatural troubles . . .'

Thirteen

JANE MARRIOTT MARCHED into Sarah's office in the Fontwell surgery the following morning after the last patient had left and deposited herself firmly in a chair. Sarah glanced at her. 'You're looking very cross,' she remarked as she signed off some paperwork.

'I feel cross.'

'What about?'

'You.'

Sarah folded her arms. 'What have I done?'

'You've lost your compassion.' Jane tapped a stern finger against her watch. 'I know I used to wig you about the length of time you spent on your patients, but I admired you for the trouble you took. Now, suddenly, they're in and out like express trains. Poor old Mrs Henderson was almost in tears. "What have I done to upset Doctor?" she asked me. "She hardly had a kind word for me." You really mustn't let this business over Mathilda get to you, Sarah. It's not fair on other people.' She drew an admonishing breath. 'And don't tell me I'm only the receptionist and you're the doctor. Doctors are fallible, just like the rest of us.'

Sarah pushed some papers about her desk with the point of her pencil. 'Do you know what Mrs Henderson's first words to me were when she came in? "I reckon it's safe to come back to you, Doctor, seeing as how it was that bitch of a daughter what done it." And she lied to you. I didn't have a *single* kind word for her. I told her the truth for once, that the only thing wrong with her is an acidulated spleen which could be cured immediately if she looked for the good in people instead of the bad.' She wagged the pencil under Jane's nose. 'I am rapidly coming to the conclusion that Mathilda was right. This village is one of the nastiest places on earth, peopled entirely by ignorant, evil-minded bigots with nothing better to do in their lives than sit and pass judgement on anyone who doesn't conform to their commonplace, petty-minded stereotypes. It's not compassion I've lost, it's my blinkers.'

Jane removed the pencil from Sarah's grasp before it could lodge itself in her nostril. 'She's a lonely old widow, with little or no education, and she was trying in her very ham-fisted way to say sorry for ever having doubted you. If you haven't the generosity of spirit to make allowances for her clumsy diplomacy then you are not the woman I thought you were. And for your information, she now thinks she is suffering from a very severe condition, namely acidulated spleen, which you are refusing to treat. And she's put that down to the cuts in the Health Service and the fact that, as an old woman, she is now considered expendable.'

Sarah sighed. 'She wasn't the only one. They're all cock-a-hoop because they think Joanna did it and I resent them using me and my surgery to score points off her.' She pulled her fingers through her hair. 'Because that's what today was

all about, Jane, a sort of childish yah-boo-sucks at their latest victim, and if Jack hadn't decided to play silly buggers, then there wouldn't have been so much for them to gossip about.'

'Don't you believe it,' said Jane tartly. 'What they can't get any other way they make up.'

'Hah! And you have the nerve to haul me over the coals for cynicism!'

'Oh, don't assume I'm not just as irritated as you are by their silliness. Of course I am, but then I don't expect anything else. They haven't changed just because Mathilda's died, you know, and I must say it's a bit rich accusing Mrs Henderson of only seeing the bad in people when the greatest exponent of that has just left you a small fortune. Mrs Henderson's view of people is positively saintly compared with Mathilda's. *She* really did have an acidulated spleen.'

'All right. Point taken. I'll drop in on Mrs H. on my way home.'

'Well, I hope you'll be gracious enough to apologize to her. Perhaps I'm being over-sensitive but she did seem so upset, and it's not like you to be cruel, Sarah.'

'I feel cruel,' she growled. 'As a matter of interest, do you talk to the male doctors like this?'

'No.'

'I see.'

Jane bridled. 'You don't see anything. I'm fond of you. If your mother were here she would be saying the same things. You should never allow events to sour your nature, Sarah. You leave that particular weakness to the Mathildas of this world.'

Sarah felt a surge of affection for the elderly woman, whose apple cheeks had grown rosy with indignation. Her mother, of course, would say no such thing, merely purse her lips and declare that she had always known Sarah was sour at heart. It took someone with Jane's generosity to see that other people were diplomatically inept, or weak, or disillusioned. 'You're asking me to betray my principles,' she said mildly.

'No, my dear, I'm asking you to stand by them.'

'Why should I condone Mrs Henderson calling Joanna a murderess? There's no more evidence against her than there was against me, and if I apologize it's a tacit acceptance.'

'Nonsense,' said Jane stoutly. 'It's courtesy towards an old lady. How you deal with Joanna is a different matter altogether. If you don't approve of the way the village is treating her then you must demonstrate it in a very public way so that no one is in any doubt of where your sympathies lie. But,' her old eyes softened as they rested on the younger woman, 'don't take your annoyance out on poor Dolly Henderson, my dear. She can't be expected to see things as you and I do. She never enjoyed our liberal education.'

'I will apologize.'

'Thank you.'

Sarah suddenly leaned forward and planted a kiss on the other's cheek.

Jane looked surprised. 'What was that for?'

'Oh, I don't know.' Sarah smiled. 'Standing in for my mother, perhaps. I wonder sometimes if the stand-ins aren't rather better at the job than the real thing. Mathilda did it,

too, you know. She wasn't *all* acidulated spleen. She could be just as sweet as you when she wanted to be.'

'Is that why you're looking after Ruth? As a sort of quid pro quo?'

'Don't you approve?'

Jane sighed. 'I don't approve or disapprove. I just feel it's a little provocative in the circumstances. Whatever your reasons for doing it, the village has put the worst interpretation on those reasons. You do know they're saying that Joanna's about to be arrested for the murder of her mother, and that's why Ruth has gone to live with you?'

'I hadn't realized it was quite that bad.' Sarah frowned. 'God, they're absurd. Where do they get this rubbish from?'

'They put two and two together and make twenty.'

'The trouble is' – she paused – 'there's nothing much I can do about it.'

'But, my dear, all that's required is an explanation of why Ruth is with you,' Jane suggested, 'and then you can knock these rumours on the head. There must be one, after all.'

Sarah sighed. 'It's up to Ruth to explain, and at the moment she's not in a position to do that.'

'Then invent one,' said Jane bluntly. 'Give it to Mrs Henderson when you see her this afternoon and it'll be all round the village by tomorrow evening. Fight fire with fire, Sarah. It's the only way.'

Mrs Henderson was touched by Dr Blakeney's apology for her bad temper in the surgery, thought it very handsome of her to take the trouble to come out to her cottage, and

quite agreed that if you'd been up all night looking after a seventeen-year-old showing all the symptoms of glandular fever, you were bound to be shirty the next day. Mind, she didn't quite understand why Ruth had to stay with Dr Blakeney and her husband in the circumstances. Wouldn't it be more fitting for her to remain with her mother? Much more fitting, agreed Sarah firmly, and Ruth would prefer it too, of course, but, as Mrs Henderson knew, glandular fever was an extremely painful and debilitating viral infection, and because of the likelihood of its recurring if the patient wasn't cared for properly and bearing in mind this was Ruth's A level year, Joanna had asked Sarah to take her in and get her back on her feet again as quickly as possible. In the circumstances, what with Mrs Gillespie's will and all (Sarah looked suitably embarrassed), she could hardly refuse, could she?

'Not when you're the one what's got all the money,' was Mrs Henderson's considered retort, but her rheumy eyes clouded in puzzlement. 'Ruth going back to Southcliffe then, when she's better, like?'

'Where else would she go?' murmured Sarah unblushingly. 'As I said, it's her A level year.'

'Well, I never! There's some lies being told and no mistake. Who killed Mrs Gillespie, then, if it weren't you and it weren't the daughter?'

'God knows, Mrs Henderson.'

'Happen he does, too, so it's a shame He doesn't pass it on. He's causing a lot of bother by keeping the information to Hisself.'

'Perhaps she killed herself.'

'No,' said the old woman decidedly. 'That I'll never

believe. I don't say as I liked her very much but Mrs Gillespie was no coward.'

Sarah knew Joanna was in Cedar House, despite the stubborn silence that greeted her ringing of the doorbell. She'd seen the set white face in the shadows at the back of the dining-room and the brief flicker of recognition before Joanna slipped into the hall and out of sight. Rather more than her refusal to answer the door, it was her flicker of recognition that fuelled Sarah's anger. Ruth was the issue here, not Mathilda's will or Jack's shenanigans, and while she might have sympathized with Joanna's reluctance to open the door to the police, she could not forgive the barricading of it against the person Joanna knew was sheltering her daughter. Sarah set off grimly down the path that skirted the house. What kind of woman, she wondered, put personal enmity before concern for her daughter's welfare?

In her mind's eye, she pictured the portrait Jack was working on. He had trapped Joanna inside a triangular prism of mirrors, with her personality split like refracted light. It was an extraordinary depiction of confused identity, the more so because for each image there was a single image reflected back from the huge encompassing mirror that bordered the canvas. Sarah had asked him what the single image represented. 'Joanna as she wants to be seen. Admired, adored, beautiful.'

She pointed to the prism images. 'And what are they?'

'That's the Joanna she's suppressing with drugs,' he said. 'The ugly, unloved woman who was rejected by mother,

husband and daughter. Everything in her life is illusion, hence the mirror theme.'

'That's sad.'

'Don't go sentimental on me, Sarah, or on her either for that matter. Joanna is the most self-centred woman I have ever met. I guess most addicts are. She says Ruth rejected her. That's baloney. It was Joanna who rejected her because Ruth cried whenever Joanna picked her up. It was a vicious circle. The more her baby cried the less inclined she was to love it. She claimed Steven rejected her because he was revolted by the pregnancy, but in the next sentence she admitted she couldn't stand the way he fussed over Ruth. It was she, I think, who rejected him.'

'But why? There must be a reason for it.'

'I suspect it's very simple. The only person she loves or is capable of loving is herself and because her swollen belly made her less attractive in her own eyes, she resented the two people responsible for it, namely her husband and her baby. I'll put money on the fact that she's the one who found the pregnancy repulsive.'

'Nothing's ever that simple, Jack. It could be something quite serious. Untreated post-natal depression. Narcissistic personality disorder. Schizophrenia even. Perhaps Mathilda was right, and she *is* unstable.'

'Maybe, but if she is, then Mathilda was entirely to blame. From what I can gather, she kowtowed to Joanna and Joanna's histrionics from day one.' He gestured towards the painting. 'When I said that everything in her life is illusion, what I meant was: everything is false. This is the fantasy she wants you to believe, but I'm ninety-nine per

cent certain she doesn't believe it herself.' He laid his forefinger on the central triangle of the prism, which as yet contained nothing. 'That's where the real Joanna will be, in the only mirror that can't reflect her stylized image of herself.'

Clever stuff, thought Sarah, but was it true? 'And what is the real Joanna?'

He stared at the painting. 'Utterly ruthless, I think,' he said slowly, 'utterly and completely ruthless about getting her own way.'

The kitchen door was locked but the key that Mathilda had hidden under the third flowerpot to the right was still there and, with an exclamation of triumph, Sarah pounced on it and inserted it into the Yale lock. It was only after she'd opened the door and was removing the key to lay it on the kitchen table that she wondered if anyone had told the police that entry into Cedar House was that easy if you knew what was under the flowerpot. *She* certainly hadn't, but then she had forgotten all about it until the need to get in had jogged her memory. She had used it once, months ago, when Mathilda's arthritis was so bad that she hadn't been able to get out of her chair to open the front door.

Gingerly, she laid the key on the table and stared at it. Intuition told her that whoever had used the key last had killed Mathilda Gillespie, and she didn't need to be Einstein to work out that if their fingerprints had been on it she had just destroyed them with her own. 'Oh, Jesus!' she said with feeling.

'How dare you come into my house without asking,' announced Joanna in a tight little voice from the hall doorway.

Sarah's glare was so ferocious that the other took a step backwards. 'Will you get off your ridiculous high horse and stop being so pompous,' she snapped. 'We're all in deep shit here and the only thing you ever do is stand on your wretched dignity.'

'Stop swearing. I detest people who swear. You're worse than Ruth and she has a mouth like a sewer. You're not a lady. I can't understand how my mother put up with you.'

Sarah drew a deep angry breath. 'You're unreal, Joanna. Which century do you think you're living in? And what is a lady? Someone like you who's never done a hand's turn in her life but passes muster because she doesn't utter profanities?' She shook her head. 'Not in my book it isn't. The greatest lady I know is a seventy-eight-year-old Cockney who works with the down-and-outs in London and swears like a trooper. Open your eyes, woman. It's the contribution you make to society that earns you respect, not a tight-arsed allegiance to some outmoded principle of feminine purity that died the day women discovered they weren't condemned to a life of endless pregnancy and child-rearing.'

Joanna's lips thinned. 'How did you get in?'

Sarah nodded towards the table. 'I used the key under the flowerpot.'

Joanna frowned angrily. 'Which key?'

'That one, and don't touch it, whatever you do. I'm sure whoever killed your mother must have used it. Can I borrow the phone? I'm going to call the police.' She brushed past Joanna into the hall. 'I'll have to ring Jack as well, tell him

I'm going to be late. Do you mind? Presumably the cost will come out of your mother's estate.'

Joanna pursued her. 'Yes, I do mind. You've no business to force your way in. This is my house and I don't want you here.'

'No,' said Sarah curtly, picking up the phone on the hall table, 'according to your mother's will, Cedar House belongs to me.' She flicked through her diary for Cooper's telephone number. 'And you're only in it because I've balked at evicting you.' She held the receiver to her ear and dialled Learmouth Police Station, watching Joanna as she did so. 'But I'm rapidly changing my mind. Frankly, I see no reason why I should show you more consideration than you're prepared to show your own daughter. Detective Sergeant Cooper, please. Tell him it's Dr Blakeney and it's urgent. I'm at Cedar House in Fontwell. Yes, I'll hold.' She put her hand over the mouthpiece. 'I want you to come home with me and talk to Ruth. Jack and I are doing our best but we're no substitute for you. She needs her mother.'

A small tic flickered at the side of Joanna's mouth. 'I resent your interference in matters that don't concern you. Ruth is quite capable of looking after herself.'

'My God, you really are unreal,' said Sarah in amazement. 'You couldn't give a shit, could you?'

'You are doing this deliberately, Dr Blakeney.'

'If you're referring to my swearing, then, yes, you're dead right I am,' said Sarah. 'I want you to be as shocked by me as I am by you. Where's your sense of responsibility, you *sodding* bitch? Ruth didn't materialize out of thin air. You and your husband had a *fucking* good time when you made her, and don't forget it.' Abruptly she transferred her

attention to the telephone. 'Hello, Sergeant, yes, I'm at Cedar House. Yes, she's here, too. No, there's no trouble, it's just that I think I know how Mathilda's murderer got in. Has anyone told you she kept a key to the kitchen door under a flowerpot by the coal bunker at the back? I know, but I forgot about it.' She pulled a face. 'No, it's not still there. It's on the kitchen table. I used it to get in.' She held the receiver away from her ear. 'I did not do it on purpose,' she said coldly after a moment. 'You should have searched a bit more thoroughly at the beginning then it wouldn't have happened.' She replaced the receiver with unnecessary force. 'We've both got to stay here until the police come.'

But Joanna's composure had abandoned her. 'GET OUT OF MY HOUSE!' she screamed 'I WILL NOT BE SPOKEN TO LIKE THIS IN MY HOUSE!' She ran up the stairs. 'YOU WON'T GET AWAY WITH IT! I'LL REPORT YOU TO THE MEDICAL COUNCIL! MUD STICKS. I'LL TELL THEM YOU MURDERED MR STURGIS AND THEN MY MOTHER.'

Sarah followed in her wake, watched her run into the bathroom and slam the door, then lowered herself to the floor and sat cross-legged outside it. 'Tantrums and convulsions may have worked a treat with Mathilda but they sure as hell aren't going to work with me. GODDAMMIT!' she roared suddenly, putting her mouth to the oak-panelled door. 'You're a forty-year-old middle-aged woman, you stupid cow, so act your age.'

'DON'T YOU DARE SPEAK TO ME LIKE THAT!'

'But you get up my nose, Joanna. I have only contempt for someone who can't function unless they're doped stupid.' Tranquillizers was Jack's guess.

No answer.

'You need help,' she went on matter-of-factly, 'and the best person to give it to you is based in London. He's a psychiatrist who specializes in all forms of drug addiction but he won't take you on unless you're willing to give up. If you're interested I'll refer you, if you're not then I suggest you prepare yourself for the long term consequences of habitual substance abuse on the human body, beginning with the one thing you don't want. You will get old very much quicker than I will, Joanna, because your physical chemistry is under constant attack and mine isn't.'

'Get out of my house, Dr Blakeney.' She was beginning to calm down.

'I can't, not till Sergeant Cooper gets here. And it's not your house, remember, it's mine. What are you on?'

There was a long, long silence. 'Valium,' said Joanna finally. 'Dr Hendry prescribed it for me when I came back here after Steven died. I tried to smother Ruth in her cot, so Mother called him in and begged him to give me something.'

'Why did you try to smother Ruth?'

'It seemed the most sensible thing to do. I wasn't coping terribly well.'

'And did tranquillizers help?'

'I don't remember. I was always tired, I remember that.'

Sarah believed her, because she could believe it of Hugh Hendry. Classic symptoms of severe post-natal depression, and instead of giving the poor woman anti-depressants to lift her mood, the idiot had effectively shoved her into a state of lethargy by giving her sedatives. No wonder she found it so difficult to get on with Ruth, when one of the tragic consequences of post-natal depression, if it wasn't

treated properly, was that mothers found it difficult to develop natural loving relationships with their babies whom they saw as the reason for their sudden inability to cope. God, but it explained a lot about this family if the women had a tendency to post-natal depression. 'I can help you,' she said. 'Will you let me help you?'

'Lots of people take Valium. It's perfectly legal.'

'And very effective in the right circumstances and under proper supervision. But you're not getting yours from a doctor, Joanna. The problems of diazepam addiction are so well documented that no responsible practitioner would go on prescribing them for you. Which means you've got a private supplier somewhere and the tablets won't be cheap. Black market drugs never are. Let me help you,' she said again.

'You've never been afraid. What would you know about anything if you've never been afraid?'

'What were you afraid of?'

'I was afraid to go to sleep. For years and years I was afraid to go to sleep.' She laughed suddenly. 'Not any more, though. She's dead.'

The doorbell rang.

Sergeant Cooper was in very tetchy mood. The last twenty-four hours had been frustrating ones for him and not just because he had had to work over the weekend and miss Sunday lunch with his children and grandchildren. His wife, tired and irritable herself, had delivered the inevitable ticking-off about his lack of commitment to his family. 'You

should put your foot down,' she told him. 'The police force doesn't own you, Tommy.'

They had held Hughes overnight at Learmouth Police Station but had released him without charge at lunchtime. After a persistent refusal the previous afternoon to say anything at all, he had reverted that morning to his previous statement, namely that he had been driving around aimlessly before returning to his squat. He gave the time for his return as nine o'clock. Cooper, dispatched by Charlie Jones to interview the youths who shared the squat with him, had come back deeply irritated.

'It's a set-up,' he told the DCI. 'They've got his alibi off pat. I spoke to each one in turn, asked them to give me an account of their movements on the evening of Saturday, the sixth of November, and each one told me the same story. They were watching the portable telly and drinking beer in Hughes's room when Hughes walked in at nine o'clock. He stayed there all night, as did his van which was parked in the road outside. I did not mention Hughes once, nor imply that I was at all interested in him or his blasted van. They offered the information gratuitously and without prompting.'

'How could they know he'd told us nine o'clock?'

'The solicitor?'

Charlie shook his head. 'Very unlikely. I get the impression he doesn't like his client any more than we do.'

'Then it's a prearranged thing. If questioned, Hughes will always give nine o'clock as the time he returns to the squat.'

'Or they're telling the truth.'

Cooper gave a snort of derision. 'No chance. They were scum. If any of them were tamely watching telly that night, I'm a monkey's uncle. Far more likely, they were out beating up old ladies or knifing rival football supporters.'

The Inspector mulled this over. 'There's no such thing as an alibi applicable in all situations,' he said thoughtfully. 'Not unless Hughes always makes a habit of committing crimes after nine o'clock at night, and we know he doesn't do that, because Ruth stole her grandmother's earrings at two thirty in the afternoon.' He fell silent.

'So what are you saying?' asked Cooper when he didn't go on. 'That they're telling the truth?' He shook his head aggressively. 'I don't believe that.'

'I'm wondering why Hughes didn't produce this alibi yesterday. Why did he keep mum for so long if he knew his mates were going to back him up?' He answered his own question slowly. 'Because his solicitor forced my hand this morning and demanded to know the earliest time that Mrs Gillespie might have died. Which means Hughes had already told him he was in the clear from nine o'clock, and hey presto, out comes his alibi.'

'How does that help us?'

'It doesn't,' said Jones cheerfully. 'But if it was the set-up you say it is, then he must have done something else that night that required an alibi from nine o'clock. All we have to do is find out what it was.' He reached for his telephone. 'I'll talk to my oppo in Bournemouth. Let's see what he can come up with on the crime sheet for the night of Saturday, November the sixth.'

The answer was nothing.

Nothing, at least, that remotely fitted the modus operandi of David Mark Hughes.

Hence Cooper's tetchiness.

He tut-tutted crossly at Sarah as he examined the key on the table. 'I thought you had more sense, Dr Blakeney.'

Sarah held on to her patience with an effort, remembering Jane's admonishment not to let events sour her nature. 'I know. I'm sorry.'

'You'd better hope we do raise someone else's fingerprints, otherwise I might be inclined to think this was a stunt.'

'What sort of stunt?'

'A way of leaving your fingerprints on it legitimately.'

She was way ahead of him. 'Assuming I was the one who used it to get in and kill Mathilda and had forgotten to wipe my fingerprints off it at the time, I suppose?' she said tartly.

'Not quite,' he said mildly, 'I was thinking more in terms of a Good Samaritan act on behalf of someone else. Who have you unilaterally decided is innocent this time, Dr Blakeney?'

'You're not very grateful, Cooper,' she said. 'I needn't have told you about it at all. I could have put it back quietly and kept my mouth shut.'

'Hardly. It has your fingerprints all over it and someone would have found it eventually.' He glanced at Joanna. 'Did you really not know it was there, Mrs Lascelles?'

'I've already told you once, Sergeant. No. I had a key to the front door.'

There was something very odd going on between her

and Dr Blakeney, he thought. The body language was all wrong. They were standing close together, arms almost touching, but they seemed unwilling to look at each other. Had they been a man and a woman, he'd have said he'd caught them in flagrante delicto; as it was, intuition told him they were sharing a secret although what that secret was and whether it had any bearing on Mrs Gillespie's death was anyone's guess.

'What about Ruth?'

Joanna shrugged indifferently. 'I've no idea but I wouldn't think so. She's never mentioned it to me, and I've only ever known her use her front door key. There's no sense in coming all the way round the back if you can get in through the front. There's no access on this side.' She looked honestly puzzled. 'It must be something Mother started recently. She certainly didn't do it when I was living here.'

He looked at Sarah who spread her hands in a gesture of helplessness. 'All I know is that the second or third time I came to visit her, she didn't answer the door, so I walked round to the french windows and looked into the drawing-room. She was completely stuck, poor old thing, quite unable to push herself out of her chair because her wrists had packed up on her that day. She mouthed instructions through the glass. "Key. Third flowerpot. Coal bunker." I imagine she kept it there for just that kind of emergency. She worried all the time about losing her mobility.'

'Who else knew about it?'

'I don't know.'

'Did you tell anyone?'

Sarah shook her head. 'I can't remember. I may have

mentioned it in the surgery. It was ages ago, anyway. She started responding very well to the new medication I gave her and the situation didn't recur. I only remembered it when I came round the back this afternoon and saw the flowerpots.'

Cooper took a couple of polythene bags out of his pocket and used one to inch the key off the table into the other. 'And why did you come round the back, Dr Blakeney? Did Mrs Lascelles refuse to let you in at the front?'

For the first time Sarah glanced at Joanna. 'I don't know about refusing. She may not have heard the bell.'

'But it was obviously something very urgent you needed to discuss with her or you wouldn't have been so determined to get in. Would you care to let me in on what that was? Presumably it concerns Ruth.' He was too old and experienced a hand to miss the look of relief on Joanna's face.

'Sure,' said Sarah lightly. 'You know my views on education. We were discussing Ruth's future schooling.'

She was lying, Cooper thought, and he was startled by the fluency with which she did it. With an inward sigh, he made a mental note to review everything she had told him. He had believed her to be an honest, if naïve, woman, but the naïvety, he realized now, was all on his side. There was no fool like an old fool, he thought bitterly.

But then silly old Tommy had fallen a little in love.

There is no truer saying than 'Revenge is a dish best eaten cold.' It is so much sweeter for the waiting, and my only regret is that I cannot broadcast my triumph to the world. Sadly, not even to James, who is duped but does not know it.

This morning I heard from my bank that he has cashed my cheque for £12,000 and has therefore by default agreed to the insurance settlement. I knew he would. Where money is concerned James has the intemperate greed of a child. He spends it like water because cash in hand is the only thing he understands. Oh, to be a fly on the wall and see how he's living, but I can guess, anyway. Drink and sodomy. There was never anything else in James's life.

I am £36,500 richer today than I was yesterday, and I glory in it. The cheque from the insurance company for the various items stolen from the safe over Christmas while Joanna and I were in Cheshire came to an astonishing £23,500, the bulk of which was for the set of diamond jewellery belonging to my grandmother. The tiara alone was insured for £5,500, although I imagine

it was worth more than that as I have not had it valued since Father's death. Extraordinary to have such a windfall for items I, personally, would not be seen dead in. There is nothing so ugly or heavy as ornate Victorian jewellery.

By contrast, James's clocks are anything but vulgar, probably because it was his father who bought them and not James. I took them to Sotheby's to be valued and discovered they are worth more than double the £12,000 they were insured for. Thus, after paying James £12,000, I retain £11,500 from the insurance cheque and have effectively purchased from my contemptible husband a fine investment, valued at £25,000.

As I said, revenge is a dish best eaten cold . . . .

Fourteen

EARLIER THAT afternoon, a tall, distinguished-looking man was shown into Paul Duggan's office in Poole. He gave his name as James Gillespie and calmly produced his passport and his marriage certificate to Mathilda Beryl Gillespie to prove it. Aware that he had dropped something of a bombshell, he lowered himself on to a vacant chair and clasped his hands around the handle of his walking-stick, studying Duggan with amusement from beneath a pair of exuberant white eyebrows. 'Bit of a shock, eh?' he said. Even from the other side of the desk, the smell of whisky on his breath was powerful.

The younger man examined the passport carefully, then placed it on the blotting-pad in front of him. 'Unexpected, certainly,' he said dryly. 'I had assumed Mrs Gillespie was a widow. She never mentioned a husband or,' he laid a careful stress upon the next syllable, '*ex*-husband still living.'

'Husband,' grunted the other forcefully. 'She wouldn't. It suited her better to be thought a widow.'

'Why did you never divorce?'

'Never saw the need.'

'This passport was issued in Hong Kong.'

'Naturally. Out there forty years. Worked in various banks. Came back when I realized it was no place to end my days. Too much fear now. Peking's unpredictable. Uncomfortable for a man of my age.' He spoke in clipped staccato sentences like someone in a hurry or someone impatient with social niceties.

'So why have you come to see me?' Duggan watched him curiously. He was striking to look at, certainly, with a mane of white hair and an olive complexion, etched with deep lines around his eyes and mouth, but closer examination revealed an underlying poverty beneath the superficial air of prosperity. His clothes had once been good, but time and usage had taken their toll and both the suit and the camel-hair coat were wearing thin.

'Should have thought it was obvious. Now she's dead – reclaiming what's mine.'

'How did you know she was dead?'

'Ways and means,' said the other.

'How did you know I was her executor?'

'Ways and means,' said the other again.

Duggan's curiosity was intense. 'And what is it that you wish to reclaim?'

The old man took a wallet from his inside pocket, removed some folded sheets of very thin paper and spread them on the desk. 'This is an inventory of my father's estate. It was divided equally amongst his three children on his death forty-seven years ago. My share was those items marked with the initials JG. You will find, I think, that at least seven of them appear on your inventory of Mathilda's estate. They are not hers. They never were hers. I now wish to recover them.'

Thoughtfully, Duggan read through the documents. 'Precisely which seven items are you referring to, Mr Gillespie?'

The huge white eyebrows came together in a ferocious scowl. 'Don't trifle with me, Mr Duggan. I refer, of course, to the clocks. The two Thomas Tompions, the Knibbs, the seventeenth-century mahogany long case, the Louis XVI Lyre clock, the eighteenth-century "pendule d'officier" and the crucifix clock. My father and grandfather were collectors.'

Duggan steepled his hands over the inventory. 'May I ask why you think any of these things appear on the inventory of Mrs Gillespie's estate?'

'Are you telling me they don't?'

The solicitor avoided a direct answer. 'If I understood you correctly you've been absent from this country for forty years. How could you possibly know what might or might not have been in your wife's possession the day she died?'

The old man snorted. 'Those clocks were the only things of value I had, and Mathilda went to a great deal of trouble to steal them from me. She certainly wouldn't have sold them.'

'How could your wife steal them if you were still married?'

'Tricked me out of them, then, but it was still theft.'

'I'm afraid I don't understand.'

Gillespie removed an airmail letter from his wallet and handed it across the desk. 'Self-explanatory, I think.'

Duggan unfolded the letter and read the terse lines. The address was Cedar House and the date was April 1961.

Dear James,
I am sorry to have to tell you that during a burglary here over Christmas much of value was stolen, including your collection of clocks. I have today received a cheque in settlement from the insurance company and I enclose their invoice, showing that they sent me a total of £23,500. I also enclose a cheque for £12,000 which was the insured value of your seven clocks. You bought my silence by leaving the clocks with me, and I am reimbursing you only because I fear you might return one day to claim them. You would be very angry, I think, to discover I'd cheated you a second time. I trust this means we will not need to communicate again.
Yours, Mathilda.

Duggan's amiable face looked up in bewilderment. 'I still don't understand.'

'They weren't stolen, were they?'

'But she gave you twelve thousand pounds for them. That was a small fortune in 1961.'

'It was fraud. She told me the clocks were stolen when they weren't. I accepted the money in good faith. Never occurred to me she was lying.' He tapped his walking-stick angrily on the floor. 'Two ways of looking at it. One, she stole the clocks herself and defrauded the insurance company. A crime, in my book. Two, other things were stolen to the value of twenty-three and a half thousand and she saw an opportunity to take the clocks off me. Also a crime. They were my property.' His ancient mouth turned down at the corners. 'She knew their value, knew they'd be the best asset she had. Been to Sotheby's myself. Rough

estimate, of course, with only descriptions in the inventory to go by, but we're talking over a hundred thousand at auction, probably a great deal more. I want them back, sir.'

Duggan considered for a moment. 'I don't think the situation is quite as clear-cut as you seem to think, Mr Gillespie. There's a burden of proof here. First, you have to show that Mrs Gillespie deliberately defrauded you; second, you have to show that the clocks in Mrs Gillespie's estate are the precise clocks that were left to you by your father.'

'You've read both inventories. What else could they be?'

For the moment, Duggan avoided the question of how James Gillespie knew there was an inventory of Mathilda's estate or what was on it. Once broached, it was going to be a very unpleasant can of worms. 'Similar clocks,' he said bluntly. 'Maybe even the same clocks, but you will have to prove she didn't buy them back at a later stage. Let's say the collection was stolen, and she passed on the compensation to you as she was supposed to. Let's say, then, that she set out to replace the collection because she had developed an interest in horology. She could quite legitimately have used her own money to buy similar clocks at auction. In those circumstances, you would have no claim on them at all. There is also the undeniable fact that you had a duty, encumbent on you as the owner, to establish to your satisfaction that the money you were paid in 1961 represented a full and fair settlement by the insurance company for the theft of your goods. In accepting twelve thousand pounds, Mr Gillespie, you effectively did that. You abandoned the clocks to sail to Hong Kong, accepted handsome compensation for them without a murmur, and only wish to reclaim them now because after forty years you

believe they might have been worth hanging on to. I will admit that this is a grey area, which will require Counsel's opinion, but off the top of my head, I'd say you haven't a leg to stand on. It's an old saying, but a true one. Possession is nine tenths of the law.'

Gillespie was not so easily intimidated. 'Read her diaries,' he growled. 'They'll prove she stole them off me. Couldn't resist boasting to herself, that was Mathilda's trouble. Put every damn thing on those miserable pages, then read them over and over again to remind herself how clever she was. Wouldn't have left out a triumph like this. Read the diaries.'

The younger man kept his face deliberately impassive. 'I will. As a matter of interest, do you know where she kept them? It'll save me the trouble of looking for them.'

'Top shelf of the library. Disguised as the works of Willy Shakespeare.' He took a card from his wallet. 'You're a solicitor, Mr Duggan, so I'm trusting you to be honest. That's where I'm staying. Expect to hear from you on this in a couple of days or so. Grateful if you'd treat it as a matter of urgency.' He levered himself to his feet with his walking-stick.

'I'd much prefer to deal through your solicitor, Mr Gillespie.'

'I don't have one, sir.' He spoke with a touching dignity. 'My pension won't allow it. I am relying on you being a gentleman. Presumably they still exist in this wretched country. Precious little else does.' He made his way to the door. 'Perhaps you think I treated Mathilda badly by deserting her and the child. Perhaps you think I deserved to be stolen from. Read the diaries. She'll tell you herself what really happened.'

Duggan waited until the door had closed, then reached for the telephone and dialled Learmouth Police Station.

The information about Mathilda's diaries was telephoned through to Cooper as he was about to leave Cedar House. He replaced the receiver with a frown. He'd been over that house from top to bottom, and he was as sure as he could be that there were no handwritten diaries in the library or anywhere else. 'Sorry, ladies, I shall have to trespass on your time a little longer. Will you come with me, please?'

Puzzled, Joanna and Sarah followed him across the hall and into the library.

'What are you looking for?' asked Joanna as he stood staring at the top shelf.

He reached up and tapped the thick mahogany ledge that ran, like its fellows, across the width of the wall. 'Do either of you see the collected works of William Shakespeare up here?'

'They're all over the place,' said Joanna dismissively. 'Which particular edition are you looking for?'

'The one that's supposed to be on this shelf.' He glanced at her. 'Your mother's diaries. I'm told she kept them on the top shelf, disguised as the works of William Shakespeare.'

Joanna looked genuinely surprised. 'What diaries?'

'Our information is that she kept a record of everything that happened to her.'

'I didn't know.'

'The informant was very positive.'

Joanna gestured helplessly. 'I didn't know,' she said again.

'Who's your informant?' asked Sarah curiously.

Cooper was watching Joanna as he spoke. 'James Gillespie,' he said. 'Mrs Lascelles's step-father.'

This time the look of surprise lacked conviction. It was left to Sarah to make the obvious response. 'I thought he abandoned Mathilda years ago,' she said thoughtfully. 'How would he know whether she kept diaries or not? Anyway, he's in Hong Kong, or that's what my receptionist told me.'

'Not any more, Dr Blakeney. According to Mrs Gillespie's solicitor, he's living in Bournemouth.' He addressed Joanna. 'We'll have to search the house again, and I'd prefer it if you were here while we did so.'

'Of course, Sergeant. I'm not planning to go anywhere. This is my house, after all.'

Sarah caught her gaze. 'What about Ruth? You can't just abandon her.'

'Ruth must learn to fend for herself, Dr Blakeney.' She gave an eloquent little shrug. 'Perhaps you should have considered the consequences a little more carefully before you persuaded Mother to change her will. You must see that it's quite impossible for me to support her as things stand at the moment.'

'It's emotional support she needs, and that won't cost you a bean.'

'There's nothing I could say to her that wouldn't make matters worse.' Joanna's pale eyes stared unwinkingly at Sarah. 'She's had more opportunities than I ever had and she's chosen to throw them away. You do realize she was

stealing from Mother for months before this sordid little episode at school.' Her mouth thinned unpleasantly. 'You can't imagine the resentment I've felt since Miss Harris telephoned to explain why Ruth was being expelled. Have you any idea of the money that's been wasted on that child's education?'

'Miss Harris has given you a very one-sided view of what happened,' said Sarah carefully, aware that Cooper was all ears beside her. 'You must see that it's only fair to hear Ruth's side as well, at least give her the chance to demonstrate that what happened wasn't entirely her fault.'

'I've lived with my daughter on and off for nearly eighteen years, and I know exactly who's to blame. Ruth is quite incapable of telling the truth. You would be very foolish to assume otherwise.' She smiled very slightly. 'You may tell her that she knows where I am if she wants me, although please make it very clear that, unless this business of the will is settled satisfactorily, then she can expect no help from me either in terms of her continuing education or of her living expenses.'

This woman was using Ruth as a bargaining chip, thought Sarah in disgust, but she reminded herself that in her own way Joanna was as desperate as Ruth. She tried again. 'Money isn't the issue here, Joanna, the only issue is that your daughter would like to see you. She's too frightened to come to Cedar House because the man who persuaded her to steal knows this address and has made threats against her. Please, please, will you come with me to Mill House and talk to her there? She isn't lying, but she's deeply disturbed about everything that's happened and

needs reassurance that you haven't rejected her. She has spent most of her time sitting by the telephone, hoping and praying that you would call. I don't think you have any idea how deeply she cares for you.'

There was the briefest of hesitations – *or was that wishful thinking on Sarah's part?* 'You took her in, Dr Blakeney, so I suggest you deal with her. I can't begin to condone anything she's done. Worse, I'm inclined to think it was she who murdered my mother. She's quite capable of it. Please don't be in any doubt about that.'

Sarah shook her head in disbelief. 'Ah, well, perhaps it's better this way. The one thing Ruth doesn't need at the moment is you downloading your hypocritical crap on her. You're tarred with exactly the same brush, or have you forgotten the mess you were in when Mathilda rescued you?' She shrugged. 'I'd made up my mind to turn the bequest down and let you and Ruth have a fair crack at convincing a court you had more rights than the donkeys. Not any more. You'll have to fight me for it now, and you'll be fighting your corner alone because I intend to put money in trust for Ruth so that she doesn't lose out whatever happens.' She walked to the door, flashing Cooper one of the sweet smiles that made his elderly heart race around like a young spring lamb. 'If it's of any interest to you, Sergeant, I am still of the opinion that Joanna did not kill Mathilda. Arthritis or no arthritis, Mathilda would have legged it for the hills the minute this bitch came near her.'

Well, well, Cooper thought, gazing after her as she stormed across the hall, there was passion in Dr Blakeney

after all. But he wished he knew what had happened to Ruth that was making her and Jack so angry.

Cadogan Mansions, implying as it did something grand and impressive, was a misnomer for the shabby neglect of the purpose-built block that greeted Cooper the following morning. Sixties architecture, drab, square and unstylish, squeezed into a gap between two suburban villas and constructed solely to provide extra accommodation at minimum cost for maximum profit. How very different towns might look, Cooper always thought, if planners had been prosecuted instead of praised for their urban vandalism.

He climbed the utilitarian stairs and rang the bell of number seventeen. 'Mr James Gillespie?' he asked of the rugged old man who poked his nose round the door and gusted stale whisky in his face. Cooper flipped open his warrant card. 'DS Cooper, Learmouth Police.'

Gillespie's eyebrows beetled aggressively. 'Well?'

'May I come in?'

'Why?'

'I'd like to ask you some questions about your late wife.'

'Why?'

Cooper could see this conversation dragging on interminably. He opted for the direct approach. 'Your wife was murdered, sir, and we have reason to believe you may have spoken to her before she died. I understand that you have been living abroad for some years, so perhaps I should remind you that you are obliged by British law to assist us in any way you can with our enquiries. Now, may I come in?'

'If you must.' He seemed quite unruffled by the policeman's bald statement but led the way past a room with a bed in it to another room containing a threadbare sofa and two plastic chairs. There was no other furniture and no carpets, but a piece of net curtaining was draped in the windows to give a modicum of privacy. 'Expecting bits and pieces from Hong Kong,' he barked. 'Should arrive any day. Camping out meanwhile. Sit down.' He lowered himself on to the sofa, trying somewhat clumsily to hide the empty bottle that lay on the floor at his feet. The room was frowsty with whisky, urine and unwashed old man. The front of his trousers was saturated, Cooper saw. Tactfully, he took out his notebook and concentrated his attention on that.

'You didn't seem very surprised when I told you your wife was murdered, Mr Gillespie. Did you know already?'

'Heard rumours.'

'Who from?'

'My brother. We used to live in Long Upton once. He still knows people there. Hears things.'

'Where does he live now?'

'London.'

'Could you give me his name and address?'

The old man thought about it. 'No harm, I suppose. Frederick Gillespie, Carisbroke Court, Denby Street, Kensington. Won't help you, though. Doesn't know any more than I do.'

Cooper flicked back through the pages of his notebook till he came to Joanna Lascelles's address. 'Your step-daughter lives in Kensington. Does your brother know her?'

'Believe so.'

Well, well, well, thought Cooper. A panorama of intriguing possibilities opened up in front of him. 'How long have you been back in England, Mr Gillespie?'

'Six months.'

The bits and pieces from Hong Kong were eyewash, then. Nothing took that long these days to be freighted round the world. The old boy was destitute. 'And where did you go first? To your brother? Or to your wife?'

'Spent three months in London. Then decided to come back to my roots.'

Frederick couldn't put up with an incontinent drunk. It was guesswork, of course, but Cooper would put money on it. 'And you saw Joanna during that time and she told you that Mathilda was still living in Cedar House.' He spoke as if it were something he had established already.

'Nice girl,' said the old man ponderously. 'Pretty, like her mother.'

'So you went to see Mathilda.'

Gillespie nodded. 'Hadn't changed. Rude woman still.'

'And you saw the clocks. The ones she told you had been stolen.'

'Solicitor's talked, I suppose.'

'I've just come from Mr Duggan. He informed us of your visit yesterday.' He saw the old man's scowl. 'He had no option, Mr Gillespie. Withholding information is a serious offence, particularly where a murder has occurred.'

'Thought it was suicide.'

Cooper ignored this. 'What did you do when you realized your wife had lied to you?'

Gillespie gave a harsh laugh. 'Demanded my property

back, of course. She found that very amusing. Claimed I'd accepted money in lieu thirty years ago and no longer had an entitlement.' He searched back through his memory. 'Used to hit her when I lived with her. Not hard. But I had to make her frightened of me. It was the only way I could stop that malicious tongue.' He fingered his mouth with a trembling hand. It was mottled and blistered with psoriasis. 'I wasn't proud of it and I never hit a woman again, not until—' He broke off.

Cooper kept his voice level. 'Are you saying you hit her when she told you you couldn't have your property back?'

'Smacked her across her beastly face.' He closed his eyes for a moment as if the recollection pained him.

'Did you hurt her?'

The old man smiled unpleasantly. 'I made her cry,' he said.

'What happened then?'

'Told her I'd be putting the law on to her and left.'

'When was this? Can you remember?'

He seemed to become suddenly aware of the urine stains on his trousers and crossed his legs self-consciously. 'The time I hit her? Two, three months ago.'

'You went there at other times then?'

Gillespie nodded. 'Twice.'

'Before or after you hit her?'

'After. Didn't want the law on her, did she?'

'I don't follow.'

'Why would you? Doubt you saw her till she was dead. Devious, that's the only way to describe Mathilda. Devious and ruthless. Guessed I'd fallen on hard times and came

here the next day to sort something out. Talked about a settlement.' He picked at the scabs on his hand. 'Thought I wouldn't know what the clocks were worth. Offered me five thousand to leave her alone.' He fell silent.

'And?' Cooper prompted when the silence lengthened.

The old eyes wandered about the empty room. 'Realized she'd pay more to avoid the scandal. Went back a couple of times to demonstrate how vulnerable she was. She was talking fifty thousand the day before she died. I was holding out for a hundred. We'd have got there eventually. She knew it was only a matter of time before someone saw me and recognized me.'

'You were blackmailing her.'

Gillespie gave his harsh laugh again. 'Mathilda was a thief. D'you call it blackmail to negotiate back what's been stolen from you? We understood each other perfectly. We'd have reached an agreement if she hadn't died.'

Cooper allowed his revulsion to get the better of him. 'It seems to me, sir, you wanted to have your cake and eat it too. You deserted her forty years ago, left her to fend for herself with a baby, snatched up what the clocks were worth in nineteen sixty-one, spent the whole lot' – he looked pointedly at the empty bottle – 'probably on booze, repeated the exercise with everything else you've ever earned and then came home to leech off the woman you'd abandoned. I'd say it's arguable who was the greater thief. If the clocks were so important to you, why didn't you take them with you?'

'Couldn't afford to,' said Gillespie dispassionately. 'Put together enough for my passage. Nothing left over to freight the clocks.'

'Why didn't you sell one to pay for the freight of the others?'

'She blocked it.' He saw the scepticism in Cooper's expression. 'You didn't know her, man, so don't make judgements.'

'Yet by your own admission you used to beat her to make her frightened of you. How could she stop you selling your own property? You'd have thrashed her.'

'Maybe I did,' he growled. 'Maybe she found another way to stop me. You think I was the first one to try blackmail? She was a past master at it.' He touched his lips again and this time the tremor in his hands was more marked. 'We reached an accommodation, the essence of which was no scandal. She'd let me leave for Hong Kong on the condition that there was no divorce and she kept the clocks. Mutual insurance, she called them. While she housed them, she could be sure of my silence. While I owned them I could be sure of hers. They were worth a bob or two, even in those days.'

Cooper frowned. 'What silence were you buying?'

'This and that. It was an unhappy marriage, and you washed your dirty linen in public when you divorced in those days. Her father was an MP, don't forget.'

She let me leave for Hong Kong . . . Strange use of words, thought Cooper. How could she have stopped him? 'Were you involved in something criminal, Mr Gillespie? Were the clocks a quid pro quo for her not going to the police?'

He shrugged. 'Water under the bridge now.'

'What did you do?'

'Water under the bridge,' the old man repeated stub-

bornly. 'Ask me *why* Mathilda had to buy my silence. That's a damn sight more interesting.'

'Why then?'

'Because of the baby. Knew who the father was, didn't I?'

Water under the bridge, thought Cooper sarcastically. 'You told Mr Duggan that your wife kept diaries,' he said, 'that they were on the top shelf of her library disguised as the collected works of William Shakespeare. Is that correct?'

'It is.'

'Did you see them when you went to Cedar House or did Mrs Gillespie tell you about them?'

Gillespie's eyes narrowed. 'You saying they're not there now?'

'Will you answer my question, please. Did you see them or are you relying on something Mrs Gillespie told you?'

'Saw them. Knew what to look for, see. I had the first two volumes bound for her as a wedding present. Gave her another eight with blank pages.'

'Could you describe them, Mr Gillespie?'

'Brown calfskin binding. Gold lettering on the spines. Titles courtesy Willy Shakespeare. Ten volumes in all.'

'What sort of size?'

'Eight inches by six inches. An inch thick or thereabouts.' He wrung his hands in his lap. 'They're not there, I suppose. Don't mind telling you, rather relying on those diaries. They'll prove she set out to defraud me.'

'So you read them?'

'Couldn't,' the old man grumbled. 'She never left me alone long enough. Fussed around me like a blasted hen.

But the proof'll be there. She'd've written it down, just like she wrote everything else.'

'Then you can't say for sure they were diaries, only that there were ten volumes of Shakespeare on the top shelf which bore a resemblance to some diaries you'd bought for her forty-odd years ago.'

He pursed his lips obstinately. 'Spotted them the first time I was there. They were Mathilda's diaries all right.'

Cooper thought for a moment. 'Did Mrs Lascelles know about them?'

Gillespie shrugged. 'Couldn't say. I didn't tell her. Don't believe in emptying the armoury before I have to.'

'But you told her you weren't her father?'

He shrugged again. 'Someone had to.'

'Why?'

'She was all over me. Wouldn't leave me alone. Pathetic really. Seemed wrong to let her go on believing such a fundamental lie.'

'Poor woman,' murmured Cooper with a new compassion. He wondered if there was anyone who *hadn't* rejected her. 'I suppose you also told her about the letter from her natural father.'

'Why not? Seemed to me she has as much right to the Cavendish wealth as Mathilda had.'

'How did you know about it? It was written after you left for Hong Kong.'

The old man looked sly. 'Ways and means,' he muttered. But he saw something in Cooper's eyes that caused him to reflect. 'There was talk in the village when Gerald topped himself,' he said. 'Word got about he'd written a letter which his brother managed to suppress. Suicide' – he shook

his head – 'wasn't the done thing in those days. William hushed it up for the sake of the family. I heard the stories at the time and suggested Joanna look for the letter. Stood to reason what would be in it. Gerald was a sentimental half-wit bound to've mentioned his bastard. Couldn't've resisted it.'

'And perhaps you reached an accommodation with Mrs Lascelles as well. You'd testify in court to her real paternity if she kept you in clover for the rest of your life. Something like that?'

Gillespie gave a dry chuckle. 'She was a great deal more amenable than her mother.'

'Then why did you bother to go on negotiating with Mrs Gillespie?'

'Didn't rate Joanna's chances much, not against Mathilda.'

Cooper nodded. 'So you killed your wife to improve the odds.'

The dry chuckle rasped out again. 'Wondered when you'd pull that one out of the hat. Didn't need to. If she didn't kill herself, then rather think my step-daughter did it for me. She was mighty put out to discover that her mother played the tart with her great-uncle.' Abruptly, like some guilty secret he'd decided to unburden, he fished a full bottle of whisky from where it was tucked down behind the sofa cushions, unscrewed the cap and held it to his mouth. 'Want some?' he asked vaguely after a moment, waving the bottle in Cooper's direction before placing it between his lips again and half-draining it in huge mouthfuls.

The Sergeant, whose experience of drunks was consider-

able after years of plucking them out of the gutter in sodden heaps, watched in amazement. Gillespie's tolerance levels were extraordinary. In two minutes he had consumed enough neat spirit to put most men on their backs, and the only effect it seemed to have on him was to reduce the tremors in his hands.

'We're having difficulty establishing a motive for your wife's murder,' Cooper said slowly. 'But it seems to me yours is rather stronger than most.'

'Bah!' Gillespie snorted, his eyes bright now with alcoholic affability. 'She was worth more to me alive. I told you, she was talking fifty thousand the day before she died.'

'But you didn't keep your side of the bargain, Mr Gillespie. That meant your wife was free to reveal why you had to abscond to Hong Kong.'

'Water under the bridge,' came his monotonous refrain. 'Water under the bloody bridge. No one'd be interested in my little peccadillo now, but there's a hell of a lot'd be interested in hers. The daughter, for a start.' He raised the bottle to his mouth again, and the shutters went down.

Cooper couldn't remember when anyone or anything had disgusted him quite so much. He stood up, buttoning depression about himself with his coat. If he could wash his hands of this terrible family, he would, for he could find no saving graces in any of them. What's bred in the bone comes out in the flesh, and their corruption was as rank as the stench in that room. If he regretted anything in his life it was being on shift the day Mathilda's body was found. But for that, he might have remained what he had always believed he was – a truly tolerant man.

Unnoticed by Gillespie, he retrieved the empty bottle from the floor with his fingertips and took it with him.

Jack studied the address that Sarah had patiently cajoled out of Ruth. 'You say it's a squat, so how do I get him outside alone?'

She was rinsing some cups under the cold water tap. 'I'm having second thoughts. What happens if you end up in traction for the next six months?'

'It couldn't possibly be worse than what I'm suffering already,' he murmured, pulling out a chair and sitting on it. 'There's something wrong with the spareroom bed. It's giving me a stiff neck. When are you going to boot Ruth out and let me back where I belong?'

'When you've apologized.'

'Ah, well,' he said regretfully, 'a stiff neck it is then.'

Her eyes narrowed. 'It's only an apology, you bastard. It won't kill you. Stiff-necked says it all, if you ask me.'

He gave an evil grin. 'It's not the only thing that's stiff. You don't know what you're missing, my girl.'

She glared at him. 'That's easily cured.' With a swift movement she upended a cupful of freezing water into his lap. 'It's a pity Sally Bennedict didn't do the same.'

He surged to his feet, knocking the chair backwards. 'Jesus, woman,' he roared, 'will you stop trying to turn me into a eunuch!' He gripped her round the waist and lifted her bodily into the air. 'You're lucky we've got Ruth in the house,' he growled, twisting her sideways and holding her head under the running tap, 'otherwise I might be tempted

to show you how ineffectual cold water is on a deprived libido.'

'You're drowning me,' she spluttered.

'Serves you right.' He set her on her feet again and turned off the tap.

'You asked for passion,' she said, dripping water over the quarry tiles. 'Don't you like it now that you've got it?'

He tossed her a towel. 'Hell, yes,' he said with a grin. 'The last thing I wanted was a wife who understood. I will not be patronized, woman.'

She shook her head in fury, splattering the kitchen with droplets. 'If one more person calls me patronizing,' she said, 'I will do them some damage. I am *trying* to be charitable towards some of the most useless and self-indulgent egotists it has ever been my misfortune to meet. And it's bloody difficult.' She rubbed her hair vigorously with the towel. 'If the world was made up of people like me, Jack, it would be paradise.'

'Well, you know what they say about paradise, old thing. It's heaven until the horned viper pops his head out from under the fig leaf and spots the moist warm burrow under the bushes. After that all hell breaks loose.'

She watched him pull on his old donkey jacket and take a torch from the kitchen drawer. 'What are you planning to do exactly?'

'Never you mind. What you don't know can't incriminate you.'

'Do you want me to come with you?'

His dark face split into a grin. 'What for? So you can stitch him back together again when I've finished with him?

You'd be a liability, woman. Anyway, you'd be struck off if we were caught, and someone's got to stay with Ruth.'

'You will be careful, won't you?' she said, her eyes dark with concern. 'In spite of everything, Jack, I am really very fond of you.'

He touched a finger to her lips. 'I'll be careful,' he promised.

He drove slowly up Palace Road, located number twenty-three and the white Ford transit outside it, made a circuit of the block and drew into a space which gave him an unobstructed view of the house but was far enough away from it not to attract attention to himself. Yellow lamplight gleamed along the street, throwing pools of shadow amongst the houses, but few people were abroad at eight o'clock on a cold Thursday evening in late November, and only once or twice did his heart jump at the unexpected appearance of a dark-clad figure on the pavement. An hour had passed when a dog emerged into a swathe of light ten yards from the car and began to rootle amongst some garbage by a dustbin. It was only after several minutes of watching that Jack realized it wasn't a dog at all but an urban fox, scavenging for food. So prepared was he for a long wait, and so entranced by the delicate scratchings of the fox, that he missed the door of number twenty-three opening. Only the noise of laughter alerted him to the fact that something was going down. With narrowed eyes, he watched a group of young men piling into the back of the van, saw the doors slam and a figure disappear round the side.

Impossible to tell if it was Hughes. Ruth had described him as tall, dark and handsome, but, as all cats are black in the night, so all young men look the same from thirty yards distant on a winter's evening. Jack, gambling on something else she had said, that the van was his and he always drove it, pulled out behind it as it drove away.

The doctor has written 'heart failure' as the cause of Father's death. I had difficulty keeping a straight face when I read it. Of course he died of heart failure. We all die of heart failure. Mrs Spencer, the housekeeper, was suitably distraught until I told her I'd keep her on while she looked about for another niche for herself. After that she rallied with surprising speed. That class has little loyalty to anything except money.

Father looked very peaceful in his chair, his whisky glass still clasped in his hand. 'Taken in his sleep' according to the doctor. How very, very true, in every respect. 'He drank far more than was good for him, my dear. I did warn him about it.' He went on to assure me that I need have no fears about him suffering. I made an appropriate response, but thought: What a pity he hadn't. He deserved to suffer. Father's worst fault was his ingratitude. James was really very lucky. Had I realized how easy it was to get rid of drunks, well, well . . . enough said.

Unfortunately, Joanna saw me. The wretched child woke up and came downstairs just as I was removing

the pillow. I explained that Grandpa was ill and that the pillow was to make him more comfortable, but I have the strangest feeling she knows. She refused to go to sleep last night, just lay looking at me with that very unnerving stare of hers.

But what possible significance could a pillow have for a two-year-old . . .

Fifteen

HALF AN HOUR later and well into the better side of town, the van drew to a halt in the shadows of an expensive-looking house to pick up the wide-eyed adolescent girl waiting there. The hairs began to crawl on the back of Jack's neck. He watched her climb with gawky eagerness into the passenger seat, and he knew that she was as unprepared as Ruth had been for the surprise that Hughes had waiting for her in the back.

The van took the coast road east towards Southbourne and Hengistbury Head and, as the traffic thinned, Jack allowed the distance between it and him to lengthen. He toyed with one possibility after another – should he stop to call the police and risk losing the van altogether? – should he ram the van and risk injuring himself and the girl? – should he try to deter them by drawing in beside them when they parked, at the risk of their driving off and giving him the slip? He discarded each idea in turn, seeing only their weaknesses, and suddenly felt a deep regret that he hadn't brought Sarah with him. He had never wanted the comfort of her friendship quite so desperately.

The van turned into a deserted car park on the sea front,

and more by instinct than design Jack killed his lights thrust the gears into neutral and freewheeled to a stop beside the kerb some fifty yards behind it. Every detail of what happened next was lit by a cold, clear moon, but he knew what to expect because Ruth had described Hughes's MO in all too graphic detail. The driver, Hughes for a certainty, flung open his door and jumped out on to the tarmac, dragging the girl after him. There was the briefest of scuffles before he pinioned her in his arms and carried her, kicking and struggling, to the back of the van. He was laughing as he wrenched the rear door open and flung her like a sack of potatoes into the lit interior. The square of light shone out briefly before he closed the doors and strolled away towards the sea shore, lighting a cigarette as he went.

Jack could never explain afterwards why he did what he did. In retrospect he could only really remember his fear. His actions were governed entirely by instinct. It was as if faced with a crisis, normal reason deserted him and something primeval took over. He focused entirely on the child. The need to help her was paramount, and the only method that presented itself was to open the van doors and physically remove her from danger. He eased into first gear and motored gently towards the transit, watching Hughes as he did so to see if he picked up the throb of the engine above the wash of the waves against the shore. Apparently not. The man stooped lazily to gather stones from the beach and send them spinning out across the black water.

Jack coasted to a halt behind the van and left the engine purring while he unbuckled his belt, drawing it from around his waist and wrapping the end about his fist. He took the

heavy rubber torch in his other hand, clicked open the door and slipped out on to the tarmac, sucking in great draughts of air to still the thudding of his heart.

In the distance, Hughes turned round, took in the situation at a glance, and started to pound up the beach.

Adrenaline plays tricks. It floods the body to galvanize it into colossal and spontaneous effort, but the mind observes what happens in slow motion. Thus time, that most relative of phenomena, ceases to exist in any meaningful way, and what Jack would for ever insist took several minutes, in reality took seconds. He burst the van doors open and brought the torch down on the head of the man nearest him, bellowing like a bull. The startled white face of another youth turned towards him and Jack flicked the belt across it in a vicious backhand swipe, crooking his elbow round the first man's neck as he did so and pulling him backwards on to the tarmac. He released his hold and brought the torch round in a scything arc to smash under the chin of the face he'd whipped, toppling the youth off balance into thin air behind him.

The three men left in the van, two holding the girl down, the other bare-arsed on top of her, were frozen into shocked immobility. The violence of the onslaught was so extreme, the noise of Jack's continuous roaring so disorientating, that he was on top of them before they could register what was happening. He used the hand holding the belt to grip the hair of the bastard raping the girl, wrenched his head up and swung the torch in a mighty forehand smash into the wide-eyed, frightened face. Blood erupted from the broken nose in a stream, and the youth slithered sideways with a whimper of pain.

'GET OUT!' Jack shouted at the girl who was scrambling to her knees in terror. 'GET IN THE CAR!' He whipped the belt back and sliced it through the air into the eyes of a boy who was struggling to his feet in the corner. 'YOU BLOODY LITTLE SHITS!' he roared. 'I'M GOING TO KILL YOU.' He brought his boot down on the unprotected groin of the rapist and turned like a madman on the only youth he hadn't touched. With a cry of terror, the boy cowered away, his arms held protectively above his head.

Perhaps, after all, reason hadn't entirely deserted Blakeney. He abandoned the torch and the belt, flung himself precipitately out of the van, bundled into the car after the girl, and roared it into motion, tugging the door closed as he did so. He saw Hughes too late to avoid him as he careered across the tarmac, and caught him a glancing blow with the offside wing, bouncing him into the air like a rag-doll. Jack's anger was out of control, a red frenzy that pounded in his head like cannon-fire. Spinning the wheel, he turned the vehicle in a tight circle and headed back towards the crouching figure, switching on the headlights with a lazy flick of his fingers to catch Hughes's terrified face in the glare as he prepared to mow him down.

He had no idea what stopped him doing it. Perhaps it was the girl's screams. Perhaps his anger abated as rapidly as it had surged into life. Perhaps, quite simply, his humanity triumphed. Instead, he slewed the car to a screaming halt, slammed the door into the man's body and leapt out to wind his fist around the long hair and drag Hughes to his feet. 'Into the back, sweetheart,' he said to the girl, 'as fast as you can.' She was too terrified not to obey and slid in

hysterics between the seats. 'Now, you, in,' he said, yanking down on the hair and shoving his knee into the small of Hughes's back, 'or, so help me, I'll break your filthy neck now.'

Hughes believed him. As the lesser of two evils, he allowed himself to be thrust face-down across the seat and sighed as Jack's heavy weight descended across his legs. The car raced into life again, screaming across the tarmac as Jack forced it into gear, the door slamming shut when it impacted against another flying figure. 'PUT YOUR SEAT BELT ON!' he yelled at the screaming girl. 'IF THIS BASTARD MOVES A MUSCLE I'M GOING TO PILE THE SIDE WHERE HIS HEAD IS INTO THE BIGGEST BRICK WALL I CAN FIND.' He changed up, swung out on to the road and set off at a blistering pace through Southbourne with his hand clamped over the horn. If there was any justice in this cess-pit of a world, someone would get the police out before the Ford transit caught up with him.

There was some justice left in the England Rupert Brooke died for. The local police received seventeen 999 calls in three minutes, twelve from elderly widows living alone, four from outraged men, and one from a child. They all reported the same thing. Joy-riders were turning the quiet tree-lined streets of their suburb into a death-trap.

Jack's car and the pursuing white transit were ambushed as they tore on to the main road leading into Bournemouth city centre.

*

The phone rang in Mill House at eleven thirty that night. 'Sarah?' Jack barked down the wire.

'Hi,' she countered with relief. 'You're not dead then.'

'No. I'm under sodding arrest,' he shouted. 'This is the one telephone call I'm allowed to make. I need help PDQ.'

'I'll come straight away. Where are you?'

'The bastards are going to charge me with joy-riding and rape,' he said furiously, as if she hadn't spoken. 'They're fucking *cretins* here, won't listen to a word I say. Goddammit, they've banged me up along with Hughes and his animals. The poor kid they were having a go at in the back of the van's completely hysterical and thinks I'm one of them. I keep telling them to contact Cooper but they're such bloody morons they won't listen to me.'

'Okay,' she said calmly, trying to make what she could of this alarming speech, 'I'll get Cooper. Now tell me where you are.'

'Some shit-hole in the middle of Bournemouth,' he roared. 'They're about to take swabs off my fucking penis.'

'The address, Jack. I need the address.'

'WHERE THE HELL AM I?' he bellowed at someone in the room with him. 'Freemont Road Police Station,' he told Sarah. 'You'll have to bring Ruth, too,' he said with regret. 'God knows, I never meant to involve her but she's the only one who knows what happened. And get Keith as well. I need a solicitor I can trust. They're all bloody fascists in this place. They're talking about frigging paedophile rings and conspiracies and Christ knows what else.'

'Calm down,' she said sternly. 'Keep your mouth shut

till I get there and, for God's sake, Jack, don't lose your temper and hit a policeman.'

'I already have, dammit. The bastard called me a pervert.'

It was well after two o'clock when Sarah, Cooper and Ruth finally arrived bleary-eyed at Freemont Road. The night Sergeant at Learmouth had been adamant in his refusal either to contact Cooper or to give Sarah his home phone number when she put through an urgent call requesting to speak to him. 'DS Cooper is not on duty, madam,' was his measured response. 'If you have a problem, you deal with me or wait until tomorrow morning when he will be on duty.' It was only when he was faced with her angry presence in front of his desk, threatening him with questions in Parliament and court action for negligence, that he was moved to contact the Detective Sergeant. The counter-blast from Cooper's end, not in the best of moods, anyway, after being woken up from a deep sleep, left him shaken. He grumbled away to himself for the rest of his shift. Sod's law said that it didn't matter how considerate a chap tried to be, he was always in the wrong.

Keith, even more irritable than Cooper to be dragged from the arms of Morpheus far away in London, perked up a little to hear that Jack was under arrest for joy-riding and rape. 'Good God,' he said with cynical amusement, 'I had no idea he was so active. I thought he preferred spectator sports.'

'It's not funny, Keith,' said Sarah curtly. 'He needs a solicitor. Can you come down to Bournemouth?'

'When?'

'Now, you oaf. They're taking swabs off him at this very minute.'

'Did he do it?'

'What?'

'The rape,' said Keith patiently.

'No, of course he didn't,' she spluttered angrily. 'Jack's not a rapist.'

'Then there's nothing to worry about. The swabs will prove he hasn't been in contact with the victim.'

'He says they think he's part of a paedophile ring. They may charge him with conspiracy to rape even if they can't charge him with the actual offence.' She sighed. 'At least I think that's what he said. He's very angry and it was all a bit garbled.'

'What on earth's he been up to?'

'I don't know yet,' she said through gritted teeth. 'Just get your arse down here, will you, and earn some of the fortune we've paid you over the years.'

'I'm not much of a criminal lawyer, you know. You might do better to get hold of a specialist from down there. I could give you some names out of the book.'

'He asked for you, Keith. He said he wants a solicitor he can trust, so – ' her voice rose ' – for God's sake will you stop arguing and get in your car. We're wasting time. He's at Freemont Road Police Station in Bournemouth.'

'I'll be there as soon as I can,' he promised. 'In the meantime, tell him to keep quiet and refuse to answer any questions.'

Easier said than done, thought Sarah ruefully, as she and Ruth were given chairs to sit on while Cooper was taken into an interview room. When the door opened, they heard

Jack in full spate. '*Look*, how many times do you have to be *told*? I was rescuing her from being raped, not bloody raping her myself. Jesus wept!' His fist pounded on the table. 'I will not talk to morons. Doesn't anyone in this piss-pot have a measurable IQ?' He gave a whoop of relief. 'Hallelujah! Cooper! Where the hell have you been, you bastard?' The door closed again.

Sarah leant her head against the wall with a sigh. 'The trouble with Jack,' she said to Ruth, 'is he never does anything by halves.'

'He wouldn't be here at all if it wasn't for me,' the girl said wretchedly, washing her hands over and over in her lap. She was so nervous she could barely keep her breathing under control.

Sarah glanced at her. 'I think you should be rather proud of yourself. Because of you he obviously stopped someone else getting the treatment you were given. That's good.'

'Not if they think Jack was involved.'

'Cooper will set them straight.'

'Does that mean I won't have to say anything? I don't want to say anything.' The words came out in a rush. 'I'm so frightened,' she said simply, tears welling tragically in the huge dark eyes. 'I don't want anyone to know' – her voice shook – 'I'm so ashamed.'

Sarah, who had had to use a very heavy hand in the shape of emotional blackmail to get her this far, balked at using any more. The girl was in a highly emotional state already, desperately seeking to justify her mother's indifference because then she could justify her own indifference to the growing foetus inside her. But she couldn't justify it, of course, and that made her guilt about wanting an abortion

all the stronger. There was no logic to human psychology, thought Sarah sadly. She had said nothing about her visit to Cedar House, merely offered to drive Ruth over to Fontwell. 'In fairness,' she had said, 'all your mother knows is that you've been expelled for going out to meet your boyfriend. I'm sure she'll be sympathetic if you tell her the truth.' Ruth shook her head. 'She wouldn't,' she whispered, 'she'd say I got what I deserved. She used to say it to Granny about her arthritis.' Her face had pinched in pain. 'I wish Granny hadn't died. I did love her, you know, but she died thinking I didn't.' And what could Sarah say to that? She had never come across three people so intent on destroying each other, and themselves.

She put her arm now around the girl's thin shoulders and hugged her tight. 'Sergeant Cooper will sort it out,' she said firmly, 'and he won't force you to say anything you don't want to.' She gave her throaty chuckle. 'He's far too nice and far too soft which is why he's never made Inspector.'

But the law, like the mills of God, grinds slow but exceeding small, and Sarah knew that if any of them emerged unscathed at the end of their brush with it, it would be a miracle.

'You realize, Dr Blakeney, we could charge you with being an accessory before the fact,' said an irate Inspector. 'You knew when you helped your husband get hold of Hughes's address that he planned to do something illegal, didn't you?'

'I wouldn't answer that,' said Keith.

'No, I did not,' said Sarah stoutly. 'And what's illegal

about preventing a brutal rape? Since when was rescuing somebody a chargeable offence?'

'You're in the wrong ballpark, Doctor. We're talking attempted murder, GBH, abduction, driving without due care and attention, assault on a police officer. You name it, it's down here. Your husband's an extremely dangerous man and you sent him off after Hughes, knowing full well that he was liable to lose control of his temper if confronted. That's a fair summary, isn't it?'

'I wouldn't answer that,' said Keith automatically.

'Of course it isn't,' she snapped. '*Hughes* is the extremely dangerous man, not Jack. What would you have done if you knew a young girl was about to be brutally attacked by five zombies who are so degenerate and uneducated they'll do anything their sadistic leader tells them to do?' Her eyes flashed. 'Don't bother to answer. I know exactly what you'd have done. You'd have crept off with your tail between your legs to the nearest telephone to dial nine-nine-nine, and never mind the damage that was done to the child in the meantime.'

'It's an offence to withhold information from the police. Why did you not inform us about Miss Lascelles's rape?'

'I really do advise you not to answer that question,' said Keith wearily.

'Because we gave her our word we wouldn't. Why on earth do you think Jack went out tonight if we could have told the police everything?'

Keith held up his hand to forestall the Inspector. 'Any objections to switching off the tape while I confer with my client?'

The other man eyed him for a moment then consulted

his watch. 'Interview with Dr Blakeney suspended at 3.42 a.m.' He spoke abruptly, then pressed the 'stop' button.

'Thanks. Now, will you explain something to me, Sarah?' Keith murmured plaintively. 'Why did you drag me all the way down here if neither you nor Jack will listen to a word I say?'

'Because I'm so bloody angry, that's why. They should be grateful to Jack; instead they're condemning him.'

'The Inspector's paid to make you angry. That's how he gets his results, and you're making this very easy for him.'

'I object to that remark, Mr Smollett. I am paid, among other things, to try and get at the truth when a criminal offence has occurred.'

'Then why don't you stop bull-shitting,' suggested Keith amiably, 'and deal in straightforward fact? I can't be the only one here who's bored stiff with all these idiotic threats of criminal prosecution. Of course you can charge Mr Blakeney if you want to, but you'll be a laughing-stock. How many people these days would have bothered to go in and do what he did with only a belt and a torch as protection?' He smiled faintly. 'We're a non-involvement society these days, where heroism is confined to the television screens. There was a case the other day where a woman was sexually assaulted by two men in full view of several taxi-drivers at a taxi rank, and not a single one of them lifted a finger to help her. Worse, they wheeled up their windows to block out her screams for help. Should I infer from your attitude towards Mr Blakeney that that is the sort of behaviour you approve of in our so-called civilized society?'

'Vigilante behaviour is just as dangerous, Mr Smollett.

For every case of non-involvement you cite, I can cite another where rough justice has been meted out on innocent people because a lynch mob decides arbitrarily who is or is not guilty. Should I infer from your attitude that you approve of the kangaroo-court approach to justice?'

Keith acknowledged the point with a nod. 'Of course not,' he said honestly, 'and had Mr Blakeney taken a private army with him I'd be on your side. But you're on very thin ice describing him as a lynch mob. He was one man, faced with an impossible decision – to act immediately to stop the rape or to abandon the girl to her fate while he drove off to summon assistance.'

'He would never have been there at all had he and his wife not conspired together to withhold the information about Miss Lascelles. Nor for that matter would Hughes and his gang have been able to subject the young lady Mr Blakeney rescued to the terror she was put through, for the simple reason that they would all have been under lock and key charged with the rape of Miss Lascelles.'

'But Miss Lascelles has told you categorically that she would have been too frightened to say anything to the police, assuming the Blakeneys had reported what she told them. She lives in terror of Hughes carrying out his threat to rape her again the minute he's set free, and there's no guarantee, even now, that she – or tonight's victim – will find the courage to give the evidence in court that will convict him. Your best bet, quite frankly, is Jack Blakeney's testimony. If he remains strong, which he will, Ruth will gain courage from his example, and if the other girl and her parents are made aware of just what they owe him, then she, too, may find the courage to speak out. By the same

token, if you insist on pursuing these charges against Blakeney, then you can kiss goodbye to any co-operation from two terrified young women. Quite reasonably they will conclude that justice is on Hughes's side and not on theirs.'

The Inspector shook his head. 'What none of you seems able to grasp,' he said irritably, 'is that if we fail to charge Mr Blakeney we make the prosecution case against Hughes so much harder. His defence will have a field day in court pointing up the contrast between police leniency towards the *admitted* violence of a middle-class intellectual and police harshness towards the *alleged* violence of an unemployed navvy. Hughes was outside the van, remember, when the rape was taking place, and he's sitting there now claiming he had no idea what was going on. The lad who was raping the girl when your client burst into that van is only fifteen, a juvenile, in other words, who can be sentenced to detention but not to custody in an adult prison. The oldest boy there, if we exclude Hughes, is eighteen and his age will be taken into account at his trial. At the moment, they're all shell-shocked and fingering Hughes as the instigator and prime mover, but by the time they come to trial it will have become a bit of harmless fun that was the girl's idea and which Hughes knew nothing about because he had wandered off for a walk along the beach. The worst of it is, Mr Blakeney will have to testify to that in court because he saw him doing it.' He rubbed his tired eyes. 'It's a mess, frankly. God knows if we will ever succeed in bringing a conviction. Without clear evidence of intent I can see Hughes getting off scot-free. His MO is to manipulate youngsters into doing his dirty work while he stands

aloof and collects the money, and once these boys realize how short their sentences are going to be because the law is relatively powerless against juveniles, they'll stop grassing him up. I'm so confident of that, I'd lay my last cent on it.'

There was a long silence.

Sarah cleared her throat. 'You're forgetting the girls,' she said. 'Won't their evidence carry weight?'

The Inspector's smile was twisted. 'If they're not too frightened to testify, if they don't collapse under cross-examination, if their stealing isn't used by the defence to blacken their characters, if the speed with which they were prepared to spread their legs for Hughes doesn't lose them the sympathy of the jury.' He shrugged. 'Justice is as fickle as fate, Dr Blakeney.'

'Then release him now and be done with it,' she said coldly. 'I mean, let's face it, it's going to be a damn sight easier to fill your productivity quota by prosecuting Jack than by having to put the counselling effort into bringing thieving little tarts up to scratch. Perhaps you should ask yourself why none of these girls felt confident enough to come to the police in the first place?' Her eyes narrowed angrily as she answered her own question. 'Because they believed everything Hughes told them, namely that *he* would always be acquitted, and *they* would always be left to fend for themselves. He was right, too, though I'd never have guessed it if I hadn't heard it from you.'

'He'll be charged and hopefully he'll be held on remand, Dr Blakeney, but what happens at trial is out of my hands. We can do our best to prepare the ground. We cannot, unfortunately, predict the outcome.' He sighed. 'For the moment, I have decided to release your husband without

charge. I shall be taking advice, however, which means we may decide to proceed against him at a later date. In the meantime, he will be required to remain at Mill House in Long Upton and, should he wish to travel anywhere, he must advise Detective Sergeant Cooper of his intentions. Is that clear?'

She nodded.

'In addition, please note that if he ever involves himself again in similar activities to those he engaged in tonight, he will be charged immediately. Is that also clear?'

She nodded.

The Inspector's tired face cracked into a smile. 'Off the record, I rather agree with Mr Smollett here. Your husband's a brave man, Doctor, but I'm sure you knew that already.'

'Oh, yes,' said Sarah loyally, hoping that her expression was less sheepish than it felt. For as long as she'd known him Jack had always maintained the same thing. All men were cowards but it was only a few, like himself, who had the courage to admit it. She was beginning to wonder if there were other aspects of his character that she had misjudged so completely.

Father rang today to give me the inquest verdict on Gerald's death. 'They've opted for misadventure, thank God, but I had to pull every string in the book to get it. That damned Coroner was going to bring in suicide if he could.' Poor Father! He could never have shown his face in the House again if his brother had killed himself. Heaven forbid! What stigma is still attached to suicide, particularly amongst the upper classes. Nothing is so bad as the ultimate weakness of taking one's own life.

I am naturally delighted with the verdict, if somewhat piqued to have my brilliance overlooked. There is an extraordinary urge to confess, I find, if only to draw attention to what one has achieved . . . I won't, of course.

Gerald was putty in my hands when it came to writing the codicil because I told him he'd go to prison for raping his niece if he didn't. 'Lord, what fools these mortals be!' The only purpose of the codicil was to convince the idiot solicitor that Gerald had committed suicide when he discovered whose child Joanna really was. Once persuaded, he alerted Father to the fact that a document detailing Gerald's incest existed, and they both performed to perfection. They made such a song-

and-dance about pulling their various strings in order to suppress any hint that Gerald might have done away with himself that everyone, including the Coroner, was in no doubt that he had. It is all so very amusing. My only regret is that I had to involve Jane, but I am not unduly concerned about that. Even if she does have any suspicions, she won't voice them. She can't afford to, but in any case no one has questioned where Gerald acquired his barbiturates, or if they have I suspect Father has claimed them as his. He's so drunk most of the time, he probably believes they were.

Father's relief was short-lived. I told him I had a signed carbon copy of the codicil in my possession and he became apoplectic at the other end of the wire. He calls it blackmail. I call it self-preservation . . .

Sixteen

Two faxes were waiting on Cooper's desk when he arrived at the station later that morning. The first was brief and to the point:

> Fingerprints on Yale key, ref: TC/H/MG/320, identified as belonging to Sarah Penelope Blakeney. 22 point agreement. No other prints. Fingerprints on bottle, ref: TC/H/MG/321 agree in 10, 16 and 12 points respectively with prints located in Cedar House on desk (room 1), chair (room 1), and decanter (room 1). Full report to follow.

The second fax was longer and rather more interesting. After he had read it, Cooper went off in search of PC Jenkins. It was Jenkins, he recalled, who had done most of the tedious legwork around Fontwell in the days following Mrs Gillespie's death.

'I hear you've been busy,' said Charlie Jones, dunking a ginger biscuit into a cup of thick white coffee.

Cooper sank into an armchair. 'Hughes, you mean.'

'I'm going down there in half an hour to have another bash at him. Do you want to come?'

'No thanks. I've had more than enough of Dave Hughes and his fellow-lowlife to last me a lifetime. You wait till you see them, Charlie. Kids, for Christ's sake. Fifteen-year-olds who look twenty-five and have a mental age of eight. It scares me, it really does. If society doesn't do something to educate them and match a man's brain to a man's body, we haven't a hope of survival. And the worst of it is, it's not just us. I saw a ten-year-old boy on the telly the other day, wielding a machine gun in Somalia as part of some rebel army. I've seen children in Ireland throwing bricks at whichever side their bigoted families tell them to, adolescent Palestinian boys strutting their stuff in balaclavas, negro lads in South Africa necklacing each other because white policemen think it's a great way to get rid of them, and Serbian boys encouraged to rape Muslim girls the way their fathers do. It's complete and utter madness. We corrupt our children at our peril, but by God we're doing a fine job of it.'

Charlie eyed him sympathetically. 'Not just a busy night, obviously, but an exhausting one, too.'

'Forget *in vino veritas*,' said Cooper acidly. '*In insomnio veritas* is more like it. I wake up in the early hours of the morning sometimes and see the world as it really is. A bear garden, with religious leaders twisting souls on one side, power-corrupt politicians twisting minds on the other side, and the illiterate, intolerant masses in the middle baying for blood because they're too uneducated to do anything else.'

'Stop the world I want to get off, eh?'

'That's about the size of it.'

'Are there no redeeming features, Tommy?'

Cooper chuckled. 'Sure, as long as no one reminds me of Hughes.' He passed the first fax across the desk-top. 'Gillespie never left the sitting-room, apparently, and the key's a dead-end.'

Jones looked disappointed. 'We need something concrete, old son, and quickly. I'm being pushed to drop this one and concentrate on something that will get a result. The consensus view is that, even if we do manage to prove it was murder, we're going to have the devil's own job bringing a prosecution.'

'I wonder where I've heard that before,' said Cooper sourly. 'If things go on like this, we might as well pack it in and let the anarchists have a go.'

'What about the diaries? Any progress there?'

'Not really. The search was a wash-out, but then I knew it would be. I went through every book in the library the first time we searched Cedar House.' He frowned. 'I had a word with Jack and Ruth last night, but they're claiming ignorance as well, although Jack does remember Mrs Gillespie being in a paddy one day because she said her books were being disturbed.' He fingered his lip. 'I know it's hypothetical but, let's say the diaries did exist and that someone was looking for them, then that might at least explain why the books were disturbed.'

Charlie snorted. 'Hellishly hypothetical,' he agreed, 'and quite unprovable.'

'Yes, but if whoever was looking for them found them, then it might explain why they've been removed.' He took pity on Charlie's baffled expression. 'Because,' he said patiently, 'they could tell us who murdered her and why.'

Charlie frowned. 'You're clutching at straws. First, convince me they existed.'

'Why would James Gillespie lie?'

'Because he's a drunk,' said Charlie. 'You don't need any better reason than that.'

'Then why was Mathilda in a paddy because her books were being disturbed? Explain that, or are you suggesting Jack's lying, too?'

Charlie registered this second use of 'Jack' with an inward sigh. When would the silly fellow learn that it was his inability to keep his distance that scuppered his chances every time? *Unprofessional. Cannot remain objective*, was what Jones's predecessor had written on Cooper's last assessment. 'She must have guessed who it was,' he said. 'It's a narrow field in all conscience. Why didn't she tackle them about it?'

'Perhaps she did. Perhaps that's why she was murdered.' Cooper tapped the fax with his forefinger. 'The key complicates it, though. If whoever it was knew about that, then they could have let themselves in without her knowing. The field becomes much wider then.'

'I suppose you've considered that Gillespie's our man, and only mentioned the diaries to you because he thought everyone else would have known about them.'

'Yes. But why would he take them away and deny all knowledge if he's expecting them to prove she diddled him over the clocks?'

'Double bluff. He read them, discovered they proved the exact opposite, so destroyed them in order to keep his claim alive, then topped her to give himself a free run with Mrs Lascelles who he thought was going to inherit.'

Cooper shook his head. 'It's a possibility, I suppose, but it doesn't feel right. If he stole them himself because he knew they'd destroy his chances of any money, how could he be sure no one else had read them first? It's too iffy, Charlie.'

'It's *all* too iffy, frankly,' said the Inspector dryly. 'If the diaries existed – if the searcher *knew* they existed – if there was something incriminating in them – if he or she knew about the key . . .' He fell silent, dunking his biscuit again. 'There are two things I don't understand. Why did Mrs Gillespie leave all her money to Dr Blakeney and why did her murderer put the scold's bridle on her head and deck it out with nettles and daisies? If I knew the answers to those two questions, I could probably tell you who killed her. Otherwise I'm inclined to make do with a verdict of suicide.'

'I think I know why she left the money to Dr Blakeney.'

'Why?'

'I reckon it was a Pontius Pilate exercise. She'd done a lousy job herself bringing up her daughter and granddaughter, knew they'd destroy themselves with jealous infighting if she left the money to them, so passed the buck to the only person she'd ever got on with and respected. Namely Dr Blakeney. I think she hoped the doctor would succeed where she hadn't.'

'Sentimental twaddle,' said the Inspector amiably. 'And all because you're reasoning backwards, from the effect you see to the cause you imagine a normal person would wish to achieve. Try reasoning forwards. She was a bloody-minded, mean and vicious old woman, who not only acquired a fortune through blackmail and creative insurance scams but also loathed and despised everyone around her for most of her life. Why, having sown nothing but discord

for sixty years, did she suddenly endow an easy-going, pleasant stranger with a fortune? Not for the sake of harmony, that's for sure.' The Inspector's eyes narrowed thoughtfully. 'I can go along with the scold's bridle as a sort of symbolic drawing attention to the final curbing of a peculiarly unpleasant tongue, but I cannot go along with the idea that the leopard suddenly changed its spots when it came to making the will.'

'You can't ignore the Blakeneys' view of her character, Charlie. According to them, she was a much pleasanter person than anyone else credited her with being. My guess is they gave her room to breathe, didn't demand anything and the real Mathilda blossomed.' He paused for a moment and took stock. 'Think about this. We've been dwelling on the symbolism of the scold's bridle, largely because of Ophelia's "nettles, daisies and long purples", but look at it in practical terms instead. They were used to keep women quiet, and perhaps the reason she was wearing it was as simple as that. Her murderer didn't want her alerting the next-door neighbours by screaming her head off, so shoved that contraption on her head and then adorned it with flowers to give it a mystical – but misleading – significance.'

Jones steepled his fingers under his chin. 'But she must have taken the barbiturates first or she'd have struggled when the bridle was put on and there'd have been scratches on her face. If she was so doped up that she didn't bother to fight it, then why put it on at all?'

'Do what you told me to do and reason forwards. You want to kill a woman by making it look like suicide, but the neighbours are too close for comfort so you need a method of keeping her quiet in case the barbiturates aren't as

effective as you hope. A belt and braces job in other words. You can't use tape or Elastoplast because it'll leave a mark on the skin, and you're canny enough not to use a gag in case bits of fabric are found in the mouth during the post mortem, so you pitch on something you can leave in place which has its own significance to the victim, and you trust to luck that the police will put it down as a macabre example of self-condemnation. Then you carry her to the bath, clasp your hands over hers while you slit each wrist, drop the knife to the floor and leave her to die, knowing that even if she does struggle back to consciousness, the bridle will prevent her calling for help.'

Jones nodded. 'It sounds feasible, but why bother with the bath and the Stanley knife at all? Why not simply overdose her on sleeping pills and kill her that way?'

'Because there weren't enough, presumably, and even if there were, they're very unreliable. Supposing Ruth had come back the next morning and found the old lady still alive. It might have been possible to pump her out and revive her. Plus, of course, Ophelia drowned herself which may have inspired the idea.' He smiled self-consciously. 'I've read the play to see if there are any clues in it and a blood-thirsty piece it is, too. There's no one left standing by the end.'

'Did you find any clues?'

'No.'

'I'm not surprised. It was written four hundred years ago.' Jones tapped his pencil against his teeth. 'I can't see that any of this makes much difference, frankly. You're still describing someone who knew her intimately, which is what we've believed from the start. The only new pieces of

information are the discovery of the key and the absence of the diaries. I admit the key may mean that her murderer came in uninvited, but it still had to be someone very close to her or she'd have screamed her head off. And there's so much intimate detail involved – the Stanley knife, the sleeping pills, her yen for Shakespeare, the scold's bridle. Whoever it was probably even knew there were nettles and daisies in her garden *and* where to find them in the dark. And someone *that* close means the Blakeneys, the Lascelles women or Mr and Mrs Spede.'

Cooper took the second fax from his notebook and spread it on the desk. 'According to the fingerprint tests we made, bearing in mind I told the lab to get a move on so these results will have to be double-checked for accuracy, they've made tentative identifications on four of the prints in that house, excluding Mrs Gillespie herself, Mrs Spede, the Blakeneys, Mrs and Miss Lascelles and now James Gillespie. The four are . . .' he ran his finger slowly down the page, 'the Reverend Matthews, matched in ten points with print located on hall mirror; Mrs Orloff, matched in sixteen points with print located on kitchen worktop and in fourteen points with print found on kitchen door; Mrs Spencer, matched in twelve points with print on hall door; and, lastly, Mrs Jane Marriott, matched in eighteen points with two prints on desk in library and one on stair newel post.' He looked up. 'Mrs Orloff is her neighbour. Mrs Spencer runs the local shop and Mrs Marriott is the receptionist at the Fontwell surgery. What's interesting is that the Reverend Matthews, Mrs Orloff and Mrs Spencer all admitted quite happily that they had been inside the house in the week before Mrs Gillespie died. Mrs Marriott

didn't. According to Jenkins who interviewed her when he was going door to door, she said she hadn't been near Cedar House for years.'

With careless disregard for the restrictions placed on his movements by the Bournemouth police, Jack waited until Sarah had left for work then set off for Fontwell on the old bicycle that Geoffrey Freeling's next-of-kin had abandoned in the garage. His car was in the pound at Freemont Road and looked like remaining there indefinitely until a decision was reached on whether or not to prosecute him, but he was deeply suspicious about their motives for holding it. They had claimed it was material evidence, but he saw Keith's devious hand at work behind the Inspector. It's unreasonable to expect Dr Blakeney to guard her husband for you, so deprive Jack of his wheels, and he may stay put. For once he was grateful to Smollett's lingering partiality for his wife.

Ruth was dead to the world upstairs, worn out by the mental and physical stress that had taken its toll of her all too meagre reserves the previous night, but he left a note on the kitchen table in case she woke up and panicked to find him gone: 'You're quite safe with Hughes in the nick,' it read, 'but don't answer the door to anyone, just in case. Back soon, love Jack.'

'Mrs Marriott?' Cooper leant on the receptionist's counter in the empty surgery and held up his warrant card. 'DS Cooper, Learmouth Police.'

Jane smiled automatically. 'How can I help you, Sergeant?'

'I'd like a word or two in private, if that's possible.'

'It's private enough here for the moment,' she said. 'The only thing likely to disturb us is the telephone. Would you care for a cup of coffee?'

'Thank you. White, two sugars, please.'

She busied herself with the kettle.

'We've had some interesting results from our fingerprint tests,' said Cooper to her back. 'One way and another the evidence points to quite a few people visiting Mrs Gillespie before she died. You, for example.'

Jane became very still suddenly. 'I hoped you wouldn't find out,' she admitted after a moment, plucking invisible fluff from her jumper. 'And then, of course, you invited us all to give examples of our fingerprints. It was very difficult to know what to do then. Should I confess that I'd told a lie the first time or sit it out in the hopes I hadn't touched anything?'

'Why didn't you want us to know you'd been to Cedar House?'

'Because you'd have asked me my reason for going.'

He nodded. 'Which was?'

She turned back to the coffee cups and poured out the water. 'It had nothing to do with Mathilda's death, Sergeant. It was a very private matter.'

'I'm afraid that really won't do, Mrs Marriott.'

She pushed a cup across the counter and placed the sugar bowl and a spoon beside it. 'Will you arrest me if I refuse to tell you?'

He chuckled good-humouredly. 'Not immediately.'

'When?'

He sidestepped the question. 'If I say to you that, as long as what you tell me really does have no bearing on Mrs Gillespie's death, it will go no further than these four walls, will you trust me enough to keep my word?' He held her gaze with his. 'You've no idea of the sort of publicity you'll face if I have to take you in for questioning. Once the press have their teeth into you, they don't let go easily.'

Jane's plump homely face took on a very bleak expression. 'How Mathilda would adore this if she were still alive,' she said. 'She loved making trouble.'

'You knew her well then.'

'Too well.'

'And you didn't like her?'

'I couldn't bear her. I tried to avoid her as far as I could but that wasn't very easy once I started working here, what with phone calls demanding a doctor's visit and requests for repeat prescriptions.'

'Yet you went to see her?'

'I had to. I saw James coming out of her house the day before she died.' She held a hand to her bosom. 'It was such a shock. I thought he was in Hong Kong.' She fell silent.

'Tell me about it,' Cooper prompted gently.

'You wouldn't understand,' said Jane with conviction. 'You didn't know Mathilda.'

Jack was in a very bad mood by the time he reached Cedar House. He hadn't ridden a bicycle in years, and four miles along rutted country lanes on something that should have been condemned to the scrap heap years ago had given him

sore balls and the sort of trembling thighs that would have disgraced a nonagenarian. He abandoned the bicycle against a tree in the Cedar Housing Estate, vaulted the fence and ran lightly across the grass to the kitchen window. For reasons of his own, he had no intention of announcing his presence by approaching across the gravel or using the front doorbell.

He tapped lightly but persistently on the window pane, and after a minute or two, Joanna appeared in the doorway that led from the kitchen into the hall. 'What do you want?'

He read her lips, rather than heard the words, and gestured towards the back door. 'Let me in,' he mouthed, his voice barely above a whisper.

Jane's eyes narrowed as she looked back down the corridors of time. 'You see, you can't assess Mathilda on what people tell you now. They've forgotten how beautiful she was as a young woman, how witty she was and how many men desired her. She was the most eligible girl around – her father was the MP, her uncle was a wealthy bachelor – ' she shrugged ' – she could have married anybody.'

'Then why didn't she?'

'At the time everyone assumed she was hanging on for something better, a title perhaps, or a stately home with acres, but I always thought there was more to it than that. I used to watch her at parties and it was very clear to me that, while she enjoyed flirting and being the centre of attention, she couldn't bear men touching her.' She fell silent.

'Go on,' Cooper prompted after a moment or two.

'It wasn't until ten years later when my husband and I met James in Hong Kong and he told us the truth about Joanna's parentage that it made sense.' She sighed. 'Not that I've ever really understood exactly what happened because, of course, child abuse and incest were kept under wraps in those days. James believed she encouraged Gerald, but I never did. It's the one area where I always felt sorry for her. She was emotionally crippled by it, I think.'

'So you've known for a long time that Mrs Lascelles wasn't James Gillespie's daughter?'

'Yes.'

'Did Mrs Gillespie know you knew?'

'Oh, yes.'

'Didn't that worry her?'

'She knew I wouldn't tell anyone.'

'How could she know?'

'She just did,' said Jane flatly.

What was it James Gillespie had called it? Mutual insurance.

Without warning, as the back door closed behind him, Jack's huge hand circled Joanna's throat and drove her through the kitchen and into the hall. 'Didn't what happened to Mathilda teach you anything, you silly bitch?' he said in a savage undertone.

Cooper took out a cigarette, remembered where he was and put it back again. 'Was it you who was friendly with Mr Gillespie, or your husband?' he asked Jane.

'Paul and he went through the war together, but I'd known him a long time as well.'

'Why did it shock you so much to see him coming out of Cedar House that day?'

'I'd always hoped he was dead.' She sighed. 'I know you've seen him. Sarah told me. Did he tell you anything?'

'About what, Mrs Marriott?'

She gave a tired smile. 'You'd know if he'd told you, Sergeant.'

'Then I don't think he can have done,' he said honestly. 'But you're obviously afraid he will, so wouldn't it be better coming from you? I presume it's something that only you, he and Mathilda were privy to. You were confident she wouldn't say anything because you could reveal the truth about Joanna's father, but he's a different matter. You have no hold over him, which is why you were so shocked to see him back in England and why you went to see Mathilda, to find out if he was going to spill the beans. Am I right?'

Joanna showed only the slightest flicker of alarm before she relaxed against the wall and stared into his eyes with a look of triumph. 'I knew you'd come back.'

He didn't say anything, just searched her beautiful face and marvelled again at its absolute perfection. It was the face of the Madonna in Michelangelo's Pietà, the face of a mother gazing down in quiet contemplation on the body of her adored son, a study of such simple purity that it had brought tears to his eyes when he first saw it. For years, he had wondered about the woman behind the Madonna. Was she real? Or was she something fabulous that Michelangelo

had conjured from his own imagination? Until Joanna, he had believed she must have existed in the eye of her creator because only an artist could have made a thing of such immeasurable beauty. Now he held it beneath his hand and knew that its conception had been as random and as accidental as his own. He closed his eyes to stem the tears that threatened to well again.

Jane nodded unhappily. 'James blackmailed me for five years after we returned home from Hong Kong. In the end, I paid him over ten thousand pounds, which was all the money my mother left me.' Her voice shook. 'He stopped when I sent him copies of my bank statement which showed I had nothing more to give him, but he warned me he'd come back.' She was silent for a moment, striving for control. 'I never saw or heard from him again until that awful day when he came out of Cedar House.'

Cooper studied her bent head with compassion. He could only assume she'd had an affair that James and Mathilda Gillespie had found out about, but why was it so hard to confess to all these years on? 'Everyone has skeletons somewhere in their closet, Mrs Marriott. Mine still bring a blush to my cheeks when I think about them. But do you really think your husband would hold yours against you after thirty-odd years?'

'Oh, yes,' she said honestly. 'Paul always wanted children, you see, and I could never give him any.'

Cooper waited for her to go on but, when she didn't, he prompted her gently: 'What do children have to do with it?'

'Paul had an affair with Mathilda and Mathilda got pregnant. That's why James went to Hong Kong. He said it was the last straw, that he might have coped with Gerald's incestuous bastard but not with Paul's love child as well.'

Cooper was very taken aback. 'And that's what James was blackmailing you over?' But no, he thought, that didn't make sense. It was the adulterous husband who paid the blackmailer not the deceived wife.

'Not about the affair,' said Jane. 'I knew all about that. Paul told me himself after he resigned. He was Sir William's agent and used to stay with James and Mathilda in their flat in London whenever he had business in town. I don't think the affair was anything more than a brief infatuation on both their parts. She was bored with the tedious domestic routine of washing nappies and keeping house and he . . .' she sighed, 'he was flattered by the attention. You really must try to understand how captivating Mathilda could be, and it wasn't just beauty, you know. There was something about her that drew men like magnets. I think it was the remoteness, the dislike of being touched. They saw it as a challenge, so when she let her guard down for Paul, he fell for it.' She gave a sad little smile. 'And I understood that, believe me. It may sound odd to you but there was a time – when we were young – when I was almost as in love with her as he was. She was everything I always wanted to be and never was.' Her eyes filled. 'Well, you know how attractive she could be. Sarah fell in love with her, just the way I did.'

*

'Show me how much you love me, Jack.' Joanna's voice, soft and husky, was a lover's caress.

Gently his fingers smoothed the white column of her throat. How could someone so ugly be *so* beautiful? She made a mockery of the wonder of creation. He raised his other hand to the silver-gold hair and, with a violent twist, wrapped the strands around his palm and jerked her head backwards with his fingers still clamped about her throat. 'I love you this much,' he said quietly.

'You're hurting me.' This time her voice rose in alarm.

He tightened his grip on her hair. 'But I enjoy hurting you, Joanna.' His voice echoed through the emptiness of the hall.

'I don't understand,' she cried out, her voice rasping against his fingers on her larynx. 'What do you want?' She saw something in his eyes that brought the fear leaping into hers. 'Oh, my God. It was you who killed my mother.' She opened her mouth to scream but only a thread of sound came out as the pressure on her throat tightened.

'I'm sorry if I'm being particularly slow on the uptake,' said Cooper apologetically, 'but I don't quite see what hold James Gillespie could have had over you that would prompt you to pay him ten thousand pounds. If you already knew about the affair from your husband—' he broke off. 'It was something to do with the pregnancy, presumably. Did you not know about that?'

She compressed her lips in an effort to hold back tears. 'Yes, I did. It was Paul who never knew.' She drew another

deep sigh. 'It's so awful. I've kept it secret for so long. I wanted to tell him but there was never a good time. Rather like the lie I told your constable. At what point do you come clean, as it were?' She touched her fingers to her lips in a gesture of despair. 'Being a father. It was all he ever wanted. I prayed and prayed that we would have children of our own, but of course we never did . . .' She tailed off into silence.

Cooper put a large, comforting hand over hers. He was completely at sea here, but was reluctant to press too hard in case she clammed up on him. 'How did you know about the pregnancy if your husband didn't?'

'Mathilda told me. She rang me and asked me to go to London, said if I didn't she'd make sure the whole of Fontwell knew about her and Paul. He'd written her some letters and she said she'd make them public if I didn't do what she wanted.'

'What did she want?'

It was some moments before she could speak. 'She wanted me to help her murder the baby when it came.'

'Good God!' said Cooper with feeling. And she must have done it, he thought, or James Gillespie would never have been able to blackmail her.

There was the sound of footsteps on the gravel outside and a ring on the doorbell. 'Joanna!' called Violet's high-pitched, nervous voice. 'Joanna! Are you all right, dear? I thought I *heard* something.' When she received no answer, she called again: 'Is someone with you? Do answer, please.' Her voice rose even higher. 'Duncan! Duncan!' she called.

'There *is* something wrong. I know there is. You must call the police. I'm going to get help.' Her footsteps skittered away as she ran towards the gate.

Jack stared down into Joanna's drawn and haunted face, then lowered her with surprising gentleness on to the nearest chair. 'You don't deserve it, but you were luckier than your mother,' was all he said, before walking off towards the kitchen and the back door.

Joanna Lascelles was still screaming when Duncan Orloff, in a state of complete panic, used a sledgehammer to break open the front door and confront whatever awaited him in the hall of Cedar House.

'And did you help her?' Cooper asked with a calm that belied his true feelings.

She looked wretched. 'I don't know – I don't know what she did – I can only guess.' She wrung her hands in distress. 'She didn't say anything in so many words. She just asked me to steal some sleeping pills – barbiturates – from my father's dispensary. She said they were for her because she couldn't sleep. I hoped – I thought – she was going to kill herself – and I was glad. I hated her by that time.'

'So you got her the pills?'

'Yes.'

'But she didn't kill herself.'

'No.'

'But you said she wanted you to help her kill the baby.'

'That's what I thought for ten years.' The long-held-back tears oozed slowly from between her lids. 'There was only Joanna, you see. The other baby might never have

existed. I didn't think it had ever existed.' She held a shaking hand to her face. 'I thought I'd helped her kill it – and then in Hong Kong, James kept asking me how Gerald could have killed himself with barbiturates, because no doctor would have prescribed them for him, and I realized it was Gerald she'd wanted to kill all along, and I'd given her the means to do it.' She took out a handkerchief and blew her nose. 'I was so *shocked* that James guessed what I'd done. I think he'd always known, though. In many ways, he and Mathilda were very alike.'

Cooper sought desperately to break this down into manageable proportions. There were so many unanswered questions. 'Why would no doctor prescribe barbiturates for Gerald Cavendish? I've checked the coroner's report. There was no question of murder, only a choice between misadventure and suicide.'

'Gerald was . . .' Jane sought for the right word, 'feeble-minded, I suppose, like the Spedes, but today they call it educationally subnormal. It's why the property was kept intact for William. Mathilda's grandfather was afraid Gerald would give it away to anyone who asked for it. But I've never really understood how Mathilda came to sleep with him. He was a very pathetic person. I've always assumed her father forced her into it to protect his legacy somehow, but James said it was all Mathilda's idea. I don't believe that. James hated her so much he'd have said anything to blacken her.'

Cooper shook his head in bewilderment. How uneventful his own life had been, compared with the agonies of this grey-haired motherly soul who looked as if butter wouldn't melt in her mouth. 'Why did you visit James Gillespie in

Hong Kong if your husband had had an affair with his wife? There can't have been much love lost between the three of you in all conscience.'

'We didn't or at least not like that. We had no idea James had gone to Hong Kong. Mathilda never told us – why would she? – and we moved away from here after the affair and went to live in Southampton. I became a teacher and Paul worked for a shipping company. We put it all behind us, and then Paul had to go to Hong Kong on business and took me with him for a holiday.' She shook her head. 'And almost the first person we met when we arrived was James. The expatriate community was so small' – she raised her hands in a gesture of helplessness – 'we were bound to meet him. If we'd only known he was there, we'd never have gone. Fate is very cruel, Sergeant.'

He couldn't argue with that. 'Then why did you come back here to live, Mrs Marriott, knowing that Mrs Gillespie was in Cedar House? Weren't you tempting fate a second time?'

'Yes,' she said simply, 'but what could I do about it? Paul knows nothing of any of this, Sergeant, and he's dying – slowly – of emphysema. We kept our house here – it was his parents' house and he was too fond of it to sell it, so we let it out to tenants – and then five years ago, he was retired on health grounds and he begged me to let us come home.' Her eyes flooded again. 'He said I needn't worry about Mathilda, that the only thing he had ever felt for her was compassion, while the only woman he had ever loved was me. How could I tell him then what had really happened? I still thought his baby was dead.' She held her handkerchief to her streaming eyes. 'It wasn't until I went to Cedar

House and asked Mathilda about James that she told me she'd put the baby up for adoption.' She buried her face in her hands. 'It was a boy and he's still alive somewhere.'

Cooper pondered the sad ironies of life. Was it providence, God or random selection that made some women fertile and some barren? With a deep reluctance he took her back to the day Mathilda died, knowing there was little chance that what she told him could ever remain a secret.

I am pregnant again, sickeningly and disgustingly pregnant. Barely six months after giving birth to one bastard, I am carrying another. Perhaps James's drunken rages will achieve some good purpose by bringing on a miscarriage. He weeps and rants in turn, screaming insults at me like a fishwife, intent, it seems, on trumpeting my 'whorishness' to the entire building. And all for what? A brief, unlovely affair with Paul Marriott whose clumsy, apologetic gropings were almost past endurance. Then, why, Mathilda?

Because there are days when I could 'drink hot blood, and do such bitter business as the day would quake to look on'. Paul's priggishness annoyed me. He talked about 'dear Jane' as if she mattered to him. Mostly I think about death – the baby's death, James's death, Gerald's death, Father's death. It is, after all, such a final solution. Father connives to keep me in London. He tells me Gerald has sworn to marry Grace if I return. The worst of it is, I believe him. Gerald is so very, very frightened of me now.

I paid a private detective to take photographs of

James. And, my, my, what photographs they are! 'The fitchew nor the soiled horse goes to't with such a riotous appetite.' And in a public lavatory too. If the truth be told, I am rather looking forward to showing them to him. What I did was merely sinful. What James does is criminal. There'll be no more talk of divorce, that's for sure, and he'll go to Hong Kong without a murmur. He has no more desire than I to have his sexual activities made public.

Really, Mathilda, you must learn to use blackmail to better effect on Gerald and Father . . .

Seventeen

HUGHES, WHO WAS suffering from sleep deprivation and niggling doubts about the continued obedience of the youngsters he had so successfully controlled, was subdued when he faced Chief Inspector Charlie Jones across the table in the interview room at Freemont Road Police Station. Like Cooper, he was in pessimistic mood. 'I suppose you've come to stitch me up for the old cow's murder,' he said morosely. 'You're all the same.'

'Ah, well,' said Charlie in his lugubrious fashion, 'it makes the percentages look better when the league tables get published. We're into business culture in the police force these days, lad, and productivity's important.'

'That stinks.'

'Not to our customers it doesn't.'

'What customers?'

'The law-abiding British public who pay handsomely for our services through their taxes. Business culture demands that we first identify our client base, next, assess its needs, then, finally, respond in a satisfactory and adequate manner. You already represent a handsome profit on the balance sheet. Rape, conspiracy to rape, abduction, holding without

consent, conspiracy to hold without consent, assault, sexual assault, theft, conspiracy to commit theft, handling stolen goods, corruption, conspiracy to pervert the course of justice – ' he broke off with a broad smile – 'which brings me to Mrs Gillespie's murder.'

'I knew it,' said Hughes in disgust. 'You're gonna fucking frame me for it. Jesus! I'm not saying another word till my brief gets here.'

'Who said anything about framing you?' demanded Charlie plaintively. 'It's a little co-operation I'm after, that's all.'

Hughes eyed him suspiciously. 'What do I get in return?'

'Nothing.'

'Then it's no.'

Charlie's eyes narrowed to thin slits. 'The question you should have asked me, lad, is what do you get if you don't co-operate? I'll tell you. You get my personal assurance that not a stone will be left unturned until I see you convicted and sent down for the abduction and rape of a child.'

'I don't do children,' Hughes sneered. 'Never have done. Never will. And you won't get me for rape neither. I've never raped a girl in my life. I've never needed to. What those other punks did is their affair. I had no idea what was going on.'

'For an adult male to sleep with a thirteen-year-old girl is rape. She's under age and therefore too young to give consent for what's done to her.'

'I've never slept with a thirteen-year-old.'

'Sure you have, and I'll prove it. I'll work every man under me until he drops in order to turn up just one little

girl, *virgo intacta* before you raped her, who lied to you about her age.' He gave a savage grin as a flicker of doubt crossed Hughes's face. 'Because there'll be one, lad, there always is. It's an idiosyncrasy of female psychology. At thirteen, they want to pass for sixteen, and they do. At forty, they want to pass for thirty, and by God they can do that, too, because the one damn thing you can be sure about the female of the species is that she never looks her age.'

Hughes fingered his unshaven jaw. 'What sort of co-operation are you talking about?'

'I want a complete run-down on everything you know about Cedar House and the people in it.'

'That's easy enough. Fuck all's the answer. Never went in. Never met the old biddy.'

'Come on, Dave, you're a pro. You sat outside in your van over the months, waiting while Ruth did her stuff inside. You were her chauffeur, remember, turned up day after day during the holidays to give her a good time. How did she know you were there if you couldn't signal to her? Don't kid me you weren't close enough to watch all the comings and goings in that place.'

Hughes shrugged. 'Okay, so I saw people from time to time, but if I don't know who they were, how's it gonna help you?'

'Did you ever watch the back of the house?'

The man debated with himself. 'Maybe,' he said guardedly.

'Where from?'

'If you're aiming to use this against me, I want my brief.'

'You're in no position to argue,' said Charlie impatiently.

'Where were you watching it from? Outside or inside the garden?'

'I sometimes used to park the van in the housing estate at the side. Ruth reckoned it was safer, what with all the yuppies living there. Wives commuting to work along with their husbands so no one in during the day,' he explained obligingly. 'There's some rough ground next to the fence round Cedar House garden, easy enough to hop over and watch from the trees.'

The Inspector took an ordnance survey map out of his briefcase. 'The Cedar Estate?' he asked, tapping the map with his forefinger.

Hughes sniffed. 'Probably. Ruth said the land once belonged to the house before the old lady sold it off for cash, though Christ knows why she didn't flog the rest while she was about it. What she want with a massive garden, when there's people living on the streets? Jesus, but she was a tight-fisted old bitch,' he said unwarily. 'All that frigging money and no one else got a bloody look-in. Is it true she left the lot to her doctor or was Ruth just spinning me a yarn?'

Charlie stared him down. 'None of your business, lad, but I'll tell you this for free. Ruth didn't get a penny because of what you forced her to do. Her grandmother took agin her when she started stealing. But for you, she'd have had the house.'

Hughes was unmoved. 'Shouldn't have been so quick to open her legs then, should she?'

Charlie looked at the map again, fighting an urge to hit him. 'Did you ever see anyone go in through the back door?'

'The cleaner used to sweep the step now and again. Saw the woman from next door pottering about in her bit and the old boy sunning himself on his patio.'

'I mean strangers. Someone you wouldn't have expected.'

'I never *saw* anyone.' He put unnatural emphasis on the verb.

'Heard then?'

'Maybe.'

'Where were you? What did you hear?'

'I watched Mrs Gillespie go out in her car one day. Thought I'd take a look through the windows, see what was there.'

'Was Ruth with you?'

He shook his head. 'Back at school.'

'Refusing to co-operate, presumably, so you had to find out for yourself what was worth stealing. You were casing the place.'

Hughes didn't answer.

'Okay, what happened?'

'I heard the old lady coming round the path so I dived behind the coal bunker by the kitchen door.'

'Go on.'

'It wasn't her. It was some other bastard who was nosing around like me.'

'Male? Female?'

'An old man. He knocked on the back door and waited for a bit, then let himself in with a key.' Hughes pulled a face. 'So I legged it.' He saw the triumph on Jones's face. 'That what you wanted?'

'Could be. Did he have the key in his hand?'

'I wasn't looking.'

'Did you hear anything?'

'The knocking.'

'Anything else?'

'I heard a stone being moved after the knocking.'

The flowerpot. 'How do you know it was a man if you weren't looking?'

'He called out. "Jenny, Ruth, Mathilda, are you there?" It was a man all right.'

'Describe his voice.'

'Posh.'

'Old? Young? Forceful? Weak? Drunk? Sober? Pull your finger out, lad. What sort of impression did you get of him?'

'I already told you. I reckoned it was an old man. That's why I thought it was *her* coming back. He was really slow and his voice was all breathy, like he had trouble with his lungs. Or was very unfit.' He thought for a moment. 'He might have been drunk, though,' he added. 'He had real trouble getting the words out.'

'Did you go round the front afterwards?'

Dave shook his head. 'Hopped over the fence and went back to the van.'

'So you don't know if he came by car?'

'No.' A flash of something – *indecision?* – crossed his face.

'Go on,' prompted Jones.

'I'd never swear to it, so it's not evidence.'

'What isn't?'

'I was listening, if you get my meaning. He gave me a hell of a shock when I heard him coming so I reckon I'd've heard a car if there'd been one. That gravel at the front makes a hell of a row.'

'When was this?'

'Middle of September. Thereabouts.'

'Okay. Anything else?'

'Yeah.' He fingered his shoulder gingerly where Jack's car door had slammed into it. 'If you want to know who killed the old biddy then you should talk to the bastard who dislocated my fucking arm last night. I sussed him the minute I saw his face in the light. He was forever sniffing round her, in and out that place like he owned it, but he made damn sure Ruth wasn't there at the time. I spotted him two or three times up by the church, waiting till the coast was clear. Reckon he's the one you should be interested in if it's right what Ruth told me, that the old woman's wrists were slit with a Stanley knife.'

Charlie eyed him curiously. 'Why do you say that?'

'He cleaned one of the gravestones while he was waiting, scraped the dirt out of the words written on it. And not just the once neither. He was really fascinated by that stone.' He looked smug. 'Used a Stanley knife to do it, too, didn't he? I went and read it afterwards . . . "Did I deserve to be despised, By my creator, good and wise? Since you it was who made me be, Then part of you must die with me." Some bloke called Fitzgibbon who snuffed it in 1833. Thought I'd use it myself when the time came. Kind of hits the nail on the head, wouldn't you say?'

'You won't be given the chance. They censor epitaphs these days. Religion takes itself seriously now the congregations have started to vanish.' He stood up. 'A pity, really. Humour never harmed anyone.'

'You interested in him now then?'

'I've always been interested in him, lad.' Charlie smiled mournfully. 'Mrs Gillespie's death was very artistic.'

Cooper found the Inspector enjoying a late pint over cheese and onion sandwiches at the Dog and Bottle in Learmouth. He lowered himself with a sigh on to the seat beside him. 'Feet playing you up again?' asked Charlie sympathetically through a mouthful of bread.

'I wouldn't mind so much,' Cooper grumbled, 'if my inside had aged at the same rate as my outside. If I felt fifty-six, it probably wouldn't bug me.' He rubbed his calves to restore the circulation. 'I promised the wife we'd take up dancing again when I retired, but at this rate we'll be doing it with Zimmer frames.'

Charlie grinned. 'So there's no truth in the saying: you're as old as you feel?'

'None whatsoever. You're as old as your body tells you you are. I'll still feel eighteen when I'm a bed-ridden ninety-year-old and I still won't be able to play football for England. I only ever wanted to be Stanley Matthews,' he said wistfully. 'My dad took me to watch him and Blackpool win the FA cup in 1953 as a sixteenth birthday present. It was pure magic. I've never forgotten it.'

'I wanted to be Tom Kelley,' said Charlie.

'Who's he?'

The Inspector chuckled as he wiped his fingers on a napkin. 'The photographer who persuaded Marilyn Monroe to pose nude for him. Imagine it. Marilyn Monroe entirely

naked and you on the other side of the lens. Now, that really would have been magic.'

'We're in the wrong business, Charlie. There's no charm in what we do.'

'Mrs Marriott hasn't raised your spirits then?'

'No.' He sighed again. 'I made a promise to her, said we wouldn't use what she told me unless we had to, but I can't see at the moment how we can avoid it. If it doesn't have a bearing on the case, then I'm a monkey's uncle. First, Joanna Lascelles was not Mrs Gillespie's only child. She had another one thirteen, fourteen months later by Mrs Marriott's husband.' He ran through the background for Charlie's benefit. 'Mrs Marriott believed Mrs Gillespie killed the baby when it was born, but on the morning of the sixth, Mrs Gillespie told her it had been a boy and that she'd put it up for adoption when it was born.'

Charlie leaned forward, his eyes bright with curiosity. 'Does she know what happened to him?'

Cooper shook his head. 'They were screaming at each other, apparently, and that little tit-bit was tossed out by Mrs Gillespie as she closed the door. Mrs Marriott says Mathilda wanted to hurt her, so it might not even be true.'

'Okay. Go on.'

'Second, and this is the real shocker, Mrs Marriott stole some barbiturates from her father's dispensary which she says Mathilda used to murder Gerald Cavendish.' He detailed what Jane had told him, shaking his head from time to time whenever he touched on James Gillespie's part in the tragedy. 'He's evil, that one, blackmails everyone as far as I can judge. The wretched woman's terrified he's going to broadcast what he knows.'

'Serves her right,' said Charlie unsympathetically. 'What a corrupt lot they all were, and they say it's only recently the country started going to pot. You say she went to see Mrs Gillespie on the morning of the murder. What else did Mrs Gillespie tell her?'

'Murder?' queried Cooper with a touch of irony. 'Don't tell me you agree with me at last?'

'Get on with it, you old rogue,' said Jones impatiently. 'I'm on the edge of my seat here.'

'Mrs Gillespie began by being very cool and composed, told Mrs Marriott that the whole matter was out of her hands and that she wasn't prepared to pay the sort of money James was demanding from her. As far as she was concerned she didn't care any more what people said or thought about her. There had never been any doubt that Gerald committed suicide and if Jane wanted to own up to stealing drugs from her father, that was her affair. Mathilda would deny knowing anything about them.' He opened his notebook. '"I'm more sinned against than sinning," she said and advised Mrs Marriott that, in the matter of the baby, things would get worse before they got better. She went on to say that Mrs Marriott was a fool for keeping her husband in the dark all these years. They had a terrible row during which Mrs Marriott accused Mrs Gillespie of ruining the lives of everyone she had ever had contact with, at which point Mrs Gillespie ordered her out of the house with the words: "James has been reading my private papers and knows where the child is. It's quite pointless to keep quiet any longer." She then told Mrs Marriott it was a boy and that she'd put it up for adoption.' He closed the notebook. 'My bet is the "private papers" were the diaries and things were

going to get worse because Mrs Gillespie had made up her mind to acknowledge her illegitimate child and spike James's guns.' He rubbed his jaw wearily. 'Not that that scenario really makes a great deal more sense than it did before. We'd more or less decided that whoever was reading the diaries was the same person who stole them and murdered the old lady, and I still say James Gillespie wouldn't have drawn our attention to the diaries if he was the guilty party. The psychology's all wrong. And what motive did he have for killing her? She was far more valuable alive as a blackmail victim. Let's face it, it wasn't just the business of the baby he could hold over her, it was her uncle's murder as well.'

'But he probably couldn't prove that, not so long afterwards, and you're making too many assumptions,' said Charlie slowly. '"I'm more sinned against than sinning",' he echoed. 'That's a line from *King Lear*.'

'So?'

'King Lear went mad and took to wandering in the fields near Dover with a crown of weeds on his head because his daughters had deprived him of his kingdom and his authority.'

Cooper groaned. 'I thought it was Ophelia who had the crown of weeds.'

'Hers were coronet weeds,' corrected Jones with idle pedantry. 'It was Lear who wore the crown.' He thought of the epitaph on the Fontwell tombstone. 'By God, Tommy, there's a lovely symmetry about this case. Jack Blakeney's been using a Stanley knife to clean inscriptions in Fontwell.'

Cooper scowled at him. 'How many pints have you had?'

Charlie leaned forward again, his keen eyes scouring Cooper's face. 'I studied *King Lear* at school. It's a hell of a play. All about the nature of love, the abuse of power, and the ultimate frailties of the human spirit.'

'Just like *Hamlet* then,' said Cooper sourly. '*Othello*, too, if it comes to that.'

'Of course. They were all tragedies with death the inevitable consequence. King Lear's mistake was to misinterpret the nature of love. He gave more weight to words than to deeds and partitioned his kingdom between two of his daughters, Goneril and Regan, whom he believed loved him but who, in reality, despised him. He was a tired old man who wanted to relinquish the burdens of state and live the rest of his life in peace and tranquillity. But he was also extremely arrogant and contemptuous of anyone's opinions but his own. His rash assumption that he knew what love was sowed the seeds of his family's destruction.' He grinned. 'Not bad, eh? Damn nearly verbatim from an essay I wrote in the sixth form. And I loathed the flaming play at the time. It's taken me thirty years to see its merits.'

'I came up with *King Lear* a few days ago,' remarked Cooper, 'but I still don't see a connection. If she'd divided her estate between Mrs Lascelles and Miss Lascelles there'd have been a parallel then.'

'You're missing the point, Tommy. *King Lear* was the most tragic of all Shakespeare's plays and Mrs Gillespie knew her Shakespeare. Dammit, man, she thought everything he wrote was gospel. There was a third child, don't forget, who was turned off without a penny.' He surged to his feet. 'I want Jack Blakeney in the nick in half an hour.

Be a good fellow and bring him in. Tell him your boss wants to talk to him about Mrs Gillespie's adopted son.'

What neither of them knew was that Jack Blakeney had been arrested at Mill House, half an hour previously, following the Orloffs' 999 call and Joanna Lascelles's hysterical assertions that he had not only tried to kill her but had admitted killing her mother.

The Inspector learnt of it as soon as he arrived back from lunch. Cooper was informed by radio and ordered to return post haste. He took time out, however, to sit for five minutes in depressed disillusion in a deserted country lane. His hands were shaking too much to drive with any competence, and he knew, with the awful certainty of defeat, that his time was over. He had lost whatever it was that had made him a good policeman. Oh, he had always known what his superiors said about him, but he had also known they were wrong. His forte had been his ability to make accurate judgements about the people he dealt with, and whatever anyone said to the contrary, he was usually right. But he had never allowed his sympathies for an offender and an offender's family to stand in the way of an arrest. Nor had he seen any validity in allowing police work to dehumanize him or destroy the tolerance that he, privately, believed was the one thing that set man above the animals.

With a heavy heart, he fired the engine and set off back to Learmouth. He had misjudged both the Blakeneys. Worse, he simply couldn't begin to follow Charlie Jones's

flights of fancy over *King Lear* or comprehend the awful symmetry behind inscriptions and Stanley knives. Hadn't Mr Spede told him that the Stanley knife on the bathroom floor was the one from the kitchen drawer? The crown he thought he understood. Whoever had decked out Mrs Gillespie in nettles had seen the symbolic connection between her and *King Lear*. How then had Ophelia come to lead them up the garden path? *Coronet weeds,* he recalled, and Dr Blakeney's reference to them in the bathroom.

An intense sadness squeezed about his heart. Poor Tommy Cooper. He was, after all, just an absurd and rather dirty old man, entertaining fantasies about a woman who was young enough to be his daughter.

An hour later, Inspector Jones pulled out the chair opposite Jack and sat down, switching on the tape recorder and registering date, time and who was present. He rubbed his hands in anticipation of a challenge. 'Well, well, Mr Blakeney, I've been looking forward to this.' He beamed across at Cooper who was sitting with his back to the wall, staring at the floor. 'The Sergeant's whetted my appetite with what he's told me about you, not to mention the reports of your contretemps with the police in Bournemouth and this latest little fracas at Cedar House.'

Jack linked his hands behind his head and smiled wolfishly. 'Then I hope you won't be disappointed, Inspector.'

'I'm sure I won't.' He steepled his fingers on the table in front of him. 'We'll leave Mrs Lascelles and the Bournemouth incident to one side for the moment because I'm more interested in your relationship with Mrs Gillespie.' He

looked very pleased with himself. 'I've deciphered the floral crown that she was wearing in her bath. Not Ophelia at all, but King Lear. I've just been looking it up. Act IV, Scene IV where Cordelia describes him as "Crown'd with rank fumiter and furrow weeds, With burdocks, hemlock, nettles, cuckoo-flow'rs". And then Scene VI, a stage direction. "Enter Lear, fantastically dressed with weeds." Am I right, Mr Blakeney?'

'It did occur to me that Ophelia was a very unlikely interpretation. I guessed Lear when Sarah described the scene to me.'

'And Lear certainly makes more sense.'

Jack cocked his irritating eyebrow. 'Does it?'

'Oh, yes.' He rubbed his hands in gleeful anticipation. 'It goes something like this, I think. Lear had two vile daughters, Goneril and Regan, and one loving daughter, Cordelia. Cordelia he banished because she refused to flatter him with hollow words; Goneril and Regan he rewarded because they were deceitful enough to tell lies in order to get their share of his wealth. For Goneril and Regan, read Joanna and Ruth Lascelles. For Cordelia, read the son Mrs Gillespie put up for adoption, i.e. the one she banished who never received a penny from her.' He held Jack's gaze. 'Now, in the play, Cordelia comes back to rescue her father from the brutality her sisters are inflicting upon him, and I think it happened in real life, too, though purely figuratively speaking of course. Neither Joanna nor Ruth were *brutal* to Mrs Gillespie, merely desperately disappointing.' He tapped his forefingers together. 'Cordelia, the adopted son whom Mathilda had long since given up on, reappears miraculously to remind her that love does still exist for her, that she is

not as embittered as she thought she was and that, ultimately, she has produced at least one person who has qualities she could be proud of. How am I doing, Mr Blakeney?'

'Imaginatively.'

Charlie gave a low laugh. 'The only question is, who is Cordelia?'

Jack didn't answer.

'And did he come looking for his mother or was it pure chance that brought him here? Who recognized whom, I wonder?'

Again Jack didn't answer, and Charlie's brows snapped together ferociously. 'You are not obliged to answer my questions, Mr Blakeney, but you would be very unwise to forget that I am investigating murder and attempted murder here. Silence won't help you, you know.'

Jack shrugged, apparently unmoved by threats. 'Even if any of this were true, what does it have to do with Mathilda's death?'

'Dave Hughes told me an interesting story today. He says he watched you clean a gravestone in the cemetery at Fontwell, claims you were obviously so fascinated by it that he went and read it after you'd gone. Do you remember what it says?'

'"George Fitzgibbon 1789–1833. Did I deserve to be despised, By my creator, good and wise? Since you it was who made me be, Then part of you must die with me." I looked him up in the parish records. He succumbed to syphilis as a result of loose living. Maria, his wretched wife, died of the same thing four years later and was popped into the ground alongside George, but she didn't get a tomb-

stone because her children refused to pay for one. There's a written epitaph in the record instead and hers is even better. "George was lusty, coarse and evil, He gave me pox, he's with the devil." Short, and to the point. George's was ridiculously hypocritical by contrast.'

'It all depends who George thought his creator was,' said Charlie. 'Perhaps it was his mother he wanted to take to hell with him.'

Idly Jack traced a triangle on the surface of the table. 'Who told you Mathilda had an adopted son? Someone reliable, I hope, because you're building a hell of a castle on their information.'

Jones caught Cooper's eye, but ignored the warning frown. As Cooper said, their chances of respecting Jane Marriott's confidences were thin. 'Mrs Jane Marriott, whose husband was the boy's father.'

'Ah, well, a *very* reliable source then.' He saw the gleam of excitement in the Inspector's eyes and smiled with genuine amusement. 'Mathilda was not my mother, Inspector. If she had been I'd have been thrilled. I loved the woman.'

Charlie shrugged. 'Then Mrs Gillespie lied about having a son, and it's your wife who's Cordelia. It has to be one or other of you or she wouldn't have made that will. She wasn't going to make Lear's mistake and bequeath her estate to the undeserving daughters.'

Jack looked as if he were about to deny it, then shrugged. 'I imagine Mathilda told Jane Marriott it was a boy out of spite. She never referred to her by name, always called her that "prissy creature at the surgery". It was cruel of her, but then Mathilda was usually cruel. She was a deeply unhappy woman.' He paused to collect his thoughts. 'She told me

about her affair with Paul after I'd finished her portrait. She said there was something missing from the painting, and that that something was guilt. She was absolutely racked with it. Guilt for having given up the baby, guilt for not being able to cope, guilt for blaming the second baby's adoption on Joanna's crying, ultimately, I suppose, guilt for her inability to feel affection.' Briefly he fell silent again. 'Then Sarah turned up out of the blue and Mathilda recognized her.' He saw the look of incredulity on Charlie Jones's face. 'Not immediately and not as the baby she'd given away, but gradually as the months went by. There were so many things that matched. Sarah was the right age, her birthday was the same day as the baby's birthday, her parents had lived in the same borough in London where Mathilda's flat was. Most importantly she thought she detected a likeness in Sarah's and Joanna's mannerisms. She said they had the same smile, the same way of inclining their heads, the same trick of looking at you intently while you speak. And from the start Sarah took Mathilda as she found her, of course, the way she takes everyone, and for the first time in years Mathilda felt valued. It was a very potent cocktail. Mathilda was so convinced she'd found her lost daughter that she approached me and commissioned me to paint the portrait.' He smiled ruefully. 'I thought my luck had changed but all she wanted, of course, was an excuse to find out more about Sarah from the only person available who knew anything of value.'

'But you didn't know that while you were painting her?'

'No. I did wonder why she was so interested in us both, what our parents were like, where they came from, if we had brothers and sisters, whether or not I got on with my

in-laws. She didn't confine herself to Sarah, you see. If she had, I might have been suspicious. As it was, when she finally told me that Sarah was her lost child, I was appalled.' He shrugged helplessly. 'I knew she couldn't be because Sarah wasn't adopted.'

'Surely that was the first thing Mrs Gillespie asked you?'

'Not in so many words, no. She never put anything as directly as that.' He shrugged again in the face of the Inspector's scepticism. 'You're forgetting that no one in Fontwell knew about this child, except Jane Marriott, and Mathilda was far too proud to give the rest of the village a glimpse of her clay feet. She was looking for a private atonement, not a public one. The closest we ever came to it was when she asked me if Sarah had a good relationship with her mother and I said, no, because they had nothing in common. I can even remember the words I used. I said: "I've often wondered if Sarah was adopted because the only explanation for the disparity between the two of them in looks, words and deeds is that they aren't related." I was being flippant, but Mathilda used it to build castles in the air. Rather as you're doing at the moment, Inspector.'

'But she'd made up her mind before you started painting that portrait, Mr Blakeney. If I remember correctly she began consulting Mr Duggan about the will in August.'

'It was like a faith,' said Jack simply. 'I can't explain it any other way. She needed to make amends to the child who'd had nothing, and Sarah had to be that child. The fact that the ages, birthdays and mannerisms were pure coincidence was neither here nor there. Mathilda had made up her mind and all she wanted from me was the gaps filled in.' He ran his fingers through his hair. 'If I'd known

sooner, then I'd have disabused her, but I didn't know, and all I achieved, quite unwittingly, was to fuel the belief.'

'Does Dr Blakeney know any of this?'

'No. Mathilda was adamant she never should. She made me promise to keep it to myself – she was terrified Sarah would treat her differently, stop liking her, even reject her completely – and I thought, thank God, because this way no one gets hurt.' He rubbed a hand across his face. 'I didn't know what to do, you see, and I needed time to work out how to let Mathilda down gently. If I'd told her the truth, there and then, it would have been like taking the baby away from her all over again.'

'When was this, Mr Blakeney?' asked Charlie.

'About two weeks before she died.'

'Why did she tell you, if she didn't want anyone to know?'

Jack didn't answer immediately. 'It was the portrait,' he said after a moment. 'I took it round to show it to her. I still had some work to do on it but I wanted to see what her reaction was so that I could paint that into the picture. I've had some amazing responses in the past: anger, shock, vanity, irritation, disappointment. I record them all beneath my signature so that anyone who understands the code will know what the subject thought about my treatment of his or her personality. It's a sort of visual joke. Mathilda's reaction was intense grief. I've never seen anyone so upset.'

'She didn't like it?' suggested Charlie.

'The exact opposite. She was weeping for the woman she might have been.' His eyes clouded in reflection. 'She said I was the first person who had ever shown her compassion.'

'I don't understand.'

Jack glanced across at the Sergeant who was still sitting staring at the floor. 'Tommy does,' he said. 'Don't you, my old friend?'

There was a brief pause before Cooper raised his head. 'The gold at the heart of the picture,' he murmured. 'That was Mathilda as she was in the beginning before events took over and destroyed her.'

Jack's dark eyes rested on him with affection. 'Goddammit, Tommy,' he said, 'how come I'm the only one to appreciate your qualities? Does anything escape you?'

When I told Father I was pregnant, he fainted. It was an extraordinary example of craven cowardice. Gerald, by contrast, was rather pleased. 'Is it mine, Matty?' he asked. Perhaps I should have been offended, but I wasn't. I found his delight in what he'd achieved rather touching.

Father is all for an abortion, of course, and not just because of the potential scandal. He says the baby will be even more of an imbecile than Gerald. I have refused. Nothing will induce me to go near a backstreet abortionist which is all Father is offering me. He says he knows of somebody in London who will do it for a small fee, but I don't trust him an inch and will not entrust my life to some incompetent woman with knitting needles and gin. In any case, if the child's as defective as Father's suggesting, then it will not survive long. Gerald is only with us in all conscience because his silly mother nursed him devotedly for years.

Every cloud has its silver lining. Gerald has never been easier to manage than he is at the moment. The knowledge that I am carrying his baby has wiped all

memories of Grace from his mind. It means I shall have to marry to give the baby legitimacy, but James Gillespie is tiresome in his approaches, and will marry me tomorrow if I agree. Father says James is homosexual and needs a wife to give himself respectability, but as I need a husband for the same reason, I can no doubt tolerate him for the few months till the baby's born.

I have told Father to put a brave face on it, something the silly man is incapable of doing, and to let me and James have the use of his flat in London. Once the baby is born I shall return home. Father will stay at his club on the rare – now, very rare – occasions when he is sober enough to attend a debate at the House. He wept his drunken tears this evening and said I was unnatural, claiming all he had ever wanted me to do was be sweet to Gerald and keep him happy.

But it was Grace who introduced Gerald to sex, not I, and Father knows it. And how was I supposed *to keep a sexually active imbecile happy? By playing bridge? By discussing Plato? Dear God, but I have such contempt for men. Perhaps I* am *unnatural . . .*

Eighteen

JONES DRUMMED his fingers impatiently on the table. 'You told the Sergeant you were with an actress in Stratford the night Mrs Gillespie was murdered. You weren't. We've checked. Miss Bennedict said' – he consulted a piece of paper – 'she'd see you in hell before she allowed you near her again.'

'True.' He gave an amiable grin. 'She didn't like the portrait I did of her. She's had it in for me ever since.'

'Then why give her as your alibi?'

'Because I'd already told Sarah that's where I was, and she was listening when the Sergeant asked me.'

Charlie frowned but let this pass. 'Where were you then, if you weren't in Stratford?'

'Cheltenham.' He linked his hands behind his neck and stared at the ceiling.

'Can you prove it?'

'Yes.' He reeled off a phone number. 'Sarah's father's house. He will confirm that I was there from six o'clock on the Friday evening until midday on the Sunday.' He flicked a lazy glance at the Inspector. 'He's a JP, so you can be fairly sure he won't be lying.'

'What were you doing there?'

'I went on the off-chance that he had something I could show Mathilda that would prove Sarah wasn't her daughter. I knew I could talk fairly freely without him blabbing about it. If I'd approached her mother, she'd have been on the phone to Sarah like a shot and then the cat would have been out of the bag with Sarah demanding to know why I wanted proof she wasn't adopted. By the same token, she'd have asked me why I was going to see her father, so I told her I was staying with Sally to put her off the scent.' He looked suddenly pensive. 'Not the most intelligent thing I've ever done.'

Charlie ignored this. 'Did her father give you proof?'

'No. He said he hadn't got anything and that I'd have to talk to her mother. I was planning to bite the bullet and go the next weekend, but, by the Monday, Mathilda was dead and it didn't matter any more.'

'And you still haven't told your wife?'

'No.'

'Why not?'

'I promised Mathilda I wouldn't,' he said evenly. 'If she'd wanted Sarah to know what she believed, she'd have told her herself on the video.'

'Any idea why she didn't?'

Jack shrugged. 'Because she wasn't going to tell her in life either, I suppose. She had too many secrets which she thought would be exposed if she claimed Sarah as her own – and let's face it, she was right. Look what Tommy's unearthed already.'

'It would have been unearthed anyway. People were

bound to ask questions the minute they heard she'd left her money to her doctor.'

'But she wouldn't have expected the police to be asking them because she didn't know she was going to be murdered. And, as far as I can make out, from what Sarah has told me of the video, she did the best she could to warn Joanna and Ruth off putting in a counter-claim by dropping enough heavy hints about their lifestyles to give Sarah's barrister a field day if the thing ever went to court.' He shrugged again. 'The only reason either of them feels confident about challenging it now is because Mathilda was murdered. Whatever they've done pales into insignificance beside that.'

Cooper rumbled into life behind him. 'But the video is full of lies, particularly in relation to her uncle and her husband. Mrs Gillespie implies she was the victim of them both, but Mrs Marriott tells a very different story. She describes a woman who was ruthless enough to use blackmail and murder when it suited her. So which is true?'

Jack swung round to look at him. 'I don't know. Both probably. She wouldn't be the first victim to strike back.'

'What about this business of her uncle's feeble-mindedness? She described him on the video as a drunken brute who raped her when she was thirteen, yet Mrs Marriott says he was rather pathetic. Explain that.'

'I can't. Mathilda never talked to me about it. All I know is that she was deeply scarred by her inability to love and when I showed her the portrait with the scarring represented by the scold's bridle, she burst into tears and said I was the first person to show her any compassion. I chose to

interpret that as meaning that I was the first person to see her as a victim, but I could have been wrong. You'll have to make up your own mind.'

'We wouldn't have to if we could find her diaries,' said Cooper.

Jack didn't say anything and the room fell silent with only the whirr of the tape to disturb the complete bafflement that at least two of those present were experiencing. Jones, who had approached this interview in the confident expectation that Jack Blakeney would spend tonight in a police cell, was falling prey to the same crippling ambivalence that Cooper had always felt towards this man.

'Why did you tell Mrs Lascelles this morning that you murdered her mother if you already had an alibi for the night Mrs Gillespie died?' he asked at last, rustling the papers in front of him.

'I didn't.'

'She says in this report that you did.'

'I didn't.'

'She says you did.'

'She said what she believed. That's a different thing entirely.'

Jones pondered for a moment. He had a nasty feeling that he would receive almost as dusty an answer to his next question, but he put it anyway. 'Why did you try to murder Mrs Lascelles?'

'I didn't.'

'She says, and I'm quoting, "Jack Blakeney forced me against the wall and started to strangle me. If Violet hadn't interrupted him, he'd have killed me." Is she lying?'

'No. She's telling you what she believes.'

'But it's not true.'

'No.'

'You weren't trying to strangle her?'

'No.'

'I have to tell you, Mr Blakeney, that according to this report she had the marks of a stranglehold on her neck when the car that answered the nine–nine–nine call arrived at Cedar House. Therefore someone did try to strangle her, and she says that someone was you.' He paused, inviting Jack to answer. When he didn't, he tried a different approach. 'Were you in Cedar House at approximately ten thirty this morning?'

'Yes.'

'Did you put your hand about Mrs Joanna Lascelles's throat?'

'Yes.'

'Is she justified in believing that you were trying to strangle her?'

'Yes.'

'Were you trying to strangle her?'

'No.'

'Then explain it to me. What the hell were you doing?'

'Showing you lot where you've been going wrong again. Mind you, it's not the most sensible thing I've done, and I wouldn't have done it at all if I hadn't been so pissed off by that jerk of an Inspector last night.' His eyes narrowed angrily at the memory. 'I don't give a toss about myself, matter of fact I rather hope he decides to prosecute and give me my day in court, but I do care about Sarah and I care very much indeed at the moment about Ruth. He treated them both like shit and I made up my mind then

that enough was enough. Joanna's past saving, I suspect, but her daughter isn't, and I want the poor kid free to put this bloody awful mess behind her.' He took a deep angry breath. 'So I sat up last night and did what you should have done, worked out who killed Mathilda and why. And believe me it wasn't difficult.'

Charlie did believe him. Like Cooper, he was beginning to find Jack irresistible. 'Mrs Lascelles,' he said with conviction. 'She's always been top of the list.'

'No, and I satisfied myself of that this morning. I agree she's quite capable of it. She has an almost identical personality to her mother, and if Mathilda could murder to get what she wanted, then Joanna could, too. You don't grow up in an atmosphere of extreme dysfunction and emerge normal at the end of it. But Joanna's relationship with Mathilda was very ambivalent. Despite everything, I suspect they were actually rather fond of each other. Perhaps, quite simply, their fondness was based on mutual understanding, the devil you know being more acceptable than the devil you don't.'

'All right,' said Charlie patiently. 'Then who did kill Mrs Gillespie?'

'I can't prove it, that's your job. All I can do is take you through what I worked out last night.' He took a moment to organize his thoughts. 'You've concentrated entirely on Sarah, me, Joanna and Ruth,' he said, 'and all because of the will. Not unreasonable in the circumstances – but if you take us out of the equation then the balance of probability shifts. So let's assume she wasn't killed for money and take it from there. Okay, I don't believe she was killed in anger

either. Anger is a violent, hot-blooded emotion and her death was too well planned and too meticulous. Too symbolic. Whoever murdered her may well have been angry with her, but it wasn't done because someone's patience had finally run out.' He glanced at Jones who nodded. 'Which leaves what? Hatred? She was certainly disliked by a lot of people but as none of them had killed her before, why decide to do it then? Jealousy?' He shrugged eloquently. 'What was there to be jealous of? She was a virtual recluse, and I can't believe Jane Marriott stored her jealousy for years to have it erupt suddenly in November. So, at the risk of stating the obvious, Mathilda must have been murdered because someone wanted her out of the way.'

Jones had difficulty keeping the sarcasm out of his voice. 'I think we can agree on that,' he said.

Jack stared at him for a moment. 'Yes, but *why*? Why did someone want her out of the way? What had she done or what was she going to do that meant she had to be killed? That's the question you've never asked, not outside the context of the will at least.'

'Because I don't find it quite so easy, as you apparently do, to ignore it.'

'But it *is* just a will. Thousands of people make them every week and thousands of people die every week. The fact that Mathilda's was unusually radical becomes completely irrelevant if you absolve Joanna, Ruth, Sarah and me of her death. No one else is directly affected by the way she chose to leave her money.'

Cooper cleared his throat. 'It's a good point, Charlie.'

'All right,' he conceded. 'Why *was* she killed then?'

'I don't know.'

Charlie raised his eyes to heaven. 'God give me strength!' he growled savagely.

Cooper chuckled quietly to himself. 'Get on with it, Jack, before you give the poor man apoplexy,' he suggested. 'We're all running out of patience on this one. Let's take it as read that the will wasn't the motive and that neither the Lascelles women nor you and your wife were involved. Where does that leave us?'

'With Mathilda wearing the scold's bridle. Why? And why did it have half a hedgerow carefully entwined through it? Isn't that what persuaded you it wasn't suicide?'

Cooper nodded.

'Then the logical conclusion has to be that the murderer never intended you to think it *was* suicide. I mean we're not talking about a moron here, we're talking finesse and careful planning. My guess is that someone knew Mathilda thought Sarah was her daughter, knew that both Mathilda and Joanna had been conditioned by the scold's bridle in their childhoods, knew that Joanna was a florist and knew, too, that "scold's bridle" was Mathilda's nickname for Sarah. Hence the contraption on her head and the *King Lear* imagery. If you put all that together with the fact that Ruth was in the house that day, then the aim must surely have been to focus your attention on Sarah, Joanna and Ruth – Lear's three daughters in other words. And that's exactly what happened, even if it was the will that set you thinking along those lines because you mistook the symbolism for Ophelia's coronet weeds. You mustn't forget how close Mathilda played the will to her chest. As far as anyone knew, Joanna and Ruth were going to share the estate

between them. Sarah's possible claim as the long-lost daughter was nothing but a wild card when the murder took place so, for the murderer, it came as a sort of bonus.'

Charlie frowned. 'I still don't understand. Were we supposed to arrest one of them? And which one? I mean, was your wife indicated because of the scold's bridle, was Joanna indicated because of the flowers, or was Ruth indicated because she was there?'

Jack shrugged. 'I'd say that's the whole point. It doesn't matter a damn, just so long as you focus your attention on them.'

'But why?' snarled Charlie through gritted teeth.

Jack looked helplessly from him to Cooper. 'There's only one reason that I can see, but maybe I've got it all wrong. Hell dammit!' he exploded angrily. 'I'm not an expert.'

'Confusion,' said Cooper stoutly, a man ever to be relied upon. 'The murderer wanted Mrs Gillespie dead and confusion to follow. And why would they want confusion to follow? Because it would be much harder to proceed with any kind of normality if the mess surrounding Mrs Gillespie's death wasn't sorted out.'

Jack nodded. 'Sounds logical to me.'

It was Charlie's turn to be lost in Cooper's flights of fancy. 'What normality?'

'The normality that follows death,' he said ponderously. 'Wills in other words. Someone wanted the settling of Mrs Gillespie's estate delayed.' He thought for a moment. 'Let's say she was about to embark on something that someone else didn't like, so they stopped her before she could do it. But let's say, too, that whatever it was could be pursued by her beneficiary the minute that beneficiary came into the

estate. With a little ingenuity, you throw a spanner in the works by pointing a finger at the more obvious legatees and grind the process to a halt. How does that sound?'

'Complicated,' said Charlie tartly.

'But the pressure was to stop Mathilda,' said Jack. 'The rest was imaginative flair which might or might not work. Think of it as a speculative venture that could, with a little bit of luck, produce the goods.'

'But that brings us right back to square one,' said Cooper slowly. 'Whoever killed her knew her very well and, if we jettison the four who knew her best, then we're left with – ' he pressed his fingers to his eyes in deep concentration, 'Mr and Mrs Spede, Mr and Mrs Marriott, and James Gillespie.'

'You can do better than that, Cooper,' said Jack impatiently. 'The Spedes are simple souls who could never have dreamt up the *Lear* symbolism in a million years; Paul and Jane Marriott have avoided Mathilda like the plague for years so probably couldn't have found their way around her house, let alone known where she kept the Stanley knife; and, as far as I understand it, if what Duggan told Sarah is true, rather than trying to delay the processing of the will, James Gillespie is doing the exact opposite and pressing for the controversy to be settled so that he can lay claim to the clocks.'

'But there isn't anyone else.'

'There is, and I proved it this morning.' He hammered his fist on the table. 'It's Ruth's involvement that should have alerted you. Someone knew she was in the house that day and could therefore figure as a suspect. You've been chasing around in circles since you found out about it, but Sarah says you only learnt she was there because you

received an anonymous letter. So who sent it?' He slammed his palm on the table at Cooper's blank expression. 'Who tried to rescue Joanna this morning?'

Violet Orloff opened her front door and stared at the piece of polythene-encased paper that Detective Sergeant Cooper was holding in front of him. He turned it round to read it aloud. '"Ruth Lascelles was in Cedar House the day Mrs Gillespie died. She stole some earrings. Joanna knows she took them. Joanna Lascelles is a prostitute in London. Ask her what she spends her money on. Ask her why she tried to kill her daughter. Ask her why Mrs Gillespie thought she was mad." Would we be right in assuming you wrote this, Mrs Orloff?' he enquired in his friendly way.

'Duncan did, but we were only trying to *help*,' she said breathily, looking from him to the tall figure of Charlie Jones behind him, the collar of whose thick sheepskin jacket was pulled up about his comfortably sad face. She took heart from their mutual lack of hostility. 'I know we probably ought to have come in person, but it's so *difficult*.' She gestured vaguely in the direction of the other part of the house. 'We are neighbours, after all, and Duncan does so hate unpleasantness.' She smiled tentatively. 'But when a murder's been committed – I mean, one can't expect the police to solve it if people who know things stay quiet. It seemed more *tactful*, somehow, not to get involved personally. You do understand, don't you?'

'Perfectly,' said Charlie with an encouraging smile, 'and we're very grateful to you for the trouble you took.'

'That's all right then. I *told* Duncan it was important.'

'Didn't he agree with you?'

She glanced cautiously over her shoulder, then pulled the door to behind her. 'I wouldn't put it quite like *that*,' she said. 'He's grown so lazy since we came here, won't stir himself, won't have his routines upset, can't bear what he calls aggravations. He says he's earned a peaceful retirement and doesn't want it *upset* by lots of bother. He's very unfit, of course, which doesn't help, but I can't help feeling that it isn't good to be so' – she struggled for the right word – '*unenterprising*.'

'Mrs Gillespie's death must have been a shock then, what with the police tramping about the house, and Mrs Lascelles and her daughter coming back.'

'He hasn't *enjoyed* it,' she admitted, 'but he did see there was nothing we could do about it. Don't get so het up, he told me. A little patience and it will all blow over.'

'Still, it must be very unsettling,' said Cooper, 'worrying about what's going to happen to Cedar House now that Mrs Gillespie's dead. Presumably it will be sold, but you won't have any control over who it's sold to.'

'That's just what *I* said. Duncan would go mad with noisy children next door.' She lowered her voice. 'I know one shouldn't take pleasure in other people's misfortune, but I can't deny it's a relief to have Joanna and Dr Blakeney at loggerheads over the will. They're going to court about it, you know, and as Duncan said, that sort of thing takes years.'

'And in the meantime the house will stand empty?'

'Well, *exactly*.'

'So it's definite that Mrs Lascelles intends to contest the will?'

'Oh, yes.'

'She told you that?'

She looked guilty again. 'I heard her and the doctor talking in the drawing-room. I don't make a habit of listening, not as a general rule, but . . .' She left the rest of the sentence unsaid.

'You've been worried and you needed to know what's going on,' suggested Charlie helpfully.

'Well, *exactly*,' she said again. 'Someone has to take an interest. If it's left to Duncan, we'll only know what sort of neighbours we've got when they're living next to us.'

'Like Mrs Gillespie, you mean. I suppose you knew a lot about her one way and another.'

Violet's mouth pinched disapprovingly. 'Not through choice. I don't think she ever realized just how piercing her voice was. Very *strident*, you know, and she was so convinced that her opinions *mattered*. I never really listened, to tell you the truth, but Duncan found her amusing from time to time, particularly when she was being rude on the telephone, which she was, often. She took people to task about the most *trivial* things and she thought they couldn't hear her, you know, unless she shouted. She was a very silly woman.'

Charlie nodded, as if in agreement. 'Then I'm surprised you didn't hear anything the night she died. She must have spoken to her murderer, surely?'

Violet's face flushed a dull red. 'She didn't, you know. Duncan never heard a sound.'

He pretended not to notice her embarrassment. 'And what about you, Mrs Orloff? Did you hear anything?'

'Oh, dear,' she wailed, 'it's not as though it's a *crime*

though you'd think it was the way Duncan carries on. I have a tot or two of whisky of an evening, really nothing very much. Duncan's a teetotaller and doesn't approve, but as I always say, where's the harm in it? Mathilda's done it for years – it's unnatural not to, she always said – and she drank far more than I do.' She dropped her voice again. 'It's not as though I'm an *alcoholic*.'

'Good *lord* no,' said Charlie effusively, picking up the loaded speech patterns. 'If I didn't drink enough to send myself to sleep every night, I'd be a nervous wreck come the morning.'

'Well, exactly,' came the repetitive refrain. 'But I do nod off in front of the television, and, of course, I *did* the night Mathilda died. Hardly surprising really since I spent the day in Poole with my sister, and I find that very tiring now. You see, I'm not as young as I used to be, and I won't deny I've been worrying ever since, did Mathilda call for help? Duncan *swears* she didn't but, you know, he's so anti getting involved in anything that he'd have persuaded himself it was just Mathilda being irritating.'

'Any idea what time you nodded off?' asked Cooper, showing more interest in the state of his shoes than in her answer.

'*Very* early,' she said in a whisper. 'We'd just finished supper and sat down to watch *Blind Date*, and the next thing I knew Duncan was shaking me and telling me I was snoring and it was annoying him because it was spoiling *Match of the Day*. Goodness, but I was tired. I went to bed and slept like a *log* till the morning, and I can't help feeling that if I'd only stayed awake, I might have been able to do something for poor Mathilda.'

And that of course was true.

Charlie gestured towards the door. 'May we talk to your husband now, Mrs Orloff?'

'Is that necessary? He won't be able to tell you anything and it'll just make him *grumpy* for the rest of the day.'

'I'm afraid it is.' He produced a paper from his pocket with an air of apology. 'We also have a warrant to search your house, but I assure you, we'll be as careful as we can.' He raised his voice. 'Bailey! Jenkins! Watts! Show yourselves, lads. We're ready to go.'

Quite bewildered by this sudden turn of events, Violet stood meekly to one side while Jones, Cooper and three DCs filed into her hallway. Behind their backs, she crept away with the stealth of a guilty person into the kitchen.

Duncan's small eyes watched the two senior policemen closely as they eased into the cramped living-room, but otherwise he showed remarkably little concern at this sudden invasion of his privacy. 'Forgive me if I don't get up,' he said courteously, 'but I find I'm not as mobile as I used to be.' He waved towards a delicate two-seater sofa, inviting them to sit down. They declined with equal courtesy, afraid of breaking it under their combined weight. 'I've met Detective Sergeant Cooper but I don't know you, sir,' he said, examining Charlie with interest.

'Detective Chief Inspector Jones.'

'How do you do.'

Charlie inclined his head in a brief salute. He was assailed with doubt as he looked at the fat old man in the oversized armchair, his huge stomach overhanging his thighs like the

meat from a split sausage skin. Could such ungainly bulk have performed the delicate artistry of Mrs Gillespie's murder? Could he even have abstracted himself from this room without waking his wife? He listened to the shallow wheezing breaths, each one a battle against the smothering pressure of flesh, and recalled Hughes's description of the man who had used the key to open the back door. *His voice was all breathy like he had trouble with his lungs.* 'Was Mrs Gillespie aware that you knew about the key under the flowerpot?' he asked without any attempt at preamble.

Duncan looked surprised. 'I don't understand you, Inspector.'

'No matter. We have a witness who can identify you. He was there when you let yourself in one morning in September.'

But Duncan only smiled and shook his fat cheeks in denial. 'Let myself in where?' There was a sound above them as one of the DCs moved a piece of furniture across the floor, and Duncan's gaze shifted to the ceiling. 'What exactly is all this in aid of?'

Charlie produced the warrant and handed it to him. 'We are searching these premises for Mrs Gillespie's diaries or, more likely, the remains of Mrs Gillespie's diaries. We have reason to believe you stole them from the library of Cedar House.'

'How very peculiar of you.'

'Are you denying it?'

He gave a low chuckle. 'My dear chap, of course I'm denying it. I didn't even know she kept diaries.'

Charlie changed tack. 'Why didn't you tell my Sergeant on the Monday after the murder that Miss Ruth Lascelles

had been in Cedar House during the afternoon? Or indeed that Mrs Jane Marriott had had a row with her in the morning?'

'How could I tell him something I didn't know myself?'

'If you were here, Mr Orloff, you could not have avoided knowing. Jane Marriott describes her confrontation with Mrs Gillespie as a screaming match and Ruth says she rang the doorbell because she left her key at school.'

'But I wasn't here, Inspector,' he said affably. 'I took the opportunity of my wife's absence in Poole to go for a long walk.'

There was a gasp from the doorway. 'Duncan!' declared Violet. 'How can you tell such lies? You *never* go for walks.' She advanced into the room like a small ship under sail. 'And don't think I don't know *why* you're lying. You can't be bothered to assist the police in their enquiries, just like you haven't been bothered all along. Of *course* he was here, and of *course* he will have heard Jane and Ruth. We *always* heard Ruth when she came back. She and her grandmother couldn't be in a room together without arguing, any more than she can be in a room with her mother without arguing. Not that I altogether blame her. She wants love, poor child, and neither Mathilda nor Joanna were capable of such an emotion. The only people Mathilda had any fondness for were the Blakeneys, you know, the artist and his wife. She used to laugh with *them*, and I think she even took her clothes off for *him*. I heard her in her bedroom, being very coy and silly, saying things like "Not bad for an old woman" and "I was beautiful once, you know. Men competed for me." And that was true, they *did*. Even Duncan loved her when we were all much younger. He denies it now, of

course, but I knew. All us girls knew we were only second best. Mathilda played so hard to get, you see, and that was a challenge.' She paused for breath and Cooper, who was beside her, smelt the whisky on her lips. He had time to feel sadness for this little woman whose life had never blossomed because she had lived it always in the shade of Mathilda Gillespie.

'Not that it *matters*,' she went on. 'Nothing matters that much. And it's years since he lost interest. You can't go on loving someone who's rude all the time, and Mathilda was always rude. She thought it was funny. She'd say the most appalling things, and *laugh*. I won't pretend we had a close relationship, but I did feel sorry for her. She should have done something with her life, something interesting, but she never did and it made her bitter.' She turned a severe gaze on her husband. 'I know she used to *tease* you, Duncan, and call you Mr Toad, but that's no reason not to help find her murderer. Murder is inexcusable. And I can't help feeling, you know, that it was *particularly* inexcusable to put that beastly scold's bridle on her head. You were very upset when she put it on you.' She turned back to Charlie. 'It was one of her horrible jokes. She said the only way Duncan would ever lose weight was if he had his *tongue* clamped, so she crept up behind him one day when he was asleep in the garden with his mouth open and popped that horrid rusty thing over his head. He nearly *died* of shock.' She paused for another breath but this time she had run out of steam and didn't go on.

There was a long silence.

'I suppose that's how you put it on her,' murmured

Charlie finally, 'when she was already asleep, but I'd be interested to know how you gave her the barbiturates. The pathologist estimates four or five and she would never have taken that many herself.'

Duncan's gaze rested briefly on his wife's shocked face, before shifting to Cooper's. 'Old women have two things in common,' he said with a small smile. 'They drink too much and they talk too much. You'd have liked Mathilda, Sergeant, she was a very amusing woman, although the memory of her was a great deal more attractive than the real thing. It was a disappointment coming back. Age has few compensations, as I think I told you.' His pleasant face beamed. 'On the whole I prefer male company. Men are so much more predictable.'

'Which is convenient,' remarked Cooper to the Blakeneys in Mill House kitchen that evening, 'since he'll probably spend the rest of his life in prison.'

'Assuming you can prove he did it,' said Jack. 'What happens if he doesn't confess? You'll be left with circumstantial evidence, and if his defence has any sense they'll go all out to convince the jury Mathilda committed suicide. You don't even know why he did it, do you?'

'Not yet.'

'Doesn't Violet know?' asked Sarah.

Cooper shook his head, thinking of the wretched woman they'd abandoned at Wing Cottage, wringing her hands and protesting there must be some mistake. 'Claims she doesn't.'

'And you didn't find the diaries?'

'We never really expected to. He'd have destroyed them long ago.'

'But there's so much unexplained,' said Sarah in frustration. 'How did he get her to take the sleeping pills? Why did he do it? Why didn't Violet wake up? Why didn't he tell you Ruth had been there if he wanted her implicated? And then the bit I really don't understand – why on earth did Jane have a row with Mathilda that day?'

Cooper glanced at Jack, then took out his cigarettes. 'I can make a guess at some answers,' he said, planting a cigarette in the side of his mouth and flicking his lighter to the tip. 'Both Mathilda and Violet liked a tipple in the evening and they both drank whisky. I think the chances are it was Mathilda who first introduced Violet to it, made it respectable as it were in the face of Duncan's disapproval, but in any case Violet was certainly in the habit of dozing off in her armchair. The night Mathilda died, Violet went out for the count during *Blind Date* which comes on at six thirty or thereabouts, woke up briefly some time after ten o'clock, when Duncan shook her and told her she was snoring through *Match of the Day*, went up to bed and slept like the dead for the rest of the night.' He tapped ash into his cupped palm. 'That was definitely no doze. That was a barbiturate-induced stupor which is why Duncan leaving the room wouldn't have wakened her. I think he greeted Violet when she got home after a tiring day in Poole with a stiff whisky, laced with sleeping tablets, waited till she fell asleep, then trotted next door and used the same concoction on Mathilda. She kept the drink in the kitchen. How simple

just to say: Don't stir yourself. Let me do the honours and get you a top-up.'

'But where did he get the sleeping pills from? He's on my list and I've never prescribed any for him or Violet.'

'Presumably he used the ones you prescribed for Mrs Gillespie.'

Sarah looked doubtful. 'When could he have taken them, though? Surely she'd have noticed if any were missing.'

'If she did,' he said dryly, 'then she probably assumed it was her own daughter who was responsible. With Mrs Lascelles's sort of dependence she must have been raiding her mother's drug cupboard for years.'

Jack looked thoughtful. 'Who told you?'

'As a matter of fact, you did, Jack. But I wasn't too sure what she was on until we searched the house yesterday for the diaries. She's not very good at hiding things, but then she's damn lucky she hasn't fallen foul of the police before. She will, though, now that the money's dried up.'

'I didn't tell you anything.'

Cooper tut-tutted. 'You've told me everything you know about Mrs Lascelles, right down to the fact that you, personally, despise her. I stood and looked at her portrait while we were discussing Othello and Iago, and all I could see was a desperately weak and fragmented character whose existence – ' he used his hands to depict a border ' – depends on external stimulation. I compared the pallid colours and the distorted shapes of Joanna's portrait with the vigour of Mathilda's and Sarah's and I thought, you've painted a woman without substance. The only reality you perceive is a reflected reality, in other words, a personality

that can only express itself artificially. I guessed it had to be drink or drugs.'

'You're lying through your teeth,' said Jack bluntly. 'That bastard Smollett told you. Dammit, Cooper, even I didn't see all that and I painted the bloody picture.'

Cooper gave a deep chuckle. 'It's all there, my friend, believe me. Mr Smollett told me nothing.' His face sobered. 'But you had no business withholding that information, either of you, not in a murder enquiry.' He looked at Sarah. 'And you should never have confronted her with it the other afternoon, if you don't mind me saying so, Doctor. People like that are shockingly unpredictable and you were alone in the house with her.'

'She's not on LSD, Cooper, she's on Valium. Anyway, how do you know I confronted her with it?'

'Because I'm a policeman, Dr Blakeney, and you were looking guilty. What makes you think she's on Valium?'

'She told me she was.'

Cooper raised his eyes to heaven. 'One day, Dr Blakeney, you will learn not to be so gullible.'

'Well, what is she on then?' demanded Jack. 'I guessed tranquillizers, too. She's not injecting. I sketched her in the nude and there wasn't a mark on her.'

'It depends what you were looking for. She's rich enough to do the thing cleanly. It's dirty needles and dirty lavatories that cause most of the problems. Where did you look anyway? Arms and legs?' Jack nodded. 'The veins around her groin?'

'No,' he admitted. 'I was having enough trouble as it was, I didn't want to encourage her by staring at the damn thing.'

Cooper nodded. 'I found half a pharmacy under her floorboards, including tranquillizers, barbiturates, amphetamines and sizeable quantities of heroin and syringes. She's chronically addicted, I'd say, presumably has been for years. And, I'll tell you this for free, her mother's allowance alone couldn't possibly have funded what she'd got stashed away, and nor could fancy flower arranging. I think Duncan and Violet's anonymous letter said it all, Joanna is a high-class prostitute turning tricks to fund a very expensive habit, begun, I would guess, when she married Steven Lascelles.'

'But she looks so . . .' Sarah sought for the right word, 'unsullied.'

'Not for much longer,' said Cooper cynically. 'She's about to discover what it's like to live in the real world where there's no Mathilda to keep the coffers topped up. It's when you get desperate that you start getting careless.' He patted Sarah's hand. 'Don't waste your sympathy on her. She's been a taker all her life and, rather belatedly, her mother has forced her to face up to it.'

Of all absurd things, Gerald has developed a conscience. 'No more, Matty, please,' he said, bursting into tears. 'We'll go to hell for what we've done.' The ingratitude of the man beggars belief. Does he think I get any pleasure from being pawed by a drooling half-wit? It's Father's doing, of course. He lost his temper yesterday and started calling Gerald names. Now Gerald says he's going back to the slut down the road who first seduced him, and this time he says he'll marry her. 'Grace will give Gerry a baby, Matty,' he blubbered, 'and Gerry wants a baby.' Why, oh why, was my grandfather so stupid? How much more sensible it would have been to weather the embarrassment of certifying Gerald than to pretend to the world he was normal.

I sought out Father in the library, drunk as usual, and told him bluntly that Gerald wasn't playing any more. 'You're such a fool,' I stormed at him. 'Grace won't be bought off a second time. Don't imagine she hasn't guessed by now that she'll get more by marrying Gerald than by taking your bribes.' Father cringed

away from me as he always does. 'It's not my fault,' he whined, 'it's your grandfather's fault. He should have mentioned me by name in his will instead of referring to Gerald's nearest male relative.' I could have murdered him then. The same old story, never his fault, always someone else's. But in one way he's right. Why did my grandfather create a trust to prevent his idiot first-born disposing of his wealth without clarifying that my father must inherit afterwards? And why did it not occur to him that Gerald might repeat the terms of the will parrot-fashion to any scheming little bitch who cared to listen? Grace must have worked out by now that Gerald is worth marrying just to produce a son who will inherit everything. I suppose my grandfather had no idea that imbeciles were so interested in sex nor, indeed, that they were capable of fathering children.

I made Father wear the scold's bridle all evening and he's promised to hold his tongue in future. Gerald, of course, whimpered in the corner, afraid that I would make him wear it, too, but I promised that if we heard no more talk of going to live with Grace, I would be nice to him. Now he is pliable once more.

How strange it is that these two, without a brain between them, can see the scold's bridle for the humiliation it is, while Duncan, who has some pretensions to intelligence, is disgustingly excited by it. For Gerald and Father it is a necessary penance for the sins they wish to commit. For Duncan, it is a fetish that unlocks his potency. He is invariably aroused by wearing it. But what a gutless worm he is. He begs me on his knees to marry him while he allows Violet and her parents to

continue with the marriage arrangements. He is not prepared to risk losing her miserable dowry, unless he is first assured of mine.

I could never marry a man who takes pleasure in his own humiliation, for then there would be no pleasure left to me. I can only love them when they cringe. Still, it is odd how many men find cruelty attractive. Like dogs, they lick the hand that whips them. Poor Violet. I have planted fantasies in Duncan's mind that she can never satisfy. Well, well, what a very amusing thought that is. I really couldn't bear to see them happy. But then I can't bear to see anybody happy . . .

Nineteen

SARAH TOPPED UP their wine glasses and viewed the empty bottle with a wry look. 'Thank God my poison is legal,' she murmured. 'I know damn well I need an external stimulant to make the miseries bearable. Did you take her heroin off her, Cooper? She'll be in a desperate state if you did.'

'No,' he admitted, 'but you can keep that information to yourselves.'

'You're a very kind man,' she told him.

'I'm a realist,' he corrected her. 'If Joanna had murdered her mother then I was in a stronger position keeping what I knew up my sleeve than showing my hand before I had to. She would have been very vulnerable to police questioning if we could have charged her with possession and murder both at the same time.'

'You're such a bad liar,' said Sarah fondly. 'You're not going to charge her at all. Will you even tell her you know?'

But Cooper sidestepped that question. 'We were talking about how Duncan murdered Mathilda,' he said. 'So where were we?'

'With Mathilda being immensely suspicious when he

came through the back door uninvited and offered to top up her whisky,' said Sarah dryly.

'Oh, yes, well he wouldn't have gone that way. He'd have rung the front door bell. It was quite safe. Violet wasn't going to hear anything, not if she was snoring her head off in front of the television, and I'm sure he had a very convincing reason for knocking on Mathilda's door at seven o'clock on a Saturday evening. He did know a great deal about her life, after all, any bit of which he could tap into as an excuse. She would have to have been deeply paranoid to lock her door against a neighbour she saw almost every day.' Absent-mindedly, he tapped more ash into his palm then turned it upside down to scatter it on the floor. 'Once he'd given her the whisky, and watched her drink it, he made his excuses and left. He's a cautious man and he didn't know how effective the sedative would be, plus he needed to be sure Violet really was dead to the world and hadn't heard the bell ringing. Presumably if he'd found her semi-conscious, he'd have abandoned the project as being too dangerous and, by the same token, he wanted Mathilda well and truly under before he put the scold's bridle over her head.

'From then on, it would all have been very straightforward. He checked on Violet, donned a pair of gloves, collected the appropriate weeds from the garden – he wouldn't have done that during daylight hours in case someone saw him and put two and two together when they heard about Mathilda's flower arrangement. Then he let himself in again, this time through Mathilda's back door, took the Stanley knife from the kitchen drawer, checked Mathilda was asleep, took the weeds, the knife and the

scold's bridle upstairs where he left them on the dressing-table, filled the bath, then went back down to collect Mathilda. All he had to do was scoop her up in his arms, put her on the lift, take her upstairs and undress her.

'The time would have been approximately nine thirty, we think, which has made the pathologist very happy. He always favoured earlier rather than later, particularly as Mathilda wouldn't have died immediately.' He cast about in his mind again for the thread of where he had been. 'Right, so once he'd undressed her, he placed her in the warm bath, put the scold's bridle on her head, slit her wrists and then arranged the nettles and daisies in the head-band, probably using the sponge to wedge the gap. Then all he had to do was leave the whisky glass beside the empty sleeping-pill bottle, remove the diaries, wipe the key clean for safety's sake and replace it, before going home to Violet and the television. He undoubtedly took the poor woman to task the next morning over her drinking being so bad that she'd passed out the night before, or she might have told us earlier that she'd been asleep instead of going along with Duncan's story that there had been no sound from next door.' He massaged his chin. 'She's a very pliable woman and, in fairness to her, it obviously never occurred to her that he could have murdered Mathilda. I think she prompted him to write us the anonymous letter because she felt so guilty about letting Mathilda down.' He flicked a glance at Jack. 'She overheard her crying that time you went round to show her the painting, and she's convinced herself that if she'd only spoken to her then she might have prevented the murder.'

He saw the look of puzzled enquiry on Sarah's face, and

ploughed on relentlessly. 'As far as Ruth and Jane are concerned, Duncan didn't want to tell us about them being in Cedar House that day because he couldn't afford to draw attention to how much could be heard through the walls. But Violet gave him the perfect opportunity to involve Ruth when she overheard a row between Joanna and Ruth in their hall. She consulted Duncan about the wisdom of reporting it and, while he flatly refused to let her come in person, to avoid any unpleasantness, as he put it, he didn't object to an anonymous letter, although he insisted on wearing gloves to avoid us tracing it through the finger-prints. Violet thought that was *very* exciting,' he concluded with heavy irony.

'It's odd that Mathilda never mentioned hearing them,' said Jack. 'It's the sort of thing that would have driven her mad.'

'Mrs Orloff says she spoke very clearly and decisively, so perhaps she was a little deaf, and if she never heard them, it wouldn't occur to her that they could hear her. In any case, as soon as they realized just how much could be overheard, I suspect they tempered their own volume. It's interesting to watch them. He speaks just above a whisper and when-ever she gets excited, he frowns at her and she drops her voice.'

'I suppose that's how he found out about the key,' said Sarah slowly. 'When Mathilda told me where it was that day. He must have heard her.'

Cooper nodded.

'How did he know about the diaries?'

'According to Violet, she often used to talk to herself when no one was there, so I'm guessing she read them

aloud. Otherwise, he stumbled on them by accident when he was looking for something else.' He frowned. '*He*'s not going to tell us, that's for sure. He's just sitting there at the moment denying everything and challenging us to give one good reason why he would suddenly want to murder a woman he had known for fifty years, when scarcely one cross word had been exchanged between them in all that time. And Violet supports him on that. She says Duncan is far too lazy either to take offence or give it, so Mathilda very quickly got bored with trying to provoke any sort of reaction out of him.'

'He's got you by the short and curlies,' remarked Jack with reluctant admiration. 'You won't get very far with "trying to delay the passage of the will" as a convincing motive for murder. Even if the Prosecution's prepared to run with it, I can't see a jury accepting it. Have you really no idea at all why he wanted her dead? Surely Violet must know something.'

'She's very distressed at the moment. The DCI hopes a little tender care from a sympathetic policewoman will help jog her memory, but, if you want my opinion, she's being genuinely honest when she says she doesn't know. She's a funny little person, seems to live in a world of her own most of the time, talks nineteen-to-the-dozen but doesn't listen. I suspect most of what went on inside Cedar House was just background noise to her.' He glanced from one to the other of them. 'All of which is why I'm here. I need to talk to Ruth. She mentioned that her grandmother wrote her a letter shortly before she died, and it occurred to me that there might have been something in there which might help us.'

'If it's the same one she told me about, then she tore it up,' said Sarah.

'Still, she'll remember what was in it. I really do need to talk to her.'

Sarah shook her head firmly. 'Not now, Cooper. She's paranoid about the police at the moment, what with last night, and Jack being carted off in handcuffs at lunchtime. Okay, I know none of it's your fault, but you've got to show her a little compassion.'

'Don't make me insist,' he begged. 'I really don't have a choice on this one. We can't hold Duncan indefinitely without some very concrete evidence and, once he walks, he'll be free to tidy up anything we've missed.'

She sighed and took one of his large hands in hers. 'Look, I'm going to tell you something that, strictly speaking, I shouldn't because it's Ruth's secret and not mine, but I'd trust you with my life, Cooper, so I think I can trust you with Ruth's.' She gave the hand a quick squeeze before releasing it to reach across for Jack's, her eyes creasing with affection. 'Why do you think this silly sod has been charging about like a bull in a china shop? He says what he's done is rational and sensible. You and I know it isn't. Rather belatedly, he's discovered that he has some very powerful paternal feelings which, because he's the generous soul he is, he does not intend to limit to his own offspring. He is acting in lieu of Ruth's dead father because he wants her to know that there is someone in this shitty world who loves her.'

Jack raised her fingers to his lips. 'Two people,' he corrected her.

She held his gaze for a moment. 'Two people,' she

agreed. She took her hand away and transferred her attention back to Cooper. 'Ruth is so vulnerable at the moment that if she's put under any more pressure, then I can guarantee she'll withdraw from reality in the way that Joanna clearly has done and Mathilda probably did as well. It's almost as if there's a self-destructive gene in the family that triggers the withdrawal.' She shook her head. 'Whatever it is, Ruth is not going the same way, not if Jack and I can prevent it. She's pregnant, Cooper. I know she doesn't look it, but she's almost at the legal cut-off point, and if she doesn't make up her mind very quickly about having the pregnancy terminated, then she'll have to go through with it. Jack was trying to buy her the peace and quiet she needs to reach a decision, because as yet she hasn't had the chance to do it.'

Cooper absorbed all this in grave silence. 'Are you helping her reach her decision?' he asked at last.

'I've given her all the information I can, but I don't like to say, do this or do that. It's her mother's role to give advice but Joanna doesn't even know about the rape, let alone about the pregnancy.'

'Hmm,' grunted Cooper, pursing his lips in deep thought. 'Well, I certainly don't intend to add to the poor girl's problems,' he said at last. 'I'm sure her grandmother wouldn't demand justice for herself before consideration for her granddaughter. If she was that way inclined she'd have reported Ruth for thieving when she was still alive.' He stood up and buttoned his coat about him, preparatory to leaving. 'But, if you'll forgive the impertinence, Dr Blakeney, you must take your responsibilities as her adopted mother, temporary or otherwise, a great deal more

seriously. It's no good giving her information and leaving it up to her to decide, without making it very clear that you believe it's in her best interests to have an abortion. The chances are she'll scream and yell, say you don't love her and don't care tuppence for her feelings, but parenting is not about patting oneself on the back for being understanding and liberal, it's about guidance, education and training to help the child you love become a man or woman you can respect.' He nodded a friendly goodbye and made for the door, only to pause as he saw Ruth in the shadows of the hall.

'I've been listening,' she said, her wretched eyes full of tears. 'I'm sorry. I didn't mean to.'

'There, there,' said Cooper, gruff with embarrassment, pulling a large white handkerchief from his pocket and offering it to her. 'I'm the one who should apologize. I'd no business to interfere.'

Her eyes brimmed again. 'I don't mind about what you said. I was thinking – if only – you said you wished your children had had my opportunities – do you remember?'

He nodded. He had indeed said that, he thought with chagrin.

'Well, I was just thinking – I wish' – she gave him a watery smile – 'I wish I'd had theirs. I hope they appreciate you, Sergeant Cooper.' She took a letter from her pocket and gave it to him. 'It's Granny's,' she said. 'I didn't throw it away, but I couldn't show it to you because she talks about my stealing.' A tear splashed on to her hand. 'I really did love her, you know, but she died thinking I didn't, and that's almost worse than everything else.'

'Yes,' he said gently, 'I'm sure it is, because there's nothing you can do to mend it.'

'Not ever.'

'Well, as to ever – that I couldn't say. In this life, the best any of us can do is learn from our mistakes and try not to make them again. We're none of us infallible, Ruth, but we owe it to ourselves and to those around us to act with whatever wisdom we possess. Otherwise, how will mankind ever improve?'

She pressed her lips together to hold back the tears. 'And you think it would be wise for me to have an abortion?'

'Yes,' he said with absolute honesty, 'I do.' He placed his broad palm against her stomach. 'At the moment you're not quite old enough or tough enough to be mother and father to another human being, and you're too riddled by guilt over your grandmother, and what you see as your betrayal of her, to give this baby away to someone else.' He smiled rather shyly. 'That's not to say I expect you to agree with me or that I'll turn my back on you if you decide to have your baby. Dr Blakeney's quite right when she says it's your choice. But I'd rather see you pregnant when you've lived a little and found a man you can love who loves you, too. Then your babies will be wanted and you'll be free to be the kind of mother you want to be.'

She tried to thank him, but the words wouldn't come, so Cooper took her in his arms instead and held her tight. Behind them, Sarah turned a tear-streaked face to Jack. 'Remind me of this,' she whispered, 'whenever I get complacent. I've just learnt how little I really know.'

My dear Ruth [Mathilda had written], Your mother and I have fallen out over a letter written by my uncle Gerald Cavendish shortly before he died, making Joanna his heir. She is threatening to take me to court over it because she believes she can use it to overturn my father's will. She won't succeed, but I have been unable to convince her of that. She feels understandably aggrieved and wants to punish me. I realize now there has been too much secrecy within this family and so I am writing to you now to acquaint you with the knowledge she already has, because I do not want you to learn about it from her. She will not, I think, tell you kindly. James Gillespie was not your mother's father. Gerald Cavendish was. I realize how shocked you will be by this information but I urge you to do what I have done all these years and see it as something that happened which should not be regretted. You may find this hard to believe but, despite everything, I have always been fond of your mother, as indeed I have been fond of you.

I am faced now with a difficult choice. I am aware, my dear, that you have been stealing from me for some months. I am aware, too, that your mother has given up on life and prefers the twilight world of drug dependency and the casual relationships that give her the illusion of being loved without the ties of responsibility. You are both allowing yourselves to be abused by men and, in view of my own history, I find that deeply disheartening. I realize I have failed you, and have decided, therefore, to set you both free to make your own decisions about your futures.

My intention is to make over a lump sum to you and your mother on your eighteenth birthday, the amount to

be apportioned in the ratio 2:1, with your mother receiving double your share. Perhaps it is something I should have done a long time ago, but I was reluctant to give up what I have worked so hard for in the Cavendish name. As things are now, I see that a name is nothing unless the individuals who bear it stand above their peers, for it is not the accident of our births that makes us great but our individual characters. By setting you and your mother free to lead your lives as you choose, I hope to give you the chance to prove yourselves, just as others – those less fortunate – have already done.

In conclusion, should anything happen to me and you find yourself in need of a friend, then I urge you to talk to Dr Sarah Blakeney, my GP, who will give you nothing but good advice whatever the situation you find yourself in.

With love, Granny.

Cooper placed the letter in front of Detective Chief Inspector Jones. 'I've been asking myself where she was going to get the money from to give lump sums to Mrs and Miss Lascelles if she'd already made a will giving everything to Dr Blakeney.'

Charlie scanned the page rapidly. 'Did you come up with an answer?'

'I reckon it's on the video, if we'd only known what to look for. Do you remember when she was talking to Ruth towards the end and she mentioned her promise to leave the girl Cedar House before Ruth's behaviour of the last six months had persuaded her to change her mind? Okay, well

immediately after that she went on to say something like: "You'd have had the choice either to sell up or stay but you'd have sold because the house would have lost its charms for you once the estate was approved." Or words to that effect.'

Charlie nodded.

'I assumed the phrase "once the estate was approved" referred to the goods and chattels being handed over to Joanna as part of her share.'

'Go on.'

'I think now she was talking about an estate of houses. She was planning to sell off the garden for development. How else could she raise a lump sum for the Lascelles women and still be able to leave Cedar House and its contents to Dr Blakeney? Just imagine the impact that would have had on Duncan Orloff. A man who can't bear the thought of noisy children next door sure as hell isn't going to sit tamely by and watch his garden turned into a building site.'

'Prove it,' said Duncan placidly. 'Name the developer. Explain why there's no correspondence with this mythical company. Good grief, man, she wouldn't even have got planning permission for such an enterprise. The days of unravelling the green belt are long gone. They're knitting it back together now just as fast as they can. There's electoral mileage in the environmental vote and none at all in speculative vandalism.'

All of which, thought Charlie gloomily, was true. It was

left to Cooper to bring a dose of common sense to the situation.

The following morning, after lengthy consultations with the local borough planning officer, he presented himself at Howard & Sons, building contractors of Learmouth since 1972. A middle-aged secretary, agog with curiosity at this unexpected appearance of a plain-clothes policeman in their midst, ushered him with some ceremony into the office of Mr Howard Snr.

Mr Howard, a thickset elderly man with a scattering of grizzled grey hairs, looked up from a set of plans with a frown. 'Well, Sergeant? What can I do for you?'

'I understand your company was responsible for the Cedar Estate development in Fontwell. It was built ten years ago. Do you recall it?'

'I do,' barked the other. 'What of it? Who's complaining?'

'No one, as far as I know,' said Cooper placidly.

He waved to a chair. 'Sit down, man. You can't be too sure about anything these days. It's a dog-eat-dog world where litigation's the name of the game and the only people who get fat are the solicitors. I had a letter this morning from a tight-fisted bastard who's refusing to pay what he owes because he says we're in breach of contract by putting in one less electric socket than the plans called for. It makes you sick.' He beetled ferocious eyebrows. 'So what's your interest in Cedar Estate?'

'You bought the land for it from a Mrs Mathilda Gillespie of Cedar House, Fontwell.'

'I did. Blood-sucking old bitch she is, too. Paid far more for it than I should have done.'

'*Was*,' Cooper corrected him. 'She's dead.'

Howard eyed him with sudden interest. 'Is that so? Ah, well,' he murmured without regret, 'it comes to us all in the end.'

'In her case rather prematurely. She was murdered.'

There was a short silence. 'And what does that have to do with the Cedar Estate?'

'We're having difficulty establishing a motive. One idea that suggests itself,' he declared ponderously, 'is that she was planning to continue her successful venture with you by selling off the rest of her garden for development. From consultations I've had with the planning department, I understand some sort of second phase has always been on the cards, but this would have made her very unpopular in certain quarters and might have inspired the murder.' He hadn't missed the gleam of interest in the sharp old eyes opposite. 'Have you had any recent correspondence with her on the subject, Mr Howard?'

'Only negative.'

Cooper frowned. 'Could you explain that?'

'She approached us with a view to going forward. We made an offer. She rejected it.' He grunted with annoyance. 'Like I told you, she was a blood-sucking old bitch. Wanted far more for the land than it's worth. The building trade's been through the worst recession in its history and prices have plummeted. I wouldn't mind so much if it wasn't down to us in the first place that she was even in a position to develop the damn thing.' He glared at Cooper as if Cooper were responsible for Mathilda's rejection. 'It was us

who established the sodding outline permission on her garden ten years ago which is why we left access space on the south-east boundary. First refusal on the second phase if she decided to go ahead was part of the original contract and she had the gall to turn us down.'

'When was this? Can you remember?'

'The day she turned us down? Bonfire night, November the fifth.' He chuckled suddenly. 'I told her to stick a rocket up her arse and she hung up on me. Mind, I'd said many worse things first time round – I don't mind my Ps and Qs for anyone – and she always came back.'

'You saw her in person?'

'Telephone. She meant it, though, wrote a couple of days later confirming. Claimed she was in no hurry and was prepared to wait for the prices to go back up again. It's in the file, along with a copy of our offer.' The gleam of interest was back in his eyes. 'Still, if she's dead, her heirs might be interested, eh? It's a fair offer. They won't get better from anyone else.'

'Her will's being contested,' said Cooper apologetically. 'I imagine it will be some time before ownership of the property is proved. May I see her letter?'

'Don't see why not.' He pressed the intercom and demanded the Gillespie file. 'So who killed her then?'

'No one's been charged as yet.'

'Well, they do say planning disputes bring out the worst in people. Bit extreme to murder someone over it though. Eh?'

'Any murder's extreme,' said Cooper.

'A few houses more or less. It's hardly a motive.'

'People fear the unexpected,' said Cooper phlegmatically.

'I sometimes think that's the root cause of all murders.' He looked towards the door as the secretary popped in with an orange folder. 'The boat rocks and the only solution is to kill the person who's rocking it.'

Howard opened the file and selected a sheet from the top. 'There you are.' He handed it across.

Cooper examined it carefully. It was dated Saturday, November 6th, and typed. As Howard had said, it confirmed her refusal to proceed until prices improved. 'When did you say you got this?'

'Couple of days after the phone call.'

'That would have been a Sunday.'

'The Monday then, or maybe the Tuesday. We don't work weekends, not in the office at least.'

'Did she always type her letters?'

'Don't remember her ever doing it before.' He looked back through the file. 'Copper-plate script every time.'

Cooper thought of her letter to Ruth. That had been written in a beautiful hand. 'Have you any other letters from her? I'd like to compare the signatures.'

Howard licked a finger and flicked over the pages, removing several more sheets. 'You think someone else wrote it?'

'It's a possibility. There's no typewriter in her house and she was dead by the Saturday night. When could she have had it done?' He placed the pages side by side on the desk and squinted at the subscriptions. 'Well, well,' he said with satisfaction, 'the best laid schemes – you've been very helpful, Mr Howard. May I take these with me?'

'I'll want photocopies for my records.' He was consumed

with curiosity. 'Never occurred to me it wasn't kosher. What's wrong with it then?'

Cooper placed a finger on the typed letter's signature. 'For a start, he's dotted his "i"s' – he pointed to the others – 'and she hasn't. His "M" is too upright and the "G" runs on to the following "i".' He chuckled. 'The experts are going to have a field day on this. All in all it's a very cack-handed effort.'

'Bit of a fool, is he?'

'Arrogant, I'd say. Forgery is an art like any other. It takes years of practice to be any good.'

'I've a forensic team sifting through a dustbin full of Violet's old cinders,' Charlie told Cooper when he returned to the nick, 'and they tell me they've found the diaries. Or what's left of them at least. There's the odd scrap of paper but several quite substantial pieces of what they say is the calf-skin binding. They're still looking. They're confident of finding at least one scrap with her writing on it.' He rubbed his hands together.

'They might look for scraps of typed paper while they're about it, preferably with a Howard & Sons imprint,' said Cooper, producing his sheaf of letters. 'They made her a formal offer for her land on the first of November, and we certainly didn't find it when we went through her papers. The chances are Orloff swiped an entire file. Howard Snr has a stack of correspondence relating to Cedar Estate, and there wasn't a damn thing on the subject anywhere in the house. If there had been we might have twigged a bit sooner.'

'No one's fault but her own. I suppose she learnt never to trust anyone which is why she played everything so close to her chest. She said it all in her letter to Ruth, "there's been too much secrecy within this family". If she'd mentioned her plans to the solicitor even, she'd probably be alive now.'

'Still, we didn't ask the right questions, Charlie.'

The Inspector gave a dry laugh. 'If the answer's forty-two, then what's the Ultimate Question? Read *The Hitch Hiker's Guide to the Galaxy*, old son. It's harder to ask the right question than it is to come up with the answer, so don't lose any sleep over it.'

Cooper, who somewhat belatedly was trying to improve his reading, took out his notebook and jotted down the title. At the very least, it had to be more palatable than *Othello* which he was struggling through at the moment. He tucked his pencil back into his pocket and took Charlie through his conversation with the developer. 'It was six weeks of hard negotiating the first time before he and she could agree on a price. She used to horse-trade over the phone, apparently, rejecting every offer until he came up with one she could accept. Poor old soul,' he said with genuine feeling. 'Orloff must have thought his ship had come in when he heard her doing it the second time round. She made it so easy for him.' He tapped the typed letter. 'All he had to do was get rid of her and post that off the next day. Howard claims he and his sons lost interest immediately because he'd made it clear to her on more than one occasion that the bottom had dropped out of the market and he wasn't in a position to offer her any more.'

Charlie picked up the letter and examined it. 'There was

a portable typewriter on the desk in his sitting-room,' he recalled. 'Let's get the lads out there to make a quick comparison for us. He's put all his effort into forging her signature and forgotten that typewriters have signatures, too.'

'He'd never make it that easy for us.'

But he had.

'Duncan Jeremiah Orloff . . . formally charged with the murder of Mathilda Beryl Gillespie . . . Saturday, November sixth . . .' The voice of the Duty Officer droned on relentlessly, making little impact on Cooper who knew the formula off by heart. Instead, his mind drifted towards an elderly woman, drained of her lifeblood, and the rusted iron framework that had encased her head. He felt an intense regret that he had never known her. Whatever sins she had committed, it would, he felt, have been a privilege.

'. . . request that you be refused bail because of the serious nature of the charges against you. The magistrates will order an immediate remand into custody . . .'

He looked at Duncan Orloff only when the man beat his fat little hands against his breast and burst into tears. It wasn't his fault, he pleaded, it was Mathilda's fault. Mathilda was to blame for everything. He was a sick man. What would Violet do without him?

'Collapse of stout party,' muttered the Duty Officer under his breath to Cooper, listening to the rasping, anguished breaths.

A deep frown creased Cooper's pleasant face. 'By heaven, she deserved better than you, she really did,' he said to

Orloff. 'It should have been a brave man who killed her, not a coward. What gave you the right to play God with her life?'

'A brave man wouldn't have had to, Sergeant Cooper.' He turned haunted eyes towards the policeman. 'It wasn't courage that was needed to kill Mathilda, it was fear.'

'Fear of a few houses in your garden, Mr Orloff?'

Duncan shook his head. 'I am what I am' – he held trembling hands to his face – 'and it was she who made me. I have spent my adult life shunning the woman I married in favour of fantasies about the one I didn't, and you cannot live in hell for forty years without being damaged by it.'

'Is that why you came back to Fontwell, to relive your fantasies?'

'You can't control them, Sergeant. They control you.' He fell silent.

'But you returned five years ago, Mr Orloff.'

'I asked nothing from her, you know. A few shared memories perhaps. Peace even. After forty years I expected very little.'

Cooper eyed him curiously. 'You said you killed her out of fear. Was that what you fantasized about? Being so afraid of her that you could bring yourself to kill her?'

'I fantasized about making love,' he whispered.

'To Mathilda?'

'Of course.' He gathered his tears in the palms of his hands. 'I've never made love to Violet. I couldn't.'

Good God, thought Cooper with disgust, did the man have no pity at all for his poor little wife? 'Couldn't or wouldn't, Mr Orloff? There is a difference.'

'Couldn't.' The word was barely audible. 'Mathilda did

certain things' – he shivered like a man possessed – 'which Violet was offended by' – his voice broke – 'it was less unpleasant for both of us if I paid for what I wanted.'

Cooper caught the Duty Officer's gaze above Duncan's head, and gave a cynical laugh. 'So this is going to be your defence, is it? That you murdered Mathilda Gillespie because she gave you a taste for something only prostitutes could supply?'

A thready sigh puttered from the moist lips. 'You never had cause to be afraid of her, Sergeant. She didn't own you because she didn't know your secrets.' The sad eyes turned towards him. 'Surely it's occurred to you that when we bought Wing Cottage our solicitor discovered the outline planning permission on the remaining Cedar House land? We went ahead with the purchase because Mathilda agreed to a clause in the contract, giving us a power of veto over any future decision.' He gave a hollow laugh. 'I blame myself because I knew her so much better than Violet ever did. The clause was worth less than the paper it was written on.' Briefly, he pressed his lips together in an effort to control himself. 'She was obliged to tell me about her approach to Howard because she was going to need my signature on the final document, but when I told her that Violet and I would object to the proposed plan, which put the nearest house ten yards from our back wall, she laughed. "Don't be absurd, Duncan. Have you forgotten how much I know about you?"'

When he didn't go on, Cooper prompted him. 'She was going to blackmail you into signing?'

'Of course.' He placed his damp palms to his breasts. 'We were in the drawing-room. She left me for a couple of

minutes to fetch a book from the library, and when she came back she read extracts to me.' Distress wheezed from him in quickened breaths. 'It was one of her diaries – full of such terrible lies and obscenity – and not just about me – Violet, too – intimate details that Violet had told her when she was tipsy. "Do you want me to photocopy this, Duncan, and spread it round the village?" she asked. "Do you want the whole of Fontwell to know that Violet is still a virgin because the demands you made of her on your wedding night were so disgusting that she had to lock herself in the bathroom?"' – his voice faltered – 'she was very entertained by it all – couldn't put the book down once she'd started – read me pieces about the Marriotts, the vicar, the poor Spedes – everyone.' He fell silent again.

'So you went back later to read the others?' suggested Cooper.

Duncan shrugged helplessly. 'I was desperate. I hoped I'd find something I could use against *her*. I doubted there'd be anything of value in the early ones, simply because I'd have to find independent proof to challenge her, and, bar references to Joanna's drug addiction, Ruth's stealing and her belief that Sarah Blakeney was the daughter she'd had by Paul Marriott, the later ones were simply a catalogue of her dislikes. They were the product of a diseased mind, and she used them, I think, as a channel for expunging her poison. If she hadn't been able to express herself on paper' – he shook his head – 'she was quite mad, you know.'

'Still,' said Cooper ponderously, 'murder was an extreme solution, Mr Orloff. You could have used her daughter's and her granddaughter's problems against her. She was a

proud woman. She wouldn't have wanted those made public, surely?'

The sad eyes fixed on him again. 'I never planned to murder her, or not till that Saturday morning when Jane Marriott went to see her. I intended to threaten her with divulging what I knew to Dr Blakeney. But as I told you, it was fear that killed her. A brave man would have said: "publish and be damned".'

He had lost Cooper. 'I don't understand.'

'She told Jane Marriott that things would get worse before they got better because she knew James had been reading her private papers – it never occurred to her it was me – then she went on to say that she had no intention of keeping quiet any longer.' He wrung his hands. 'So, of course, I went round the minute Jane left and asked her what she meant by "she had no intention of keeping quiet any longer"?' His face was grey with fatigue. 'She picked up the scold's bridle and taunted me with it. "Mathilda Cavendish and Mathilda Gillespie did not write their diaries for fun, Duncan. They wrote them so that one day they could have their revenge. They will not be gagged. I shall see to that."' He paused. 'She really was mad,' he insisted, 'and she knew it. I said I'd call a doctor for her so she laughed and quoted *Macbeth* at me. "More needs she the divine than the physician."' He raised his hands in a gesture of surrender. 'And I thought how all of us, who would be destroyed by her diaries, needed the divine more than the physician, and I made up my mind during that terrible afternoon to play . . . God.'

Cooper was deeply sceptical. 'But you must have planned

it all in advance because you stole the sleeping pills beforehand.'

He sighed. 'They were for me – or Violet – or both of us.'

'So what made you change your mind?'

'Sergeant, I am, as you rightly say, a coward and I realized that I could not destroy the diaries without destroying her as well. *She* was the poison, the diaries were only the outward manifestation. At least I have allowed all the others to keep their dignity.'

Cooper thought of the ones he cared about, Jack and Sarah, Jane and Paul Marriott; Ruth above all.

'Only if you plead guilty, Mr Orloff, otherwise this will all come out in court.'

'Yes. I owe Violet that much,' he said.

After all, it is easy to manipulate a man if all he wants is something as worthless as love. Love is easily given when it is the body that's invaded and not the mind. My mind can withstand anything. I am Mathilda Cavendish and what does Mathilda care when the only thing she feels is contempt?

Man, proud man,
Drest in a little brief authority,
Most ignorant of what he's most assur'd,
His glassy essence, like an angry ape,
Plays such fantastic tricks before high heaven,
As make the angels weep.

If angels weep Mathilda sees no sign of it. They do not weep for me . . .

Twenty

JANE MARRIOTT replaced the telephone receiver and held a shaking hand to her lips. She walked through to the living room where her invalid husband was dozing quietly in the bright winter sunshine which poured through the window. She sat beside him and took her hand in his. 'That was Sergeant Cooper on the phone,' she said. 'James Gillespie was found dead in his flat this morning. A heart attack, they think.'

Paul didn't say anything, only stared out across the garden.

'He says there's nothing to worry about any more, that no one need ever know. He also said' – she paused briefly – 'he also said that the child was a girl. Mathilda lied about your having a son.' She had told him everything after her return home from the surgery the day Sergeant Cooper had questioned her.

A tear squeezed from between his lids. 'I'm so sorry.'

'For James?'

'For – everything. If I'd known—' He fell silent.

'Would it have made a difference, Paul?'

'We could have shared the burden, instead of you bearing it alone.'

'It would have destroyed me,' she said honestly. 'I couldn't have coped with you knowing that Mathilda had had your child.' She studied his face closely. 'As time went by, you would have thought more of her and less of me.'

'No.' His marbled hand clutched at hers. 'She was in every sense of the word a brief madness so, even if I'd known about the child, it wouldn't have changed anything. I have only ever loved you.' His eyes grew damp. 'In any case, my dear, I think your first instincts were right, and that Mathilda would have killed the baby. We can none of us put any faith in what she said. She lied more often than she told the truth.'

'Except that she left her money to Sarah,' said Jane in a rush, 'and Sergeant Cooper said the baby was a girl. Suppose Sarah—?' She broke off and squeezed his hand encouragingly. 'Nothing's ever too late, Paul. Would it do any harm, do you think, to ask a few tactful questions?'

He looked away from her eager face and, in Cooper's earlier footsteps, traced the fickleness of fate. He had lived his life believing he was childless, and now, at the age of seventy, Jane had told him he was a father. But of whom? Of a son? Of a daughter? Or had Mathilda lied about this as she had lied about so much else? For himself, it hardly mattered – he had long since come to terms with being childless – but for Jane, Mathilda would always cast a long and spiteful shadow. There were no guarantees that Sarah Blakeney was his daughter, no guarantees even that the child, if it existed at all, would welcome the intrusion of parents into its life, and he couldn't bear to see Jane's hopes dashed in this as surely as her hope in his fidelity had been

dashed. In the end, wasn't it better to live with the illusion of happiness than the awful certainty of trust betrayed?

'You must promise me you will never say anything.' He laid his head against the back of the chair and struggled for breath. 'If I am her father, then Mathilda never told her, or I'm sure she would have come here of her own accord.' His eyes filled with tears. 'She has a loving father already who has done a fine job – a very fine job – in bringing her up. Don't force her to choose between us, my dearest one. Rejections are such painful things.'

Jane smoothed the thinning hair from his forehead. 'Perhaps, after all, some secrets are best kept secret. Shall we share this one together and dream a little from time to time?' She was a wise and generous woman who, just occasionally, acknowledged that it was Mathilda's treachery that had given her insights into herself and Paul that she hadn't had before. After all, she thought, there was less to mourn now than there was to celebrate.

Joanna sat where her mother had always sat, in the hard-backed chair beside the french windows. She tilted her head slightly to look at Sergeant Cooper. 'Does Dr Blakeney know you're telling me this?'

He shook his head. 'No. I rather hope you'll make the first move by offering to drop your challenge to the will if she agrees to honour your mother's intentions as set out in her letter to Ruth. A little oil on troubled waters, Mrs Lascelles, goes a very long way and it's in everyone's interests to put this sad affair behind you and go back to London where you belong.'

'In Dr Blakeney's certainly, not in mine.'

'I was thinking more of your daughter. She's very young still, and her grandmother's death has distressed her a great deal more than you realize. It would be' – he sought for a word – 'helpful if you pursued an amicable settlement rather than a continued and painful confrontation. Barristers have a nasty habit of unearthing details that are best left buried.'

She stood up. 'I really don't wish to discuss this any more, Sergeant. It's none of your business.' The pale eyes hardened unattractively. 'You've been seduced by the Blakeneys just as my mother was, and for that reason alone I will not negotiate amicably with them. I still find it incomprehensible that you haven't charged Jack Blakeney with assault, or, for that matter, Ruth with theft, and I intend to make sure my solicitor raises both those issues with your Chief Constable. It's quite clear to me that Dr Blakeney, ably abetted by my daughter, is using her husband and you to pressure me into leaving this house so that she can gain vacant possession of it. I will not give her the satisfaction. The longer I remain, the stronger my title to it.'

Cooper chuckled. 'Do you even have a solicitor, Mrs Lascelles? I hope you don't because you're wasting your money if that's the sort of advice he's giving you.' He pointed to the chair. 'Sit down,' he ordered her, 'and thank your daughter and the Blakeneys for the fact that I am not going to arrest you now for the illegal possession of heroin. I'd like to, make no mistake about that, but as I said before it's in everyone's interests, not least your own, if Dorset is shot of you. I should, by rights, pass on what I know to the Metropolitan Police but I won't. They'll find out anyway

soon enough because, even with the capital sum Dr Blakeney pays you, you'll be quite incapable of managing. There'll be no more monthly cheques, Mrs Lascelles, because there's no old lady left to terrorize. What did you do to her to make her pay?'

She was staring out of the window but it was a long time before she answered. 'I didn't have to do anything, except be her daughter. She assumed I was like her, and that made her afraid of me.'

'I don't understand.'

She turned round to fix him with her strangely penetrating gaze. 'I watched her murder her father. She was terrified I was going to do the same to her.'

'Would you have done?'

She smiled suddenly and her beauty dazzled him. 'I'm like Hamlet, Sergeant, "but mad north-north-west". You probably won't believe me but I was always more frightened that she would kill me. I've been sleeping quite well recently.'

'Will you go back to London?'

She shrugged. 'Of course. "When a man is tired of London, he is tired of life." Have you read Samuel Johnson, Sergeant? He was a great deal wittier than Shakespeare.'

'I will now, Mrs Lascelles.'

She turned back to the window and its wonderful view of the cedar of Lebanon that dominated the garden. 'I suppose if I fight Dr Blakeney you'll pass on what you know about me to the Metropolitan Police.'

'I'm afraid I will.'

She gave a low laugh. 'Mother was always very good at

blackmail. It's a pity you never met her. Will the Blakeneys look after Ruth, Sergeant? I wouldn't want her to starve.'

Which was, thought Cooper, the closest she would ever come to expressing affection for her daughter. 'They certainly plan to keep her with them in the short term,' he told her.

('Ruth will need all our emotional support,' Sarah had said, 'and that includes yours, Cooper, if she's to get through the abortion and Dave Hughes's trial.' 'And if Hughes is acquitted?' Cooper asked. 'He won't be,' said Sarah firmly. 'Three more girls have agreed to testify against him. Women have plenty of courage, you know, when they're not pinned to the ground with knives held to their throats.')

'And in the long term?' Joanna asked him.

'Assuming the will isn't challenged, then Dr Blakeney will set up a trust fund for Ruth at the same time as she makes you a gift of the money your mother intended you to have.'

'Will she sell off the garden to do it?'

'I don't know. She told me this morning that Cedar House would make rather a fine nursing home.'

Joanna gripped her arms angrily. 'Mother must be turning in her grave to think the old ladies of Fontwell will be looked after at her expense. She couldn't stand any of them.'

Cooper smiled to himself. There really was a beautiful irony about it all, particularly as the first customer would probably be poor, bewildered Violet Orloff.

*

Jack watched Sarah out of the corner of his eye as he sat at his easel putting the finishing touches to the portrait of Joanna. She was staring aimlessly out of the window towards the wooded horizon, her forehead pressed against the cool glass. 'Penny for them,' he said at last.

'Sorry?' She turned to glance at him.

'What were you thinking about?'

'Oh, nothing, just – ' she shook her head – 'nothing.'

'Babies?' he suggested, without the usual trace of irony.

She moved into the centre of the room and stared at the painting of Mathilda. 'All right, yes, I was, but you needn't worry. It wasn't in hopeful anticipation. I was thinking that you've been right all along and that having babies is a mug's game. They bring you nothing but heartache and, frankly, I'd as soon play it safe and spare myself the anguish.'

'Pity,' he murmured, rinsing his brush in turpentine and wiping it on the kitchen roll, 'I was just getting acclimatized to the whole idea.'

She kept her voice deliberately light. 'I can take your jokes on most things, Jack, but not where babies are concerned. Sally Bennedict destroyed any credibility you might have on the subject the day she destroyed your little mistake.'

He looked very thoughtful. 'As a matter of interest, am I being singled out because I'm a man or are you planning to lay that same guilt-trip on Ruth in years to come?'

'That's different.'

'Is it? Can't see it myself.'

'Ruth wasn't two-timing her husband,' she muttered through gritted teeth.

'Then we aren't talking about babies, Sarah, and whether

or not I have the right to change my mind, we are talking about infidelity. Two different things entirely.'

'In your book, maybe. Not in mine. Committing yourself to a person is no different from committing yourself to a belief. Why, if you couldn't bear to impregnate your wife, were you so unconcerned about impregnating your mistress?' Two spots of colour flared high on her cheekbones, and she turned away abruptly. 'Let bygones be bygones. I don't want to talk about it any more.'

'Why not?' he said. 'I'm having a hell of a good time.' He linked his hands behind his head and grinned at her rigid back. 'You've put me through hell these last twelve months. You yank me out of London without a "by your leave" or a "do you mind?". Stick me in the middle of nowhere with a "take it or leave it, Jack, you're only my shit of a husband".' His eyes narrowed. 'I've put up with Cock Robin Hewitt strutting his stuff about my kitchen, leering at you and treating me like something the dog threw up. I've smiled while mental midgets pissed on my work, because I'm just the bum who likes nothing better than scrounging off his wife. And on top of all that I've had to listen to Keith Smollett lecturing me on your virtues. In all that time only one person, and this includes you, ever treated me as if I were human – and that was Mathilda. But for her, I'd have walked out in September and left you to stew in your own complacent juice.'

She kept her back towards him. 'Why didn't you?'

'Because, as she kept reminding me, I'm your husband,' he growled. 'Jesus, Sarah, if I didn't think what we had was worth something, why would I have married you in the first

place? I didn't have to, for Christ's sake. No one held a gun to my head. I wanted to.'

'Then why—?' She didn't go on.

'Why did I get Sally pregnant? I didn't. I never even slept with the horrible little bitch. I painted her portrait because she thought I was going places after the Bond Street dealer clinched my one and only sale.' He gave a hollow laugh. 'She wanted to hitch her wagon to a rising star, the way she's hitched it to every other rising star she's ever met. Which is what I painted, of course – a lazy parasite with pretensions to greatness. She has hated me ever since. If you'd told me she was claiming me as the father of her unwanted baby I'd have set you straight, but you didn't trust me enough to tell me.' His voice hardened. 'You sure as hell trusted her, though, and you didn't even like the bloody woman.'

'She was very plausible.'

'OF COURSE SHE WAS PLAUSIBLE!' he roared. 'She's a *fucking* actress, and I use the word advisedly. When are you going to open your eyes, woman, and see people in the round, their dark sides, their bright sides, their strengths, their weaknesses? Dammit, you should have let your passions go, clawed my miserable eyes out, slashed my balls – *anything* – if you thought I'd two-timed you.' His voice softened. 'Don't you love me enough to hate me, Sarah?'

'You bastard, Blakeney,' she said, turning round and raking him from head to toe with glittering eyes. 'You will never know how unhappy I've been.'

'And you have the nerve to accuse me of being self-centred. What about my unhappiness?'

'Yours is easily cured,' she said.

'It damn well isn't.'

'It damn well is.'

'How?'

'A little massage to ease the stiffness and then a kiss to make it better.'

'Ah,' he said thoughtfully, 'well, it's certainly a start. But bear in mind the condition's chronic and needs repeated applications. I do not want a relapse.'

'It'll cost you, though.'

He eyed her through half-closed lids. 'I thought it sounded too good to be true.' He dug in his pocket. 'How much?'

She cuffed him lightly across the head. 'Information only. Why did Mathilda have a row with Jane Marriott on the morning she died? Why did Mathilda cry when you showed her your painting? And why did Mathilda leave me her money? I know they're all related, Jack, and I know Cooper knows the answer. I saw it in his eyes last night.'

'No massage if you don't get the answer, I suppose.'

'Not for you. I'll offer it to Cooper instead. One of you is bound to tell me in the end.'

'You'd kill the poor old chap. He goes into spasms if you touch his hand.' He drew her down on to his lap. 'It won't make it any easier if I tell you,' he warned. 'In fact it'll make it harder. I know you too well.' Whatever guilt she felt now, he thought, would be nothing compared with the agonies of wondering if she had unwittingly conned Mathilda into believing she was adopted. And what would it do to her relationship with Jane Marriott? Knowing Sarah, she would feel duty-bound to tell Jane the truth, and push the poor

woman away with a surfeit of honesty. 'I made Mathilda a promise, Sarah. I really don't want to break it.'

'You broke it when you told Cooper,' she pointed out.

'I know, and I'm not happy about it, any more than I was happy about breaking my promise to Ruth.' He sighed. 'But I really did have no option. He and the Inspector were convinced the will was the motive for Mathilda's murder and I had to explain why she made it.'

Sarah stared at Mathilda's portrait. 'She made it because she was buying her rite of passage into immortality and she didn't trust Joanna or Ruth to deliver the goods for her. They would have squandered the money while she trusted me to build the "something worthwhile in her memory".' She sounded bitter, Jack thought. 'She knew me well enough to know I wouldn't spend a bequest on myself, particularly one to which I felt I had no right.'

'She wasn't that cynical, Sarah. She made no secret of her fondness for you.'

But Sarah was still absorbed in the portrait. 'You haven't explained,' she said suddenly, 'why you went to stay with Sally that weekend?' She turned to look at him. 'But that was a lie, wasn't it? You went somewhere else.' She put her small hands on his shoulders. 'Where, Jack?' She shook him when he didn't answer. 'It had something to do with Mathilda's weeping and, presumably, her will, too, though you didn't know it at the time.' He could almost hear her mind working. 'And whatever it was required your absence for that weekend without my knowing where you were going.' She searched his face. 'But for all she knew she would live for another twenty years, so why tell you

something now that wouldn't have any real impact until after she was dead?'

'She didn't intend to tell me. I was a very reluctant recipient of her confession.' He sighed. Sooner or later, he realized, Sarah would find out that he had stayed with her father and why he had gone there. 'A year or so after Joanna was born, she had a second daughter by Paul Marriott, whom she put up for adoption. For all sorts of reasons she persuaded herself that you were her lost daughter, and she told me she'd changed her will in your favour.' He gave a wry smile. 'I was so shocked that I didn't know what to do. Say nothing and let you inherit under false pretences? Tell her the truth and shatter her illusions? I decided to put the decision on hold while I went to see if your father had something I could show her.' He shook his head ironically. 'But when I got back Mathilda was dead, the police were searching around for a murder motive, and I was the only person who knew Mathilda had left you a fortune. It was a nightmare. All I could see was that you and I would be arrested for conspiracy unless I kept my mouth shut. We couldn't prove I hadn't told you about the will, and you had no alibi.' He gave a low laugh. 'Then out of the blue you offered me my marching orders and I realized the best thing I could do was grab them with both hands and leave you thinking I was a miserable bastard. You were so hurt and angry that, for once in your life, you didn't try to hide your emotions, and Cooper received a hefty dose of transparent honesty. You showed him everything from shock about the will to complete bewilderment that I'd been able to paint Mathilda's portrait without your knowing.' He

laughed again. 'You got us both off the hook without even realizing what you were doing.'

'Thanks very much,' she said tartly. 'And what would have happened if I'd been overjoyed to see the back of you?'

His face split into an evil grin. 'Well, just in case, I took out an insurance policy by moving in with Joanna. She's better-looking than you so you were bound to be jealous.'

'Bollocks.' But she didn't elaborate on whether it was the looks or the jealousy that was evoking her scorn. 'Did Mathilda tell Jane she'd had Paul's child? Was that what the row was about?'

He nodded. 'But she told her it was a boy.'

It was Sarah's turn to sigh. 'Then I doubt it's even true. She could have fantasized a baby just as easily as she fantasized her uncle's suicide' – she shrugged – 'or had an abortion or smothered the poor little thing at birth. I think it just suited her to resurrect the fantasy in order to create a thoroughly guilty and embarrassed legatee whose strings she could pull after she was dead.' She turned back to examine the portrait again. 'She used and abused us all, one way and another, and I'm not sure I want to be manipulated by her any more. What do I say to Jane and Paul if they ask me why she left me her money?'

'Nothing,' he said simply. 'Because it's not your secret, Sarah, it's mine. Duncan did her one good service by destroying her diaries. It leaves you free to build a memorial to her in any shape or form you like. In ten years, Fontwell will see her only as a generous benefactress because there'll be no evidence to prove otherwise.' He cupped her face in his hands. 'Don't abandon her now, sweetheart. Whatever

her motives were and whatever she did, she entrusted you with her redemption.'

'She should have entrusted it to you, Jack. I think she probably loved you more than anyone in her whole life.' Dampness glistened along her lashes. 'Does she deserve to have people think well of her?'

He touched her tears with the tip of his finger. 'She deserves a little pity, Sarah. In the end that's all any of us deserve.'

This is the diary of Mathilda Beryl Cavendish. It is my story for people to read when I am dead. If anyone finds it they should take it to the police and make sure Father is hanged. He made me do something wicked today and when I said I was going to tell the vicar, he locked me in the cupboard with the scold's bridle on my head. I WAS BLEEDING. *He cries a lot and says it is Mother's fault for dying. Well, I think it's Mother's fault, too.*

It was my birthday yesterday. Father says I am old enough and that Mother would not mind. She knew about men's needs. I am not to tell ANYONE *or he will use the bridle.* OVER AND OVER AGAIN.

Mother should never have done such things, then Father would not do them to me. I am only ten years old.

I HATE HER. I HATE HER. I HATE HER . . .

THE ECHO

Minette Walters

'It was the smell that Mrs Powell noticed first. Slightly sweet. Slightly unpleasant ... It shocked her badly to find a dead man huddled on sheets of flattened cardboard in the corner, his head slumped on his knees.'

Who was Billy Blake, other than a homeless alcoholic who wandered the streets? Why was he found dead from starvation in one of the richest areas of one of the richest capitals in the world? And why did he die in the garage of wealthy architect Amanda Powell, without once calling for her help?

Having thwarted press interest at the time, six months on from the bizarre tragedy Amanda is suddenly eager to talk to journalist Michael Deacon. She seems to have developed a strange obsession with her dead visitor, and Deacon's curiosity – both about her and her motives in trying to establish Billy's true identity – is intense . . .

What follows here is an early scene from the novel.

MRS POWELL was certainly immaculately groomed but she was twenty years short of late fifties. She was also far too controlled ever to display the sorts of emotion that Lisa was hoping for. She greeted them with a brisk, professional courtesy before showing them into an impeccable sitting-room which smelt of rose-petal pot-pourri and had the clean, spare look of designer minimalism. She clearly liked space, and Deacon rather approved of the cream leather and chrome chairs and sofa that formed an island about a low glass coffee table in the middle of a russet-coloured carpet. Beyond them an expanse of window, framed by draped but undrawn curtains, looked across the Thames to the lights on the other side. There was very little else in the room: only a series of glass shelves above tinted glass cabinets which clearly contained a stereo system; and three canvases – one white, one grey and one black – which adorned the wall opposite the shelves.

He nodded towards them. 'What are they called?'

'The title's in French. *Gravure à la manière noire.* It means mezzotint in English. They're by Henri Benoit.'

'Interesting,' he said, glancing at her, although it wasn't

clear if he was referring to the canvases or to the woman herself.

In fact he was thinking that her taste in interior design sat rather oddly with her choice of house. It was an uninteresting brick box on a new estate in the Isle of Dogs which would probably be billed in estate agents' jargon as 'an exclusive development of detached executive homes with views of the river'. He guessed the house to be about five years old, with three bedrooms and two reception rooms, and put its value at well outside an average price range. But why, he wondered, would an obviously wealthy woman with interesting taste choose something so characterless when, for the equivalent money, she could have had a spacious flat anywhere in the heart of London? Perhaps she liked detached houses, he thought rather cynically. Or views of the river. Or perhaps *Mr* Powell had chosen it.

'Do sit down,' she said gesturing towards the sofa. 'Can I get you something to drink?'

'Thank you,' said Lisa, who'd taken an instant dislike to her. 'Black coffee would be nice.' In the scheme of feminine competition, Mrs Powell oozed success. She appeared to have everything – even femininity – and Lisa looked around for something to criticize.

'Mr Deacon?'

'Do you have anything stronger?'

'Of course. Whisky, brandy, beer?'

'Red wine?' he suggested hopefully.

'I've a 1984 Rioja open. Would that do?'

'It would. Thank you very much.'

Mrs Powell disappeared down the corridor and they heard her filling the kettle in the kitchen.

'What's with black coffee, Smith,' murmured Deacon, 'when there's alcohol on offer?'

'I thought we were supposed to be behaving ourselves,' she whispered. 'And, for Christ's sake, don't start smoking. There are no ashtrays. I've already looked. I don't want you putting her back up before she agrees to the photographs.'

He watched her critical appraisal of the room. 'What's the verdict?'

'JP was right about everything except her age and her husband. *She*'s the stockbroker. I'll bet the Mrs is a courtesy title to give her some status in a male-dominated world. There's no sign of a man living here. It's all too uncomfortable and it doesn't half stink of roses. She probably sprayed the room before we arrived.' She turned her mouth down. 'I hate women who do that. It's a kind of one-upmanship. They want to prove their house is cleaner than yours.'

He lifted an amused eyebrow. 'Are you jealous?'

'What's to be jealous of?' she hissed.

'Success,' he murmured, holding a finger to his lips as they heard Mrs Powell returning.

'If you want to smoke,' she said, passing a coffee cup to Lisa and a glass of red wine to Deacon, 'I'll find you an ashtray.' She put her own wine glass on the table near an armchair and looked at them both.

'No, thank you,' said Lisa, thinking of JP's instruction.

'Yes, please,' said Deacon, doubting he could stand the scent of rose petals for an hour. He wished Lisa hadn't mentioned them. Once noticed, the smell was cloying, and he was reminded of the second Mrs Deacon who had plundered his very mediocre fortune in order to dowse herself in Chanel No. 5. It had been the shorter of his two

marriages, lasting a mere three years before Clara had cleared off with a twenty-year-old toyboy and rather too much of her husband's capital. He took the china saucer Mrs Powell handed him, then placed a cigarette between his lips and lit it. The smell of burning tobacco immediately swamped the roses, and Deacon felt guilt and satisfaction in equal measures. He left the cigarette jutting from his mouth as he took a tape recorder and a notebook from his pocket and placed them on the table in front of him. 'Do you mind if I record what you say?'

'No.'

He set the tape in motion and reluctantly broached the subject of photographs. 'We'd like a small visual to accompany the piece, Mrs Powell, so have you any objections to Lisa photographing you?'

She stared at him as she sat down. 'Why would you want photographs of me if you're planning to write about Billy Blake, Mr Deacon?'

Why indeed? 'Because in the absence of pictures of Billy, which we've established don't exist,' he lied, transferring the cigarette to the ashtray, 'I'm afraid you're the next best thing. Is that a problem for you?'

'Yes,' she said flatly. 'I'm afraid it is. I've already told you I have no intention of being used by your magazine.'

'And, as I told you, Mrs Powell, I don't make a habit of using people.'

She had ice-blue eyes which reminded him of his mother's, and that was a shame, he thought, because in other respects she was quite attractive. 'Then surely you agree that it's absurd to illustrate an article on poverty and the homeless with a picture of a woman who lives in an

expensive house in an expensive part of London.' She paused for a moment, inviting him to speak. When he didn't she went on: 'In fact, there *are* pictures of Billy Blake. I have two which I'm prepared to lend you. One is a mugshot from when he was first arrested and the other was taken in the mortuary. Either would illustrate poverty better than a photograph of me.'

Deacon shrugged but didn't say anything.

'You said you were interested in Billy.'

She sounded put out, he thought, and that made him curious, for he'd been a journalist long enough to recognize that Mrs Powell was keener to tell her story than he was to hear it. *But why now, when she had refused to talk to the press at the time?* That question intrigued him. 'No pictures of you, no story, I'm afraid,' he said, reaching forward to switch off the tape. 'Editor's instructions. I'm sorry to have wasted your time, Mrs Powell.' He looked with regret at his untouched wine. 'And your Rioja.'

She watched him as he began to gather his bits and pieces together, clearly weighing something in her mind. 'All right,' she said abruptly, 'you can take your photographs. Billy's story needs to be told.'

'Why?' He shot the word at her as he depressed the record button a second time.

It was a question she had prepared for. The words came out so fluently that he was sure she'd rehearsed the answer in advance. 'Because we're in terrible trouble as a society if we assume that any man's life is so worthless that the manner of his death is the only interesting thing about him.'

'That's a fine sentiment,' he said mildly, 'but hardly very newsworthy. People die in obscurity all the time.'

'But why starve to death? Why here? Why does nobody know anything about him? Why had he told the police he was twenty years older than he actually was?' She searched his face intently. 'Aren't you at all curious about him?'

Of course! Curiosity wormed like a maggot in his brain, but he was far more interested in her than he was in the man who had died in her garage. *Why, for example, did she take Billy's death so personally that she was prepared to be exploited in order to have his story publicized?* 'Are you sure you didn't know him?' he suggested with apparent indifference.

Her surprise was genuine. 'No. Why would I need answers if I'd known him?'

He opened his notebook on his lap, and wrote: *Why does anyone need answers about a complete stranger six months after his death?* 'Which would you prefer,' he asked, 'that Lisa takes her photographs before we talk or while we're talking?'

'While.'

He waited as Lisa unzipped her bag and removed her camera. 'Do you have a Christian name, Mrs Powell?'

'Amanda.'

'Do you prefer Amanda Powell or Mrs Powell?'

'I don't mind.' She frowned into the camera lens.

'A smile would be better,' said Lisa. She snapped the shutter. Click. 'That's great.' Click. 'Could you look at the floor? Good.' Click. 'Keep your eyes cast down. That's really touching.' Click, click.

'Go on, Mr Deacon,' said the woman curtly. 'I'm sure you don't want me to be sick over my own carpet.'

He grinned. 'I prefer Deacon or Mike. How old are you?'

'Thirty-six.'

'What do you do for a job?'

She glanced at him as Lisa took another photograph. 'I'm an architect.'

'On your own or with a firm?'

'I'm with W. F. Meredith.' Click.

Not bad, he thought. Meredith was about as good as you could get. 'What are your political affiliations, Amanda?'

'None.'

'How about off the record?'

She gave a faint smile which Lisa caught. 'The same.'

'Do you vote?' She caught him watching her, and he looked away.

'Of course. Women fought long and hard to give me that right.'

'Are you going to tell me which party you usually vote for?'

'Whichever I think will do the least damage.'

'You seem to have little time for politicians. Is there a particular reason for that or is it just *fin-de-siècle* depression?'

The faint smile again as she reached for her wine glass. 'Personally, I'd hesitate to qualify a huge abstract concept like *fin-de-siècle* depression with "just", but for the purposes of your article it's as truthful as anything else.'

He wondered what it would be like to kiss her. 'Are you married at the moment, Amanda?'

'Yes.'

'What does your husband do?'

She raised the glass to her lips, momentarily forgetting the camera lens pointing at her, then lowered it with a frown as Lisa took another photograph. 'My husband wasn't here when I found the body,' she said, 'so what he does is irrelevant.'

Deacon caught the look of amused cynicism on Lisa's face. 'It's human interest,' he countered lightly. 'People will want to know what sort of man a successful architect is married to.'

Perhaps she realized that his curiosity was personal, or perhaps, as Lisa had guessed, there *was* no Mr Powell. In either case, she refused to expand on the matter. 'It was I who found the body,' she repeated, 'and you have my details already. Shall we continue?'

The pale eyes, so like his mother's, rested on Deacon's craggy face too long for comfort, and his mild fantasy about kissing her shifted from harmless fun to sadistic revenge. He could imagine what JP's reaction was going to be to the paucity of information that he'd managed to drag out of her so far. *Name, rank and number.* And he had little optimism that the photographs would be any better. Her features were so controlled that she might as well be a poker-faced prisoner of war backed against a wall. He wondered if fires had ever burned in her cool little face, or if her life had been entirely passionless. Predictably, the idea excited him.

'All right,' he agreed, 'let's talk about finding the body. You said you were shocked. Can you describe the experience for me? What sort of thoughts went through your mind when you saw him?'

'Disgust,' she said, careful to keep her voice neutral. 'He

was behind a stack of empty boxes in the corner and he'd covered himself in an old blanket. The smell was really quite awful once I'd pulled it away from him. Also, his body fluids had seeped out all over the floor.' Her mouth tightened in sudden distaste and she blinked as the flash of the camera stung her eyes. 'Afterwards, when the police told me that he'd died of self-neglect and malnutrition, I kept wondering why he'd made no attempt to save himself. It wasn't just that I found him beside my chest freezer' – she gestured unhappily towards the window – 'everyone's so affluent on this estate that even the dustbins have perfectly edible food in them.'

'Any ideas?'

'Only that he was so weak by the time he found my garage that he hadn't the energy to do more than crawl into the corner and hide himself.'

'Why would he want to hide?'

She studied him for a moment. 'I don't know. But if he wasn't hiding, why didn't he try to attract my attention? The police think he must have entered the garage on the Saturday, because his only opportunity to get inside was when I went to the shops that afternoon and left the doors unlocked for half an hour.' In so far as she was capable of showing emotion, she did. Her hand flickered nervously towards her mouth before she remembered the camera and dropped it abruptly. 'I found his body on the following Friday and the pathologist estimated he'd been dead five days. That means he was alive on the Sunday. I could have helped him if he'd called out and let me know he was there. So why didn't he?'

'Perhaps he was afraid.'

'Of what?'

'Being turned over to the police for trespass.'

She shook her head. 'Certainly not that. He had no fear of the police or of prison. I understand he was arrested quite regularly. Why should this time have been any different?'

Deacon made shorthand notes on his pad to remind himself of the nuances of expression that crossed her face as she talked about Billy. *Anxiety. Concern. Bewilderment even.* Curiouser and curiouser. *What was Billy Blake to her that he could inspire emotion where her husband couldn't?* 'Maybe he was just too weak to attract your attention. Presumably the pathologist can't say if he was conscious on the Sunday?'

'No,' she said slowly, 'but I can. There was a bag of ice-cubes in the freezer. Someone had opened it, and it certainly wasn't me, so I presume it must have been Billy. And one corner of the garage had been urinated in. If he was strong enough to move around the garage, then he was strong enough to bang on the connecting door between the garage and my hall. He must have known I was here that weekend because he could have heard me. The door's not thick enough to block out sound.'

'What did the police make of that?'

'Nothing,' she said. 'It made no difference to the pathologist's verdict. Billy still died of malnutrition whether through wilful self-neglect or involuntary self-neglect.'

He lit another cigarette and eyed her through the smoke. 'How much did the cremation cost you?'

'Does the amount matter?'

'It depends how cynical you believe the average reader

to be. He might think you're being coy about the figure because you want everyone to assume you spent more.'

'Five hundred pounds.'

'Which is a great deal more than you would have given him alive?'

She nodded. Click. 'If I'd met him as a beggar in the street, I'd have thought I was being generous if I gave him five pounds.' Click. Click. She glanced with irritation at Lisa, looked as if she were about to say something, then thought better of it. Her face took on its closed expression again.

'You said yesterday that you felt you owed him something. What exactly?'

'Respect, I suppose.'

'Because you felt he hadn't been shown any in life?'

'Something like that,' she admitted. 'But it sounds ridiculously sentimental when it's put into words.'

He wrote for a moment. 'Do you have a religion?'

She turned away as another flash exploded in her eyes. 'Surely she's taken enough by now?'

Lisa kept the camera lens on her face. 'Just a couple more shots with the eyes cast down, Amanda.' Click. 'Yes, that's really nice, Amanda.' Click. 'More compassion maybe.' Click. 'Great, Amanda.' Click, click, click.

Deacon watched increasing irritation gather in the woman's eyes. 'All right, Smith. Let's call a halt, shall we?'

'How about a few more in the garage?' suggested the girl, reluctant to waste the end of the film. 'It won't take a minute.'

Mrs Powell stared into the blood-red depths of her glass before taking a sip. 'Be my guest,' she said without raising

her head. 'The keys are on the table in the hall, and the light comes on automatically when the garage door is lifted. I don't use the connecting door any more.'

'I meant a few more of you,' said Lisa. 'I'll need you to come with me. If it's cold and damp out there, a few atmospheric shots could be really good. More in tune with a wino dying of starvation.'

The woman's stillness following this remark persuaded Lisa she hadn't been listening. She tried again. 'Five minutes, Amanda, that's all we'll need. You might like to stand near where you found him, look a bit upset, that sort of thing.'

The only sound in the room was the ticking of a clock on the mantelpiece, and it grew louder as Mrs Powell's silence lengthened. She seemed to Deacon to be waiting for something, and he held his breath and waited with her. It startled him to hear her speak. 'I'm sorry,' she said to the girl, 'but you and I are very different animals. I could no more pose weepy-eyed over where Billy died than I could wear your fuck-me clothes or your fuck-me make-up. You see, I'm neither so vulgar nor so desperate to be noticed.'

There were too many sibilants in the last sentence, and her careful diction abandoned her. With a slight shock, Deacon realized she was drunk.